THE MAHABHARATA

PRAISE FOR THE SERIES

'The modernization of language is visible, it's easier on the mind, through expressions that are somewhat familiar. The detailing of the story is intact, the varying tempo maintained, with no deviations from the original. The short introduction reflects a brilliant mind. For those who passionately love the Mahabharata and want to explore it to its depths, Debroy's translation offers great promise . . .'

—*Hindustan Times*

'[Debroy] has really carved out a niche for himself in crafting and presenting a translation of the Mahabharata . . . The book takes us on a great journey with admirable ease.'

—*Indian Express*

'The first thing that appeals to one is the simplicity with which Debroy has been able to express himself and infuse the right kind of meanings . . . Considering that Sanskrit is not the simplest of languages to translate a text from, Debroy exhibits his deep understanding and appreciation of the medium.'

—*The Hindu*

'Overwhelmingly impressive . . . Bibek is a truly eclectic scholar.'

—*Business Line*

'Debroy's lucid and nuanced retelling of the original makes the masterpiece even more enjoyably accessible.'

—*Open*

'The quality of translation is excellent. The lucid language makes it a pleasure to read the various stories, digressions and parables.'

—*Tribune*

'Extremely well-organized, and has a substantial and helpful Introduction, plot summaries and notes . . . beautiful example of a well thought-out layout which makes for much easier reading.'

—*Book Review*

'The dispassionate vision [Debroy] brings to this endeavour will surely earn him merit in the three worlds.'

—*Mail Today*

'Thoroughly enjoyable and impressively scholarly . . .'

—*DNA*

'Debroy's is not the only English translation available in the market, but where he scores and others fail is that his is the closest rendering of the original text in modern English without unduly complicating the readers' understanding of the epic.'

—*Business Standard*

'The brilliance of Ved Vysya comes through.'

—*Hindustan Times*

THE MAHABHARATA

Volume 7
(Sections 73 to 77)

Translated by
BIBEK DEBROY

PENGUIN BOOKS
An imprint of Penguin Random House

PENGUIN BOOKS

USA | Canada | UK | Ireland | Australia
New Zealand | India | South Africa | China

Penguin Books is part of the Penguin Random House group of companies whose addresses can be found at global.penguinrandomhouse.com

Published by Penguin Random House India Pvt. Ltd
7th Floor, Infinity Tower C, DLF Cyber City,
Gurgaon 122 002, Haryana, India

First published by Penguin Books India 2013
This edition published 2015

10 9 8 7 6 5 4 3 2

ISBN 9780143425205

Typeset in Sabon by Eleven Arts, New Delhi
Printed at Repro Knowledgecast Limited, India

www.penguin.co.in

For my wife, Suparna Banerjee (Debroy),
who has walked this path of dharma with me

Ardha bhāryā manuṣyasya bhāryā śreṣṭhatamaḥsakhā
Bhāryā mulam trivargasya bhāryā mitram mariṣyataḥ
Mahabharata (1/68/40)

Nāsti bhāryāsamo bandhurnāsti bhāryasamā gatiḥ
Nāsti bhāryasamo loke sahāyo dharmasādhanaḥ
Mahabharata (12/142/10)

Contents

FAMILY TREE

Bharata/Puru Lineage

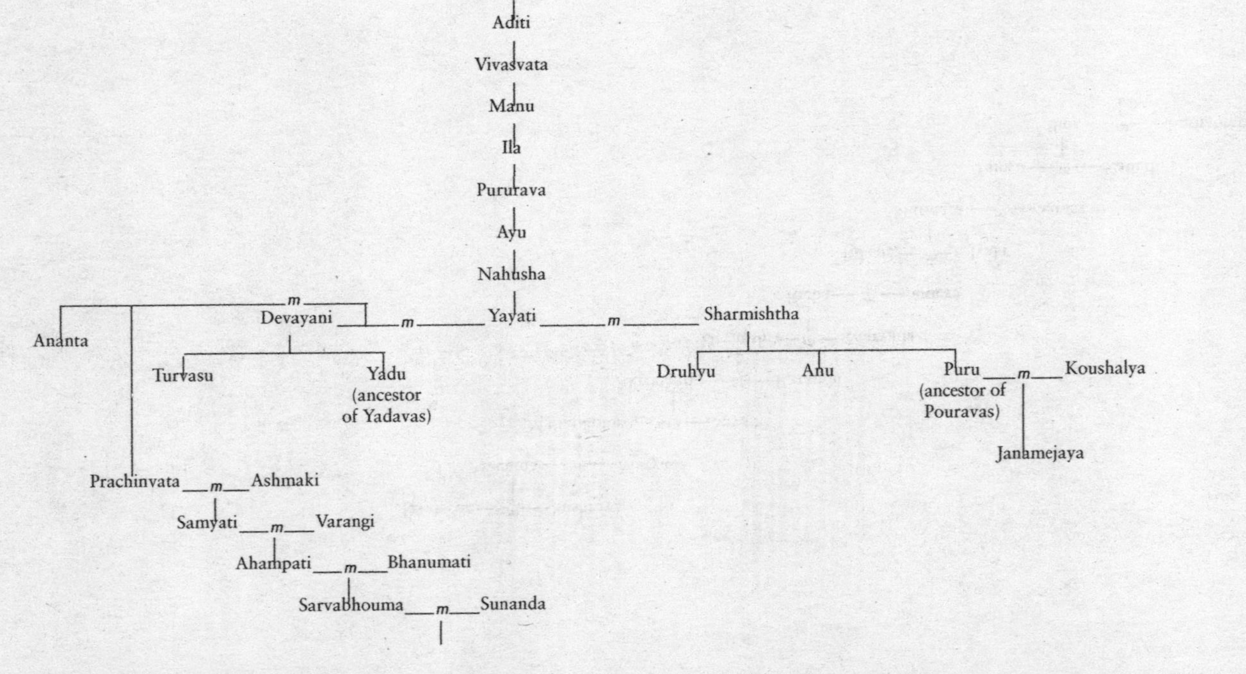

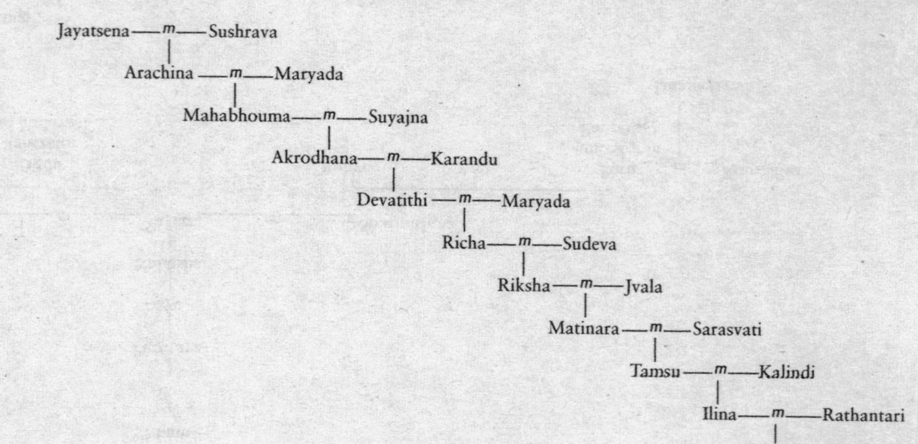
Jayatsena—m—Sushrava
Arachina—m—Maryada
Mahabhouma—m—Suyajna
Akrodhana—m—Karandu
Devatithi—m—Maryada
Richa—m—Sudeva
Riksha—m—Jvala
Matinara—m—Sarasvati
Tamsu—m—Kalindi
Ilina—m—Rathantari

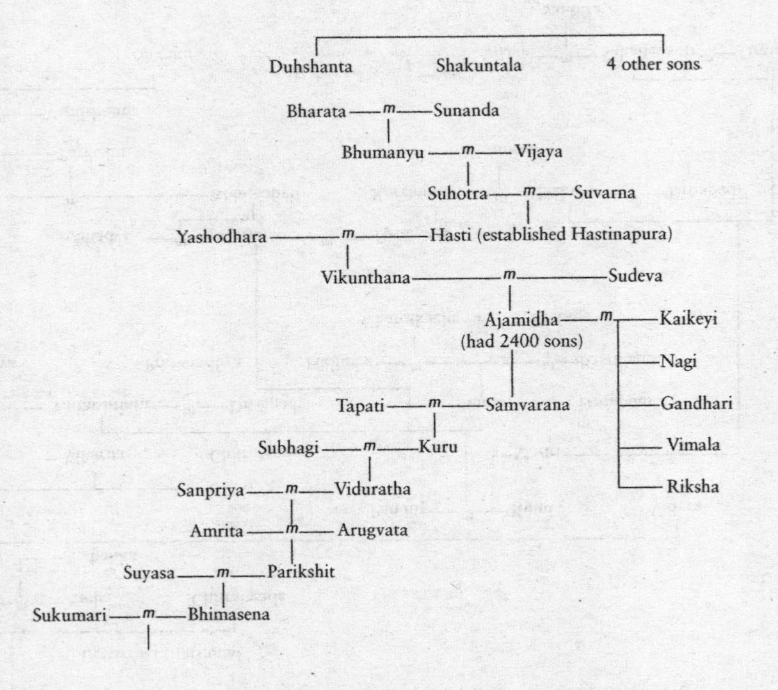

Duhshanta
Shakuntala
4 other sons
Bharata
m
Sunanda
Bhumanyu
m
Vijaya
Suhotra
m
Suvarna
Yashodhara
m
Hasti (established Hastinapura)
Vikunthana
m
Sudeva
Ajamidha
(had 2400 sons)
m
Kaikeyi
Nagi
Gandhari
Vimala
Riksha
Tapati
m
Samvarana
Subhagi
m
Kuru
Sanpriya
m
Viduratha
Amrita
m
Arugvata
Suyasa
m
Parikshit
Sukumari
m
Bhimasena

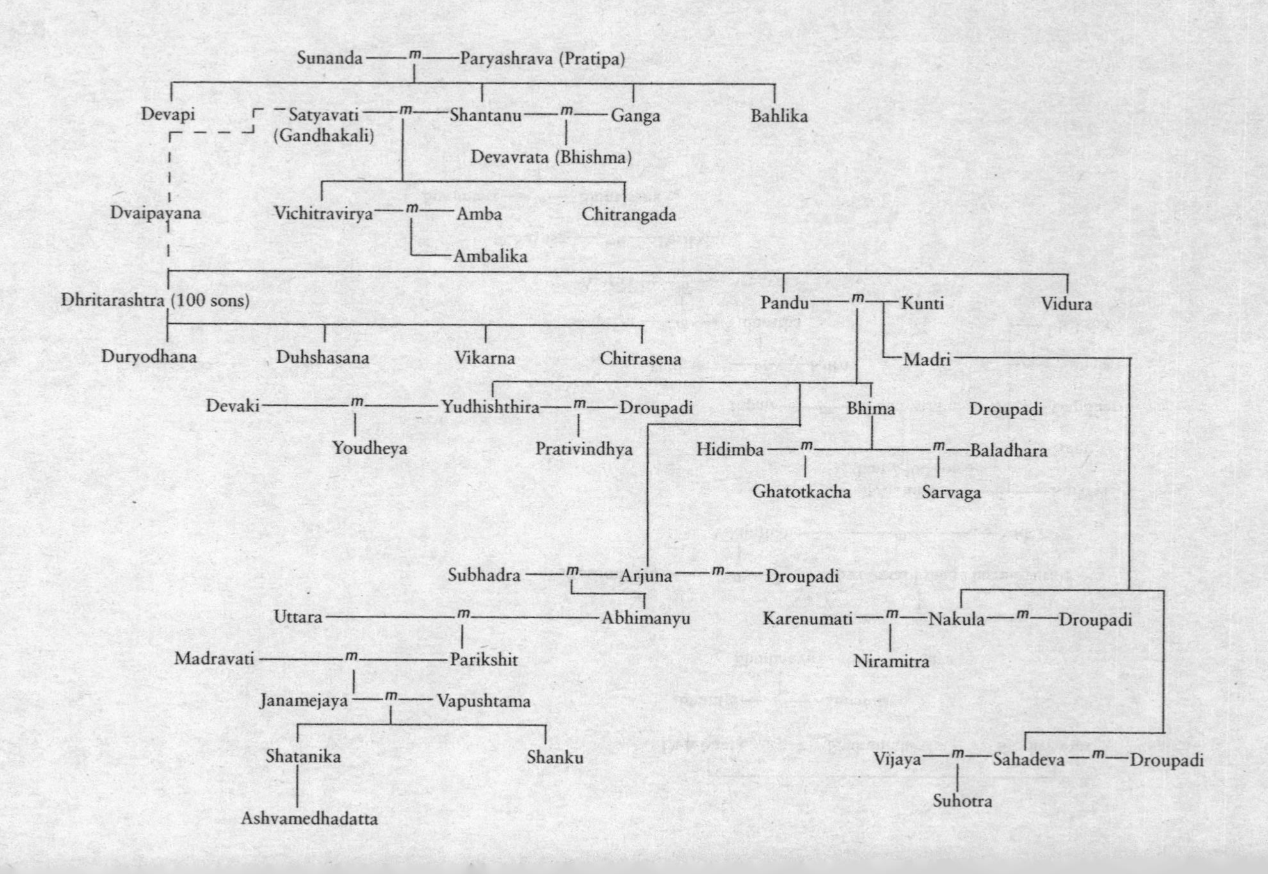
Sunanda
m
Paryashrava (Pratipa)
Devapi
Satyavati
(Gandhakali)
m
Shantanu
m
Ganga
Bahlika
Devavrata (Bhishma)
Dvaipayana
Vichitravirya
m
Amba
Chitrangada
Ambalika
Dhritarashtra (100 sons)
Pandu
m
Kunti
Vidura
Duryodhana
Duhshasana
Vikarna
Chitrasena
Madri
Devaki
m
Yudhishthira
m
Droupadi
Bhima
Droupadi
Youdheya
Prativindhya
Hidimba
m
m
Baladhara
Ghatotkacha
Sarvaga
Subhadra
m
Arjuna
m
Droupadi
Uttara
m
Abhimanyu
Karenumati
m
Nakula
m
Droupadi
Madravati
m
Parikshit
Niramitra
Janamejaya
m
Vapushtama
Shatanika
Shanku
Vijaya
m
Sahadeva
m
Droupadi
Suhotra
Ashvamedhadatta

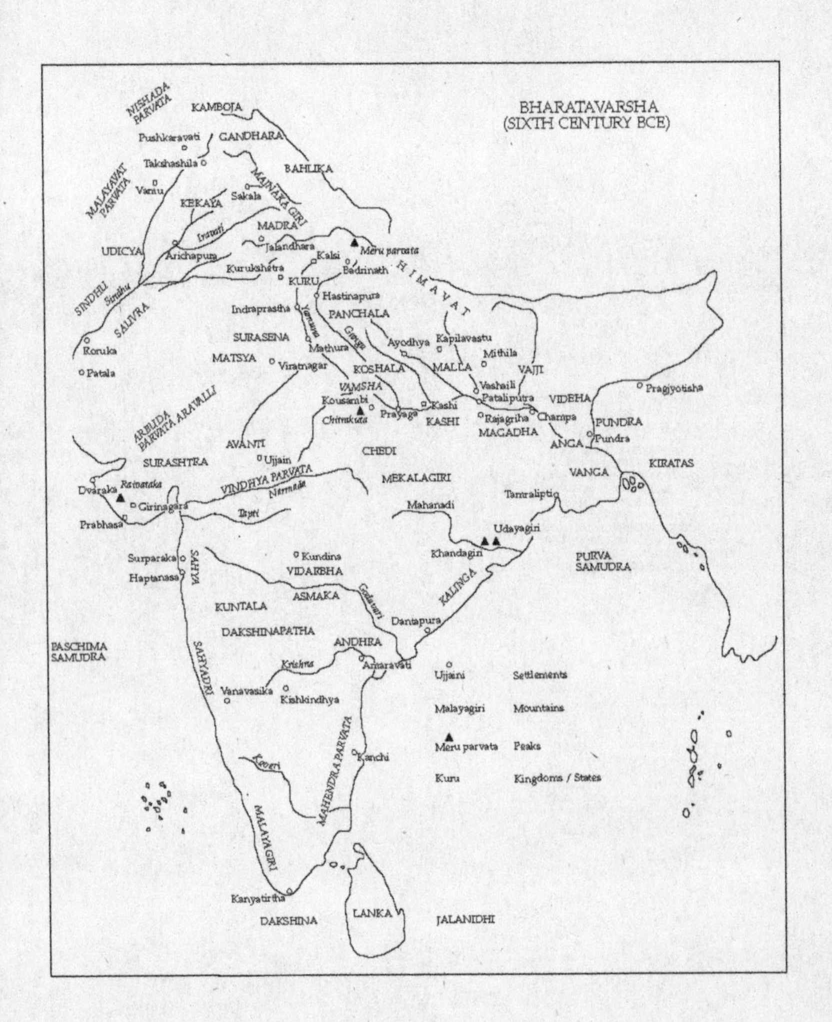
BHARATAVARSHA
(SIXTH CENTURY BCE)
NISHADA PARVATA
KAMBOJA
Pushkaravati
GANDHARA
Takshashila
BAHLIKA
MALAYAVAT PARVATA
Varnu
MAINAKA GIRI
Sakala
KEKAYA
MADRA
Iravati
UDICYA
Arichapura
Jalandhara
Meru parvata
Kalsi
Badrinath
Kurukshetra
KURU
HIMAVAT
SINDHU
Sindhu
Hastinapura
Indraprastha
SAUVIRA
PANCHALA
Yamuna
SURASENA
Ganga
Roruka
Mathura
Ayodhya
Kapilavastu
Mithila
MATSYA
Viratnagar
KOSHALA
MALLA
VAJJI
Patala
VAMSHA
Vashaili
Pataliputra
Pragjyotisha
Kousambi
Chitrakuta
Prayaga
Kashi
VIDEHA
ARBUDA PARVATA ARAVALLI
KASHI
Rajagriha
Champa
MAGADHA
PUNDRA
Pundra
AVANTI
ANGA
SURASHTRA
Ujjain
CHEDI
KIRATAS
VINDHYA PARVATA
VANGA
MEKALAGIRI
Dvaraka
Raivataka
Narmada
Tamralipti
Girinagara
Mahanadi
Tapti
Prabhasa
Udayagiri
Khandagiri
Surparaka
SAHYA
Kundina
PURVA SAMUDRA
VIDARBHA
Haptanasa
Godavari
KALINGA
KUNTALA
ASMAKA
Dantapura
DAKSHINAPATHA
ANDHRA
PASCHIMA SAMUDRA
SAHYADRI
Krishna
Amaravati
Ujjaini
Settlements
Vanavasika
Kishkindhya
Malayagiri
Mountains
MAHENDRA PARVATA
Meru parvata
Peaks
Kaveri
Kanchi
Kuru
Kingdoms / States
MALAYAGIRI
Kanyatirtha
DAKSHINA
LANKA
JALANIDHI

Acknowledgements

Carving time out from one's regular schedule and work engagements to embark on such a mammoth work of translation has been difficult. It has been a journey of six years, ten volumes and something like 2.25 million words. Sometimes, I wish I had been born in nineteenth-century Bengal, with a benefactor funding me for doing nothing but this. But alas, the days of gentlemen of leisure are long over. The time could not be carved out from professional engagements, barring of course assorted television channels, who must have wondered why I have been so reluctant to head for their studios in the evenings. It was ascribed to health, interpreted as adverse health. It was certainly health, but not in an adverse sense. Reading the Mahabharata is good for one's mental health and is an activity to be recommended, without any statutory warnings. When I embarked on the hazardous journey, a friend, an author interested in Sanskrit and the Mahabharata, sent me an email. She asked me to be careful, since the track record of those who embarked on unabridged translations of the Mahabharata hasn't always been desirable. Thankfully, I survived, to finish telling the tale.

The time was stolen in the evenings and over weekends. The cost was therefore borne by one's immediate family, and to a lesser extent by friends. Socializing was reduced, since every dinner meant one less chapter done. The family has first claim on the debt, though I am sure it also has claim on whatever merits are due. At least my wife, Suparna Banerjee (Debroy) does, and these volumes are therefore dedicated to her. For six long years, she has walked this path of dharma along with me, providing the conducive home cum family environment that made undistracted work possible. I suspect Sirius has no claim on the merits, though he has been remarkably patient at the times when he has been curled up near my feet and I have been translating away. There is some allegory there about a dog keeping company when the Mahabharata is being read and translated.

Most people have thought I was mad, even if they never quite said that. Among those who believed and thought it was worthwhile, beyond immediate family, are M. Veerappa Moily, Pratap Bhanu Mehta and Laveesh Bhandari. And my sons, Nihshanka and Vidroha. The various reviewers of different volumes have also been extremely kind and many readers have communicated kind words through email and Twitter, enquiring about progress.

Penguin also believed. My initial hesitation about being able to deliver was brushed aside by R. Sivapriya, who pushed me after the series had been commissioned by V. Karthika. And then Sumitra Srinivasan became the editor, followed by Paloma Dutta. The enthusiasm of these ladies was so infectious that everything just snowballed and Paloma ensured that the final product of the volumes was much more readable than what I had initially produced.

When I first embarked on what was also a personal voyage of sorts, the end was never in sight and seemed to stretch to infinity. There were moments of self-doubt and frustration. Now that it is all done, it leaves a vacuum, a hole. That's not simply because you haven't figured out what the new project is. It is also because characters who have been part of your life for several years are dead and gone. I don't mean the ones who died in the course of the actual war, but the others. Most of them faced rather tragic and unenviable ends. Along that personal voyage, the Mahabharata changes you, or so my wife tells me. I am no longer the person I was when I started it, as an individual. That sounds cryptic, deliberately so. Anyone who reads the Mahabharata carefully is bound to change, discount the temporary and place a premium on the permanent.

To all those who have been part of that journey, including the readers, thank you.

The original ten volumes were published sequentially, as they were completed, between 2010 and 2014.

Introduction

The Hindu tradition has an amazingly large corpus of religious texts, spanning Vedas, Vedanta (*brahmanas*,[1] *aranyakas*,[2] Upanishads,), Vedangas,[3] *smritis*, Puranas, dharmashastras and *itihasa*. For most of these texts, especially if one excludes classical Sanskrit literature, we don't quite know when they were composed and by whom, not that one is looking for single authors. Some of the minor Puranas (Upa Purana) are of later vintage. For instance, the Bhavishya Purana (which is often listed as a major Purana or Maha Purana) mentions Queen Victoria.

In the listing of the corpus above figures itihasa, translated into English as history. History doesn't entirely capture the nuance of itihasa, which is better translated as 'this is indeed what happened'. Itihasa isn't myth or fiction. It is a chronicle of what happened; it is fact. Or so runs the belief. And itihasa consists of India's two major epics, the Ramayana and the Mahabharata. The former is believed to have been composed as poetry and the latter as prose. This isn't quite correct. The Ramayana has segments in prose and the Mahabharata has segments in poetry. Itihasa doesn't quite belong to the category of religious texts in a way that the Vedas and Vedanta are religious. However, the dividing line between what is religious and what is not is fuzzy. After all, itihasa is also about attaining the objectives of *dharma*,[4]

[1] Brahmana is a text and also the word used for the highest caste.

[2] A class of religious and philosophical texts that are composed in the forest, or are meant to be studied when one retires to the forest.

[3] The six Vedangas are *shiksha* (articulation and pronunciation), *chhanda* (prosody), *vyakarana* (grammar), *nirukta* (etymology), *jyotisha* (astronomy) and *kalpa* (rituals).

[4] Religion, duty.

artha,[5] *kama*[6] and *moksha*[7] and the Mahabharata includes Hinduism's most important spiritual text—the Bhagavad Gita.

The epics are not part of the *shruti* tradition. That tradition is like revelation, without any composer. The epics are part of the *smriti* tradition. At the time they were composed, there was no question of texts being written down. They were recited, heard, memorized and passed down through the generations. But the smriti tradition had composers. The Ramayana was composed by Valmiki, regarded as the first poet or *kavi*. The word kavi has a secondary meaning as poet or rhymer. The primary meaning of kavi is someone who is wise.

And in that sense, the composer of the Mahabharata was no less wise. This was Vedavyasa or Vyasadeva. He was so named because he classified (*vyasa*) the Vedas. Vedavyasa or Vyasadeva isn't a proper name. It is a title. Once in a while, in accordance with the needs of the era, the Vedas need to be classified. Each such person obtains the title and there have been twenty-eight Vyasadevas so far.

At one level, the question about who composed the Mahabharata is pointless. According to popular belief and according to what the Mahabharata itself states, it was composed by Krishna Dvaipayana Vedavyasa (Vyasadeva). But the text was not composed and cast in stone at a single point in time. Multiple authors kept adding layers and embellishing it. Sections just kept getting added and it is no one's suggestion that Krishna Dvaipayana Vedavyasa composed the text of the Mahabharata as it stands today.

Consequently, the Mahabharata is far more unstructured than the Ramayana. The major sections of the Ramayana are known as *kanda*s and one meaning of the word kanda is the stem or trunk of a tree, suggesting solidity. The major sections of the Mahabharata are known as *parva*s and while one meaning of the word parva is limb or member or joint, in its nuance there is greater fluidity in the word parva than in kanda.

The Vyasadeva we are concerned with had a proper name of Krishna

[5] Wealth. But in general, any object of the senses.
[6] Desire.
[7] Release from the cycle of rebirth.

Dvaipayana. He was born on an island (*dvipa*). That explains the Dvaipayana part of the name. He was dark. That explains the Krishna part of the name. (It wasn't only the incarnation of Vishnu who had the name of Krishna.) Krishna Dvaipayana Vedavyasa was also related to the protagonists of the Mahabharata story. To go back to the origins, the Ramayana is about the solar dynasty, while the Mahabharata is about the lunar dynasty. As is to be expected, the lunar dynasty begins with Soma (the moon) and goes down through Pururava (who married the famous apsara Urvashi), Nahusha and Yayati. Yayati became old, but wasn't ready to give up the pleasures of life. He asked his sons to temporarily loan him their youth. All but one refused. The ones who refused were cursed that they would never be kings, and this includes the Yadavas (descended from Yadu). The one who agreed was Puru and the lunar dynasty continued through him. Puru's son Duhshanta was made famous by Kalidasa in the Duhshanta–Shakuntala story and their son was Bharata, contributing to the name of Bharatavarsha. Bharata's grandson was Kuru. We often tend to think of the Kouravas as the evil protagonists in the Mahabharata story and the Pandavas as the good protagonists. Since Kuru was a common ancestor, the appellation Kourava applies equally to Yudhishthira and his brothers and Duryodhana and his brothers. Kuru's grandson was Shantanu. Through Satyavati, Shantanu fathered Chitrangada and Vichitravirya. However, the sage Parashara had already fathered Krishna Dvaipayana through Satyavati. And Shantanu had already fathered Bhishma through Ganga. Dhritarasthra and Pandu were fathered on Vichitravirya's wives by Krishna Dvaipayana.

The story of the epic is also about these antecedents and consequents. The core Mahabharata story is known to every Indian and is normally understood as a dispute between the Kouravas (descended from Dhritarashtra) and the Pandavas (descended from Pandu). However, this is a distilled version, which really begins with Shantanu. The non-distilled version takes us to the roots of the genealogical tree and at several points along this tree we confront a problem with impotence/sterility/death, resulting in offspring through a surrogate father. Such sons were accepted in that day and age. Nor was this a lunar dynasty problem alone. In the Ramayana, Dasharatha of the solar dynasty also had an infertility problem, corrected through a sacrifice. To return to the genealogical tree, the Pandavas won the Kurukshetra war. However, their five sons through Droupadi were killed. So was Bhima's son Ghatotkacha, fathered on Hidimba. As was Arjuna's son Abhimanyu, fathered on Subhadra. Abhimanyu's son Parikshit inherited the throne in Hastinapura, but was killed by a serpent. Parikshit's son was Janamejaya.

Krishna Dvaipayana Vedavyasa's powers of composition were remarkable. Having classified the Vedas, he composed the Mahabharata in 100,000 shlokas or couplets. Today's Mahabharata text doesn't have that many shlokas, even if the Hari Vamsha (regarded as the epilogue to the Mahabharata) is included. One reaches around 90,000 shlokas. That too, is a gigantic number. (The Mahabharata is almost four times the size of the Ramayana and is longer than any other epic anywhere in the world.) For a count of 90,000 Sanskrit shlokas, we are talking about something in the neighbourhood of two million words. The text of the Mahabharata tells us that Krishna Dvaipayana finished this composition in three years. This doesn't necessarily mean that he composed 90,000 shlokas. The text also tells us that there are three versions to the Mahabharata. The original version was called Jaya and had 8,800 shlokas. This was expanded to 24,000 shlokas and called Bharata. Finally, it was expanded to 90,000 (or 100,000) shlokas and called Mahabharata.

Krishna Dvaipayana didn't rest even after that. He composed the eighteen Maha Puranas, adding another 400,000 shlokas. Having composed the Mahabharata, he taught it to his disciple Vaishampayana. When Parikshit was killed by a serpent, Janamejaya organized a snake-sacrifice to destroy the serpents. With all the sages assembled there, Vaishampayana turned up and the assembled sages wanted to know the story of the Mahabharata, as composed by Krishna Dvaipayana. Janamejaya also wanted to know why Parikshit had been killed by the serpent. That's the background against which the epic is recited. However, there is another round of recounting too. Much later, the sages assembled for a sacrifice in Naimisharanya and asked Lomaharshana (alternatively, Romaharshana) to recite what he had heard at Janamejaya's snake-sacrifice. Lomaharshana was a *suta*, the sutas being charioteers and bards or raconteurs. As the son of a suta, Lomaharshana is also referred to as Souti. But Souti or Lomaharshana aren't quite his proper names. His proper name is Ugrashrava. Souti refers to his birth. He owes the name Lomaharshana to the fact that the body-hair (*loma* or *roma*) stood up (*harshana*) on hearing his tales. Within the text therefore, two people are telling the tale. Sometimes it is Vaishampayana and sometimes it is Lomaharshana. Incidentally, the stories of the Puranas are recounted by Lomaharshana, without Vaishampayana intruding. Having composed the Puranas, Krishna Dvaipayana taught them to his disciple Lomaharshana. For what it is worth, there are scholars who have used statistical tests to try and identify the multiple authors of the Mahabharata.

As we are certain there were multiple authors rather than a single one, the question of when the Mahabharata was composed is somewhat pointless. It wasn't composed on a single date. It was composed over a span of more than 1000 years, perhaps between 800 BCE and 400 ACE. It is impossible to be more accurate than that. There is a difference between dating the composition and dating the incidents, such as the date of the Kurukshetra war. Dating the incidents is both subjective and controversial and irrelevant for the purposes of this translation. A timeline of 1000 years isn't short. But even then, the size of the corpus is nothing short of amazing.

***

Familiarity with Sanskrit is dying out. The first decades of the twenty-first century are quite unlike the first decades of the twentieth. Lamentation over what is inevitable serves no purpose. English is increasingly becoming the global language, courtesy colonies (North America, South Asia, East Asia, Australia, New Zealand, Africa) rather than the former colonizer. If familiarity with the corpus is not to die out, it needs to be accessible in English.

There are many different versions or recensions of the Mahabharata. However, between 1919 and 1966, the Bhandarkar Oriental Research Institute (BORI) in Pune produced what has come to be known as the critical edition. This is an authenticated text produced by a board of scholars and seeks to eliminate later interpolations, unifying the text across the various regional versions. This is the text followed in this translation. One should also mention that the critical edition's text is not invariably smooth. Sometimes, the transition from one shloka to another is abrupt, because the intervening shloka has been weeded out. With the intervening shloka included, a non-critical version of the text sometimes makes better sense. On a few occasions, I have had the temerity to point this out in the notes which I have included in my translation. On a slightly different note, the quality of the text in something like Dana Dharma Parva is clearly inferior. It couldn't have been 'composed' by the same person.

It took a long time for this critical edition to be put together. The exercise began in 1919. Without the Hari Vamsha, the complete critical edition became available in 1966. And with the Hari Vamsha, the complete critical edition became available in 1970. Before this, there were regional variations in the text and the main versions were available from Bengal, Bombay and the south. However, now, one should stick to the critical edition, though there are occasional instances where there are reasons for dissatisfaction with what the scholars of the Bhandarkar Oriental Research Institute have accomplished. But in all fairness, there are two published versions of the critical edition. The first one has the bare bones of the critical edition's text. The second has all the regional versions collated, with copious notes. The former is for the ordinary reader, assuming he/she knows Sanskrit. And the latter is for the scholar. Consequently, some popular beliefs no longer find a place in the critical edition's text. For example, it is believed that Vedavyasa dictated the text to Ganesha, who wrote it down. But Ganesha had a condition before accepting. Vedavyasa would have to dictate continuously, without stopping. Vedavyasa threw in a counter-condition. Ganesha would have to understand each couplet before he wrote it down. To flummox Ganesha and give himself time to think, Vedavyasa threw in some cryptic verses. This attractive anecdote has been excised from the critical edition's text. Barring material that is completely religious (specific hymns or the Bhagavad Gita), the Sanskrit text is reasonably easy to understand. Oddly, I have had the most difficulty with things that Vidura has sometimes said, other than parts of Anushasana Parva. Arya has today come to connote ethnicity. Originally, it meant language. That is, those who spoke Sanskrit were Aryas. Those who did not speak Sanskrit were mlecchas. Vidura is supposed to have been skilled in the mlechha language. Is that the reason why some of Vidura's statements seem obscure? In similar vein, in popular renderings, when Droupadi is being disrobed, she prays to Krishna. Krishna provides the never-ending stream of garments that stump Duhshasana. The critical edition has excised the prayer to Krishna. The never-ending stream of garments is given as an extraordinary event. However, there is no intervention from Krishna.

How is the Mahabharata classified? The core component is the couplet or shloka. Several such shlokas form a chapter or *adhyaya*. Several adhyayas form a parva. Most people probably think that the Mahabharata has eighteen parvas. This is true, but there is another 100-parva classification that is indicated in the text itself. That is, the adhyayas can be classified either according to eighteen parvas or according to 100 parvas. The table (given on pp. xxiii–xxvi), based on the critical edition, should make this clear. As the table shows, the present critical edition only has ninety-eight parvas of the 100-parva classification, though the 100 parvas are named in the text.

Eighteen-parva classification	*100-parva classification*	*Number of adhyayas*	*Number of shlokas*
(1) Adi	1) Anukramanika[8]	1	210
	2) Parvasamgraha	1	243
	3) Poushya	1	195
	4) Pouloma	9	153
	5) Astika	41	1025
	6) Adi-vamshavatarana	5	257
	7) Sambhava	65	2394
	8) Jatugriha-daha	15	373
	9) Hidimba-vadha	6	169
	10) Baka-vadha	8	206
	11) Chaitraratha	21	557
	12) Droupadi-svayamvara	12	263
	13) Vaivahika	6	155

[8] Anukramanika is sometimes called anukramani.

Eighteen-parva classification	*100-parva classification*	*Number of adhyayas*	*Number of shlokas*
	14) Viduragamana	7	174
	15) Rajya-labha	1	50
	16) Arjuna-vanavasa	11	298
	17) Subhadra-harana	2	57
	18) Harana harika	1	82
	19) Khandava-daha	12	344
		Total = 225	Total = 7205
(2) Sabha	20) Sabha	11	429
	21) Mantra	6	222
	22) Jarasandha-vadha	5	195
	23) Digvijaya	7	191
	24) Rajasuya	3	97
	25) Arghabhiharana	4	99
	26) Shishupala-vadha	6	191
	27) Dyuta	23	734
	28) Anudyuta	7	232
		Total = 72	Total = 2387
(3) Aranyaka	29) Aranyaka	11	327
	30) Kirmira-vadha	1	75
	31) Kairata	30	1158
	32) Indralokabhigamana	37	1175
	33) Tirtha-yatra	74	2293
	34) Jatasura-vadha	1	61
	35) Yaksha-yuddha	18	727
	36) Ajagara	6	201
	37) Markandeya-samasya	43	1694
	38) Droupadi-Satyabhama-sambada	3	88
	39) Ghosha-yatra	19	519
	40) Mriga-svapna-bhaya	1	16
	41) Vrihi-drounika	3	117
	42) Droupadi-harana	36	1247
	43) Kundala-harana	11	294
	44) Araneya	5	191
		Total = 299	Total = 10239
(4) Virata	45) Vairata	12	282
	46) Kichaka-vadha	11	353
	47) Go-grahana	39	1009
	48) Vaivahika	5	179
		Total = 67	Total = 1736

Eighteen-parva classification	*100-parva classification*	*Number of adhyayas*	*Number of shlokas*
(5) Udyoga	49) Udyoga	21	575
	50) Sanjaya-yana	11	311
	51) Prajagara	9	541
	52) Sanatsujata	4	121
	53) Yana-sandhi	24	726
	54) Bhagavat-yana	65	2055
	55) Karna-upanivada	14	351
	56) Abhiniryana	4	169
	57) Bhishma-abhishechana	4	122
	58) Uluka-yana	4	101
	59) Ratha-atiratha-samkhya	9	231
	60) Amba-upakhyana	28	755
		Total = 197	Total = 6001
(6) Bhishma	61) Jambukhanda-vinirmana	11	378
	62) Bhumi	2	87
	63) Bhagavad Gita	27	994
	64) Bhishma vadha	77	3947
		Total = 117	Total = 5381
(7) Drona	65) Dronabhisheka	15	634
	66) Samshaptaka-vadha	16	717
	67) Abhimanyu-vadha	20	643
	68) Pratijna	9	365
	69) Jayadratha-vadha	61	2914
	70) Ghatotkacha-vadha	33	1642
	71) Drona-vadha	11	692
	72) Narayanastra-moksha	8	538
		Total = 173	Total = 8069
(8) Karna	73) Karna-vadha	69	3870
(9) Shalya	74) Shalya-vadha	16	844
	75) Hrada pravesha	12	664
	76) Tirtha yatra	25	1261
	77) Gada yuddha	11	546
		Total = 64	Total = 3315
(10) Souptika	78) Souptika	9	515
	79) Aishika	9	257
		Total = 18	Total = 771

Eighteen-parva classification	*100-parva classification*	*Number of adhyayas*	*Number of shlokas*
(11) Stri	80) Vishoka	8	194
	81) Stri	17	468
	82) Shraddha	1	44
	83) Jala-pradanika	1	24
		Total = 27	Total = 713
(12) Shanti	84) Raja-dharma	128	4509
	85) Apad-dharma	39	1560
	86) Moksha Dharma	186	6935
		Total = 353	Total = 13006
(13) Anushasana	87) Dana Dharma	152	6450
	88) Bhishma-svargarohana	2	84
		Total = 154	T otal = 6493
(14) Ashva-medhika	89) Ashvamedhika	96	2743
(15) Ashra-mavasika	90) Ashrama-vasa	35	737
	91) Putra Darshana	9	234
	92) Naradagamana	3	91
		Total = 47	Total = 1061
(16) Mousala	93) Mousala	9	273
(17) Mahapra-sthanika	94) Maha-Prasthanika	3	106
(18) Svargarohana	95) Svargarohana	5	194
Hari Vamsha	96) Hari-vamsha	45	2442
	97) Vishnu	68	3426
	98) Bhavishya	5	205
		Total = 118	Total = 6073
Grand total = 19	Grand total = 98 (95 + 3)	Grand total = 2113 (1995 + 118)	Grand total = 79,860 (73787 + 6073)

Thus, interpreted in terms of BORI's critical edition, the Mahabharata no longer possesses the 100,000 shlokas it is supposed to have. The figure is a little short of 75,000 (73,787 to be precise). Should the Hari Vamsha be included in a translation of the Mahabharata? It doesn't quite belong. Yet, it is described as a *khila* or supplement to the Mahabharata and BORI includes it as part of the critical edition, though in a separate volume. In this case also, the translation of the Hari Vamsha will be published in a separate and independent volume. With the Hari Vamsha, the number of shlokas increases to a shade less than 80,000 (79,860 to be precise). However, in some of the regional versions the text of the Mahabharata proper is closer to 85,000 shlokas and with the Hari Vamsha included, one approaches 95,000, though one doesn't quite touch 100,000.

Why should there be another translation of the Mahabharata? Surely, it must have been translated innumerable times. Contrary to popular impression, unabridged translations of the Mahabharata in English are extremely rare. One should not confuse abridged translations with unabridged versions. There are only five unabridged translations—by Kisori Mohan Ganguly (1883–96), by Manmatha Nath Dutt (1895–1905), by the University of Chicago and J.A.B. van Buitenen (1973 onwards), by P. Lal and Writers Workshop (2005 onwards) and the Clay Sanskrit Library edition (2005 onwards). Of these, P. Lal is more a poetic trans-creation than a translation. The Clay Sanskrit Library edition is not based on the critical edition, deliberately so. In the days of Ganguly and Dutt, the critical edition didn't exist. The language in these two versions is now archaic and there are some shlokas that these two translators decided not to include, believing them to be untranslatable in that day and age. Almost three decades later, the Chicago version is still not complete, and the Clay edition, not being translated in sequence, is still in progress. However, the primary reason for venturing into yet another translation is not just the vacuum that exists, but also reason for dissatisfaction with other attempts. Stated more explicitly, this translation, I believe, is better and more authentic—but I leave it to the reader to be the final judge. (While translating 80,000 shlokas is a hazardous venture, since Ganguly and Dutt were Bengalis, and P. Lal was one for many purposes, though not by birth, surely a fourth Bengali must also be pre-eminently qualified to embark on this venture!)

A few comments on the translation are now in order. First, there is the vexed question of diacritical marks—should they be used or not? Diacritical marks make the translation and pronunciation more accurate, but often put readers off. Sacrificing academic purity, there is thus a conscious decision to avoid diacritical marks. Second, since diacritical marks are not being used, Sanskrit words and proper names are written in what seems to be phonetically natural and the closest—such as, Droupadi rather than Draupadi. There are rare instances where avoidance of diacritical marks can cause minor confusion, for example, between Krishna (Krishnaa) as in Droupadi[8] and Krishna as in Vaasudeva. However, such instances are extremely rare and the context should make these differences, which are mostly of the gender kind, clear. Third, there are some words that simply cannot be translated. One such word is dharma. More accurately, such words are translated the first time they occur. But on subsequent occasions, they are romanized in the text. Fourth, the translation sticks to the Sanskrit text as closely as possible. If the text uses the word Kounteya, this translation will leave it as Kounteya or Kunti's son and not attempt to replace it with Arjuna. Instead, there will be a note explaining that in that specific context Kounteya refers to Arjuna or, somewhat more rarely, Yudhishthira or Bhima. This is also the case in the structure of the English sentences. To cite an instance, if a metaphor occurs towards the beginning of the Sanskrit shloka, the English sentence attempts to retain it at the beginning too. Had this not been done, the English might have read smoother. But to the extent there is a trade-off, one has stuck to what is most accurate, rather than attempting to make the English smooth and less stilted.

As the table shows, the parvas (in the eighteen-parva classification) vary widely in length. The gigantic Aranyaka or Shanti Parva can be contrasted with the slim Mousala Parva. Breaking up the translation into separate volumes based on this eighteen-parva classification therefore doesn't work. The volumes will not be remotely similar in size. Most translators seem to keep a target of ten to twelve volumes when translating all the parvas. Assuming ten volumes, 10 per cent means roughly 200 chapters and 7000 shlokas. This works rather well for Adi Parva, but collapses thereafter. Most translators therefore have Adi Parva as the first volume and then handle the heterogeneity

[9] Krishna or Krishnaa is another name for Droupadi.

across the eighteen parvas in subsequent volumes. This translation approaches the break-up of volumes somewhat differently, in the sense that roughly 10 per cent of the text is covered in each volume. The complete text, as explained earlier, is roughly 200 chapters and 7,000 shlokas per volume. For example, then, this first volume has been cut off at 199 chapters and a little less than 6,500 shlokas. It includes 90 per cent of Adi Parva, but not all of it and covers the first fifteen parvas of the 100- (or 98-) parva classification.

* * *

The Mahabharata is one of the greatest stories ever told. It has plots and subplots and meanderings and digressions. It is much more than the core story of a war between the Kouravas and the Pandavas, which everyone is familiar with, the culmination of which was the battle in Kurukshetra. In the Adi Parva, there is a lot more which happens before the Kouravas and the Pandavas actually arrive on the scene. In the 100-parva classification, the Kouravas and the Pandavas don't arrive on the scene until Section 6.

From the Vedas and Vedanta literature, we know that Janamejaya and Parikshit were historical persons. From Patanjali's grammar and other contemporary texts, we know that the Mahabharata text existed by around 400 BCE. This need not of course be the final text of Mahabharata, but could have been the original text of Jaya. The Hindu eras or *yuga*s are four in number—Satya (or Krita) Yuga, Treta Yuga, Dvapara Yuga and Kali Yuga. This cycle then repeats itself, with another Satya Yuga following Kali Yuga. The events of the Ramayana occurred in Treta Yuga. The events of the Mahabharata occurred in Dvapara Yuga. This is in line with Rama being Vishnu's seventh incarnation and Krishna being the eighth. (The ninth is Buddha and the tenth is Kalki.) We are now in Kali Yuga. Kali Yuga didn't begin with the Kurukshetra war. It began with Krishna's death, an event that occurred thirty-six years after the Kurukshetra war. Astronomical data do exist in the epic. These can be used to date the Kurukshetra war, or the advent of Kali Yuga. However, if the text was composed at different points in time, with additions and interpolations, internal consistency in astronomical data is unlikely. In popular belief, following two alternative astronomers, the Kurukshetra war has been dated to 3102 BCE (following Aryabhatta) and 2449 BCE (following Varahamihira). This doesn't mesh with the timelines of Indian history. Mahapadma Nanda ascended the throne in 382 BCE, a historical fact on which there is no dispute. The Puranas have genealogical lists. Some of these state that 1050 years elapsed between Parikshit's birth and Mahapadma Nanda's ascension. Others state that 1015 years elapsed. (When numerals are written in words, it is easy to confuse 15 with 50.) This takes Parikshit's birth and the Kurukshetra war to around 1400 BCE. This is probably the best we can do, since we also know that the Kuru kingdom flourished between 1200 BCE and 800 BCE. To keep the record straight, archaeological material has been used to bring forward the date of the Kurukshetra war to around 900 BCE, the period of the Iron Age.

As was mentioned, in popular belief, the incidents of the Ramayana took place before the incidents of the Mahabharata. The Ramayana story also figures in the Mahabharata. However, there is no reference to any significant Mahabharata detail in the Ramayana. Nevertheless, from reading the text, one gets the sense that the Mahabharata represents a more primitive society than the Ramayana. The fighting in the Ramayana is more genteel and civilized. You don't have people hurling rocks and stones at each other, or fighting with trees and bare arms. Nor do people rip apart the enemy's chest and drink blood. The geographical knowledge in the Mahabharata is also more limited than in the Ramayana, both towards the east and towards the south. In popular belief, the Kurukshetra war occurred as a result of a dispute over land and the kingdom. That is true, in so far as the present text is concerned. However, another fight over cattle took place in the Virata Parva and the Pandavas were victorious in that too. This is not the place to expand on the argument. But it is possible to construct a plausible hypothesis that this was the core dispute. Everything else was added as later embellishments. The property dispute was over cattle and not land. In human evolution, cattle represents a more primitive form of property than land. In that stage, humankind is still partly nomadic and not completely settled. If this hypothesis is true, the Mahabharata again represents an earlier period compared to the Ramayana. This leads to the following kind of proposition. In its final form, the Mahabharata was indeed composed after the Ramayana. But the earliest version of the Mahabharata was composed before the earliest version of the Ramayana. And the events of the Mahabharata occurred before the events of the Ramayana, despite popular belief. The proposition about the feud ending with Virata Parva illustrates the endless speculation that is possible with the Mahabharata material. Did Arjuna, Nakula and Sahadeva ever exist? Nakula and Sahadeva have limited roles to play in the story. Arjuna's induction could have been an attempt to assert Indra's supremacy. Arjuna represents such an integral strand in the story (and of the Bhagavad Gita), that such a suggestion is likely to be dismissed out of hand. But consider the following. Droupadi loved Arjuna a little bit more than the others. That's the reason she was denied admission to heaven. Throughout the text, there are innumerable instances where Droupadi faces difficulties. Does she ever summon Arjuna for help on such occasions? No, she does not. She summons Bhima. Therefore, did Arjuna exist at all? Or were there simply two original Pandava brothers—one powerful and strong, and the other weak and useless in physical terms. Incidentally, the eighteen-parva classification is clearly something that was done much later. The 100-parva classification seems to be older.

The Mahabharata is much more real than the Ramayana. And, therefore, much more fascinating. Every conceivable human emotion figures in it, which is the reason why it is possible to identify with it even today. The text itself states that what is not found in the Mahabharata, will not be found anywhere else. Unlike the Ramayana, India is littered with real places that have identifications with the Mahabharata. (Ayodhya or Lanka or Chitrakuta are identifications that are less certain.) Kurukshetra, Hastinapura, Indraprastha, Karnal, Mathura, Dvaraka, Gurgaon, Girivraja are real places: the list is endless. In all kinds of unlikely places, one comes across temples erected by the Pandavas when they were exiled to the forest. In some of these places, archaeological excavations have substantiated the stories. The war for regional supremacy in the Ganga–Yamuna belt is also a plausible one. The Vrishnis and the

Shurasenas (the Yadavas) are isolated, they have no clear alliance (before the Pandavas) with the powerful Kurus. There is the powerful Magadha kingdom under Jarasandha and Jarasandha had made life difficult for the Yadavas. He chased them away from Mathura to Dvaraka. Shishupala of the Chedi kingdom doesn't like Krishna and the Yadavas either. Through Kunti, Krishna has a matrimonial alliance with the Pandavas. Through Subhadra, the Yadavas have another matrimonial alliance with the Pandavas. Through another matrimonial alliance, the Pandavas obtain Drupada of Panchala as an ally. In the course of the royal sacrifice, Shishupala and Jarasandha are eliminated. Finally, there is yet another matrimonial alliance with Virata of the Matsya kingdom, through Abhimanyu. When the two sides face each other on the field of battle, they are more than evenly matched. Other than the Yadavas, the Pandavas have Panchala, Kashi, Magadha, Matsya and Chedi on their side. The Kouravas have Pragjyotisha, Anga, Kekaya, Sindhu, Avanti, Gandhara, Shalva, Bahlika and Kamboja as allies. At the end of the war, all these kings are slain and the entire geographical expanse comes under the control of the Pandavas and the Yadavas. Only Kripacharya, Ashvatthama and Kritavarma survive on the Kourava side.

Reading the Mahabharata, one forms the impression that it is based on some real incidents. That does not mean that a war on the scale that is described took place. Or that miraculous weapons and chariots were the norm. But there is such a lot of trivia, unconnected with the main story, that their inclusion seems to serve no purpose unless they were true depictions. For instance, what does the physical description of Kripa's sister and Drona's wife, Kripi, have to do with the main story? It is also more real than the Ramayana because nothing, especially the treatment of human emotions and behaviour, exists in black and white. Everything is in shades of grey. The Uttara Kanda of the Ramayana is believed to have been a later interpolation. If one excludes the Uttara Kanda, we generally know what is good. We know who is good. We know what is bad. We know who is bad. This is never the case with the Mahabharata. However, a qualification is necessary. Most of us are aware of the Mahabharata story because we have read some version or the other, typically an abridged one. Every abridged version simplifies and condenses, distills out the core story. And in doing that, it tends to paint things in black and white, fitting everything into the mould of good and bad. The Kouravas are bad. The Pandavas are good. And good eventually triumphs. The unabridged Mahabharata is anything but that. It is much more nuanced. Duryodhana isn't invariably bad. He is referred to as Suyodhana as well, and not just by his father. History is always written from the point of view of the victors. While the Mahabharata is generally laudatory towards the Pandavas, there are several places where the text has a pro-Kourava stance. There are several places where the text has an anti-Krishna stance. That's yet another reason why one should read an unabridged version, so as not to miss out on these nuances. Take the simple point about inheritance of the kingdom. Dhritarashtra was blind. Consequently, the king was Pandu. On Pandu's death, who should inherit the kingdom? Yudhishthira was the eldest among the brothers. (Actually, Karna was, though it didn't become known until later.) We thus tend to assume that the kingdom was Yudhishthira's by right, because he was the eldest. (The division of the kingdom into two, Hastinapura and Indraprastha, is a separate matter.) But such primogeniture was not universally clear. A case can also be established for Duryodhana, because he was Dhritarashtra's son. If primogeniture was the rule, the eldest son of the Pandavas was Ghatotkacha, not Abhimanyu. Before both were killed, Ghatotkacha should have had a claim to the throne. However, there is no such suggestion anywhere. The argument that Ghatotkacha was the son of a rakshasa or demon will not wash. He never exhibited any demonic qualities and was a dutiful and loving son. Karna saved up a weapon for Arjuna and this was eventually used to kill Ghatotkacha. At that time, we have the unseemly sight of Krishna dancing around in glee at Ghatotkacha being killed.

In the Mahabharata, because it is nuanced, we never quite know what is good and what is bad, who is good and who is bad. Yes, there are degrees along a continuum. But there are no watertight and neat compartments. The four objectives of human existence are dharma, artha, kama and moksha. Etymologically, dharma is that which upholds. If one goes by the Bhagavad Gita, pursuit of these four are also transient diversions. Because the fundamental objective is to transcend these four, even moksha. Within these four, the Mahabharata is about a conflict of dharma. Dharma has been reduced to *varnashrama* dharma, according to the four classes (*varna*s) and four stages of life (*ashrama*s). However, these are collective interpretations of dharma, in the sense that a Kshatriya in the *garhasthya* (householder) stage has certain duties. Dharma in the Mahabharata is individual too. Given an identical situation, a Kshatriya in the garhasthya stage might adopt a course of action that is different from that adopted by another Kshatriya in the garhasthya stage, and who is to judge what is wrong and what is right? Bhishma adopted a life of celibacy. So did Arjuna, for a limited period. In that stage of celibacy, both were approached by women who had fallen in love with them. And if those desires were not satisfied, the respective women would face difficulties, even death. Bhishma spurned the advance, but Arjuna accepted it. The conflict over dharma is not only the law versus morality conflict made famous by Krishna and Arjuna in the Bhagavad Gita. It pervades the Mahabharata, in terms of a conflict over two different notions of dharma. Having collectively married Droupadi, the Pandavas have agreed that when one of them is closeted with Droupadi, the other four will not intrude. And if there is such an instance of intrusion, they will go into self-exile. Along comes a Brahmana whose cattle have been stolen by thieves. Arjuna's weapons are in the room where Droupadi and Yudhishthira are. Which is the higher dharma? Providing succour to the Brahmana or adhering to the oath? Throughout the Mahabharata, we have such conflicts, with no clear normative indications of what is wrong and what is right, because there are indeed no absolute answers. Depending on one's decisions, one faces the consequences and this brings in the unsolvable riddle of the tension between free will and determinism, the so-called karma concept. The boundaries of philosophy and religion blur.

These conflicts over dharma are easy to identify with. It is easy to empathize with the protagonists, because we face such conflicts every day. That is precisely the reason why the Mahabharata is read even today. And the reason one says every conceivable human emotion figures in the story. Everyone familiar with the Mahabharata has thought about the decisions taken and about the characters. Why was life so unfair to Karna? Why was Krishna partial to the Pandavas? Why didn't he prevent the war? Why was Abhimanyu killed so unfairly? Why did the spirited and dark Droupadi, so unlike the Sita of the Ramayana, have to be humiliated publicly?

* * *

It is impossible to pinpoint when and how my interest in the Mahabharata started. As a mere toddler, my maternal grandmother used to tell me stories from *Chandi*, part of the Markandeya Purana. I still vividly recollect pictures from her copy of *Chandi*: Kali licking the demon Raktavija's blood. Much later, in my early teens, at school in Ramakrishna Mission, Narendrapur, I first read the Bhagavad Gita, without understanding much of what I read. The alliteration and poetry in the first chapter was attractive enough for me to learn it by heart. Perhaps the seeds were sown there. In my late teens, I stumbled upon Bankimchandra Chattopadhyay's *Krishna Charitra*, written in 1886. Bankimchandra was not only a famous novelist, he was a brilliant essayist. For a long time, *Krishna Charitra* was not available other than in Bengali. It has now been translated into English, but deserves better dissemination. A little later, when in college, I encountered Buddhadeb Bose's *Mahabharater Katha*. That was another brilliant collection of essays, first serialized in a magazine and then published as a book in 1974. This too was originally in Bengali, but is now available in English. Unlike my sons, my first exposure to the Mahabharata story came not through television serials but comic books. Upendrakishore Raychowdhury's Mahabharata (and Ramayana) for children was staple diet, later supplanted by Rajshekhar Basu's abridged versions of both epics, written for adults. Both were in Bengali. In English, there was Chakravarti Rajagopalachari's abridged translation, still a perennial favourite. Later, Chakravarthi Narasimhan's selective unabridged translation gave a flavour of what the Mahabharata actually contained. In Bengal, the Kashiram Das version of the Mahabharata, written in the seventeenth century, was quite popular. I never found this appealing. But in the late 1970s, I stumbled upon a treasure. Kolkata's famous College Street was a storehouse of old and second-hand books in those days. You never knew what you would discover when browsing. In the nineteenth century, an unabridged translation of the Mahabharata had been done in Bengali under the editorship of Kaliprasanna Singha (1840–70). I picked this up for the princely sum of Rs 5. The year may have been 1979, but Rs 5 was still amazing. This was my first complete reading of the unabridged version of the Mahabharata. This particular copy probably had antiquarian value. The pages would crumble in my hands and I soon replaced my treasured possession with a republished reprint. Not longer after, I acquired the Aryashastra version of the Mahabharata, with both the Sanskrit and the Bengali together. In the early 1980s, I was also exposed to three Marathi writers writing on the Mahabharata. There was Iravati Karve's *Yuganta*. This was available in both English and in Marathi. I read the English one first, followed by the Marathi. The English version isn't an exact translation of the Marathi and the Marathi version is far superior. Then there was Durga Bhagwat's *Vyas Parva*. This was in Marathi and I am not aware of an English translation. Finally, there was Shivaji Sawant's *Mritunjaya*, a kind of autobiography for Karna. This was available both in English and in Marathi. Incidentally, one should mention John Smith's excellent abridged translation, based on the Critical Edition, and published while this unabridged translation was going on.

In the early 1980s, quite by chance, I encountered two shlokas, one from Valmiki's Ramayana, the other from Kalidasa's *Meghadutam*. These were two poets separated by anything between 500 to 1,000 years, the exact period being an uncertain one. The shloka in *Meghadutam* is right towards the beginning, the second shloka to be precise. It is the first day in the month of Ashada. The yaksha has been cursed and has been separated from his beloved. The mountains are covered with clouds. These clouds are like elephants, bent down as if in play. The shloka in the Valmiki Ramayana occurs in Sundara Kanda. Rama now knows that Sita is in Lanka. But the monsoon stands in the way of the invasion. The clouds are streaked with flags of lightning and garlanded with geese. They are like mountain peaks and are thundering, like elephants fighting. At that time, I did not know that elephants were a standard metaphor for clouds in Sanskrit literature. I found it amazing that two different poets separated by time had thought of elephants. And because the yaksha was pining for his beloved, the elephants were playing. But because Rama was impatient to fight, the elephants were fighting. I resolved that I must read all this in the original. It was a resolution I have never regretted. I think that anyone who has not read *Meghadutam* in Sanskrit has missed out on a thing of beauty that will continue to be a joy for generations to come.

In the early 1980s, Professor Ashok Rudra was a professor of economics in Visva-Bharati, Santiniketan. I used to teach in Presidency College, Kolkata, and we sometimes met. Professor Rudra was a left-wing economist and didn't think much of my economics. I dare say the feeling was reciprocated. By tacit agreement, we never discussed economics. Instead, we discussed Indological subjects. At that point, Professor Rudra used to write essays on such subjects in Bengali. I casually remarked, 'I want to do a statistical test on the frequency with which the five Pandavas used various weapons in the Kurukshetra war.' Most sensible men would have dismissed the thought as crazy. But Professor Rudra wasn't sensible by usual norms of behaviour and he was also a trained statistician. He encouraged me to do the paper, written and published in Bengali, using the Aryashastra edition. Several similar papers followed, written in Bengali. In 1983, I moved to Pune, to the Gokhale Institute of Politics and Economics, a stone's throw away from BORI. *Annals of the Bhandarkar Oriental Research Institute (ABORI)* is one of the most respected journals in Indology. Professor G.B. Palsule was then the editor of ABORI and later went on to become Director of BORI. I translated one of the Bengali essays into English and went and met Professor Palsule, hoping to get it published in ABORI. To Professor Palsule's eternal credit, he didn't throw the dilettante out. Instead, he said he would get the paper refereed. The referee's substantive criticism was that the paper should have been based on the critical edition, which is how I came to know about it. Eventually, this paper (and a few more) were published in ABORI. In 1989, these became a book titled *Essays on the Ramayana and the Mahabharata*, published when the Mahabharata frenzy had reached a peak on television. The book got excellent reviews, but hardly sold. It is now out of print. As an aside, the book was jointly dedicated to Professor Rudra and Professor Palsule, a famous economist and a famous Indologist respectively. Both were flattered. However, when I gave him a copy, Professor Rudra said, 'Thank you very much. But who is Professor Palsule?' And Professor Palsule remarked, 'Thank you very much. But who is Professor Rudra?'

While the research interest in the Mahabharata remained, I got sidetracked into translating. Through the 1990s, there were abridged translations of the Maha Puranas, the Vedas and the eleven major Upanishads. I found that I enjoyed translating from the Sanskrit to English and since these volumes were well received, perhaps I did do a good job. With Penguin as publisher, I did a translation of the Bhagavad Gita, something I had always wanted to do. *Sarama and Her Children*, a book on attitudes towards dogs in India, also with Penguin, followed. I kept thinking about doing an unabridged translation of the Mahabharata and waited to muster up the courage. That courage now exists, though the task is daunting. With something like two million words and ten volumes expected, the exercise seems open-ended. But why translate the Mahabharata? In 1924, George Mallory, with his fellow climber Andrew Irvine, may or may not have climbed Mount Everest. They were last seen a few hundred metres from the summit, before they died. Mallory was once asked why he wanted to climb Everest and he answered, 'Because it's there.' Taken out of context, there is no better reason for wanting to translate the Mahabharata. There is a steep mountain to climb. And I would not have dared had I not been able to stand on the shoulders of the three intellectual giants who have preceded me—Kisori Mohan Ganguli, Manmatha Nath Dutt and J.A.B. van Buitenen.

Bibek Debroy

Karna Parva

Karna Parva continues with the account of the war. After Drona's death, Karna is instated as the commander of the Kourava army. Karna is the commander for two days, days sixteen and seventeen. In the 18–parva classification, Karna Parva is the eighth. In the 100–parva classification, Karna Parva constitutes Section 73. Karna Parva has sixty-nine chapters. In the numbering of the chapters in Karna Parva, the first number is a consecutive one, starting with the beginning of the Mahabharata. And the second number, within brackets, is the numbering of the chapter within Karna Parva.

Karna Parva

Karna Parva continues with the account of the war. After Drona's death, Karna is instated as the commander of the Kourava army. Karna is the commander for two days, the sixteenth and seventeenth. In the 18-parva classification, Karna Parva is the eighth. In the 100-parva classification, Karna Parva constitutes Section 73. Karna Parva has seventy chapters. In the numbering of the chapters in Karna Parva, the first number is a cumulative one, starting with the beginning of the Mahabharata. And the second number, within brackets, is the numbering of the chapter within Karna Parva.

SECTION SEVENTY-THREE

Karna-Vadha Parva

This parva has 3,870 shlokas and sixty-nine chapters.

Chapter 1151(1): 49 shlokas
Chapter 1152(2): 20 shlokas
Chapter 1153(3): 14 shlokas
Chapter 1154(4): 108 shlokas
Chapter 1155(5): 110 shlokas
Chapter 1156(6): 46 shlokas
Chapter 1157(7): 42 shlokas
Chapter 1158(8): 45 shlokas
Chapter 1159(9): 35 shlokas
Chapter 1160(10): 36 shlokas
Chapter 1161(11): 41 shlokas
Chapter 1162(12): 71 shlokas
Chapter 1163(13): 25 shlokas
Chapter 1164(14): 64 shlokas
Chapter 1165(15): 43 shlokas
Chapter 1166(16): 38 shlokas
Chapter 1167(17): 120 shlokas
Chapter 1168(18): 76 shlokas
Chapter 1169(19): 75 shlokas
Chapter 1170(20): 32 shlokas
Chapter 1171(21): 42 shlokas
Chapter 1172(22): 61 shlokas
Chapter 1173(23): 54 shlokas
Chapter 1174(24): 161 shlokas
Chapter 1175(25): 11 shlokas
Chapter 1176(26): 74 shlokas
Chapter 1177(27): 105 shlokas
Chapter 1178(28): 66 shlokas
Chapter 1179(29): 40 shlokas
Chapter 1180(30): 88 shlokas
Chapter 1181(31): 68 shlokas
Chapter 1182(32): 84 shlokas
Chapter 1183(33): 70 shlokas
Chapter 1184(34): 42 shlokas
Chapter 1185(35): 60 shlokas
Chapter 1186(36): 40 shlokas
Chapter 1187(37): 38 shlokas
Chapter 1188(38): 42 shlokas
Chapter 1189(39): 38 shlokas
Chapter 1190(40): 130 shlokas
Chapter 1191(41): 7 shlokas
Chapter 1192(42): 57 shlokas
Chapter 1193(43): 78 shlokas
Chapter 1194(44): 55 shlokas

Chapter 1195(45): 73 shlokas
Chapter 1196(46): 48 shlokas
Chapter 1197(47): 14 shlokas
Chapter 1198(48): 15 shlokas
Chapter 1199(49): 115 shlokas
Chapter 1200(50): 65 shlokas
Chapter 1201(51): 110 shlokas
Chapter 1202(52): 33 shlokas
Chapter 1203(53): 14 shlokas
Chapter 1204(54): 29 shlokas
Chapter 1205(55): 73 shlokas
Chapter 1206(56): 58 shlokas
Chapter 1207(57): 69 shlokas
Chapter 1208(58): 28 shlokas
Chapter 1209(59): 45 shlokas
Chapter 1210(60): 33 shlokas
Chapter 1211(61): 17 shlokas
Chapter 1212(62): 62 shlokas
Chapter 1213(63): 83 shlokas
Chapter 1214(64): 32 shlokas
Chapter 1215(65): 45 shlokas
Chapter 1216(66): 65 shlokas
Chapter 1217(67): 37 shlokas
Chapter 1218(68): 63 shlokas
Chapter 1219(69): 43 shlokas

Vadha *means killing and the section is named after the killing of Karna. It is also simply known as Karna Parva. After Drona's death, Karna is made the overall commander. Bhima kills Kshemadhurti (the king of Kuluta), Satyaki kills Vinda and Anuvinda from Kekaya, Droupadi's sons kill Chitrasena and Chitra from Abhisara, Arjuna kills Dandadhara and Danda from Magadha, Ashvatthama kills Pandya, and Arjuna kills large numbers of the enemy (primarily the* samshaptakas[1]*). On the seventeenth day, on Karna's request, Duryodhana asks Shalya to be Karna's charioteer. Bhima kills Karna's son, Satyasena and some of Duryodhana's brothers, Kripa kills Suketu from Panchala, and Arjuna, Bhima and Karna kill many of the enemy. Uttamouja kills Sushena, Karna's son. Karna kills many warriors on the Pandava side and, in an inconsistent statement, Satyaki kills Sushena, Karna's son. Bhima kills some of Duryodhana's brothers. In a major highlight of the war, Bhima kills Duhshasana*

[1]Samshaptakas are warriors who have taken an oath and these warriors (primarily the Trigartas) take an oath to die or kill Arjuna.

and drinks his blood. Arjuna kills Vrishasena, Karna's son. Finally, Arjuna kills Karna.

Chapter 1151(1)

Vaishampayana said, 'O king! After Drona had been killed, the kings, with Duryodhana at the forefront, were extremely anxious in their minds. They went to Drona's son. They sorrowed and were dispirited because the infinitely energetic Drona had been killed. In their grief, they surrounded the son of Sharadvati.[2] For some time, they comforted him by recounting the reasons given in the sacred texts. However, once night arrived, those lords of the earth went to their own camps. But, in particular, the son of the *suta*,[3] King Suyodhana, Duhshasana and Shakuni could not sleep. In their camps, the Kouravyas and the lords of the earth found no cheer. They thought of that terrible destruction and could not sleep. Together,[4] they spent the night in Duryodhana's camp and thought about the extremely fierce enmity that they had unleashed on the great-souled Pandavas. They had oppressed Krishna[5] at the time of gambling with the dice and had brought her to the assembly hall. They thought of that and repented. They became extremely anxious. They thought of the hardships the Parthas had confronted on account of the gambling match. O king! As they thought about these difficulties, the moment seemed to last for a hundred years. Then, the clear morning dawned and they went through the prescribed rites. O descendant of the Bharata lineage! All of them performed these necessary tasks and having performed these necessary tasks, they were somewhat reassured. When the sun arose, they instructed

[2]Ashvatthama's mother was Sharadvati or Kripi, the daughter of Sharadvata.

[3]Karna.

[4]This is a reference to Karna, Duryodhana, Duhshasana and Shakuni.

[5]Krishnaa, Droupadi.

that the soldiers should be yoked and departed. Karna was made the overall commander and the auspicious ceremonies were performed. The foremost among brahmanas were praised and given vessels full of curds, clarified butter, parched rice, golden coins, cattle, gold and extremely expensive garments. Bards, raconteurs and minstrels prayed that their victory and prosperity might increase. O king! In similar fashion, the Pandavas also performed all the morning rites. O king! Making up their minds to fight, they emerged from their camps. As the Kurus and the Pandavas wished to kill each other, a tumultuous battle commenced and it made the body hair stand up. O king! When Karna was the overall commander, the battle between the Kuru and Pandava soldiers lasted for two days. It was wonderful to see. After having caused a great slaughter of the enemy in the battle, Vrisha[6] was brought down by Phalguna, while all the sons of Dhritarashtra looked on. Sanjaya then went to the city of Nagasahvya[7] and told Dhritarashtra everything that had transpired in Kurujangala.'[8]

Janamejaya said, 'Having heard that Drona had been killed by the enemy in the battle, the aged king, Ambika's son,[9] had been overcome by supreme grief. O supreme among brahmanas! On hearing that Karna, Duryodhana's well-wisher, had been slain, he must have been miserable. How could he sustain his life? The king's hopes for the victory of his sons had been based on him. On hearing that he had been killed, how could Kouravya sustain his life? Even when there is a hardship, I think that it is very difficult for men to die, since, despite hearing that Karna had been slain, the king did not give up his life. O brahmana! That was also true of Shantanu's aged son,[10] Bahlika, Drona, Somadatta and Bhurishrava. Many other well-wishers, sons and grandsons were also brought down. O brahmana! On hearing this, I think that it must have been very

[6]Karna.

[7]Another name for Hastinapura.

[8]Another name for Kurukshetra.

[9]Dhritarashtra was the son of Ambika.

[10]Bhishma.

difficult for the king to remain alive. O one rich in austerities! Tell me everything about this in detail. I am not satisfied with hearing about the great conduct of my ancestors.'

Vaishampayana said, 'O great king! When Karna was slain, with a distressed mind, Gavalgana's son[11] set out in the night for Nagapura,[12] on horses that were as fleet as the wind. He reached Hastinapura with great anxiety in his mind. He went to Dhritarashtra's place, where, the number of well-wishers had declined.[13] He saw the king, who was overcome by lassitude and was devoid of energy. Joining his hands in salutation, he bowed his head at the king's feet. He worshipped Dhritarashtra, lord of the earth, in accordance with the prescribed rites. He then spoke these words. "Alas! I am Sanjaya. O lord of the earth! Are you happy? You have confronted this state because of your own sins. I hope you are not confounded now. You did not follow the beneficial advice of Vidura, Drona, Gangeya[14] and Keshava. Are you distressed when you remember that? In the assembly hall, Rama, Narada and Kanva spoke beneficial words to you, but you did not accept them.[15] Are you distressed when you remember that? Remembering that the well-wishers who were engaged in your welfare, with Bhishma and Drona as the foremost, have been killed by the enemy in the battle, are you distressed?" Having been thus addressed, the king joined his hands in salutation before the son of the suta.[16] He sighed deeply. Oppressed by sorrow he spoke these words. "O Sanjaya! The brave Gangeya, who was well versed in the use of divine weapons, has been brought down. So has the great archer, Drona, and my mind is severely distressed. The energetic one[17]

[11]Sanjaya was Gavalgana's son.

[12]Another name for Hastinapura, *naga* and *hasti* both mean elephant.

[13]They were out fighting, but the sense is more of them having been killed.

[14]Ganga's son, Bhishma.

[15] Rama means Parashurama. These incidents have been described in Section 54 (Volume 4).

[16]Sanjaya was the son of a suta (charioteer).

[17]Bhishma, who was one of the eight Vasus born on earth. There are eight Vasus. According to the Mahabharata, they are descended from Brahma. The

was born from the Vasus. The armoured one slaughtered ten thousand *ratha*s. He has been killed by Yajnasena's son, Shikhandi, who was protected by the Pandaveyas. My mind is severely distressed. Bhargava gave supreme weapons to the great-souled one and when he was a child, Rama himself taught him Dhanurveda.[18] It is through his favours that the immensely strong Kounteya princes and many other lords of the earth became *maharatha*s. Drona was a great archer and unwavering in his aim. On hearing that he has been killed by Dhrishtadyumna in the battle, my mind is severely distressed. In the three worlds, there was no man who was his equal in the sacred texts.[19] On hearing that Drona had been killed, what did those on my side do? Using his valour, the great-souled Pandava Dhananjaya dispatched the army of the samshaptakas to Yama's abode. The *narayana* weapon used by Drona's intelligent son was repulsed.[20] After this, and when the remainder of the army was slain and driven away, what did those on my side do? I think that they must have been immersed in an ocean of grief. When Drona was killed, they must have been like people on an ocean whose boat had been shattered. O Sanjaya! What were the facial complexions of Duryodhana, Karna, Bhoja Kritavarma, Shalya, the king of Madra, Drona's son, Kripa, my remaining sons and the others when the soldiers fled? Tell me that. O son of Gavalgana! Tell me everything, exactly as it happened in the battle. Tell me everything about the Pandaveyas and those on my side." Sanjaya replied, "O venerable one! On hearing what

---

names of the eight Vasus vary from one text to another. According to the Mahabharata, the names are Anala (alternatively Agni), Dhara (Prithvi elsewhere), Anila (alternatively Vayu), Aha (Antariksha elsewhere), Pratyusha (Aditya elsewhere), Prabhasa (Dyaus elsewhere), Soma (alternatively Chandrama) and Dhruva. Bhishma had taken a vow to kill ten thousand warriors every day.

[18]Bhargava is Parashurama, also referred to as Rama. In Section 60 (Volume 5), there is a reference to Bhishma having been taught by Parashurama and having received weapons from him. Dhanurveda is the art of fighting.

[19]Since the text says *shaastra* (sacred texts), there may be a typo. *Shastra* (weapons) fits better.

[20]Drona's son was Ashvatthama. The use of the divine narayana weapon has been described in Section 72 (Volume 6).

transpired between the Pandaveyas and the Kouraveyas, you should not be distressed. This is destiny and your mind should not be full of grief. Sometimes, what should not happen, happens to a man. And sometimes, what should happen, does not. Therefore, learned ones do not grieve over that which has not been obtained, or what has been obtained." Dhritarashtra said, "O Sanjaya! On hearing this, my mind is not distressed. I think this is because of what destiny has ordained earlier. Tell me what you wish to."'

Chapter 1152(2)

'Sanjaya said, "When Drona, the great archer, was killed, your maharatha sons became pale in their faces. They grieved and were bereft of their senses. O lord of the earth! All of them held weapons in their hands, but were silent. They were oppressed by grief and did not look at each other, or speak to each other. O descendant of the Bharata lineage! On seeing that they were so distressed, your soldiers were also miserable and glanced upwards, extremely terrified. O Indra among kings! The weapons of those who remained were smeared in blood. On seeing that Drona had been brought down, these dropped from their hands. O descendant of the Bharata lineage! O great king! But some[21] still hung down from their hands and were seen to be like stars in the firmament. O great king! They were stationed there, dispirited and bereft of enterprise. On seeing his own army in that state, King Duryodhana spoke these words. 'I am fighting on the basis of the valour in your arms. Depending on this, I have challenged the Pandaveyas to this battle. With Drona having been killed in the battle, I discern that you are distressed. All the warriors who are fighting in the battle are being killed. When fighting in a battle, there may be victory, or there may be death. What is strange about this? Face all the directions

[21]Weapons.

and fight. Behold the great-souled warrior Karna Vaikartana in the battle. The immensely strong and great archer is roaming around, possessing divine weapons. Dhananjaya, Kunti's son, is frightened of fighting with him. He always retreats before that wrathful one, like small animals before a lion. The immensely strong Bhimasena possesses the strength of ten thousand elephants. But in a human battle, he was reduced to a miserable state.[22] The brave Ghatotkacha knew the use of maya. Using the divine weapon, the invincible spear, in the battle, he killed him and roared loudly.[23] The intelligent one's valour is difficult to cross. He is unwavering in his aim. You will witness the inexhaustible strength in his arms in the battle today. You will behold both the great-souled Radheya and Drona's son act against the Pandu and Panchala soldiers. All of you are brave, wise and born in noble lineages. You will witness each other's good conduct and skill in the use of weapons today.' O great king! When the king had spoken in this way, the immensely strong Vaikartana Karna roared like a lion. As all of them looked on, he fought with the Srinjayas, Panchalas, Kekayas and Videhas and caused great destruction, releasing hundreds of showers of arrows from his bow. They seemed to be linked head to tail, like a flock of bees. The spirited one afflicted the Panchalas and Pandavas. He killed thousands of warriors and was brought down by Arjuna."'

Chapter 1153(3)

Vaishampayana said, 'O great king! On hearing this, Dhritarashtra, Ambika's son, was seen to be overcome by

[22]Karna subdued Bhimasena without resorting to divine weapons. This has been described in Section 69 (Volume 6).

[23]This has been described in Section 70 (Volume 6). Karna killed Ghatotkacha with the invincible spear.

great grief. He thought that Suyodhana had already been killed. He lost his senses and fell down on the ground, like an elephant that had lost its consciousness. That supreme among kings was senseless and fell down on the ground. O supreme among the Bharata lineage! A great lamentation arose among the women. That sound filled the earth, everywhere. The Bharata women were immersed in a great and terrible ocean of grief. O bull among the Bharata lineage! Gandhari approached the king. All those from the inner quarters[24] lost their senses and fell down on the ground. O king! At this, Sanjaya comforted those distressed ones. Miserable, copious quantities of tears flowed from their eyes. He repeatedly assured the trembling women. In every direction, they were like plantain trees that had been whirled by a storm. Vidura sprinkled the Kourava king, the lord who had wisdom for his sight,[25] with water and comforted him. O king! He slowly regained his senses and saw the ladies. O lord of the earth! The king seemed to be mad and stood there, silently. He reflected for a long time and sighed repeatedly. He censured his sons in many ways and applauded the Pandavas. He censured his own intelligence and that of Shakuni Soubala. He thought for a long time and trembled repeatedly. The king then used his mind to restrain himself. Resorting to patience, he asked Sanjaya, the suta who was the son of Gavalgana. "O Sanjaya! I have heard the words that you have spoken to me. O suta! Has my son, Duryodhana, already gone to Yama's abode? O Sanjaya! Tell me everything accurately, even if you have told it to me earlier." O Janamejaya! Having been thus addressed by the king, the suta replied, "O king! The great archer, Vaikartana, was killed, with his maharatha sons and brothers and so were the sons of other sutas.[26] In the battle, Duhshasana was killed by the illustrious and angry Pandava Bhimasena, who drank his blood."'

[24]The women.

[25]Dhritarashtra was blind.

[26]Karna was brought up by a charioteer named Adhiratha and is known as the son of a suta.

Chapter 1154(4)

Vaishampayana said, 'O great king! On hearing these words, Dhritarashtra, Ambika's son, became anxious. His senses were overcome with grief. He spoke to the suta, Sanjaya. "O son![27] All this is the result of my evil policy. My mind and my soul are overcome. On hearing that Vaikartana has been killed, the sorrow is tearing out my inner organs. He was skilled in the use of supreme weapons. This is like a stake and I wish to cross the ocean of grief. Among the Kurus and the Srinjayas, who are the ones who remain alive and who are dead?"

'Sanjaya replied, "O king! Shantanu's son[28] was brought down. He was unassailable and powerful. He killed ten thousand Pandava warriors for each of ten days. The great archer, Drona, was invincible. The one with the golden chariot roamed around amidst the Panchala rathas and killed warriors. Thereafter, he was slain. Having slain half the soldiers[29] who remained after the slaughter by the great-souled Bhishma and Drona, Vaikartana Karna was killed. O great king! The immensely strong, Prince Vivimshati, killed hundreds of warriors from the Anarta region. He was then killed in the battle. Remembering the duty of kshatriyas, your brave son, Vikarna, stood stationed, facing the enemy, though he was without mounts and without weapons. Bhimasena remembered the diverse and extremely terrible hardships caused by Duryodhana and his own pledge and brought him down.[30] Having performed extremely difficult deeds, the immensely strong princes from Avanti, Vinda and Anuvinda, went to Vaivasvata's abode.[31] O king! The immensely

[27]The word used is *tata*. Though this means son, it is affectionately used towards anyone who is younger or junior.

[28]Bhishma. There is a great deal of inconsistency in the names that follow.

[29]On the Pandava side.

[30]Bhima pledged to kill Duryodhana and all his brothers. However, so far, there has been no mention of Vivimshati having been killed. In describing the deaths of Duryodhana's brothers, there is lack of consistency in the text. Vikarna was killed in Section 69 (Volume 6), though he is mentioned again in Section 70 (Volume 6).

[31]Vinda and Anuvinda were killed by Arjuna in Section 69 (Volume 6). Vaivasvata is Yama.

valorous Jayadratha was the foremost among those from the Sindhu kingdom. The brave one controlled ten kingdoms and he was always obedient to your instructions. Having vanquished eleven *akshouhini*s with his sharp arrows, Arjuna killed him.[32] Duryodhana's son was spirited and invincible in battle. He followed his father's instructions and was brought down by Subhadra's son.[33] Duhshasana's son was brave and possessed strength of arms. He prided himself in battle and was dispatched to Yama's abode by Droupadi's sons.[34] Bhagadatta was the lord of the *kiratas*[35] and those who dwelt along the shores of the ocean. He had dharma in his soul and was the revered and beloved friend of the king of the gods. That lord of the earth was always devoted to the dharma of kshatriyas. Through Dhananjaya's valour, he went to Yama's abode.[36] O king! The immensely illustrious and brave Bhurishrava, son of the Kourava Somadatta, was killed by Satyaki in the battle.[37] Shrutayu from Ambashtha was a foremost archer among the kshatriyas. He fearlessly roamed around in the battle and was killed by Savyasachi.[38] O great king! Your son, Duhshasana, was skilled in the use of weapons and was invincible in battle. He was brought down by Bhimasena.[39] O king!

[32]Jayadratha was Dhritarashtra's son-in-law and was killed by Arjuna in Section 69 (Volume 6). The Sindhus, Souviras and Shibis seemed to be more like a confederation of assorted kingdoms. Hence, the reference to ten kingdoms. An akshouhini is a large army and consists of 21,870 chariots, 21,870 elephants, 65,610 horses and 109,350 soldiers on foot. Since the entire Kourava army consisted of eleven akshouhinis and since the war is not yet over, this only means that Arjuna defeated them, not killed them.

[33]Subhadra's son is Abhimanyu. He killed Duryodhana's son, Lakshmana, in Section 67 (Volume 6).

[34]So far, there is no information about Duhshasana's son having been killed by Droupadi's sons.

[35]Hunters.

[36]Bhagadatta was Indra's friend. He was killed by Arjuna in Section 66 (Volume 5).

[37]Bhurishrava was killed by Satyaki in Section 69 (Volume 6).

[38]Arjuna killed Shrutayu from Ambashtha in Section 69 (Volume 6). Savyasachi was Arjuna's name.

[39]However, Duhshasana has not yet been killed.

Sudakshina possessed many thousands of wonderful armies of elephants. Savyasachi slew him in the battle.[40] The lord of Kosala killed many hundreds of the enemy and through the valour of Subhadra's son, was sent to Yama's abode.[41] Having fought with many warriors and Bhimasena, Chitrasena, your maharatha son, was brought down by Bhimasena.[42] The handsome and brave son of the king of Madra increased the terror of his enemies. He wielded a sword and a shield and was brought down by Subhadra's son.[43] The immensely energetic Vrishasena was Karna's equal in battle. He was swift in the use of weapons and did not deviate from his aim. Dhananjaya remembered Abhimanyu's death and the pledge that he had made and while Karna looked on, used his valour to send him to Yama's abode.[44] Shrutayu, lord of the earth, was firm in his enmity towards the Pandavas. Reminding him of that enmity, Partha brought him down.[45] O venerable one! O king! Rukmaratha, Shalya's son, was brave. He was the son of Sahadeva's maternal uncle, but was nevertheless killed by his brother in the battle.[46] The aged King Bhagiratha and Brihatkshatra of Kekaya were brave and powerful, but despite their supreme valour, they were killed.[47] O king! Bhagadatta's son was immensely strong and wise. He was brought down by Nakula, who roamed in the battle like a hawk. Your grandfather Bahlika, with all the others from Bahlika,

[40]Sudakshina of Kamboja was killed by Arjuna in Section 69 (Volume 6).

[41]Abhimanyu killed Brihadbala, the king of Kosala, in Section 67 (Volume 6).

[42]Chitrasena was killed by Bhima in Section 69 (Volume 6).

[43]Shalya was the king of Madra and his son was Rukmaratha. Rukmaratha was killed by Abhimanyu in Section 67 (Volume 6).

[44]Vrishasena was Karna's son. However, he has not yet been killed.

[45]This Shrutayu (distinct from the Shrutayu from Ambashtha) was killed by Arjuna in Section 69 (Volume 6).

[46]Since Rukmaratha was killed by Abhimanyu, there is an inconsistency. Shalya was Madri's brother and Sahadeva's maternal uncle. Thus, Rukmaratha and Sahadeva were brothers.

[47]Brihatkshatra was killed by Drona in Section 69 (Volume 6). We do not know about Bhagiratha.

[48]Bahlika was Pratipa's son and was killed by Bhima in Section 70 (Volume 6). Pratipa had three sons, Devapi, Bahlika and Shantanu. Shantanu was

was sent to Yama's abode through Bhimasena's valour.[48] O king! Jayatsena was Jarasandha's immensely strong son. That descendant of Magadha was slain by Subhadra's great-souled son in the battle.[49] O king! Your sons, Durmukha and maharatha Duhsaha, prided themselves on their valour. Bhimasena killed them with his club.[50] Having performed excellent deeds, maharatha Durmarshana, Durvishaha and Durjaya went to Yama's eternal abode. The suta Vrishavarma was your adviser and was extremely valorous. Because of Bhimasena's valour, he went to Yama's abode. The king possessed the strength of ten thousand elephants and had a large army of ten thousand elephants. With his followers, he was killed by Pandu's son, Savyasachi.[51] O great king! There were two thousand Vasatis, skilled in striking and the brave Shurasenas. All these warriors were killed. The Abhishahas were armoured. They could strike and were mad with insolence. They were slain, together with the best of rathas from among the Shibis and the Kalingas. There were those who were reared in Gokula. They were extremely well versed in fighting. Many thousands of them arrayed themselves as masses of samshaptakas. All of them approached Partha and went to Vaivasvata's eternal abode.[52] O great king! The kings Vrishaka and Achala were your brothers-in-law and those brave ones fought in your cause. They were killed by Savyasachi.[53] O great king! King Shalva was famous because of his terrible deeds and his acts as a great archer. He was brought down by Bhimasena.[54] O great king! Together with

---

Dhritarashtra's grandfather and so, by extension, was Bahlika. However, that Bahlika would have been too old to take part in the battle.

[49]We do not know anything about Jayatsena having been killed. In Section 67 (Volume 6), Abhimanyu killed Ashvaketu from Magadha.

[50]Durmukha and Durjaya were killed by Bhima in Section 69 (Volume 6). There is no information yet about the deaths of Duhsaha, Durmarshana and Durvishaha.

[51]The name of this king is not indicated.

[52]Arjuna killed the samshaptakas in Section 66 (Volume 5).

[53]Vrishaka and Achala were Shakuni's brothers and were killed by Arjuna in Section 66 (Volume 5).

[54]If this is Shala (not Shalva), he was killed by Satyaki in Section 70 (Volume 6).

Brihanta, Oghavan was valiant in the battle, for the sake of their friends. They have gone to Vaivasvata's eternal world.[55] O lord of the earth! In that fashion, Kshemadhurti was the best among rathas. O king! In the battle, he was killed through Bhimasena's club.[56] King Jalasandha was immensely strong and a great archer. He performed extremely great deeds in the battle and was killed by Satyaki.[57] Alayudha, Indra among the *rakshasa*s, possessed charming asses as his mounts. Through Ghatotkacha's valour, he went to Yama's abode.[58] The ones descended from Radheya,[59] the son of the suta, and all his maharatha brothers and all the Kekayas were killed by Savyasachi. The Malavas, Madraka and Dravidas were terrible in their valour. O venerable one! There were the Mavellakas, the Tundikeras, the Savitriputrakas, the Anchalas, those from the east, north, west and the south. Large numbers of infantry and tens of thousands of horses were slain. When the horses and best of elephants were killed, chariots wandered around. There were those who were reared in noble lineages and made the best of efforts at the right time. They had standards, weapons, every kind of garment and ornament and were brave. O king! Partha, never exhausted in his deeds, killed them in the battle. There were others who were infinitely strong, wishing to kill each other.[60] In the battle, there were many other kings, with their followers. O king! They were killed in thousands. I will now tell you what you have asked me. Such was the carnage when Karna and Arjuna clashed against each other. It was like the great Indra against Vritra,[61] or Rama against Ravana. It was like Mura being brought down and slain by Krishna in a battle, or the brave Kartavirya, indomitable in battle, being killed by Bhargava Rama in an encounter, together with his kin and relatives, after an extremely great and terrible fight that is famous in the three

[55]So far, we have no information about these deaths.

[56]Section 69 (Volume 6) says that Kshemadhurti was killed by Brihatkshatra.

[57]Section 69 (Volume 6).

[58]Section 70 (Volume 6).

[59]Radheya is Karna's name.

[60]This is left implicit. They were killed in the battle.

[61]Vritra was a demon killed by Indra.

worlds.[62] O king! In that fashion, in a duel, Karna, supreme among strikers and indomitable in battle, was killed by Arjuna, together with his advisers and relatives. He was the main cause behind the enmity and he was the one on whom the sons of Dhritarashtra depended for their victory. O king! The Pandavas have accomplished what they could not have contemplated earlier. O great king! However, your relatives who were your well-wishers had told you about this. That is the reason this great catastrophe has arisen now. O king! Your sons desired the kingdom and you concurred with their wishes. Ill action was practised and the fruits of that have arrived."

'Dhritarashtra said, "O son![63] You have so far recounted the names of those on my side who have been killed by the Pandavas.[64] O Sanjaya! Tell me about the Pandaveyas who have been killed by those on my side."

'Sanjaya replied, "The sons of Kunti were valiant in the battle. They possessed great spirits and immense strength. Bhishma brought down their warriors, with their relatives and their advisers. In a battle, Satyajit possessed valour and strength that was Kiriti's equal. He was unwavering in his aim and he was killed by Drona in the encounter.[65] Virata and Drupada were aged and fought valiantly, for the sake of their friends. With their sons, those kings were killed in the battle by Drona. Though a child, he was revered in battle and the lord was as unassailable as Savyasachi, Keshava or Baladeva. He was skilled in fighting and performed great deeds. Though he was alone, he was surrounded by six enemies who were rathas. They were incapable of withstanding Bibhatsu, but brought down Abhimanyu.[66] Though he

[62]Mura was the general of the demon Narakasura and was killed by Krishna. Hence, Krishna is known as Murari, or Mura's enemy. Bhargava Rama is Parashurama and he killed Kartavirya Arjuna.

[63]The word used is tata.

[64]Since Brihatkshatra (killed by Drona) has been mentioned, this is not entirely correct.

[65]Drona killed Satyajit in Section 66 (Volume 5). Kiriti is Arjuna's name. Drupada and Virata were killed by Drona in Section 71 (Volume 6).

[66]Abhimanyu was killed in Section 67 (Volume 6). Though he was surrounded by seven great warriors, he killed one of them (Brihadbala) before he was slain.

was deprived of his chariot, the brave one remained established in the dharma of kshatriyas. O great king! Subhadra's son was killed by Duhshasana's son in the battle. Brihanta, the great archer, was skilled in the use of weapons and indomitable in battle. Through Duhshasana's valour, he went to Yama's abode. The kings Maniman and Dandadhara were unassailable in battle and fought valiantly for the sake of their friends. They were brought down by Drona. King Anshuman of Bhoja was a maharatha. Because of the valour of Bharadvaja's son, with his soldiers, he went to Yama's abode. Chitrayudha was wonderful in fighting and performed great deeds. He exhibited his valour in wonderful modes and was killed by Karna in the battle. The Kekaya warriors were firm in fighting and were Vrikodara's equals. Brother brought down brother and they were slain through the valour of the Kekayas.[67] Janamejaya fought with a club. That powerful one hailed from the mountainous regions. O great king! He was brought down by your son, Durmukha. The Rochamanas[68] were tigers among men and were like blazing planets. O king! Drona shot arrows into the sky and killed them simultaneously. O lord of the earth! There were kings who fought back valiantly. They performed extremely great deeds and went to Vaivasvata's eternal abode. Purujit Kuntibhoja was Savyasachi's maternal uncle.[69] In the battle, he won many worlds for himself and was killed by Drona's arrows. Abhibhu, the king of Kashi, was surrounded by many from Kashi. Vasudana's son made him give up his body in the battle. The valiant Yudhamanyu and Uttamouja were infinitely energetic. In the battle, those brave ones killed hundreds and were then themselves slain. O venerable one! Kshatradharma and Kshatravarma from Panchala were supreme archers. Drona made them go to Yama's abode. O king! O descendant of the Bharata lineage! Kshatradeva, Shikhandi's son, was chief among warriors and

[67]The Kekayas were divided in the war. While most fought on the side of the Kouravas, five Kekaya brothers fought on the side of the Pandavas.

[68]The dual is used, so there were two Rochamanas.

[69]Purujit Kuntibhoja is the same individual. Kuntibhoja was Kunti's father and Kuntibhoja's son was Purujit. Purujit Kuntibhoja means Purujit, the son of Kuntibhoja. Purujit was thus Arjuna's maternal uncle.

was killed in the battle by your grandson, Lakshmana.[70] Suchitra and Chitradharma were father and son and were maharathas. They roamed around with great valour and were killed by Drona in the battle. O great king! O great king! Vardhakshemi performed great deeds in the battle. O great king! He was brought down by the Kourava Bahlika. O great king! Dhrishtaketu was a foremost ratha among the Chedis. Having performed great deeds, he went to Vaivasvata's eternal abode. O father![71] In that fashion, Satyadhriti performed great deeds. He fought valiantly for the sake of the Pandavas and went to Yama's abode. Suketu, lord of the earth, was Shishupala's son. The warrior killed many enemies in the battle and was then slain by Drona. The brave Satyadhriti,[72] the valiant Madirashva and the valorous Suryadatta were killed by Drona's arrows. O great king! Shrenimana fought valiantly and having performed great deeds, went to Vaivasvata's eternal abode. O king! Magadha,[73] the destroyer of enemy heroes, fought valiantly and powerfully and was killed in the battle by Bhishma. Vasudana performed extremely great deeds in the battle. Because of the valour of Bharadvaja's son, he went to Yama's abode. There were many other maharathas on the side of the Pandavas. They were slain through Drona's valour. This is what you had asked me."

'Dhritarashtra said, "O supreme among eloquent ones! The foremost of soldiers on my side have been killed. O suta! I think the remnants will also be destroyed. What is the point of remaining alive? You have told me about the names of the ones who have been killed. I think that the ones who are still alive will also ascend to heaven. That is my view."

'Sanjaya replied, "O king! Drona's son is still alive. He is a brave maharatha who is skilled and swift in the use of his arms. He is firm in wielding weapons and his fists are also firm. He is valiant and spirited. Drona, supreme among brahmanas, gave him many

[70]Lakshmana was Duryodhana's son.

[71]The word used is tata. Though this means father, it is affectionately used towards anyone who is senior.

[72]Satyadhriti is mentioned again.

[73]This means Sahadeva, Jarasandha's son.

valuable weapons that are wonderful, sparkling and of four different types.[74] This includes divine weapons. He is still stationed, desiring to fight for your sake. Bhoja Kritavarma is skilled in the use of weapons. He resides in the Anarta region and is the son of Hridika.[75] He is a maharatha and is foremost among the Satvatas. He is still stationed, desiring to fight for your sake. O king! Sharadvata Goutama[76] is immensely strong and can fight in many wonderful ways. He possesses a wonderful bow that is capable of withstanding a great burden. He has grasped it and is stationed, desiring to fight. Artayani[77] does not tremble in the battle and is the first among the soldiers who are on your side. He has abandoned the Pandaveyas, who are the sons of his sister. The spirited one wishes to make his pledge come true, that he will sap the energy of the son of the suta in the battle. This is the promise that he made to Ajatashatru earlier. Shalya is unassailable and is Shakra's equal in valour. He is stationed, desiring to fight for your sake. The king of Gandhara[78] is united with his own army, which comes from Sindhu, Kamboja, Vanayu, Bahlika and other mountainous and unnamed regions. He is stationed, desiring to fight for your sake. O Indra among kings! Your son Kurumitra is also stationed. He is foremost among the Kurus and is on his chariot, with a blazing complexion that is like that of the sun or the fire. He is as dazzling and resplendent as the sun. Duryodhana is immensely valiant and is with the best of soldiers. He is in the

[74]Weapons are of five types—*mukta* (those that are released from the hand, like a *chakra*), *amukta* (those that are never released, like a sword), *muktamukta* (those that can be released or not released, like a spear), *yantramukta* (those that are released from an implement, like an arrow) and *mantramukta* (magical weapons unleashed with incantations). If one leaves out mantramukta or divine weapons, there are four kinds of weapons.

[75]Anarta was the kingdom of the Yadavas in the northern part of Gujarat. Kritavarma was a Yadava and Satvata is a term for the Yadavas.

[76]Kripa, Sharadvata's son and descended from the Goutama lineage.

[77]Shalya. Shalya's sister was Madri. Ajatashatru is Yudhishthira's name and Shakra is Indra's name. In Section 49 (Volume 4), Shalya sided with the Kouravas, but promised Yudhishthira that he would sap Karna's energy in the battle.

[78]Shakuni.

midst of an army of elephants. His chariot is decorated with gold and he is stationed in the battle, desiring to fight. In the midst of the kings, Chitravarma is blazing in gold.[79] He is brave among men and is resplendent. His complexion is like that of a lotus, or a flame that is without smoke. He is shining, like the sun emerging from clouds. Your sons, the brave Satyasena and Sushena, have swords and shields in their hands. They are cheerfully stationed in the battle, together with Chitrasena, and wish to fight. The princes of the Bharata lineage, Chitrayudha, Shrutakarma, Jaya, Shala, Satyavrata and Duhshala are modest. However, they are powerful and are stationed, wishing to fight. The lord of Kaitavya is proud of his valour.[80] From one battle to another, that prince kills his enemies. He is advancing with infantry, horses, elephants and chariots. He is stationed in the battle, desiring to fight for your sake. The brave Shrutayu and Shrutayudha[81] and the valiant Chitrangada and Chitravarma, foremost among men, are stationed. They are proud strikers, who are unwavering in their aim. Karna's son, the great-souled Satyasena, is stationed in the battle, wishing to fight. O Indra among kings! Karna has two other supreme sons who are dexterous in the use of their hands. They are stationed. They desire to fight for your sake and are at the heads of two large armies that are impatient. O king! These and others are the foremost warriors. They are infinite in their power. For the sake of victory, the king of the Kurus is stationed in the midst of an army of elephants, like the great Indra."

'Dhritarashtra said, "You have accurately described to me those who are still alive, on our side and that of the enemy. From this, I can understand what is obvious, about which side will triumph."'

[79]The names that follow are the names of Duryodhana's brothers. However, there is often a problem with these names, because of lack of consistency. For example, Chitrasena has been killed in Section 69 (Volume 6).

[80]There is no kingdom named Kaitavya. This is probably an adjective, drawing on *kaitava*, which means gambling and deceit. This is usually associated with Shakuni, but Shakuni has already been mentioned. This is thus a probable reference to Uluka, Shakuni's son.

[81]However, these two have already been killed in Section 69 (Volume 6).

Vaishampayana said, 'Dhritarashtra, Ambika's son, realized that the foremost among the warriors on his side had been killed and that only a little bit of his army remained. Having heard this and having spoken thus, he was overcome by confusion and sorrow and his senses were benumbed. He became unconscious for a while and then said, "O Sanjaya! Wait. O son! Having heard this extremely unpleasant news, my mind is anxious." The lord of the earth lost his senses and fell down.'

Chapter 1155(5)

Janamejaya asked, 'O foremost among brahmanas! On hearing that Karna had been killed in that battle and that his sons had run away, how was that Indra among kings assured and what did he say? Because of the great disaster that confronted his sons, he suffered from supreme grief. What did he say at that time? I am asking you. Tell me.'

Vaishampayana replied, 'He heard of Karna's death, which was unbelievable and extraordinary. It was so terrible that it paralysed all beings, as if Mount Meru had moved. It was as if the senses of the immensely wise Bhargava[82] had got confused, or that Indra, the performer of terrible deeds, had been defeated and shattered by his enemies. It was as if the immensely radiant sun had fallen down from the sky onto the earth, or the unthinkable drying up of the waters from the ocean. It was as extraordinary as the earth, the sky and all the directions being destroyed. It was as if both good and evil deeds had become fruitless. Dhritarashtra, the lord of men, used his intelligence to skilfully think about this. With Karna killed, he thought that his side had been destroyed and came around to the view that all the other beings would similarly be destroyed. He was

[82]This Bhargava means Shukra, the preceptor of the demons and the fount of wisdom. Shukra was the son of the sage Bhrigu.

scorched by the flames of sorrow and his heart could find no solace. His soul was shattered and he sighed in distress. He was extremely miserable and lamented. O great king! Dhritarashtra, Ambika's son, lamented in woe.

'Dhritarashtra said, "O Sanjaya! Adhiratha's son was brave. He was like a lion or an elephant in his valour. His shoulders were like that of a bull. His eyes, gait and voice were like those of a bull. He was a bull and like a bull. He was young and was capable of withstanding the *vajra*. He did not retreat from a battle, even if the adversary were to be the great Indra. Because of his bowstring twanging against his palms and because of the shower of his arrows, chariots, horses, men and elephants could not stand before him in a battle. He was mighty-armed and without decay. He was the slayer of large numbers of the enemy. Depending on him, Duryodhana ventured to provoke an enmity with the immensely strong sons of Pandu. How could Karna, best of rathas, have been brought down by Partha in the battle? He was capable of withstanding valour that is impossible to counter. How could that tiger among men have been killed? Depending on the strength of his own arms, he never showed any reverence towards Achyuta,[83] Dhananjaya or the Vrishnis. 'The wielders of the Sharnga and Gandiva bows[84] are undefeated. When they are together, on their divine chariot, I will alone bring them down in the battle.' He always spoke these words to the wicked and evil Duryodhana, who was afflicted by desire for the kingdom and was confused because of his greed for what was undesirable. He is the one who defeated powerful enemies who were extremely difficult to vanquish—the Gandharas, the Madrakas, the Matsyas, the Trigartas, the Tanganas, the Shakas, the Panchalas, the Videhas, the Kunindas, the Kashis, the Kosalas, the Suhmas, the Angas, the Pundras, the Nishadas, the Vangas, the Kichakas, the Vatsas, the Kalingas, the Taralas, the Ashmakas and the Rishikas. In earlier times, using his strength, the brave one defeated all of these in battles. Just as Uchchaihshrava[85] is supreme among

[83]The one without decay, Krishna's name.

[84]Krishna and Arjuna respectively.

[85]The name of Indra's horse, which arose from the churning of the ocean.

horses, Vaishravana[86] is supreme among *yakshas*[87] and the great Indra is supreme among gods, Karna was supreme among those who could strike. Having obtained and pacified him through riches and honours, the king of Magadha wished to fight with all the kshatriyas on earth, with the exception of the Kouravas and the Yadavas.[88] On hearing of Karna's death in the duel with Savyasachi, I am immersed in an ocean of grief. It is as if I am on an ocean without a boat. I think that my heart cannot be shattered and must be harder than the vajra. I have heard about the defeat of my kin, matrimonial allies and friends. O suta! Other than an unfortunate one like me, which other man in the world would not have given up his life? I wish for poison, or fire. I desire to fall down from the summit of a mountain. O Sanjaya! I am incapable of bearing this misery and hardship."

'Sanjaya replied, "O king! In prosperity, lineage, fame, austerities and learning, the virtuous ones regard you to be the equal of Yayati, Nahusha's son. You are like a maharshi in your learning and are accomplished in your deeds. Find solace inside your own self. Do not give way to this sorrow in your mind."

'Dhritarashtra said, "I think that destiny is supreme. Shame on manliness, it is futile. Karna was the equal of Rama[89] and has been killed in this battle. He killed Yudhishthira's soldiers and the Panchalas who roamed around in their chariots. With his showers of arrows, the maharatha scorched all the directions. In the battle, he confounded the Parthas, like the wielder of the vajra against the asuras. How can he have been killed? How can he lie down, like a tree that has been shattered by the storm? I do not see an end to my sorrows and seem to be in an endless ocean. My anxiety is increasing. It is terrible. The desire to die is increasing. I have heard about Karna's death and Phalguna's[90] victory. But I do not think that Karna's death is believable. It is certain that my heart has the essence of the vajra. It

[86]Kubera.

[87]Yakshas are semi-divine species and companions of Kubera, the god of treasure.

[88]This is the story of an alliance between Jarasandha and Karna that does not figure in the Critical edition.

[89]Parashurama.

[90]Phalguna is Arjuna's name.

is extremely firm. On hearing about the death of Karna, tiger among men, it has not been shattered. It is certain that, from earlier times, destiny has ordained an extremely long life for me. I am extremely miserable. But despite hearing about Karna's death, I am still alive. O Sanjaya! I am without well-wishers now and shame on this life. O Sanjaya! I have been reduced to this reprehensible state today. I am wicked in my understanding. Everyone will grieve over my miserable state. Earlier, I used to be honoured by the entire world. O suta! Having been defeated, how can I bear to remain alive? O Sanjaya! I have faced hardships and have moved from pain to greater pain. There was Bhishma's death and then that of the great-souled Drona. With the son of the suta having been killed in the battle, I do not see any remnants left. O Sanjaya! It was he who would have enabled my sons to tide over this great enmity. The brave one released many arrows and has been slain in the battle. When that bull among men has been killed, what is the point of my remaining alive? There is no doubt that the *atiratha*[91] was afflicted by arrows and fell down from his chariot. It was like the summit of a mountain, shattered by the vajra. There is no doubt that he is lying down, adorning the earth, blood flowing from his wounds. He is like a crazy elephant, brought down by another elephant. He was the strength of the sons of Dhritarashtra and fear for the Pandavas. Karna was revered by all archers and has been slain by Arjuna. The brave and great archer granted my sons freedom from fear. The brave one has been killed and is lying down, like Bala by Shakra.[92] Duryodhana's wishes are now like a lame one desiring to walk, the wishes of a poor man being satisfied, or a thirsty man without drops of water. We thought of one thing when performing our deeds, but it has turned out to be something else. Destiny is powerful and time is extremely difficult to transgress.

'"O suta! What about my son, Duhshasana? When he was killed, was he running away? Was he weak, distressed in his soul and devoid of manliness? O son! Did he display inferior conduct in the battle?

[91]An unrivalled warrior, whose valour is unlimited, greater than a maharatha.

[92]Indra (Shakra) killed a demon named Bala.

Was the brave one killed like other kshatriyas on our side have been slain? Yudhishthira's words have always been against war. They were like diet and medicine, but the foolish Duryodhana did not accept them. Bhishma was lying down on a bed of arrows and desired a drink. The extremely great-souled Partha pierced the surface of the earth. O son! On seeing the fountain of water that was created by the Pandava, the mighty-armed one spoke about peace with the Pandavas. 'Be pacified. Let there be peace and let the hostilities of the war end. With fraternal feelings, enjoy the earth with the sons of Pandu.'[93] My son did not act in accordance with those words and is no doubt sorrowing now. What the far-sighted one stated in his words has now transpired. O Sanjaya! My advisers have been killed and my sons have been slain. I have been reduced to this state because of the gambling match, like a bird without wings. O Sanjaya! Boys cheerfully grasp birds in sport and having severed their wings, let them go. But because their wings have been severed, they cannot fly away. I have been reduced to that state, like a bird without wings. I am destitute and weak in every way. I am without relatives and kin. I am miserable and have come under the subjugation of my enemies. Which direction will I turn to? For the sake of Duryodhana's prosperity, the lord[94] conquered the earth. He was valorous, but has been vanquished by the capable and brave Pandavas. When the great archer, Karna, was killed in the battle by Kiriti, which brave ones surrounded him? O Sanjaya! Tell me that. When he was slain by Pandava in the battle, I hope he was not abandoned and alone. O brave one! Earlier, you have told me how the valiant ones were brought down. Bhishma, supreme among wielders of all weapons, did not fight back and was brought down in the battle by Shikhandi's supreme arrows. Similarly, Drona, the great archer, cast aside his weapons in the battle and immersed himself in yoga. O Sanjaya! He was already pierced with many arrows and Dhrishtadyumna, Drupada's son, raised his sword and slew him. Both of them were

[93]This incident has been described towards the end of Section 64 (Volume 5). Bhishma addressed Duryodhana.

[94]Karna.

killed through a weakness, especially through deceit. That is what I have heard about the way Bhishma and Drona were brought down. Even the wielder of the vajra himself would not have been able to kill Bhishma and Drona in a battle, provided the fight took place through fair means. I tell you this truthfully.

'"Karna must have unleashed many divine weapons. The brave one was Indra's equal. How could death have touched him in the battle? He possessed a divine spear that was as radiant as lightning. It was decorated with gold and was capable of killing the enemy. Purandara gave him that in exchange for the earrings.[95] Among the arrows in his quiver, there was a divine arrow, decorated with gold. It was lying there and was smeared with sandalwood paste. It had a serpent in its mouth and the slayer of enemies did not use it.[96] The brave one ignored maharathas like Bhishma and Drona and learnt the extremely terrible *brahmastra* from Jamadagni's son.[97] When the mighty-armed one saw that Drona and the others were afflicted by the arrows released by Subhadra's son, he used his arrows to sever his[98] bow. Bhimasena possessed the strength of ten thousand elephants and the speed of the wind. But the one without decay deprived him of his chariot and laughed at his brother.[99] He conquered Sahadeva with straight-tufted arrows. But having deprived him of his chariot, he took compassion on him and knowing about dharma, did not kill him.[100] Ghatotkacha, Indra among the rakshasas, used a thousand different kinds of maya and was crazy in the battle. But he destroyed all those and killed him with the spear that he had obtained from Shakra. For all these days, Dhananjaya has been frightened of fighting

[95]That spear could kill only one person and was used to kill Ghatotkacha, in Section 70 (Volume 6).

[96]This jumps the gun. In Section 19 (Volume 2), in the course of burning down the Khandava forest, Arjuna destroyed the serpents. Ashvasena, a serpent who escaped, vowed vengeance on Arjuna and became an arrow in Karna's quiver.

[97]Parashurama.

[98]Abhimanyu's.

[99]Since Karna was Kunti's son, Bhima was his brother.

[100]Karna had given word to Kunti that barring Arjuna, he would not kill any of the other Pandavas.

a duel with him. The brave one was like an elephant. How could he have been killed in the battle? His chariot must have been shattered. His bow must have been fragmented. His weapons must have been exhausted. Otherwise, how could he have been killed by the enemy? When Karna brandished his gigantic bow, who was capable of standing against him in the battle? In the battle, he released terrible arrows and divine weapons. Who could defeat that tiger among men? He was like a tiger in his force. It is certain that his bow must have been shattered. His chariot must have got stuck in the ground. Else, his weapons must have got exhausted, since you have told me that he has been killed. Without these being destroyed, I can see no other reason for his death. 'Until I have killed Arjuna, I will not wash my feet.' This is the extremely terrible vow that the great-souled one took. In the forest, Dharmaraja Yudhishthira was always terrified of him. The bull among men could not sleep for thirteen years.[101]

'"When my son forcibly brought the wife of the Pandus to the assembly hall, he depended on the valour and bravery of the great-souled one. While the Pandavas looked on, in the midst of that assembly hall, in the assembly of the Kurus, he[102] had spoken to Panchali. 'You are the wife of slaves. You think that arrows released from Gandiva have the touch of the fire. O Krishna! They are no longer your husbands.' He said this while Partha looked on. O Sanjaya! Depending on the strength of his own arms, not for a single moment was he frightened of the Parthas, their sons, or of Janardana. O son! I do not think that he could have been killed even by the gods, with Vasava,[103] even if they had angrily rushed against him, not to speak of the Pandavas. When he touched the bowstring with his finger-guards, which man was capable of standing before Adhiratha's son?[104] It is possible for the earth to be deprived of the blazing rays of the sun or the moon. However, that Indra among men did not retreat from a battle and his death is impossible. The wicked

[101]The period of exile.

[102]Karna. Panchali is Droupadi or Krishnaa.

[103]Vasava is Indra's name.

[104]Karna was reared by a suta named Adhiratha.

one, evil in his intelligence,[105] obtained him as an aide and with his brother, Duhshasana, rejected Vasudeva's desirable proposal.[106]

'"On seeing that Karna, with the shoulders of a bull, has been brought down and on seeing that Duhshasana has been killed, I think that my son must be grieving. On hearing that Vaikartana has been killed in a duel with Savyasachi and on witnessing the victory of the Pandavas, what did Duryodhana say? He heard that Durmarshana and Vrishasena[107] had been killed in the battle. He saw the army was shattered and was being slaughtered by the maharathas. The kings were unwilling to fight and were running away. On seeing that the rathas were routed, I think that my son must be grieving. He is extremely insolent and wrathful because of his childish intelligence. On seeing that the army had lost its enterprise, what did Duryodhana say? On seeing that Bhimasena had killed his brother in the battle and had drunk his blood, what did Duryodhana say? With the king of Gandhara,[108] he had proclaimed in the assembly hall, 'Karna will kill Arjuna in the encounter.' On seeing him slain, what did he say? Earlier, having deceived the Pandavas in the gambling match, Shakuni Soubala had rejoiced. O son! On seeing Karna killed, what did he say? On seeing that Karna had been slain, what did the great archer, Hardikya Kritavarma, the maharatha of the Satvata lineage, say? Drona's son is intelligent. Brahmanas, kshatriyas and vaishyas worship him, for the sake of learning about *dhanurveda*. He is young, handsome, qualified, beautiful and immensely illustrious. O Sanjaya! On learning that Karna had been killed, what did Ashvatthama say? O son! Sharadvata Kripa is the preceptor in dhanurveda and possesses supreme knowledge.[109] When Karna was killed, what did he say? Shalya, the great archer and the king of Madra, is the adornment of any assembly. It is destiny that he did everything so

[105]Meaning Duryodhana.

[106]For peace, described in Section 54 (Volume 4).

[107]Karna's son.

[108]Shakuni.

[109]Before Drona arrived, Kripa taught the Kouravas and the Pandavas the art of fighting.

that Karna might be brought down. There were kings of the earth who had come to fight. O Sanjaya! On seeing that Vaikartana had been killed, what did they say? O Sanjaya! At the time when the brave Karna, tiger among rathas and bull among men, was killed, who were the leaders of the main divisions of the army? O Sanjaya! How did Shalya, supreme among rathas and king of Madra, come to be engaged as Vaikartana's charioteer. Tell me about that. In the battle, who protected the right wheel of the son of the suta? Who protected the left wheel? Who protected the brave one from the rear? Which were the brave ones who did not abandon Karna and who were the inferior ones who ran away? When all those on our side were united, how was maharatha Karna killed? How did the brave ones among the Pandavas advance against the maharatha, creating a shower of arrows, like clouds showering down rain? There was a great and divine arrow, with a serpent at the mouth. O Sanjaya! How was it rendered unsuccessful? Tell me that. O Sanjaya! When the best of soldiers on our side have been killed, I do not see any refuge for the dispirited ones who are left. Those two brave and great archers were supreme among those on the Kuru side. On hearing of the death of Bhishma and Drona, what is the point of my remaining alive? I cannot tolerate the thought of Radheya, the ornament of a battle, being slain. The strength of his arms was equal to that of ten thousand elephants. O Sanjaya! When Drona was killed, tell me everything that took place between those brave ones among men, between the Kouravas and the enemy and how the Kounteyas prepared themselves for fighting with Karna. In the battle, how was the one without decay killed by his foes and how did he find peace?"'

Chapter 1156(6)

'Sanjaya said, "O descendant of the Bharata lineage! O great king! When Drona, the great archer was killed on that day, and the resolution of Drona's maharatha son countered,[110] the Kourava forces were driven away there. Together with his brothers, Partha[111] arranged the soldiers on their side into a *vyuha*.[112] O bull among the Bharata lineage! On discerning that he was stationed in that fashion and on seeing that his own forces were running away, your son[113] used his manliness to restrain them. O descendant of the Bharata lineage! Having stationed his own troops, he used the strength of his arms to fight with the Pandaveyas for a long time. The enemy had attained its objective and was cheerful, after having struggled for a very long time. However, since it was evening, the armies withdrew. The soldiers were withdrawn and entered their own respective camps. Having done this, the Kurus consulted with each other. They were on expensive beds, with supreme cushions and supreme beds. They were on supreme seats and comfortably lying down, were like the immortals. King Duryodhana spoke to them in conciliatory and supremely restrained tones. He addressed those great archers in words that were appropriate to the occasion. 'O best among intelligent ones! All of you, quickly tell me what your counsel is. O kings! What should be done now? What is the supreme task?' Having been thus addressed by that Indra among men, those lions among men, who were seated on their thrones, used different kinds of signs to indicate that they wished to fight. They were ready to offer their lives as oblations into the sacrifice of war. The king's face was also as radiant as the rising sun. On seeing this, the preceptor's son, who was intelligent and eloquent in words, spoke these words. 'Passion, engagement, skill and policy—these are the means to accomplish objectives. That is what the learned ones have said. However, everything depends on destiny. We had foremost among men, maharathas, on our side. They were the equals of the

[110]In Section 72 (Volume 6), Ashvatthama used the divine narayana *astra*, which was countered through Krishna's advice.

[111]Probably meaning Arjuna.

[112]A vyuha is an arrangement of troops in battle formation and there were different types of vyuhas.

[113]Duryodhana.

gods. They had good policy and were devoted, skilled and faithful. But they have been killed. However, despite this, we should not lose hope about our victory. If we use good policies, destiny will become favourable in accomplishing all our objectives. Among all these foremost men, we should make Karna the overall commander. He is endowed with all the qualities. We will then crush our enemy.' On hearing these pleasant words, Duryodhana was delighted. He thought that these auspicious and beneficial words were full of affection towards him.

'"O great king! Reassuring his mind because of the strength of his arms,[114] King Duryodhana spoke these words to Radheya. 'O Karna! I know your valour and that you are my supreme well-wisher. O mighty-armed one! But nevertheless, I will address some beneficial words towards you. O brave one! Having heard them, do what pleases you. You have always been the wisest. You are my supreme refuge. Bhishma and Drona, both atirathas, were my commanders and they have been killed. You are superior to them. Become my commander. Those great archers were aged and were partial towards Dhananjaya. O Radheya! I revered those brave ones because of your words. O son![115] In the great battle, for ten days, you saw that Bhishma, the grandfather, protected the sons of Pandu. Having laid his weapons aside in the great battle, Bhishma, the grandfather, was killed by Phalguna, who placed Shikhandi at the forefront. That immensely fortunate one was brought down and is lying down on a bed of arrows. O tiger among men! It was because of your words that Drona was placed in our forefront.[116] But because they were his students, he also protected the Parthas in the battle. Then, the aged one was swiftly killed by Dhrishtadyumna. Thinking about it, I do not see any other warrior who is your equal, because of your infinite valour, even if I include those two foremost ones who have been killed. There is no doubt that you will be able to ensure victory. You know everything about what has happened, earlier, in

[114]Meaning Duryodhana's, not Karna's.

[115]The word used is tata.

[116]That is, Drona was made the commander.

the middle, and later. You should be our leader in this battle. You should be the leader in this enterprise. Consecrate your own self in all these soldiers, like Skanda, the undecaying lord, is the general of the gods. Like that, become the protector of the soldiers of the sons of Dhritarashtra. Slay all the large numbers of the enemy, like the great Indra against the *danava*s. Knowing that you are stationed in the battle, the maharatha Pandavas, together with the Panchalas, will run away, like the danavas on seeing Vishnu. O tiger among men! Therefore, become the leader of this large army. When you station yourself and make endeavours, the Pandavas, with their advisers, the Panchalas and the Srinjayas, will be bereft of their senses. You will be like a rising sun that scorches with its energy and dispels the terrible darkness. Like that, you will drive away our enemy.' Karna replied, 'O son of Gandhari! In your presence, I have spoken these words before. O king! I will defeat the Pandavas, with their sons and with Janardana. There is no doubt that I will be your commander. O great king! Be assured. Know that I will defeat the Pandavas.' Having been thus addressed, the immensely energetic King Duryodhana arose, together with the kings, like the gods with Shatakratu.[117]

'"He instated Karna as the commander, like the immortals did to Skanda. Desirous of victory, King Duryodhana and the other kings swiftly sprinkled water, according to the prescribed rites.[118] Golden and earthen pots were filled and mantras pronounced over them. The tusks of elephants and the horns of large bulls were filled with water. There were others[119] that were decorated with gems and jewels and with fragrant perfumes and herbs. He seated himself on a seat made out of the fig tree,[120] covered with a piece of silk. He was consecrated, in accordance with the rites in the sacred texts. 'In the great battle, may you defeat Partha and Govinda, together with their followers.' O bull among the Bharata lineage! These were the benedictions pronounced by bards and brahmanas. 'Be like the rising

[117]The performer of one hundred sacrifices, Indra's name.

[118]The sprinkling of water is part of the act of consecration.

[119]Clearly, other vessels.

[120]*Udumbara*, the sacred fig tree.

sun, the destroyer of darkness through its fierce rays. May they, together with Keshava, not be able to look at your arrows. May those ungrateful ones look on them as the blazing rays of the sun. May the Parthas and the Panchalas not be able to stand before you. In a battle, you possess the knowledge of weapons and will be like the great Indra against the danavas.' Thus was the infinitely radiant Radheya consecrated. In his resplendent form, he looked like another sun. Radheya was instated as the commander by your son and goaded by destiny, he thought that his task had been accomplished. O king! Having become the commander, Karna, the destroyer of enemies, instructed that the soldiers should be yoked and should wait for the sun to rise. O descendant of the Bharata lineage! Surrounded by your sons, Karna looked dazzling there. He was like Skanda surrounded by the gods, in the *tarakamaya* battle."'[121]

Chapter 1157(7)

'Dhritarashtra asked, "O Sanjaya! Vaikartana Karna obtained the generalship and was addressed by the king himself,[122] in those gentle and fraternal words. He instructed the soldiers to be yoked and for the sun to rise. O immensely wise one! What did he do next? Tell me that."

'Sanjaya replied, "O bull among the Bharata lineage! Having ascertained Karna's views, your son instructed that the soldiers should be yoked and that musical instruments should be sounded. O venerable one! When that long night was over, a great sound of 'Array, yoke,' suddenly arose. In the army, elephants and chariots were prepared. O lord of the earth! Infantry and cavalry were readied. The spirited warriors shouted at each other. There was a large and tumultuous noise that seemed to touch heaven. Karna, the great archer

[121]The tarakamaya battle was a famous and ancient battle fought between the gods and the demons.

[122]Duryodhana.

and supreme among rathas, was seen stationed on his chariot. His flags were white and his steeds possessed the complexion of the rising sun. His bow had a golden back and his standard bore the mark of an elephant's housing. The army had quivers full of arrows and armlets. They wielded *shataghnis*,[123] bells, lances, spears, clubs and bows. In his chariot and flags, the son of the suta was seen, sparkling like a clear sun. O father![124] He blew on his conch shell, which was decorated in nets of gold. He stretched his giant bow, which was embellished with gold. O venerable one! On seeing Karna, the great archer and supreme among rathas, stationed on his chariot, like a rising sun that drives away thousands of clumps of darkness, the Kouravas, tigers among men, no longer thought about Bhishma and Drona's death. O venerable one! Urging the warriors with sounds from his conch shell, Karna made the Kourava army march out. Wishing to defeat the Pandava, Karna, the great archer and scorcher of enemies, arranged a vyuha in the form of a *makara*.[125] O king! Karna stationed himself at the makara's mouth. The brave Shakuni and maharatha Uluka were at the eyes. Drona's son was at the head. In the midst of his brothers and surrounded by a large army, King Duryodhana was at the neck. O Indra among kings! Kritavarma stationed himself along the left leg, with the narayana and *gopala* forces who were indomitable in battle.[126] O king! Goutama, for whom truth was valour, was at the right leg, surrounded by great archers from the Trigarta and southern regions. Shalya was stationed at the rear left leg, with a large army that had been raised from the Madra region. O great king! Sushena, unwavering in his resolution, was on the right, surrounded by a thousand chariots and a hundred tuskers.[127] The brave brothers and

[123]Unidentified weapon that could kill one hundred people at one go.

[124]The word used is tata.

[125]Mythical animal that can be translated as crocodile or shark.

[126]Gopalas are cowherds. The narayana and gopala soldiers were offered by Krishna to Duryodhana.

[127]This means on the rear right leg. Sushena was one of Duryodhana's brothers. However, he has already been killed by Bhima in Section 69 (Volume 6) and this is also true of Chitrasena. Therefore, Chitrasena and Chitra mentioned here were probably not Duryodhana's brothers.

kings, Chitrasena and Chitra, were at the tail, surrounded by a large army. O Indra among kings! Thus did the supreme among the best of men emerge.

'"On seeing this, Dharmaraja glanced towards Dhananjaya and said, 'O Partha! In the battle, behold the large army of the sons of Dhritarashtra. They have been arrayed by Karna and are protected by brave maharathas. The remnants of the large army of the sons of Dhritarashtra are bereft of brave ones. O mighty-armed one! It is my view that the remnants are feeble and like grass. There is only one great archer who is stationed there and that is the son of the suta. That supreme among rathas cannot be vanquished by the gods, the *asuras*, the *gandharvas*, the *kinnaras*, the giant serpents and all the mobile and immobile creatures in the three worlds. O mighty-armed one! O Phalguna! If you kill him today, you will be victorious. The stake that has been in my heart for twelve years will be uprooted. O mighty-armed one! Knowing this, construct the vyuha that you desire.' On hearing his brother's words, the Pandava with the white horses arranged the soldiers in a counter-vyuha that was in the shape of a half-moon. O king! Bhimasena stationed himself on the left flank and the immensely strong and great archer, Dhrishtadyumna, was on the right. Pandava himself was at the centre of the vyuha, with Krishna as his charioteer. With Dharmaraja, Nakula and Sahadeva were at the rear. Protected by Kiriti, Yudhamanyu and Uttamouja from Panchala protected Arjuna's wheels and did not desert him in the battle. O descendant of the Bharata lineage! The remaining brave kings armoured and stationed themselves in the vyuha, according to each one's position, enterprise and spirit. O descendant of the Bharata lineage! Thus did the Pandavas arrange themselves into a great vyuha.

'"The great archers on your side made up their minds to fight. On seeing the army in the battle, arranged into a vyuha by the son of the suta, your son and all the others on our side thought that the Pandavas had already been killed. O lord of men! In similar fashion, on seeing the Pandava soldiers arranged into a vyuha, Yudhishthira thought that the sons of Dhritarashtra and Karna had already been killed. Conch shells, kettledrums, drums, cymbals and other musical instruments were loudly sounded and the noise spread in every direction. O king! There was a loud noise in both the armies. Desiring victory, the brave ones roared like lions. There were sounds of the neighing of horses and the trumpeting of elephants. O lord of men! There were fierce sounds from the wheels of chariots. O bull among the Bharata lineage! On seeing the great archer, Karna, stationed at the front of the vyuha, no one[128] thought of Drona's loss. On both sides, the soldiers were full of great spirits and the men and elephants were cheerful. O king! Wishing to kill each other quickly, they remained stationed in the battle. O Indra among kings! Karna and Pandava were resplendent in the midst of their soldiers and were extremely angry on seeing each other stationed thus. As they advanced towards each other, the two armies seemed to be dancing around. Wishing to fight, they emerged from the flanks and smaller segments. O great king! A battle commenced between men, elephants, horses and chariots and they firmly wished to kill each other."'

Chapter 1158(8)

'Sanjaya said, "Those two armies clashed against each other, with cheerful horses, men and elephants. That great encounter was like that between the armies of gods and asuras. In that great battle, elephants, chariots, horses and infantry struck at each other, mangling bodies and destroying lives. The heads of men who were like lions were strewn around on the ground and the faces of those lions among men who were killed were like full moon, the sun, or lotuses in splendour. The heads of the warriors were severed with broad-headed and razor-sharp arrows in the shape of the half-moon, swords, lances and battleaxes. They possessed thick and long arms and these were severed by others with thick and long arms. Those thick arms were severed and fell down, with weapons and armlets still on the hands.

[128]Among the Kouravas.

With those red fingers and palms, the earth looked resplendent. It was as if five-headed serpents had been fiercely killed by Garuda. Horses, chariots, elephants and brave warriors were destroyed by the enemy and fell down. It was as if residents of heaven had been dislodged from their celestial vehicles,[129] after their sacred merits had been exhausted. In that battle, hundreds of brave and braver ones were uprooted through thick and heavy clubs, maces and bludgeons. Rathas were killed by rathas and mad elephants by other mad elephants. As they clashed in that supreme encounter, horses were brought down by horses. Rathas were destroyed by supreme rathas, elephants by horse riders and foot soldiers. Horse riders and foot soldiers were killed and lay down on that field of battle. Chariots, horses, foot soldiers and elephants were destroyed by chariots, elephants, horses and foot soldiers. Chariots, foot soldiers, elephants and horses were destroyed by men, horses, chariots and elephants. Chariots, horses and men fought against men, horses and chariots and caused a great carnage, fighting with hands, feet, weapons and chariots.

'"While those brave soldiers were being slaughtered and killed, the Parthas, with Vrikodara at the forefront, advanced against us. They were with Dhrishtadyumna, Shikhandi, Droupadi's sons, the Prabhadrakas, Satyaki, Chekitana and the Dravida soldiers. They were surrounded by a large army from the Pandyas, the Cholas and the Keralas. They were broad in the chest and long in the arms. They were tall and handsome. They were ornamented and possessed red teeth. They were like crazy elephants in their valour. They were adorned in garments of many colours and were smeared with fragrant scents. They had girded swords and nooses in their hands. They were capable of countering elephants. O king! Prepared to die, they were stationed against each other in that army. There were quivers and bows in their hands and their hair was long. They were pleasant in speech. The foot soldiers from Andhra were terrible in form and valiant and were led by Satyaki. There were other brave ones from Chedi, Panchala, Kekaya, Karusha, Kosala, Kashi and Magadha and they dashed forward. There were many

[129] *Vimanas*.

kinds of chariots, elephants, supreme horses and infantry amidst them and they could be seen to be dancing and laughing. Surrounded by supreme ones from the enemy, Vrikodara was in the midst of that large army. He was seated astride an elephant. That supreme among elephants was fierce and having been properly prepared, looked dazzling. It was like a palace atop Mount Udaya, illuminated at the peak by the rising sun.[130] His[131] supreme armour was made out of iron and he was adorned with the best of gems. He sparkled like the autumn sky, studded with stars. There was a fierce spear in his hand and it was beautifully adorned at the tip. Like the midday sun in autumn, he began to burn up the enemy.

'"Seeing that elephant from a distance, Kshemadhurti arrived, seated on another elephant.[132] He was cheerful and attacked and challenged someone who was more cheerful than he was. There was a clash between those two elephants, both of which were fierce in form. They clashed as they wished, like two mountains with trees at the top. Astride the clashing elephants, those two brave ones struck each other with their spears. The powerful ones were as dazzling as the rays of the sun and striking each other, roared. They then retreated and circled on their elephants. Both of them picked up bows and struck each other. They slapped their arms and in every direction, there was the sound of arrows. As they roared like lions, they delighted all the men. Those immensely strong lords were on elephants that raised up their trunks. As they fought, the flags whirled around in the wind. Having severed each other's bows, they roared. They showered down lances and spears, like clouds pouring down rain during the monsoon. Kshemadhurti used great force to strike Bhima between the breasts with a spear and striking him again with another six, roared. Because of those spears, Bhimasena was resplendent in

[130]Mount Udaya is believed to be the mountain from behind which, the sun rises. The sun is believed to set behind Mount Asta. The mountain is being compared to the elephant and the palace to Bhima.

[131]Bhima's.

[132]Kshemadhurti has already been killed. But this is a different Kshemadhurti, the king of Kuluta.

the field of battle. In that encounter, his body blazed with anger, like seven suns seven times.[133] Bhima carefully hurled a spear towards his enemy. It was made out of iron and possessed the complexion of the sun. It flew straight. The lord of Kuluta affixed ten arrows to his bow and shattered the spear. He then pierced Pandava with sixty more. Pandava picked up a bow that roared like a giant cloud and afflicting his enemy's elephants with his arrows, roared. Having been afflicted by the arrows of Bhimasena in the battle, the elephant did not remain there any longer, though one tried to restrain it. It was like a cloud dispelled by the wind. Bhimasena's elephant, the king of elephants, pursued it, like a cloud driven by a strong wind follows a cloud blown away by the wind. Having endeavoured to restrain his elephant, Kshemadhurti attacked Bhimasena and his elephant and pierced them with arrows. The bull among men used a razor-sharp arrow that was released well to sever his enemy's bow and oppressed his enemy's elephant. As if striking Bhima with a rod, Kshemadhurti used iron arrows to pierce the elephant everywhere in its inner organs. Before the elephant could fall down, Bhimasena descended and stationed himself on the ground. He struck down the enemy's elephant with a club. When that elephant was brought down, Kshemadhurti advanced with an upraised weapon. But Vrikodara killed him with his club. He was killed, with the sword in his hand, and having been brought down, lay down next to the elephant. He was like a lion killed by the vajra, alongside a mountain shattered by the vajra. O bull among the Bharata lineage! On seeing that the illustrious king of Kuluta had been killed, your soldiers were distressed and fled."'

Chapter 1159(9)

'Sanjaya said, "In the battle, the great archer, Karna, killed the Pandava soldiers with his straight-tufted arrows. O king! In

[133]This shloka is not very clear and is difficult to translate. But one can guess the meaning. The sun has seven horses, hence the seven suns. And Bhima has been struck by seven spears.

that fashion, in Karna's presence, the maharatha Pandavas angrily killed your son's soldiers. O king! The mighty-armed Karna killed the Pandava soldiers with iron arrows that had been polished by artisans and were like the rays of the sun. O descendant of the Bharata lineage! The elephants were afflicted by Karna's iron arrows. They roared loudly and were weakened. They lost their senses and fled in the ten directions. O venerable one! While the army was thus being slaughtered by the son of the suta, Nakula swiftly attacked the son of the suta in that great battle. Bhimasena advanced against Drona's son, who was performing extremely difficult deeds. Satyaki countered Vinda and Anuvinda from Kekaya.[134] Chitrasena, lord of the earth, advanced against Shrutakarma.[135] With a colourful standard and a colourful bow, Chitra advanced against Prativindhya. Duryodhana attacked King Yudhishthira, Dharma's son. Dhananjaya angrily attacked the large numbers of samshaptakas. When the brave ones were being killed, Dhrishtadyumna rushed against Kripa. Shikhandi attacked the undecaying Kritavarma. Shrutakirti [136]attacked Shalya. O great king! Madri's son, the powerful Sahadeva, attacked your son, Duhshasana.

'"In the encounter with Satyaki, the Kekayas showered down radiant arrows. O descendant of the Bharata lineage! Satyaki also enveloped the two from Kekaya. In the great battle, those two brothers severely struck the brave one in the chest and it was like two elephants striking another elephant with their tusks. With their armour pierced by arrows, the brothers were resplendent in the battle. O king! But they pierced Satyaki, who was truthful in his deeds, with arrows. O great king! O descendant of the Bharata lineage! However, Satyaki countered them and laughed. He shrouded them in every direction with a shower of arrows. Having been repulsed by the shower of

[134]Not to be confused with Vinda and Anuvinda from Avanti. Those two were killed by Arjuna in Section 69 (Volume 6).

[135]Prativindhya was Droupadi's son through Yudhishthira, Sutasoma through Bhima, Shrutakarma (or Shrutakirti) through Arjuna, Shatanika through Nakula and Shrutasena through Sahadeva.

[136]This should probably read Shrutasena.

arrows released by Shini's descendant, they quickly enveloped the chariot of Shini's descendant with arrows. In that great battle, Shouri severed their colourful bows.[137] In that encounter, he repulsed them with sharp arrows that were difficult to withstand. They then grasped other bows and giant arrows in their fists and roaming around with skill and dexterity, covered Satyaki. They shot giant arrows that were tufted with the feathers of herons and peacocks and were decorated. They were embellished with gold and illuminated all the directions. O king! Because of the arrows released, there was darkness in the great battle there. Those maharathas severed each other's bows. O great king! Satvata, indomitable in battle, became enraged. In that encounter, he picked up and strung another bow. With an extremely sharp *kshurapra* arrow, he severed Anuvinda's head. O king! That large head, with earrings, fell down on the ground, like Shambara's head when he was killed in the great battle.[138] On seeing that he swiftly fell down on the ground, all the Kekayas grieved. On seeing that his brave brother had been killed, the maharatha[139] strung another bow and countered Shini's descendant. He pierced Satyaki with gold-tufted spears that had been sharpened on stone.[140] The maharatha from Kekaya roared loudly and powerfully and asking Satyaki to wait, struck him in the arms and in the chest with arrows that were like the flames of fires. The wise and spirited Satvata was wounded in all his limbs by these arrows. O king! He was resplendent in that battle, like a *kimshuka*[141] with leaves. Having been pierced by the great-souled Kekaya in the battle, Satyaki laughed and pierced Kekaya with twenty-five arrows. In their excellent arms, they grasped shields that were marked with the signs of one hundred moons. Wielding the best of swords, they roamed around in that great arena. It was like

[137]While Shouri is usually used for Krishna, Shouri means Shura's descendant and Shura was a common ancestor. The Yadavas are also referred to as Satvatas.

[138]There were several demons named Shambara. Since they were killed in different battles, we don't know which of the various Shambaras is meant.

[139]Vinda.

[140]The text uses the word *shakti*, which means spear. Since these were tufted and sharpened on stone, arrows are indicated instead.

[141]Tree with red blossoms.

the immensely strong Jambha and Shakra in the battle between the gods and the asuras.[142] In the great battle, they roamed around in circles and swiftly attacked each other, wishing to kill each other in the encounter. Satvata severed Kekaya's shield into two fragments and in that way, the king also shattered Satyaki's shield. Having severed the shield that was marked with the signs of hundreds of stars, Kekaya whirled around in circles, advancing and retreating. Wielding the best of swords, Shini's descendant also roamed around in that great arena and striking sideways, severed Kekaya's head. O king! Still wearing his armour, in that great battle, the great archer from Kekaya was severed into two parts and fell down, like a mountain shattered by thunder. Having killed him in the battle, Shini's brave descendant, supreme among rathas and scorcher of enemies, quickly climbed onto Yudhamanyu's chariot. He then again ascended a different chariot that had been prepared properly. Using his arrows, Satyaki began to slaughter the large army of the Kekayas. The large army of the Kekayas was slaughtered in that battle. It abandoned the enemy in the encounter and fled in the ten directions."'

Chapter 1160(10)

'Sanjaya said, "O great king! In the encounter, Shrutakarma angrily struck Chitrasena, lord of the earth, with fifty arrows that had been sharpened on stone. The king of Abhisara[143] struck Shrutakarma with nine straight-tufted arrows and pierced his charioteer with five. In the forefront of the army, Shrutakarma became enraged. He struck Chitrasena in his inner organs with extremely sharp iron arrows. Using the opportunity,[144] the immensely

[142]Jambha was a demon killed by Indra. But there was also another demon named Jambha who was killed by Krishna or Vishnu.

[143]So we now know that this was a different Chitrasena and Chitra was his brother.

[144]In non-Critical versions, there are shlokas that say that Chitrasena became unconscious.

illustrious Shrutakirti shrouded the lord of the earth with ninety arrows. Having recovered his senses, maharatha Chitrasena severed his[145] bow with a broad-headed arrow and pierced him with seven arrows. He grasped another bow that was decorated with gold and could strike hard. Piercing Chitrasena with arrows, he made him look colourful. The youthful king was adorned with colourful garlands and was made colorful by the arrows. He looked like an ornamented youth in an assembly. In that encounter, angrily asking Shrutakarma to wait, he pierced him between the breasts with iron arrows. In the battle, Shrutakarma was pierced by those iron arrows and began to shed copious quantities of blood, like a mountain exuding red minerals. His limbs were covered in blood and he was like a picture drawn in blood. O king! In that battle, he was as resplendent as a blossoming kimshuka. O king! Having been thus struck by the enemy, Shrutakarma angrily countered the foe and severed his bow into two. O best of the Bharata lineage! Having severed his bow, the immensely illustrious Shrutakarma pierced him with three hundred iron arrows. Swiftly, he severely struck him with another sharp and broad-headed arrow and severed the great-souled one's helmeted head. Chitravarma's[146] extremely large head fell down on the ground, as if the moon was wilfully dislodged from heaven and fell down on the surface of the ground. O venerable one! On seeing that the king of Abhisara had been killed, Chitrasena's soldiers attacked with force. However, Shrutakarma, the great archer, angrily used his arrows to drive away those soldiers, like the wrathful lord of the dead[147] at the time of the destruction of all beings. Having driven them away, he roamed around there.

'"Prativindhya pierced Chitra with five swift arrows and having pierced his charioteer with three, brought down his standard with a single arrow. Chitra struck him in the chest and the arms with nine broad-headed arrows that were gold-tufted, sharpened on stone and shafted with the feathers of herons and peacocks. O descendant of

[145]Shrutakarma's.

[146]The text says Chitravarma. Either Chitravarma was another name for Chitrasena, or there is a typo.

[147]Yama.

the Bharata lineage! Prativindhya used his arrows to sever his bow and then struck that ratha with five sharp arrows. O great king! He hurled a spear towards your son.[148] It possessed a golden handle and was difficult to resist. It was terrible and was like the flame of a fire. As it descended, Prativindhya severed it with his sharp arrows. It was like the vajra frightening all beings at the end of a yuga and on seeing that this spear had been destroyed, Chitra grasped a large club. It was decorated with nets of gold and he hurled it towards Prativindhya. In that great battle, it slew his horses and his charioteer. It struck his chariot with great force and crushed it down on the ground. O descendant of the Bharata lineage! At this time, he ascended another chariot and hurled a spear that was decorated with golden bells towards Chitra. O king! O descendant of the Bharata lineage! As it descended, the great-souled Chitra seized it and flung it back towards Prativindhya. In the battle, the immensely radiant spear struck the brave Prativindhya. It pierced his right arm and fell down on the surface of the earth. Having fallen down, because of its radiance, like lightning, it lit up the spot where it had fallen down. O king! Prativindhya grasped a javelin that was decorated with gold. Wishing to kill Chitra, he angrily hurled it towards him. It pierced the armour on his body and his heart. It then swiftly penetrated the ground, like a snake entering its hole. The king was struck by that javelin and was brought down, extending his large and thick arms that were like clubs. On seeing that Chitra, the ornament of a battle, was killed, all those on your side powerfully attacked Prativindhya from all directions. They released many kinds of arrows and shataghnis with bells. They quickly enveloped him, like the sun by a mass of clouds. But in that encounter, the mighty-armed one struck them with a net

[148]The text uses the word *putra* (son) and not *poutra* (grandson). In an extended sense, Prativindhya was Dhritarashtra's grandson and assuming that putra is not a typo, the word son can also be interpreted in a broad sense. This shloka is stated such that it is not clear who is doing the hurling of the spear at whom. Given the context, Chitra must have hurled the spear towards Prativindhya. But it is also possible that Chitra from Abhisara was confused with the Chitra who was Dhritarashtra's son, in which case, 'son' makes sense and Prativindhya did the hurling of the spear.

of arrows and drove away those soldiers, like the wielder of the vajra against the asuras. O king! In the battle, those on your side were slaughtered by the Pandavas. They were violently dispersed, like the clouds by the wind. The army was slaughtered and scattered in all the directions. Drona's son alone quickly attacked the immensely strong Bhimasena. A terrible and violent clash ensued between them. It was like that between Vritra and Vasava in the battle between the gods and the asuras."'

Chapter 1161(11)

'Sanjaya said, "O king! Drona's son possessed supreme speed. He displayed his dexterity with weapons and struck Bhimasena with an arrow. He then again struck him with another ninety sharp arrows in his inner organs. He was light in the use of his hands and had seen and was knowledgeable about where the weak spots were. O king! Having been struck by the sharp arrows shot by Drona's son, Bhimasena was resplendent in that battle, like the sun with its rays. Pandava shot one thousand well-aimed arrows and enveloping Drona's son, emitted a roar like a lion. O king! In the encounter, Drona's son countered Pandava with one hundred arrows and smiling, struck him in the forehead with an iron arrow. O king! Bearing that arrow on his forehead, Pandava looked like a proud and horned rhinoceros in the forest. While Drona's son was making his efforts in the battle, the valiant Bhima also seemed to smile and struck him in the forehead with three iron arrows. With those arrows stuck to his forehead, the brahmana was resplendent. He looked like a supreme mountain with three peaks, drenched during the rains. Drona's son struck Pandava with one hundred arrows, but could not make him tremble, like the wind against a mountain. Drona's son used hundreds of other sharp arrows in the battle. However, he could not make the cheerful Pandava tremble, like the wind against a mountain.

The maharathas shrouded each other with many other showers of arrows. They were proud in the battle and roaming around on their chariots, the brave ones were resplendent. They blazed like a couple of suns that had arisen for destroying beings. Their supreme arrows were like rays and they scorched each other with these. In that great battle, they acted and counteracted each other. Without any fear, they made efforts to act and counteract. The maharathas roamed around in that battle, like tigers. The invincible arrows were like the teeth and the terrible bows were like the mouths. With nets of arrows on all sides, they became invisible. It was as if the sun or the moon in the sky was enveloped by a net of clouds. But in a short instant, those two scorchers of enemies became visible again, like the moon and the sun in the sky, freed from the net of clouds.

'"Drona's son placed Vrikodara on his right and showered down hundreds of sharp arrows, like rain pouring down on a mountain. However, Bhima was not ready to tolerate signs of his enemy being victorious. O king! Remaining on the right, Pandava began to execute circular motions, advancing and retreating. In that great battle, there was a tumultuous encounter between them. In that spot, they traversed along various circular paths. They drew their bows back to the full extent and struck each other with arrows. The maharathas made the best efforts to kill each other. In that battle, they used their arrows to try and deprive each other of their chariots. Drona's maharatha son released many great weapons and in that encounter, Pandava destroyed them with his own weapons. O great king! There was an extremely fierce battle with those weapons. It was as if there was a tremendous clash between the planets, for the sake of destroying beings. O descendant of the Bharata lineage! Those arrows were swiftly released and clashed against each other. They illuminated all the directions and the soldiers on every side. Because of the large numbers of arrows, the sky looked terrible. O king! It was as if meteors were descending to destroy beings. O descendant of the Bharata lineage! As the torrents of arrows clashed against each other, sparks of fire were generated and those blazing flames consumed both the armies. O great king! The *siddhas*[149] descended there and said, 'This encounter is superior to all other encounters. All other battles do not amount to one-sixteenth of this.[150] Such an encounter has not happened earlier, nor will it happen again. These two lords are knowledgeable and terrible in their valour. Bhima is terrible in his valour and the other one is skilled in the use of weapons. They represent the essence of valour and great is their skill. They are stationed in the battle like two Destroyers. They are like two Rudras or like two suns. In this battle, those two tigers among men have terrible forms, like two Yamas.' At that time, we repeatedly heard these words spoken by the siddhas. Among the assembled denizens of heaven, there were roars like lions, on witnessing the extraordinary and unthinkable deeds performed by them in that battle. O king! Having injured each other in that encounter, those two brave ones glanced towards each other, their eyes dilated with rage. Their eyes were red with anger. Their lips trembled in rage. They gnashed their teeth in wrath. They bit their lips in ire. The maharathas enveloped each other with showers of arrows. In that encounter, the arrows were like rain pouring from clouds. The weapons were like lightning. The maharathas pierced each other's standards and charioteers. They pierced each other's horses and struck each other. O great king! In that great encounter, they picked up two arrows and swiftly released them towards each other, wishing to kill each other. O great king! At the heads of the two armies, those two arrows blazed and struck each other, with an irresistible force that was like that of the vajra. They severely wounded each other through the force of those arrows. Those two, who were extremely valiant, sank down on the floors of their chariots. O king! While all the kshatriyas looked on, knowing that Drona's son had become unconscious, his charioteer bore him away from the field of battle. O king! In similar fashion, Pandava, the scorcher of enemies, repeatedly lost his senses and his charioteer bore him away on the chariot."'

[149]The siddhas are a semi-divine species, inhabiting the area between the sun and the earth and 88,000 in number.

[150]The text uses the word *kala*. The moon has sixteen kalas or phases and sixteen kalas constitute the whole.

Chapter 1162(12)

'Dhritarashtra said, "Describe the battle between Arjuna and the samshaptakas and also tell me about the one between the others on my side and the Pandavas."

'Sanjaya replied, "O king! Listen. I will describe the battle exactly as it happened. The brave ones fought with the enemy and this destroyed bodies and lives. Partha penetrated the mass of samshaptakas, which was like an ocean.[151] The destroyer of enemies was like a giant storm that agitated the ocean. Dhananjaya used his sharp and broad-headed arrows to slice off the heads of the brave ones. The faces were like full moons, with excellent eyes, eyebrows and teeth. He[152] quickly scattered these around on the ground, like lotuses devoid of their stalks. The faces were well formed and large and were smeared with sandalwood paste and perfumes. With weapons and armour on their bodies, they looked like five-headed serpents. In that encounter, Arjuna severed the arms of his enemies with razor-sharp arrows. With his broad-headed arrows, Pandava severed the best of charioteers, standards, bows and hands decorated with gems. O king! Arjuna shot thousands of arrows in that battle and dispatched elephants, horses and chariots, with their riders, to Yama's eternal abode. The foremost of brave ones roared like angry bulls that desired intercourse. They roared and attacked. As they were being killed, they struck him with their arrows, like bulls goring with their horns. The battle between them and him was wonderful and it made the body hair stand up. It was like one between the wielder of the vajra and the *daitya*s, for the conquest of the three worlds. With his weapons, Arjuna countered all the weapons of his enemies on every side. He swiftly pierced them with many arrows and robbed them of their lives. He shattered the poles,[153] wheels

[151]However, in Section 66 (Volume 5), Arjuna had effectively destroyed the samshaptakas.

[152]Arjuna.

[153]*Trivenu*. Literally, trivenu means something with three poles. A trivenu was a triangular piece made out of bamboo, used to provide strength to a chariot.

and axles and killed warriors, horses and charioteers. He shattered the weapons and quivers and brought down the standards. The yokes, harnesses, poles and bumpers of chariots were fragmented. The place became impassable because of the shattered yokes and the heaps of weapons. The chariots were scattered, like giant clouds by the wind. Everyone was astounded on seeing this and this, increased the terror of the enemy. Arjuna rivalled the deeds of one thousand maharathas acting together. Masses of siddhas, *devarshis*[154] and *charanas*[155] were satisfied. The drums of the gods were sounded and flowers were showered down on Keshava and Arjuna's heads. An invisible voice was heard. 'Keshava and Arjuna possess the beauty of the moon, the sun, the wind and the fire. They blaze in strength and are resplendent. Those two brave lords always dazzle. When those two brave ones are stationed on the same chariot, they are as invincible as Brahma and Ishana.[156] Those two brave lords are foremost among all beings and are Nara and Narayana.'[157] O descendant of the Bharata lineage! On witnessing this great wonder and on hearing these words, Ashvatthama controlled himself and rushed against the two Krishnas in the battle.[158]

'"He advanced against Pandava and attacked him with arrows that were like the destroyer Yama. Drona's son laughed on his chariot. In his hand, he held up an arrow and said, 'O brave one! A guest has arrived before you. If you think me to be deserving, with all your heart, grant the guest the opportunity of fighting with you.' Having been thus challenged by the preceptor's son, who wished to fight, Arjuna thought that he had been greatly honoured and spoke to Janardana. 'The samshaptakas should be killed by me, but Drona's

---

The base was towards the chariot. The other two poles were extended in the direction of the horses and were fastened to the central yoke.

[154]Divine sage.

[155]Celestial singers.

[156]Shiva.

[157]Nara and Narayana are ancient sages. Nara is identified with Arjuna and Narayana with Krishna.

[158]Krishna is also one of Arjuna's names.

son is challenging me. O great-armed one! Instruct me about which one I should do first.' Having been thus addressed, Krishna drove Partha, like Vayu taking Indra to a sacrifice, towards Drona's son, who had issued a challenge in the appropriate manner. Drona's son was single-minded in his intentions and Keshava spoke to him. 'O Ashvatthama! Be patient. Strike and bear the counter-strike. The time has come for those who live off others to repay the food they have received from their masters.[159] Brahmanas are subtle in settling disputes. Kshatriyas are coarser, resulting in victory or defeat. Because of your folly, you have asked for excellent and divine hospitality from Partha. Now be patient and receive what you have asked for from Pandava.' When Vasudeva had spoken thus, the supreme among brahmanas agreed. He pierced Keshava with sixty iron arrows and Arjuna with three. Arjuna became extremely angry at this and used three broad-headed arrows to slice down his bow. Drona's son then picked up a bow that was more terrible. He strung it in an instant and pierced Arjuna and Keshava, with three arrows for Vasudeva and one thousand for Pandava. Carefully, Drona's son shot a thousand arrows, then another one million and then ten million. He confounded Arjuna in the battle. O venerable one! He was knowledgeable about the brahman and arrows issued from his quiver, his bow, his bowstring, his fingers, his arms, his hands, his chest, his face, his nose, his eyes, his ears, his head, his limbs, his pores, his chariot and his standard. He pierced Keshava and Pandava with a great net of arrows. Drona's son roared in joy, like the rumbling of a large cloud. On hearing the roar, Pandava spoke to Achyuta.[160] 'O Madhava! Behold Drona's son's wickedness towards me. He thinks that since we have entered this chamber of arrows, we are about to be slain. But with my training and my strength, I will destroy his resolution.' The foremost among the Bharata lineage shattered each of Ashvatthama's arrows into three fragments. It was like the wind dispelling a mist.

'"Then Pandava used his fierce arrows to pierce the samshaptakas and their horses, charioteers, chariots, elephants, standards and large

[159]Since Drona and Ashvatthama obtained a livelihood from Duryodhana.

[160]The one without decay, Krishna's name.

numbers of infantry. Everyone who was a spectator there, in whatever form, thought himself to have been covered by those arrows. Arrrows of many different types were shot from Gandiva. In that battle, they killed elephants, horses and men who were within a distance of a *krosha*.[161] Broad-headed arrows severed and brought down the trunks of elephants that were mad with musth. They were sliced down, like trees in the autumn by an axe. After this, the elephants themselves, like mountains, were brought down, with their riders. It was as if the mountains were being shattered by the wielder of the vajra with his vajra. There were chariots that had been properly prepared and were like the cities of gandharvas. Well-trained and swift horses, indomitable in battle, were yoked to them. Dhananjaya showered down arrows on these enemies, ornamented horse riders, foot soldiers and horses. In that great ocean of the samshaptakas, Dhananjaya was like the sun that arises at the end of a yuga. They were difficult to dry up.[162] But with his fierce arrows that were like rays, he dried them up.

'"Drona's son was like a gigantic mountain and swiftly, he again pierced him with extremely forceful iron arrows that were as energetic as the sun, like the wielder of the vajra against a mountain. At this, the preceptor's son became wrathful and wished to fight. He advanced towards Partha, wishing to strike his horses and his charioteer with his swift arrows. But these were struck down. He[163] next released a multitude of arrows towards Ashvatthama, who was like a guest whohad arrived in a house. Abandoning the samshaptakas, Pandava attacked Drona's son, like a giver abandons the undesirable in favour of the desirable.[164] There was a clash like that between Shukra and the radiant

[161]Measure of distance equal to two miles.

[162]The image is that of an ocean.

[163]Arjuna.

[164]This translation doesn't capture the entire nuance. The words used are *pankteya* (desirable or admissible), vis-à-vis *apankteya* (undesirable or inadmissible). *Pankti* means line or row. Pankteyas are those with whom one sits down in the same row to eat. Apankteyas are those with whom one does not eat together. One will serve pankteyas first.

Angirasa.[165] It was as if Shukra and Angirasa were clashing in the sky to enter the same *nakshatra*.[166] Their flaming arrows traversed the sky and scorched each other. They terrified the worlds with those rays, like planets that had been dislodged from their positions. With an iron arrow, Arjuna severely struck Drona's son in the midst of his eyebrows and he looked as resplendent as the sun, with its rays extending upwards. The two Krishnas were also severely wounded by the hundreds of arrows shot by Ashvatthama. They looked like two suns that dazzled with their rays at the end of a yuga. Protected by Vasudeva, Arjuna released a weapon that was sharp on every side. He struck Drona's son with arrows that were like the vajra, the fire, or Vaivasvata's[167] staff. The performer of terrible deeds pierced the extremely energetic Keshava and Arjuna in the inner organs. These were arrows that were released well and were extremely fierce and forceful. Struck by these, even Death would have been pained. But Arjuna countered the arrows of Drona's son and covered him with twice that number of well-tufted arrows.

'"Having enveloped that solitary and brave one and his horses, charioteer and standard, he struck the samshaptakas again. Partha shot arrows and severed the bows, arrows, quivers, bowstrings, hands, arms, weapons held in the hands, umbrellas, standards, horses, garments, garlands, ornaments, shields, armour, wishes and all the beautiful heads of his enemies, as they were stationed there and did not retreat.[168] Those brave ones made every endeavour, stationed on well-prepared chariots, horses and elephants. But they were restrained by the large numbers of Partha's arrows and the foremost among men fell down. The heads of men were like lotuses, the sun

[165]Brihaspati is the son of the sage Angirasa and is the preceptor of the gods. Shukra is the preceptor of the demons and Brihaspati and Shukra are therefore rivals. Brihaspati is Jupiter and Shukra is Venus.

[166]One of the translations of nakshatra is constellation. It can also be translated as a star.

[167]Yama's.

[168]Samshaptakas did not retreat. The word 'wishes' needs an explanation, since, without the pun, its inclusion seems strange. Ratha is a chariot. *Manoratha* is a chariot of the mind, that is, a wish or a desire.

and the full moon. They were adorned with diadems, garlands and crowns. They were severed by broad-headed and razor-sharp arrows and arrows that were in the shape of a half-moon. They incessantly fell down on the ground. Brave ones from Kalinga, Vanga, Anga and Nishada wished to kill Pandava and rushed against him. They were astride elephants that looked like the elephant of the king of the gods. They were angry and insolent, as insolent as the enemies of the gods. Partha sliced down those elephants, their trunks and their armour and mangled their inner organs. He brought down the standards and flags, as if the one with the vajra in his hand was bringing down the peaks of mountains.

'"When they were routed, Kiriti enveloped his preceptor's son with arrows that possessed the complexion of the rising sun. It was as if a rising sun was dispelling a large net of clouds created by the wind. Countering Arjuna's arrows with his own arrows, Drona's son covered Arjuna and Vasudeva with his arrows, as if the moon and the sun were being covered in the sky by a thundering cloud at the end of the summer. Afflicted by these arrows, Arjuna directed his weapons towards those on your side and suddenly made everything dark with his arrows. He pierced all of them with his well-tufted arrows. In that encounter, no one could discern when Savyasachi picked up an arrow, affixed it and released it. One could only see that horses, elephants, foot soldiers and rathas were slain and their bodies fell down. Swiftly, Drona's son affixed ten iron arrows. He released them so quickly that they seemed to be a single arrow. They were released well and Arjuna was pierced by five and Achyuta by another five. Having been thus wounded, those two foremost of men, who were like the lord of riches[169] and Indra, began to exude blood. They were afflicted by the one who had completed his learning.[170] Some thought that they had been killed. The lord of Dasharha spoke to Arjuna. 'Why are you hesitating? Kill this warrior. If you commit the error of ignoring him, he will cause great hardship, like a disease that spreads.' Having been thus addressed by Achyuta, he was no longer

[169]Kubera.

[170]Ashvatthama.

distracted and sought to wound Drona's son with his arrows. He severed the harnesses of the horses and pierced the steeds, which then bore him[171] a long distance away. The intelligent one did not return again to fight with Partha. The one with self-control knew that the victory of the brave one from the Vrishni lineage and Dhananjaya, the best of the Angirasa lineage,[172] was certain. Reversing, Ashvatthama withdrew his horses from the field of battle, like a disease is treated through mantras, herbs and remedies and withdraws from the body. Keshava and Arjuna headed in the direction of the samshaptakas. Flags were stirred by the wind and fluttered atop their chariot, which rumbled like the clouds."'

Chapter 1163(13)

'Sanjaya said, "At this time, a loud uproar arose towards the northern side of the Pandu soldiers. The rathas, elephants, horses and foot soldiers were being slaughtered by Dandadhara. Keshava reversed the direction of the chariot, but did not stop the swift horses, which were as fast as Garuda or the wind. He told Arjuna, 'Magadha is extremely powerful and is on an elephant that can crush. He is like Bhagadatta in training and strength. Having killed him, you will then slay the samshaptakas again.' Having completed these words, he bore Partha towards Dandadhara.[173] The

[171]Ashvatthama.

[172]There is no obvious connection between Arjuna and the sage Angirasa. However, Angirasa is also described as the first man. Hence, this probably means no more than that Arjuna was the best among men.

[173]Dandadhara was a king from Magadha and he and his brother, Danda, fought on the side of the Kouravas. The Magadhas were divided in the war. Sahadeva, Jarasandha's son, fought on the side of the Pandavas. Jayatsena is also described as a son of Jarasandha. While he is usually described as having fought on the side of the Kouravas, there are also places where he is described as belonging to the Pandava side.

foremost among Magadhas was foremost in wielding the goad, just as the brilliant planet is foremost among planets.[174] He was fiercely destroying the enemy soldiers, like a brilliant planet destroying the earth.[175] His elephant was the crusher of enemy soldiers and was like an elephant of the danavas. It had been prepared well and it roared like a giant cloud. He killed thousands of rathas, horses and large numbers of elephants with his arrows. The elephant also stood on chariots and quickly crushed horses, charioteers, rathas and foot soldiers. With its front legs and its trunk, it killed elephants, like a wheel of death. Men with armour made out of steel[176] and adorned in ornaments were brought down, with their horses and foot soldiers. As those supreme ones were crushed and killed, a sound arose, like that of reeds being crushed by the wind. There were the sounds of drums, kettledrums and many conch shells at the spot, mixed with the noise of bowstrings slapping against palms. There were the roars of thousands of men, horses and elephants.

'"On his supreme chariot, Arjuna advanced against that supreme of elephants. Dandadhara struck Arjuna with twelve supreme arrows, Janardana with sixteen and each of the horses with three. He then roared and laughed. At this, Partha used broad-headed arrows to slice off his bow, with the bowstring and arrows attached, and brought down his ornamented standard. He next struck those who were protecting his feet and this enraged the lord of Girivraja.[177] His tusker's temples were shattered and it was as dark as a mass of clouds. But it was also as swift as the wind and he wished to crush Arjuna with this. He shot arrows and hurled spears at Janardana and Dhananjaya. Pandava simultaneously shot three razor-sharp

[174]The text uses the word *vikacha*, which has several meanings, including brilliant. The word also means a kind of comet. Finally, the word can mean a hairless or headless person. Using the headless angle, this part of the text has sometimes been interpreted as a reference to Ketu, who does not possess a head. In that event, this is one of the rare instances where Ketu is mentioned, Rahu having been frequently mentioned.

[175]Vikacha again.

[176]Literally, black iron, interpreted as steel.

[177]Girivraja (or Rajagriha or Rajgir) was the capital of Magadha.

arrows and severed his two arms, which were like the trunks of elephants, and his head, which had the complexion of the full moon. He then struck the elephant with one hundred arrows. Partha's arrows were decorated with gold. They struck the elephant, which was clad in golden armour. It looked like a mountain in the night, when herbs and trees burn because of a fire. Afflicted with pain, it roared like a cloud. It roamed aimlessly and then, with trembling steps, it tottered as it tried to run away. It was weakened and fell down, together with the driver. It was as if a mountain had been shattered by thunder and had fallen down.

'"When his brother was killed in the battle, Danda advanced, wishing to kill Indra's younger brother[178] and Dhananjaya. He was astride a tusker that possessed the complexion of snow and was garlanded in gold. It looked like a summit of the Himalayas.[179] He hurled three lances that were as bright as the rays of the sun towards Janardana and five towards Arjuna. Having struck them, he roared. Pandava severed his arms with extremely fierce kshurapra arrows, while they still held lances, were adorned with armlets and were smeared with sandalwood paste. They simultaneously fell down from the elephant's back and looked as beautiful as two serpents that had fallen off a mountain's peak. With an arrow that was in the shape of a half-moon, Kiriti severed Danda's head and it fell down from the elephant onto the ground. It was covered with blood and looked beautiful as it fell down, like the sun setting in the western direction. The supreme elephant possessed a white complexion and Partha pierced it with supreme arrows that blazed like the rays of the sun. It shrieked as it fell down, as if the summit of a mountain had been struck down by thunder. There were other supreme elephants that were their equals[180] and wished to obtain victory. Like those two elephants, Savyasachi carefully brought them down and that extremely large army of elephants was routed. Elephants, chariots, horses and large numbers of men dashed against each other and fell

[178]Indra's younger brother, referred to as Upendra, is Vishnu or Krishna.
[179]The elephant was white.
[180]Equal to the two elephants that had been brought down.

down in that battle. They were wounded and struck each other. They anxiously lamented and were killed. Arjuna was then surrounded by his own soldiers, like Purandara by the masses of gods. They said, 'O brave one! We were frightened of the enemy, who seemed to us to be like Death before beings. It is good fortune that you have killed him. We were immersed in terror and had you not rescued us, we would have been afflicted by the forces of the enemy. The enemy would have rejoiced. You have killed the enemy and we are now rejoicing.' Hearing these and many other conciliatory words spoken by his well-wishers, Arjuna was delighted in his mind. He then honoured the men, in accordance with what they deserved, and again headed towards the mass of samshaptakas."'

Chapter 1164(14)

'Sanjaya said, "Jishnu again returned, like the planet Angaraka[181] in its forward and retrograde motions, to kill large numbers of samshaptakas. O king! O venerable one! Men, horses, rathas and elephants were killed by Partha's arrows. They wavered, wandered around, shrieked, fell down and died. Large numbers of charioteers and chariots were flung away. There were hands, with weapons still in the hands, and arms and heads. Pandava severed them with broad-headed and razor-sharp arrows, arrows that were in the shape of a half-moon and arrows that had heads like a calf's tooth, as those enemy heroes fought against him in that battle. They fought, like a bull that desires intercourse fighting against another bull. Hundreds and thousands of brave ones descended on Arjuna. The encounter between them and him was extraordinary and it made the body hair stand up. It was as if the daityas were fighting with the wielder of the vajra for the conquest of the three worlds. Ugrayudha pierced him with three arrows that were like malignant snakes,[182] but he severed

[181]Mars.

[182]A specific type of malignant snake called *dandashuka*.

his[183] head from his body. All of them[184] became extremely angry and showered down many weapons on Arjuna, like clouds urged by the Maruts surrounding the Himalayas at the end of summer. With his own weapons, Arjuna countered all the weapons of his enemies. He used many well-directed arrows to kill all those who meant to injure him. The trivenus were shattered around their thighs. The *parshni*[185] charioteers were killed. The harnesses were torn and the poles, axles, joints and yokes of chariots were shattered. Using his arrows, Arjuna swiftly destroyed all their equipment. There were large numbers of chariots there, fragmented into pieces. They looked like the palaces of the rich, destroyed by the fire, the wind and the rain. Arrows that were like the vajra mangled the inner organs of the elephants and they fell down, resembling mansions on mountains destroyed by thunder, storm and fire. Persecuted by Arjuna, large numbers of horses and riders fell down on the ground. Their tongues lolled out. Their entrails were plucked out. They were weak. They were covered in blood. They looked terrible. Savyasachi's iron arrows struck men, horses and elephants. O venerable one! They tottered, shrieked, fell down and died. Like the great Indra against the danavas, Partha killed the inferior ones with arrows that were sharpened on stone and were like the vajra or like virulent poison. There were brave ones, with extremely expensive armour and ornaments. They possessed diverse kinds of garments and weapons. With their chariots and their standards, they were slain by Partha and forced to lie down. They were the performers of pious deeds. They were distinguished and famous. Nevertheless, they were vanquished and died. They conquered heaven because of their deeds, but their bodies lay down on the ground. The brave ones on your side attacked Arjuna's chariot. They were the leaders of many different countries and they, and

[183]Ugrayudha's.

[184]The other warriors.

[185]Parshni has different meanings. When four horses are attached to a chariot, it means one of the outside horses. It can also mean one of the two charioteers who drive the outside horses, as opposed to the main charioteer (*sarathi*), or someone who guards the axles.

their followers, were full of rage. They were on chariots and horses and the foot soldiers also desired to kill him. They quickly rushed against him, with many different kinds of weapons. Those warriors angrily showered down a large number of weapons, as if from a giant cloud. However, like the wind, Arjuna swiftly dispelled them with his sharp arrows. Using his own weapons as a bridge, Partha violently crossed that large and boatless ocean of weapons, horses, infantry, elephants and chariots.

'"Vasudeva spoke to him. 'O Partha! O unblemished one! Why are you toying with them? Crush the samshaptakas and make haste towards Karna's death.' Having been thus addressed, Arjuna swiftly struck the remaining samshaptakas. He powerfully unleashed his weapons and killed them, like Indra against the daityas. In that battle, no one could distinguish when Arjuna took out an arrow, affixed it and released it. He was that swift. As he goaded his horses, Govinda himself said that it was extraordinary. As they penetrated the soldiers, his arrows were like white and swift swans diving into a lake. The field of battle was full of the destruction of men. On seeing this, Govinda spoke to Savyasachi. 'O Partha! A great and extremely terrible destruction of the Bharatas, the earth and the kings is going on. This is because of Duryodhana's extremely evil deeds. O descendant of the Bharata lineage! Behold the bows, with golden backs, of the archers. The large armour and quivers have been dislodged. The arrows have drooping tufts and the tufts are made out of gold. The iron arrows have been washed in oil and are like snakes that have cast off their skins. The place is strewn with colourful lances and bows that are decorated in gold. The swords have handles of ivory and are embellished in gold. O descendant of the Bharata lineage! The armour and sheaths for the bows possess golden backs. The lances and spears are embellished with gold and are also decorated in gold. The giant clubs are tied in garments that are decorated with gold. The handles of the swords are made out of gold and the battleaxes are also embellished in gold. The handles of the scattered battleaxes are ornamented in gold. Lances made of iron and heavy bludgeons have fallen down.

Behold the colourful shataghnis and the large maces. There are many chakras[186] and clubs that have been scattered around in this battle. There are many kinds of weapons that were grasped by the ones who desired victory. Their bodies have been crushed by clubs and bludgeons and their heads have been smashed. Behold the thousands of elephants, horses, chariots and warriors who have been destroyed. Men, elephants and horses have been struck with arrows, lances, swords, spears, scimitars, javelins, spikes, nails and bludgeons. Their bodies have been mangled in many ways and they are covered in blood. O destroyer of enemies! They have lost their lives and are strewn around in this field of battle. Their arms are smeared with sandalwood paste and adorned with armlets and sparkling ornaments. O descendant of the Bharata lineage! The earth is resplendent with arm-guards and bracelets. The ornamented tips of the hands, with finger-guards, are scattered around.[187] The supreme heads sport gems on the headdresses and wear earrings. Those with eyes like bulls have been brought down and the earth looks dazzling. There are headless torsos covered in blood, since the heads have been severed from the bodies. O foremost among the Bharata lineage! They are scattered on the ground and it is as if the fiery flames of the fire have been pacified. Many kinds of chariots, with sparkling golden bells, have been shattered. Behold the many horses, covered in blood. The place is strewn with the white and giant conch shells of the warriors. As they lie down like mountains, the tongues of the elephants are lolling out. Sporting colourful flags of victory, warriors who fought on horses and elephants have been slain. There are excellent cushions, covers and blankets from the elephants. They are diverse and have been uprooted. So have the colourful and varied housings. Many bells have been broken, crushed by the feet of the elephants. Staffs and goads decorated with lapis lazuli have fallen down on the ground. Harnesses were decorated with gold and so were the tips of the standards that the riders

[186]If chakra has to be translated, it can only be translated as disc or discus. The chakra is Vishnu and Krishna's weapon.

[187]The hands having been severed. The heads have also been severed.

possessed. They were colourful with many kinds of gems and were polished in gold. From the horses, cushions and covers made out of the skin of *ranku* deer have fallen down on the ground. The lords among men had gems on their headdresses and golden garlands. Umbrellas are scattered around and so are fans and whisks. The faces of the kshatriyas have beautiful earrings and are as beautiful as the moon or nakshatras. The brave ones are ornamented and their beards have been clipped. Behold. Their heads are scattered around on the ground, in the mire created by blood. Behold. The men who are still alive are lamenting in every direction. O lord of the earth! There are many who are honouring you and others have been killed by your weapons. With their relatives, they are repeatedly lamenting there. Though they have been routed, there are some spirited warriors with angry faces. Driven by anger and desiring victory, they wish to advance and fight again. However, there are other proud ones who are fleeing from the spot. Their relatives have fallen down and desire water from those brave ones. O Arjuna! Some have gone in search of water and there are many who have lost their lives. It can be seen that those brave ones have lost their senses and are retreating. Having seen water, they are rushing to the spot, shouting at each other. O descendant of the Bharata lineage! Behold the ones who have expired after drinking water and the others who are drinking. Others have abandoned their beloved ones, their beloved relatives, kith and kin. In the great battle, they can be seen to be running around, here and there. O foremost among men! Behold the others. They are repeatedly gnashing their teeth and biting their lips. O Arjuna! In the great battle today, these are the deeds that you have performed. The deeds performed by you in the battle are like those of the king of the gods, or those who live in heaven.' In this way, Krishna showed Kiriti the field of battle.

'"As they were returning, they heard a loud noise from Duryodhana's army. It was mixed with the blaring of conch shells and the beating of drums and kettledrums and mingled with the fierce sound of weapons and roars of chariots, horses and elephants. Borne by horses that were as fast as the wind, Krishna penetrated that army and was surprised to see that your army was being crushed by Pandya. That foremost among warriors was using many different kinds of arrows. He was slaying the enemy, like Yama among those whose life has run out. The foremost among strikers was mangling the bodies of elephants, horses and men with his sharp arrows and was robbing them of their bodies. With many weapons and arrows, he was piercing heroes among the enemy. Pandya was killing the enemy, like Shakra against the asuras."'

Chapter 1165(15)

'Dhritarashtra said, "O Sanjaya! You have earlier spoken about that great hero, famous in the worlds. But you have not recounted his deeds in the battle. Now, in detail, recount to me that hero's valour, learning, power, bravery, expanse and pride."

'Sanjaya replied, "Drona, Bhishma, Kripa, Drona's son, Karna, Arjuna and Janardana completed their learning of archery and you think that they are the foremost among warriors. But he thinks himself to be an equal of Karna and Bhishma and does not wish to be regarded as inferior to Vasudeva and Arjuna. Such was Pandya, foremost among kings and supreme among all wielders of weapons. He was like Yama and overcame and killed Karna's soldiers. Stationed in the midst of that army of chariots, horses, foot soldiers and elephants, Pandya crushed them. He whirled them around like a potter's wheel. Pandya's arrows dispelled them, like the wind amidst a mass of clouds. The horses, charioteers, standards, rathas and warriors of the enemy were struck. Elephants were killed. Flags, standards and weapons were uprooted. The destroyer of enemies killed the elephants, together with those who guarded their feet. He killed horse riders, armed with spears, javelins and quivers. The Pulindas, Khashas, Bahlikas, Nishadas, Andhrakas, Tanganas, those from the south and the Bhojas were fierce and did not retreat from a battle. However, Pandya used his arrows to deprive them of their weapons and armour and robbed them of their lives. In that battle, Pandya used his arrows to slaughter the four divisions of the army.[188] He showed no fear. On seeing this, Drona's son fearlessly advanced towards him.

'"As he seemed to be dancing around, he,[189] best among strikers, fearlessly challenged him and spoke to him in sweet words. 'O king! O one with eyes like the petals of a lotus! You are foremost among those who are borne into a battle. You are known as someone who can withstand the vajra and you are foremost in strength and manliness. You have weapons in your hands and you are using your arms to stretch your giant bow. As you extend it with your arms, you seem to be like a large cloud. With great force, you are showering down torrents of arrows on the enemy. In this battle, with my exception, I do not see anyone who is your match in bravery. You have single-handedly crushed many chariots, elephants, foot soldiers and horses, like an extremely fierce and powerful lion kills large numbers of deer. The sky and the earth resound with the great noise of your chariot. O king! At the end of the monsoon, you are filling the earth and its crops.[190] You are taking out sharp arrows from your quiver and they are like venomous serpents. You should fight with me alone, like Andhaka fighting with Tryambaka.'[191] Having been thus addressed, he[192] agreed.

'"Asking him to strike, Drona's son struck him and Malayadhvaja struck him back with a barbed arrow. Drona's son, supreme among preceptors, smiled and struck Pandya with fierce arrows that were like the flames of fire and could penetrate the inner organs. Ashvatthama then released nine other sharp and iron arrows that were tufted with the feathers of herons and covered the ten directions. Pandya severed five of these with five sharp arrows. However, four swiftly struck his horses and robbed them of their

[188]Chariots, horses, elephants and infantry.

[189]Ashvatthama.

[190]The sense is of untimely showers destroying crops.

[191]Tryambaka, the three-eyed one, is one of Shiva's names and Shiva killed a demon named Andhaka.

[192]Pandya. Malayadhvaja was clearly his name and he was the king of Pandya. He is also described a little later as the lord of Malaya or the lord of the mountains, since Malaya is a mountain.

lives.[193] Pandya, who was as radiant as the sun, severed the bowstring of Drona's son with sharp arrows. However, Drona's son, the destroyer of enemies, fixed another string to his bow and shot thousands of arrows at Pandya. He enveloped the sky and all the directions with his torrents of arrows. Pandya, the great-souled bull among men, knew that the arrows shot by Drona's son were inexhaustible. However, he made efforts to cut down the arrows of Drona's son and then used sharp arrows to rob the ones who were protecting his chariot wheels of their lives. On seeing his dexterity, Drona's son stretched his bow into a circle and showered down arrows, like rain pouring from a cloud. O venerable one! That encounter lasted for an eighth part of a day.[194] Nevertheless, Drona's son shot as many weapons as could be carried on eight carts, drawn by eight bullocks. He was like an angry Destroyer, or like the Destroyer of the Destroyer. Almost every one who saw him there lost his senses. The preceptor's son showered down arrows like rain on the soldiers, like rain pouring on the earth, with its mountains and trees, at the end of summer. That shower of arrows released by Drona's son, who was like a cloud, was extremely difficult to withstand. Pandya swiftly countered it with a *vayavya* weapon[195] and roared like a gale. His standard was smeared with sandalwood paste and aloe and he looked like Mount Malaya. As he was roaring, Drona's son severed his standard and killed his four horses. He then killed his charioteer with another arrow. With an arrow that was in the shape of a half-moon, he severed the bow that thundered like a giant cloud and shattered the chariot into small fragments. Having countered his weapons with his own weapons and having cut down all his weapons, Drona's son found the opportunity to kill him in the battle. There was a supreme tusker that had been prepared well and its rider had been killed. As it was swiftly advancing towards him, as if against a rival, the powerful one[196] climbed onto it, roaring like a

[193]To make it clearer, Ashvatthama shot nine arrows. Five were cut down by Pandya, but the remaining four killed his horses.

[194]Three hours.

[195]Divine weapon named after Vayu, the wind god.

[196]Pandya.

lion. Stationed on it, the lord of Malaya looked like a mountain with two peaks.[197] He swiftly urged the elephant forward. He picked up a spear that was as radiant as the rays of the sun and hurled that weapon with supreme force, care and anger. The lord of the mountains hurled this towards the preceptor's son and roared. The head of Drona's son was decorated with a diadem. It was decorated with supreme gems, jewels and diamonds and adorned with excellent cloth, garlands and pearls. It was as dazzling as the sun, the moon, the planets and the fire. Being severely struck,[198] it was shattered into fragments and fell down, like a large forest when it is struck by the great Indra's vajra, or when the summit of a mountain falls down on the ground. At this, he[199] blazed with great rage, like a king of the serpents that has been struck by the foot. He picked up fourteen arrows that were capable of killing the enemy and each of these was like Yama's staff. With five, he served the feet and trunk of the elephant and with three, the king's arms and head. With six, he killed the six splendid maharathas who were following the king of Pandya. The king's arms were long and smeared with the best of sandalwood paste. They were adorned with gold, pearls, gems and diamonds. Those arms of the king fell down on the ground and writhed around like serpents that had been killed by Tarkshya.[200] His head possessed a face with the complexion of the full moon. His eyes were coppery red with rage and his nose was excellent. With its earrings, the head fell down on the ground and was as resplendent as the moon between two Vishakhas.[201] The preceptor's son was accomplished in learning and when he completed this task, your son, the king, was delighted and surrounded by his well-wishers, honoured him, like the lord of the immortals honouring Vishnu after he had vanquished Bali."'[202]

[197]He being one of the peaks and the elephant, or its head, being the other.

[198]By the spear.

[199]Ashvatthama.

[200]Tarkshya is Garuda's name.

[201]Vishakha is the sixteenth of the twenty-seven nakshatras, but is being used here as a general term for a nakshatra. That is, he was as resplendent as the moon between two nakshatras.

[202]Bali was a king of the demons who conquered the three worlds and

Chapter 1166(16)

'Dhritarashtra asked, "O Sanjaya! When Pandya was killed, what did Arjuna do in the battle, especially when the brave Karna was single-handedly driving away the enemy? Pandava is brave and accomplished in learning. He is powerful. The great-souled Shankara made all beings subservient to him.[203] That is the reason my greatest fear is from Dhananjaya, the slayer of enemies. O Sanjaya! Tell me everything that Partha did there."

'Sanjaya replied, "When Pandya was killed, Krishna quickly spoke these beneficial words to him. 'Without looking towards the king,[204] the Pandavas are retreating. To accomplish Ashvatthama's resolution, Karna is killing the Srinjayas. He is creating a great carnage there, amidst the horses, men and elephants.' The extremely unassailable Vasudeva spoke these words to Kiriti. On hearing this and on seeing that his brother was facing a great and terrible calamity, Pandava asked Hrishikesha to quickly urge the horses. Hrishikesha advanced on that chariot against those warriors.

'"O supreme among kings! Yet again, there was a terrible encounter and clash between Karna and the Pandavas and it extended Yama's kingdom. Wishing to kill each other, they swiftly grasped bows, arrows, clubs, swords, lances, spikes, maces, catapults, spears, scimitars, battleaxes, bludgeons, javelins, cutlasses, darts, slings and large hooks and descended. The whizzing of arrows and the sound of palms against bowstrings extended into the sky, the directions and the sub-directions. As they attacked, they roared and the earth resounded with the thunder of chariot wheels. Those great sounds of battle cheered them. Brave ones fought extremely terrible battles with brave ones, wishing to bring an end to the hostility. There were sounds from bowstrings, palm-guards and bows and the trumpeting of elephants. They were

dislodged Indra. In his *vamana* (dwarf) incarnation, Vishnu vanquished Bali and obtained heaven back for Indra.

[203]Shiva's boon has been described in Section 31 (Volume 2).

[204]Yudhishthira.

attacked and as they fell down, roared loudly. There were many sounds generated by the arrows and by the roars of brave ones. O descendant of the Bharata lineage! On hearing this terrible sound, some were frightened, turned pale and fell down. There were many among them who roared and showered down arrows. In the battle, Atiratha Karna crushed many of them with his arrows. With his arrows, Karna conveyed five heroes from Panchala, ten rathas and five others, with their horses, charioteers and standards, to Yama's eternal abode. Many foremost and immensely valorous warriors from the Pandus swiftly attacked Karna in that battle and surrounding him from all sides, covered the sky with their weapons. Karna agitated the enemy soldiers with his shower of arrows. He was like the leader of a herd[205] plunging into a lake full of birds and lotuses. Radheya penetrated into the midst of the enemy. He brandished his supreme bow and using his sharp arrows, began to bring down their heads. The shields and armour were shattered and the bodies were deprived of life. There was no one among them who needed the touch of a second arrow.[206] The arrows that were released from the bow crushed armour and bodies. The bowstrings and palm-guards were shattered, like horses lashed with a whip. Whenever Pandus, Srinjayas and Panchalas came within the reach of his arrows, Karna quickly struck them in the inner organs, like a lion among large numbers of deer.

'"O venerable one! The son of Panchala,[207] Droupadi's sons, the twins and Yuyudhana united and advanced against Karna. When the Kurus were severly engaged with the Pandavas and the Srinjayas, warriors advanced against each other, prepared to give up their lives in the battle. They were armoured well, with coats of mail, helmets and ornaments. The maharathas used clubs, maces and other kinds of bludgeons. They advanced fiercely, like the god wielding his staff.[208] O venerable one! They roared loudly and challenged each other. They

[205]Of elephants.

[206]That is, they were killed with the first arrow.

[207]Dhrishtadyumna.

[208]A reference to Yama.

struck each other. Struck by the others, they fell down. They vomited blood and lost their limbs, heads and eyes in the battle. Complete with teeth, but laced with blood, the faces looked like pomegranates. Though they had been brought down by weapons, they seemed to be alive. They struck each other with spears, swords, lances, catapults, nails, javelins and spikes. They were crushed and cut down by others. They also crushed and cut others down. They angrily killed and struck each other. They were brought down and killed by others. Losing their lives, they were covered with blood. They seemed to exude their own natural red juice, like sandalwood trees. Rathas were killed by rathas, elephants by elephants, men by the best of men and thousands of horses were brought down by horses. Standards, heads, umbrellas, the trunks of elephants and the arms of men were severed by razor-sharp and broad-headed arrows, arrows in the shape of a half-moon and other weapons. In that battle, men, elephants, chariots and horses were brought down. Horse riders slew brave warriors. The trunks of tuskers were severed. Flags and standards were shattered and brought down, strewn around like mountains. Foot soldiers destroyed elephants and chariots. Struck and killed, they fell down in every direction. Horse riders clashed against foot soldiers and were swiftly killed by them. In the battle, large numbers of foot soldiers were killed by horse riders and lay down. O greatly intelligent one! The faces and limbs of those who were killed looked like crushed lotuses and faded garlands. O king! The beautiful forms of elephants, horses and men looked like garments that had been sullied and therefore, became supremely hideous to see."'

Chapter 1167(17)

'Sanjaya said, "There were many excellent elephants that were urged on by your son. Wishing to kill Dhrishtadyumna, they angrily advanced against Parshata. These were among the best who fought on elephants, from the east, the south, Anga, Vanga, Pundra,

Magadha, Tamraliptaka, Mekala, Kosala, Madra, Dasharna and Nishadha. O descendant of the Bharata lineage! They were skilled in fighing with elephants and united with those from Kalinga. Arrows, spears and iron arrows showered down like rain from clouds and in that battle, all of them sprinkled Panchala, who was like a mountain. Those elephants were violently urged on against the enemy with goads and with toes prodding the flanks. As they advanced towards Parshata, he showered down iron arrows on them. O descendant of the Bharata lineage! Each of those angry elephants was like a mountain and he pierced each with ten, six or eight arrows. He was enveloped by those elephants, like clouds covering the sun. On seeing this, the Pandus and Panchalas roared. They raised sharp weapons and attacked those elephants, the arrows making music on the bowstrings. Nakula, Sahadeva, Droupadi's sons, the Prabhadrakas, Satyaki, Shikhandi and the valiant Chekitana advanced. The elephants were driven by *mlecchas*[209] and used their trunks to pick up men, horses and chariots and crush them with their feet. They pierced others with the tips of their tusks, picked them up and flung them down. Others were stuck to the tips of the tusks and looked terrible. Vanga's[210] elephant was stationed in front of him. Satyaki powerfully struck it with a fierce iron arrow. Pierced in its inner organs, it fell down. Abandoning that elephant, he[211] was about to descend from the elephant. However, Satyaki struck him on the breast with an iron arrow and made him fall down on the ground. Pundra's elephant was descending like a mobile mountain. Sahadeva carefully killed it with three iron arrows. It was deprived of its flag, its rider, its armour, its standard and its life. Having brought that elephant down, Sahadeva advanced against Anga.[212] However, Nakula asked Sahadeva to desist and himself attacked Anga. He struck him with three iron arrows that were like Yama's staff and struck the elephant with one hundred. Anga hurled eight hundred spears that were as bright as the rays of the sun.

[209]Barbarians, those who do not speak Sanskrit.

[210]The king of Vanga's.

[211]The king of Vanga.

[212]The king of Anga.

However, Nakula sliced each of these down into three fragments. Pandava then severed his head with an arrow that was in the shape of a half-moon. Having been killed, the mleccha fell down, together with the tusker. The son of their preceptor was skilled in the technique of managing elephants.[213] When he was killed, the excellent ones from Anga attacked Nakula on elephants. The best of flags fluttered and the sides[214] were decorated in gold. They looked like mountains on fire and wished to swiftly destroy the enemy. There were those from Mekala, Utkala, Kalinga, Nishadha and Tamraliptaka. Wishing to kill him, they showered down arrows and spears. They enveloped Nakula, like the sun shrouded by clouds. At this, the Pandus, the Panchalas and the Somakas were enraged. A battle commenced between those rathas and the elephants. Showers of arrows and thousands of spears were released. These shattered the temples of the elephants and penetrated their inner organs in many ways. The tusks were pierced by iron arrows and seemed to be ornamented. Sahadeva quickly killed eight giant elephants with sixty-four extremely energetic arrows and brought them down, together with their riders. Nakula, the descendant of the Kuru lineage, carefully drew his supreme bow and used many straight-flying iron arrows to kill many elephants. Shini's descendant, Panchala, Droupadi's sons, the Prabhadrakas and Shikhandi brought down many showers of arrows on the mighty elephants. The warriors on the Pandu side were like clouds full of rain and the elephants of the enemy were like mountains. Slain by those showers of arrows, they fell down, like mountains shattered by a storm of thunder. Your elephants were thus killed by the Pandus, who were like elephants among men. The soldiers[215] were soon seen like a river with shattered banks. Having thus agitated the

[213]One has to deduce what this means. The person killed was actually the prince of Anga, though referred to as the king of Anga. The king of Anga was the preceptor of all those from Anga. The Critical edition uses the expression *acharyaputra*, meaning the preceptor's son. Some non-Critical versions directly say, the son of Anga.

[214]Of the elephants.

[215]The Kourava soldiers.

soldiers,[216] the soldiers of the sons of Pandu glanced towards them and again advanced towards Karna.

'"O great king! While Sahadeva was angrily scorching your army, Duhshasana advanced against him and it was brother against brother. The kings who were there, witnessed a great battle between them and roaring like lions, waved their garments around. O descendant of the Bharata lineage! Your archer son was angry and pierced Pandu's powerful son in the chest with three arrows. O king! Sahadeva pierced your son with an iron arrow and again pierced him with seventy, striking his charioteer with three. O king! In that great battle, Duhshasana severed his bow and struck Sahadeva in the arms and the chest with seventy-three arrows. Sahadeva became wrathful and in that great encounter, grasped a sword. The foremost among warriors whirled and hurled it towards your handsome son. That great sword severed his bow, with an arrow still affixed to it. It then fell down on the ground, like a serpent that has been dislodged from the sky. The powerful Sahadeva picked up another bow and shot an arrow that was like death towards Duhshasana. That arrow was as bright as Yama's staff and descended. However, Kourava severed it into two parts with a sword that was sharp at the edges. As that sword suddenly descended in the battle, Sahadeva cut it down with sharp arrows and seemed to be laughing.[217] O descendant of the Bharata lineage! In that great battle, your son swiftly shot sixty-four arrows towards Sahadeva's chariot. O king! In that encounter, many arrows descended with force. However, Sahadeva sliced down these with five arrows each. Having countered the great arrows that were shot by your son, Madri's son released a large number of arrows. O great king! The powerful Sahadeva became angry and affixed an extremely fierce arrow that was like the Destroyer and like Death. He drew his bow back with force and shot it towards your son. O king! It penetrated his armour and his body with great force and penetrated the earth, like a snake entering a termite hill. O king!

[216]The Kourava soldiers.

[217]By excising a shloka, the Critical edition has a break in continuity here. In the missing shloka, Duhshasana hurled the sword towards Sahadeva.

Your maharatha son lost his senses. On seeing that he had lost his consciousness, his charioteer, who was frightened and himself severely wounded with sharp arrows, quickly bore him away on the chariot. O Pandu's elder brother! O king! Having defeated him in the battle, Pandava cheerfully began to crush Duryodhana's army in every direction, like an extremely angry man crushing a large number of ants. O descendant of the Bharata lineage! Thus did he wrathfully crush the Kourava soldiers.

'"O king! While Nakula was violently destroying the soldiers in the battle, Vaikartana Karna repulsed him. Nakula laughed and spoke to Karna. 'After a long time, because of the kindness of destiny, you have seen me. O wicked one! And in this battle, you have surfaced before my sight. You are the root cause of the evil, the enmity and the quarrel. It is because of your sins that those of the Kuru lineage are clashing against each other and are being destroyed. I will kill you in the battle today and become successful, devoid of fever.'[218] Having been thus addressed, the son of the suta, who was himself like a prince and also an archer, replied to Nakula. 'O child! Strike me in this battle. Let me see your manliness. O brave one! One should boast only after having performed deeds in a battle. O son![219] Those who do not speak in an encounter, but fight to the best of their strength, are known as brave. Fight with me, to the utmost of your strength and I will destroy your pride today.' Having spoken thus, the son of the suta swiftly struck Pandu's son. In that battle, he pierced him with seventy-three arrows that had been sharpened on stone. O descendant of the Bharata lineage! Having been thus pierced by the son of the suta, Nakula pierced the son of the suta back with eighty arrows that were like venomous serpents. Karna severed his bow with gold-tufted arrows that had been sharpened on stone. The supreme archer then struck Pandava with thirty arrows. Those pierced his armour and drank his blood in the battle. They were like venomous serpents that drink water after entering

[218]Mental fever.

[219]The word used is tata and it means son. But it is also used to address anyone who is younger or junior.

the earth. O great king! Nakula, the destroyer of enemy heroes, became angry at this. He picked up another bow with a back that was embellished with gold. It was extremely difficult to resist. He pierced Karna with twenty arrows and his charioteer with three. With an extremely sharp arrow that was like a razor at the tip, he severed Karna's bow. Having severed the bow, the brave one, who was regarded as a maharatha by the entire world, laughed and struck him with three hundred arrows. O venerable one! On seeing that Karna was thus afflicted by Pandu's son, all the rathas and all the gods were struck by supreme wonder. Vaikartana Karna picked up another bow and struck Nakula between the shoulder joints with five arrows. With those arrows sticking to his chest, Madri's son looked resplendent on the chariot, as if the sun was using its rays to shower radiance on the earth. O venerable one! Nakula pierced Karna with seven iron arrows and again severed the ends of his bow. In that encounter, he[220] picked up another bow that was even more powerful and enveloped Nakula and all the directions with his arrows. When the maharatha was suddenly covered with arrows released from Karna's bow, he swiftly used his own arrows to slice down those arrows. The sky was seen to be shrouded with a net of arrows and it was as if the firmament was covered with a large number of fireflies that were flitting around. Hundreds of arrows were released and covered the sky and it was as if it was full of a swarm of locusts that had been stirred up by the wind. Arrows decorated in gold descended repeatedly in an array and were as beautiful as an array of swans. When the sky was covered by the arrows, the sun was shrouded. O lord of the earth! No beings could descend and nothing could be seen.[221] In every direction, those large numbers of arrows obstructed their paths. Those two immensely fortunate ones were as resplendent as two young suns that had just arisen. The arrows released from Karna's bow slaughtered the Somakas. O Indra among kings! They were severely afflicted and pained by the

[220]Karna.

[221]That is, creatures like birds could not descend from the sky.

arrows and lost their lives. In a similar way, Nakula's arrows killed your soldiers. O king! They were driven away in all the directions, like clouds dispelled by the wind. Those two sets of soldiers were slaughtered by their large and divine arrows and withdrew from that rain of arrows, remaining only as spectators. When the men there were driven away by Karna and Pandava's arrows, those two great-souled ones started to pierce each other with their showers of arrows. In that field of battle, they displayed their divine weapons. Wishing to kill each other, they violently enveloped each other. The arrows released by Nakula were tufted with the feathers of herons and peacocks. They seemed to remain stationed there, after having enveloped Karna. O king! Both of them seemed to be in a chamber created by arrows and could not be seen. They were like the moon and the sun, enveloped during the monsoon.

'"Karna became wrathful in that battle and assumed a fiercer form. In every direction, he shrouded Pandava with showers of arrows. O king! In that encounter, Pandava was enveloped by the son of the suta. However, like the sun covered by clouds, he felt no pain. O venerable one! At this, Adhiratha's son laughed in the battle and shot hundreds and thousands of nets of arrows. The arrows of the great-souled one seemed to cover everything in a canopy of shade. Those supreme arrows were like clouds that were descending. O great king! The great-souled Karna severed his bow. He laughingly brought his charioteer down from the seat on the chariot. O descendant of the Bharata lineage! With four sharp arrows, he killed his four horses and quickly dispatched them to Yama's abode. O venerable one! Using his arrows, he swiftly shattered his chariot into tiny fragments and also destroyed his flags, the ones who protected his wheels, his standard, his sword, his shield that was decorated with the signs of one hundred moons and all his implements. O lord of the earth! His horses were slain. He was without a chariot. He was devoid of his armour. He quickly descended from his chariot and stood there, with a club. O king! That extremely terrible club was raised. However, using hundreds and thousands of arrows, the son of the suta shattered it into fragments. On seeing that he was without any weapons, Karna struck with many arrows with drooping tufts, but made sure that he did not hurt him grievously. O king! Nakula was defeated in that battle by someone who was powerful and was skilled in the use of weapons. With his senses afflicted, he suddenly fled. Radheya followed him, laughing repeatedly. O descendant of the Bharata lineage! O king! He placed the string of his bow around the neck of the one who was running away.[222] Pulled by the string of the great bow around his neck, he was as resplendent as the moon in the sky, surrounded by white clouds and decorated with Shakra's bow.[223] Karna spoke these words to him. 'The words that were spoken by you have been rendered futile. You have been repeatedly struck by me. Can you cheerfully utter them again? O Pandava! Do not fight again with those who are your superior in strength. O son! O Pandava! Fight with those who are your equals. Do not be ashamed at this. O son of Madri! Go home, or go where Krishna and Phalguna are.' O great king! Having spoken these words, he released him. O king! Though he could have been killed, the son of the suta did not kill him. O king! He remembered Kunti's words and abandoned him. O king! Having been released by the archer son of the suta, Pandava was ashamed and went towards Yudhishthira's chariot. Having been tormented by the son of the suta, he ascended that chariot and sighed, scorched by grief, like angry snakes inside a pot.

'"Having abandoned him in the battle, Karna swiftly advanced against the Panchalas. He was on a chariot with dazzling flags and drawn by horses with the complexion of the moon. O lord of the earth! When they saw the commander[224] advancing against the Panchalas on his chariot, a great uproar arose among the Pandavas. O great king! The son of the suta caused carnage there. As the sun reached its midday spot, the lord roamed and wheeled around. The

[222]Karna gave word to Kunti that he would not kill any of the Pandavas, with the exception of Arjuna. That promise has been described in Section 55 (Volume 4). The placing of the bowstring around the neck is a sign of subjugation.

[223]Shakra's bow is the rainbow.

[224]Karna.

wheels of chariots were shattered. The standards and flags of others were torn. O venerable one! The son of the suta killed charioteers and shattered the wheels. We saw the dispirited Panchalas fleeing on their chariots. Crazy elephants were terrified and roamed here and there, as if their limbs had been burnt by a conflagration in a great forest. The temples of elephants were shattered and they exuded blood. Their trunks were severed. O venerable one! Their bodies and armour were mangled, their tails were sliced down. They were like dispelled clouds, destroyed by that great-souled one. There were other elephants that were frightened because of the iron arrows and hundreds of spears. They advanced towards him, like insects towards a fire. We saw other giant elephants destroying each other. Blood flowed from their bodies, like water from the slopes of mountains. Horses lost their breastplates, the dressings on their tails and their silver, bronze and golden ornaments. Their coverings were destroyed and they lost their bridles. Whisks, spreads and quivers fell down. Brave riders, the ornaments of a battle, were killed. In that battle there, we saw supreme horses wandering around. O lord of men! We saw the best of warriors who fought on horses, with lances, swords and scimitars. They wore armour and headdresses. They were destroyed. There were chariots embellished with gold, yoked to swift horses. With the rathas swiftly slain, we saw them roaming around.[225] O venerable one! Wheels and poles were destroyed for some, wheels were shattered for others. There were others without flags and standards, or with their yokes destroyed. O lord of the earth! Deprived of everything, we saw rathas wandering around in every direction, scorched by the arrows and weapons of Surya's son.[226] There were those without weapons. And there were many with weapons, but they had been killed. We saw many foot soldiers from their side running around in every direction. They were adorned with colourful flags of many different hues, decorated with bells. There were other warriors with severed head, arms and thighs. We

[225]Dragged around by the horses.

[226]Karna, born from Kunti, was the son of the sun god, Surya.

saw the arrows released from Karna's bow sever them. We beheld those warriors confront a terrible and great calamity. They were killed by Karna's sharp arrows. In that battle, the Srinjayas were slaughtered by the son of the suta, as they advanced towards him, like insects towards a flame. In every spot there, he consumed those arrays of maharathas and the kshatriyas avoided him, taking him to be the fire that comes at the time of the destruction of a yuga. The remnants of the brave Panchala maharathas were routed and retreated. Karna pursued them from the rear, showering arrows. They were devoid of armour and standards, but the spirited one pursued them. The maharatha son of the suta tormented them with his arrows. It was like the destroyer of darkness[227] scorching beings when it has attained midday."'

Chapter 1168(18)

'Sanjaya said, "Your son, Yuyutsu, was driving away that large army.[228] Uluka asked him to wait and quickly attacked him. O king! At this, Yuyutsu used an arrow that was extremely sharp at the edges to strike Uluka, like Indra striking a mountain with his vajra. In that encounter, Uluka became angry with your son and slicing his bow down with a kshurapra arrow,[229] struck him with a barbed arrow. When his bow was severed, Yuyutsu picked up another large bow that was more forceful. O bull among the Bharata lineage! His eyes red with rage, he pierced Shakuni's son with sixty arrows. Striking his charioteer with three arrows, he pierced him[230] again. Uluka now became wrathful in the battle and piercing him with twenty arrows that were adorned with gold, severed his golden

[227]The sun.

[228]Yuyutsu was Dhritarashtra's son through a vaishya woman. He fought the war on the side of the Pandavas. Uluka was Shakuni's son.

[229]Arrow with a razor-sharp tip.

[230]Uluka.

standard. With the pole shattered, that extremely large and lofty standard fell down. O king! Blazing in gold, it fell down in front of Yuyutsu. On seeing that his standard had been uprooted, Yuyutsu became senseless with rage. He struck Uluka between the breasts with five arrows. O venerable one! O supreme among the Bharata lineage! With a broad-headed arrow that had been washed in oil, Uluka violently severed his charioteer's head. He then killed his four horses and pierced him with five arrows. Having been severely struck by that powerful one, he[231] departed on his chariot. O king! Having defeated him, Uluka swiftly advanced towards the Panchalas and the Srinjayas and began to slay them with sharp arrows.

'"O great king! Fearlessly, and in the twinkling of an eye, your son, Shrutakarma, advanced against Shatanika and deprived him of his horses, his charioteer and his chariot.[232] O venerable one! Though his horses were slain, the immensely powerful Shatanika remained stationed on his chariot and extremely angry, flung a club towards your son. O descendant of the Bharata lineage! Having reduced the chariot, together with its horses and charioteer, to ashes, it fell down with great force and shattered the earth. Those two brave ones, the extenders of the fame of the Kuru lineage, were both without chariots. They glared angrily at each other and withdrew from the battle. Frightened, your son ascended Vivitsu's chariot.[233] Shatanika quickly advanced towards Prativindhya's chariot.[234]

'"Angrily, Sutasoma[235] pierced Shakuni with sharp arrows, but could not make him tremble, like a wind against a mountain. O descendant of the Bharata lineage! On seeing his father's supreme enemy, Sutasoma enveloped him with thousands of arrows. However, Shakuni was dexterous and colourful in fighting and

[231]Yuyutsu.

[232]This doesn't quite fit. The standard listing of Duryodhana's brothers doesn't include Shrutakarma. The closest one gets is Rudrakarma. Shrutakarma or Shrutakirti is Arjuna's son, through Droupadi. Shatanika is Nakula's son.

[233]Vivitsu was one of Duryodhana's brothers.

[234]Prativindhya was Yudhishthira's son.

[235]Bhima's son through Droupadi.

wished to be victorious in that encounter. He severed those arrows with other arrows. In that battle, having countered those arrows with his sharp arrows, he angrily struck Sutasoma with three arrows. Your immensely valorous brother-in-law used his arrows to bring down his horses and his charioteer and shattered his standard into fragments. At this, all the people roared in applause. O venerable one! His horses were slain. He was without a chariot. His bow was severed. However, the archer[236] descended from the chariot, stood on the ground and picked up a supreme bow. He released gold-tufted arrows that had been sharpened on stone and enveloped your brother-in-law's chariot. The shower of arrows released by the maharatha was like a torrent of insects. But on seeing this, Soubala was not distressed and remained stationed on his chariot. The immensely illustrious one countered those arrows with a storm of his arrows. On witnessing Sutasoma's extraordinary deed of fighting on foot, while the king was on his chariot, all the warriors, and all the siddhas who were assembled in the firmament, were satisfied and honoured him. The king[237] then used sharp and extremely forceful broad-headed arrows that possessed drooping tufts to sever his bow and all his quivers. When his bow was severed in the encounter, he picked up a sword and roared. It possessed the complexion of lapis lazuli or a lotus and had an ivory handle. It was as radiant as the clear sky, and the intelligent Sutasoma whirled it around. It seemed as if he was Death himself. O great king! He had the strength and learning of fourteen techniques[238] and roamed around, violently whirling his sword in thousands of circular motions. The valiant Soubala shot arrows at him. But as they descended, he quickly severed them with his supreme sword. O great king! Soubala, the destroyer of enemy heroes, became enraged at this and shot arrows that were like venomous serpents towards Sutasoma. However, displaying his learning, strength

[236]Sutasoma.

[237]Shakuni.

[238]There were different types of motions prescribed for fighting with a sword, variously described as twenty-one, twenty-four and thirty-two.

and dexterity, the immensely radiant one, with valour like that of Tarkshya,[239] used his sword to slice them down in that battle. O king! As he was roaming around and executing circular motions, he[240] used an extremely sharp kshurapra arrow to sever that resplendent sword. Thus sliced down, the large sword fell down violently on the ground. When the sword was severed, maharatha Sutasoma retreated six steps and hurled that part of the sword that was still in his fist. That fragment was decorated with gold and diamonds. In that encounter, it quickly severed the great-souled one's[241] bow and bowstring and fell down on the ground. After this, Sutasoma went to Shrutakirti's giant chariot. Soubala picked up another terrible bow that was extremely difficult to withstand. Using this, he attacked the Pandava soldiers and killed large numbers of the enemy. O lord of the earth! On seeing Soubala fearlessly striding around in the battle, a loud uproar arose amongst the Pandavas, when they saw that large, proud and armed soldiers were driven away by the great-minded Soubala. O king! It was like the army of the daityas being crushed by the king of the gods. In that fashion, the Pandava soldiers were destroyed by Soubala.

'"O king! Kripa countered Dhrishtadyumna in the battle, like a *sharabha*[242] in a forest, advancing and fighting against a proud elephant. O descendant of the Bharata lineage! Parshata was checked by the powerful Goutama and could not advance a single step. On witnessing Goutama's form advancing towards Dhrishtadyumna's chariot, all the beings were terrified and thought that he[243] was confronting destruction. The rathas and riders were distressed in their minds and said, 'The immensely energetic Sharadvata, supreme among men, is certainly extremely enraged at Drona's

[239]Garuda.

[240]Shakuni.

[241]Shakuni's.

[242]Sharabha has many meanings—young elephant, camel. It is also a mythical animal with eight legs, believed to be stronger than a lion. In this context, one probably means the mythical animal.

[243]Dhrishtadyumna.

killing. He is intelligent and skilled in the use of divine weapons. Will Dhrishtadyumna be safe today from Goutama? Will this entire army be freed from this great danger? The brahmana will kill all of us together. His severe form is seen to be like that of the Destroyer. In this encounter, he will follow the footsteps of Bharadvaja's son. The preceptor[244] is light in the use of his hands and is always victorious in battle. He possesses the valour of weapons and is angry as well. It can be seen that Parshata is now extremely reluctant to fight.' These and other words were spoken by those on your side and on the side of the enemy. O king! Kripa Sharadvata breathed angrily and enveloped Parshata, who was immobile, in all his inner organs. In that encounter, he was struck by the great-souled Goutama. He was supremely confounded in that battle and did not know what he should do. His charioteer said, 'O Parshata! Are you fine? I have never seen you face such a difficulty in a battle. These arrows shot by that foremost among brahmanas are capable of penetrating the inner organs and are directed at your inner organs. It is sheer fortune that you have escaped. I will withdraw the chariot from the spot, like the force of a river driven back by the ocean. Your valour has been destroyed by this brahmana and I think that he cannot be killed.' O king! At this, Dhrishtadyumna gently spoke these words. 'O son![245] My mind has gone numb and there is sweat on my body. Behold! My body is overcome by lassitude and my body hair is standing up. O charioteer! Abandon the brahmana in the battle and slowly go to the spot where Achyuta, Arjuna and Bhimasena are, so that I may obtain safety in the battle. In my view, that is what we should do.' O great king! At this, the charioteer urged the horses towards the spot where the great archer, Bhima, was fighting with your soldiers. O venerable one! On seeing that Dhrishtadyumna's chariot was going away, Goutama followed it and showered hundreds of arrows. The scorcher of enemies repeatedly blew on his conch shell. He drove away Parshata, like the great Indra against Shambara.

[244]Kripa was the preceptor of the Pandavas and the Kouravas before Drona turned up.

[245]The word used is tata.

'"The invincible Shikhandi was responsible for Bhishma's death. In the battle, Hardikya[246] smiled repeatedly and repulsed him. Shikhandi advanced against the maharatha from the Hridika lineage and struck him between the shoulder joints with five sharp and iron arrows. Kritavarma became angry and struck him with sixty swift arrows. O king! The maharatha smiled and severed his[247] bow with a single arrow. Drupada's powerful son then grasped another bow and enraged, asked Hardikya to wait. O Indra among kings! He shot ninety arrows that were gold-tufted and extremely forceful. But they were repulsed by his[248] armour. On seeing that they were repulsed and fell down on the ground, the powerful one used an extremely sharp kshurapra arrow to sever his bow. When the bow had been severed, he[249] was like a bull with shattered horns and he[250] angrily struck him in the arms and the chest with eighty arrows. Though he was angry, Kritavarma was mangled by these arrows. The lord picked up another stringed bow and affixing arrows, struck Shikhandi in the shoulder with those supreme arrows. With those arrows sticking to his shoulders, Shikhandi looked beautiful. He was like a giant tree, with sparkling branches and sub-branches. Having severely pierced each other, they were both covered with blood. They were as resplendent as bulls that had wounded each other with their horns. Those two maharathas made supreme efforts to kill each other. They roamed around on their chariots, executing a thousand circular motions. O great king! In that battle, Kritavarma pierced Parshata with seventy arrows that were gold-tufted and had been sharpened on stone. In that encounter, Bhoja, supreme among strikers, quickly released a terrible arrow that was capable of robbing life. O king! Severely struck by this, he[251] quickly lost his consciousness. He suddenly lost his senses and grasped the pole of

[246]Kritavarma, Hridika's son.

[247]Shikhandi's.

[248]Kritavarma's.

[249]Kritavarma.

[250]Shikhandi.

[251]Shikhandi.

his standard. His charioteer took the supreme of rathas away from the battle. Tormented by Hardikya's arrows, he sighed repeatedly. O lord! Drupada's brave son was defeated. At this, the Pandava soldiers were slaughtered and fled in all directions."'

Chapter 1169(19)

'Sanjaya said, "O great king! The one on the white horses[252] killed your soldiers, like the wind scattering a mass of cotton in every direction. The Trigartas, Shibis, Kouravas, Shalvas, samshaptakas and the army of narayanas combined and attacked him. O descendant of the Bharata lineage! There were Satyasena, Satyakirti, Mitradeva, Shrutanjaya, Soushruti, Chitrasena and Mitravarma. In that battle, the king of Trigarta was surrounded by his brothers and sons. They were great archers and wielded many kinds of weapons while fighting. In that battle against Arjuna, they released a storm of arrows. They attacked in that encounter, like waves agitated by the wind in the ocean. Hundreds and thousands of warriors attacked Arjuna, but all of them encountered their destruction, like serpents at the sight of Tarkshya.[253] O king! But though they were killed in that battle, they did not abandon Pandava. They were scorched, like insects in a fire.

'"In that battle, Satyasena pierced Pandava with three arrows, Mitradeva with sixty-three, Chandradeva with seven, Mitravarma with seventy-three, Soushruti with five, Shatrunjaya with twenty and Susharma with nine arrows. He[254] killed King Shatrunjaya with arrows sharpened on stone. He severed Soushruti's helmeted head from his body. He swiftly used arrows to convey Chandradeva to Yama's eternal abode. O great king! When the other maharathas endeavoured against him, he struck them with five arrows each.

[252]Arjuna.
[253]Garuda.
[254]Arjuna.

Satyasena became angry in that battle. He roared like a lion and hurled a giant spear towards Krishna. It was extremely terrible and was made completely out of iron. It pierced the great-souled Madhava's left arm and penetrated the ground. O lord of the earth! Madhava was thus pierced by the spear in that great battle, and the whip and the reins fell down from his hand. However, the immensely illustrious one picked up the whip and the reins again and drove the horses towards Satyasena's chariot. On seeing that Vishvaksena[255] had been pierced, the immensely strong Partha Dhananjaya struck Satyasena with sharp arrows. In the forefront of that army, with extremely sharp arrows, he severed the king's large head, adorned with earrings, from his body. O venerable one! He then struck and killed Chitravarma with sharp arrows and used a sharp *vatsadanta* arrow to kill his charioteer. He angrily brought down hundreds and thousands from that mass of samshaptakas with hundreds of arrows. With a kshurapra arrow that was silver-tufted, the great-souled and immensely illustrious one severed King Mitradeva's head. In wrath, he struck Susharma between his shoulder joints. At this, all the samshaptakas surrounded Dhananjaya. They angrily showered him with weapons and roared in the ten directions. Jishnu, who was like Shakra in his valour, was oppressed by them. The maharatha, whose soul was immeasurable, released the *aindra*[256] weapon. O lord of the earth! Thousands of arrows were released from this. In that encounter, standards, bows, chariots and their flags, quivers with their arrows, axles, yokes, wheels, harnesses, seatings, bumpers and whips were shattered. In that battle, rocks rained down, with a shower of lances. There were clubs, maces, lances and spears. O venerable one! Shataghnis with wheels and arms and thighs fell down, with necklaces, armlets and bracelets. O descendant of the Bharata lineage! There were golden necklaces and body armour, with umbrellas, whisks and heads adorned with crowns. O lord of the earth! A great sound could be heard there. There were heads ornamented with earrings, with faces like the full moon. They could

[255]Krishna.

[256]Divine missile named after Indra.

be seen lying there, like stars in the firmament. The slain bodies could be seen on the ground. They had excellent garlands and excellent garments and were smeared with sandalwood paste. At that time, the fierce field of battle looked like a city of the gandharvas. Immensely strong princes and kshatriyas were killed. Elephants and swift horses were brought down on the ground. In that battle, they were heaped around like mountains and it became difficult to pass. As the great-souled Pandava slew a large number of the enemy and elephants with his broad-headed arrows, there was no path for him. As he roamed around in that battle, in that red-coloured mud, it was as if the wheels of his own chariot were sinking in distress. But though the wheels seemed to sink, his horses possessed great energy and had the speed of the mind and the wind. They exerted a great effort and dragged along Pandu's archer son, as he killed those soldiers. None of them could remain stationed in the battle and most of them retreated. In that battle, Jishnu defeated large numbers of samshaptakas. O great king! He was resplendent, like a blazing fire without any smoke.

'"O great king! Yudhishthira shot a large number of arrows and King Duryodhana fearlessly received him himself. On seeing that your immensely strong son was violently descending, Dharmaraja asked him to wait and pierced him. He[257] pierced him back with nine sharp arrows and, extremely angry, struck his charioteer with a broad-headed arrow. At this, King Yudhishthira shot thirteen arrows at Duryodhana. They were gold-tufted and sharpened on stone and possessed stone heads. The maharatha[258] killed his four horses with four arrows and with a fifth, severed his charioteer's head from his body. With a sixth, he brought down the king's standard; with a seventh, his bow; and with an eighth, his sword, on the ground. With five more arrows, Dharmaraja severely struck the king. With the horses slain, your son descended from his chariot. He was stationed on the ground and was in supreme danger. On seeing that he was overcome by this calamity, Karna, Drona's son, Kripa and the others collectively rushed there, wishing to save the king. O king! At this,

[257]Duryodhana.
[258]Yudhishthira.

all the sons of Pandu surrounded Yudhishthira in the battle and an encounter commenced.

'"In that great battle, thousands of trumpets were sounded. O lord of the earth! As the Panchalas clashed against the Kouravas, a tumultuous sound arose. Men clashed against men and elephants against supreme elephants. Rathas clashed against rathas and horses against horse riders. O great king! Duels could be witnessed in that encounter. As supreme weapons were used, the sight was wonderful and unthinkable. They wished to kill each other and fought with great force, killing each other in that battle and following the vow of warriors. In that encounter, for a short while, no one attacked from the rear and it was beautiful to see. O king! But it soon became crazy and no one followed codes of honour. As they roamed around in the field of battle, rathas attacked elephants and dispatched them to Yama, using straight-tufted arrows. Elephants attacked horses and brought down large numbers of them there, fiercely driving them away. O king! Having driven away large numbers of horses, the elephants were intoxicated with their strength and gored them with their tusks or severely crushed them. In that battle, they pierced horse riders and horses with their tusks. Others picked them up powerfully and flung them down with great force. In every direction, there were elephants that were struck by foot soldiers in their weak spots. They uttered fierce woes of lamentation and fled in the ten directions. In that great battle, foot soldiers were violently driven away. In the field of battle, there were many who quickly discarded their ornaments. Having determined that this was a sign, the giant elephants picked up those expensive ornaments and pierced them.[259] Other elephants were severely wounded in their temples and the bases of their tusks by lances and spears. Others were sorely and fiercely struck along their sides with clubs hurled by rathas and horse riders. They were shattered and fell down on the ground. There were other giant elephants that powerfully brought charioteers and horse riders down on the ground, with their armour and their flags. O venerable

[259]The elephant riders discerned that the flinging away of ornaments was a sign of victory and pierced the foot soldiers.

one! In that great battle, some elephants assumed terrible forms. They approached rathas and picking them up, hurled them down violently. Giant elephants were killed by iron arrows and brought down. They lay down on the ground, like mountain peaks shattered by thunder. In the battle, warriors encountered warriors and struck each other with their fists. They dragged and seized each other by the hair. Others sought to use their arms and flung the foe down on the ground. They placed their feet on their chests and cheerfully severed their heads. O great king! With their feet, some kicked those that were already dead. Others used weapons to sever the bodies of those who were alive but dying. O descendant of the Bharata lineage! In that spot, warriors fought great fights with their fists. They fiercely seized each other by the hair and there were others who only wrestled. In that battle, there were many who were killed with weapons while they were fighting with another and were therefore ignorant.[260] The warriors were thus engaged in that frightful encounter. Hundreds and thousands of headless torsos stood there. The weapons and armour were red. And in that great arena, so were the garments. Thus did that great and fierce battle rage on and filled the universe with a sound like that of violent waves. O king! Oppressed by arrows, they could not distinguish those on one's own side from that of the enemy. O great king! Desiring victory, the kings fought as they should and killed those who advanced against them, whether they were from their own side or from the side of the enemy. As they advanced, the warriors on both sides were anxious. O great king! The chariots were shattered and the elephants were brought down. The horses were brought down and the men fell. The earth was covered with flesh, blood and mud and became impassable. O great king! In a short instant, there were currents of blood. Karna killed the Panchalas and Dhananjaya killed the Trigartas. O king! Bhimasena killed the Kurus and their entire army of elephants. O great king! In this way, there was carnage among the soldiers of the Kurus and the Pandavas, as they clashed in the afternoon, desiring a great victory."'

[260]Because they were fighting with another person, they were ignorant that they were being attacked by a third party.

Chapter 1170(20)

'Dhritarashtra said, "O Sanjaya! I have heard from you about many fierce and terrible sorrows that are difficult to tolerate and about the destruction of my sons. O suta! From what you have told me and from the way the war is going on, it is my firm view that the Kouravas don't exist any more. In that great battle, Duryodhana was deprived of his chariot. What did Dharma's son do then and what did the king[261] do in return? How did the battle that makes the body hair stand up rage in the afternoon? O Sanjaya! You are skilled. Tell me all this in detail."

'Sanjaya replied, "The soldiers fought in accordance with their different divisions. O lord of the earth! Your son resorted to another chariot. He was overcome by great rage, like a venomous snake. O descendant of the Bharata lineage! On seeing Dharmaraja Yudhishthira, Duryodhana quickly told his charioteer, 'O charioteer! Drive and swiftly take me to the spot where Pandava is. The king is resplendent in his armour there and an umbrella is held aloft his head.' Having been thus instructed by the king, in that encounter, the charioteer drove that supreme chariot towards King Yudhishthira. Yudhisthira was also angry and maddened, like an excellent bull. He instructed his charioteer to go to the spot where Suyodhana was. The best of rathas, those two brave brothers who were immensely valorous, clashed against each other, armoured and invincible in battle. In the battle, those two great archers mangled each other with their arrows. O venerable one! In that encounter, with a broad-headed arrow that was sharpened on stone, King Duryodhana severed the bow of the one who observed dharma in his conduct. Yudhishthira could not tolerate this conduct and became enraged. In front of the army, Dharma's son cast aside that severed bow and, his eyes red with rage, picked up another bow and severed Duryodhana's standard and bow. He[262] picked up another bow and pierced Pandava back.

[261]Duryodhana.

[262]Duryodhana.

Extremely angry, they showered down arrows on each other. They wished to defeat each other and were as enraged as lions. They struck each other and roared like bulls. The maharathas roamed around, glancing at each other. O great king! They drew their bows back to the complete extent and wounded each other. They were as resplendent as flowering kimshukas. O king! They roared repeatedly at each other, like lions. In that great battle, they made sounds with the slapping of their palms and the twangs of their bows. O great king! Those best of rathas blew on their conch shells and severely wounded each other. King Yudhishthira angrily struck your son in the chest with three arrows that were irresistible and had the force of the vajra. Your son quickly pierced the king back, using five sharp arrows that were gold-tufted and sharpened on stone. O descendant of the Bharata lineage! King Duryodhana hurled a lance. It was sharp, made completely out of iron and like a giant meteor. On seeing it descend violently, Dharmaraja used sharp arrows to powerfully shatter it into three fragments and then pierced him with seven arrows. That extremely expensive lance fell down, with its golden handle, blazing like a giant meteor with trails of fire. O lord of the earth! On seeing that the lance had been destroyed, your son struck Yudhishthira with nine sharp and broad-headed arrows. The foremost among scorcher of enemies[263] was powerfully and severely struck and quickly affixed an arrow in Duryodhana's direction. The immensely strong and valiant king affixed the arrow on his fierce bow and angrily released it at the king.[264] That arrow struck your maharatha son. Having robbed the king of his senses, it penetrated the ground. Duryodhana became angry at this and forcefully raised a club. He advanced against Pandava, wishing to bring an end to the feud.[265] With that upraised club, he was like Yama with a staff in his hand. On seeing this, Dharmaraja hurled a giant spear towards your son. It blazed and was immensely powerful, flaming like a giant meteor. As he[266] was stationed on his

[263]Yudhishthira.

[264]The two kings being Yudhishthira and Duryodhana respectively.

[265]If Yudhishthira was killed, the feud would end.

[266]Duryodhana.

chariot, it pierced his armour in the great battle. Severely wounded and struck in the chest, he lost his senses and fell down.

'"Kritavarma swiftly approached your son, as the king was immersed in an ocean of hardship. Bhima also grasped a giant club that was decorated with gold and in that battle, powerfully advanced against Kritavarma. Thus the battle raged between those on your side and the enemy."'

Chapter 1171(21)

'Sanjaya said, "Those on your side placed Karna at the forefront. They were invincible in battle and the encounter commenced again, like that between the gods and the asuras. There was the sound of elephants, chariots, men, horses and conch shells and that of many weapons descending. Elephants, rathas and foot soldiers, with their leaders, were cheered by this and descended and struck each other. The riders used arrows, battleaxes, supreme swords, spikes and many different kinds of arrows. In that great battle, there were elephants, chariots, horses, the best of men and the vehicles of the men. The ground was beautiful, strewn with the heads of men. The faces possessed the complexion of the lotus, the sun or the moon. The teeth were white. The mouths, eyes and noses were excellent. They were adorned with beautiful crowns and earrings. Thousands of elephants, men and horses were killed with hundreds of clubs, maces, spears, javelins, nails, catapults and bludgeons. A river of blood began to flow. The slain and wounded men, rathas, horses and elephants were terrible to look at. Because that large army was destroyed in the cause, it was like the kingdom of the lord of the ancestors[267] when there is a destruction of beings.

'"O god among men! Your soldiers and your sons looked like the sons of the gods, when, in the forefront of the battle, those bulls

[267]Yama is the lord of the ancestors.

among the Kurus advanced against Shini's descendant.[268] That army was extremely beautiful and was fierce in its sentiments. It was full of the best of men, horses, chariots and elephants. It was like the soldiers of the immortals or the asuras and made a sound like the salty ocean. The son of the sun[269] was like the lord of the gods in his valour. As a warrior, he was equal to the best among the thirty gods. He attacked the foremost among the Shini lineage with arrows that blazed like the rays of the sun. In that encounter, the bull among the Shini lineage quickly used many kinds of arrows, which were as resplendent as venomous snakes, and enveloped the supreme among men,[270] with his chariot, his horses and his charioteer. Vasusena[271] was oppressed because of the arrows of the bull among the Shinis, and the atirathas and well-wishers on your side quickly advanced towards that bull among rathas,[272] together with their elephants, chariots, horses and foot soldiers. That force was as large as the ocean. But it was quickly driven away by the enemy, the friends of Drupada's son,[273] and there was a great destruction of men, rathas, horses and elephants.

'"The best of men, Arjuna and Keshava, performed their religious ceremonies and worshipped Lord Bhava[274] in accordance with the proper rites. They set their minds on killing the enemy and swiftly rushed against your army. The chariot roared like a cloud and the flags and standard fluttered in the wind. It was drawn by white horses. On seeing it advance towards them, like Death, they[275] were distressed in their minds. Arjuna stretched Gandiva and seemed to dance around in the battle. He showered arrows and covered the sky, the directions and the sub-directions. There were chariots that were like celestial vehicles, equipped with machines, weapons and standards. Using his arrows,

[268]Satyaki.

[269]Karna.

[270]Karna.

[271]Karna's name.

[272]Karna.

[273]This is a roundabout away of referring to the Pandavas, Drupada's son presumably meaning Dhrishtadyumna.

[274]Shiva.

[275]The Kourava soldiers.

he destroyed these, together with their charioteers, like a wind driving away clouds. There were elephants with triumphant standards and weapons and those who controlled these elephants. There were horse riders, horses and foot soldiers. Using his arrows, he conveyed them to Yama's eternal abode. The maharatha was angry and unassailable, like Yama. Duryodhana advanced against him alone and struck him with his arrows. However, Arjuna used seven arrows to strike his bow, his charioteer, his standard and his horses.[276] With another arrow, he then brought down his umbrella. He then affixed a ninth arrow, with the desire of killing Duryodhana. However, Drona's son shattered that supreme arrow into seven fragments. Pandava then used supreme arrows to destroy the bow of Drona's son and also killed his horses. He then severed Kripa's fierce bow. Having severed Hardikya's bow and standard and killed his horses, he cut down Duhshasana's supreme bow and attacked Radheya. At this, Karna abandoned Satyaki and struck Arjuna with three arrows. He then pierced Krishna with twenty arrows and struck Partha with three more. However, Satyaki advanced against Karna and pierced him with sharp arrows, first with ninety-nine fierce arrows and yet again with one hundred. All the foremost among the Pandus oppressed Karna—Yudhamanyu, Shikhandi, Droupadi's sons, the Prabhadrakas, Uttamouja, Yuyutsu, the twins and Parshata.[277] The Chedis, Karushas, Matsyas, Kekayas and their armies, the powerful Chekitana and Dharmaraja, excellent in his vows—these rathas, horses, elephants and foot soldiers who were fierce in their valour—surrounded Karna in that battle and released many kinds of weapons. All of them devoted themselves to killing Karna and addressed him in fierce and eloquent words. Karna used his sharp arrows to cut down those numerous showers of weapons. He destroyed all of them, like a wind breaks down trees. One saw Karna angrily use his storm of arrows to destroy rathas, elephants and their riders, horses and their riders. The Pandu forces were slaughtered by Karna's energy. Most of them lost their weapons and their bodies were wounded. They retreated. Then, Arjuna himself countered Karna's

[276]With four horses, there is a total of seven targets.
[277]Parshata means Dhrishtadyumna.

weapons with his own weapons. He enveloped the directions, the sky and the earth with his showers of arrows. Those arrows descended like clubs and bludgeons. Some were like shataghnis and others were as fierce as the vajra. The soldiers, the foot soldiers, horses, rathas and elephants, were destroyed. They closed their eyes, uttered woes of lamentation and fled distractedly in different directions. In that battle, horses, men and elephants were destroyed. The soldiers were killed by the arrows and terrified, fled.

'"Thus did they engage in battle, desiring victory. The sun approached Mount Asta.[278] O great king! In particular, there was darkness and dust. We could not see anything, favourable or unfavourable. O descendant of the Bharata lineage! The great archers were frightened of fighting in the night. With all their horses, they therefore withdrew.[279] O king! When the Kouravas departed at the end of the day, the Parthas were delighted in their minds at having obtained victory and also left for their own camps. They showed contempt for the enemy by sounding many kinds of musical instruments, roaring like lions, dancing and praising Achyuta and Arjuna. When the brave ones and all the soldiers retreated, all the lords of men pronounced benedictions on the Pandaveyas. Having retreated, the Kurus and the Pandavas were cheerful. The lords of men went to their camps in the night and rested. Large numbers of yakshas, *rakshas*, *pishachas* and carnivorous beasts went to that terrible field of battle, which was like Rudra's dancing arena."'

Chapter 1172(22)

'Dhritarashtra said, "Arjuna killed all of us easily, as he wished. I don't think Yama would have escaped, had he attacked him in a battle. O fortunate one! Partha robbed single-handed. Single-

[278]The mountain behind which the sun sets.

[279]That is, the Kouravas withdrew.

handed, he satisfied Agni.[280] He vanquished the earth single-handed and made all the powerful kings offer tribute.[281] Single-handedly, using his divine bow, he killed the *nivatakavachas*.[282] He fought single-handedly with Sharva, who was in the form of a hunter.[283] He protected the Bharatas single-handed and satisfied Bhava.[284] Fierce in his energy, he single-handedly defeated all those on my side. They[285] should not be censured. Tell me what they did next."

'Sanjaya replied, "They were killed, wounded and shattered. They were deprived of their armour and the vehicles that bore them in war. Their voices were distressed. Those insolent ones grieved and were defeated by the enemy. The Kouravas went to their camps and sought counsel and advice from each other. They were like serpents that had been defanged and had lost their poison, having then been trod on by the foot. Karna angrily spoke to them, sighing like a snake. He rubbed one hand against another hand and glanced towards your son.[286] 'Arjuna is always firm, skilled and persevering. He understands and when the time is right, Adhokshaja[287] instructs him. We were deceived by him today, because of that sudden shower of weapons. O lord of the earth! But tomorrow, I will destroy all his intentions.'[288] Thus addressed by him, the supreme among kings gave his assent. Having cheerfully spent the night, they emerged to do battle. They saw that Dharmaraja had constructed an invincible vyuha, which the foremost among the Kurus had constructed according to the injunctions of Brihaspati

[280]In the burning of the Khandava forest, described in Section 19 (Volume 2).

[281]A reference to the conquest of the earth, described in Section 23 (Volume 2).

[282]This has been described in Section 35 (Volume 3).

[283]Sharva and Bhava are Shiva's names. This is a reference to the incidents of Section 31 (Volume 2).

[284]The protection of the Bharatas is a reference to the gandharva incident of Section 39 (Volume 3).

[285]The Kouravas.

[286]Duryodhana.

[287]Vishnu's name, meaning one who is beyond the senses.

[288]Though not explicitly stated, this is being said by Karna.

and Ushanas.[289] At this, Duryodhana remembered Karna, whose shoulders were like that of a bull. He was in control of his soul and could counteract the deeds of others. He was Purandara's equal in a battle and as strong as the masses of Maruts. Karna was like Kartyavirya[290] in his valour and the king's mind turned towards him. The son of a suta was a great archer, and in a hardship, one turns towards a relative.

'Dhritarashtra said, "In that miserable situation, your minds turned towards Vaikartana Karna. Did you look towards him, like those afflicted with cold glance towards the sun? After the retreat was over, the battle commenced again. O Sanjaya! How did Vaikartana Karna fight then? How did all the Pandavas fight there, with the son of a suta? The mighty-armed Karna could single-handedly kill the Parthas and the Somakas. It is my view that the valour of Karna's arms is equal to that of Shakra and Vishnu. The great-souled one's weapons and valour are extremely terrible. He saw that Duryodhana was severely afflicted by the Pandavas and he also saw that the sons of Pandu were extremely powerful in that great battle. Yet again, in the battle, the proud Duryodhana had relied on Karna to defeat the Parthas, their sons and Keshava. It is a great sorrow that the powerful Karna could not overcome the sons of Pandu in the encounter. There is no doubt that destiny is supreme. The consequences of that terrible gambling match have arrived now. Alas! These terrible miseries are the result of what Duryodhana did. O Sanjaya! I am bearing all these extremely fierce stakes. O son![291] Soubala[292] was revered as one who knew about policy. O Sanjaya! Though this is named a battle, it is a gambling match that is going on. I am always hearing about my sons being killed and defeated. There is no one who is capable of countering the Pandavas in battle and they are immersing themselves, as if in the midst of a crowd of women. Destiny is certainly most powerful."

[289]Brihaspati and Shukra (Ushanas) are respectively the preceptors of the gods and the demons.

[290]Kartavirya Arjuna.

[291]The word used is tata.

[292]Shakuni.

'Sanjaya said, "Those deeds have been done and you are thinking about them now. Those deeds should not have been done. But thinking about them brings destruction. The deeds that you did are long distant from memory. You did what should not have been done, and you did not think then about what would be obtained, and what would not be obtained, from those deeds. O king! You have been told several times not to fight with the Pandavas. O lord of the earth! But because of your delusion, you did not accept that advice about the Pandavas. You performed many terrible deeds against the sons of Pandu. It is because of what you did that this terrible destruction of kings is taking place. O bull among the Bharata lineage! But all that has transpired. Do not sorrow about it. O one without decay! Listen to a detailed account of the terrible destruction that happened.

'"When night was over and it was morning, Karna went to the king. Meeting Duryodhana, the mighty-armed one said, 'O king! I will clash against Pandu's illustrious son today. Either I will kill that brave one, or he will kill me. O lord of the earth! O king! Because of the many things that Partha and I have done, this clash between me and Arjuna has not taken place earlier. O lord of the earth! I am speaking these words in accordance with my wisdom. Listen to them. O descendant of the Bharata lineage! I will not return without having killed Partha in battle. The foremost of our soldiers have been killed and I am the one who will be stationed in battle. Partha will attack me, now that I am without Shakra's spear.[293] O lord of men! Therefore, listen to what is beneficial. The valour of my weapons is equal to the energy of Arjuna's. Savyasachi is not my equal in fighting against great warriors, dexterity, shooting from a distance, skill and the use of weapons. My bow, Vijaya, is supreme among all weapons. Vishvakarma[294] constructed it for Indra's sake. It was with this that Shatakratu vanquished large numbers of daityas. In the ten directions, the daityas were confounded because of its roar. Shakra

[293]Indra (Shakra) gave Karna a spear that would kill only one person. In Section 70 (Volume 6), it was used up to kill Ghatotkacha.

[294]The architect of the gods.

gave that revered weapon to Bhargava and Bhargava gave that divine and supreme bow to me.[295] With this, I will fight against the mighty-armed Arjuna, foremost among victorious ones, like Indra fighting in a battle against all the assembled daityas. Rama[296] gave me this terrible bow and it is superior to Gandiva. It was with this bow that he[297] conquered the earth twenty-one times. Bhargava told me about this bow's divine deeds and Rama gave it to me. I will use it to fight against Pandava. O Duryodhana! I will delight you and your relatives today. I will kill the brave Arjuna, foremost among victorious ones, in the battle. O king! The entire earth, with its mountains, forests, islands and oceans, will be yours, for your sons and your grandsons to be established in, without any opposition. There is nothing that I cannot accomplish today, especially if it is something that brings you pleasure, just as one who has controlled his soul and follows dharma is certain to obtain success. Like a tree against fire, he will not be able to stand against me in the battle. But I must certainly tell you how I am inferior to Phalguna. His bowstring is divine and his large quivers are inexhaustible. He possesses a celestial and supreme bow and Gandiva is invincible in battle. I also possess a supreme, great and divine bow known as Vijaya. O king! Therefore, in the matter of bows, I am superior to Partha. Listen to how that brave Pandava is superior to me. His reins are held by Dasharha, who is revered by all the worlds. His divine chariot is decorated with gold and was given to him by Agni. O brave one! It is impenetrable in every way and his horses are as swift as thought. His standard is divine and, with the resplendent ape atop it, causes wonder. Krishna, the creator of the universe, protects that chariot. Though I am inferior to him in these respects, I still wish to fight with Pandava. But this brave Shalya, the ornament of assemblies, is his[298] equal. If he acts as my charioteer, there will certainly be victory. Shalya is incapable of being resisted by the enemy. Therefore, let him be my charioteer. Let a large

[295]Karna studied weapons under Parashurama (Bhargava).

[296]Parashurama.

[297]Parashurama.

[298]Krishna's.

number of carts bear iron arrows that are shafted with the feathers of vultures. O Indra among kings! Let supreme horses be yoked to the best of chariots. O bull among the Bharata lineage! Let these always follow me from the rear. Through these, my qualities will be superior to those of Partha. Shalya knows more about horses than Krishna, and I am superior to Arjuna. Just as Dasharha, the destroyer of enemy heroes, knows about the minds of horses, maharatha Shalya also knows about horses. There is no one who is equal to the king of Madra in the strength of his arms. Just as there is no archer who is equal to me in weapons, there is no one who is equal to Shalya in knowledge of horses. In this fashion, my chariot will become superior to that of Partha's. O great king! O scorcher of enemies! I have told you what I desire. Please do this. Let all these wishes of mine be satisfied. O descendant of the Bharata lineage! You will then see what I accomplish in this battle. In every way, I will vanquish all the Pandavas, when they advance against me.' Duryodhana replied, 'O Karna! I will do everything that you have thought of. O son of a suta! Chariots, with implements and horses, will follow you. There will be many carts, bearing iron arrows tufted with the feathers of vultures. O Karna! We, and all these kings, will follow you.' O great king! Having spoken thus, your powerful son went to the king of Madra and spoke these words to him."'

Chapter 1173(23)

'Sanjaya said, "O great king! Your son spoke these words to the king of Madra. He went humbly to him and spoke these affectionate words to him. 'O one who observes truthful vows! O immensely fortunate one! O one who increases the hardship of enemies! O lord of Madra! O one who is brave in battle! O one who is terrible to enemy soldiers! O supreme among eloquent ones! You have heard Karna's words. I am seeking you out among all these lions among kings. This is for Partha's destruction and for my welfare. O best of rathas! O one with an excellent mind! You should accept the task of being a charioteer. There is no one in the worlds who is your equal in holding the reins. Protect Karna in every way, like Brahma protects Shankara. Krishna is Partha's adviser and he is supreme in holding the reins. In that fashion, always protect Radheya. Bhishma, Drona, Kripa, Karna, you, the valiant Bhoja, Shakuni Soubala, Drona's son and I are our strength. O leader of an army! In that fashion, we were divided into nine divisions. The divisions of the great-souled Bhishma and Drona no longer exist. They slew my enemy, more than the two parts that were allotted to them.[299] But those two tigers among men were old and were killed through deceit. O unblemished one! Having performed extremely difficult deeds for us, they have gone to heaven. In that way, in this battle, many other tigers among men have been slain by the enemy. In that way, in this encounter, there are many on our side who have ascended to heaven, giving up their lives, striving to the best of their capacity and performing good rites. The mighty-armed Karna alone remains, engaged in our welfare. O tiger among men! And you are there, a maharatha in all the worlds. O lord of Madra! That is the reason my hopes of victory are still great. Krishna is foremost among those who hold Partha's reins in battle. O king! In the battle, he is engaged in protecting Partha. You have witnessed the deeds that he has performed. Earlier, in an encounter, Arjuna has never killed enemies in this fashion.[300] O lord of Madra! But you have seen how he has killed and driven away in this battle. O immensely radiant one! Yours and Karna's divisions are left. In the battle, unite with Karna and bear that share. O venerable one! Surya and Aruna are seen to destroy the darkness.[301] In that way, destroy the Kounteyas, with the Panchalas and the Srinjayas. Karna is foremost among rathas. You are foremost among men. When there is a clash, there is no one in

[299]The enemy was divided into nine shares, with each of these nine warriors taking care of his share.

[300]Because Krishna is with Arjuna, Arjuna has become stronger.

[301]While Aruna is also a name for the sun, more specifically, Aruna is the sun's charioteer.

the worlds who is your equal. Varshneya protects the Pandavas in every situation. In that way, in this battle, protect Vaikartana Karna. O lord of the earth! If you are the charioteer of the horses, he will be unassailable in a battle by Shakra and all the gods, not to speak of the Pandaveyas. Do not doubt these words of mine.'

'"Hearing these words of Duryodhana, Shalya was filled with anger. His brows furrowed into three lines. He repeatedly whirled his hands around. His large eyes were red with rage. The mighty-armed Shalya was proud of his lineage, prosperity, knowledge and strength. He spoke these words. 'O son of Gandhari! You are insulting me and it is certain that you suspect me. Without any hesitation, you have asked me to act as a charioteer. You regard Karna to be superior to us and have honoured and praised him. But I have never regarded Radheya as my equal in battle. O lord of the earth! Instruct me to assume a burden that is greater than my share. Having defeated them in battle, I will return to the place I have come from. O descendant of the Kuru lineage! I will fight single-handedly with them. As I consume the enemies in the battle, behold my valour today. O Kouravya! It is not proper for a man to advance with an injury in his heart. Do not doubt me and do not enjoin me in this way. You should not act so as to insult me in the battle. Behold my thick arms. They are capable of withstanding the vajra. Behold my colourful bow and these arrows, which are like venomous serpents. Behold my chariot. Well-trained horses that are as swift as the wind have been yoked to it. O son of Gandhari! Behold my club. It has been decorated with strips of golden garments. If I am angry, I can split the earth and shatter the mountains. O lord of the earth! I can dry up the oceans with my energy. O king! Knowing that I am capable of oppressing the enemy in this way, why are you instructing me to be the charioteer of Adhiratha's inferior son in the battle? O Indra among kings! You should not employ me on such a lowly task. Since I am superior, I have no interest in following the commands of that wicked person. A superior person has arrived with affection and obedience. If one makes such a person subject to the commands of an inferior one, one commits the crime of confusing the inferior with the superior. Brahma created brahmanas from his mouth and kshatriyas from his chest. He created vaishyas from his thighs and shudras from his feet. That is what has been heard. O descendant of the Bharata lineage! Because of mixture among the varnas, those who are other than the four varnas, *pratiloma* and *anuloma*, have been generated.[302] It has been said in the sacred texts that kshatriyas are protectors. They accumulate wealth and distribute it. Pure brahmanas act as officiating priests, study and receive.[303] Brahmanas have been established on earth for the sake of gratifying people. Agriculture, animal husbandry and donations are always the tasks of vaishyas. It has been decreed that shudras are the servants of brahmanas, kshatriyas and vaishyas. It has been decreed that sutas are the servants of brahmanas and kshatriyas. They are not the servants of shudras.[304] O unblemished one! Therefore, listen to my words. I am one whose head has been consecrated.[305] I have been born in a lineage of *rajarshi*s. I am famous as a maharatha and should be served by bards and minstrels. O destroyer of enemy forces! Since I am such a person, I have no interest in being the charioteer of the son of the suta in battle. Having been thus humiliated, I will never fight. O son of Gandhari! I am seeking your permission now, because I wish to return to the place that I have come from.' Having spoken these words, Shalya, tiger among men and the ornament of an assembly, was angry and quickly stood up in the midst of those kings.

'"However, your son restrained him, with affection and great respect. He spoke sweet and conciliatory words that were capable of achieving every object. 'O Shalya! There is no doubt that it is exactly as you have said. O lord of men! But I have an objective. Please listen to it. O king! Karna is not superior to you and I have never doubted you. The king who is the lord of Madra will never do something that is false. Your ancestors, the best of men, always spoke the truth. It is

[302]Pratiloma means against the natural order and applies to progeny where the mother is superior in varna to the father. Anuloma applies to progeny where the father is superior in varna to the mother.

[303]Receive gifts.

[304]Unless shudras are being equated with sutas, it is possible that there is a typo here and the text should read, 'they are not the servants of sutas'.

[305]By sprinkling with sacred water.

my view that this is the reason you are known as Artayani.[306] O one who deserves honours. That is the reason, on this earth, you are like a stake to enemies.[307] O lord of the earth! That is the reason you are known by the name of Shalya. You have given away a large quantity of donations earlier. O one who knows about dharma! Therefore, for my sake, do what you have promised to do earlier. Radheya and I are not more valiant than you, that I am asking you to be the charioteer of those foremost of horses in the battle. Just as the world thinks that Karna is superior to Dhananjaya in qualities, the world thinks that Shalya is superior to Vasudeva. O bull among men! Karna is superior to Partha in weapons. And you are superior to Krishna in the knowledge of horses and in strength. The great-minded Vasudeva knows about the heart of horses. O king of Madra! But there is no doubt that you are twice as knowledgeable as him." Shalya replied, "O son of Gandhari! O Kourava! Since, in the midst of the soldiers, you have said that I am superior to Devaki's son, I am pleased with you. Therefore, I will be the charioteer of the illustrious Radheya, while he fights with the foremost of the Pandavas. O brave one! It shall be as you wish. O brave one! But let this be clear to Vaikartana, what when the time is right, I will be free to speak disrespectful words to him." O king! O descendant of the Bharata lineage! O supreme among the Bharata lineage! Together with Karna, your son told the king of Madra that it would be this way.'

Chapter 1174(24)

'"Duryodhana said, 'O lord of Madra! Listen once more to what I am about to tell you. O lord! This is an account of the ancient battle that took place between the gods and the *asura*s.

[306]Artayani was Shalya's name. Artayana means someone who is the refuge of one who is distressed and Artayani means a descendant of Artayana.

[307]There is a pun that a translation cannot capture. The word shalya means stake.

The great rishi, Markandeya, told my father about this. O supreme among rajarshis! I will recount it, without leaving anything out. You should listen to it, without doubting its veracity.

'"'The gods and the asuras engaged with each other in a mighty battle. O king! At first, there was the encounter known as Tarakamaya.[308] It has been heard by us that the daityas were then defeated by the gods. O king! When the daityas were defeated, Taraka's three sons, Taraksha,[309] Kamalaksha and Vidyunmali, resorted to fierce austerities and established themselves in supreme control. O scorcher of enemies! They oppressed their bodies with austerities. O king! Because of their control, austerities and rules, the grandfather[310] was pleased with them and offered them supreme boons. O king! They were united in asking for the boon that all beings would always be unable to kill them. They wanted this from the grandfather of all the worlds. The god who is the lord and master of all the worlds told them, "O asuras! There is nothing like immortality and not being killed by anyone. Ask for any other boon that pleases you." At this, they consulted among themselves for a long time and then, bowing down before the lord who is the master of the worlds, spoke these words, "O god! O grandfather! Please grant us this boon. With your favours, we will dwell in three cities above the earth and roam around in this world. O unblemished one! Once, every one thousand years, those cities will merge with one another and become one. O illustrious one! When they have merged, if a supreme among gods slays us with a single arrow, let that be the means of our death." Having agreed to this, the god[311] left for heaven.

'"'Having obtained the boon, they were pleased and consulted each other about constructing the three cities. They asked the great asura Maya, who was accomplished in everything. He was without decay and was worshipped by the daityas and the

[308]There are different stories about the Tarakamaya battle. In this version, it is named after the demon Taraka.

[309]Subsequently referred to as Tarakaksha.

[310]Brahma.

[311]Brahma.

danavas.[312] Using his own austerities, the intelligent Maya created those three cities, one of gold, another of silver and another of black iron. O lord of the earth! The one that was of gold was resplendent in heaven, the one of silver in the firmament and the one of iron on earth. They were such that they circled. Each was a hundred *yojana*s in length and breadth and possessed houses, mansions and many walls and gates.[313] The roads had many qualities and they were also spacious. There were many kinds of palaces, adorned with gates. O king! Each of those cities had a different king. The great-souled Tarakaksha possessed the expensive city of gold, Kamalaksha the silver one and Vidyunmali the iron one. Those three daitya kings swiftly attacked the three worlds with their energy. They spoke these words. "Who is the one who is known as Prajapati?"[314] There were no heroes to rival them and the foremost among danavas went and united with them, in tens of millions. They sought refuge in those three inaccessible cities, desiring great wealth. When they were thus united, Maya gave them everything they wanted. Resorting to him, all of them lived there, without any fear. If any resident of the three cities desired anything in his mind, using his powers of illusion, Maya immediately satisfied that wish. Tarakaksha had an immensely strong son named Hari. He went through supreme austerities and satisfied the grandfather. Having satisfied the god, he asked for a boon. "Let there be a lake in our city. When those killed with weapons are flung into it, let them emerge with life and greater strength." Having obtained the boon, Tarakaksha's brave son, Hari, constructed a lake there. O lord! It was capable of reviving the dead. In whatever form and in whatever attire a daitya was slain, once he was thrown there, he became alive in that form. Having obtained them back, those in Tripura[315] began to oppress all the worlds. They obtained success through their great austerities and extended the fear of the gods. O king! They never suffered from destruction in a battle. At this, they were overcome by avarice and delusion and were bereft

[312]Maya was the architect of the demons.

[313]A yojana is a measure of length, between 8 and 9 miles.

[314]Prajapati is Brahma's name.

[315]Tripura means three cities.

of their senses. They shamelessly uprooted everything that had been established. Everywhere, they drove away the gods and their companions. They roamed around at will, insolent because of the boon they had obtained, through all the celestial forests and other regions loved by the residents of heaven and the sacred and revered hermitages of rishis. The evil-acting danavas did not show respect towards anyone.

'""O scorcher of enemies! All the gods united and went to the grandfather, to tell him about the depredations caused by those who were not *suras*.[316] They bowed their heads in obeisance before him and told him everything. They asked the illustrious grandfather about a means for their destruction.[317] On hearing this, the illustrious god told the gods, "The asuras are evil-souled and hate the gods. Those who commit crimes against you, also oppress me. There is no doubt that I am neutral among beings. But those who are against dharma must be killed. I am firmly telling you this. You elect Sthanu Ishana Jishnu, the performer of undecaying deeds.[318] O Adityas! He will save you and kill the ones who are not suras." Having heard his words, with Shakra at the forefront, the gods placed Brahma ahead of them and sought refuge with the one who bears the mark of a bull. They performed supreme austerities and praised the eternal *brahman*. With the rishis, the ones who knew about dharma gave up all their souls to Bhava.[319] With eloquent words, they praised the one who grants freedom from fear in all situations that cause fear. He is the great-souled one who is the soul of everything. He pervades everything with his soul. They[320] knew special austerities and many kinds of yoga to control the soul. They knew about the techniques of *sankhya*, so that the soul could always be controlled.[321] They then

[316]The suras are gods. Those who are not suras are the asuras.

[317]The destruction of the demons.

[318]These are Shiva's names. Sthanu means the one who is immoveable or motionless. Ishana means the splendid lord. Jishnu means the victorious one.

[319]Shiva's name, meaning the excellent one.

[320]The gods.

[321]While sankhya is a school of philosophy, it can loosely be translated as knowledge of the soul.

beheld Ishana, the consort of Uma, in his mass of energy. He has no equal in the worlds. He is devoted to vows and is without blemish. He is the single illustrious one, though they had thought of him in many different forms. On seeing the form of the great-souled one, whom they had thought of in many different forms in their own souls, all of them were astounded and glanced at each other in great wonder. He is the lord who is in all beings. He is the one without origin and is the lord of the universe. On seeing him, all the gods and brahmarshis bowed their heads down on the ground. Shankara welcomed them with words of benediction over them and asked them to arise. The illustrious one smiled and said, "Tell me why you have come." Having obtained permission from Tryambaka,[322] their hearts were assured. They told Bhava, "O lord! We bow down. We bow down before you. We bow down before the one who is the god of all the gods. You are the archer. You are the one who is supremely angry. You are the one who destroyed the sacrifice of Prajapati.[323] You are the one who is worshipped by all Prajapatis. We bow down before you. We praise you. We praise the one who is praised by those who are about to die. You are the one who is red. You are Rudra. You are the one with the blue throat. You are the one with the trident. You are the one who cannot be repulsed. You are the one with the eyes of a deer. You are the one who fights with the best of weapons. You are unassailable. You are the seed. You are the brahman. You are a brahmachari. You are Ishana. You are the one who cannot be measured. You are the one who controls. You are dressed in skin. You are always engaged in austerities. You are tawny. You are the one who observes vows. You are the one who is attired in skin. You are the father of Kumara. You are three-eyed. You wield the best of weapons. You destroy the afflictions of those who seek refuge. You destroy masses of those who hate brahmanas. You are the lord of trees. You are the lord of men. We bow down before you. You are the lord of cattle. You are always the lord of sacrifices. We bow down before you. We bow down before you.

[322]The three-eyed one, Shiva.

[323]Here, Prajapati means Daksha. Shiva destroyed Daksha's sacrifice.

O Tryambaka! Fierce in your energy, you are in front of all the soldiers. O god! We worship you, in our thoughts and our deeds. Be pacified." At this, the illustrious one was gratified and welcomed and honoured them. He asked, "Let the reason for your fright be dispelled. Tell me what I should do for you." The great-souled one granted a boon to the masses of ancestors, gods and rishis. Brahma honoured Shankara and spoke these words for the welfare of the worlds. "O lord of the gods! Through your favours, I have obtained the status of Prajapati. Having been thus established, I have granted a great boon to the danavas. Because of that, they are transgressing all norms of respect. You are the lord of the past, the present and the future. Other than you, there is no one who can destroy those wicked ones. Show your favours to the gods and grant this to the residents of heaven. O lord of the gods! O wielder of the trident! Show your favours and kill the danavas."

'"'The illustrious one replied, "All your enemies should be killed. That is my view. But I cannot kill them alone. Those who hate the gods are capable. Therefore, all of you should unite. Use the energy of my weapons to fight against the enemy in battle. Unity offers great strength."

'"'The gods said, "We think that their energy and strength is double that of ours. We think that we have already witnessed their energy and their strength."

'"'The illustrious one replied, "Those who have committed crimes against you and are wicked must always be killed. Accept half of my energy and strength and kill all those enemies."

'"'The gods said, "O Maheshvara! We will not be able to bear half of your energy. But with half of our united strength, you can kill the enemies."'

'"Duryodhana said, 'O supreme among kings! The gods accepted what the lord of the gods had said.[324] All of them gave him half of their energy and he became superior. The god became the strongest among all the strong ones. From that time, Shankara came to be

[324]The Critical edition excises an intervening shloka. In that, Shiva agreed to accept half the energy and strength of the gods.

known as Mahadeva.[325] Mahadeva said, "Armed with the bow and the arrow, I will station myself on my chariot and kill the enemies of the residents of heaven. Therefore, all of you attend to my chariot and my bow and arrows. Behold, as I bring them down on the surface of the earth."

'"'The gods said, "Let all forms be gathered from everywhere in the three worlds. O lord of the gods! Using that, we will construct an immensely energetic and resplendent chariot for you, which will be fashioned by Vishvakarma with his intelligence."

'"'The tigers among the gods then constructed the chariot.[326] The goddess earth, garlanded with large cities and with mountains, forests, islands and all the beings, became the seat for the charioteer. Mandara[327] was the axle and Mahanadi[328] became the flank. The directions and the sub-directions became the entourage around the chariot. The flaming planets were the *anukarsha*[329] and the stars were the bumpers. Dharma, artha and kama united to become the *trivenu*.[330] Many kinds of herbs and many trees, with flowers and fruit, became the seat for the charioteer. The sun and the moon became wheels of that supreme chariot. Day and night were the auspicious flanks, ahead and to the rear. The ten lords of the nagas, with Dhritarashtra[331] as the foremost, constituted the shaft. The sky was the yoke and Samvartaka and Balahaka were the leather coverings for the yoke.[332] Fortitude, understanding, permanence and humility were the staffs. The planets, nakshatras, stars and the colourful firmament were the leather coverings. The guardians of the

[325]The great god.

[326]This is Duryodhana continuing his account.

[327]Mount Mandara.

[328]The river.

[329]It is not obvious what an anukarsha is. It is something that was used to attract or pull and may have been some kind of hook.

[330]Trivenu means three bamboo poles. One doesn't know what part of the chariot this is, except that it is clearly a joint.

[331]Not to be confused with the Kourava Dhritarashtra.

[332]Samvartaka and Balahaka are the names of clouds that appear at the time of the destruction of the universe.

world, the lords of the gods, the water, the dead and wealth,[333] were made the horses. Sinivali, Anumati, Kuhu and Raka, all excellent in their vows, were made the yokes and harnesses around the necks of the mounts, for use by the rider.[334] Action, truth, austerities and prosperity were made the reins. The mind became the base and Sarasvati[335] the track for the chariot. Many beautiful and colourful flags were whirled around by the wind. With lightning and Indra's bow fastened to the chariot, it blazed in radiance. O great king! Thus was the supreme of chariots prepared there. O tiger among men! The gods prepared it, for crushing those who hated them. Shankara placed the best of his weapons on the chariot. Having made the firmament the flagstaff for his chariot, he placed the mark of the bull there. Brahma's staff, Yama's staff, Rudra's staff and Fever became the protectors of the chariot and faced all the directions. The great-souled Atharvan and Angirasa became the protectors of the chariot wheels. [336] Rig Veda, Sama Veda and the Puranas were in the front. Itihasa[337] and the Yajur Veda protected the rear. Divine words and learning surrounded it from all sides. O Indra among kings! *Vashatkara*[338] was the goad there. O king! The syllable *Om* was at the forefront and made it look radiant. He[339] made the year, with its six seasons, his bow. He made the night that destroys men the undecaying bowstring. Vishnu, Agni and Soma were the arrows. Agni and Soma constitute the entire universe and it is said that Vishnu is the universe. Vishnu is the illustrious one's soul and Bhava's infinite energy. That is the reason they[340] could not bear the touch of Hara's

[333]Indra, Varuna, Yama and Kubera respectively.

[334]Sinivali is the day before the new moon. Anumati is the day before the full moon. Kuhu is the day of the new moon and Raka is the day of the full moon. These are also the names of goddesses associated with those days.

[335]Meaning speech.

[336]Famous sages.

[337]Itihasa means the two epics and the Puranas. Since the Puranas have already been mentioned, it means only the two epics here.

[338]The exclamation 'vashat' made at the time of offering an oblation.

[339]Shiva.

[340]The asuras.

bowstring. On that arrow, the lord released his fierce and virulent fire of anger, generated from the intolerable wrath of Bhrigu and Angirasa. Nilalohita, Dhumra and Krittivasa looked terrible.[341] He blazed like ten thousand suns, amidst a mass of flaming energy. Hara is the vanquisher of those who can be defeated with difficulty. He is the slayer of those who hate Brahma. He is always the protector and the destroyer. He is the refuge of dharma and adharma. He was surrounded by large numbers of terrible and fierce beings who were horrible in form. Surrounded by large numbers of these, the illustrious Sthanu was resplendent. O king! The entire world and universe is established in his limbs and all mobile and immobile objects were beautiful. It was a wonderful sight. On seeing that the chariot was ready, he donned divine armour and picked up his bow and arrow. He grasped the celestial arrows that were generated through Soma, Vishnu and Agni. O king! O supreme among kings! The gods instructed the lord of the wind to blow sacred fragrances. Mahadeva ascended the chariot and terrified the gods. When he ascended, the earth and heaven trembled. The granter of boons was beautiful, with his sword, arrows and bow.

'"'He smiled and asked the masses of gods, "Who will be my charioteer?" The gods replied, "O lord of the gods! There is no doubt that whoever you employ, will be your charioteer." He told the gods again, "You decide who is superior to me. Decide this yourselves and make him the charioteer." Having heard the words of the great-souled one, the gods went to the grandfather and having obtained his reassurance, spoke these words. "O god! We have done everything that you asked us to, for destroying the enemies of the thirty gods. The one with the bull on his banner is completely pleased with us. We have constructed a chariot and equipped it with many wonderful weapons. But we do not know who should be the charioteer of that supreme chariot. Therefore, let the best of the gods be appointed as the charioteer. O god! O lord! You should ensure that the words

[341]Shiva's names. Nilalohita means the one who is blue-red. Dhumra means the one who is dark-red or covered in smoke. Krittivasa means the one who is attired in skin.

that you spoke become successful. O illustrious one! You told us earlier that you would do that which would be beneficial for us. You should act in accordance with that. The supreme of chariots has parts from all the gods. It is irresistible and will drive away the enemy. The one with the Pinaka in his hand is the warrior. He is ready and will strike terror among the danavas. The four Vedas have become the best of steeds. With all the mountains, the earth is the great-souled one's chariot. The nakshatras have obediently become the ornaments. But we do not see a charioteer for that warrior. O god! O grandfather! When such are the chariot, the horses and the warrior, the charioteer must be someone who is special in every way, just as the armour, the weapons and the bow are. But except you, we do not see someone who can be a charioteer. O lord! You are the one who is superior to the gods in all the qualities. Ascend swiftly as a charioteer and control those supreme horses." It has been heard, that in this fashion, the gods bowed down their heads before the grandfather who is the lord of the three worlds and sought his favours, so that he might become the charioteer. Brahma said, "O residents of heaven! There is nothing false in everything that you have said. I will control the horses when Kapardin[342] fights." The illustrious god, the grandfather who was the creator of the worlds, was appointed by the gods as the charioteer of the great-souled Ishana. When he swiftly ascended the chariot, worshipped by the worlds, the horses, which possessed the speed of the wind, quickly lowered their heads and sank down on their knees on the ground. Maheshvara also ascended. The great grandfather of the three worlds successfully grasped the reins and urged those horses, which possessed the speed of thought and the wind. When the granter of boons[343] ascended and left in the direction of the asuras, the lord of the universe[344] smiled and said, "Excellent! Wonderful! O god! Go to the spot of the daityas. Urge the horses diligently. Behold the strength of my my arms today. I will slay the enemies in the battle."

[342]Shiva's name, the one with the matted hair.

[343]Brahma.

[344]Shiva.

At this, he[345] urged the horses, which were as fleet as the wind. O king! He went towards the city that was protected by the daityas and the danavas.

"''Sharva[346] strung the bow and affixed the arrow. He affixed the *pashupata* weapon and thought of Tripura. O king! Having stationed himself there, he angrily stretched his bow. At that point, the cities united and became one. The three cities united and became one and a tumultuous sound of delight arose among the great-souled gods. All the masses of gods, siddhas and supreme rishis became full of joy and uttered words of praise, signifying victory. Tripura manifested itself before the one who wanted to slay the asuras, the god whose form was indescribable and fierce and whose energy was intolerable. The illustrious one, the lord of the worlds, drew his celestial bow. The one who is the essence of the three worlds released the arrow towards Tripura. He consumed the large numbers of asuras and flung them into the western ocean. Thus, Tripura was burnt and the remaining danavas scorched by the angry Maheshvara for the welfare of the three worlds. The one with three eyes then pacified the flames that resulted from his wrath and said, "Do not reduce the world to ashes." At this, nature, the gods, the worlds and the rishis returned to their natural states and satisfied the infinitely energetic Sthanu with eloquent words of grave import. On receiving the permission of the illustrious one, all of them returned to where they had come from. Having accomplished their objective, the gods, with Prajapati at the forefront, were satisfied. Thus did the illustrious Brahma, the grandfather who is the controller of the worlds, control the horses, and you should do the same for the great-souled Radheya. O tiger among kings! There is no need to debate whether you are especially superior to Krishna, Karna and Phalguna. O unblemished one! He[347] is like Rudra in a battle and you are like Brahma. Like the asuras, if the two of you are united, you can vanquish my enemies. O Shalya! Act so that Karna can swiftly oppress and slay Kounteya, the one

[345]Brahma.

[346]Shiva.

[347]Karna.

with the white horses, with Krishna as his charioteer. Karna, the kingdom and our foundation is based on you.

'"'There is another account I will tell you about. Listen to it. A brahmana who knew about dharma recounted it in my father's presence. Hear these wonderful words, full of reasons, deeds and objectives. O Shalya! Do what must be done and do not reflect. The immensely energetic Jamadagni was born in the lineage of the Bhargavas. He had a famous son named Rama,[348] with energy and all the qualities. So that he might be able to please Bhava and obtain weapons, he performed terrible austerities. He was cheerful in his soul, controlled and restrained his senses. At this, Mahadeva was satisfied and pleased by his devotion. Shankara knew what was in his mind and showed himself. The god said, "O Rama! I am satisfied with you. O fortunate one! I know what you wish for. If you purify your soul, you will get everything that you want. When you become pure, I will give you all the weapons. O Bhargava! Those weapons burn down a person who is incapable and undeserving." Having been thus addressed by the god of the gods who wields a trident, Jamadagni's great-souled son bowed his head in obeisance and told the lord, "O lord of the gods! If you think that I am a person who is capable of bearing those weapons, you should give me those weapons, since I have always served you." He performed austerities and resorted to control and discipline. He worshipped, offered gifts and sacrifices and honoured him with oblations and mantras. He worshipped Sharva for a large number of years. Mahadeva was satisfied with the great-souled Bhargava. In the presence of the gods, he spoke about his[349] many qualities. "Rama is firm in his vows and is always devoted to me." The lord, the destroyer of enemies, was pleased and spoke about his qualities in many different ways, in the presence of the gods and the ancestors. At this time, the daityas became extremely powerful. Because of their insolence and delusion, they afflicted the residents of heaven. At this, all the gods united and made up their minds to kill them. They made every effort to kill the enemy, but were

[348]Parashurama.

[349]Parashurama's.

incapable of vanquishing them. The gods then went and spoke to Maheshvara. They pleased him with their devotion and asked him to kill the large numbers of the enemy. Having obtained a promise from the god that the enemies would be destroyed, the gods summoned Bhargava Rama. Shankara told him, "O Bhargava! For the sake of the welfare of the worlds and to please me, kill the enemies of the assembled gods." Rama replied, "O lord of the gods! O Maheshvara! Without the weapons, what strength do I possess, that I should kill the danavas? All of them are accomplished in the use of weapons and are indomitable in battle." The god said, "On my instructions, go. You will kill the danavas. Having vanquished the enemy, you will obtain many qualities." Having heard these words, he agreed wholeheartedly. Rama offered benedictions and left in the direction of the danavas. He killed the enemies of the gods, who were proud, insolent and powerful. Bhargava struck them with the touch of the vajra. The danavas inflicted wounds on the body of Jamadagni's son, supreme among the brahmanas. However, at Sthanu's touch, all those wounds disappeared. The illustrious god was pleased at his deed and granted boons to the great-souled Bhargava, who was knowledgable about the brahman. The god of the gods, the wielder of the trident, was pleased and said, "From the descent of the weapons, there are wounds on your body. O descendant of the Bhrigu lineage! These prove the superhuman deed you have achieved. As you desired, accept these divine weapons from me." He obtained the weapons and all the boons that he wished for. Having obtained these diverse objects, Rama lowered his head before Shiva. The immensely ascetic one took the permission of the lord of the gods and departed. This is the ancient account that was told by the rishi.

"''Bhargava imparted all his knowledge of dhanurveda to the great-souled Karna, tiger among men, having been extremely pleased with him. O king! Had Karna not been a deserving person, the descendant of the Bhrigu lineage would not have given him those celestial weapons. I therefore think that Karna cannot have been born in the lineage of a suta. I think that he is the son of a god, born in the lineage of kshatriyas. The maharatha is long in his arms and possessed earrings and armour. How can a doe give birth to such a tiger? Behold his thick arms, which are like the trunk of a king of elephants. Behold his thick chest, capable of withstanding all enemies.'"'

Chapter 1175(25)

'"Duryodhana said, 'Thus did the illustrious god, the grandfather of all the worlds, become the charioteer, when Rudra was the ratha. It is a duty for the charioteer of a chariot to be braver than the ratha. O tiger among men! Therefore, you should control the horses in the battle.'"

'Sanjaya said, "At this, Shalya, the lord of Madra, was delighted and embraced your son. He spoke these words to Duryodhana, the slayer of enemies. 'O king! O son of Gandhari! O handsome one! If this is what you think, I will do everything that brings pleasure to you. O best of the Bharatas! I will perform whatever task I am thought to be fit for. With my entire heart, I will bear the burden of any task. For the sake of what is beneficial, I may speak words to Karna, pleasant and unpleasant. You and Karna should pardon all of them.' Karna replied, 'O king of Madra! Like Brahma for Ishana and like Keshava for Partha, may you always serve us for our benefit.' Shalya said, 'There are four kinds of conduct not followed by those who are *arya*s—self-censure, self-glorification, speaking ill of others and adulation of others. O learned one! I will speak words for your own good. They may be full of self-praise. But listen to them attentively. O lord! In knowledge, skills of medication, controlling and avoiding distractions,[350] I am like Matali, fit to be Shakra's charioteer. O unblemished one! O son of a suta! When you are engaged in warring with Partha in the battle, I will guide your horses. Do not be anxious on that account.'"'

[350]All of this is with reference to horses.

Chapter 1176(26)

'"Duryodhana said, 'O Karna! This king of Madra will act as your charioteer. He is superior to Krishna and is like Matali, the charioteer of the king of the gods. Just as Matali controls the horses yoked to Hari's[351] chariot, Shalya will control the ones that are yoked to yours. With you as the warrior on that chariot and with the king of Madra as the charioteer, it is certain that this foremost of chariots will vanquish Partha in the battle.'"

'Sanjaya said, "Duryodhana then spoke again to the spirited king of Madra. 'O king! Control these supreme horses in the battle. Protected by you, Radheya will defeat Dhananjaya.' O descendant of the Bharata lineage! Having been thus addressed, he[352] agreed and ascended the chariot. When Shalya approached, Karna was delighted in his mind and spoke to the charioteer. 'O charioteer! Swiftly prepare my chariot and equip it.' That supreme and victorious chariot was like a city of the gandharvas. Having prepared it, the lord[353] brought it and said, 'May you be victorious.' Karna, foremost among rathas, worshipped the chariot in accordance with the prescribed rites. It had earlier been sanctified by a priest who was knowledgeable about the brahman. He circumambulated it carefully and prayed to the sun. The king of Madra was nearby and he asked him to climb onto it first. That great and supreme chariot of Karna's was unassailable. The immensely energetic Shalya ascended, like a lion atop a mountain. O king! On seeing that Shalya was stationed, Karna ascended his supreme chariot, like the sun atop clouds tinged with lightning. Ascended on the same chariot, they were like Aditya and Agni together.[354] They were as resplendent as clouds in the firmament, tinged with Surya and Agni together. Those two brave ones, supreme among resplendent ones, were praised. They were like Indra and Agni, praised by priests and assisting priests at a sacrifice. Shalya

[351]Hari is one of Indra's names.

[352]Shalya.

[353]Shalya.

[354]The sun god and the fire god respectively.

controlled the horses. Karna stood on the chariot and extended his terrible bow, like the sun in its halo. On the best of chariots, Karna, tiger among men, with his arrows like rays, looked like the sun on Mandara.

'"The infinitely energetic and immensely brave Radheya was on the chariot and ready to leave. Duryodhana spoke these words. 'O brave one! O Adhiratha's son! Drona and Bhishma were incapable of accomplishing this extremely difficult task in the battle, while all the archers looked on. Accomplish it. I have always been convinced in my mind that maharatha Bhishma and Drona would kill Arjuna and Bhimasena. O brave one! They were unable to accomplish that valiant deed in this great battle. O Radheya! Like the one with the vajra in his hand, accomplish that task. O Radheya! Seize Dharmaraja, or kill Dhananjaya, Bhimasena and the twins who are the sons of Madri. O fortunate one! May you be victorious. O bull among men! Depart. Reduce all the soldiers of the sons of Pandu to ashes.' Thousands of trumpets and tens of thousands of drums were sounded. The sound of those musical instruments was like the sound of clouds in the sky.

'"Accepting those words and stationed on the chariot, the supreme of rathas, Radheya, addressed Shalya, who was skilled in fighting. 'O mighty-armed one! Urge the horses, so that I can kill Dhananjaya, Bhimasena, the twins and King Yudhishthira.[355] O Shalya! Let Dhananjaya behold the strength of my arms today, when I shoot hundreds and thousands of arrows shafted with the feathers of herons. O Shalya! I will unleash supremely energetic arrows today, for the destruction of the Pandavas and for Duryodhana's victory.' Shalya replied, 'O son of a suta! Why do you disrespect the Pandavas? All of them are great archers and know about all the weapons. All of them are maharathas. They do not retreat, are immensely fortunate. They cannot be vanquished and truth is their valour. They are capable of generating fear in Shatakratu himself. O Radheya! When you hear the twang of Gandiva in battle, like the

[355]However, Karna had sworn to Kunti that he would not kill any of the Pandavas, other than Arjuna.

tumultuous sound of thunder, you will no longer speak in this way.' O lord of men! Disregarding the words spoken by the king of Madra, Karna glanced towards Shalya and asked him to proceed.

'"O scorcher of enemies! On seeing that the great archer, Karna, was stationed and ready to fight, all the Kouravas were filled with delight and let out a roar. There was the sound of drums and kettledrums. There was the sound of arrows and the roars uttered by those spirited ones. Those on your side emerged to do battle, resolved to die, rather than retreat. As Karna advanced, the warriors were delighted. O king! The earth trembled and let out a mighty roar. The seven great planets and the sun seemed to be moving. Showers of meteors could be seen and the directions seemed to be blazing. Thunder descended and fierce winds began to blow. Large numbers of animals and birds kept your army to the right, signifying great fear.[356] When Karna advanced, his horses fell down on the ground. Bones showered down from the sky, portending fear. The weapons seemed to be blazing and the standards trembled. O lord of the earth! The mounts released tears. O venerable one! These, and many other ominous signs, were seen there. They signified the extremely terrible destruction of the Kouravas. However, because they were confounded by destiny, none of them paid any attention to these. On seeing the son of the suta advance, all the men on earth cried out for his victory. The Kouravas thought that the Pandavas had already been vanquished.

'"Vaikartana Vrisha, elephant among rathas and the slayer of enemy heroes, was stationed on his chariot. He thought of the deaths of the brave Bhishma and Drona and blazed like a fire. On seeing Partha's unequalled deeds, he was consumed by pride and insolence. He blazed in anger and sighing deeply, spoke these words to Shalya. 'When I am stationed on my chariot with my bow and enraged, I will not be frightened of the great Indra, with the vajra in his hand. On seeing that Bhishma and the best of others are lying down, do not be anxious. They[357] were like the great Indra and Vishnu.

[356]Therefore, the animals and birds were to the left and the left is inauspicious.
[357]Meaning Bhishma and Drona.

They were unmatched and unblemished. They were the ones who crushed the best of chariots, horses and elephants. It was as if they could not be slain, but they were killed by the enemy. Nevertheless, I am not alarmed in this battle. The preceptor was a bull among brahmanas and was knowledgeable about great weapons. On seeing the extremely powerful kings, with their men, horses, elephants and chariots, slain by arrows, why did he not kill all of them in the battle? O Kurus! Remembering Drona in the great battle, I am telling you this truthfully. Listen to me. Other than me, there is no one who is capable of withstanding Arjuna, when he advances in the battle, in the form of a fierce Death. Drona possessed learning, serenity, strength, fortitude, great weapons and good policy. When that great-souled one had to succumb to death, I think that all the others are distressed now. When I think about it, there is nothing in this world that is certain. Everything is always the outcome of action. When the preceptor has been brought down, who can proudly say with certainty that he will be alive till today's sunrise?[358] There is no doubt that weapons, strength, valour, deeds, good policy and supreme weapons cannot ensure human happiness, since the preceptor has been slain by the enemy in battle. His energy was like that of the sun or the fire. He was equal to Vishnu and Purandara in valour. He was always like Brihaspati and Ushanas[359] in policy. He was extremely difficult to withstand, but weapons could not save him. Our women and children are weeping. The manliness of the sons of Dhritarashtra has been defeated. O Shalya! Know that I have to accomplish the task. Therefore, advance towards the soldiers of the enemy, where the Pandava king who is unwavering in his aim and Bhimasena and Arjuna are stationed. There are Vasudeva, the Srinjayas, Satyaki and the twins. Who, other than me, can withstand them? O lord of Madra! Therefore, advance swiftly in the battle, towards the Panchalas, Pandavas and Srinjayas. I think that I will kill those assembled ones in the battle, or follow Drona's lead.[360] O Shalya! Do

[358]These events are happening just before sunrise on the seventeenth day.

[359]Shukracharya.

[360]That is, die.

not think that I will not advance into the midst of those brave ones. I cannot tolerate this dissension among friends.[361] I will give up my life and follow Drona. Whether wise or foolish, when one's lifespan is over, one cannot escape with one's life and advances into Yama's mouth. O learned one! Therefore, I will advance against Partha. I cannot negate my destiny. O king! The son of Vichitravirya's son[362] has always been kind towards me. To accomplish his objective and attain his end, I will give up my beloved pleasures and my life, which is so difficult to abandon. This expensive chariot is covered with the skins of tigers. Its axles don't make a sound. The three frames are golden and the trivenu is made out of silver. It is yoked to excellent horses. Rama[363] gave it to me. O Shalya! Behold the colourful bows, standard, clubs, arrows with fierce forms, flaming sword, supreme weapons and the white conch shell that has a fierce sound. It[364] has flags and clatters like the sound of the thunder. It is yoked to white horses and is adorned with superb quivers. Stationed on this chariot, I will use my force to slay Arjuna, bull among rathas, in the battle. Even if Death, the destroyer of everything, diligently protects the son of Pandu in the encounter, I will engage with him and kill him in the encounter, or follow the path to Yama, along which, Bhishma has led. Even if Yama, Varuna, Kubera, Vasava, together with all their followers, unite to protect Pandava in this battle, I will defeat him. What is the need to speak more?'

'"On hearing the words of the one who was delighted at the prospect of battle and was bragging, the valiant king of Madra showed him disrespect and laughed at him. To restrain him, he gave him the following reply. 'O Karna! Desist. Refrain from such bragging. You are delighted and are saying that which should not be said. Where is Dhananjaya, supreme among men? And where are you, an extremely stupid person? The abode of the Yadus was

[361]Referring to the quarrel between Karna and Shalya.

[362]Duryodhana. Duryodhana is Dhritarashtra's son and Dhritarashtra is Vichitravirya's son.

[363]Parashurama. That is, Parashurama gave Karna the chariot.

[364]The chariot.

protected by Upendra.[365] It was like heaven, protected by the king of the immortals. Who other than Arjuna, supreme among men, could have violently abducted that beautiful lady, while he looked on?[366] He has a power and valour like that of the king of the gods. Where is the man, other than Arjuna, who at the time of the slaughter of the animal, could have challenged Bhava, the lord of all lords and the creator of the three worlds, to a battle?[367] To honour Agni, Jaya[368] vanquished asuras, gods, giant serpents, men, birds, pishachas, yakshas and rakshasas with his arrows and gave him the oblations he desired.[369] Do you remember how Dhritarashtra's son was seized by the enemy and was freed by that supreme among men, using arrows that were as bright as the rays of the sun? In that wilderness, he killed large numbers of the enemy. You were the first to run away then. Do you remember how Dhritarashtra's quarrelsome son was freed and the Pandava defeated large numbers of those who travel through the skies?[370] At the time of the seizure of the cattle, all of them, though they possessed large numbers of forces and mounts, were vanquished by that supreme of men. The preceptor, the preceptor's son and Bhishma were also there. Why did you not defeat Arjuna then?[371] This supreme and excellent encounter has presented itself now, for the sake of your destruction. O son of a suta! If you do not run away, because of fear of the enemy, you will be slain today, when you advance to fight.' The lord of Madra spoke many such harsh

[365]Upendra is Indra's younger brother, that is, Vishnu. Here, it means Krishna.

[366]This is a reference to the abduction of Subhadra, Krishna's sister, described in Section 17 (Volume 2).

[367]This is a reference to Arjuna's duel with Shiva, described in Section 31 (Volume 2).

[368]Arjuna's name.

[369]This is a reference to the burning of Khandava, described in Section 19 (Volume 2).

[370]The gandharvas travel through the sky. This is a reference to the gandharvas capturing the Kouravas, described in Section 39 (Volume 3).

[371]This is a reference to the Kourava attempt to seize Virata's cattle, described in Section 47 (Volume 4).

words cheerfully, praising your enemy. Vrisha, the leader of the Kuru forces, became supremely enraged and spoke these words to the lord of Madra. 'Let it be that way. Even if it is that way, why are you praising him, when a battle is about to commence between him and me? If he defeats me in this great battle, will it be said that the words uttered by you have been spoken well?' The lord of Madra agreed with this and did not say anything in reply. Wishing to fight, Karna asked the lord of Madra to depart. The ratha left in the direction of the enemy with the white horses, with Shalya as his charioteer. He killed enemies in the battle, like the sun destroying darkness. Karna was on a chariot yoked to white horses, covered with the skins of tigers. He left cheerfully. He saw the standards of the Pandavas and quickly asked about where Dhananjaya was."'

Chapter 1177(27)

'Sanjaya said, "Karna left, delighting your army. He told every Pandava soldier that he saw, 'Today, I will grant the one who points out to me the great-souled one on the white horses, whatever boon he desires for. If he thinks that is not enough, I will again give a cart full of jewels to the one who tells me about Dhananjaya. If the man who shows Arjuna to me thinks that is not enough, I will again give him six carts full of gold, drawn by bulls that are like elephants. I will again give him one hundred ornamented women. They will be virgins,[372] with necklaces of gold, and skilled in singing and dancing. If the man who shows me Arjuna thinks that this is not enough, I will give him another boon of five hundred white horses. They will have golden harnesses and be decorated with bejewelled ornaments. I will give him another eight hundred well-trained horses. I will give the person who tells me about Dhananjaya a golden and

[372]The word used is *shyama*. This means dark. But it also means a woman who hasn't had a child or hasn't been exposed to intercourse.

sparkling chariot that is yoked to supreme horses from the Kamboja region. I will give him another boon of six hundred elephants that have golden harnesses and are adorned with golden necklaces. They have been born in the frontier regions and have been trained well by those who are skilled in elephants. If the man who shows me Arjuna thinks that this is not enough, I will give him another boon that he will desire himself. I possess sons, wives and riches. If he desires these, I will again give them to him. I will give the person who shows me Keshava and Arjuna all their riches, after having killed the two Krishnas.' In the battle, having spoken these and many other words, Karna blew on his supreme conch shell. It had been generated from the ocean and produced a wonderful sound. O great king! Having heard these words of the son of the suta, which were appropriate to his character, Duryodhana and all his followers were delighted. At this, drums and kettledrums were sounded in every direction. Together with the musical instruments, there were roars like lions and the trumpeting of elephants. O king! O bull among the Bharata lineage! These sounds arose among the soldiers. The sounds made by the delighted warriors mingled with these.

'"The soldiers were delighted and Radheya, the afflicter of enemies, was about to plunge himself into the ocean of battle. The king of Madra laughed and addressed him in these words. 'O son of a suta! When a man shows you Dhananjaya, do not, in your insolence, give him six golden bulls that are like elephants. Like a child, you are giving away riches as if you are Vaishravana.[373] O Radheya! Even if you do not make an effort, you will see Dhananjaya today. Like an extremely foolish person, you are unnecessarily giving them away. Because of your delusion, you do not realize the sins of giving to the undeserving. With the many riches that you propose to give away, you are capable of performing many sacrifices. O suta! Perform sacrifices. Because of your delusion and your intolerance, you desire to kill the two Krishnas. But we have not heard of two lions being brought down by a jackal. You desire what should not be desired. Clearly, you have no well-wishers, since they are not

[373]Kubera.

restraining you from swiftly falling into a fire. You do not know what should be done when. There is no doubt that you have been ripened by time.[374] A man who desires to be alive should not speak such words that should not be listened to. You are like someone wishing to cross an ocean with his arms, with a stone tied around his neck. Or you are like someone who wishes to fall down from the peak of a mountain. If you wish to ensure your own welfare, fight with Dhananjaya from the midst of this battle formation, with all the warriors, and well protected. I am saying this for the welfare of Dhritarashtra's son and not from malice towards you. If you wish to remain alive, pay attention to the words spoken by me.'

'"Karna replied, 'I wish to encounter Arjuna in the battle on the basis of my own valour and not by relying on others. You are an enemy in the disguise of a friend and are trying to frighten me. No one is capable of restraining me from my resolution today, not even Indra himself, with an upraised vajra. What can a mortal seek to do?'"

'Sanjaya said, "When Karna had finished speaking, Shalya, the lord of Madra, wished to provoke Karna further and again spoke these words to him. 'Forceful arrows will be released from Phalguna's arms and unleashed from his bowstring. They will descend on you, sharp at the tip and shafted with the feathers of herons. It is then that you will regret advancing against Arjuna. Partha will grasp his celestial bow. Savyasachi will scorch the soldiers and oppress you with his sharp arrows. O son of a suta! You will regret it then. You are like a child supine on a mother's lap, who wishes to touch the one who removes water.[375] Because of your delusion, you wish to vanquish the resplendent Arjuna today, who is stationed on his chariot. It is as if you are rubbing the extremely sharp edges of a trident against all your limbs. O Karna! Today, you are wishing to fight with Arjuna, whose deeds are extremely sharp. This is like the childish folly of a spirited but small deer, who wishes to challenge a large and maned lion. O son of a suta! Your challenge to Arjuna

[374]And are ready to be plucked.

[375]The sun.

now is like that challenge. O son of a suta! Do not challenge that prince, who is extremely valorous and is like a lion. You should be like a fox in the forest, satisfied with some meat. Do not challenge Partha today and be destroyed. O Karna! Your challenging Partha in a battle will be like a rabbit challenging a mighty elephant with tusks like ploughs and with a shattered temple. You will be like a child, striking a cobra, with great poison and full sacs, in a hole with a stick. Your desire to fight with Partha is like that. O Karna! Pandava is a lion among men. Like a stupid jackal, you are shouting at a maned and angry lion. For the sake of its own downfall, a small bird challenges the spirited Suparna, Vinata's son, supreme among birds.[376] O Karna! You are like that against Partha Dhananjaya. You wish to cross the terrible ocean, the abode of all the waters, on a raft, at a time when the moon is rising and its waves are turbulent and full of thousands of fish. He is a bull with sharp horns. His neck is as thick as a drum. He is a striker. O Karna! Like a small calf, you are challenging that Partha Dhananjaya to a fight. A large cloud makes a mighty noise and pours down desired rain on the world. Arjuna is like a cloud among men and you are croaking back at him, like a frog. From its own house, a dog barks at a tiger that is roaming in the forest. O Karna! Like that, you are barking at Dhananjaya, tiger among men. O Karna! Dwelling in a forest and surrounded by rabbits, a jackal thinks itself to be a lion, until it actually sees a lion. O Radheya! Like that, you think yourself to be a lion. But you do not see Dhananjaya, tiger among men, the crusher of enemies. You think yourself to be a tiger until you see the two Krishnas on a single chariot, like the sun and the moon. O Karna! Until you hear the roar of Gandiva in the great battle, till then, you are capable of speaking as you wish. You will hear that tiger[377] roar and make the ten directions resound with the clatter of his chariot and the twang of his bow. You will then become a jackal. You have always been a jackal and Dhananjaya has always been a lion. O foolish one! Because of your hatred towards those who are valiant, you have always seemed

[376]Meaning Garuda.

[377]Arjuna.

to be a jackal. Because of your own deeds and your strengths and weaknesses, you and Partha are known to be like a rat to a cat, a dog to a tiger, a fox to a lion and a rabbit to an elephant.'

'"Thus rebuked by the infinitely energetic Shalya, whose words were like darts to him,[378] Radheya became extremely angry and spoke to Shalya. 'O Shalya! Qualities, and the absence of qualities, are known to those with qualities, not to those without qualities. You have always been devoid of qualities. How will you know the difference between qualities and the lack of qualities? O Shalya! I know about Arjuna's great weapons, anger, valour, bow and arrows. You do not know their true nature. In that way, I know my valour and Pandava's valour. O Shalya! Knowing that, I have challenged him to a battle. I am not like an insect that heads towards a fire. O Shalya! I possess this arrow. It is well tufted and will drink blood. It has been washed excellently in oil and has been decorated well. It is lying alone in this quiver. It is lying down in sandalwood powder and has been worshipped by me for many years. This is extremely poisonous and is a serpent.[379] It is capable of slaying large numbers of men, horses and elephants. It is powerful and extremely terrible and is capable of shattering body armour and bones. In my wrath, I can use this to shatter the giant Mount Meru. Listen to me. I am saying this truthfully. I will never release this at anyone other than Phalguna and Krishna, the son of Devaki. O Shalya! I will use this arrow against Vasudeva and Dhananjaya. I will be extremely angry and fight with them. That will be an act that is worthy of me. Among all those of Vasudeva's lineage, Lakshmi[380] is vested in Krishna. Among all the sons of Pandu, victory is vested in Partha. When those two advance, how can one retreat? Those two tigers among men are united and stationed on a chariot, and will advance against me, who is single-handed. O Shalya! Behold my good lineage then. They are

[378]There is a pun, because the word *shalya* means dart.

[379]The serpent Ashvasena survived the conflagration in Khandava, described in Section 19 (Volume 2). To wreak vengeance on Arjuna, he hid himself in the tip of an arrow that Karna would use in the battle.

[380]That is, prosperity.

unvanquished cousins, one the son of a maternal uncle and the other one the son of a father's sister.[381] You will see them killed by me, like two gems on a single thread. Arjuna's Gandiva, Krishna's chakra and Tarkshya and the ape on the standards[382] only generate fear among cowards. O Shalya! They generate delight in me. You are evil in nature. You are stupid. You do not know about great battles. You are overcome with terror and have spoken a lot of words because of your fright. I do not know why you are praising them, perhaps because you have been born in a wicked country. Having killed them in the battle, I will slay you, with your relatives. You have been born in a wicked country and are evil in intelligence. You are inferior and the worst among kshatriyas. If you are a well-wisher, why are you frightening me about the two Krishnas, like an enemy? Today, I will be stationed in battle and either I will kill them, or they will kill me. I am not scared of the two Krishnas. I know my own strength. I will single-handedly slay one thousand Vasudevas and one hundred Phalgunas. O one who is born in a wicked country! Do not speak. Women, children, aged ones and those who have completed their studies often say something about the evil-souled ones from Madraka[383] and it has become a universal saying. O Shalya! I will tell you that saying. Listen. In the assemblies of the kings, this is what the brahmanas also recounted earlier. O foolish one! Listen attentively to this and then forgive me, or render a reply. A Madraka is always one who hates those who are his friends. One who always hates, is a Madraka. There are no good feelings in a Madraka. He is inferior in words and is the worst among men. A Madraka is always inferior in his soul. He always lies and is never straight. We have heard it said that wickedness exists among Madrakas. Fathers, mothers, sons, mothers-in-law, fathers-in-law, maternal uncles, sons-

[381]Arjuna's mother (Pritha/Kunti) and Krishna's father (Vasudeva) were brother and sister. Therefore, Krishna is the son of Arjuna's maternal uncle. Arjuna is the son of Krishna's father's sister.

[382]Tarkshya is Garuda. Vishnu/Krishna has Garuda on his standard and Arjuna has an ape on his standard.

[383]Madraka is the same as Madra.

in-law, daughters, brothers, grandsons, kin, friends, others who have arrived, male servants and female servants mingle together. Noble women, according to their own wishes, mingle with men, known and unknown. In their homes, even the better ones always eat coarse grain and other undesirable food. They drink liquor,[384] eat the flesh of cows and dance and laugh. The songs don't have proper rhymes. They indulge in satisfying desire. They speak to each other, incoherent in desire. How can there be dharma there? Among those who have been ruined, the Madrakas are known as the performers of wicked deeds. It is said that one should have neither enmity, nor friendship, with Madrakas. One should not mix with Madrakas, because Madrakas are always fickle. Contact with Madrakas is futile, like purity among those from Gandhara, just as oblations proffered at a sacrifice are destroyed if the king is himself both the sacrificer and the priest. A brahmana who performs ceremonies[385] for shudras confronts destruction. Like that, one who hates brahmanas always confronts destruction. One who mixes with Madrakas is also destroyed, as if from the poison of a scorpion. I have pacified everything with mantras from the Atharva Veda. Wise ones who have been stung by a scorpion and have been afflicted by different types of poison, resort to medicines in this way.[386] This is seen to be the truth. O learned one! Keep quiet and listen to more of my words. Women who are intoxicated by liquor cast off their clothes and dance around. They do not follow restraints and indulge in sexual

[384]More specifically, *sidhu*, liquor made from molasses. Actually, the negative nuance doesn't seem to be on liquor, but on the fact that it is made from molasses.

[385]*Samskara*. There are thirteen samskaras or sacraments. The list varies a bit. But one list is *vivaha* (marriage), *garbhalambhana* (conception), *pumshavana* (engendering a male child), *simantonnayana* (parting the hair, performed in the fourth month of pregnancy), *jatakarma* (birth rites), *namakarana* (naming), *chudakarma* (tonsure), *annaprashana* (first solid food), *keshanta* (first shaving of the head), *upanayana* (sacred thread), *vidyarambha* (commencement of studies), *samavartana* (graduation) and *antyeshti* (funeral rites).

[386]Shalya's words are being compared to the bite of a scorpion.

intercourse, following the dictates of desire. O Madraka! You are the son of one such. How can you talk about dharma? There are inferior women who urinate like camels and buffaloes. They are devoid of shame, and shamelessly do this everywhere. You are the son of one such person. How can you talk about dharma? If asked for collyrium, a Madraka woman scratches her buttocks and unwilling to give it, speaks these terrible words. "No. I will not give any collyrium. I would rather give my beloved instead. On every occasion, I will give up my son. But I will not give the collyrium." Madraka women are ignoble. They are large. They are without modesty and are hairy. They eat a lot and are without any purity. That is what is generally heard. I, and others, are capable of recounting many such things about them, from the ends of their hair to the tips of their toes. How can the Madrakas and the Sindhu-Souviras know about dharma? They have been born in a wicked country. They are mlecchas. They do not know anything about dharma. The most important dharma for a kshatriya is that he should be slain and should lie down on the ground, honoured by the virtuous. That is what we have heard. It is my prime wish that, in this release and clash of weapons, I should be killed and should go to heaven. I am also the beloved friend of Dhritarashtra's intelligent son. My life and the riches that I posssess are for him. O one who has been born in a wicked country! It is evident that you have been bought by the Pandavas. That explains your action towards us, always like that of an enemy. Like a person who is knowledgeable about dharma cannot be dissuaded by an atheist, I am headed towards this battle and cannot be dissuaded by hundreds of people like you. Like a deer that is sweating, you are welcome to lament or thirst. But I am established in the conduct of kshatriyas and you are incapable of frightening me. My preceptor, Rama,[387] had earlier told me about the ends obtained by the lions among men who gave up their lives and did not retreat from battle. I remember that. I am ready to save those on our side and kill the enemy. Know that I am established in this conduct, like the supreme Pururava. O Madraka! I do not see anyone

[387]Parashurama.

in the three worlds who is capable of dissuading me from that objective. That is my view. Knowing this, why have you spoken such a lot, trying to terrify me? O worst of the Madrakas! I will not slay you now and give your body to predatory creatures. O Shalya! That is because of my friendship with Dhritarashtra's son, to avoid censure and because I am patient. Those are the three reasons that you are still alive. O king of Madra! But if you speak such words yet again, I will bring down your head with this club, which is like a vajra. O one who has been born in a wicked country! Today, people will hear and see either that Karna has killed the two Krishnas, or that Karna has been slain by them.' O lord of the earth! Having spoken these words, Radheya again fearlessly addressed the king of Madra, asking him to proceed."'

Chapter 1178(28)

'Sanjaya said, "O venerable one! On hearing the words of Adhiratha's son, who delighted himself in battle, Shalya again spoke to Karna, citing an example. 'You seem to be like one who is intoxicated with liquor. But whether you are like that or not, and irrespective of your intoxication, as a well-wisher, I will try to cure you. O Karna! I will tell you about the story of the crow. Listen to me. O wicked one! O worst of the lineage! On hearing this, do what you wish. O Karna! O mighty-armed one! I do not recollect a single taint in me, as a result of which you wish to kill an unblemished one like me. Had you known what was good for you, you would certainly have listened to my words, especially because I am your charioteer and the king's[388] well-wisher. The even and uneven terrain, the strengths and weaknesses of the chariot, the fatigue and perspiration of the horses and the charioteer, the knowledge of the weapons, the cries of animals and birds, what is burdensome

[388]Duryodhana's.

and what is extremely burdensome,[389] antidotes to wounds from weapons, the use of different weapons in battle and knowledge of portents—all of these are known to me. And I am familiar with this chariot. O Karna! Therefore, let me recount the example to you once more. On the other side of the ocean, there lived a vaishya and he possessed a lot of riches and foodgrains. He performed sacrifices, was generous and quiet and established in the deeds he ought to perform.[390] He was pure. He had many sons whom he loved and he was compassionate towards all beings. Without any fear, he dwelt in the kingdom of a king who observed dharma. His illustrious sons were young. There was a crow that lived there and it subsisted on many kinds of leftover food. The young sons of the vaishya always gave it meat, curds, milk, *payasam*,[391] honey and butter. The crow subsisted on the leftovers that were given by the young sons of the vaishya. It became insolent and showed no respect to birds that were its equal or superior. Once, it so happened that swans descended on the other side of the ocean. They were cheerful in their hearts and could go anywhere at will. Their speed was like that of Garuda. On seeing the swans, the young boys spoke to the crow. "O bird! You are superior to all the winged birds." The one who was born from an egg was thus addressed by those who were of limited intelligence. Because of his stupidity and insolence, he regarded those words to be true. He asked those who could travel long distances[392] who among them was the swiftest in speed. The swans could travel long distances. But because of insolence and evil intelligence, the crow that fed on leftovers challenged that bird to a test of flight. On hearing these words of the crow, the swans that had assembled there, powerful and supreme birds, began to laugh. Those birds, which could go anywhere at will, spoke these words to the crow. "We are swans that roam the earth. We live in Lake Manasa. Among birds, we are always revered as those that can travel long distances. A swan is powerful.

[389]For the horses to bear.

[390]Appropriate for a vaishya.

[391]Rice mixed with milk and sugar.

[392]The swans.

Its limbs are like a vajra. It can travel a great distance. O evil-minded one! You are a crow. How can you issue such a challenge? O crow! How will you fly with us?" They laughed and told him that. Because of the limited intelligence of its species, the stupid crow repeatedly questioned the words of the swans. Eventually, it replied, "There is no doubt that I will fly in one hundred and one different kinds of ways. I will fly each span of a hundred yojanas in a beautiful and varied way. I will rise up and swoop down. I will circle and fly straight. I will fly slowly and I will fly fast. I will fly diagonally. I will traverse slowly. I will whirl around. I will move gently and fast. I will then fly extremely fast and even faster than that. I will swoop down and rise up again. Forward, backwards and sideways, I will show many techniques of flight. I will show all these to you. Behold my strength." Having been thus addressed by the crow, one of the swans laughed. The swan spoke these words to the crow. "Listen to me. O crow! There is no doubt that you will fly in one hundred and one different kinds of ways. I will however fly in the only way that all the birds know. O crow! That is the way I will fly, because I do not know any other. O red-eyed one! You fly in whichever way you think appropriate." At this, the crows who had assembled there began to laugh. "How will the swan fly in only one kind of way and defeat flight in one hundred different ways?" They began to fly, one in one technique, and the other used one hundred and one flying techniques. Powerful and swift in strength, the swan and the crow flew. The swan and the crow flew, rivalling each other. The one that could fly anywhere[393] flew. The crow also flew. Each flew so as to cause wonder in the rival and praised his own deeds. The crow flew in a myriad and colourful ways. On seeing this, the assembled crows were delighted and started to caw loudly. The swans laughed at them and uttered many unpleasant words. From one instant to another, they[394] repeatedly rose up and swooped down. Descending and ascending, they were on the tops of trees and on the ground. They uttered many kinds of noises, signifying their victory. O venerable

[393]The swan.

[394]The swan and the crow involved in the match.

one! With that single and gentle motion, the valiant swan continued to fly and for an instant, it seemed as if it had been defeated by the crow. Slighting the swans, the crows spoke these words. "The swan that rose up into the sky is clearly being defeated." On hearing these words, the swan flew in a westward direction. It increased its speed and flew over the ocean, Varuna's abode. At this, fear penetrated the crow and it lost its senses. It did not see any islands or trees, where it could descend and rest, when it was tired. "When I am tired, where will I descend in this ocean of water? This ocean is the abode of a large number of beings and is intolerable. There are many large beings that reside here and it is superior to the sky."[395] O worst of your lineage! The ocean is superior to everything in depth. O Karna! It is as limitless as the sky. The ocean is impossible to conquer. O Karna! Given its extremely long distance, what could a crow do? In a short while, the swan travelled a long distance. It could not leave the crow behind and glanced back at it. Having overtaken the crow, the one that could travel anywhere at will glanced back at it.[396] Seeing that it was exhausted, the swan wished to rescue the one who was sinking and remembered the vows observed by righteous people. It said, "You repeatedly spoke about many different kinds of flight. You should not speak about these techniques of flight. They are a mystery to us. O crow! What is the name of this pattern of flight that you are now being forced to fly? Your wings and your beak are repeatedly touching the water. You are touching the waters of the ocean with your wings and your beak. O crow! You are extremely exhausted and you will suddenly fall down."

'"'The swan said, "O crow! You spoke about one hundred and one different techniques of flight. Earlier, you spoke about many techniques. All of those have come to nought now."

'"'The crow replied, "O swan! Having fed on leftovers, I became insolent. I thought myself to be the equal of Suparna.[397] I showed disrespect to many other crows and all birds. I seek my life back

[395]The crow is thinking this.

[396]The swan waited for the exhausted crow to catch up.

[397]Garuda.

from you. Take me to the shores of an island. O swan! Let me obtain assurance and let me return to my country again. I will never show disrespect to anyone again. Save me."

"'"It was distressed and spoke in this way.[398] Devoid of its senses, it lamented. Submerged in the great ocean, it cawed. The crow was drenched in water and faced a great hardship. The swan picked it up with its feet and gently raised it onto its[399] back. O Karna! The swan made the crow, bereft of its senses, climb astride its back. They again quickly flew to the island where the match had started. Having placed the bird down there, it comforted it.[400] The swan, as swift as thought, then flew away to the country it wished to. This is what happened to the crow that fed on leftovers from a vaishya household. There is no doubt that you have subsisted on leftovers from the sons of Dhritarashtra. O Karna! That is the reason you show disrespect to all those who are your equal and superior. You were protected by Drona, Drona's son, Kripa, Bhishma and the other Kouravas in Virata's city. Partha was single-handed. Why didn't you kill him then?[401] All of you were distressed and vanquished by Kiriti, like jackals defeated by a lion. Where was your valour then? When you saw that your brother was defeated and killed by Savyasachi, while all the brave ones among the Kurus looked on, you were the first to run away.[402] O Karna! Like that, when you were attacked by the gandharvas in Dvaitavana,[403] you abandoned all the Kurus and were the first to run away. Partha killed and defeated the gandharvas, with Chitrasena at the forefront, in battle. O Karna! He freed Duryodhana and his wife. Then again, in earlier times, in the assembly of the kings, Rama[404] himself spoke about the power of Partha and Keshava.In the presence of the kings, Bhishma and

[398]This is Shalya speaking again.

[399]The swan's.

[400]The swan comforted the crow.

[401]The seizure of the cattle, described in Section 47 (Volume 4).

[402]Arjuna killed three of Karna's brothers in Section 66 (Volume 5).

[403]The incident described in Section 39 (Volume 3).

[404]Parashurama, this is a reference to Section 54 (Volume 4).

Drona have always said that the two Krishnas cannot be killed. You have heard that. I have only told you a little bit about how Dhananjaya is superior to you in various ways, like a brahmana is superior to all other beings. You will soon see that expensive chariot and Vasudeva's son and Pandava Dhananjaya stationed on it. Those two bulls among men are famous among gods, asuras and humans. They are renowned among men because of their radiance and you are like a firefly. O son of a suta! Know this to be your state. Those two lions among men, Achyuta and Arjuna, will destroy you. Do not indulge in self-praise.'"'

Chapter 1179(29)

'Sanjaya said, "Adhiratha's son heard these unpleasant words spoken by the lord of Madra. But he was not pacified and spoke to Shalya. 'Everything about Arjuna and Vasudeva is known to me. Shouri's skill in driving Arjuna's chariot, Pandava's strength and great weapons are just as you have said and are known to me. O Shalya! But you have not directly seen this.[405] They are invincible and foremost among the wielders of weapons. However, without being overcome with fear, I will fight with the two Krishnas. I am suffering from greater torment because of Rama. That supreme brahmana has cursed me. In earlier times, wishing to obtain a divine weapon from Rama, I lived with him, in the disguise of a brahmana. O Shalya! For the sake of Phalguna's welfare, the king of the gods caused an obstruction there.[406] He penetrated my thigh and entered my body in the distorted form of an insect. Because of fear of my preceptor, I did not move.[407] On waking up, the brahmana saw this.

[405]That is, Shalya has heard about these accounts, but without being present there himself.

[406]Arjuna was Indra's son.

[407]At that time, Parashurama was sleeping, with his head on Karna's thigh. Karna was scared of waking Parashurama up.

The maharshi asked me who I was and on learning that I was a suta, he cursed me.[408] "O suta! You have obtained this weapon through a deception. Therefore, when it is time to perform a task, it will not manifest itself before you.[409] When it is the time for your death, it will go elsewhere." The brahman can certainly not be present in a person who is not a brahmana. "O father![410] In this fierce and tumultuous battle today, I have forgotten that powerful weapon. The powerful and unfathomable lord of the waters dashes forward, to submerge many beings. The ocean is like a mighty mountain. But the shoreline repulses that immeasurable object. In this world, Kunti's son is the foremost among those who stretch bowstrings. He will release a mass of arrows that can't be resisted. They will be shafted and will penetrate the inner organs, slaying heroes. However, I will counter him in the battle. He is supremely strong amongst those who are strong. He possesses great weapons. He will shoot from an extremely long distance and will be like the fierce ocean. The kings will be submerged in his waves of arrows. But, like the shoreline, I will withstand Partha's arrows. I think that he has no equal among men who wield the bow. But I will fight with him in the battle today, though he is capable of vanquishing the gods and the asuras in a battle. Behold my extremely terrible battle with him today. Pandava is extremely proud and desires to fight. He will advance against me with his superhuman and great weapons. In the battle, I will counter his weapons with my own weapons. I will bring down Partha with my supreme arrows. I will scorch like the rays of the sun. I will blaze like the illustrious one's rays. Like clouds gather around the dispeller of the darkness, I will envelop Dhananjaya with my arrows. A flaming fire has trails of smoke. Its energy scorches all the worlds. But like clouds pacify that fire, I will quench Partha with my arrows in the

[408]A brahmana wouldn't have been able to bear the pain from an insect drilling through. Karna was cursed because he studied under Parashurama under the pretext of being a brahmana.

[409]These were divine weapons. When summoned, they manifested themselves before the user.

[410]The word used is tata. It means father, but is affectionately used towards anyone who is senior.

battle. The fierce wind god is powerful and destroys with a storm. The angry and intolerant Dhananjaya is like that. But, in the battle, I will withstand him like the immobile Himalayas. He is skilled and knows about the circular motions of a chariot. He is always foremost among those who are borne in a battle. He is supreme among all archers in the world. However, I will withstand that Dhananjaya in the battle. I think that there is no archer who is equal to him among men. I know that he has withstood the entire earth. But today, I will encounter him in the battle. Savyasachi vanquished all the beings, together with the gods, in the region known as Khandava. Which other man, with me being an exception, can fight with him and seek to protect his own life? I will cheerfully speak about Pandava's manliness in an assembly of kshatriyas. O stupid one! O one who has lost his senses! Why are you telling me about Arjuna's manliness? Those who are forgiving always forgive an inferior and cruel person who speaks harsh and unpleasant words. I can kill one hundred who are like you. However, because I am forgiving and bearing the appropriate time in mind, I am forgiving you. For Pandava's sake, you have spoken unpleasant words. You have censured me, like a stupid person who performs evil deeds. I did not deserve it. Yet, you have used your tongue to lash me. You are one who hates friends. One with whom one walks seven paces is a friend.[411] The present time is full of death and is extremely terrible. Duryodhana has chosen this to advance in battle. I desire that his objectives are accomplished. But you act as if to counter them, as if you are one who doesn't love him. A friend delights a friend, and always does that which brings him pleasure. He frees him, honours him and shares in his delight. This is what the brahmanas have said earlier. Towards Duryodhana, I tell you that all these traits exist in me. An enemy always chastises and sharpens his weapons. He causes injury, makes us sigh and distresses us. These many harmful qualities are seen in an enemy and almost all of these exist in you. You are showing them towards me. For the sake of accomplishing Duryodhana's objective and for bringing him pleasure, for the sake of bringing glory to myself and for the sake of

[411]Seven paces or *saptapada*. This is symbolic.

accomplishing what the gods want,[412] I will endeavour to fight with Pandava and Vasudeva. Behold my deeds today. Behold my supreme weapons today, brahmastra and other divine and human weapons. I will cushion the one whose valour is fierce, like a supreme elephant killing another crazy elephant. For the sake of victory, I will use my mental powers to hurl the brahmastra at Partha. It is unrivalled and is victorious. In the battle, he will not be able to escape from it, unless my wheels get stuck in uneven terrain. O Shalya! Know that I will not be frightened, even if Vaivasvata[413] with his staff, Varuna with his noose, the lord of riches[414] with his club, Vasava with his vajra, or any other assassin advances against me. Therefore, I have no fear of Partha or Janardana. Today, there will be a clash between me and those two enemies. However, a brahmana told me, "Your miserable wheel will be stuck in the ground and you will confront great fear in your heart, when you are fighting in a battle." Since then, I have greatly suffered from fright at the brahmana's words. O Shalya! The brahmana was a store of austerities and I had unconsciously used my arrows to kill the calf that had been born from his *homa* cow,[415] while it was roaming around amongst people. I gave that foremost among brahmanas seven hundred tusked elephants and hundreds of servants and servant-maids. But he was not satisfied with me. To obtain the favours of that supreme among brahmanas, I brought fourteen thousand black cows, each with a white calf. I offered him a beautiful house, with every object of desire, and all the riches I possessed. I honoured him with all this, but he did not wish to receive them. I had committed a crime and begged him, so that I might remedy it. However, he told me, "O suta! What I have uttered will certainly happen. It cannot be falsified. If I utter a falsehood, beings will be killed and I will commit a sin. Therefore, to protect

[412]Actually, the text uses the word god in the singular. But that doesn't make it clear which god is meant. The use of the plural seems to convey the sense better.

[413]Yama.

[414]Kubera.

[415]Homa means oblations into the fire. The homa cow thus produced milk products used for such oblations.

dharma, I have no interest in speaking a falsehood. You must perform atonement for causing violence towards what provides a brahmana sustenance. There is no one in this world who can make my words false and you should accept them." Though you have censured me, because I am a well-wisher, I have told you this. I know that you are the one who is censuring me. But be quiet and listen to what I will tell you next.'"'

Chapter 1180(30)

'Sanjaya said, "O great king! Radheya again addressed the king of Madra, the scorcher of enemies. He restrained him and spoke these words. 'O Shalya! You have spoken to me about instances. However, your words are incapable of terrifying me in this battle. Even if all the gods, together with Vasava, fight against me, even then, I will not be frightened, not to speak of Partha and Keshava. I am incapable of being frightened by words alone. Know that the person you are capable of terrifying in a battle is someone else. O evil-minded one! You have spoken a lot of harsh words to me. That is the strength of inferior people. You are incapable of comprehending my qualities. O venerable one! Karna was not born so as to be frightened. I have been born for valour and for fame. O lord of Madra! Listen attentively to what I had heard in Dhritarashtra's presence. Honouring Dhritarashtra, brahmanas recounted the ancient and wonderful accounts of many kingdoms and many kings. An aged one, foremost among brahmanas, recounted ancient tales and spoke these words of ill repute about those from the lands of Bahlika and Madra. "They are cast out from the region of the Himalayas and are despised in the region of the Ganga. That is also true of those who live in the central regions, around the Sarasvati, the Yamuna and Kurukshetra, the five rivers[416] and with Sindhu as the sixth. It

[416]The five rivers of the Punjab.

is one's dharma to avoid the impure Bahlikas, who are outside these regions. From the days of my youth, I remember that the kings of their lineage had a fig tree named Govardhana and a quadrangular spot named Subhanda near the gate.[417] Because of some secret work, I had to live with the Bahlikas then. Because I dwelt among them, their conduct is known to me. There is a city named Shakala, a river named Apaga that flows downwards and a lineage of the Bahlikas named Jartika.[418] Their conduct is severely censured. They drink liquor made from grain and molasses. They eat the flesh of cows, laced with garlic. They eat bread mixed with meat and fried barley that has not been sowed.[419] They are devoid of good conduct. Intoxicated, the women throw away their garments and laugh, sing and dance in the cities, and outside the walls, without garlands and unguents. Intoxicated, they sing many songs, in voices that are like those of asses and camels. They freely summon others.[420] When their husbands and lords are killed, they call out their names in intoxication and say, 'Alas! Alas!' However, those wicked ones do not observe sacred occasions and continue to scream and dance. A chief among the Bahlikas lived among those women who made such uproar, and then dwelt for some time in Kurujangala. Cheerless in his mind, he said, 'She is large and fair.[421] She is attired in a thin blanket. When it is time for lying down, she must be thinking about the Bahlika who now lives among the Kurus. When will I cross the river Shatadru and the beautiful Iravati and go to my own country, where I will see those handsome women with large bodies? Those fair women have

[417]It is not evident why this should be reprehensible. It is sometimes suggested that the quadrangular spot was for slaughtering cattle and Subhanda was a store for liquor. Though possible, this doesn't follow.

[418]While the Bahlikas were originally from Bactria, there was a settlement around Punjab. Shakala is identified with Sialkot. The river Apaga is identified as Chandrabhaga (Chenab). Jat is believed to be derived from Jartika. The Madras lived in close proximity to the Bahlikas.

[419]That is, the barley has been bought from others.

[420]To acts of intercourse.

[421]This is a reference to his mistress.

circles of red arsenic on their limbs and black collyrium on their heads.[422] Those beautiful ones are attired only in skins and are sporting. When will I obtain happiness among those intoxicated ones, who have the sounds of asses, camels and mules? There will be the sounds of drums, kettledrums and conch shells. There is joy in the forest paths there, full of *shami*, *pilu* and *karira* trees. I will live amongst those who eat cakes ground with wheat and coarse meal. When will I be prosperous and strong along those paths, which echo to the many sounds of our oppression and banditry?'[423] The evil-souled Bahlikas are inferior and outcasts in this way. Which man would like to and dwell amidst them, even for an instant?" Thus did the brahmana describe the Bahlikas, whose conduct is vile. Whether it is their good qualities or bad, you possess one-sixth of those. Having said this, the virtuous brahmana began to speak again. This is what he said about the ill-mannered Bahlikas. Listen. "In the large city of Shakala, a rakshasa lady always used to sing every night, on the fourteenth day of the dark lunar fortnight,[424] to the sound of drums. When will those songs be announced and when will I sing in Shakala again?[425] When will I satiate myself with the flesh of cows and drink the great liquor made from molasses? Having drunk the liquor made from molasses, I will be with the large and ornamented women. I will wash my mouth after eating copious quantities of the meat of sheep, laced with onions, and also the flesh of boars, fowl, cows, asses and camels. Those who do not eat the flesh of sheep, are born in vain." Drunk with liquor, thus do the residents of Shakala, young and old, cry out. How can there be good conduct among them? O Shalya! Know this and be surprised. I will tell you more. This is what another brahmana told us in the assembly of the Kurus. "There is a forest of pilu trees in the spot where the five rivers

[422]The red arsenic is probably on their foreheads and the collyrium on their eyes.

[423]The idea is that the Bahlikas are robbers and bandits. They descend on passers-by along those forest paths and rob them.

[424]*Krishna chaturdashi*.

[425]It is a bit odd for the brahmana to say this. It will soon be clear that this is actually a quote.

flow—Shatadru, Vipasha, Iravati as the third, Chandrabhaga and Vitasta. As the sixth, Sindhu flows outside that region. There is a country named Aratta[426] there, where dharma has been destroyed. One should not go there. The gods, the ancestors and the brahmanas do not receive offerings from those who are outcasts, those born from servants and those from the land of Videha,[427] who do not sacrifice. It has been heard that those from Bahlika have destroyed all dharma." The learned brahmana also said this in the assembly of the virtuous. "Bahlikas eat from vessels made out of wood and clay, in which, coarse meal has been ground and which have been licked by dogs. They have no revulsion at this. They drink the milk of sheep, camels and asses. They drink and eat preparations made from these. Inter-caste sons are born there and those contemptible ones drink every kind of milk and eat everything. The learned say that the Bahlikas known as Aratta must always be avoided." O Shalya! You are certain to know this. But I will tell you more. In the gathering of the Kurus, in the assembly hall, another brahmana said the following. "Having drunk milk in the spot known as Yugandhara, how can one go to the place without decay? Having bathed in Bhutilaya, how can one go to heaven? That is the spot where five rivers issue from the mountains and flow. A noble person should not dwell among the Aratta-Bahlikas for even two days. In Vipasha, there are two pishachas named Bahi and Hlika. They were not created by Prajapati, and the Bahlikas are their offspring. One must avoid those without dharma—Karashkaras, Mahishakas, Kalingas, Kikatas, Atavis, Karkotakas and Virakas." He had gone on a *tirtha* and had spent a single night under a shami tree.[428] He was addressed by a *rakshasi*, whose hips were as broad as a mortar. "Those from the land known as Aratta, the people known as Bahlika and those who reside in the Sindhu-Souvira region are generally reviled."[429] O

[426]There is speculation about the location of Aratta, the name also occurring in Sumerian stories.

[427]The Critical edition may have erred here. Non-critical versions say Bahlika, which fits the context more than Videha.

[428]This is a reference to the brahmana, who was addressed by the rakshasi.

[429]This seems to be the rakshasi speaking.

Shalya! You are certain to know this. But I will tell you more. Listen with an attentive mind to everything that is spoken by me. On an earlier occasion, a skilled brahmana came to our house as a guest. Witnessing our conduct, the skilled one was delighted and said, "I have lived for a long time on a single peak of the Himalayas. I have seen many different countries, where diverse kinds of dharma are followed. But I have never seen a country where all the subjects act against dharma. All of them professed dharma to be what those learned in the Vedas have proclaimed it to be. I have always travelled in many countries, where different kinds of dharma are followed. O great king! However, having gone to the Bahlikas, I learnt the following. There, one first becomes a brahmana and then becomes a kshatriya. Thereafter, one becomes a vaishya, a shudra, a Bahlika, and finally a barber. Having become a barber, one once again becomes a brahmana. Having become a brahmana there, one is once again born as a slave. In every family, there is only one virtuous brahmana. Everyone else follows one's desires. The Gandharas, the Madrakas and the Bahlikas possess limited intelligence. That is what I heard there, about the admixture of dharma. Having travelled throughout the entire earth, I heard about this catastrophe among Bahlikas." O Shalya! You are certain to know this. But I will tell you more. These were the censorious words that another one spoke to me about the Bahlikas. In earlier times, a virtuous lady was abducted by some bandits from Aratta. They displayed adharma towards her. Consequently, she cursed them. "I am young. I have relatives. But against dharma, you have had intercourse with me.[430] Therefore, all the women in your lineages will be ignoble. O worst among men! You will not be able to escape from the consequences of your terrible act." The Kurus, the Panchalas, the Shalvas, the Matsyas, the Naimishas, the Kosalas, the ones from Kashi, the Angas, the Kalingas, the Magadhas and the immensely fortunate Chedis know about eternal dharma. In many countries, even those who have outwardly deviated know about virtue. Among the Matsyas, those from the lands of Kuru and Panchala and especially those from Naimisha and

[430]The bandits raped her.

Chedi, the virtuous ones lived according to ancient dharma. But this is not true of the Madras from the land of the five rivers. They are false in their tongues. O king! Knowing all this about dharma, be quiet. O Shalya! Be like those who cannot speak. You are the protector and the king of those people. Therefore, you have one-sixth share in their good and evil deeds. Or else, since you do not protect them, you only have a share in their evil deeds. A king who protects the good deeds of his subjects obtains a share in those good deeds. In earlier times, the eternal dharma was revered in all countries. But on seeing the dharma practised in the land of the five rivers, the grandfather[431] cried, "Shame!" They are outcasts. They are born from servants. They are the performers of wicked deeds. That is the reason the grandfather condemned the dharma in the land of the five rivers. Though they followed their own dharma and that of their varna, he did not honour it.[432] O Shalya! You are certain to know this. But I will tell you more. A rakshasa named Kalmashapada[433] was about to be submerged in a pond and said, "Begging is filth for a kshatriya. Falsehood is filth for a brahmana. Bahlikas are the filth of the earth. The women of Madra are the filth among women." When the traveller of the night[434] was being submerged in the pond, a king saved him. Listen to what he[435] said when he was asked. "Mlecchas are filth among men. Boxers are filth among mlecchas. Eunuchs are filth among boxers. Kings who act as officiating priests are the filth among eunuchs. Among kings who act as officiating priests, the Madrakas are filth. If you do not save me, all of that filth will be yours." The rakshasa spoke those supreme words as antidote, when a person's valour has been destroyed by the poison of a rakshasa. The Panchalas follow the brahman. The Kouraveyas follow their own dharma. The Matsyas observe truth and the Shurasenas

[431]Brahma.

[432]Because the dharma followed was wrong.

[433]Kalmashapada's story has been recounted in Section 11 (Volume 1). In that account, Kalmashapada was a king who was possessed by a rakshasa.

[434]The rakshasa.

[435]The rakshasa.

perform sacrifices. Those from the eastern regions are like slaves and those from the southern regions are contemptible. The Bahlikas are thieves and those from Surashtra are of mixed breed. Shame on those from Aratta and the land of the five rivers. They are ungrateful and steal the property of others. They are addicted to drinking liquor and have intercourse with the wives of their preceptors. Those from Panchala, Kuru, Naimisha and Matsya know about dharma. The aged ones from Kalinga, Anga and Magadha follow the virtuous path of dharma. With the fire god at the forefront, the gods reside in the eastern direction. The south is protected by the ancestors and Yama, the perfomer of auspicious deeds. The west is protected by Varuna, who takes care of other powerful gods there. The illustrious Soma is in the north, along with Brahma and the brahmanas. The rakshasas and pishachas are there in the Himalayas and the guhyakas in Gandhamadana. It is certain that Vishnu Janardana protects all the beings in the world.[436] The Magadhas understand signs, the Kosalas from what they see. The Kurus and Panchalas understand even if the speech is partly uttered, the Shalvas understand only when everything is spoken. Those who live in mountainous and hilly regions are coarse. O king! The Yavanas know everything, the Shuras especially so. The mlecchas follow their own signs. Other inferior people understand nothing. The Bahlikas, and not just the Madrakas, are against anything that has been undertaken. O Shalya! You are like that and you should not venture to give me a reply. Knowing this, keep quiet. You should not try to contradict me. Do not make me kill Keshava and Arjuna after I have killed you first.'

'"Shalya said, 'O Karna! Abandoning of the distressed and the sale of wives and sons is prevalent among those from Anga. You are the lord of that region. Bhishma enumerated the list of rathas and atirathas.[437] At that time, he recounted your vices and you were angry. Do not be angry. Brahmanas can be found everywhere. Kshatriyas can also be found everywhere. O Karna! So can vaishyas and shudras, and women who are virtuous and good in their vows. Men always

[436]Through omission, the Bahlikas are not protected by anyone.

[437]This has been described in Section 59 (Volume 4).

sport with other men and laugh at them, trying to hurt each other. In every country, there are those who are addicted to intercourse. Everyone is always skilled in detecting another one's faults. No one knows his own faults, or knowing them, is confounded.'"

'Sanjaya said, "Karna did not say anything in reply and Shalya faced the direction of the enemy. Radheya smiled again and urged him to drive."'

Chapter 1181(31)

'Sanjaya said, "Karna saw the unmatched vyuha of the enemy Parthas, protected by Dhrishtadyumna. It was capable of resisting the arrays of foes. He advanced, roaring like a lion and making his chariot clatter. The earth trembled from the sound of musical instruments. That scorcher of enemies, irresistible in battle, seemed to be trembling in rage. O bull among the Bharata lineage! The immensely energetic one constructed a counter vyuha. He began to kill the Pandava soldiers, like Maghavan against the asuras. Placing Yudhishthira on his right, he advanced towards him."

'Dhritarashtra asked, "O Sanjaya! How did Radheya construct a counter vyuha against the Pandavas? The brave Dhrishtadyumna was at the forefront and they were protected by Bhimasena. O Sanjaya! Who were stationed at the flanks and the extreme flanks of my army? How were the others divided and where were they stationed? How did the sons of Pandu construct a counter vyuha against us? How did that extremely extensive and extremely terrible battle commence? When Karna advanced against Yudhishthira, where was Bibhatsu then? In Arjuna's presence, who is capable of attacking Yudhishthira? In earlier times, he single-handedly vanquished all the beings in Khandava. Wishing to remain alive, who other than Radheya is capable of fighting with him?"

'Sanjaya replied, "Listen to the construction of the vyuha and how Arjuna arrived there. The kings on both sides arrayed themselves and fought the battle there. O king! Sharadvata Kripa, the spirited Magadhas and Satvata Kritavarma were stationed on the right flank. On their extreme flank were Shakuni and maharatha Uluka. Those soldiers were protected by fearless horse riders from Gandhara, armed with sparkling lances, and invincible ones from the mountainous regions. They were like a storm of locusts and as fierce-looking as pishachas. There were thirty-four thousand samshaptaka rathas who did not retreat. They were fierce in battle and protected the left flank. Your sons assembled together, wishing to kill Krishna and Arjuna. The Kambojas, Shakas and Yavanas were on their extreme flank. On the instructions of the son of the suta, they were there, with their chariots, horses and infantry, and challenged Arjuna and the immensely strong Keshava. Karna armoured and stationed himself at the head of the vanguard. His armour and armlets were colourful. He was garlanded and protected the front of the army. He was protected by his extremely wrathful sons, supreme among all the wielders of weapons. As he drew his bow at the head of the army, the brave one[438] was resplendent. Ready to fight, the mighty-armed Duhshasana was surrounded by soldiers and stationed himself at the rear of the vyuha. He was as resplendent as the sun and the fire. He was handsome and his eyes were tawny. He was astride a mighty elephant. O great king! King Duryodhana was himself behind him. He was protected by his brothers, Chitrashva and Chitrasena.[439] He was also protected by the immensely valorous Madras and Kekayas. O great king! He was as resplendent as Shatakratu, with the gods. Ashvatthama, the foremost maharathas among the Kurus, elephants that were always crazy and brave mlecchas stationed themselves behind that army of chariots and followed it. They looked like clouds that poured. There were standards that signified victory and supreme and blazing weapons. Stationed on horses, the riders were as beautiful as mountains

[438] Karna.

[439] As has been mentioned before, there is a consistency problem with the names of Duryodhana's minor brothers. Chitrasena has already been killed in Section 69 (Volume 6).

covered with trees. Thousands of foot soldiers guarded the feet of the elephants. Those brave ones were armed with lances and swords and did not retreat. There were ornamented riders, chariots and elephants. That vyuha was as resplendent as one of the gods or the asuras. The learned leader arrayed it well, according to the norms of Brihaspati. That mighty vyuha seemed to dance, causing fear in the hearts of the enemy. Wishing to fight, foot soldiers, horses, chariots and elephants issued forth from the flanks and extreme flanks, like clouds during the monsoon.

'"On seeing Karna stationed at the forefront of the army, King Yudhishthira spoke to Dhananjaya, the single brave one who was capable of killing all enemies. 'O Arjuna! Behold the mighty vyuha that Karna has constructed for this battle. The arrays of soldiers are blazing along its flanks and extreme flanks. On seeing this large army of the enemy, adopt such measures as are decreed by policy, so that we are not overcome.' O king! Thus addressed by the king, Arjuna joined his hands in salutation and replied, 'Everything will be done as you wish. It shall not be otherwise. O descendant of the Bharata lineage! I will act so that they can be killed. I will act so as to destroy and kill the foremost among them.'

'"Yudhishthira said, 'With that objective, you advance against Radheya, Bhimsena against Suyodhana, Nakula against Vrishasena, Sahadeva against Soubala, Shatanika against Duhshasana, the bull among the Shini lineage against Hardikya,[440] Dhrishtadyumna against Drona's son and I myself against Kripa. Let Droupadi's sons[441] and Shikhandi advance against the remaining sons of Dhritarashtra. Let the others on our side kill the enemy.'"

'Sanjaya said, "Thus addressed by Dharmaraja, Dhananjaya agreed. He instructed his own soldiers and himself advanced to the front of the army. As that chariot advanced, it was extremely wonderful to behold. Yet again, Shalya spoke to Adhiratha's son, invincible in battle. 'The chariot with the white horses is advancing, with Krishna as the charioteer. Kounteya is advancing, slaying the

[440]Satyaki and Kritavarma respectively.

[441]However, Shatanika, Nakula's son, has already been mentioned.

enemy. He is the one about whom you had asked. The great and tumultuous sound of the axles of the chariot can be heard. A dust is arising and has covered the sky. O Karna! The earth is trembling because of the axles of the chariot. A large and violent wind seems to be blowing on both sides of your army. Predatory beasts are howling and small animals are emitting a terrible sound. O Karna! Behold. This is extremely horrible and gives rise to fear. The body hair stands up. A headless torso that is like a cloud has enveloped the sun. Behold. Herds of many different kinds of animals are howling in all the directions. Powerful and proud tigers are glancing in the direction of the sun. Behold. Thousands of herons and vultures have assembled together. They are seated, fiercely facing each other, as if they are engaged in a conversation. O Karna! The white horses yoked to your giant chariot have turned pale. The arrows are blazing and the standard is trembling. Behold. The horses are extremely large and possess great speed. But they are quivering, though they are as handsome as flowing Garudas in the sky. From these portents, it is evident that the earth will be covered with kings. O Karna! They will be slain and will lie down, in hundreds and thousands. The tumultuous sound of conch shells can be heard and it makes the body hair stand up. O Radheya! There are sounds of drums and double-drums in every direction. There are the whizzing sounds of many kinds of arrows and the roars of men, horses and chariots. O Karna! Listen to the sound produced from the bowstrings and palms of those great-souled ones. O Karna! Behold Arjuna's chariot. It has been constructed by an aristan and is decorated with golden flags that have many hues. As they are stirred by the wind, they are resplendent. The flags are decorated with golden moons, stars and suns and are adorned with bells. They are like flashes of lightning in a cloud. There are other golden penants that are being stirred by the wind. Those flags are on the chariots of the great-souled Panchalas. They are slaying elephants, horses, rathas, infantry and warriors on your side. The tips of their standards can be seen. The twang of their bowstrings can be heard. Today, you will see the brave one with the white horses, with Krishna as his charioteer. He will slay the enemy in the battle. He is the one about whom you had asked. O Karna! Today, you will see Vasudeva and Arjuna stationed on a single chariot. Those two tigers among men are red-eyed and are the scorchers of foes. Varshneya is his charioteer and Gandiva is his bow. O Radheya! If you are successful in killing him, you will be our king. He has been challenged by the samshaptakas and has departed in their direction. In the battle, that powerful one is creating a great carnage among the enemy.' When Karna was thus addressed by the lord of Madra, he became extremely angry and said, 'Look. The angry samshaptakas have attacked him from every direction. Partha cannot be seen and is shrouded, like the sun by the clouds. O Shalya! Immersed in that ocean of grief, Arjuna will perish.'

'"Shalya replied, 'Who can slay Varuna with water or the fire with kindling? Who can grasp the wind, or drink up the great ocean? I think that causing hardship to Partha in a battle is equally tough. No one is capable of vanquishing Arjuna, not even Indra, with the gods and the asuras. Be satisified with your words and be cheerful in your mind. No matter what your wishes are, you cannot be victorious in this encounter. There may be someone who can raise the earth with his two arms, or consume all the beings with his anger. That person may bring down the gods from heaven. No one other than him can defeat Arjuna in a battle. Behold Kunti's brave son. Bhima is unsullied in his deeds. The mighty-armed one is radiant and is stationed like Mount Meru. He is perpetually angry, remembering the enmity that has endured for a long time. The valiant Bhima is stationed in the battle, desiring victory. Dharmaraja Yudhishthira is foremost among those who uphold dharma. The conqueror of enemy cities, the performer of good deeds, is stationed against the enemy in the battle. Nakula and Sahadeva, the brothers who are tigers among men, have been born from the Ashvins. They are stationed in the battle and are extremely difficult to defeat. Behold the five sons of Krishna,[442] who are like five mountains. They are stationed, wishing to fight and all of them are Arjuna's equal in a battle. These are the sons of Drupada, with Dhrishtadyumna at

[442]Krishnaa, Droupadi.

the forefront. Those brave ones are stationed and are supremely energetic. Satyajit is the youngest among them.'[443]

'"While those two lions among men were conversing in this way, the armies clashed against each other, like the fierce waters of the Ganga and the Yamuna."'[444]

Chapter 1182(32)

'Dhritarashtra asked, "O Sanjaya! When the arrayed armies clashed against each other, how did Partha advance against the samshaptakas and Karna against the Pandavas? You are skilled in narrating. Please tell me everything about the battle. I am never satisfied with hearing about the valour of the brave ones in battle."

'Sanjaya replied, "Because of the evil policies of your son, Arjuna created a vyuha as a counter vyuha, having seen that the large army of the enemy had been stationed. That large army[445] was full of horse riders, elephants, foot soldiers and chariots. With Dhrishtadyumna at the forefront, its formation was magnificient. Parshata's horses had the complexion of pigeons and he was as resplendent as the moon and the sun. With his bow, he was like Death personified. Droupadi's sons were stationed next to Parshata, wishing to fight. With terrible bodies, they followed him, like large numbers of stars after the moon.

'"In the battle, on seeing that the samshaptakas were arranged in a formation, Arjuna angrily attacked them, stretching the bow named Gandiva. Wishing to kill him, the samshaptakas also attacked Partha. They were firm in their resolution of obtaining victory and preferred

[443]There is a problem with translating this. The text uses the word *hina*, which should be translated as vile, inferior, or left out. Since there is no reason for Satyajit to be so described, we have translated this as youngest.

[444]Though not explicitly stated, this is Sanjaya speaking again.

[445]Of the Pandavas.

death to retreat. Those brave ones advanced against Arjuna and they possessed large numbers of horses, crazy elephants and chariots. The clash between them and Kiriti was tumultuous. We have heard about his encounter with the nivatakavachas[446] and it was like that. Partha sliced down the heads of thousands of the enemy and brought down chariots, horses, standards, elephants, foot soldiers, the leaders of rathas, arrows, bows, swords, chakras and battleaxes, in addition to arms with upraised weapons and other weapons that had not yet been raised. He was submerged in that large whirlpool of soldiers, like an eddy that swirls in the nether regions. The samshaptakas were delighted that his chariot was thus submerged and roared. But Bibhatsu slaughtered the ones who were in front of him, those that were further away, those that were to the rear, those that were to the right and those that were to the left. He was like an angry Rudra amidst animals.

'"O venerable one! The battle that commenced between the Panchalas, the Chedis and the Srinjayas and those who were on your side was extremely terrible. Kripa, Kritavarma and Shakuni Soubala were with soldiers who were cheerful, but extremely enraged. They were strikers who could bring down arrays of chariots. Those bravest of the brave were irresistible in battle and fought with the Kosalas, the Kashis, the Matsyas, the Karushas, the Kekayas and the Shurasenas. That fierce battle destroyed bodies and sins. Those brave shudras, vaishyas and kshatriyas obtained dharma, heaven and fame. O bull among the Bharata lineage! With his brothers, Duryodhana protected the foremost among the Kurus and the maharathas from Madra. In that battle, the Pandavas, the Panchalas and Satyaki fought with Karna, who was protected by the brave ones among the Kurus. Karna used his sharp arrows to slaughter that large army and crushed the best of chariots. He then afflicted Yudhishthira. He[447] severed the arrows, weapons and bodies of thousands of the enemy, thus ensuring heaven and fame for them and greatly delighting those on his side."

[446]Described in Section 35 (Volume 3).

[447]Karna.

'Dhritarashtra asked, "O Sanjaya! How did Karna penetrate the army of the Parthas, create that destruction of men and afflict the king? Tell me everything about this. Who were the foremost among the Parthas who fought against Karna and resisted him? Whom did Adhiratha's son have to crush before afflicting Yudhishthira?"

'Sanjaya replied, "On seeing that the Parthas, with Dhrishtadyumna at the forefront, were stationed, Karna, the destroyer of enemies, spiritedly attacked the Panchalas. O great king! Like swans heading towards the giant ocean, desiring victory, the Panchalas also quickly rushed against him. There was the blare of thousands of conch shells, piercing the heart. From either side, there was the fierce sound of drums. There were the sounds of many musical instruments and the noise emitted by elephants, horses and chariots. The brave ones roared like lions and it became terrible. It was as if the earth, with its mountains, trees and oceans, the sky, with clouds tossed around by the wind, and the firmament, with its moon, planets and nakshatras, seemed to be whirled around because of that sound. All the beings thought that the sound was distressing. Those that possessed limited spirit died and fell down. Karna was extremely enraged and swiftly released his weapons. He slaughtered the Pandava soldiers, like Maghavan against the asuras. He quickly penetrated the Pandava chariots and shot his arrows, killing seventy-seven of the foremost among the Prabhadrakas. The best of rathas next used twenty-five sharp arrows that were well tufted to kill twenty-five Panchala rathas. He used gold-tufted iron arrows that were capable of penetrating bodies to slaughter hundreds and thousands of Chedis. He performed superhuman deeds in that encounter. O great king! The Panchalas advanced on their chariots and surrounded him from all sides. O descendant of the Bharata lineage! Affixing five arrows that were extremely difficult to withstand, Vaikartana Vrisha Karna killed five Panchalas. O descendant of the Bharata lineage! In that encounter, he killed the Panchalas Bhanudeva, Chitrasena, Senavindu, Tapana and Shurasena. In that great battle, while the brave Panchalas were being slaughtered by the arrows, great lamentations arose among the Panchalas. Those lamentations covered all the directions and Karna swiftly killed them with his arrows. O venerable one! The protectors of Karna's chariot wheels were his invincible sons, Sushena and Satyasena, who were ready to give up their lives in the fight. Karna's eldest son, maharatha Vrishasena, himself protected him from the rear and guarded Karna's back. Wishing to kill Radheya, the strikers, Dhrishtadyumna, Satyaki, Droupadi's sons, Vrikodara, Janamejaya, Shikhandi, the brave ones among the Prabhadrakas, the Chedis, the Panchalas and the armoured Matsyas attacked him. They showered down many kinds of arrows and weapons. They showered down and oppressed him, like clouds pouring down on a mountain during the rainy season. O king! Wishing to save their father, the strikers who were Karna's sons and other brave ones on your side, repulsed those valiant ones.

'"Sushena severed Bhimasena's bow with a broad-headed arrow. He then pierced Bhima in the chest with seven iron arrows and roared. Having picked up another bow that was firmer, Vrikodara, who was terrible in his valour, strung it and severed Sushena's bow. He angrily pierced him with nine arrows and seemed to be dancing around. He swiftly pierced Karna with seventy-three sharp arrows. While all his well-wishers looked on, he struck Karna's son, Satyasena, with ten arrows and brought him down, together with his horses, charioteer, standard and weapons. His beautiful face was like the full moon. The head was struck down with a kshurapra arrow and was like a lotus severed from its stalk. Having killed Karna's son, Bhima again afflicted those on your side. He severed the bows of Kripa and Hardikya and oppressed them. He pierced Duhshasana with three iron arrows and Shakuni with six. The lord deprived Uluka and Patatri of their chariots.[448] He next picked up an arrow and said, 'O Sushena! You have been killed.' However, Karna severed this and struck him[449] with three arrows. At this, Bhima picked up another arrow that was well shafted and extremely energetic. He released this at Sushena, but Vrisha severed that too. Wishing to save his son and cruelly desiring to kill the cruel one,[450] Karna again struck Bhimasena

[448]Both Uluka and Patatri were Shakuni's sons.

[449]Bhima.

[450]Bhima.

with seventy-three arrows. Sushena picked up another supreme bow that was capable of bearing a greater load. He struck Nakula, in the arms and in the chest, with five arrows. Nakula pierced him back with twenty firm arrows that were capable of bearing a great load and roared powerfully, causing fright to Karna. O great king! At this, maharatha Sushena pierced him with ten swift arrows and used a kshurapra arrow to quickly sever his bow. Nakula became senseless with anger and picked up another bow. In that encounter, he repulsed Sushena with many arrows. O king! That slayer of enemy heroes enveloped all the directions with his arrows. Having killed Sushena's charioteer, he pierced him with three arrows. Using three broad-headed arrows, he shattered his firm bow into three fragments. Sushena became senseless with rage and picked up another bow. He pierced Nakula with sixty arrows and Sahadeva with seven. That extremely wonderful and fierce battle was like that between the gods and the asuras. Wishing to kill each other, they quickly struck each other with arrows. Satyaki killed Vrishasena's charioteer with three arrows. With a broad-headed arrow, he severed his bow and struck his horses with seven. He shattered his standard with an arrow and struck him in the chest with three. Thus struck, he[451] became senseless on his chariot, but raised himself in a short while. Wishing to slay Shini's descendant, he rushed against him with a sword and a shield. Satyaki also swiftly rushed against Vrishasena and used ten arrows, with heads like the ears of a boar, to strike his sword and shield. Duhshasana saw that he[452] was without a chariot and devoid of weapons. He quickly picked him up on his own chariot and then made him ascend another chariot. Thus, maharatha Vrishasena stationed himself on another chariot. The invincible one fought for Karna's sake and again protected his rear. Shini's descendant struck Duhshasana with ninety-nine swift arrows. Having deprived him of his charioteer, horses and chariot, he struck him in the forehead with three arrows. At this, he[453] ascended another chariot that had been

[451]Vrishasena.
[452]Vrishasena.
[453]Duhshasana.

duly prepared earlier, and stationing himself within Karna's army, began to fight with the Pandus. Dhrishtadyumna pierced Karna with ten arrows. Droupadi's sons pierced him with seventy-three and Yuyudhana with seven. Bhimasena pierced him with sixty-four arrows and Sahadeva with five. Nakula pierced him with three hundred arrows, Shatanika with seven, the brave Shikhandi with ten and Dharmaraja with one hundred. O Indra among kings! These, and many other, brave ones desired victory.

'"In the great battle, they struck the son of the suta, the great archer. The son of the suta pierced each of them back with ten arrows. The brave one, the destroyer of enemies, roamed around on his beautiful chariot and struck them back. O great king! We witnessed the valour of the weapons and the dexterity of the great-souled Karna. It was extraordinary. One did not witness a gap between the maharatha's picking up an arrow, affixing it and releasing it. The sky, the firmament, the earth and the directions were quickly enveloped by his arrows. It was as if the sky was covered with beautiful red clouds. With the bow in his hand, the powerful Radheya seemed to be dancing around. Everyone who struck him was pierced back with three times the number of arrows. Yet again, he pierced each of them, with their horses, charioteers, standards and umbrellas, with ten arrows each and roared. They had to yield and let him pass. The great archer Radheya, the afflicter of enemies, drove them away with his showers of arrows and without any hindrance, penetrated the king's[454] division. He slaughtered three hundred Chedi rathas who refused to retreat. Radheya then used sharp arrows to strike Yudhishthira. O king! The Pandavas, Shikandi and Satyaki wished to save the king from Radheya and surrounded him. And all the soldiers on your side surrounded Karna, the great archer who was irresistible in battle, in every direction. O lord of the earth! The roar of many kinds of musical instruments arose. The brave and unretreating ones roared like lions. Without any fear, the Kurus and the Pandavas clashed again. Yudhishthira was at the forefront of the Parthas and the son of the suta was at our head."'

[454]Yudhishthira's.

Chapter 1183(33)

'Sanjaya said, "Karna penetrated the soldiers and attacked Dharmaraja. He was surrounded by thousands of chariots, elephants, horses and infantry. The enemy hurled thousands of diverse weapons at Vrisha. But without any fear, he used hundreds of fierce arrows to strike these down. He cut down their heads, arms and thighs. In every direction, they were killed and fell down on the ground. The others were shattered and fled. The Dravidas, the Andhakas and the Nishadas were again rallied by Satyaki. In that battle, wishing to kill him, they attacked Karna with their infantry. Struck by Karna's arrows, they lost their arms and helmets. They fell down simultaneously on the ground, like a forest of *shala* trees that had been struck down. In this way, hundreds, thousands and tens of thousands of warriors lost their lives. Their bodies fell down on the ground and they filled the directions with their fame. In that battle, Vaikartana Karna was like Yama. The Pandus and Panchalas tried to counter him, like a disease with mantras and herbs. He repulsed them and again attacked Yudhishthira, like an irresistible disease that cannot be countered by mantras and herbs. However, though he wished to advance against the king, he was held back by the Pandus, the Panchalas and the Kekayas. It was like death not being able to conquer those who know about the brahman.

'"Yudhishthira, the slayer of enemy heroes, was some distance away from Karna, who had been checked. His eyes red with rage, he said, 'O Karna! O Karna! Your eyesight is in vain. O son of a suta! Listen to my words. You have always sought to rival the illustrious Phalguna in battle. You have always devoted yourself to the views of Dhritarashtra's son and have opposed us. Today, exhibit the strength, the valour and the enmity towards the Pandus. Based on your great manliness, display all of those today. In this great battle today, I will destroy the love you bear towards fighting.' O great king! Having thus addressed Karna, Pandu's son smiled and used ten sharp and gold-tufted arrows to pierce him. O descendant of the Bharata lineage! The son of the suta, scorcher of enemies and great archer, pierced him back with nine vatsadanta arrows[455] and laughed. In the battle, the brave and great-souled one then used two razor-sharp and straight-tufted arrows to slay the two Panchalas who were protecting his chariot wheels.[456] Those two brave ones had been resplendent along Dharmaraja's flanks. Along his chariot, they had been like Punarvasu by the side of the moon.[457] However, Yudhishthira again pierced Karna with thirty arrows and struck both Sushena and Satyasena with three arrows each.[458] He pierced Shalya with ninety arrows and the son of the suta with seventy-three arrows. He struck each of the ones who were protecting his horses with three arrows each. At this, Adhiratha's son laughed and brandished his bow. He pierced the king with a broad-headed arrow, pierced him again with another sixty arrows and laughed. Then, the brave ones among the Pandus rushed towards Yudhishthira. Wishing to save him from the son of the suta, they struck Karna with arrows. Among these were Satyaki, Chekitana, Yuyutsu, Pandya, Dhrishtadyumna, Shikhandi, Droupadi's sons, the Prabhadrakas, the twins, Bhimasena, Shishupala's son, the Karushas, the remaining Matsyas, the Kekayas and those from Kashi and Kosala. These spirited and brave ones countered Vasushena. Janamejaya from Panchala pierced Karna with sharp arrows—*varahakarna*s, *naracha*s, *nalika*s, vatsadantas, *vipatha*s, kshurapras and *atakamukhas*.[459] Wielding many fierce weapons, chariots, elephants, horses and riders surrounded and attacked Karna from every direction, wishing to kill him.

[455]Arrows that had heads like the tooth of a calf.

[456]The two Panchalas who were protecting Yudhishthira's chariot wheels. In shlokas excised in the Critical edition, their names are given as Chandradeva and Dandadhara.

[457]Punarvasu is the seventh of the twenty-seven nakshatras. However, Punarvasu is actually a double star, Castor and Pollux in the constellation Gemini.

[458]Since Satyasena has already been killed, there is an inconsistency.

[459]Varahakarnas have heads like a boar's ear, narachas are iron arrows, nalikas are hollow arrows, vatsadantas have heads like a calf's tooth, vipathas are large arrows, kshurapras are sharp as razors and atakamukhas have heads that roam around freely (probably meaning multiple heads).

'"He was attacked from every direction by the best among the Pandavas. At this, he invoked brahmastra and enveloped the directions with his arrows. The fire that was Karna had valour and anger and his arrows flamed greatly. Consuming the Pandavas, who were like a forest, he resplendently roamed around in that battle. The great-souled and wonderful archer repulsed all those great weapons. He laughed and used his arrows to sever the bow of that Indra among men.[460] In that battle, in the twinkling of an eye, he affixed ninety sharp arrows with drooping tufts and penetrated the king's armour. That armour was decorated with gold. As it fell down, it looked dazzling, like clouds tinged with lightning and tossed around by the wind, when penetrated by the sun. Having fallen off the limbs of that Indra among men, the armour looked beautiful, like celestial clouds in the night sky, ornamented with gems.[461] Devoid of armour and wounded by arrows, Partha was covered with blood. He angrily hurled a lance that was completely made out of iron towards Adhiratha's son. While it blazed through the sky, he[462] cut it down with seven arrows. It was severed by the great archer's arrows and fell down on the ground. At this, Yudhishthira struck Karna in the arms, the forehead and the chest with four javelins and roared delightedly. With blood flowing from his body, Karna was enraged and sighed like a snake. He struck down Pandava's standard with a broad-headed arrow and pierced him with three more. He struck down his quivers and shattered his chariot into tiny fragments. With his parshni charioteers slain, Partha retreated. He was incapable of remaining in front of the evil-minded Karna. Radheya pursued him and touched him on the shoulder with his hand. O king! He laughed at him and spoke disparaging words to Pandava. 'You have been born in a famous lineage and are established in the dharma of kshatriyas. How is it that you are seeking to protect your life in this great battle and are abandoning this encounter with the enemy? I don't think you know the dharma of kshatriyas well. That is my

[460]Yudhishthira.

[461]There is implicit imagery of the stars.

[462]Karna.

view. You possess the strength of the brahman and are devoted to studying and the task of performing sacrifices. O Kounteya! Do not fight again and do not advance against brave ones. Do not speak unpleasant words towards them. Do not advance towards a great battle.' Having said this, the immensely strong one released Partha. He began to slaughter the Pandava soldiers, like the wielder of the vajra against the asuras. O king! That lord of men fled in shame. On seeing that the king was departing, the Chedis, the Pandavas, the Panchalas, maharatha Satyaki, Droupadi's brave sons and the Pandavas who were the sons of Madri followed the undecaying one. On seeing that Yudhishthira's army was unwilling to fight, Karna pursued them from the rear, together with the brave Kurus. There was the sound of conch shells and drums and the twang of bows. The sons of Dhritarashtra roared like lions.

'"O Kouravya! Yudhishthira swiftly climbed onto Shrutakirti's chariot.[463] Dharmaraja Yudhishthira saw that his[464] strength was like that of Death and that he was slaying thousands of warriors. At this, he[465] became angry. Instructed by the king, all the maharatha Pandavas, with Bhimasena at the forefront, attacked your sons. O descendant of the Bharata lineage! The warriors raised a tumultuous sound there. Here and there, there were elephants, horses, chariots, foot soldiers and weapons. 'Arise. Strike. Advance towards death.' As they killed each other in that field of battle, these were the words the warriors spoke to each other. Because of the shower of arrows, it was as if the sky was covered by the shadow of clouds. The best of men clashed against each other and killed each other. In that battle, penants, standards and umbrellas were brought down. Horses, charioteers and warriors were destroyed. Those lords were slain. They lost their limbs and their bodies and fell down shattered on the ground. Supreme elephants looked like the lofty summits of mountains. Their riders were slain and they fell down, like mountains shattered by the thunder. Armour, ornaments and bodies

[463]Shrutakirti (or Shrutakarma) was the son of Arjuna and Droupadi.

[464]Karna's.

[465]Yudhishthira.

were mangled, shattered and dispersed. In thousands, horses fell down, with their brave riders. The limbs of warriors were scattered. Elephants, horses and rathas were slain. Thousands of arrays of foot soldiers were crushed by enemy heroes. Everywhere, the earth was strewn with the heads of fierce warriors. Their eyes were copper coloured and dilated. Their faces were like the lotus and the moon. As on earth, a sound could be heard in the sky. There were large numbers of apsaras on celestial vehicles and they sounded musical instruments. They welcomed the thousands of brave ones who were headed in their direction, after having been killed by the valiant enemy. The masses of apsaras made them ascend the celestial vehicles and bore them away. On beholding this great and extraordinary marvel in person, the brave ones were delighted in their minds. They desired to obtain heaven and angrily struck each other. In that battle, rathas fought a wonderful battle with rathas. Infantry fought with infantry, elephants with elephants and horses with horses. Thus did the battle continue, causing carnage among elephants, horses and men. The dust raised by the soldiers covered everything. Those on the same side slew each other. And those on the enemy's side slew each other. In the battle, they pulled each other by the hair. They fought with teeth and with nails. They fought with fists in an encounter that destroyed bodies and sins. Thus did the battle continue, destructive of elephants, horses and men. A river of blood was created from the bodies of men, horses and elephants. It carried away many fallen bodies of men, horses and elephants. There were the bodies of men, horses and elephants and there were men, horse riders and elephant riders. That extremely terrible river had currents of blood and its mud was red. It bore along the bodies of men, horses and elephants and increased the fear of those who were cowards. Desiring victory, some went over to the other side.[466] There were others who were submerged in it and sank and swam. All their limbs were covered with blood. Their armour, weapons and garments became red. O bull among the Bharata lineage! Some bathed in it. Others drank the water and lost their senses. There were chariots, horses, men,

[466]They died.

elephants, weapons, ornaments, garments and armour of those who were slain, or were being slain. The earth, the sky, the firmament and the directions were generally seen to be red. Smell, touch and taste became red in form. Above this, there were the sounds raised by those who were engaged. O descendant of the Bharata lineage! In general, the soldiers were overcome by great distress.

'"The soldiers, with Bhimasena at the forefront, and brave rathas with Satyaki at the forefront, again attacked your soldiers, who had already been routed. The great-souled ones descended with such great force that it was irresistible. O king! The large army of your sons retreated. The chariots, horses and men were scattered. Their armour and mail were in disarray. Their weapons and bows were dislodged. Your soldiers were agitated and driven away in different directions. They were like a herd of elephants, afflicted by lions in a great forest."'

Chapter 1184(34)

'Sanjaya said, "O king! On seeing that your soldiers were being driven away by the Pandavas, your son loudly tried to rally them. In that battle, the flanks, the distant flanks, the even more distant flanks and the right wings of the the Kurus raised their weapons and attacked Bhima. O great king! On seeing that the army of the sons of Dhritarashtra was running away, Karna asked Shalya, the adornment of a battle, to drive towards Vrikodara, on the foremost of horses that possessed the complexion of swans. Those horses reached Bhimasena's chariot and engaged. On seeing that Karna had approached, Bhima was full of anger. O bull among the Bharata lineage! He made up his mind to destroy Karna. He told brave Satyaki and Parshata Dhrishtadyumna, 'Protect King Yudhishthira, who has dharma in his soul. In my sight, he escaped from a great calamity. In front of me, for the sake of Duryodhana's pleasure, the evil-minded Radheya deprived the king of all his garments.[467] O Parshata! Today, I will bring an end to that misery. In the battle, I will kill Karna, or he will kill me. Either will happen in this extremely terrible battle. I am telling you this truthfully. Today, I am handing over the king in trust to you. Do not be anxious. But protect him in every way.' Having said this, the mighty-armed one headed in the direction of the chariot of Adhiratha's son. He roared loudly like a lion and this made all the directions resound.

'"On seeing that Bhima, who delighted in a battle, was swiftly advancing, the lord who was the king of Madra spoke to the son of the suta. 'O Karna! Behold the enraged and mighty-armed descendant of the Pandava lineage. He has conquered his wrath for a long time and certainly wishes to release it towards you. O Karna! I have never seen him in such a form earlier, not even when Abhimanyu and rakshasa Ghatotkacha were killed. In his ire, he is capable of resisting the three worlds. The form that he has assumed is like the resplendent fire of destruction.' O king! While the lord of Madra was speaking these words to Radheya, Vrikodara, flaming in his anger, attacked Karna. On seeing that Bhima, who delighted in fighting, had thus arrived, Radheya laughed and spoke these words to Shalya. 'O lord of Madra! O lord! There is no doubt that the words that you have spoken to me now about Bhimasena are true. Vrikodara is brave, valiant and angry. He is indifferent towards protecting his body and his life and is superior in strength. When he lived in disguise in the city of Virata, for the sake of bringing pleasure to Droupadi, resorting only to his arms, he secretly killed Kichaka and his followers.[468] He is senseless with anger and armoured now. He is stationed in the forefront of this battle. He is roaming around in this battle, like Death with a staff, and wishes to do something. I have also harboured a desire for a long time, that either I will kill Arjuna in a battle, or Dhananjaya will kill me. Now that Bhima has advanced against me, perhaps that wish may come true today. If I kill Bhimasena or deprive him of his chariot, and Partha advances against me, that will be fortunate. Please do whatever needs to done,

[467]This is a reference to the gambling match.

[468]This has been described in Section 46 (Volume 4).

quickly.' On hearing the words of the great-souled Radheya, Shalya spoke these words to the son of the suta. 'O mighty-armed one! Advance against the immensely strong Bhimasena. If you restrain Bhimasena, you may be able to reach Phalguna. O Karna! The desire that you have harboured in your heart for a long time, may well be accomplished. I am telling you this truthfully.' Having been thus addressed, Karna again spoke to Shalya. 'Arjuna will kill me in the battle, or I will kill Dhananjaya. Fix your mind on the battle. Drive. Drive there.' O lord of the earth! Having been thus instructed, Shalya swiftly drove the chariot to the spot where Bhima, the great archer, was driving away the army. At this, there was the extremely loud noise of trumpets and drums. O Indra among kings! This arose as Karna and Bhima clashed.

'"The powerful Bhimasena was extremely angry. He was invincible and drove your soldiers away in different directions, using sharp and sparkling iron arrows. O lord of the earth! O great king! That fierce battle between Karna and Pandava was tumultuous and terrible in form. O Indra among kings! In an instant, Pandava attacked Karna. On seeing that he was descending, Karna Vaikartana Vrisha angrily struck him between the breasts with an iron arrow. The one who was immeasurable in his soul again covered him with a shower of arrows. Having been thus pierced, he enveloped the son of the suta with arrows. He pierced Karna with nine sharp arrows with drooping tufts. Karna used his arrows to sever his bow into two fragments from the middle. When he was deprived of his bow, he struck him between the breasts with extremely sharp iron arrows that were capable of penetrating all armour. O king! Vrikodara picked up another bow and struck the son of the suta with extremely sharp arrows that were capable of penetrating the inner organs. He roared powerfully and made heaven and earth tremble. Karna struck him with twenty-five iron arrows, like a maddened and proud elephant attacked in the forest with flaming torches. With his limbs mangled by the arrows, Pandava became senseless with rage. His eyes were coppery red with anger and intolerance and he wished to kill the son of the suta. His bow was extremely powerful and supreme and capable of bearing a great load. He affixed an arrow that was capable of shattering mountains. The son of the wind god[469] powerfully stretched the bow back, all the way up to his ears. Wishing to kill Karna, the great archer angrily released the arrow. Having been thus released by the powerful one, the arrow, with a sound like that of the vajra or thunder, struck Karna in that battle, with a force like that of the vajra against a mountain. O extender of the Kuru lineage! Thus struck by Bhimasena, the son of the suta, the leader of an army, lost his senses and sank down on the floor of his chariot. On seeing that the son of the suta had lost his senses, the lord of Madra bore Karna, the adornment of a battle, away on the chariot. When Karna was defeated, the large army of the sons of Dhritarashtra was driven away by Bhimasena, like an army of the danavas by Indra."'

Chapter 1185(35)

'Dhritarashtra said, "O Sanjaya! This deed performed by Bhima was extremely difficult to accomplish. He brought down the mighty-armed Karna from the seat of his chariot. There is only one person who can kill the Srinjayas and the Pandavas in the battle and that is Karna. O suta! That is what Duryodhana has repeatedly told me. On seeing that Radheya had been defeated by Bhima in the battle, what did my son, Duryodhana, do next?"

'Sanjaya replied, "O king! On seeing that Radheya, the son of the suta, was beaten back in that great battle, he[470] addressed the large army of his brothers. 'O fortunate ones! Swiftly go and protect Radheya. He confronts a hardship and has been submerged in the fathomless ocean that is Bhimasena.' Having been thus instructed by the king, they wished to kill Bhimasena and attacked him in great anger, like insects heading towards a flame. Shrutayudha, Durdhara, Kratha, Vivitsu, Vikata, Soma, Nishangi, Kavachi, Pashi, Nanda,

[469] Bhima.

[470] Duryodhana.

Upanandaka, Dushpradharsha, Subahu, Vatavega, Suvarchasa, Dhanurgraha, Durmada, Satva and Soma[471]—these were valiant and extremely powerful. They attacked Bhimasena with chariots and surrounded him from every direction. They released a storm of arrows, of many different forms, from every direction. O lord of men! Your sons quickly descended on the immensely strong Bhimasena and attacked him. He killed five hundred rathas and fifty other rathas who advanced against him. He angrily severed Vivitsu's head with a broad-headed arrow. It had earrings and a helmet and was like the full moon. O great king! Severed by Bhima, it fell down on the ground. O lord! On seeing that their brave brother had been killed, in that battle, all of them attacked Bhima, who was terrible in his valour, from all directions. In that great battle, Bhima, terrible in his valour, used other broad-headed arrows to rob the lives of two more of your sons in the encounter. O king! They fell down on the ground, like trees that had been uprooted by a tempest. They were Vikata and Soma, who were like ones born from the wombs of the gods. Swiftly, Bhima used an extremely sharp iron arrow to convey Kratha to Yama's eternal abode. Slain, he fell down on the ground. O lord of men! Fierce sounds of lamentation arose there. O king! Your archer sons were being slain there. Agitating your soldiers in the battle, the immensely strong Bhimasena conveyed Nanda and Upananda[472] to Yama's abode. Your sons were terrified and lost their senses. On seeing Bhimsena in that battle, like Yama the Destroyer, they fled.

'"On seeing that your sons had been killed, the great-minded son of the suta again went to the spot where Pandava was, on horses that possessed the complexion of swans. O great king! The king of Madra swiftly drove those horses towards Bhimasena's chariot and powerfully engaged with him. O lord of men! O great king! The clash that ensued between Karna and Pandava was fierce. It

[471]The names of Duryodhana's brothers. Not only is there an inconsistency about which of Duryodhana's minor brothers was killed when, there is also inconsistency about the names of Duryodhana's minor brothers.

[472]Identical with Upanandaka.

was tumultuous and terrible in form. O great king! On seeing those two maharathas clash against each other, my mind was certainly anxious to know what would transpire today. O Indra among kings! However, Karna laughed and didn't have to make a great effort. In a short instant, he deprived Bhima, whose deeds were terrible, of his chariot. O best of the Bharatas! Despite being deprived of his chariot, the one who was like the wind god, laughed. The mighty-armed one descended from his supreme chariot, with a club in his hand. O king! Bhima, the striker and scorcher of enemies, assumed a terrible form and violently killed seven hundred elephants. He knew about the inner organs and struck them at the base of their tusks, their eyes, their temples and their loins. Having severely struck them in their inner organs and killed them, he roared. They fled in fear, but were again rallied back by the riders. They surrounded him, like clouds around the sun. However, using his club, he killed and brought down seven hundred elephants on the ground, with their riders, weapons and flags, like a mass of clouds driven away by the wind. There were extremely strong elephants that belonged to Subala's son.[473] In the battle, Kounteya again brought down five hundred and two of these. He fiercely crushed one hundred chariots and a hundred foot soldiers that belonged to the enemy. They were killed by Pandava in the battle, while your army looked on. They were scorched by the sun and by the great-souled Bhima. Your soldiers began to shrink, like a strip of leather held above a fire. O bull among the Bharata lineage! Those on your side were terrified because of their fear of Bhima. In that encounter, they were driven away by Bhima in the ten directions. There were five hundred other rathas. With shields and armour, they cheerfully and swiftly attacked Bhima, showering him with arrows from every direction. With his club, Bhima brought down all those rathas and charioteers, with their flags, standards and weapons, like Vishnu against the asuras. On Shakuni's instructions, three thousand riders who prided themselves on their bravery, advanced against Bhima, with lances, swords and spears in their hands. He was the destroyer of enemy heroes and

[473]Shakuni.

spiritedly counter-attacked those horse riders. He roamed around in diverse motions and killed and brought them down. When they were thus oppressed by him, a great and tumultuous sound arose in every direction. O descendant of the Bharata lineage! It was as if a clump of reeds was being severed with a sword. Having slain three thousand supreme horses that belonged to Subala's son, he ascended a chariot and angrily attacked Radheya.

'"O king! In that battle, Karna enveloped Dharma's son, the scorcher of enemies, with arrows and brought down his charioteer. On seeing that he[474] was fleeing from the encounter on his chariot, the maharatha pursued him and released swift arrows that were shafted with the feathers of herons. When the fleeing king was thus enveloped with arrows, the son of the wind god angrily covered heaven and earth with his net of arrows. Radheya, the destroyer of enemies, swiftly repulsed him. In every direction, he enveloped Bhima with sharp arrows. O descendant of the Bharata lineage! Karna was in front of Bhimasena's chariot. Satyaki, whose soul was immeasurable, placed himself at the side and attacked Karna, severely afflicting him with arrows. Those two bulls among archers[475] clashed against each other and spiritedly released colourful and dazzling arrows. O Indra among kings! Those terrible nets of arrows released by them could be seen to fiercely stretch out in the sky, like the red backs of cranes. Because of the thousands of arrows released by them, we could not see the radiance of the sun, the sky, the directions, or the sub-directions. O king! It was midday and the great radiance of the sun was scorching. But all that seemed to be dispelled by the storm of arrows that Karna and Madhava[476] shot.

'"On seeing that Soubala, Kritavarma, Drona's son, Adhiratha's son and Kripa were engaged with the Pandavas, the Kurus returned again. O lord of the earth! When they descended, a fierce sound arose. It was like the terrible sound made by oceans during the rainy season. On beholding each other in that great battle, both armies were

[474]Yudhishthira.
[475]Karna and Satyaki.
[476]Satyaki.

anxious. But they were also extremely delighted at having engaged with each other. When the sun attained its midpoint, the battle commenced. Nothing like this has been seen earlier, nor heard of. A large army violently clashed against another large army in that battle. It was as if a large store of water was heading powerfully towards the ocean. There was an extremely loud roar as those two armies clashed against each other. It was as if the waters in the ocean were roaring loudly. Thus, those two armies powerfully clashed against each other. They became one, like two rivers meeting each other. O lord of the earth! A battle that was fierce in form commenced. The Kurus and the Pandavas engaged, desiring extremely great fame. O king! O descendant of the Bharata lineage! The Kurus roared out loudly to each other there and many different kinds of noises were heard. In that encounter, the warriors were heard to revile the fathers, the mothers, the deeds and the conduct of their adversaries. In the battle, they were seen to censure each other. O king! I formed the view that their lifespans had run out. On seeing the angry forms of those immensely energetic ones, I was overcome by a great fear about what would transpire. O king! The Pandava and Kourava maharathas began to wound and kill each other with sharp arrows."'

Chapter 1186(36)

'Sanjaya said, "O great king! The kshatriyas wished to kill each other. They bore feelings of enmity towards each other and slew each other in the battle. O great king! Large numbers of chariots, throngs of horses, masses of men and numerous elephants clashed against each other in every direction. There were clubs, maces, *kanapas*,[477] lances, catapults; and *bhushundis*[478] were seen to move everywhere. They descended in that extremely fierce battle.

[477]Unidentified weapon made out of iron.

[478]Unidentified weapon, probably something like a mallet that was tied to a rope.

In every direction, showers of arrows descended like locusts. In the encounter, elephants clashed against elephants and killed each other. Horses clashed against horses, chariots against chariots, infantry against large numbers of infantry and large numbers of horses against horses. O king! In that encounter, foot soldiers, chariots, elephants, rathas, elephants, horses and elephants were seen to swiftly crush the other three kinds of forces.[479] The brave foot soldiers roared at each other. That terrible encounter was like a sacrificial spot for animals. O descendant of the Bharata lineage! Covered in blood, the earth was beautiful. It was as if the earth was covered by large numbers of *shakragopa* insects during the monsoon.[480] The earth was as beautiful as a young lady[481] dressed in a white garment that had been dyed with saffron.[482] With the colourful flesh and blood, it seemed to be decorated in gold. Heads, arms and thighs were severed. O descendant of the Bharata lineage! Earrings and ornaments were dislodged. Golden necklaces and armour were dislodged from the bodies of the archers. With large numbers of flags, they fell down on the ground. Elephants engaged with elephants and gored each other with the tips of their tusk. Wounded by the tusks, the elephants looked beautiful. Their limbs were covered with blood and they looked like mobile mountains full of minerals, with red chalk flowing down their sides. The elephants destroyed many lances hurled by their opponents, including those that were still held horizontally in the hands. With their armour destroyed by iron arrows, those supreme elephants looked dazzling. O great king! They were like mountains deprived of clouds at the onset of winter. The best of elephants were pierced with gold-tufted arrows. O venerable one! They looked like beautiful mountain tops, lit with torches. Some elephants, as large as mountains, were struck by other

[479]This shloka is not composed very well and there is repetition. The four kinds of forces are elephants, horses, chariots and infantry. What is meant is that each of these fought against the other three kinds of forces.

[480]Shakragopas are cochineal insects, crimson in colour.

[481]The word used is shyama. While the word also means dark, in this context, it means a lady who has not given birth, or is not married, and is therefore a virgin. Therefore, we have used the word young.

[482]Because of the blood.

elephants and fell down on the ground. They fell down in that battle, like mountains with wings.[483] Other elephants were struck by arrows and oppressed by their wounds. These fled. With their temples and frontal globes shattered, they shrieked and fell down in that great battle. There were others that emitted terrible roars like lions. O king! There were others that shrieked and ran hither and thither. Horses with golden harnesses and trappings were killed by the arrows and weakened. They screamed and ran in the ten directions. Others that were afflicted and rendered unconscious, fell down on the ground. Oppressed by the arrows and javelins, they screamed in many different kinds of ways. O venerable one! Men were slain there. They screamed and fell down on the ground. O descendant of the Bharata lineage! Others saw their relatives, fathers, grandfathers and others running away from the enemy. On seeing this, they called out the names of their lineages and their own names and summoned each other. O great king! Bedecked with golden ornaments, their arms were severed and having fallen, or while falling down, were immobile or writhed. Thousands of these fell down on the ground and quivered. In that battle, they quivered powerfully, like serpents. O lord of the earth! Those arms were like the bodies of serpents, smeared with sandalwood. Drenched with blood, they were as beautiful as golden standards. A fierce encounter ensued in every direction. Without recognizing,[484] they fought and killed each other. Because of that descent of weapons, the earth was covered with dust. O king! Since everything was covered in darkness, one could not differentiate those on one's own side from that of the enemy. A terrible and large river with currents of blood, fierce in form, was created there and began to flow. The severed heads were like rocks. The hair constituted weeds and moss. It was full of the best of bows and arrows and large numbers of bones. Flesh constituted the mud and mire. There were extremely terrible currents of blood. The river that was created there extended Yama's kingdom. That river was fearsome in form and conveyed them to Yama's abode. It generated fear in the

[483]That is, with the wings lopped off. At one point, mountains were believed to have possessed wings.

[484]Without being able to differentiate friend from foe.

minds of the kshatriyas who submerged and immersed themselves in it. O tiger among men! Carnivorous beasts roared in various places there. That horrible field of battle looked like the city of the lord of the dead.[485] In every direction, large numbers of headless torsos were seen to rise up. Satisified with the flesh and the blood, large numbers of demons danced around. O descendant of the Bharata lineage! They drank the blood there. They drank the marrow. Satiated with the fat and the marrow, crows, vultures and smaller crows were seen to run around. O king! In that battle, the brave ones cast aside all fear, though it is difficult to give that up. They resorted to the vow of warriors and performed their tasks without any fear. There were large numbers of arrows and lances on the field of battle and it was infested with innumerable predatory beasts. The brave ones roamed around there, displaying their manliness. O descendant of the Bharata lineage! They made each other listen to their names and lineages. In the encounter, they recounted the names of their fathers and their families. O lord of the earth! In diverse ways there, the warriors made others listen to these. They attacked each other, with spears, javelins and battleaxes. An extremely terrible battle commenced, fearsome in form. The Kourava army was weakened, like a shattered boat on the ocean."'

Chapter 1187(37)

'Sanjaya said, "O venerable one! O king! While the kshatriyas immersed themselves in that battle, the tremendous roar of Gandiva was heard in that encounter, when Pandava was engaged in creating carnage among the samshaptakas, the Kosalas and the narayana army.[486] In that encounter, the samshaptakas were

[485]Yama.

[486]The narayana army was given by Krishna to Duryodhana and an army of gopalas (cowherds) is also mentioned. In Section 49 (Volume 4), Duryodhana and Arjuna had to choose between an unarmed and neutral Krishna and his army. Arjuna opted for Krishna and Duryodhana for the narayana army. In

intolerant and desired victory. From every direction, they showered down arrows on Partha's head. O king! However, the lord spiritedly withstood that violent shower. Plunging into the battle, Partha slaughtered the best of rathas. He assaulted that army of chariots with arrows that had been sharpened on stone and were tufted with the feathers of herons. In that battle, Partha approached maharatha Susharma.[487] The foremost of rathas brought down a shower of arrows on him and the samshaptakas did the same to Partha, who was stationed in the battle. Susharma pierced Partha with nine swift arrows and Janardana in the right arm with three arrows. O venerable one! O king! With another broad-headed arrow, he pierced the large standard that had been fashioned by Vishvakarma, with the best of apes astride it. At this, the ape let out a large and fierce roar. On hearing this, your army was terrified. O king! That beautiful army became immobile. It was like Chitraratha's grove, full of many flowers.[488] O best of the Kuru lineage! Having regained their senses, the warriors drenched Arjuna with their arrows, like clouds on a mountain. All of them surrounded maharatha Pandava. O descendant of the Bharata lineage! Swiftly and powerfully, they attacked his horses, his chariot wheels and his chariot and roared like lions. O great king! Some of them seized Keshava by his mighty arms, while others seized Partha, as he was cheerfully stationed on his chariot. In the field of battle, Keshava flung his arms around and brought all of them down, like an elephant against a wicked elephant. In the encounter, on seeing that Keshava had been oppressed on the chariot, Partha became angry. He attacked and brought down many maharathas and innumerable foot soldiers who had climbed onto the chariot. He covered all the warriors who were nearby with arrows that were meant for fighting at close quarters.

---

descriptions of the war, the narayana army is often mentioned in conjunction with the samshaptakas, though the two are different. The samshaptakas were warriors, mostly from Trigarta, who had sworn to die rather than retreat. Arjuna destroyed most of the samshaptakas in Section 66 (Volume 6).

[487]The king of Trigarta.

[488]Chitraratha was the king of the gandharvas.

'"In that battle, he then spoke to Keshava. 'O Krishna! O mighty-armed one! Behold. Those large numbers of samshaptakas wished to perform an extremely terrible deed against me and have been slaughtered in thousands. O bull among the Yadu lineage! With my exception, there is no man on earth who is capable of withstanding such a terrible attack, at close quarters, on the chariot.' Having spoken thus, Bibhatsu blew on Devadatta.[489] Krishna blew on Panchajanya, filling heaven and earth. O great king! On hearing the blare of those conch shells, the army of the samshaptakas wavered. They were extremely terrified. Pandava, the destroyer of enemy heroes, repeatedly invoked the naga weapon and tied down their feet.[490] Partha tied down their feet in the battle. O king! With their feet tied down by the great-souled Pandava, they became immobile, as if they were made out of stone. The descendant of the Pandu lineage then slaughtered those immobile warriors, just as in ancient times, Indra had killed the daityas in the battle with Taraka.[491] Slaughtered in the battle, they abandoned the best of chariots and threw away all their weapons. O Indra among kings! On seeing that the army had thus been tied down, maharatha Susharma quickly invoked the Suparna weapon.[492] Suparna birds descended and devoured the serpents. O king! On seeing the birds, the serpents fled. O lord of the earth! Having been freed from the thongs on the feet, the army looked as beautiful as the sun, which warms all beings, when it has been freed from a mass of clouds. O venerable one! Having been freed, the warriors released large numbers of arrows and large numbers of weapons towards Phalguna's chariot. Having used his own shower of great weapons to sever that shower of arrows, Vasava's son, the destroyer of enemy heroes, remained stationed on his chariot in the field of battle. O king! Susharma used arrows with drooping tufts to pierce Arjuna in the chest and pierced him

[489]The name of Arjuna's conch shell. The name of Krishna's conch shell is Panchajanya.

[490]Naga is a serpent. Their feet were tied down with serpents.

[491]Taraka was a demon who was eventually killed by Kartikeya.

[492]Suparna is Garuda, the enemy of serpents.

again with three other arrows. Having been severely wounded and pained, he sank down on the floor of his chariot. When he regained his senses, the one with the white horses, immeasurable in his soul and with Krishna as his charioteer, quickly invoked the aindra weapon.[493] O venerable one! Thousands of arrows were created from it and were seen to destroy men and elephants in every direction of the battle, in addition to horses, chariots and hundreds and thousands of weapons. O descendant of the Bharata lineage! When the soldiers were slaughtered, the large numbers of samshaptakas and gopalas were overcome with great fear. There was no man there who could fight back against Arjuna. While those brave ones looked on, that large army was slaughtered. Despite witnessing the slaughter and despite their valour, they remained immobile. In the battle there, Pandu's son killed ten thousand warriors. O king! He was resplendent in that battle, like a flaming fire without any smoke. O descendant of the Bharata lineage! He killed fourteen thousand foot soldiers, ten thousand rathas and three thousand tuskers. At this, the samshaptakas again surrounded Dhananjaya. They refused to retreat, and had determined to set their minds on death or victory. O lord of the earth! There was a great battle there between those on your side and the brave and powerful Pandava Kiriti."'

Chapter 1188(38)

'Sanjaya said, "O venerable one! Kritavarma, Kripa, Drona's son, the son of the suta, Uluka, Soubala and the king[494] and his brothers saw that the army was afflicted because of the fear of Pandu's son. It was submerged with great force, like a shattered boat in an ocean. O descendant of the Bharata lineage! However, in a short while, a battle commenced. It generated fear among cowards and increased the delight of brave ones. In the battle, Kripa

[493]Divine weapon named after Indra.

[494]Duryodhana.

released showers of arrows that moved like locusts and shrouded the Srinjayas. Shikandi was angry and quickly advanced against Goutama.[495] From every direction, he showered down a large number of arrows on the best of brahmanas. Kripa was knowledgeable about great weapons and destroyed that shower of arrows. In the encounter, he angrily pierced Shikhandi with ten arrows. Shikhandi became enraged in that battle. He severely pierced Kripa with swift arrows that were shafted with the feathers of herons. Having been severely pierced, maharatha Kripa, supreme among brahmanas, deprived Parshata[496] of his horses, charioteer and chariot. With his horses slain, the maharatha[497] descended from his chariot and grasping a sword and a shield, quickly advanced against the brahmana. On seeing him violently attack in the battle, he enveloped him with straight-tufted arrows and it was wonderful. What we witnessed was extraordinary, as if there was a torrent of rocks. O king! Shikhandi remained immobile in that encounter. O supreme among kings! On seeing that Shikhandi had been shrouded by Kripa, maharatha Dhrishtadyumna quickly counter-attacked Kripa. On seeing that Dhrishtadyumna was advancing towards Sharadvata's chariot, maharatha Kritavarma powerfully repulsed him. On seeing that Yudhishthira was advancing towards Sharadvata's chariot, together with his sons and soldiers, Drona's son countered him. Your son received the spirited maharathas Nakula and Sahadeva and countered them with showers of arrows. O descendant of the Bharata lineage! In that battle, Karna Vaikartana countered Bhimasena, the Karushas, the Kekayas and the Srinjayas. O venerable one! Meanwhile, in the encounter, Sharadvata Kripa swiftly dispatched arrows towards Shikhandi, as if wishing to burn him down. However, with his sword, he[498] repeatedly sliced down all the arrows that were embellished with gold and were shot at him from all directions, while they were still in mid-air. At this, Goutama quickly shattered Parshata's shield, which was decorated with the marks of one hundred moons, with

[495]Kripa.

[496]Shikhandi.

[497]Shikhandi.

[498]Shikhandi.

his arrows. The men roared loudly. O great king! Deprived of his shield, he attacked with the sword in his hand. But he had come under Kripa's control, like a diseased person in the mouth of death. The immensely strong one was afflicted by Sharadvata's fierce arrows. On seeing this, Suketu,[499] Chitraketu's son, spiritedly advanced. In the battle, he showered the brahmana with many sharp arrows. The one whose soul was immeasurable, dashed towards Goutama's chariot. O supreme among kings! On seeing that the brahmana, devoted to his vows, was engaged in a fight with someone else, Shikhandi quickly withdrew. O king! Suketu struck Goutama with nine arrows, pierced him again with seventy, and struck him yet again with three arrows. O venerable one! He next severed his[500] bow, with an arrow affixed to it. With another arrow, he severely struck his charioteer in the inner organs. Goutama became angry at this and picked up another new bow that was firm. He struck Suketu in all his inner organs with thirty arrows. All his limbs were weakened and he wavered on that supreme chariot. He was like a tree, trembling and moving during an earthquake. His head was adorned with flaming earrings. It had a headdress and a helmet. While he was moving, he[501] brought it down with a kshurapra arrow. That head fell down on the ground, like a piece of meat being carried by a hawk. Thereafter, the head was dislodged and fell down on the ground. O great king! When he was slain, those who followed him were frightened. They abandoned the fight with Goutama and fled in the ten directions.

'"Kritavarma repeatedly asked Parshata to wait.[502] In the battle, there was a tumultuous encounter between those from the Vrishni and Parshata lineages.[503] O king! It was like a fight between a hawk and a vulture over a piece of meat. In the battle, Dhrishtadyumna angrily struck Hardikya, Hridika's son, in the chest with nine

[499]Suketu was a prince of Panchala.

[500]Kripa's.

[501]Kripa.

[502]This Parshata is Dhrishtadyumna. All of Drupada's sons can be called Parshata.

[503]Kritavarma was from the Vrishni lineage.

arrows and afflicted him. In the encounter, Kritavarma was firmly struck by Parshata. In turn, he shrouded Parshata, his chariot and his horses, with arrows. O king! With his chariot enveloped by arrows, Dhrishtadyumna could no longer be seen. It was like the sun enveloped by clouds at the onset of the rains. Those large numbers of arrows were decorated with gold. O king! But having repulsed them with his arrows, though he was covered with wounds, Dhrishtadyumna looked resplendent in the battle. Parshata, the leader of an army, became angry and unleashed an extremely terrible shower of arrows towards Kritavarma. On seeing that violent and incessant shower of arrows descend in the encounter, Hardikya destroyed them with thousands of arrows. On seeing that the extremely irresistible shower of arrows had been countered in the battle by Kritavarma, Parshata advanced and repulsed him. He used a broad-headed arrow, sharp at the edges, to swiftly dispatch his charioteer to Yama's abode. Slain, he fell down from the chariot. Dhrishtadyumna vanquished his powerful maharatha enemy. In the battle, he then quickly countered the Kouravas with arrows. At this, the warriors on your side attacked Dhrishtadyumna. They roared like lions and a battle commenced."'

Chapter 1189(39)

'Sanjaya said, "On seeing that Yudhishthira was protected by Shini's descendant and by the brave sons of Droupadi, Drona's son cheerfully attacked him. He showered large numbers of gold-tufted and fierce arrows that had been sharpened on stone. He displayed many different kinds of motion, his learning and the dexterity of his hands. The one who was learned in the use of weapons invoked his arrows with the mantras of divine weapons and surrounded Yudhishthira in the battle. Everything was shrouded by the arrows of Drona's son and nothing could be seen. It was as if the heads of all the warriors were covered by arrows. The firmament was covered by a net of arrows and seemed to be shrouded by a golden net. O best of the Bharata lineage! It was beautiful, as if it had been covered with a canopy. O king! In that battle, enveloped by that radiant net of arrows, the sky seemed to be obstructed by arrows, as if by the shadow of clouds. Because of the arrows, the sight that we beheld there was extraordinary. As a result of the valour of Drona's son, nothing could be seen to descend on earth.[504] O great king! On beholding the dexterity of Drona's son, the maharathas there were astounded and were incapable of glancing at him. It was as if all the kings were being scorched by the sun.

'"Though Satyaki, Dharmaraja Pandava and the other soldiers made efforts, they could not withstand his valour. When the soldiers were being slaughtered, Droupadi's maharatha sons, Satyaki, Dharmaraja and the Panchalas united, abandoning their fear of death and fiercely attacked Drona's son. Satyaki pierced Drona's son with twenty-five arrows with stone heads. He again pierced him with seven iron arrows that were decorated with gold. Yudhishthira struck him with seventy-three, Prativindhya with seven, Shrutakarma with three arrows, Shrutakirti with seven arrows, Sutasoma with nine and Shatanika with nine.[505] Many other brave ones pierced him from all directions. O king! He became angry at this and sighed like a venomous serpent. He pierced Satyaki back with twenty-five arrows that had been sharpened on stone, Shrutakirti with nine, Sutasoma with five, Shrutakarma with eight and Prativindhya with three arrows. He struck Shatanika with nine arrows and Dharma's son[506] with seven. He struck each of the other brave ones with two arrows each. With sharp arrows, he severed Shrutakirti's bow. At this, maharatha Shrutakirti picked up another bow and pierced Drona's

[504]Beings like birds could not descend from the sky to the earth.

[505]These are the names of Droupadi's sons, Prativindhya through Yudhishthira, Sutasoma through Bhima, Shrutakarma through Arjuna, Shatanika through Nakula and Shrutasena through Sahadeva. Shrutakarma and Shrutakirti should be the same, in which case, the text should say Shrutasena (Sahadeva's son) instead of Shrutakirti.

[506]Yudhishthira.

son with three arrows, following this up by striking him with many other sharp arrows. O descendant of the Bharata lineage! Drona's son showered down arrows and covered the soldiers and the kings from every direction with arrows. Drona's son, immeasurable in his soul, again severed Dharmaraja's bow with three sharp arrows and laughed. O king! At this, Dharma's son picked up another giant bow and struck Drona's son in the arms and the chest with seventy arrows. In the battle, Satyaki angrily struck Drona's son and used an extremely sharp arrow that was in the form of a half-moon to sever his bow. Having done this, he roared loudly. With his bow severed, Drona's son, supreme among strong ones, hurled a lance and swiftly brought down the charioteer of Shini's descendant from his chariot. O descendant of the Bharata lineage! Drona's powerful son then picked up another bow and enveloped Shini's descendant with a shower of arrows. O descendant of the Bharata lineage! With his[507] charioteer brought down in the encounter, his horses were seen to run around here and there. With Yudhishthira at the forefront, they[508] powerfully attacked Drona's son, supreme among the wielders of weapons, and showered down sharp arrows. In that great battle, on seeing that they were rushing to the attack and adopting fierce forms, Drona's son, scorcher of enemies, laughed and received them. In that battle, Drona's maharatha son used hundreds of flaming arrows to consume the flanks of the soldiers, like a fire burning dead wood in the forest. O foremost among the Bharatas! The army of Pandu's son was afflicted by Drona's son, like the mouth of a river by a whale. O great king! On witnessing the valour of Drona's son, everyone thought that the Pandus had already been slain by Drona's son.

'"Spiritedly approaching Drona's maharatha son, Yudhishthira spoke to Drona's son, anger and intolerance flooding his mind. 'O tiger among men! Since you wish to kill me today, your name is not affection, nor is your name gratitude. A brahmana's task is austerities, donations and studying and a bow should be stretched by a kshatriya.

[507]Satyaki's.

[508]The Pandava soldiers.

You say that you are a brahmana. O mighty-armed one! While you look on, I will vanquish the Kouravas in the battle.' O great king! Having been thus addressed, Drona's son smiled. He thought about what was proper and did not say anything in reply. Without saying anything, he showered arrows on Pandava and enveloped him in the battle, like an angry Yama against beings. O venerable one! Having been thus shrouded by Drona's son, Partha abandoned that large army and swiftly departed from the spot. O king! Dharma's son, Yudhishthira, departed. However, Drona's great-minded son still remained stationed in that region. Thus, King Yudhishthira abandoned Drona's son in the great battle and advanced against your soldiers, having decided to perform cruel deeds."'

Chapter 1190(40)

'Sanjaya said, "Vaikartana himself countered and restrained Bhimasena, supported by the Panchalas, Chedis and Kekayas, with his arrows. While Bhimasena looked on, Karna angrily killed many Chedi, Karusha and Srinjaya maharathas. Bhimasena avoided Karna, supreme among rathas, and advanced against the Kourava soldiers, like a blazing fire amidst dead wood. The son of a suta, the great archer, slaughtered thousands of Panchalas, Kekayas and Srinjayas in the battle. The maharathas caused great carnage—Partha against the samshaptakas, Vrikodara against the Kouravas and Karna against the Panchalas. O king! Because of your evil counsel, those three were like fires and consumed and destroyed the kshatriyas in the encounter.

'"O foremost amongst the Bharata lineage! Meanwhile, Duryodhana was angry and struck Nakula with nine arrows, also piercing his four horses. O lord of men! Your son, immeasurable in his soul, again severed Sahadeva's golden standard with a razor-sharp arrow. O king! Nakula became enraged and struck your son with seventy-three arrows in the battle. Sahadeva pierced him with five.

Those two were the best amongst the Bharata lineage and the best among all archers. But he[509] angrily struck each of them with five arrows. O king! With other broad-headed arrows, he severed the bows of the twins and laughed, piercing them with seven arrows. Those two brave ones were resplendent in the battle, equals of the sons of the gods. They picked up other supreme bows that were as beautiful as Shakra's bow. O king! In that encounter, the two brothers proudly fought against a brother. They showered down arrows on him, like two giant clouds on a mountain. O great king! Your maharatha son became enraged and repulsed Pandu's sons, great archers, with arrows. O descendant of the Bharata lineage! In the encounter, the circle of his bow could be seen. In every direction, arrows could be seen to whiz around. The two Pandavas were enveloped by his arrows and looked beautiful, like the sun and the moon in the sky, when covered by clouds and robbed of their radiance. O great king! Those arrows were gold-tufted and sharpened on stone. Like the rays of the sun, they covered all the directions. The firmament was covered by those arrows. The forms of the twins were like that of Yama, at the time of the destruction of an era. On witnessing your son's valour, the maharathas thought that the sons of Madri had attained the presence of death. O king! At this, the great-souled commander-in-chief of the Pandavas, Parshata, went to the spot where King Suyodhana was.

'"Abandoning the valiant and maharatha sons of Madri, your son oppressed Dhrishtadyumna with arrows. O bull among men! Your son, immeasurable in his soul, was intolerant, and piercing Panchala with twenty-five arrows, laughed. O lord of the earth! Your son, immeasurable in his soul, again pierced Panchala with sixty-five arrows and roared. O venerable one! In the battle, the king used extremely sharp kshurapra arrows to sever his bow, with an arrow affixed to it, and his arm-guards. Discarding his severed bow, Panchala, the destroyer of enemies, quickly picked up a new bow that was capable of bearing a great load. The great archer, Dhrishtadyumna, was covered with wounds. But he blazed violently

[509]Duryodhana.

because of his anger, with eyes that were red as blood. He looked beautiful. Dhrishtadyumna sighed like a serpent and wishing to kill the foremost among the Bharata lineage, shot fifteen iron arrows that had been sharpened on stone. Those forceful arrows were shafted with the feathers of herons and peacocks. They penetrated the king's gold-decorated armour and entered the ground. O great king! Having been severely struck, your son looked dazzling, like a blossoming kimshuka dotted with flowers during the spring. His armour was shattered by the iron arrows. He was exhausted because of the blows. However, he angrily severed Dhrishtadyumna's bow with a broad-headed arrow. O king! Having severed the bow, the lord of the earth swiftly struck him between the eyebrows with ten arrows. These arrows had been polished by artisans and with these, his[510] face looked beautiful, like a flowering *champaka* tree visited by bees desiring honey.[511] The great-minded Dhrishtadyumna abandoned the severed bow and quickly picking up another bow, struck Duryodhana with sixteen broad-headed arrows, slaying his horses and charioteer with five arrows. With a broad-headed arrow that was embellished with gold, he sliced down his bow. With nine broad-headed arrows, Parshata severed your son's chariot, his seat, his umbrella, his lance, his sword, his club, his standard and his colourful and golden armlet, sparkling with gems and the sign of an elephant.[512] All the kings saw that the standard of the lord of the Kurus had been brought down. In the battle, Duryodhana was without a chariot and deprived of his weapons. O bull among the Bharata lineage! His brother, Dandadhara, sought to rescue his brother. O king! While Dhrishtadyumna looked on, he raised the frightened king onto a chariot and bore him away.

'"Having defeated Satyaki, the immensely strong Karna wished to save the king. In the battle, he advanced against Drona's fierce

[510]Dhrishtadyumna's.

[511]The arrows are being compared to bees.

[512]This adds up to nine arrows. One arrow was used for the bow, five for the horses and the charioteer and one for Duryodhana himself. We thus have a tally of sixteen arrows.

slayer.[513] Shini's descendant quickly pursued him from the rear, showering down arrows, like an elephant goring another elephant from the rear with its tusks. O descendant of the Bharata lineage! The great-souled warriors fought extremely fierce and great battle in the space between Karna and Parshata. The Pandava warriors, nor those on our side, desired to retreat. On seeing this, Karna swiftly advanced against the Panchalas. O best among men! At that time, there was a destruction of elephants, horses and men. When the sun attained midday, this gave rise to great fear. O great king! The Panchalas desired victory and quickly attacked Karna from all sides, like birds flocking to a tree. Adhiratha's son was spirited and sought to angrily repulse them. With fierce arrows, he clashed against those who were at the forefront—Vyaghraketu, Susharma, Shanku, the fierce Dhananjaya,[514] Shukla, Rochamana, Simhasena and Durjaya. Those valiant ones advanced forcefully on their chariots and surrounded the best of men. They angrily released many arrows towards Karna, the ornament of a battle. Those brave and powerful kings of men fought there. But Radheya killed all eight of them with sharp arrows. O great king! O king! In that encounter, the powerful son of a suta, skilled in fighting, then angrily slew many thousands of other warriors—Vishnu, Vishnukarma, Devapi, Bhadra, Danda, Chitra, Chitrayudha, Hari, Simhaketu, Rochamana,[515] maharatha Shalabha and many other maharathas amongst the Chedis. While he was slaughtering them, the body of Adhiratha's son was smeared in blood in all his limbs and he looked like the great Rudra himself. O descendant of the Bharata lineage! Many elephants were afflicted by Karna's arrows. Terrified, they fled in all the directions, causing greater destruction. Afflicted by Karna's arrows, they shrieked and fell down in the encounter, roaring in many different ways, as if mountains had been shattered by the thunder. In every direction, elephants, horses and men fell down and the earth became impassable because of the large numbers of chariots and horses. No other person

[513]Dhrishtadyumna.

[514]Not to be confused with Arjuna.

[515]The name Rochamana has already been mentioned.

on your side had performed such a deed in the battle—not Bhishma, nor Drona. O tiger among men! The son of a suta created a great destruction of elephants, chariots, horses and men. He was seen to fearlessly roam around, like a lion amidst deer. In that fashion, Karna fearlessly roamed around amidst the Panchalas. Just as large numbers of deer are driven away in diverse directions by a lion, in that way, the array of Panchala chariots was routed by Karna. On approaching a lion, a deer does not remain alive. In that way, on approaching Karna, the maharathas did not remain alive. People are usually burnt if they approach a blazing fire. O descendant of the Bharata lineage! In that way, in that battle, the Srinjayas were consumed by the fire that was Karna. O descendant of the Bharata linege! Proclaiming his name, Karna single-handedly killed many amongst the Chedis and the Panchalas who prided themselves on their bravery. O Indra among men! On witnessing Karna's valour, I thought that not a single one among the Panchalas would escape from Adhiratha's son in the battle.

'"O venerable one! Having slain the Panchalas in the battle, the powerful son of a suta angrily rushed against Yudhishthira, Dharma's son. Dhrishtadyumna and Droupadi's sons surrounded the king. The destroyer of enemies[516] was surrounded by hundreds of others—Shikhandi, Sahadeva, Nakula, Nakula's son, Janamejaya, Shini's grandson and many Prabhadrakas. In that encounter, they placed Dhrishtadyumna at their forefront. Those infinitely energetic ones looked beautiful, as they attacked Adhiratha's son with weapons. In that battle, Adhiratha's son single-handedly descended on those Chedis, Panchalas and Pandavas, like Garuda on numerous serpents.

'"In that battle, Bhimsena, the great and angry archer, single-handedly attacked the Kurus, Madras and Kekayas and looked extremely resplendent in the encounter. Elephants were struck in their inner organs by Bhima's iron arrows. With their riders slain, they fell down, making the earth tremble. Horses and their riders were slain and foot soldiers lost their lives. They were mangled and

[516]Karna.

lay down on the ground, vomiting copious quantities of blood. Thousands of rathas fell down, their weapons dislodged. Those that were not wounded lost their lives because of their fear of Bhima. The earth was strewn with chariots, horses, charioteers, foot soldiers and elephants that were destroyed by Bhimasena's arrows. O king! Duryodhana's army was afflicted because of Bhimasena's strength and though it remained there, it was dispirited and covered with wounds. In that great and tumultuous battle, it was seen to be immobile and cheerless. O king! It looked like an ocean when the waters are still. Your son's army had possessed the best of anger, valour and strength. But because of the arrows, it lost all that strength. It was covered in waves of blood and was drenched in blood. In the battle, the son of a suta angrily attacked the Pandava soldiers and the resplendent Bhimasena drove away the Kurus. There was a fierce battle there and it was extraordinary to behold.

'"In the midst of the army, having slain large numbers of samshaptakas, Arjuna, best among victorious ones, spoke to Vasudeva. 'O Janardana! This army, which was fighting, has been shattered. The samshaptaka maharathas are running away, together with their followers. They cannot bear my arrows, like deer cannot stand the sound of a lion. In the great battle, the large army of the Srinjayas has also been shattered. O Krishna! The intelligent Karna's standard, with the mark of an elephant's housing, can be repeatedly seen, resplendent in the midst of the king's soldiers. In a battle, I don't think those maharathas are capable of defeating Karna. You know about Karna's bravery and valour. Go to the spot where Karna is driving away our army. Abandon the battle here and advance against the maharatha son of a suta. O Krishna! Unless you are exhausted, do that, or whatever else you desire.' O great king! Having been thus addressed, Govinda laughed. He told Arjuna, 'O Pandava! Slay the Kouravas swiftly.' Urged by Govinda, those horses, with the complexion of swans, penetrated that large army, bearing along Krishna and Pandava. The horses were controlled by Keshava. They were white, with golden harnesses. They penetrated your army and drove it away in the four directions. When Keshava and Arjuna entered, that large army was shattered. Those two greatly resplendent ones were angry and dazzling. Their eyes were red with rage. They took delight in fighting and in that field of battle, were challenged by the enemy. They looked like the gods, the two Ashvins, summoned to a sacrifice by the officiating priests in the proper way. Since they were enraged, the speed of those tigers among men increased. In that great battle, they were like elephants enraged by the sound of slapping palms.[517] Phalguna roamed around the arrays of chariots and the numerous horses. In the midst of those formations, he was like Yama with a noose in his hand. O descendant of the Bharata lineage! On witnessing his valour in the battle, your son again urged the large numbers of samshaptakas. At this, one thousand chariots, three hundred elephants, fourteen thousand horses and two hundred thousand foot soldiers and archers attacked him in the great battle. They were known for their bravery. They were skilled. Those maharathas attacked and enveloped those two brave ones.[518] Having been thus shrouded in the battle by arrows, the destroyer of enemy forces displayed his fierce self, like Yama with a noose in his hand. Partha slaughtered the samshaptakas and became a sight worth beholding. His arrows, decorated with gold, dazzled like lightning. Kiriti incessantly covered the sky with these. Mighty arrows were released from Kiriti's arms and descended. They covered everything, with the radiance of Kadru's offspring.[519] They were gold-tufted and fierce at the tip. They were arrows with drooping tufts. Pandava, immeasurable in his soul, was seen to shoot them in all the directions. The maharatha killed ten thousand kings. Kounteya then swiftly attacked the extreme flank of the samshaptakas. Having approached the extreme flank, protected by the Kambojas, Partha crushed it with the force of his arrows, like Vasava against the danavas. Using broad-headed arrows, he swiftly servered the arms, with the hands still holding on to weapons, and the heads of those among the enemy who wished to slay him. Limbs and bodies were sliced down. Deprived

[517]The image is that of hunters pursuing and hunting wild elephants with the slapping of palms.

[518]Krishna and Arjuna.

[519]The snakes are Kadru's offspring.

of weapons, they fell down on the ground. They were shattered, like trees with many branches broken by a storm. The storm that was Arjuna destroyed elephants, horses, chariots and infantry. Sudakshina's younger brother showered down a hail of arrows on him.[520] His arms were like clubs. However, with two arrows in the shape of a half-moon, he[521] sliced off those arms. His face was like the full moon. However, with a kshurapra arrow, he severed that head. He fell down from his vehicle, exuding blood, like the summit of a mountain, when it is struck by the thunder and exudes red arsenic. Sudakshina's younger brother, from Kamboja, was seen to be slain. He was tall. His eyes were like the petals of lotuses. He was extremely handsome. He was like a golden pillar, or a golden mountain, and was shattered. Thereafter, the battle continued and it was fierce and wonderful to behold. In many different ways, the warriors fought there. The Kambojas, the Yavanas and the Shakas abandoned their horses. O lord of the earth! All of them were covered with blood and everything seemed red. Chariots lost their rathas, horses and charioteers. The riders of horses were slain. The riders of elephants were killed. The drivers of elephants were slain. O great king! They fought with each other and created a great destruction of men.

'"The great-souled Arjuna, foremost among victorious ones, destroyed the flank and the extreme flank.[522] Drona's son brandished his great bow, decorated with gold, and swiftly advanced against him. He released many terrible arrows that were like the rays of the sun. O great king! The arrows released by Drona's son descended in all the directions. They enveloped Krishna and Dhananjaya, who were stationed on the chariot. Bharadvaja's powerful descendant released hundreds of sharp arrows and in that battle, immobilized Madhava and Pandava. On seeing that the protectors of the mobile and the immobile were thus shrouded by arrows, lamentations arose everywhere, amidst the mobile and the immobile. Large numbers

[520]Sudakshina and his brother were from Kamboja. Arjuna killed Sudakshina in Section 69 (Volume 6).

[521]Arujna.

[522]Of the samshaptakas.

of siddhas and charanas assembled there from every direction and began to reflect about the welfare of the worlds. O king! I have not witnessed valour like this earlier, as Drona's son enveloped the two Krishnas with his arrows. The twang of the bow of Drona's son generated great terror in the battle. O king! It was repeatedly heard, like the roaring of a lion. He roamed around in that battle, to the left and to the right. His bowstring was as beautiful as a cloud tinged with lightning. Pandava was swift in acting and his hand was firm. However, on seeing Drona's son, he seemed to be overcome with great stupefaction. He thought that his own valour had been surpassed by the great-souled one. O king! In that battle, his[523] form was impossible to behold. O Indra among kings! In that great battle between Drona's son and Pandava, the great strength of Drona's son was seen to increase. On seeing that Kounteya was waning, Krishna was overcome with rage. O king! He sighed repeatedly with rage and glanced towards Drona's son and Phalguna in that encounter, as if burning them down with his eyes. Krishna angrily spoke to Partha, though with affection. 'O Partha! On seeing you in this encounter, I find it to be extraordinary. O descendant of the Bharata lineage! Drona's son is surpassing you today. O Arjuna! Is Gandiva not in your hand? Or are you not stationed on your chariot? Are your arms well? Is your valour still there?' Having been thus addressed by Krishna, he[524] was enraged. At a time when speed was of the essence, he quickly used fourteen broad-headed arrows to destroy the bow and chariot of Drona's son and also his standard, umbrella, flags, chariot, javelin and club. With vatsadanta arrows, he struck him severely in the shoulder joints. Having become completely unconscious, he[525] grasped the pole of his standard. To protect him from Dhananjaya, his charioteer bore him away from the field of battle. O descendant of the Bharata lineage! At that time, Vijaya, the scorcher of enemies, destroyed hundreds and thousands of your soldiers, while your brave son looked on. Thus, as they engaged with

[523]Ashvatthama's.

[524]Arjuna.

[525]Ashvatthama.

the enemy, there was the destruction of your soldiers. O king! That cruel and terrible destruction was because of your evil counsel. In that battle, Kounteya completely destroyed the samshaptakas, Vrikodara the Kurus and Vasushena the Panchalas."'

Chapter 1191(41)

'Sanjaya said, "Krishna was advancing quickly and again spoke softly to Partha. 'O Kouravya! Behold. The kings are advancing towards Pandava.[526] Behold Karna in this great arena, blazing like a fire. This Bhima is a great archer and has returned to fight again. With Dhrishtadyumna at the forefront, the others have also returned and are following him—with the Panchalas, the Srinjayas and the Pandavas leading the way. The large army of the enemy is being shattered by the returning Parthas. O Arjuna! The Kouravas who were running away have been held together by Karna. His force is like that of Yama and his valour is Shakra's equal. O Kouravya! Drona's son, supreme among the wielders of weapons, is advancing there. In the battle, maharatha Dhrishtadyumna is advancing against him.' In this way, the invincible Vasudeva described it to Kiriti. O king! Then, an extremely great and extremely fierce battle commenced. As the clash started, roars like lions' were heard. O king! Both sets of soldiers preferred death to retreat."'

Chapter 1192(42)

'Sanjaya said, "Without any fear, the Kurus and the Srinjayas started to fight again. The Parthas had Yudhishthira at the

[526]Yudhishthira.

forefront and we had Vaikartana at the forefront. There was a fierce battle between Karna and the Pandavas and it extended Yama's kingdom and made the body hair stand up. That tumultuous battle created waves of blood. O descendant of the Bharata lineage! Only a few of the samshaptakas remained. O great king! With Dhrishtadyumna and all the kings, the maharatha Pandavas rushed against Karna. They were cheerful and attacked in that battle, desiring victory. Alone in that battle, Karna received them, like a mountain receives a flood of water. Having clashed against Karna, those maharathas were shattered and beaten back in all the directions, like a flood of water against a mountain. O great king! The battle that commenced made the body hair stand up. Dhristhadyumna angrily asked Radheya to wait and struck him with an arrow with drooping tufts. The maharatha[527] brandished Vijaya, foremost among bows, and severed Parshata's bow with arrows that were like venomous serpents. He angrily struck Parshata with nine arrows. O unblemished one! The great-souled one shattered his gold-decorated armour and, covered with blood, they[528] looked as beautiful as shakragopa insects. Maharatha Dhrishtadyumna discarded his severed bow and picked up another bow. With seven straight-tufted arrows that were like venomous serpents, he pierced Karna. O king! In that fashion, Karna, the great archer, pierced Parshata, the scorcher of enemies and Drona's enemy,[529] with sharp arrows. O great king! Karna angrily dispatched a gold-decorated arrow that was like Yama's staff. O lord of the earth! O king! On seeing it suddenly descend, terrible in form, Shini's descendant displayed the lightness of his hand and shattered it into seven fragments. O lord of the earth! On seeing that the arrow had been repulsed by arrows, Karna showered arrows from every direction on Satyaki. In that encounter, he pierced him with seven iron arrows and Shini's descendant pierced him back with arrows that were decorated with gold. The battle that raged was fearful to those who saw and heard. O king! Though it was fearful in every

[527]Karna. Vijaya was the name of Karna's bow.

[528]The arrows.

[529]Dhrishtadyumna killed Drona.

direction, it was wonderful to see. O king! On witnessing the deeds of Karna and Shini's descendant in the battle, the body hair of all the beings there stood up.

'"Drona's son was extremely strong. At that time, he rushed against Parshata, the destroyer of enemies who could rob the valour of the foe. Dhananjaya was still at a distance and Drona's son angrily addressed him.[530] 'O slayer of a brahmana! Stay. Stay. You will not escape from me with your life.' Having spoken thus, the brave one swiftly struck Parshata and enveloped him with sharp arrows that were terrible in form and extremely energetic. The maharatha[531] strove to the best of his capacity. O venerable one! In the encounter, Drona's son glanced towards Parshata and in that encounter, Parshata, the slayer of enemy heroes, also glanced towards Drona's son. In the battle, Drona's son was delighted to see Parshata, the slayer of enemy heroes. But he was not greatly delighted, thinking that his own death might be before him.[532] O Indra among kings! On seeing Dhrishtadyumna stationed in the battle, Drona's brave son sighed with anger and attacked Parshata. On seeing each other, they were overcome with supreme rage. O great king! O lord of the earth! Drona's powerful son swiftly approached Dhrishtadyumna and said, 'O worst of the Panchala lineage! I will send you to death. On an earlier occasion, you committed an evil deed by killing Drona. O stupid one! You will regret that today and no longer remain hale, as long as you are stationed in the battle and not protected by Partha. I am telling you this truthfully.' Having been thus addressed, the powerful Dhrishtadyumna replied. 'I will reply to your words with my sword, which also answered your father when he endeavoured in the battle. You are a brahmana only in name. If Drona could be slain by me, why should I not use my valour and kill you in the battle?' O great king! Having spoken thus, the intolerant Parshata, the commander-in-chief, pierced Drona's son with sharp arrows. O king! In that encounter, Drona's son became wrathful and enveloped

[530]Dhrishtadyumna.

[531]Dhrishtadyumna.

[532]However, Ashvatthama was immortal.

Dhrishtadyumna from every direction with straight-tufted arrows. O great king! Shrouded by thousands of arrows everywhere, the sky, the directions and the warriors could not be seen. O king! In that fashion, while the son of a suta looked on, Parshata enveloped Drona's son, the ornament of a battle, with arrows. O great king! Meanwhile, while everyone looked on from every direction, Radheya single-handedly countered the Panchalas, the Pandavas, Droupadi's sons, Yudhamanyu and maharatha Satyaki. In the battle, Dhrishtadyumna severed the bow of Drona's son. Abandoning that bow in the battle, he picked up another bow that was powerful and terrible. O Indra among kings! Using arrows that were like venomous serpents, he sliced down Parshata's bow, javelin, club and standard and in an instant, used his arrows to destroy his horses, charioteer and chariot. His bow was severed. He was without a chariot. His horses were slain. His charioteer was killed. He grasped a giant sword and a shield that blazed like the sun and was marked with the sign of one hundred moons. O Indra among kings! However, Drona's maharatha son was brave. He was firm in using weapons and light in use of his hands. Before he[533] could descend from his chariot, he swiftly severed these with his broad-headed arrows and it was extraordinary. Dhrishtadyumna was without a chariot. His horses had been slain and his bow had been severed. O best of the Bharata lineage! The maharatha[534] tried his best. But though he tried his best, pierced him with many arrows and shattered his weapons, he could not kill him. O king! When Drona's son could not kill him with his arrows, the brave one cast aside his bow and quickly advanced towards Parshata. O king! The great-souled one attacked and descended powerfully, like Garuda descending to pick up the best of serpents.

'"At this moment, Madhava spoke to Arjuna. 'O Partha! Behold. Drona's son is making great efforts for Parshata's destruction and there is no doubt that he will kill him. O mighty-armed one! Free Parshata, the scorcher of enemies. He has reached the mouth of Drona's son, as if he is within the mouth of death.' O great king!

[533]Dhrishtadyumna.

[534]Ashvatthama.

Having said this, the powerful Vasudeva swiftly urged the horses towards the spot where Drona's son was. Those horses possessed the complexion of the moon and were urged by Keshava. As they advanced towards the chariot of Drona's son, they seemed to drink up the sky. O king! On seeing that the immensely valorous and radiant Krishna and Dhananjaya were advancing, the immensely strong one[535] made great efforts to kill Dhrishtadyumna. O lord of men! On seeing that Dhrishtadyumna was being dragged,[536] the immensely strong Partha shot arrows towards Drona's son. Those arrows were decorated with gold and dispatched from Gandiva. They severely struck Drona's son and penetrated, like serpents entering a termite hill. Drona's powerful son was devastated by those fierce arrows. Afflicted by Dhananjaya's arrows, the brave one climbed onto his chariot. He picked up his supreme bow and pierced Partha with arrows. O lord of men! At this time, the brave Sahadeva picked up Parshata, the scorcher of enemies, on his chariot and bore him away. O great king! Arjuna pierced Drona's son with arrows and Drona's son angrily struck him on the arms and the chest. Becoming enraged in that battle, Partha used an iron arrow that was like death. It was like Yama's staff and he released it towards Drona's son. Immensely radiant, it descended on the brahmana's shoulder. O great king! In that battle, because of the force of that arrow, he lost his senses. Overcome by supreme lassitude, he sank down on the floor of his chariot. O great king! On seeing Arjuna engaged in the battle, Karna repeatedly brandished his Vijaya bow. In the great battle, he desired to have a duel with Partha. On seeing that the brave one[537] had lost his senses, his charioteer used his chariot to swiftly bear the destroyer of enemies away from the field of battle. O great king! On seeing that Parshata had been freed and Drona's son afflicted, the Panchalas were delighted and became hopeful of victory. Thousands of divine musical instruments were sounded. On witnessing such terrible and extremely wonderful deeds, they roared

[535]Ashvatthama.

[536]Ashvatthama was dragging Dhrishtadyumna by the hair.

[537]Ashvatthama.

like lions. Having done this, Partha Dhananjaya spoke to Vasudeva. 'O Krishna! Proceed towards the samshaptakas. That should be my next task.' On hearing the words spoken by Pandava, Dasharha departed on the chariot that had many banners and possessed the speed of the wind or thoughts."'

Chapter 1193(43)

'Sanjaya said, "At this time, Krishna spoke these words to Partha, pointing out to Kounteya, Dharmaraja Yudhishthira. 'O Partha! Pandava, your brother, is being swiftly pursued by the immensely strong sons of Dhritarashtra. They are great archers and wish to kill him. The angry Panchalas, invincible in battle, are also following at great speed, wishing to save the great-souled Yudhishthira. O Partha! Duryodhana is the king of all the worlds. He is armoured and is following the king with an array of chariots. With his brothers, the powerful one desires to kill that tiger among men. Their touch is like that of venomous serpents and they are skilled in all manner of fighting. Wishing to kill him, these elephants, horses, chariots and foot soldiers are also advancing. The sons of Dhritarashtra are after Yudhishthira, like those after a supreme jewel. Behold. They have been checked by Satvata and the lord Bhima. They are like daityas desiring amrita, but held in check by Shakra and Agni. However, many of them are again swiftly advancing towards Pandava. Those maharathas are like waters made turbulent by the wind, rushing towards the ocean during the monsoon season. They are roaring like lions, or like clouds at the end of the summer. The powerful and great archers are brandishing their bows. I think that Yudhishthira, Kunti's son, has entered the jaws of death. The fortunate one has come under Duryodhana's subjugation and is like an oblation poured into the fire. O Pandava! The army of the sons of Dhritarashtra has been prepared properly. Even Shakra will not be able to escape, if he comes within the range of their arrows. Duryodhana, Drona's son and Sharadvata are brave. The force of Karna's arrows can shatter mountains. Duryodhana is valiant and shoots a storm of arrows quickly. When he is angry, he is like Yama. Who is capable of withstanding his force in battle? The king, the scorcher of enemies, has already been forced to retreat by Karna, who is powerful, dexterous and accomplished, and skilled in fighting. Radheya is capable of oppressing the best of the Pandavas in the battle. In addition, the brave one is with the great-souled sons of Dhritarashtra. He[538] is controlled in his soul. When he fought with them in the battle, other maharathas robbed Partha of his armour. O supreme among the Bharata lineage! The king is severely emaciated because of his fasts. He is established in the strength of the brahman, but he does not possess a great deal of strength of the kshatriya variety. O Partha! I do not think that Yudhishthira, the great king, will remain alive, even though Bhimasena is with him and is roaring intolerantly, like a lion. O scorcher of enemies! The sons of Dhritarashtra are roaring repeatedly. Desiring victory in the battle, they are blowing on their giant conch shells. O bull among the Bharata lineage! Pandaveya Yudhishthira will be killed. Karna will urge the immensely strong sons of Dhritarashtra towards Partha. He will shroud the king with *sthunakarna*, *indrajala* and pashupata and the maharathas will follow him.[539] O descendant of the Bharata lineage! It is my view that the king must be in distress. At a time when speed is of the essence, the Panchalas and the Pandavas, supreme among all wielders of weapons, are following him. They are like powerful ones dashing to save someone who has been submerged in the nether regions. O Partha! The king's flags cannot be seen. They may have been brought down by Karna's arrows, while the twins, Satyaki, Shikhandi, Dhrishtadyumna, Bhima, the lord Shatanika and all the Panchalas and Chedis looked on. O

[538]Yudhishthira.

[539]Sthunakarna is a broad-headed arrow, while pashupata is a divine weapon named after Pashupati or Shiva. Literally, indrajala means Indra's net and signifies magic or illusion.

Partha! In this battle, Karna is destroying the Pandava soldiers with his arrows, like an elephant among lotuses. O descendant of the Pandu lineage! The rathas on your side are being driven away. O Partha! Look at how the maharathas are retreating. O descendant of the Bharata lineage! In the battle, the elephants have been struck by Karna. They are shrieking and are running away in the ten directions. O Partha! Behold. Arrays of chariots are fleeing in different directions. They have been routed in the battle by Karna, the destroyer of enemies. In the battle, behold the chariot of the son of the suta roaming around here and there. He is stationed on it. He has the best of standards and it is marked with the sign of an elephant's housing. Radheya is advancing towards Bhimasena's chariot. He is showering down hundreds of arrows and slaughtering your army. Behold the Panchalas being driven away by the great-souled one. He is like Shakra destroying the daityas in a great battle. This Karna has defeated the Panchalas, Pandus and Srinjayas. He is now searching around in all the directions for you. That is my view. O Partha! Behold. He looks beautiful, as he is stretching the best of bows. Having defeated the enemy, he is like Shakra, surrounded by large numbers of gods. On witnessing Karna's valour, the Kouravas are roaring. Thousands of Parthas and Srinjayas have been frightened in the battle. In this great battle, he has wholeheartedly terrified the Pandus. O one who grants honours! Radheya is addressing all the soldiers. "O Kouravas! Attack them quickly. Advance and drive them away, so that no one among the Srinjayas can escape from this encounter with his life. Act united in this way and we will follow you." Having said this, he is advancing behind them, showering arrows. O Partha! Behold Karna in the battle. He is under a white umbrella and is as radiant as the sun behind Mount Asta. O descendant of the Bharata lineage! A white umbrella that is like the full moon and possesses a hundred spokes is held aloft his head in the battle. O lord of the earth! Karna is casting his glances around, looking for you. He will certainly make the best of efforts in this battle. O mighty-armed one! Behold him brandishing his giant bow. The immensely strong one is releasing arrows that are like venomous serpents. O one with the ape on the banner! Radheya can be seen to be headed in this direction. He is advancing for his own destruction, like an insect towards a lamp. O descendant of the Bharata lineage! On seeing that Karna is alone, Dhritarashtra's son has turned his array of chariots towards him, controlling them so as to protect him. If you desire fame, the kingdom and supreme happiness, make efforts to kill him, with all the evil-souled ones who are with him. O bull among the Bharata lineage! You have controlled your soul. Glance towards your own self. Radheya is firm in his hatred for the great-souled Yudhishthira. Accomplish the end that Radheya has set for himself. O noble one! Set your mind on fighting and repel that leader of rathas. O supreme among rathas! Five foremost rathas are powerfully advancing towards you,[540] with hundreds of others. They are strong and fierce in their energy. There are five thousand elephants and twice that number of horses. O Kounteya! Ten thousand foot soldiers are also advancing. O brave one! Protecting each other, that army is advancing towards you. Reveal your own self to the son of a suta, the great archer. O bull among the Bharata lineage! Make the best of efforts and repulse them. This Karna is extremely angry and is attacking the Panchalas. Behold his flag in the direction of Dhrishtadyumna's chariot. O scorcher of enemies! I think that he will uproot the Panchalas. O Partha! O bull among the Bharata lineage! But I will tell you something that will please you. Kouravya King Yudhishthira, Dharma's son, is alive. The mighty-armed Bhima has returned and is stationed at the head of the army. O descendant of the Bharata lineage! He is surrounded by the Srinjaya soldiers and by Satyaki. O Kounteya! In this encounter, Bhimasena and the great-souled Panchalas are slaying the Kouravas with sharp arrows. The soldiers of Dhritarashtra's son are retreating and running away from the field of battle. Slain by Bhima's forceful arrows, they are being routed. With blood flowing from their wounds, they look like the earth after a crop has been harvested. O best of the Bharatas! The army of the Bharatas[541] presents a miserable sight. O Kounteya!

[540]The names of these five are not indicated.

[541]That is, the Kourava army.

Behold. They have been forced to retreat. Bhimasena, the lord of warriors, who is like a venomous serpent, has angrily driven away the army. O Arjuna! Yellow, red, black and white flags, with the signs of stars, the moon and the sun, and many umbrellas are strewn around. There are golden and silver standards and those that are made of other metals. They have been brought down and are scattered around, and so are elephants and horses. Deprived of their lives, rathas have fallen down from their chariots. They have been slain by many-hued arrows released by the Panchalas, who are not running away. O Dhananjaya! The army of the sons of Dhritarashtra is without men, elephants, horses and chariots, and the Panchalas are spiritedly driving it away. O scorcher of enemies! The enemy's army was unassailable. But ready to give up their lives and seeking refuge with Bhimasena, they[542] are driving it away. The Panchalas are roaring, like clouds at the end of the summer. They are driving away the enemy in the battle and slaying them with arrows. O scorcher of enemies! Behold the greatness of heaven before the Panchalas.[543] They are angrily slaying the sons of Dhritarashtra, like lions against elephants. Every part of the large army of the sons of Dhritarashtra has been attacked. The force of the Panchalas is like that of swans that leave Manasa[544] for the Ganga. Kripa, Karna and other brave ones are severely trying to counter the valorous Panchalas, like bulls against bulls. However, the maharathas among the sons of Dhritarashtra are deeply submerged in Bhima's weapons. On seeing that the rathas in the great army of the sons of Dhritarashtra are distressed, the brave ones, with Dhrishtadyumna at the forefront, are slaying the enemy in thousands. Behold. The elephants have been shattered by Bhima's iron arrows and are falling down. They are like summits that have fallen down on the ground, after being struck by the vajra of the wielder of the vajra. Mighty elephants have been struck by Bhimasena's straight-tufted arrows. As they are running away, they

[542]The Panchalas.
[543]If they die in the battle, the Panchalas will ascend to heaven.
[544]Lake Manasa.

are slaying their own soldiers. Do you not know Bhima's unbearable leonine roar? O Arjuna! Desiring victory in the battle, the brave one is roaring. Astride a supreme elephant, the Nishada[545] is advancing against Pandava. He is angrily attacking him with javelins, like Yama with a staff in his hand. Bhima is roaring and breaking down those javelins with his bare hands. He has then used ten sharp iron arrows, which are like the flames of the fire, to slay him. Behold. Having slain him, the striker has again attacked other elephants that are like blue clouds and are driven by skilled drivers. Vrikodara has slain those elephants, seven at a time, with spears and javelins and has brought down their victorious standards. They have been slain and mangled with sharp arrows by Partha's elder brother. Each of ten elephants has been slain by ten sharp arrows. The roars of the sons of Dhritarashtra can no longer be heard now. They have been forced to retreat by the angry bull among the Bharata lineage,[546] who is Purandara's equal. Three akshouhinis from the sons of Dhritarashtra united against him. However, Bhimasena, lion among men, angrily countered them.' On seeing that Bhimasena had accomplished that extremely difficult deed, Arjuna slaughtered the remaining ones with his sharp arrows. O lord! Large numbers of samshaptakas were slaughtered in that battle. Bereft of sorrow and filled with delight, they became Shakra's guests. With straight-tufted arrows, Partha, tiger among men, destroyed the fourfold[547] army of the sons of Dhritarashtra."'

Chapter 1194(44)

'Dhritarashtra asked, "When Bhimasena and Pandava Yudhishthira returned and my army was slaughtered by the Pandus and the Srinjayas, when my army that was like an ocean was

[545]Obviously a king among the nishadas.

[546]Bhima.

[547]Chariots, elephants, horses and infantry.

repeatedly distressed, what was done by the Kurus? O Sanjaya! Tell me that in detail."

'Sanjaya replied, "O king! On seeing the mighty-armed Bhima, the eyes of the powerful son of a suta became red with rage. He attacked Bhimasena. O king! On seeing that your army had retreated before Bhimasena, the powerful one made great efforts to rally it. Having rallied your son's army, the mighty-armed Karna advanced against the Pandavas, who were indomitable in battle. Radheya counter-attacked the maharatha Pandavas. He brandished his bow and showered down arrows on Bhimasena, Shini's grandson, Shikhandi, Janamejaya, the powerful Dhrishtadyumna and all the Prabhadrakas. The Panchalas, tigers among men, angrily attacked your army from all sides in that battle, desiring victory. O king! In that fashion, the maharathas on your side wished to kill them and impetuously attacked the Pandava army. O tiger among men! The place was beautiful with chariots, elephants, horses, foot soldiers and standards and the armies were wonderful to see. O great king! Shikhandi advanced against Karna and Dhrishtadyumna against your son, Duhshasana, who was surrounded by a large army. Nakula advanced against Vrishasena and Yudhishthira against Chitrasena.[548] O king! In the encounter, Sahadeva attacked Uluka, Satyaki attacked Shakuni and Bhimasena the Kouravas. In the battle, Drona's maharatha son made endeavours against Arjuna. In the battle, Goutama attacked the great archer, Yudhamanyu, and Kritavarma advanced against the powerful Uttamouja. O venerable one! Single-handedly, the mighty-armed Bhimasena countered all your sons, the Kurus, together with their soldiers.

'"O great king! Shikhandi, the slayer of Bhishma, roamed around fearlessly and countered Karna with his arrows. Countered, Karna's lips quivered in rage. He struck Shikhandi between his eyebrows with three arrows. With those arrows stuck there, Shikhandi looked exceedingly beautiful. He was like a silver mountain with three peaks. In the battle, having been thus grievously struck by the son of a suta in the encounter, he pierced Karna with ninety sharp

[548]The inconsistency about Chitrasena has been mentioned earlier.

arrows. Karna slew his horses and charioteer with three arrows. The maharatha then brought down his standard with a kshurapra arrow. With his horses slain, the maharatha, the scorcher of enemies,[549] jumped down from his chariot and angrily flung a javelin towards Karna. O descendant of the Bharata lineage! In the battle, Karna cut that down with his arrows and then mangled Shikhandi with nine sharp arrows. Shikhandi, supreme among men and supreme among victorious ones, avoided the arrows released from Karna's bow and retreated quickly.

'"O great king! Karna then scattered the Pandu soldiers, like a mass of cotton by the speed of a mighty wind. O great king! Dhrishtadyumna was afflicted by your son and struck Duhshasana between the breasts with three arrows. O venerable one! Duhshasana pierced his left arm with a sharp, gold-tufted and broad-headed arrow with drooping tufts. O descendant of the Bharata lineage! Thus pierced, Dhrishtadyumna became fierce in his wrath and angrily dispatched an arrow towards Duhshasana. O lord of the earth! The arrow released by Dhrishtadyuma descended with great force, but your son sliced it down with three arrows. He then used another seventeen broad-headed and gold-decorated arrows to strike Dhrishtadyumna in the arms and in the chest. O venerable one! Becoming angry, Parshata severed his bow with an extremely sharp kshurapra arrow and people roared in applause. O bull among the Bharata lineage! Your son picked up another bow and showered a storm of arrows from every direction on Dhrishtadyumna. On witnessing the valour of your great-souled son, the warrior, in the battle, the large numbers of siddhas and apsaras smiled.

'"O scorcher of enemies! Thus the battle raged between those on your side and that of the enemy. It was fierce, as terrible in form as the destruction of all beings at the end of a yuga. Vrishasena pierced Nakula with five iron arrows and stationing himself near his father,[550] pierced him again with three arrows. Nakula became angry and laughed at Vrishasena. He then pierced him firmly in the chest

[549]Shikhandi.

[550]Vrishasena was Karna's son.

with an extremely sharp iron arrow. Having been severely struck by the powerful enemy, the destroyer of foes struck his adversary with twenty arrows and was pierced back with five. Those two bulls among men shot thousands of arrows at each other and, supported by their respective soldiers, enveloped each other. O lord of the earth! On seeing that the soldiers of the sons of Dhritarashtra were fleeing, the son of a suta followed them and powerfully checked them. O venerable one! When Karna had withdrawn, Nakula advanced against the Kouravas. In the battle, Karna's son also abandoned Nakula and swiftly went to the spot where Radheya was.

'"In the battle, the angry Uluka was checked by Sahadeva. The powerful Sahadeva slew his four horses and conveyed his charioteer towards Yama's abode. O lord of the earth! At this, Uluka, loved by his father, descended from his vehicle and swiftly joined the army of the Trigartas.

'"Satyaki pierced Shakuni with twenty sharp arrows and severing Soubala's standard with a broad-headed arrow, laughed. O king! The powerful Soubala became enraged in that battle. Having shattered Satyaki's armour, he again brought down his golden standard and pierced him back with sharp arrows. O great king! He[551] brought down his charioteer with three arrows and swiftly used other arrows to convey his mounts to Yama's eternal abode. O bull among the Bharata lineage! Maharatha Shakuni suddenly alighted from his chariot and swiftly ascended that of Uluka. He was quicky borne away from Satyaki, who was skilled in fighting. O king! In that battle, Satyaki attacked your soldiers with great force and shattered the formation. O lord of the earth! Your soldiers were enveloped by arrows shot by Shini's descendant and were quickly scattered in the ten directions. They lost their lives and fell down.

'"Your son[552] countered Bhimasena in the battle. But in an instant, Bhima deprived that lord of men of his horses, charioteer, chariot and standard. This satisfied the charanas. At this, he withdrew from Bhimasena's presence. Wishing to kill the single-

[551]Satyaki.

[552]Though not clearly stated, this seems to be Duryodhana.

handed Bhimasena, all the Kuru soldiers let out a mighty roar and attacked him.

'"Yudhamanyu attacked Kripa and quickly severed his bow. Kripa, supreme among the wielders of weapons, picked up another bow. He brought down Yudhamanyu's standard, charioteer, umbrella and bow on the ground. Maharatha Yudhamanyu withdrew on another chariot. Hardikya was terrible in his valour and Uttamouja suddenly shrouded him with arrows, like clouds raining down on a mountain. O scorcher of enemies! O lord of the earth! The encounter between them was extremely great and terrible. I have not seen anything like that earlier. O king! In that battle, Kritavarma pierced Uttamouja in the chest and he sank down on the floor of his chariot. His charioteer bore the best of rathas away on his chariot. O king! The Pandu soldiers were then quickly routed."'

Chapter 1195(45)

'Sanjaya said, "O king! Surrounded by a large array of chariots, Drona's son swiftly descended on the spot where the king[553] was. On seeing him violently descend, the brave Partha,[554] with Shouri as his aide, violently checked him, like the shoreline against the abode of makaras. O great king! At this, Drona's powerful son became enraged and enveloped Arjuna and Vasudeva with arrows. The maharathas saw that the two Krishnas were afflicted. The Kurus saw this and were overcome by great wonder. Arjuna seemed to smile and invoked a divine weapon. O descendant of the Bharata lineage! In the battle, the brahmana countered it. Wishing to kill, whichever weapon Pandava used in the battle was baffled by Drona's son, the great archer, in the encounter. O king! A terrible clash with weapons ensued. We saw Drona's son in that encounter,

[553]Yudhishthira.
[554]Arjuna.

like Death with a gaping mouth. Having enveloped the directions and the sub-directions with his arrows, he struck Vasudeva in the right arm with three arrows. Arjuna slew all the horses of the great-souled one and in the encounter, made the earth flow with a river of blood. Arrows released from Partha's bow killed rathas and brought them down. Freed from their yokes, horses were seen to run around here and there. On witnessing the deeds performed by Partha, Drona's son, the ornament of a battle, countered Krishna[555] in that encounter and covered him from every direction with sharp arrows. O great king! In the battle, Drona's son used another arrow to strike Arjuna in the chest. O descendant of the Bharata lineage! Having been severely struck in the battle by Drona's son, he picked up a terrible club and hurled it towards Drona's son. That club was decorated with gold and descended. However, Drona's son suddenly shattered it and people applauded. O king! Shattered into many fragments by the arrows of Bharadvaja's son, it fell down on the ground, like a mountain that has been shattered by the wind god. In the encounter, Arjuna pierced Drona's son with ten arrows and used a broad-headed arrow to bring down his charioteer from his seat on the chariot. Drona's son, swift in his valour, controlled the mounts himself and swiftly enveloped the two Krishnas with arrows. We beheld that wonderful sight. He controlled and drove the horses and fought with Phalguna. O king! In the battle, all the warriors applauded this feat. When Drona's son advanced before Phalguna in the encounter, Jaya[556] used a kshurapra arrow to slice down the harnesses that yoked the horses to the chariot. Driven by the force of the arrows, the horses fled. O descendant of the Bharata lineage! A loud uproar arose amidst your troops. Having obtained victory, the Pandavas drove away your soldiers. Desiring victory, they released sharp arrows from every direction. O great king! The large army of the sons of Dhritarasthra was repeatedly routed by the brave ones, who were urged on by the prospect of victory.

[555]Krishna is also one of Arjuna's names and this Krishna is clearly Arjuna.

[556]Arjuna's name.

'"O great king! Your sons, colourful in fighting, Shakuni Soubala and the great-souled Karna looked on. O lord of men! But they were unable to rally the large army of your sons. Afflicted in every way, they no longer remained in the battle. O great king! The warriors fled here and there. On seeing this, the large army of your sons was terrified and, extremely anxious, ran away. The son of a suta repeatedly asked them to remain. However, slain by the great-souled ones, the soldiers did not stay there. O great king! Desiring victory, the Pandavas roared repeatedly, having seen that the army of the sons of Dhritarashtra was running away in various directions. At this, Duryodhana spoke these affectionate words to Karna. 'O Karna! Behold. The soldiers have been severely oppressed by the Pandavas. Though you are here, they are frightened and are running away in every direction. O mighty-armed one! O destroyer of enemies! Knowing this, do what must be done. O bull among men! O brave one! Driven away by the Pandavas in the battle, thousands of warriors are calling out to you alone.' Hearing these important words spoken by Duryodhana, Radheya, the descendant of the suta lineage, spoke these words to the lord of Madra. 'O lord of men! Behold the valour of my arms and my weapons. In the battle today, I will kill all the Panchalas, together with the Pandus. O tiger among men! O lord of men! Drive the horses well.' Having spoken these words, the powerful and brave son of a suta, picked up Vijaya, his ancient and excellent bow. O great king! Having strung it, he repeatedly rubbed the string. He asked the warriors to return.

'"The immensely strong one with an immeasurable soul took a pledge of truth and invoked the *bhargava* weapon.[557] O king! In the great battle, thousands, millions, billions and crores of extremely sharp arrows issued from it. They were extremely terrible and blazed, shafted with the feathers of herons and peacocks. The Pandava soldiers were mangled and nothing could be seen. O lord of the earth! Great sounds of lamentation arose among the Panchalas. In the encounter, they were afflicted by the power of the bhargava weapon. O king! Elephants and men were brought down in thousands. O

[557]Divine weapon obtained from Bhargava, that is, Parashurama.

tiger among men! Chariots and horses were strewn around in every direction. O king! The slain were strewn around here and there and the earth trembled. The entire large army of the Pandavas was agitated. Karna alone was the foremost among warriors. He was like a fire without smoke. O tiger among men! That scorcher of enemies consumed the enemy and was resplendent. Having been slain by Karna, the Panchalas and the Chedis became unconscious. They were like elephants in a forest conflagration. O tiger among men! Those best among men lamented loudly. In the field of battle, loud woes of the terrified ones could be heard. O king! Terrified, they fled in different directions. There was the great sound of lamentation there, like that made by beings at the time of a flood. O venerable one! They were seen to be slaughtered there by the son of a suta. All the beings, including those belonging to an inferior species,[558] were frightened. The Srinjayas were slaughtered in the battle by the son of a suta and repeatedly cried out to Arjuna and Vasudeva. They were unconscious, like those in the city of the king of the dead, calling out to the king of the dead.[559]

'"At this, Kunti's son, Dhananjaya, spoke to Vasudeva. 'Behold the extremely terrible bhargava weapon. O Krishna! O mighty-armed one! Behold the valour of the bhargava weapon. There is no means of countering that weapon in a battle. O Krishna! Behold the angry son of a suta in the great battle. The brave one is like Yama and has performed a terrible deed. He is repeatedly casting extremely terrible glances towards me. I do not see any means of running away from Karna in this battle. If a man remains alive in a battle, there may be victory, or there may be defeat. O Hrishikesha! For the sake of victory, how can one be victorious if one is dead?' O venerable one! Janardana wished to leave to see Yudhishthira and thought that Karna would be overcome with exhaustion in the battle.[560] Krishna told Arjuna, 'The king[561] has been severely wounded. O best among

[558]Other than men, animals.

[559]Yama is the king of the dead.

[560]That is, Krishna wanted to wait until Karna was exhausted.

[561]Yudhishthira.

the Kuru lineage! Let us reassure him first and you will kill Karna after that.' Dhananjaya also wished to see the king who had been afflicted with arrows. On Keshava's instructions, he abandoned the battle and quickly departed on his chariot. Kounteya left, because he wished to see Dharmaraja. Though he looked at all the soldiers, he could not see his elder brother anywhere. O descendant of the Bharata lineage! Having fought with Drona's son and having defeated the descendant of Bhrigu lineage,[562] whom even the wielder of the vajra found difficult to withstand in battle, he departed. He defeated Drona's son, the wielder of a fierce bow. He thus accomplished an extremely difficult deed.

'"Dhananjaya, irresistible to enemies, then glanced towards his own soldiers. The bravest of the brave, who were battling at the forefronts of their divisions, were delighted to see Savyasachi. They were famous because of their earlier deeds and he instructed the rathas to be stationed with their divisions. However, the garlanded Kiriti did not see the eldest of the warriors, his brother Ajamidha.[563] He quickly approached Bhima and asked, 'How is the king? Where is the king?' Bhima replied, 'King Yudhishthira, Dharma's son, has retreated. His limbs have been mangled by Karna's arrows. I doubt that he is alive.' Arjuna said, 'Therefore, you should quickly go and find out about the king, supreme among the Kurus. Having been severely pierced by Karna's arrows, there is no doubt that the king has gone to his camp. When it was night,[564] though he was severely and grievously struck by Drona, the spirited one remained, desiring victory, and waited until Drona had been killed. In the battle today, the generous eldest among the Pandavas, has faced a disaster because

[562]Ashvatthama. But this must be a typo. Ashvatthama was descended from the Bharadvaja lineage, not the Bhrigu lineage. The Critical edition states 'the son of Bhrigu'. Instead of Bhrigu, other versions say *guru*. This fits, because Ashvatthama was Arjuna's preceptor's son.

[563]Ajamidha is one of Yudhishthira's names. Ajatashatru (one without enemies) is also one of Yudhishthira's names.

[564]This is a reference to fighting throughout the night, described in Section 70 (Volume 6).

of Karna. O Bhima! Quickly go and find out about him. I will remain here and restrain the large numbers of the enemy.' Bhima replied, 'O magnaminous one! O bull among the Bharata lineage! You go and find out how the king is. O Arjuna! If I go there, these brave ones[565] will say that I am frightened.' At this, Arjuna told Bhimasena, 'The samshaptakas are arranged in a counter-formation against me. Without killing them, it is not possible for me to abandon these large numbers of the enemy.' Bhimasena told Arjuna, 'O brave one amongst the Kuru lineage! In this encounter, I will rely on my valour and fight against all the samshaptakas. O Dhananjaya! Go.' In the midst of the enemy, he[566] heard these extremely difficult words of assurance given by Bhimasena, his brother. Wishing to leave and see the best of the Kuru lineage,[567] he then spoke these words to the best of the Vrishni lineage. 'O Hrishikesha! Drive the horses and let us leave this ocean of chariots. O Keshava! I wish to see King Ajatashatru.' Before urging the horses, the foremost among the Dasharha lineage spoke these words to Bhima. 'O brave one! For you, the task to be accomplished now is not at all wonderful. O Bhima! I am leaving. Slay these masses of the enemy.' O king! O Indra among kings! Hrishikesha then went to the spot where King Yudhishthira was, urging the steeds that were Garuda's equal to a greater and greater speed, having stationed Bhimsena, the scorcher of enemies, in the counter-formation and having given Vrikodara instructions about the fight. Those two, the best of men, approached the king, who was lying down alone. They descended from the chariot and bowed in obeisance at Dharmaraja's feet.[568] On seeing that the bull among men was well, those two bulls among men, the two Krishnas, were filled with delight, like the two Ashvins on seeing Vasava. The king honoured them, like the fire god, the Ashvins, or the preceptor greeting Shakra and Vishnu when the great asura Jambha

[565]Referring to the Kouravas.

[566]Arjuna.

[567]Yudhishthira.

[568]Krishna was also younger to Yudhishthira.

was killed.[569] Thinking that Karna had been killed, Dharmaraja Yudhishthira was delighted and addressed those two scorchers of enemies in a voice that was choking with joy."'

Chapter 1196(46)

'Sanjaya said, "On seeing the great-spirited Keshava and Arjuna arrive together, he thought that Adhiratha's son had been killed in the battle by the wielder of Gandiva. O bull among the Bharata lineage! Kounteya, the destroyer of enemies, greeted them in extremely affectionate words and, honouring them, smiled.

'"Yudhishthira said, 'O Devaki's son! Welcome. O Dhananjaya! Welcome. I am extremely delighted to see Achyuta and Arjuna together. Since neither of you is injured, how was your battle with the maharatha?[570] He is like virulent poison in a battle and is skilled in the use of all weapons. He is the leader of all the sons of Dhritarashtra and is their armour and their mail. He was protected by the archers Vrishasena and Sushena. The invincible and immensely valorous one had learnt weapons from Rama[571] himself. He was the protector of the sons of Dhritarashtra and advanced at the forefront of their army. He was the one who killed enemy soldiers. He is the one who crushed large numbers of the enemy. He was engaged in Duryodhana's welfare and was always ready to rise up against us. In a great battle, he could not be assailed even by the gods, together with Vasava. In his energy and his strength, he was like the wind and the fire. He was as deep as the nether regions and brought joy to his well-wishers. By killing Karna in the great battle, you have brought an end to my enemies. It is through good fortune that you have come to

[569]The preceptor in question is Brihaspati, the preceptor of the gods. The asura Jambha is sometimes described as having been killed by Indra, sometimes by Vishnu, and sometimes by Indra and Vishnu together.

[570]Karna.

[571]Parashurama.

me, like two immortals after killing an asura. O Achyuta! O Arjuna! I fearlessly fought a battle with him today. He was like an enraged Yama, wishing to slay all beings. He brought down my standard and slew my parshni charioteers. While Yuyudhana looked on, I was rendered without a chariot and without horses. Dhrishtadyumna, the brave twins, Shikhandi, Droupadi's sons and all the Panchalas looked on. O mighty-armed one![572] Having defeated large numbers of the enemy, the immensely valorous Karna vanquished me in the great battle, though I strove to my utmost. He pursued me in the battle and spoke many harsh words. There is no doubt that he defeated the best among the warriors. O Dhananjaya! It is because of Bhimasena's powers that I am still alive. There is no need to speak a lot. That humiliation was overwhelming. O Dhananjaya! I have been frightened about him for thirteen years. I was not able to sleep at night. Nor could I be happy during the day. O Dhananjaya! Because of my enmity towards him, it was as if I was burning. I was like a rhinoceros or an elephant, knowing that it was going to die.[573] O lord! I continuously thought about the time when he would go to Yama. How would I bring about Karna's destruction in the battle? O Kounteya! Whether I was awake or sleeping, Karna was always in front of me. I saw him everywhere. The entire universe was full of Karna. O Dhananjaya! Wherever I went, I was frightened of Karna. And wherever I went, I saw him stationed in front of me. I was forced to run away from that brave one in the battle. O Partha! I was defeated, with my horses and my chariot and he let me escape with my life. What is the point of remaining alive? What again is the point of the kingdom? I have been shamed by Karna, the ornament of a battle. What was not obtained by me earlier in the battle with Bhishma, Kripa and Drona, has been obtained by me in the encounter with the maharatha son of a suta. O Kounteya! That is the reason I am asking you about your welfare now. Tell me everything about how Karna has been slain by you. His valour in a battle is like that

[572]Though both Krishna and Arjuna are present, Yudhishthira is specifically speaking to Arjuna.

[573]The image is of old elephants or rhinos, which retire from the group to die.

of Shakra. His bravery is like that of Yama. He is like Rama[574] in weapons. How was he killed? He is famous as a maharatha. He is skilled in every method of fighting. Among all the wielders of the bow, he is the only man who is the foremost. O lord of the earth! He was always honoured by Dhritarashtra and his sons for your sake.[575] How was Radheya killed by you? O Arjuna! Among all the warriors, Dhritarashtra always used to regard Karna, bull among men, as the cause of your death in battle. O tiger among men! How was he killed by you in the encounter? O Bibhatsu! Tell me everything about how Karna has been killed by you. O tiger among men! In the sight of his comrades and well-wishers, did you sever his head, like a tiger against a *ruru* deer? In the battle, the son of a suta was searching for you and looked in every region and every direction. In the battle, Karna wished to give a bull-elephant to anyone who pointed you out. Has he been brought down by your extremely sharp arrows shafted with the feathers of herons? Having been killed by you in the battle, is the evil-souled son of a suta lying down on the surface of the earth? Perhaps you have brought me supreme delight today, by killing the son of a suta in the battle. Intoxicated with his pride, the son of a suta looked everywhere for you. He prided himself on his valour. Having clashed against you in the battle today, has he been killed by you? For your sake, he was prepared to give others a golden chariot and the best of elephants yoked to that chariot.[576] He always sought to challenge you in an encounter. O son![577] Has that wicked one indeed been killed by you in the battle? He was always crazy with insolence about his bravery and he spoke about it in the assembly of the Kouravas. He was always dear to Suyodhana. Has that evil one been killed by you today? When he clashed against you, were red arrows released from your bow, like birds? That wicked one's body has been mangled and he is lying down today. Has the arm of Dhritrarashtra's son been broken? Full of insolence, he always prided

[574]Parashurama.

[575]That is, as a counter to Arjuna.

[576]Karna promised these to the person who would point Arjuna out.

[577]The word used is tata.

himself in the midst of the kings, delighting Duryodhana. Because of his delusion, he said, "I will slay Phalguna." Has that ratha been killed by you? The one with limited intelligence said that he would not wash his feet as long as Partha was alive.[578] He always observed that vow. O Shakra's son! Has Karna been killed by you today? In the assembly hall, in the midst of the brave Kurus, the evil-minded Karna spoke to Krishna[579] and said, "O Krishna! Why don't you abandon the Pandavas? They have fallen and are extremely feeble. They have been deprived of their spirits." For your sake, Karna took a pledge that he would not return without having slain Krishna and Partha. Is the one with wicked intelligence lying down, his body mangled with arrows? The clash between the Srinjayas and the Kouravas and the state I was reduced to then are known to you. Having clashed against you, has he been slain by you today? Have you released flaming arrows from Gandiva towards that extremely evil-minded one? He possessed earrings on his head, given to him by the sun god.[580] Has Savyasachi really severed that head in the battle? O brave one! When he released arrows in my direction, I thought about Karna's death. Have you today accomplished what I thought about, by bringing down Karna? Protected by Karna, Suyodhana was full of insolence and looked down on us. Having clashed against you today, has Suyodhana's valour been destroyed? In earlier times, in the assembly hall and in the presence of the kings, he called us sterile sesamum seeds earlier.[581] Has the evil-minded and intolerant son of a suta encountered you in the battle and been killed by you? In earlier times, when Yajnaseni was won by Soubala,[582] the evil-souled son of a suta laughed at us and, laughing at her, said that she should be brought. Has he been killed by you today? When the grandfather, the best wielder of weapons on earth, classified him as only half a ratha,

[578]Karna took this vow in Section 39 (Volume 3).

[579]Krishnaa, Droupadi.

[580]However, in Section 43 (Volume 3), Karna donated these to Indra.

[581]This incident has been described in Section 27 (Volume 2).

[582]This is a reference to the gambling match, described in Section 27 (Volume 2). Yajnaseni is Droupadi's name.

the one with limited intelligence censured him.[583] Has Adhiratha's evil-souled son been killed by you? The fire of intolerance has always blazed in my heart and has been fanned by the breeze of humiliation. Having clashed against the wicked one, have you quenched it today? O Phalguna! Tell me and pacify me.'"'

Chapter 1197(47)

'Sanjaya said, "Having heard the angry words spoken about Adhiratha's great-souled son by the king who followed dharma, the unassailable Jishnu, whose valour was infinite and whose spirit was never depressed, spoke these words to Yudhishthira. 'O king! When I fought with the samshaptakas today, Drona's son suddenly stationed himself in front of me and at the forefront of the Kuru soldiers. He released arrows that were like venomous serpents. On seeing my chariot, which was like a cloud, the soldiers from Ambashtha were ready to die. O foremost among kings! I killed five hundred of those and advanced against Drona's son. He stretched his bow back all the way up to his ears and aimed many arrows. He possessed the strength of learning and weapons and showered down, like a dark cloud. In the battle, I could not distinguish between his affixing an arrow and releasing it. Drona's son circled around in that battle, sometimes to the left and sometimes to the right. Drona's son pierced me with five sharp arrows and Vasudeva with another five. In an instant, and without any gap, I struck him with thirty arrows that were like the vajra. Blood began to flow from all over his body. Those soldiers had been overcome by me and their bodies were overflowing with blood. On seeing this, he[584] entered the array of chariots that belonged to the son of a suta. The warriors were overcome and the soldiers were

[583]The grandfather is Bhishma and the reference is to the listing of maharathas and rathas, described in Section 59 (Volume 5).

[584]Ashvatthama.

devastated. Warriors, horses and elephants were running away. On seeing this, Karna swiftly dispatched fifty supreme rathas against me. After having killed them and avoided Karna, I have quickly come here to see you. On seeing Karna, all the Panchalas are filled with fright and are like cattle driven away by a lion. The Prabhadrakas are being driven away by Karna, as if they have entered the mouth of a large fish. O king! Having clashed against Karna, the Prabhadrakas are like those who have entered Death's gaping mouth. Come and see me and the son of a suta fight, striving for victory. O descendant of the Bharata lineage! Desiring heaven and the worlds,[585] six thousand princes and rathas have immersed themselves. O foremost among kings! I will engage with the son of a suta in battle, like the wielder of the vajra against Vritra. O descendant of the Bharata lineage! If you wish to see it, there will be a fierce battle today between me and the son of a suta. O king! I will engage in a battle with Karna and kill him today, together with his relatives. O lion among men! There are ends meant for those who make a pledge and do not keep it. If I fail, let that end be mine. I am inviting you. Tell me that victory in the battle will be mine. In front of us, the sons of Dhritarashtra are about to devour Bhima. O lion among kings! I will slay the son of a suta today, together with all the large numbers of enemy soldiers.'"

Chapter 1198(48)

'Sanjaya said, "On hearing that the immensely valorous Karna was still alive, the infinitely energetic Partha[586] became angry with Phalguna. Tormented by Karna's arrows, Yudhishthira spoke these words to Dhananjaya. 'In Dvaitavana, you should have said, "O king! I am not interested in fighting with Karna." O Partha! Had you said that, at the right time, we would have thought of other arrangements. O brave one! But you promised me that you would kill that powerful

[585]The worlds hereafter.

[586]Yudhishthira.

one. You have brought us into the midst of enemies and then you have shattered us by flinging us down on the ground. O Arjuna! We showered down many blessings on you and we expected many things that would be beneficial for us. O prince! All of that has been rendered unsuccessful, like an upper garment expecting fruits, but obtaining flowers instead.[587] Like a fish hook covered with flesh, or like impure food covered with pure food, I can only see worthless things in you. We desired the kingdom. But we are faced with destruction in the form of the kingdom. O evil-minded one! On the seventh day after you were born, an invisible voice spoke to Pritha[588] from the sky. "The son that has been born to you will be like Vasava in his valour. He will triumph over all the brave enemies. He will be infinitely energetic and will defeat large numbers of gods and all the beings in Khandava. He will vanquish the Madras, the Kalingas and the Kekayas and in the midst of the kings, kill the Kurus. There will be no archer who will be superior to him. No being will be born who will be able to defeat him. This noble one will bring all the beings under his subjugation and will accomplish all kinds of learning. He will be as handsome as the moon and as swift as the wind. He will be like Meru in fortitude and like the earth in forgiveness. He will possess the radiance of the sun and the prosperity of the lord of riches.[589] He will be like Shakra in his valour and like Vishnu in his strength. This great-souled son that has been born to Kunti will be like Aditi's son Vishnu,[590] the slayer of all enemies. He will bring victory to his own and slay the enemy. He will be famous and infinitely energetic and will be the originator of a lineage." This was heard from the sky, on the slopes of the Shatashringa mountains.[591] The ascetics heard the words that were spoken. This is what was spoken about you. But it

[587]The explanation has to be deduced. An upper garment has been held under a tree, expecting fruit to fall. Instead, there are flowers.

[588]Kunti.

[589]Kubera.

[590]All the gods are sons of Aditi, who was married to the sage Kashyapa.

[591]When Pandu and Kunti and Madri left for the forest, the Pandavas were born on the slopes of the Shatashringa mountain. This has been described in Section 7 (Volume 1).

has not come to pass. The gods have certainly uttered a falsehood. I heard words of praise spoken about you by the supreme of rishis and have always honoured you. I did not know that you were affectionate towards Suyodhana. Nor did I know that you feared Adhiratha's son. You are borne on a vehicle that has been created by Tvashtra.[592] Its axles rattle. The ape sits astride your auspicious standard. You have girded a sword that is decorated with gold. Gandiva bow is as long as a palm tree. O Partha! Keshava drives you. How have you withdrawn as a result of your fear of Karna? O evil-souled one! Had you given the bow to Keshava and become his charioteer in the battle, then Keshava would have slain the fierce Karna, like the lord of the Maruts[593] bringing down Vritra with his vajra. It would have been better had you not been born in Pritha's womb, but had been aborted in the fifth month itself. O prince! O evil-souled one! That would have been better than withdrawing from the field of battle.'"'

Chapter 1199(49)

'Sanjaya said, "Having been thus addressed by Yudhishthira, Kounteya, borne on the white horses, angrily grasped his sword, wishing to kill the bull among the Bharata lineage. On witnessing his wrath, Keshava, who knew about thoughts, spoke. 'O Partha! Why have you grasped your sword in this way? O Dhananjaya! I do not see anyone here with whom you need to fight. All the sons of Dhritarashtra have been devastated by the intelligent Bhima. O Kounteya! You withdrew to seek the king. King Yudhishthira is cheerful and well. You have seen that tiger among men, whose valour is like that of a tiger. This is a time for rejoicing. Why are you overcome by anger? O Kounteya! I do not see anyone here who should be killed by you. Why have you quickly taken up this

[592]Vishvakarma, the architect of the gods.

[593]Indra is the lord of the Maruts.

large sword? O Kounteya! I am asking you about this. What do you wish to do? O one who is extraordinary in valour! You have angrily grasped this supreme sword.' Having been thus addressed by Krishna, Arjuna glanced towards Yudhishthira. He sighed like a serpent and told Govinda, 'If anyone asks me to hand over Gandiva to someone else, I will slice off his head. That has been my secret vow. O infinitely valorous one! You have heard what the king with the miserable soul told me in your presence. O Govinda! I have no interest in pardoning him. Therefore, I will kill the king who is always scared about deviating from dharma. I will kill that supreme among men and protect my pledge. O descendant of the Yadu lineage! That is the reason I have picked up the sword. I will kill Yudhishthira and repay my debt to the cause of truth. O Janardana! In that way, I will be without sorrow and without fever. Now that such an occasion has arisen, what do you think? O father![594] You know everything about the universe, its past and its future. I will do whatever you ask me to.'

'"Krishna replied, 'O Partha! I now know that you have never attended to those who are old. O tiger among men! You have fallen prey to wrath at the wrong time. O Dhananjaya! No one who knows about the gradations of dharma acts in this way. Thinking something to be a duty, you are engaging in a task that is not a duty. O Partha! It is the worst of men who performs tasks that should not be performed. You should follow the dharma that wise ones have resorted to. They certainly spoke about this in detail to those who approached them.[595] O Partha! The man who does not know about these decrees and about the determination of what should be done and what should not be done, is certainly confounded. You are acting in that foolish way. It is always difficult to clearly know what should be done and what should not be done. Everything can be known through the sacred texts, but you are not acquainted with them. Based on your ignorance, you think that you are following

[594]The word used is tata. Though it means father, it is affectionately used towards anyone who is senior or elder.

[595]Such as disciples and students.

dharma and that you are acting in accordance with dharma. O Partha! You say that you are for dharma. But you do not understand that the killing of a living being is a sin. O son![596] Not killing living beings is the best course of action. That is my view. One can utter a falsehood, but one should never indulge in violence. The king, your eldest brother, is knowledgeable about dharma. How can you, like an ordinary man, kill that best of men? O descendant of the Bharata lineage! It has been said that one must not kill someone who is not fighting, someone who is without weapons, someone who is reluctant to fight, someone who is running away, someone who has sought sanctuary and someone who has joined his hands in salutation. The learned do not approve of killing such people. O Partha! In earlier times, you took that vow of yours when you were a child. Because of that, you now wish to undertake an act that is full of adharma. O Partha! How can you rush to kill your superior? Remember dharma. The course of dharma needs to be reflected about. It is subtle and difficult to follow. O bull among the Bharata lineage! I will tell you about the mysteries of dharma. Bhishma told you about this and so did Yudhishthira, who knows about dharma, kshatta Vidura and the illustrious Kunti. O Dhananjaya! I will tell you about the details. Listen. One who speaks the truth is virtuous. There is nothing superior to truth. However, it is extremely difficult to understand how one should base oneself on truth. Sometimes, truth should not be spoken. And sometimes, a lie should be spoken. When all one's possessions are being robbed, one should utter a lie. One should also utter a lie when one's life is in danger, or at the time of a marriage. Those are the times when falsehood becomes truth and truth becomes falsehood. A person who is always based on truth is but a child. A person who can differentiate between truth and falsehood can alone follow dharma. Isn't it wonderful that a man can become wise even after performing an extremely terrible deed? Like Balaka, he can obtain great merits, even though he has killed a blind being. And

[596]The word used is tata. Though it means son, it is affectionately used towards anyone who is junior or younger.

even though one strives for great virtue, one may commit a great sin, like Koushika, who lived along rivers.'

'"Arjuna said, 'O illustrious one! So that I may gain knowledge, tell me about these accounts, about Balaka and his connection with a blind being, and about Koushika, who lived near rivers.'

'"Krishna replied, 'O descendant of the Bharata lineage! Balaka was a person who hunted animals. He went to kill animals for his son and his wife, not to satisfy any desire. He looked after his blind mother and father and other dependents. He was always devoted to his own dharma. He was always truthful and not malicious. One day, though he made a lot of effort to search for animals, he could find none. Finally, he saw a carnivorous beast drinking water, using smell for its sight.[597] Though he had not seen such an animal before, he killed it. Immediately, a shower of flowers fell down from the sky. Apsaras began to sing and charming musical instruments were sounded. Celestial vehicles descended from heaven, to take that hunter of animals away. O Arjuna! Because of its austerities, that animal had been granted a boon by the self-creating one[598] that it would be able to kill all beings, but would be blind. He killed the beast that had made up its mind to kill all beings. That is the reason Balaka went to heaven. The dharma of the gods is extremely difficult to comprehend. There was a brahmana named Koushika. He was an ascetic and extremely learned. He lived at a confluence of rivers, far away from villages. He had taken a vow that he would always speak the truth. O Dhananjaya! Because he always spoke the truth, he became famous. At that time, scared of robbers, some people entered the forest. The cruel robbers made every effort to follow in their footsteps. They approached Koushika, who always spoke the truth, and asked, "O illustrious one! There were many people. What path have they taken? You are being asked in the name of truth. If you know, tell us." Having been asked, Koushika spoke to them truthfully. "This forest has many trees, creepers and lantanas and they have entered it." Those cruel men sought them out and killed

[597]That is, the animal was blind.

[598]Brahma.

them. So it has been heard. Koushika committed great adharma by speaking what should not have been said. He suffered great hardships in hell, because he did not know about the subtleties of dharma. He was just like a foolish person who does not possess a great deal of learning and does not ask the elders about the divisions of dharma, so that his great confusion can be resolved. Such indeed are the signs and indications. Supreme knowledge is extremely difficult and some try to obtain it through arguments. There are many other people who hold that dharma is only what is in the sacred texts. I will not contradict this, but everything is not laid down there. The words of dharma have been laid down for the propagation of beings. Dharma is so called because it holds everything up.[599] Dharma upholds beings. Whatever has this property of holding up is certainly dharma. There are those who wish that it should be otherwise. For those who desire otherwise, free yourself from them, without speaking a lot. There is no need to speak to them. If you have to speak to them, or if they are suspicious if you do not speak to them, it is better to utter a falsehood. That will be like speaking the truth. When life is in danger, at the time of marriage, when the entire lineage or all the riches are about to be destroyed and at the time of amusements, it is better to utter a lie. Those who know about the true nature of dharma do not see any adharma there. When one takes an oath to free oneself from an association with robbers, it is better to utter a lie. That is like speaking the truth. If one can, one should never give up one's riches to them. If one gives riches to the wicked, it is the giver that is afflicted. Therefore, a falsehood uttered for the sake of dharma does not amount to speaking a lie. These are the signs and indications and I have instructed you about them properly. O Partha! Having heard this, tell me if Yudhishthira should be killed.'

'"Arjuna said, 'You have spoken like an immensely wise one! You have spoken like an immensely intelligent one. Your words are those that will ensure our welfare. You are like our mother. You are like our father. O Krishna! You are our supreme refuge and these

[599]This is the etymological meaning of dharma, from the root *dhri*, meaning to hold up.

words have been spoken by you. There is nothing in the three worlds that is not known to you. You also know everything about supreme dharma. I think that Pandava Dharmaraja Yudhishthira cannot be killed. At this point in time, please tell me what I should do. Listen also to something else that is going on in my mind. O Dasharha! O Keshava! My vow is known to you. If there is any man who tells me, "O Partha! Give your Gandiva to someone else who is superior to you in weapons," I must kill him. Bhima also said he would kill anyone who called him an eunuch. O lion among the Vrishni lineage! In your presence, the king has asked me to hand over my bow. O Keshava! If I kill him, I will not be able to remain in the world of the living even for a short instant. O best among those in the world! O best among those who uphold dharma! O Krishna! Tell me how my pledge remains true and yet, Pandava remains alive. Provide me with the appropriate counsel.'

'"Vasudeva replied, 'The king was exhausted. In particular, in the battle, he was wounded by the large numbers of sharp arrows that Karna shot at him. O Partha! That is the reason he spoke harsh words to you. Karna is the stake in the battle today.[600] If he is slain, the Kurus will be vanquished. That is what the king, Dharma's son, thought. When a person suffers great shame, it is said, that though alive, such a person is dead. You have always honoured the king, together with Bhima and the twins, and so have the foremost and aged men in this world. You should offer him a trifling insult. O Partha! Address the king as "*tvam*".[601] O descendant of the Bharata lineage! Having been thus addressed, a senior will be as good as dead. O Kounteya! Act in this way towards Dharmaraja Yudhishthira. O extender of the Kuru lineage! Adopt this path of adharma. This supreme learning has been laid down in the sacred texts of Atharva and Angiras.[602] Men

[600]The image is that of a gambling match.

[601]In English, 'tvam' and '*bhavan*' will both be translated as you. But 'tvam' is used for someone younger, equal or junior. 'Bhavan' connotes greater honour and is used towards someone who is older or senior. So far, Arjuna has addressed Yudhishthira as 'bhavan'. 'Tvam' will be an insult.

[602]Famous sages.

must always follow this superior course, without thinking about it. O Pandava! Having been addressed by you as "tvam", Dharmaraja will think that he has been killed. You can later worship his feet and speak soft and conciliatory words to Partha.[603] The Pandaveya king, your brother, is wise and will never be angered. O Partha! You will be freed from uttering a falsehood and will not have to kill your brother. You can then cheerfully slay Karna, the son of a suta.'"

'Sanjaya said, "Having been thus addressed by Janardana, Partha applauded what his well-wisher had told him. And Arjuna used harsh words towards Dharmaraja, the likes of which he had never spoken earlier. 'O king! You[604] should not censure me about having withdrawn, since you have yourself been stationed more than one krosha away from the battle. You should not censure Bhima either. He is fighting with the foremost of the warriors. At this time, he has been afflicted by the enemies in the battle and has slain brave kings. He has killed more than one thousand elephants, emitting fierce roars like a lion. The brave one has performed an extremely difficult deed. You[605] have never done anything like this. He has jumped down from his chariot. With a supreme club, he has slaughtered horses, men and elephants in the battle. Using his supreme sword and broken parts of chariots and his bow, he destroyed horses, chariots, steeds[606] and elephants belonging to the enemy. Then again, intolerant and brave, he struck and killed with his feet and his hands. He is immensely strong and like Vaishravana[607] and Yama. He slew the enemy, as only he can. That Bhimasena has the right to censure me, but not you, who have always been protected by your well-wishers. Bhima is single-handedly agitating the sons of Dhritarashtra, their maharathas, elephants and the best of horses. That scorcher of enemies has the right to reprimand me. He is killing large numbers of the enemy, Kalingas, Vangas, Angas, Nishadas,

[603]Yudhishthira. Both Yudhishthira and Arjuna are Partha, Pritha's son.

[604]In Sanskrit, 'tvam', that being the point.

[605]'Tvam' again.

[606]The text has the word horses twice.

[607]Kubera.

Magadhas and is always as angry as a dark-blue cloud. He is like an elephant and has the right to speak to me. At the right time, he is riding on his chariot and brandishing his bow, with his fists full of arrows. The brave one is releasing a shower of arrows in the great battle, like a torrent of rain from a cloud. The learned say that speech is the strength of the best of brahmanas and strength of arms that of kshatriyas. O descendant of the Bharata lineage! You are cruel and your strength is in speech. You think that I am also like you. I have always sought to act for your benefit, with my wives, sons and with my own life and soul. And you have struck a person like me with the arrows of your words. Therefore, we will never be able to obtain any happiness from you. I have killed maharathas for your sake. But you lie down on Droupadi's bed and slight me. O descendant of the Bharata lineage! You are suspicious and cruel. Therefore, we will never be able to know any happiness through you. O lord among men! He[608] was always devoted to the truth and in the battle, for the sake of your welfare, himself told you about the means of his death. Protected by me, Drupada's great-souled and brave son, Shikhandi, killed him. Since you are addicted to the vice of gambling, I am not delighted at the prospect of your winning back the kingdom. There are many sins associated with gambling and it is against dharma. You heard Sahadeva recount them.[609] But you have always been addicted to that practice of wicked ones and that is the reason all of us have been reduced to this hardship. O Indra among kings! It was because of your gambling that the kingdom was lost and our difficulties are due to you. O king! O unfortunate one! Therefore, do not anger us by using these cruel words against us again.' Savyasachi, who was firm in his wisdom, made him listen to these harsh words. But the son of the king of the gods repented this and sighed repeatedly, unsheathing his sword.

'"On seeing this, Krishna asked, 'Why have you unsheathed your sword, which sparkles like the sky, again? Tell me truthfully and I will give you an answer. I will tell you how you can accomplish your

[608]Bhishma.

[609]It is not obvious why Sahadeva is being singled out.

objective.' Having been thus asked by the supreme of men, he was extremely distressed and spoke these words to Keshava. 'I will kill myself, because I have acted in a wicked way.'[610] In an attempt to pacify Partha, the best among the upholders of dharma spoke these words to Dhananjaya. 'O Partha! Tell him about your own qualities now. Thereby, you will kill yourself today.'[611] Dhananjaya, Shakra's son, approved of Krishna's words and, lowering his bow, spoke these words to Yudhishthira, supreme among those who uphold dharma. 'O king! O god among men! Listen. There is no other archer who is my equal, except the god who wields Pinaka.[612] I am revered even by that great-souled one. In an instant, I can destroy the universe, with its mobile and immobile objects. O king! It is I who vanquished all the directions and the kings there and brought them under your subjugation. The *rajasuya* sacrifice that you completed, with donations, and the divine assembly hall that you obtained, were because of my infinite energy.[613] The arrows have left marks on my palms, when I affixed arrows to the bow in battle. The soles of my feet bear the marks of arrows and a standard.[614] That is the reason someone like me cannot be defeated in a battle. I have slain those from the north. I have killed those from the west. I have restrained those from the east. I have destroyed those from the south. There are only a few of the samshaptakas who remain. I have destroyed half of the entire army. O king! The soldiers of the Bharatas, with an army like that of the gods, have been slain by me and are lying down. I will use weapons to kill only those who know about weapons. That is the reason I have not reduced the world to ashes.' Having said this, Partha again spoke to Yudhishthira, supreme among the upholders of dharma. 'O king! Know this. Today, Radha[615] will lose

[610]Because Arjuna has spoken harsh words to Yudhishthira.

[611]Because self-praise is like killing one's own self.

[612]Shiva. Pinaka is the name of Shiva's bow or trident.

[613]The conquest, sacrifice and coronation, described in Sections 23 and 24 (Volume 2).

[614]Arjuna was born with these signs.

[615]Radha, wife of the suta Adhiratha, reared Karna. Thus, Radha was Karna's mother.

her son, or Kunti will lose me. O king! Be pacified and pardon the the words that I have spoken. In due course, you will understand what I have told you.'[616] The foremost one pacified the king, who was capable of withstanding all enemies. He stood there, and then again spoke these words. 'I will wholeheartedly try to kill the son of a suta and extricate Bhima from the battle. O king! My life is devoted to ensuring your pleasure. Know that this is the truth.' Having said this, Kiriti, blazing in his energy, touched his feet and then stood up and said, 'All this will come to pass very quickly and I will then return to you.'

'"On hearing the harsh words of his brother, Phalguna, Dharmaraja Pandava raised himself[617] and with his heart filled with misery, spoke these words to Partha. 'O Partha! I have not acted in a way that virtuous ones do. That is the reason we are confronted with this extremely terrible calamity. Therefore, sever my head today. I am the worst of men and the exterminator of my lineage. I am wicked and addicted to evil. I am stupid in my intelligence. I am lazy and a coward. I am a man who disrespects those who are superior. What is the point of following a harsh one like me for a long time? I am wicked and I will retire to the forest today. Without an inferior one like me, let all of you be happy. The great-souled Bhimasena is fit to be a king. What will a eunuch like me do with a kingdom? I am incapable of again listening to such harsh words, spoken by you in anger. Let Bhima be the king. O brave one! Having been insulted, what is the purpose of my remaining alive?' Having said this, the king suddenly arose from his bed and prepared to leave for the forest. Vasudeva bowed down to him and said, 'O king! You know that the wielder of Gandiva is devoted to the truth and is famous for Gandiva. Any man in the world who asks him to give Gandiva to another, will be slain by him and lose his body. You spoke such words to him. O lord of the earth! Wishing to preserve the truth of Partha's pledge, I asked him to show disrespect towards you. It is said that disrespect towards one's seniors is equivalent to death. O

[616]Once Arjuna has killed Karna.

[617]He was lying down on a bed.

mighty-armed one! O king! I asked him to cross you and you should pardon both Partha and me. O great king! Both of us are seeking refuge with you. O king! We are bowing in obeisance before you and you should pardon us. Today, the earth will drink the blood of the wicked Radheya. I know this to be the truth. Today, the son of a suta will be slain. Today, the one whose death you desire will pass beyond his span of life.' Having heard Krishna's words, Dharmaraja Yudhishthira respectfully raised Hrishikesha and joining his hands in salutation, affectionately spoke these words. 'It is exactly as you have said. I have been guilty of a transgression. O Govinda! I have been taught by you. O Madhava! I have been saved by you. O Achyuta! Today, we have been saved by you from a terrible calamity and fear. We were immersed in an ocean of hardship and you have been our protector. We were confused by our terrible ignorance today and have crossed it. Both[618] of us were submerged in an ocean of grief and sorrow and your intelligence has been the raft. O Achyuta! We have an adviser. We have a protector and we have crossed it.'"'

Chapter 1200(50)

'Sanjaya said, "Having heard the words spoken by Krishna to the noble Yudhishthira, Partha became cheerless in his mind, since he had committed a wicked deed. Vasudeva laughed and spoke to him. 'O Partha! How would you have felt had you, established in dharma, used you sharp sword to slay Dharma's son? You have only spoken to the king and are overcome by this lassitude. O Partha! Had you killed the king, what would you have done next? It is extremely difficult to know dharma, especially by those who are stupid in their understanding. You are scared of dharma and there is no doubt that you would have suffered greater misery. Had you killed your elder brother, you would have gone to a terrible hell. The

[618]Yudhishthira and Arjuna.

king is foremost among those who uphold dharma. He is devoted to dharma. Pacify the best of the Kurus now. That is my view. Once you pacify him devotedly, King Yudhishthira will be pleased. We can then swiftly advance towards the chariot of the son of a suta to fight. Karna is extremely difficult to defeat. But he will be killed by your sharp arrows. O one who grants honours! Dharma's son will be filled with great delight. O mighty-armed one! It is my view that the time has come for this. Having accomplished this task, your objective will be attained.' O great king! O unblemished one! At this, filled with shame, Arjuna touched Dharmaraja's feet with his head. He repeatedly said, 'O foremost among the Bharata lineage! Forgive me. O king! Pardon what I have spoken because of my fear about dharma.' O bull among the Bharata lineage! Dharmaraja Yudhishthira saw that Dhananjaya, the destroyer of enemies, was prone at his feet and was weeping.

'"King Dharmaraja raised his brother, Dhananjaya. Having embraced him with affection, the lord of the earth wept. Those two immensely radiant brothers wept for a long time. Having overcome their sorrow, those two tigers among men became cheerful again. He affectionately inhaled the fragrance of Pandava's head.[619] Filled with great delight, he smiled and spoke to Jaya.[620] 'O mighty-armed one! O great archer! Though I made every effort in the battle, while all the soldiers looked on, Karna used his arrows to deprive me of my armour, my standard, my bow, my javelin, my horses and my club. O Phalguna! Having known and seen his deeds in the battle, I have been overcome with great grief and am no longer fond of remaining alive. O brave one! If you do not kill the son of a suta today, I will give up my life. What is the point of my remaining alive?' O bull among the Bharata lineage! Having been thus addressed, Vijaya replied, 'O king! O best of men! O lord of the earth! Through your favours, I swear on you, Bhima and the twins that I will slay Karna in the battle today, or be killed by him. I swear on my weapons that I will bring him down on the ground.' Having spoken these words

[619]Yudhishthira inhaled the fragrance of Arjuna's head.

[620]Jaya is one of Arjuna's names, as is Vijaya.

to the king, he spoke these words to Madhava. 'O Krishna! There is no doubt that I will slay Karna in the battle today. O fortunate one! With your blessings, the death of that evil-souled one is certain.' O supreme among kings! Having been thus addressed, Keshava spoke to Partha. 'O foremost among the Bharata lineage! You are capable of doing this. O maharatha! This has always been my desire. I have always thought about the means whereby you can kill Karna in the battle.' The intelligent Madhava again spoke to Dharma's son. 'O Yudhishthira! You should console Bibhatsu. With your permission, he will kill the evil-souled Karna today. O descendant of the Pandava lineage! On hearing that you were afflicted by Karna's arrows, we returned here to ascertain your welfare. O king! It is through good fortune that you are well and have not been seized. O unblemished one! For the sake of Bibhatsu's victory, console him.' Yudhishthira replied, 'O Partha! O Bibhatsu! O Pandava! Come and embrace me. You spoke beneficial words to me. You have been forgiven by me. O Dhananjaya! I give you permission to go and kill Karna. O Partha! Do not be angry at the terrible words that I have spoken to you.' O king! O venerable one! At this, Dhananjaya bowed his head down before his elder brother and grasped his feet with his hands. The king raised the sorrowing one and embraced him.

'"He inhaled the fragrance of his head and again spoke these words. 'O Dhananjaya! O mighty-armed one! I have been greatly honoured by you. May you again attain victory and eternal greatness.' Arjuna replied, 'Radheya is evil in his deeds and insolent about his strength. I will approach him in the battle and slay him, and his relatives, with arrows. He stretched a firm bow and afflicted you with arrows. Karna will reap the terrible consequence of that deed today. O lord of the earth! Having slain Karna today, I will return to you. I will give you the good news and follow you. I tell you this truthfully. Without killing Karna today, I will not return I am touching your feet and telling you this truthfully.' Having pacified Dharmaraja, Partha was cheerful in his mind. Prepared to kill the son of a suta, Partha spoke to Govinda. 'Prepare the chariot again and yoke the best of horses. Let the great chariot be equipped with all the weapons. Get horse riders to cover the well-trained horses. Let all kinds of equipment quickly be arranged on the chariot.' O great king! Having been thus addressed by the great-souled Phalguna, Krishna told Daruka,[621] 'Do everything that Arjuna, foremost among the Bharatas and best among all archers, has asked to be done.' O supreme among kings! Having been instructed by Krishna, Daruka yoked and covered the chariot, which scorched the enemy, with the skins of tigers. The chariot was yoked by the great-souled Daruka. He[622] sought Dharmaraja's leave and the blessings of the brahmanas. With auspicious rites and benedictions, he ascended that supreme chariot. The immensely wise King Dharmaraja Yudhishthira blessed him, supremely delighted at the prospect of Karna's death.

'"O descendant of the Bharata lineage! On seeing the great archer depart, all the beings thought that Karna had already been slain by the great-souled Pandava. O king! On every side, all the directions sparkled. O lord of men! At that time, blue jays, *shatapatras*[623] and curlews circumambulated the descendant of the Pandu lineage. There were many other sacred and auspicious male birds. [624] They were cheerful in form and seemed to urge Arjuna to hurry to the field of battle. O lord of the earth! Herons, vultures, crows and wild crows advanced in front of him, wishing to devour,[625] and signified an ominous portent. The signs were good and auspicious for Partha. They signified the destruction and death of Karna's soldiers. As Partha advanced, he perspired copiously. He was extremely anxious about how he would accomplish his objective.

[621]Krishna's charioteer.

[622]Arjuna.

[623]We have deliberately not translated shatapatra. Literally, it means a bird with one hundred feathers and can stand for a parrot, a woodpecker or a crane. Since this circumambulation took place in a clockwise direction (*pradakshina*), this was an auspicious sign.

[624]The text says *pumnamam* and it is difficult to pin this bird down. Literally, this should be translated as a bird name *pum*. However, this isn't an easily identifiable bird and pum also means male. Perhaps that itself was an auspicious sign.

[625]These carnivorous birds fed on dead bodies.

'"On seeing that Partha was overcome with anxiety as he proceeded, Madhusudana spoke to the wielder of Gandiva. 'O wielder of Gandiva! With this bow, you have defeated those in battle, whom no other man is capable of vanquishing. We have seen many brave ones, equal to Shakra in their valour. Having encountered you in a battle, those brave ones have attained the supreme objective. O venerable one! Whether it is Drona, Bhishma, Bhagadatta, Vinda and Anuvinda from Avanti, Sudakshina from Kamboja, Shrutayusha and the immensely valorous Achyutayusha, none of them have been able to do anything against you. There is no one who can withstand you. You possess celestial weapons. You are dexterous and strong. O Arjuna! You aim, strike and hit the target with yoga. You are not confused in a battle and know about what must be done. You are capable of killing all the gods and asuras, together with everything mobile and immobile. O Partha! There is no warrior or man on this earth who is equal to you in a battle. There are kshatriyas who pick up bows and are invincible in battle. But I have not seen, or heard of, anyone like you among them, or among the supreme gods. Brahma, the creator of all beings, constructed the extremely wonderful Gandiva.[626] O Partha! This is what you use to fight and that is the reason there is no one who is your equal. O Pandava! However, I must speak words that are beneficial for you. O mighty-armed one! Do not think lightly of Karna. He is the ornament of a battle. Karna is strong and insolent. He is skilled in weapons and a maharatha. He is accomplished and colourful in fighting. He knows about time and place.[627] He is like the fire in his energy. He is like the wind in his speed. He is like Yama in his anger. The powerful one is capable of withstanding a lion. The mighty-armed one's chest is one *aratni* in breadth.[628] He is extremely difficult to defeat. He is very proud and brave. He is extremely valiant and handsome. He has all the

[626]This is slightly inaccurate. Gandiva was created by the brahman, though Brahma owned it for one thousand years.

[627]With reference to fighting.

[628]Aratni is a measure of distance, the length of an elbow, that is, a cubit. It is thus eighteen inches long.

qualities of a warrior and is terrible to his enemies. He has always hated the Pandavas and has been engaged in the welfare of the sons of Dhritarashtra. Radheya cannot be killed by any enemy, even the gods, including Vasava. In my view, you are the only exception. Today, slay the son of a suta. All the warriors made out of flesh and blood, and even the gods, are incapable of defeating him in a battle, even if they were to unite. The evil-souled one is wicked in intelligence. He is cruel. His evil intelligence has always been used to bring injury to the Pandaveyas. He has opposed the Pandaveyas. Kill Karna today and accomplish your objective. He thinks himself to be brave, as does the wicked Suyodhana. He is the root of all wickedness. O Dhananjaya! Defeat the son of a suta.'"'

Chapter 1201(51)

'Sanjaya said, "Keshava, immeasurable in his soul, again spoke these words to Arjuna, who, in every way, had firmed up his resolution to kill Karna. 'O descendant of the Bharata lineage! Today is the seventeenth day[629] of this extremely terrible destruction of men, elephants and horses. Those on your side possessed an extremely large army and so did the enemy. O lord of the earth! Having clashed against each other in the battle, only remnants are left on both sides. O Partha! The Kouravas possessed innumerable elephants and horses. Having encountered you as an enemy, they have been destroyed in the field of battle. All these Panchalas, the Srinjayas and the others are unassailable. They united and stationed themselves with the Pandavas. O slayer of enemies! Protected by you, the Panchalas, the Pandavas, the Matsyas, the Karushas, the Chedis and the Kekayas caused a great destruction of the enemy. O son![630] In a battle, who is capable of vanquishing the assembled Kouravas,

[629]Of the battle.

[630]The word used is tata.

other than the maharatha Pandavas, who are protected by you in the encounter? You are capable of defeating the gods, asuras and men in a battle, even if the three worlds rise up against you, not to speak of the army of the Kouravas. O tiger among men! Who other than you was capable of vanquishing King Bhagadatta, who was Vasava's equal? O Partha! O unblemished one! This large army has been protected by you and all the kings are incapable of even glancing at it. O Partha! It is because they have always been protected by you that Dhrishtadyumna and Shikhandi could bring down Bhishma and Drona in the battle. O Partha! Otherwise, in the battle, how could those two maharatha Panchalas have defeated Bhishma and Drona in an encounter? They were like Shakra in their valour. In a battle, who could have withstood Shantanu's son,[631] Drona, Vaikartana, Kripa, Drona's son, Somadatta's son,[632] Kritavarma, Saindhava,[633] the king of Madra and King Suyodhana? They were brave and skilled in the use of weapons in a battle. None of them retreated. They were the leaders of akshouhinis. They were fierce, angry and unassailable in a battle. Many arrays have been destroyed. Horses, chariots and elephants have been exhausted. There were fierce and intolerant kshatriyas from many kingdoms. O descendant of the Bharata lineage! There were Govasas, Dasamiyas, Vasatis, Vratyas, Vatadhanas and the proud Bhojas. O descendant of the Bharata lineage! That large army was destroyed in Brahmakshetra.[634] Having clashed against you, they advanced towards death, with their horses, chariots and elephants. There were Tukharas, Yavanas, Khashas, Darvabhisaras, Daradas, Shakas, Ramathas, Tanganas, Andhrakas, Pulindas, Kiratas who are terrible in their valour, mlecchas, those from the mountainous regions and those who live on the boundaries of the ocean. They were fierce and the performers of terrible deeds. They were insolent, delighted in battle and were strong, with firm fists. For Suyodhana's sake, they angrily sided with the Kurus. O scorcher of enemies! Other

[631]Bhishma.
[632]Bhurishrava.
[633]Jayadratha.
[634]Being used as a synonym for Kurukshetra.

than you, no one else was capable of defeating them in a battle. We saw the immensely strong formations of the sons of Dhritarashtra being destroyed. Without you as a protector, which man could have advanced against that? That army, covered with dust, looked like a swollen ocean. O lord! Protected by you, the angry Pandavas shattered and destroyed it. Jayatsena, the lord of Magadha, was immensely strong. Since he was killed in the battle by Abhimanyu, seven days have passed.[635] There were ten thousand elephants, terrible in their deeds, which followed the king.[636] Bhima killed them with his club. Using his great force, he destroyed hundreds of other elephants and chariots. O son![637] Thus did the extremely fearful battle continue. O Pandava! Having encountered Bhimasena and you, with their horses, chariots and elephants, the Kouravas went to the world of the dead. O Partha! The vanguard of the army was destroyed by the Pandavas. O venerable one! Bhishma showered down fierce arrows. He was skilled in the use of harsh weapons and enveloped and killed the Chedis, the Kashis, the Panchalas, the Karushas, the Matsyas and the Kekayas with his arrows. Arrows issued from his bow and mangled the bodies of the enemy. Those gold-tufted arrows covered the entire sky. Having followed the tenth direction, they slew horses, rathas and elephants.[638] Those arrows were released so that they avoided those nine undesirable directions. Bhishma slaughtered your troops for ten days. He emptied the seats of chariots and killed horses, elephants and steeds.[639] He showed a form in battle that was like that of Rudra or Upendra.[640] He afflicted the Pandava soldiers and caused great destruction. He slaughtered kings from Panchala,

[635]However, this incident has not been mentioned earlier, when that day's fighting was being described.

[636]Duryodhana.

[637]The word used is tata.

[638]There are ten directions. The arrows followed the tenth direction and didn't deviate to the other nine. This is an indirect way of saying that the arrows found their mark.

[639]The word horse figures twice in the text.

[640]Vishnu.

Chedi and Kekaya. He destroyed the Pandava army, which teemed with men, horses and elephants. It was as if he was rescuing the wicked Suyodhana, who was submerged in an ocean without a raft. He roamed around in the battle, scorching like the sun. The Srinjayas and the other kings were incapable of glancing towards him. Desiring victory, he roamed around in the battle. However, the Pandavas made every effort and attacked him violently. He single-handedly drove the Pandavas and the Srinjayas away in the encounter and came to be regarded as the only one who was brave. Shikhandi was protected by you and killed the maharatha, tiger among men, with his sharp and straight-tufted arrows. The grandfather was brought down in that way and is lying down on a bed of arrows. O tiger among men! Having encountered you, he was like a crow clashing against a vulture. Drona fought fiercely for five days, destroying the army of the enemy. He constructed a vyuha in the great battle and brought down maharathas. The maharatha protected Jayadratha in the battle. When fighting took place during the night,[641] he was as fierce as Yama and consumed beings. Bharadvaja's powerful and brave son clashed against Dhrishtadyumna and attained the supreme objective. Today is the second day after that. On that day's battle, had you not checked the enemy in the encounter, the son of a suta and the other rathas, Drona would not have been killed. You restrained the entire army of the sons of Dhritarashtra. O Dhananjaya! That is how Parshata killed Drona in the battle. Which other kshatriya would have been able to accomplish this in the battle? O Partha! That is also the way you accomplished the death of Jayadratha. You countered the large army and killed the brave kings. King Saindhava was killed through the strength of your weapons and your energy. The kings know that the death of the king of Sindhu was extraordinary. O Partha! But since you know that you are a maharatha, it wasn't that wonderful. O descendant of the Bharata lineage! If all these kshatriyas clash against you, I think they will be tormented by you and killed on a single day. That is my view. O Partha! With the likes of Bhishma and

[641]On the fourteenth day, the fighting continued throughout the night. This has been described in Section 70 (Volume 6).

Drona killed, this extremely fierce army of the sons of Dhritarashtra can be regarded as having lost all its brave warriors in the battle. The best of warriors have been destroyed. Horses, men and elephants have been killed. The army of the Bharatas is like the sky without radiance, devoid of the sun, the moon and the stars. O Partha! Because of Bhima's valour, the army has been devastated in the battle, like the army of the asuras through Shakra's valour in ancient times.

""'Other than those who have been slain, only five maharathas remain—Ashvatthama, Kritavarma, Karna, the lord of Madra and Kripa. O tiger among men! If you kill those five maharathas today, you will destroy the enemies and give the kingdom, with its islands and cities, to the king. Let Partha,[642] whose energy and prosperity are infinite, obtain the earth, with its sky, waters, the nether regions, mountains and large forests. Just as Vishnu killed daityas and danavas in earlier times, you will give the earth to the king, like Hari[643] to Shakra. With the enemies slain by you today, the Panchalas will rejoice, like the gods when the danavas were slain by Vishnu. Do not honour your preceptor Drona, foremost among men, and show compassion towards Ashvatthama, or show mercy towards Kripa because of the honour due to a preceptor, or show excessive respect towards your relatives and honour your brothers,[644] or encounter Kritavarma and don't convey him to Yama's abode, or clash against your mother's brother, Shalya, the lord of Madra,[645] and not strike him down and kill him because of compassion. Karna is evil-minded and extremely injurious towards the Pandavas. O best of men! Kill him today with your sharp arrows. This is your supreme task and there is nothing wrong in it. We applaud this and there is no sin attached to it. O unblemished one! O Arjuna! Whether it was the attempt to burn down your mother with her sons in the night,[646] or

[642]Yudhishthira.

[643]Vishnu.

[644]The Kouravas.

[645]Madri was the mother of Nakula and Sahadeva and Arjuna's mother by extension.

[646]This is a reference to the episode of the house of lac, described in Section 8 (Volume 1).

whatever Suyodhana attempted towards you in the course of the gambling match, the evil-souled Karna was the root of all that. Suyodhana always thought that he would be saved by Karna and angrily tried to seize me too.[647] O one who grants honours! It is the firm belief of that Indra among men, Dhritarashtra's son, that Karna will certainly defeat all the Parthas in battle. O Kounteya! Though Dhritarashtra's son knew about your strength, he found pleasure in a conflict with you because he depended on Karna. Karna has always said, "I will defeat the assembled Parthas, Vasudeva and the kings in the great battle." The evil-minded one has encouraged Dhritarashtra's evil-souled son and roared in the assembly hall. O descendant of the Bharata lineage! Kill Karna today. In all the evil acts that Dhritarashtra's son has done towards you, in all of these, the evil-souled and extremely wicked Karna has been present. Subhadra's brave son had the eyes of a bull. We saw him killed by six cruel maharathas on the side of the sons of Dhritarashtra.[648] The brave maharatha made Drona, Drona's son and Kripa tremble. The maharatha made elephants and chariots bereft of men. His shoulders were like that of a bull and he brought fame to the Kuru and Vrishni lineages. He deprived steeds of horse riders and foot soldiers of weapons and lives. He destroyed the soldiers and maharathas. He conveyed large numbers of men, horses and elephants to Yama's eternal abode. Subhadra's son advanced, scorching the army with his arrows. O friend! O lord! I tell you truthfully that my limbs burn at the thought that even then, the evil-souled Karna attacked him. In that battle, he was unable to remain in front of Abhimanyu. He was mangled by the arrows of Subhadra's son. He was unconscious and blood flowed from his body. He blazed and sighed in rage. However, afflicted by the arrows, he retreated. He retreated and lost all enterprise. He gave up all hope of remaining alive. He was supremely unconscious in that battle and exhausted because of the blows. Hearing the appropriate, but cruel, words of Drona in the battle then, Karna severed his bow. When he was devoid

[647]When Krishna came as a messenger, described in Section 54 (Volume 4).
[648]Abhimanyu was killed in Section 67 (Volume 6).

of weapons in that battle, five maharathas, skilled in deceit, killed him with their showers of arrows. In front of the Pandaveyas and the Kurus, Karna spoke harsh and cruel words to Krishna[649] in the assembly hall. "O Krishna! The Pandavas have been destroyed and have gone to eternal hell. O wide-hipped one! O one who is sweet in speech! Choose another one as a husband. Enter Dhritarashtra's abode as a servant-maid. O one with long eyelashes! Your husbands are no longer there." He does not know about dharma and is extremely evil-minded. Those were the words that he spoke then. O descendant of the Bharata lineage! Karna spoke those wicked and sinful words in your hearing. Those were the evil one's words. Arrows decorated with gold, sharpened on stone and capable of taking away life, released by you, will pacify those words and other wicked deeds that the evil-souled one has done towards you. Let your arrows rob him of his life and pacify those and other things today. Let his limbs be touched by terrible arrows shot from Gandiva. Let the evil-souled Karna remember the words of Bhishma and Drona. Let gold-tufted iron arrows, capable of killing the enemy and with the radiance of lightning, be shot by you. Let them pierce his inner organs and drink his blood. O Arjuna! Let fierce, immensely forceful and sharp arrows be shot by you and let them penetrate his inner organs. Strike Karna with great force and convey him to Yama's eternal abode. Let all the lords of the earth see Karna brought down from his chariot, oppressed by your arrows. Let them utter woes of lamentation and let them be miserable and distressed. Let all his well-wishers see Karna prostrate, deprived of his weapons. Let them be cheerless on seeing him shattered, drenched in his own blood and lying down on the ground. The standard of Adhiratha's son is large and is marked with the sign of an elephant's harness. Let it shudder and fall down on the ground, uprooted by you with a broad-headed arrow. When the gold-decorated chariot is shattered with hundreds of your arrows, with its warrior slain, let the terrified Shalya abandon it and run away. O Dhananjaya! Let Suyodhana see that Adhiratha's son has been killed by you and give up all hope of the kingdom, or of remaining alive.

[649]Krishnaa, Droupadi.

The Panchalas are being slaughtered and driven away by Karna's sharp arrows. O best of the Bharata lineage! But wishing to serve the Pandavas, the Panchalas, Droupadi's sons, Dhrishtadyumna, Shikhandi, Dhrishtadyumna's sons, Nakula's son Shatanika, Nakula, Sahadeva, Durmukha, Janamejaya, Sudharma and Satyaki are succumbing to Karna. Karna is attacking the Panchalas in the great battle. O scorcher of enemies! Uttered by your relatives, a terrible roar can be heard. The Panchalas are not frightened. Nor are they unwilling to fight. Those maharathas, great archers, are not concerned about death in this battle. Single-handedly, Bhishma surrounded the Pandava soldiers with his torrents of arrows. But even then, the Panchalas clashed against him and did not retreat. The preceptor, Drona, was energetic and his blazing weapons were like the fire. He scorched all the archers in battle and was unassailable. Those scorchers of enemies[650] always tried to cheerfully defeat that foe in the encounter. The Panchalas will never be terrified and retreat before Adhiratha's son. The brave Panchalas spiritedly advanced against him and Karna is destroying them with his arrows, like insects before a fire. For the sake of their friends, those brave ones are advancing, ready to give up their lives. However, in the battle, Radheya is bringing destruction to hundreds of Panchalas. Karna obtained a weapon from Bhargava Rama, supreme among rishis in earlier times, and it has exhibited its extremely terrible and calamitous form. Its form is fierce and extremely terrible and it is scorching all the soldiers. Blazing in its energy, it has surrounded the large army.[651] The arrows released from Karna's bow are traversing in the field of battle. They are tormenting those on your side, like a storm of bees. O descendant of the Bharata lineage! Having encountered Karna's irresistible weapon in the battle, the weak-spirited among the Panchalas are seen to run away in all the directions. O Partha! Bhima is firm in his anger and, surrounded by the Srinjayas on all sides, is fighting with Karna. However, he is oppressed by his sharp arrows. O descendant of the Bharata lineage! The Pandavas, Srinjayas and Panchalas, will

[650]The Panchalas.

[651]Of the Pandavas.

be slain by Karna, like a body destroyed by a disease that has been neglected. Amongst all the warriors in Yudhishthira's army, with your exception, I do not see a single one who can clash against Radheya and return safely home. O bull among the Bharata lineage! Slay him with your sharp arrows today. O Partha! Act according to the oath you had taken earlier and obtain fame. O foremost among warriors! You are the one who is capable of defeating Karna and the Kouravas in battle, and no other warrior. I am telling you this truthfully. Perform the great deed of killing maharatha Karna. O Partha! O supreme among men! Be successful in your objective and be happy.'"'

Chapter 1202(52)

'Sanjaya said, "O descendant of the Bharata lineage! On hearing the words spoken by Keshava, Bibhatsu cast off his sorrow and in a short instant, became cheerful. He quickly touched the bowstring and stretched Gandiva bow for the sake of Karna's destruction. He spoke to Keshava. 'O Govinda! Protected by you, my victory is certain. You are the lord of the past, the present and the future and you are pleased with me. O Krishna! With you as my aide, I can kill the three worlds and attain the supreme world in a battle, not to speak of Karna. O Janardana! I can see that the army of the Panchalas is being driven away. I can see Karna roaming around fearlessly in the encounter. I can see Bhargava's weapon coursing in every direction. O Varshneya! It has been released by Karna, like the great vajra by Shakra. O Krishna! But as long as the earth exists, beings will talk about what will be done by me in the battle. O Krishna! Today, my arrows without barbs will convey Karna to the land of the dead. They will be released and shot from Gandiva and dispatched by my arms. Today, King Dhritarashtra will curse his intelligence, as a result of which, he instated Duryodhana in the kingdom, though he did not deserve the kingdom. O mighty-armed one! Today, Dhritarashtra will be deprived of his kingdom, his happiness, his prosperity, his kingdom, his city and his sons. Today, King Duryodhana will lose all hope of remaining alive. O Krishna! Karna will be slain. I am telling you this truthfully. On seeing Karna mangled by my arrows, the lord of men[652] will remember the words that you had spoken about peace. O Krishna! Today let Soubala know that my arrows are dice, Gandiva is the box used to throw them and my chariot the spread on which the game is played. In a battle, the son of a suta thinks that there is no other man who is equal to him on earth. Let the earth drink his blood today. Released from Gandiva, they[653] will grant Karna the supreme objective. Today, Radheya will repent the words that he spoke to Panchali. In the midst of the assembly hall, he spoke cruel words and cast aspersions on the Pandavas. They were described as sterile sesamum seeds then,[654] but will turn out to be sesamum today, when Vaikartana Karna, the evil-souled son of a suta, has been killed. He said, "I will save you[655] from fear about the sons of Pandu." My sharp arrows will render his words false. He said, "I will kill all the Pandavas and their sons." While all the archers look on, I will kill that Karna today. Resorting to his valour, the great-minded[656] son of Dhritarashtra, evil-souled and evil in his intelligence, always disregarded us. O Madhusudana! I will kill that Radheya Karna today. O Krishna! When Karna has been killed today, the sons of Dhritarashtra and the kings will be terrified and run away in different directions, like deer frightened of a lion. King Duryodhana will see the earth, with Karna killed by me in the battle today, with his sons and his well-wishers. O Krishna! On seeing that Karna has been killed, Dhritarashtra's intolerant son will know me to be the foremost among all archers in a battle. O Krishna! Today, I will repay the debt I owe to all wielders of the bow, to my anger, to

[652]Duryodhana.

[653]The arrows.

[654]In Section 27 (Volume 2), on the occasion of the gambling match.

[655]Duryodhana.

[656]This great-minded is to be interpreted in the sense of insolent, that is, this is what Duryodhana thought of himself.

the Kurus, to my arrows and to Gandiva. Today, I will free myself of the sorrow I have borne for thirteen years. O Krishna! I will kill Karna in the battle, like Maghavan against Shambara.[657] Today, when Karna has been slain in the battle, the Somaka maharathas, who wish to serve their friends in the battle, will think that their task has been accomplished. O Madhava! I do not know whether Shini's descendant will be more delighted at Karna having been killed, or at the prospect of victory. In the battle, I will kill Karna and his maharatha son and bring delight to Bhima, the twins and Satyaki. O Madhava! Having slain Karna in the great battle today, I will free myself of the debt I owe to Dhrishtadyumna, Shikhandi and the Panchalas. The wrathful Dhananjaya will be seen in the battle today, fighting with the Kouravas in the encounter and bringing down the son of a suta. In your presence, let me again indulge in self-praise. In the world, there is no one who is my equal in knowledge of dhanurveda. Where is the person who is my equal in valour? Is there anyone else who is as forgiving as me? There is no one else who is my equal in anger. With the bow in my hand and resorting to the strength of my arms, I can defeat the gods, the asuras and all the beings united together. Know that my manliness is supreme among the best. With the arrows from Gandiva, which are like rays, I alone will consume all the Kurus, Bahlikas and Kashis, with large numbers of their followers, like the fire burning dead wood at the end of winter. The arrows have left marks on my palms. An arrow is affixed to the left of the bow. The soles of my feet have the marks of a chariot and a standard. When someone like me advances into a battle, he cannot be vanquished.'"'

Chapter 1203(53)

'Sanjaya said, "Their soldiers possessed large standards and advanced, swelling in numbers. Trumpets and other musical instruments blared in the vanguard, like large masses of clouds

[657]Shambara was the name of a demon killed by Indra.

roaring at the end of summer. The mighty elephants were like clouds. There were the sounds of musical instruments, axles and the slapping of palms. The colourful weapons, decorated with gold, were like lightning. The giant chariots raised a mighty sound. Currents of blood began to flow with a great force.[658] It was full of swords and bore along the lives of kshatriyas. There was carnage of beings, cruel, like a shower at the wrong time that brings destruction. Chariots, charioteers, horses and elephants and all the other enemies were made to die by Partha's storm of arrows. He killed horses with their riders and large numbers of foot soldiers. Kripa and Shikhandi clashed against each other in the battle and Satyaki attacked Duryodhana. Shrutashrava fought with Drona's son and Yudhamanyu with Chitrasena. Uttamouja from the Srinjayas clashed against Karna's son, the ratha Sushena. Sahadeva rushed against the king of Gandhara, like a hungry lion attacking a giant bull. The young Shatanika, Nakula's son, attacked Karna's son, the young Vrishasena, with a storm of arrows. Karna's brave son struck the Panchala with many showers of arrows.[659] Madri's son, Nakula, colourful in fighting and a bull among rathas, attacked Kritavarma. Yajnasena's son, the lord of Panchala,[660] attacked Karna, the overall commander, and his soldiers. O descendant of the Bharata lineage! With the army of the Bharatas, extended by the arrays of the samshaptakas, Duhshasana attacked Bhima, supreme among wielders of weapons and unassailable because of his force, in the battle. The brave Uttamouja attacked Karna's son and severed his head, which fell down on the ground. He then roared loudly and that sound echoed in the sky. On seeing that Sushena's head had fallen down on the ground, Karna adopted a fearful form. He used extremely sharp arrows to sever his[661] horses, chariot and standard. Uttamouja used sharp arrows to strike Kripa and used a radiant sword to slay his horses and parshni charioteers. He then ascended

[658]The image is of a river.

[659]Sushena and Uttamouja. This shloka should have come earlier.

[660]Dhrishtadyumna, Yajnasena was one of Drupada's names.

[661]Uttamouja's.

Shikhandi's chariot. Shikhandi was stationed on his own chariot. On seeing that Kripa was without a chariot, Shikhandi wished to strike him with arrows. However, Drona's son repulsed him with his chariot. He saved Kripa, who was submerged, like a cow in mud. Meanwhile, Bhima was clad in golden armour and used his sharp arrows to torment the soldiers of your son. He was like the sun, at the auspicious time when it is midday."'

Chapter 1204(54)

'Sanjaya said, "While that tumultuous engagement was going on, Bhima was fighting alone and countering the army of the sons of Dhritarashtra. He was surrounded by large numbers of the enemy. In that situation of great fear, he told his charioteer, 'O charioteer! Bear me swiftly on these horses. I will send all the sons of Dhritarashtra to Yama.' Having been thus addressed by Bhimasena, the charioteer advanced with a fierce speed against the army of your son, that is, towards the army that Bhima wished to advance against. A large number of Kurus advanced against him from every direction and the enemy possessed elephants, chariots, horses and foot soldiers. With innumerable arrows, they powerfully struck the best of horses from every side. The great-souled one severed those descending arrows with his gold-tufted arrows. Those gold-tufted arrows were severed into two and three fragments by the arrows released by Bhima and fell down.[662] O king! In the midst of the kings on your side, elephants, rathas, horses and foot soldiers were slain by Bhima and roared loudly. O Indra among men! They were like mountains shattered by the thunder. The foremost among kings were shattered by Bhimasena, who was single-handed. In that encounter, they rushed against Bhima from every side, like birds in search of flowers heading towards a tree. When they attacked him, in the midst of your

[662]The enemy also had gold-tufted arrows.

soldiers, he[663]exhibited a force that was greater than the greatest. He was like the Destroyer at the time of destruction. He was the like the one who exterminates all beings, with a staff in his hand.[664] In that battle, his speed was greater than that of the greatest. Those on your side could not withstand it. It was as if the one who destroys all beings, when the time of destruction has arrived, had descended with a gaping mouth. O descendant of the Bharata lineage! In that battle, the great-souled one scorched the army of the Bharatas. They were frightened of Bhima and fled in different directions, like large masses of clouds driven away by a great wind.

'"The intelligent and powerful Bhimasena then spoke cheerfully to his charioteer again. 'O suta! Chariots and standards have assembled and are advancing towards us. Find out whether they belong to the enemy or to us. Since I am engaged in fighting, I cannot make out. I should not envelop our own soldiers with arrows. O Vishoka![665] I see the enemy on all sides and I am extremely anxious that the king[666] should not be suffering. Kiriti has not yet returned. O suta! That is the reason I am overcome by great sorrow. O charioteer! I am grieving that Dharmaraja has abandoned me in the midst of the enemy and has departed. I do not know whether he and Bibhatsu are alive or dead. That is the reason I am overcome with grief. However, I will assume a terrible form and drive away these soldiers. Once they have been destroyed, I shall rejoice. Stationed in the midst of the enemy, I will slay the assembled ones. Then, I will rejoice with you. Count all the quivers and arrows and tell me. How many arrows are still left on my chariot? What kinds are there and what is their length? O suta! Determine this and tell me.' Vishoka replied, 'O brave one! There are sixty thousand arrows, ten thousand kshurapra arrows and the same number of broad-headed arrows. O brave one! There are two thousand iron arrows. O Partha! There are three thousand

[663]Bhima.

[664]That is, Yama.

[665]Vishoka was Bhima's charioteer.

[666]Yudhishthira.

pradaras.[667] O Pandaveya! The weapons that still remain cannot be carried on six carts pulled by bullocks. Release these and others in thousands. You possess clubs, swords, your arms and other stores.' Bhima said, 'O suta! Behold. In this awful engagement today, I will shatter all the kings with my speed and force. In the encounter, my fierce arrows will be terrible in form. The sun will disappear and it will be like the world of the dead. O suta! The kings will know this today, and so will their sons, that Bhima has been submerged in this battle and has single-handedly vanquished the Kurus in the encounter. All the Kurus will be destroyed in the battle, or let the worlds know about my deeds since childhood.[668] Single-handedly, I will bring all of them down or let all of them crush Bhimasena. There are those who pronounce benedictions on virtuous deeds. Let those gods bless me. Let Arjuna, the slayer of enemies, come here, like Shakra swiftly summoned to a sacrifice. Behold. The army of the Bharatas has been shattered. Why are those Indras among men running away? It is evident that the intelligent Savyasachi, foremost among men, has shrouded the soldiers with his swift arrows. O Vishoka! Behold. The standards are being routed in the battle, and so are the large numbers of elephants, horses and infantry. The chariots are being shattered, afflicted by arrows and javelins, and so are the rathas. O suta! Behold. The Kourava soldiers are being severely slaughtered and destroyed. Dhananjaya's force is like that of the vajra, and his golden arrows, tufted with the feathers of peacocks and hawks, are devouring them. The chariots, horses and elephants are being driven away. Large numbers of foot soldiers are being crushed. All the Kouravas are confounded. The terrified elephants are running away, as if from a conflagration. O Vishoka! Sounds of lamentation are arising in the battle. Kings among elephants are emitting loud shrieks.' Vishoka replied, 'O Pandava! All your desires have come true. In the midst of the elephant arrays, the standard with the ape can be seen. Behold. Like lightning flashing amidst blue clouds, the bow is being extended there. Astride the top of

[667]A pradara is a special kind of arrow.

[668]In the event that Bhima dies.

Dhananjaya's standard, the ape can be seen from every direction. The celestial gem on the diadem is as radiant as the rays of the sun.[669] Alongside, behold the terrible and extremely loud blare of Devadatta, pale in complexion.[670] Janardana has the reins in his hand. He is driving through the army of the enemy. Behold. Next to Janardana is his chakra, increasing Keshava's fame. It is sharp at the edges and is like the sun in complexion. Its handle is like the vajra. It is always worshipped by the Yadus. O brave one! Behold.' Bhima said, 'O charioteer! Because you have pleased me greatly and given me good news, I will give you fourteen supreme villages, one hundred maidservants and twenty chariots. O Vishoka! You have given me news about Arjuna.'"'

Chapter 1205(55)

'Sanjaya said, "In the battle, hearing the clatter of chariots and roars of lions, Arjuna asked Govinda to drive the horses quickly. On hearing Arjuna's words, Govinda told Arjuna, 'I am proceeding extremely swiftly to the spot where Bhima is stationed.' The horses that were as white as snow, or conch shells, advanced. The harnesses were decorated with golds, pearls and jewels. It was as if the lord of the gods was advancing in great anger, grasping the vajra, desiring victory and wishing to kill Jambha.[671] There was a large number of chariots, horses, elephants and foot soldiers, accompanied by the whizzing sound of arrows and the clatter of hooves. The earth and the directions echoed with the sound. Angrily, they advanced against Jaya, lion among men. There was a great clash between them and Partha. That great encounter brought destruction to bodies and lives. It was like that between the asuras and the god Vishnu, supreme among victorious ones, fighting over the lordship of the three worlds.

[669]Arjuna was known as Kiriti because he wore a diadem.

[670]Devadatta was the name of Arjuna's conch shell.

[671]Jambha was a demon killed by Indra.

The diademed and garlanded one was alone. But he severed all their superior and inferior weapons. With sharp arrows that were like the razor and in the shape of a half-moon, he severed many of their heads and arms and also their umbrellas, whisks, fans and standards. Large numbers of horses, rathas, foot soldiers and elephants shrieked and fell down in diverse ways, assuming mutilated forms. They were like a forest shattered by a storm. There were giant elephants decorated with golden nets. They had been prepared for war, with standards signifying victory. They were mangled by gold-tufted arrows and looked like blazing mountains. With supreme arrows that were like Vasava's vajra, he shattered elephants, chariots and horses. He then advanced swiftly, wishing to kill Karna, just as in ancient times, the lord of the Maruts had advanced to shatter Bala.[672] O scorcher of enemies! That mighty-armed tiger among men penetrated the army of the son of a suta, like a makara entering the ocean. O king! On seeing this, those on your side attacked Pandava, with chariots and foot soldiers and a large number of elephant riders and horse riders. As they advanced against Partha, they created an extremely loud noise, like the sound made by the waters of a turbulent ocean. In the battle, those maharathas were like tigers. Ready to give up their lives and abandoning fear, they attacked that tiger among men. They descended there, showering down arrows. However, Arjuna scattered those soldiers, like clouds dispelled by a strong storm. Those large numbers of rathas were great archers and strikers. They advanced against Arjuna and pierced him with sharp arrows. However, using his arrows, Arjuna dispatched thousands of rathas, elephants and horses towards Yama's abode. In that battle, they were slaughtered by arrows released from Partha's bow. As fear was generated in the maharathas, they started to melt away. Using his sharp arrows, Arjuna conveyed four hundred brave maharathas, who were endeavouring, to Yama's abode. In the battle, they were slain by arrows of many different forms. In their fear, they abandoned Arjuna and fled in different directions. As they fled, a great uproar arose in the vanguard of the army. O fortunate one! It was like that

[672]Bala was a demon killed by Indra (lord of the Maruts).

made by the giant ocean when it dashes against a mountain. That army was severely routed and driven away by Arjuna's arrows. O venerable one! Partha then advanced in the direction of the army of the son of a suta. There was a great noise when he advanced against the enemy. It was like that made in ancient times, when Garuda descended in search of serpents.

'"On hearing that sound, the immensely strong Bhimasena was extremely delighted, because he desired to catch sight of Partha. O great king! On hearing that Partha was advancing, the powerful Bhimasena became ready to give up his life and crushed your soldiers. He was like the force of the wind. He was like the force of the wind in speed. Bhima, the powerful son of the wind god, roamed around like the wind. O Indra among kings! O lord of the earth! Your soldiers were afflicted. O great king! They were whirled around, like a shattered boat on the ocean. Bhima showed those soldiers the dexterity of his hands. He released sharp arrows and conveyed them to Yama's eternal abode. O descendant of the Bharata lineage! In the battle there, the warriors witnessed Bhima's superhuman strength. He was like the Destroyer at the time of the destruction of a yuga. O descendant of the Bharata lineage! They were afflicted by Bhimasena's terrible strength. O bull among the Bharata lineage! On seeing this, King Duryodhana spoke these words, addressing the soldiers, the great archers and the warriors. 'All of you unite in this battle and kill Bhima. Once he has been slain, I think that all the remaining soldiers will have been killed.' Accepting the instructions of your son, the kings enveloped Bhima with a shower of arrows from every direction. O king! There were many elephants and men, desiring victory. O Indra among kings! There were also chariots and horses that surrounded Vrikodara. O king! O foremost among Bharatas! Having been thus surrounded by valiant ones from every direction, the brave one was as beautiful as the moon surrounded by stars. O great king! That supreme of men looked radiant and handsome in the battle, in particular, as beautiful as Vijaya was. All those kings released showers of arrows at him. They were cruel and their eyes were red in anger. They wished to kill Vrikodara. In that battle, Bhima drove away that large army with straight-tufted arrows and emerged, like a fish in the water coming out of a net. O descendant of the Bharata lineage! He killed ten thousand elephants that refused to retreat, two hundred thousand and two hundred men, five thousand horses and one hundred rathas. Having killed them, Bhima created a river made out of blood and mire. Blood constituted the water and chariots were the eddies. It was full of crocodiles in the form of elephants. The men were the fish and horses were the sharks. Hair constituted the moss and the weeds. The trunks of the best of elephants were severed and many jewels were borne along. Thighs were alligators. The fat was the mud. It was full of many heads that were the rocks. The bows and arrows were like rafts. Clubs and maces were the flags. In the battle, a current of warriors were borne along to Yama's abode. In an instant, the tiger among men created a river that flowed downwards.[673] It was like the fierce Vaitarani, difficult for those who have not perfected their souls to cross. Wherever the spot where Pandaveya, supreme among rathas, advanced, in that spot he brought down hundreds and thousands of warriors.

'"O great king! Having seen the deeds performed by Bhimasena in the battle, Duryodhana spoke these words to Shakuni. 'O maternal uncle! Defeat the immensely strong Bhimasena in the encounter. If the immensely strong Pandaveya is vanquished, I think that our victory is ensured.' O great king! At this, the powerful Soubala advanced, surrounded by his brothers, to engage in that great battle. In the battle, he rushed against Bhimasena, whose valour was terrible. He countered the brave one, like the shoreline against the abode of makaras. Though he was restrained by sharp arrows, Bhima did not retreat. O Indra among kings! Shakuni struck him on the left flank and between the breasts with iron arrows that were gold-tufted and had been sharpened on stone. O great king! Those golden arrows, tufted with the feathers of herons and peacocks, penetrated the great-souled one's armour and sank in. In the battle, Bhima was severely pierced by those gold-decorated arrows. O descendant of the Bharata

[673]To the nether regions. The river Vaitarani flows in the nether regions and one has to cross it to reach Yama's world.

lineage! He violently shot an arrow towards Soubala. O king! As the terrible arrow arrived, the immensely strong Shakuni, the scorcher of enemies, displayed the dexterity of his hands and shattered it into one hundred fragments. O lord of the earth! When it fell down on the ground, Bhima was enraged. He laughed and severed Soubala's bow with a broad-headed arrow. The powerful Soubala cast aside that severed bow and picked up another bow and sixteen broad-headed arrows. O great king! With four of those broad-headed and straight-tufted arrows, he struck Bhima's horses and his charioteer with a fifth. O lord of the earth! He severed his standard with one and his umbrella with two. With four more, Subala's son struck his four horses.[674] O great king! At this, the powerful Bhimasena became wrathful. In that battle, he hurled a javelin that was completely made out of iron, but had a golden handle. Released from Bhima's arm, it was like the flickering tongue of a serpent. It swiftly descended on the great-souled Soubala's chariot. O lord of the earth! The javelin had been hurled by the enraged Bhimasena and was decorated with gold. But he[675] seized it and hurled it back and it penetrated the great-souled Pandava's left arm. It then fell down on the ground, like lightning descending from the sky. O great king! In every direction, the sons of Dhritarashtra let out a loud cry. However, Bhima was not prepared to tolerate those spirited roars, like those of lions. In haste, the maharatha grasped a bow and strung it. O Indra among kings! In a short while, in that battle, the immensely strong one enveloped Soubala's soldiers, who were prepared to give up their lives, with arrows. O lord of the earth! He killed his[676] four horses and his charioteer. The valiant one swiftly severed his standard with a broad-headed arrow. With the horses slain, the supreme among men abandoned his chariot. His eyes were red with rage and he stretched his bow, sighing deeply. O king! He covered Bhima from

[674]This doesn't add up to a count of sixteen. That's because the Critical edition excises some shlokas. In these, the missing arrows are used to strike Bhima.

[675]Shakuni.

[676]Shakuni's.

every direction with many arrows. However, the powerful Bhimasena countered him with force. He angrily severed his bow and pierced him with sharp arrows. O lord of men! Powerfully and extremely severely pierced by the enemy, the afflicter of enemies fell down on the ground, with only a little bit of life left in him. O lord of the earth! On discerning that he had lost his senses, your son bore him away on his own chariot, while Bhimasena looked on. On seeing that the tiger among men was taken away on the chariot, the sons of Dhritarashtra retreated. They suffered from great fear on account of Bhima and, terrified, fled in different directions. O king! When the archer Bhimasena had defeated Soubala, your son, Duryodhana, was shattered by great fear. Thinking about his maternal uncle, he fled on swift horses. O descendant of the Bharata lineage! On seeing that the king had retreated, the troops withdrew, abandoning the duels that were going on in different directions. On seeing this, all the atirathas among the sons of Dhritarashtra also retreated. Bhima quickly rushed at them, showering down many hundreds of arrows. Slaughtered by Bhima, the sons of Dhritarashtra withdrew.

'"O king! From every direction, they sought refuge with Karna, who was stationed in the battle. That greatly valiant and immensely strong one became like an island to them. O king! O tiger among men! It was as if mariners who suffered from a calamity and had a shattered boat found comfort on reaching an island. O bull among the Bharata lineage! In that way, those on your side sought refuge with Karna. O king! Having stationed themselves there, they cheered each other. They advanced to fight again, preferring to die rather than retreat."'

Chapter 1206(56)

'Dhritarashtra asked, "O Sanjaya! When the soldiers were shattered by Bhimasena in the battle, what did Duryodhana and Soubala say? What about Karna, foremost among victorious warriors, Kripa, Kritavarma, Drona's son, Duhshasana and other warriors on my side? I think that Pandaveya's valour was extremely wonderful. Did Radheya Karna, the destroyer of enemies, act towards all the Kuru warriors in accordance with his vow? O Sanjaya! On seeing that the army had been routed by the infinitely energetic Kounteya, Radheya, Adhiratha's son, remained the prosperity, the armour, the base and the hope of remaining alive. What did the warrior Karna do? What about my sons and the invincible maharatha kings? O Sanjaya! You are skilled in narrating. Tell me everything about all this."

'Sanjaya replied, "O great king! In the afternoon, while Bhimasena looked on, the powerful son of a suta began to strike all the Somakas. The extremely strong Bhima also began to uproot all the soldiers of the sons of Dhritarashtra. On seeing that the intelligent Bhimasena was driving away the army, Karna asked his charioteer to drive him towards the Panchalas. The immensely strong king of Madra, Shalya, drove the white horses, which were extremely swift, towards the Chedis, the Panchalas and the Karushas. Shalya, the destroyer of enemy troops, penetrated those soldiers. He cheerfully drove the horses to the spot where that foremost one[677] wanted him to go. The chariot was like a cloud and was covered in tiger skins. O lord of the earth! On seeing it, the Pandus and the Panchalas were terrified. The loud roar of the chariot could be heard in the great battle. Its roar was like that of a cloud, or of a mountain being shattered.

'"Karna drew his bow all the way back to his ear and slew hundreds and thousands of Pandava soldiers with hundreds of sharp arrows. While he was performing that superhuman deed in the encounter, the great archers, the Pandava maharathas, surrounded him. Shikhandi, Bhima, Parshata Dhrishtadyumna, Nakula, Sahadeva, Droupadi's sons and Satyaki surrounded him and showered down arrows, wishing to kill Radheya. In the battle, the brave Satyaki, supreme among men, pierced Karna with twenty sharp arrows in his shoulder joints. Shikhandi pierced Karna with twenty-five arrows, Dhrishtadyumna with five, Droupadi's sons with

[677]Karna.

sixty-four, Sahadeva with seven and Nakula with one hundred. In that encounter, the immensely strong and angry Bhimasena pierced him in the shoulder joints with ninety arrows with drooping tufts. Adhiratha's immensely strong son laughed. He drew back his supreme bow and released sharp arrows, afflicting them. Radheya pierced each of them back with five arrows each. The bull among men severed Satyaki's bow and standard and struck him between the breasts with nine arrows. The scorcher of enemies wrathfully pierced Bhimasena with thirty arrows and struck his charioteer with three arrows. In the twinkling of an eye, the bull among men deprived Droupadi's sons of their chariots and it was extraordinary. With straight-tufted arrows, he made all of them retreat. He killed the brave maharathas from Panchala and Chedi. O lord of the earth! In that battle, the Chedis and the Matysas were slaughtered. They rushed against Karna, who was single-handed, and struck him with torrents of arrows. The maharatha son of a suta struck those down with his sharp arrows. O descendant of the Bharata lineage! I witnessed this extraordinary deed performed by Karna. In the battle, the brave and powerful son of a suta was single-handed. O great king! However, despite those enemy warriors striving to their utmost in the encounter, he restrained the Pandaveyas with his arrows. O descendant of the Bharata lineage! All the gods, siddhas and supreme rishis were satisfied at the dexterity shown by the great-souled Karna. The great archers, the sons of Dhritarashtra, applauded that best of men. Karna was best among supreme rathas. He was foremost among all archers. O great king! Karna consumed the army of the enemy, just as a large and flaming fire burns down dead wood during the summer. Thus slaughtered by Karna and witnessing Karna's great strength, the Pandaveyas were terrified in the battle and fled here and there. In the great encounter, loud lamentations arose among the Panchalas, since they were slaughtered by the sharp arrows that were released from Karna's bow. The large army of the Pandavas was frightened at the sound. In the battle there, the enemies thought that Karna was the only warrior. Thus Radheya, the afflicter of enemies, accomplished that supremely wonderful deed. He single-handedly countered all the Pandavas and no one was capable of glancing towards him. They were like a large mass of water that dashes against a supreme mountain and is driven back. In that way, the Pandava soldiers clashed against Karna and were shattered. O king! In the battle, Karna blazed like a fire without smoke. The mighty-armed one burnt down the large army of the Pandavas. O great king! With great agility and his light arrows, the brave Karna severed the heads, with earrings, and the arms of the valiant ones. There were swords with handles of ivory. There were standards, javelins, horses and elephants. There were the parts of chariots and many kinds of flags and whisks. There were axles, yokes, harnesses and many kinds of wheels. Karna observed his vow of a warrior and shattered these into hundreds of fragments. O descendant of the Bharata lineage! Elephants and horses were slain by Karna. Because of the flesh, blood and mire, the earth assumed an impassable form. With destroyed horses, foot soldiers, chariots and elephants, one could no longer distinguish uneven terrain from plain ground. Nor could the warriors distinguish those on their own side from that of the enemy. The arrows generated from Karna's weapon created a terrible darkness. The arrows released from Radheya's bow were decorated in gold. O great king! In the battle, the Pandaveya maharathas repeatedly endeavoured, but were shrouded by Karna. O great king! The maharathas endeavoured and were submerged. They were like a herd of deer, driven away by an angry lion in the forest. The warriors who fought against Karna in the battle were greatly illustrious. But those soldiers were slaughtered, like a large number of smaller animals by a wolf.

'"Seeing that the Pandava soldiers were retreating, the great archers, the sons of Dhritarashtra, pursued them, emitting fierce roars. O Indra among kings! Duryodhana was filled with great delight. He joyfully instructed that many musical instruments should be sounded in every direction. The great archers among the Panchalas, supreme among men, were shattered. But though shattered, those brave ones returned, preferring death over retreat. O great king! The brave Radheya, scorcher of enemies and bull among men, countered and repelled them in many different kinds of ways. O descendant of the Bharata lineage! Twenty rathas among the Panchalas were slain there by Karna and so were one hundred angry enemy riders from among the Chedis. O descendant of the Bharata lineage! He emptied the seats of chariots and the backs of horses. He brought down men from the necks of elephants. He drove away the infantry. The scorcher of enemies was like the sun at midday and was impossible to look at. The son of a suta assumed as cruel a form as Yama and roamed around. O great king! In this fashion, the great archer Karna, the destroyer of large numbers of the enemy, killed men, horses, rathas and elephants and was stationed there. The immensely strong one was stationed there like the Destroyer after slaying large numbers of beings. The single-handed maharatha was stationed there, after having slain the Somakas. However, we beheld the wonderful valour of the Panchalas. Though they were slaughtered by Karna, they did not forsake the field of battle. The king,[678] Duhshasana, Sharadvata Kripa, Ashvatthama, Kritavarma and Shakuni Soubala slew the Pandava soldiers in hundreds and thousands. O Indra among kings! The brothers who were Karna's sons were also true in their valour. Those powerful ones easily fought with the Panchalas, here and there. They created a cruel and great destruction among the horses there. Despite this, the brave Pandavas, Dhrishtadyumna, Shikhandi and Droupadi's sons were enraged and attacked those on your side. In this fashion, there was destruction among the Pandavas there and also amongst those on your side, when they clashed against the immensely strong Bhima in the battle."'

Chapter 1207(57)

'Sanjaya said, "O great king! Meanwhile, in that great battle, Arjuna divided up the enemy and glanced at the enraged son of a suta. He generated a large river of blood that bore along flesh, marrow and bones. The bull among men spoke these words to Vasudeva. 'O Krishna! The standard of the son of a suta can be seen there. Bhimasena and the other maharathas are fighting there.

[678]Duryodhana.

O Janardana! Terrified of Karna, the Panchalas are being driven away. The radiant and white umbrella of King Duryodhana is there. Karna looks extremely beautiful as he is routing the Panchalas. Kripa, Kritavarma and Drona's immensely strong son are protecting the king and are protected by the son of a suta. Those on our side are unable to kill them, but they are slaying the Somakas. Shalya is stationed on his chariot, skilled in handling the reins. O Krishna! He looks extremely beautiful as he guides the horses of the chariot of the son of a suta. My wish is that you should drive my chariot to that maharatha. Without killing Karna in the battle, I will not retreat. O Janardana! Otherwise, while we look on in this battle, Radheya will exterminate the maharatha Parthas and Srinjayas.' Having been thus instructed, Keshava quickly drove the chariot towards your army, so that there might be a duel between Karna, the great archer, and Savyasachi. On Pandava's instructions, the mighty-armed Hari departed, thus providing assurance to the Pandava soldiers in every direction. O venerable one! There was the loud clatter of Pandaveya's chariot in the battle. It was like the sound of Vasava's vajra or a giant flood. There was a great roar from the chariot of Pandava, who was unwavering in his valour. Vijaya, immeasurable in his soul, advanced against your army.

'"On seeing the white horses advance, with Krishna as the charioteer, the king of Madra spoke to Karna. 'Behold the standard of the great-souled one. The chariot is coming here, with white horses and with Krishna as the charioteer. O Karna! He is slaying the enemies in the battle. He is the one about whom you had enquired. Kounteya is stationed there, touching Gandiva bow. If you can kill him today, that will be greatly beneficial for us. The army of the sons of Dhritarashtra is being routed in every direction. It is terrified of Arjuna, who is swiftly slaying large numbers of the enemy. Abandoning all the soldiers, Dhananjaya is hastening here. His body swelling with anger, I think he is coming for your sake. I do not think Partha is interested in fighting with anyone else other than you. He is blazing with anger because you have worsted Vrikodara. He has seen that you deprived Dharmaraja of his chariot and severely wounded him. Shikhandi, Satyaki, Parshata Dhrishtadyumna, Droupadi's sons, Yudhamanyu, Uttamouja and the two brothers, Nakula and Sahadeva, are looking on. O scorcher of enemies! Partha is advancing violently, alone on a chariot. His eyes are red with anger. In his rage, he wishes to kill all the archers. There is no doubt that he has abandoned all the other soldiers and is spiritedly advancing towards us. O Karna! Advance and repulse him. There is no other archer who can. I do not see any other archer in this world who is like you and can counter the angry Arjuna in a battle, like a shoreline. I do not see anyone protecting him, at the rear, or along the flanks. Behold. He is advancing alone towards you, with thoughts of success in his mind. In the battle, you are the only one who can withstand the two Krishnas in an encounter. O Radheya! It is your burden that you must fight against Dhananjaya. You are as accomplished as Bhishma, Drona, Drona's son and Kripa. Drive your chariot against Savyasachi and counter Pandava. He is like a snake with a flickering tongue. He is roaring like a bull. O Karna! He is bent on destruction, like a tiger. Slay Dhananjaya. The maharatha sons of Dhritarashtra have been driven away in the battle. In their fear of Arjuna, the kings are quickly glancing at him. There is no man other than you who can dispel the fear of the warriors who are running away in terror. O descendant of the suta lineage! There is no one other than you. In this battle, you are an island of refuge to all the Kurus. O tiger among men! They are stationed here, desiring assurance from you. You have advanced against and defeated in battle those who are invincible, those from Videha, Ambashtha, Kamboja, Nagnajit and Gandhara. O Radheya! Exert yourself now and counter Pandava and Varshneya Vasudeva, loved by Kiriti.'

"'Karna replied, 'O Shalya! You seem to be in your natural state now and amicable towards me. O mighty-armed one! It is evident that you are frightened of Dhananjaya. Behold the strength of my arms today. Behold my learning. I will single-handedly slay the large army of the Pandavas and the two Krishnas, tigers among men. I tell you this truthfully. Without killing those two brave warriors, I will not retreat. Or I will be slain by them and will lie down. Victory in a battle is uncertain. But I will be successful in my objective, whether I kill them, or whether I am killed. It is said that no one like him has been born in this world. He is supreme among rathas. That is what we have heard. I will fight against the Partha who is like that. Behold my manliness in the great battle. The foremost among rathas is advancing on his chariot. The Kourava prince is borne on swift horses. Perhaps he will convey me towards a calamity today and perhaps with Karna's death, all of this will end. This prince's hands do not sweat. They are thick and large and marks have been created on them.[679] He is firm and accomplished in the use of weapons. He is light in the use of his hands. There is no warrior who is Pandaveya's equal. He grasps many arrows tufted with the feathers of herons. He shoots them as if they were but one. They descend at the distance of one krosha and do not deviate from their aim. Where is the warrior on earth who is his equal? With Krishna as his second, the spirited atiratha Pandaveya satisfied the fire.[680] The great-souled Krishna obtained the chakra there and Pandava Savyasachi the bow Gandiva. The mighty-armed one, whose spirit does not wane, also obtained the chariot, with a fierce and loud roar. It is yoked to white horses. He obtained giant quivers that are divine in form and are inexhaustible. The bearer of oblations[681] also gave him celestial weapons. He slew the daityas in Indra's world and destroyed all the *kalakeya*s in a battle.[682] He obtained the conch shell Devadatta there. Who possesses greater fame than him on earth? He faced the immensely generous Mahadeva himself in a battle and satisfied him.[683] He thus obtained the extremely terrible pashupata, the great weapon that can destroy the three worlds. The various guardians of the world assembled and gave him weapons that have no measure. The lion among men swiftly slew in battle the assembled *kalakhanja* asuras. In Virata's city, alone on a chariot, he defeated all of us who were assembled there. He retrieved the wealth of cattle from us and robbed the maharathas of

[679]Marks from the use of weapons.

[680]At the time of the burning of the Khandava forest, described in Section 19 (Volume 2).

[681]The fire god.

[682]Described in Section 32 (Volume 2).

[683]Described in Section 31 (Volume 2).

their garments. He possesses these qualities of a valiant one and the revered Krishna is his second in the battle. Keshava is infinite in his valour. He is Narayana himself in disguise and protects him. Even if all the worlds assembled together and tried for ten thousand years, they would be incapable of describing his[684] qualities. The great-souled one possesses a conch shell, a chakra and a sword in his hands. He is Vishnu and Jishnu and the son of Vasudeva.[685] On seeing the two Krishnas together on a single chariot, both fear and valour are generated in my heart. Both of them are brave and accomplished, firm in the use of weapons. They are maharathas who can withstand anything. Phalguna and Vasudeva are like this. O Shalya! Which other person is capable of advancing against them? I will bring them down in the battle, or the two Krishnas will kill me today.'"

'Sanjaya said, "Having spoken these words to Shalya, Karna, the slayer of enemies, roared like a cloud in that battle. He approached your son and honoured him. He then spoke these words to the foremost among the Kurus who had assembled—the mighty-armed Kripa and the lord from Bhoja,[686] the king of Gandhara and his son, the son of the preceptor,[687] his younger brothers, the foot soldiers and the other horse riders and elephant riders. 'Swiftly advance against Achyuta and Arjuna from every direction and restrain them, so that they are exhausted. O kings! Then those two lords will be severely wounded and I will be able to kill them cheerfully today.' Those spirited ones agreed. Wishing to kill Arjuna, the best of the brave ones attacked, like rivers and streams full of water dashing towards the great ocean. Arjuna received them there in the battle. The enemies could not discern when he affixed supreme arrows and released them. They were oppressed by Dhananjaya's arrows. Men, horses and elephants were slain and fell down. He was as radiant as the energetic sun that arises at the end of a yuga. Gandiva was like a circular disc and the

[684]Krishna's.

[685]Jishnu means the victorious one and is not only one of Arjuna's names, but also Krishna's. Krishna's father was Vasudeva.

[686]Kritavarma.

[687]Ashvatthama.

arrows were like rays. The Kouravas were incapable of glancing towards Jaya. He was like a sun that hurts the eyes of people. Kripa, Bhoja and your son himself attacked him and shot arrows. They wished to kill him and were skilled. They shot supreme arrows in that great battle, making the best of efforts. Pandava swiftly severed those arrows and pierced each of his foes in the chest with three arrows each. Arjuna drew Gandiva back to a full circle and scorched them like the radiant sun. The arrows were like fierce rays and he was like the solar disc when it is midway between Shuchi and Shukra.[688]

'"Drona's son pierced Dhananjaya with ten supreme arrows and then struck Achyuta with three. He struck the four horses with four and released many supreme arrows at the ape.[689] While he was extending his bow to its complete extent, Dhananjaya used three arrows to sever it and sliced down his charioteer's head with a kshurapra arrow. Dhananjaya struck the four horses of Drona's son with four arrows, his standard with three and brought him down from his chariot. He[690] became angry and picked up another bow that was ornamented with diamonds and other precious stones. It had excellent joints and was as radiant as the great and supreme serpent Takshaka, resting on a mountain. The great personage placed his other weapons on the ground and strung the bow himself. Drona's son then afflicted those unvanquished and supreme men[691] with supreme arrows and pierced them from a close distance. Kripa, Bhoja and your son showered down torrents of arrows on the one who was like a sun.[692] Partha used his arrows to sever Kripa's bow, with an arrow fixed to it, and struck his horses, standard and charioteer with arrows. He enveloped your son with arrows and severing his bow and standard, roared. The powerful one slew Kritavarma's horses and severed his sparkling standard. He also slaughtered horses and charioteers, and

[688]Shukra is associated with the month of Jyaishtha and Shuchi is another name for the month of Vaishakha. Hence, this means that the sun is midway between these hot summer months.

[689]On Arjuna's standard.

[690]Ashvatthama.

[691]Arjuna and Krishna.

[692]Arjuna.

destroyed supreme elephants, horses, chariots and their standards. Your large army was shattered, like an embankment devastated by water. Dhananjaya then swiftly advanced, like Shatakratu for Vritra's death. He was followed by other chariots that raised their standards again, prepared well and ready to fight with the enemy. Maharathas Shikhandi, Shini's descendant and the twins followed Dhananjaya's chariot, countering the enemy with sharp arrows, shattering them and roaring fiercely. The brave Kurus and Srinjayas killed each other in great rage, shooting extremely energetic arrows. They were like supreme gods and asuras[693] in ancient times. They desired victory or heaven. O scorcher of enemies! Elephants, horses and chariots fell down. They roared loudly and struck each other separately with arrows that were released well. In the great battle, the supreme warriors fought with each other. The great-souled ones created darkness because of the arrows. O king! The ten directions and the sky could not be discerned. The sun's radiance was covered in darkness."'

Chapter 1208(58)

'Sanjaya said, "Dhananjaya saw that the foremost among the Kurus had attacked Bhimasena with great force and that he was submerged. O descendant of the Bharata lineage! Wishing to save him, he struck the soldiers of the son of a suta with arrows. Dhananjaya conveyed brave ones amongst the enemy to the world of the dead. Some of his nets of arrows covered the sky. Others were invisible, but killed your soldiers. He filled the sky with arrows and they seemed to be like a flock of birds. O great king! Dhananjaya was like a destroyer of the Kurus. Partha used broad-headed arrows, kshurapras and sparkling iron arrows to mangle the bodies and sever the heads. Severed bodies, dislodged armour and heads were strewn around everywhere. Foot soldiers fell down and warriors

[693]The text says suras. But this is clearly a typo and should read asuras.

were spread around. O king! Destroyed by Dhananjaya's arrows, chariots, horses, men and elephants were on the field of battle and made it look like a giant Vaitarani river. As they fought, wheels of chariots were shattered, sometimes without horses and sometimes yoked to horses. With charioteers slain, or with charioteers, chariots were scattered around on the ground. The warriors wore golden armour and golden ornaments. They were on well-trained elephants that were also armoured. The wrathful drivers angered them by urging them on towards Arjuna. Kiriti slew and brought down four hundred of these through his showers of arrows. They were like the summits of large mountains, with living beings still atop them. Struck by Dhananjaya's arrows, the elephants were strewn around on the ground. Arjuna's chariot passed through them, like the sun penetrating a mass of clouds. Elephants, men and horses were slain and many chariots were fragmented. With their armour dislodged by arrows, warriors who were fierce in battle lost their lives. Phalguna crossed over that path of battle, which was strewn around in this fashion. He stretched Gandiva and it let out a great and terrible twang. The sound was as awful as that of thunder, resounding amidst dark clouds. Struck by Dhananjaya's arrows, the army was routed. It was as if a large boat was tossed around on the ocean by a great tempest. Arrows and weapons of many forms issued out of Gandiva. They flamed like meteors and lightning and scorched your soldiers. It was like a grove of bamboos burning on a giant mountain in the night. That was how your large army seemed to blaze, oppressed by the arrows. Yours soldiers were crushed, burnt and destroyed by Kiriti. They were killed and wounded by the arrows and fled in all the directions. It was as if a herd of deer was being devoured by a conflagration in a large forest. When they were consumed by Savyasachi, such was the state of the Kurus.

'"In the battle, they abandoned the mighty-armed Bhimasena. The army of the Kurus was anxious and all of them desired to retreat. Thus, the Kurus were defeated by Bibhatsu and routed. Having clashed against Bhimasena, they were made to withdraw in a short while. Phalguna approached Bhima and consulted with him. He told him that Yudhishthira's wounds had been attended to.

Having obtained Bhimsena's permission, Dhananjaya departed. O descendant of the Bharata lineage! The earth and the sky resounded with the clatter of his chariot. Ten of your terrible sons, bulls among the enemy, and all born after Duhshasana, surrounded Dhananjaya. O descendant of the Bharata lineage! Those cruel ones seemed to dance around and attacked him with their arrows, like an elephant with flaming torches.[694] Madhusudana guided the chariot so that they were on the right side. On seeing that Arjuna was advancing towards them, those brave ones retreated. Partha swiftly used iron arrows and arrows in the shape of a half-moon to destroy their standards, chariots and bows and bring them down. He then used ten other broad-headed arrows to sever their heads.[695] The eyes were red with rage. The teeth bit the lips. Fallen down on the ground, those faces looked like stars that had been dislodged from the firmament. Ten immensely forceful, gold-tufted and broad-headed arrows brought down ten Kouravas who possessed golden clubs. When they had been pierced, the slayer of enemies departed."'

Chapter 1209(59)

'Sanjaya said, "The one with the supreme ape on his standard advanced at great speed. Ninety brave Kuru rathas wished to fight with him and attacked him. In the battle, those tigers among men surrounded Arjuna, tiger among men. However, the white horses were extremely swift and were decorated in gold. They were decorated with nets of pearls and Krishna drove it towards Karna's chariot. As Dhananjaya, the slayer of enemies, advanced towards Karna's chariot, the chariots of the samshaptakas[696] also

[694]The image is of hunters hunting a wild elephant with burning torches in their hands.

[695]Since Duryodhana and all his brothers were killed by Bhima, there is an inconsistency here and they couldn't have been Dhritarashtra's sons.

[696]Those ninety rathas had taken a vow to die rather than retreat.

followed him, showering down arrows with a desire to kill. The brave Arjuna used his sharp arrows to swiftly kill all ninety of them, with their charioteers, bows and standards. Slain by Kiriti's many different kinds of arrows, they fell down, like siddhas and their celestial vehicles from heaven, when their stores of meritorious deeds have been exhausted. O supreme among the Kuru lineage! O foremost among Bharatas! At this, the fearless Kurus attacked Phalguna, with their chariots, elephants and horses. They released weapons. Supreme and mighty elephants that belonged to your son's large army obstructed Dhananjaya in the battle. The great archers, the Kurus, used lances, swords, spears, javelins, clubs, scimitars and arrows to envelop the descendant of the Kuru lineage.[697] The Kurus showered down weapons. However, Pandava used arrows that were like the rays of the sun to strike them down. At this, on the instructions of your son, mlecchas who were astride thirteen hundred crazy elephants struck Partha from the side. They used barbed arrows, hollow arrows, iron arrows, spears, javelins, spikes, *kampana*s and catapults to afflict Partha's chariot. Having been struck by the shower of weapons released by the *yavana*s[698] on elephants, Phalguna smiled and severed those with his sharp broad-headed arrows and arrows in the form of a half-moon. All those elephants were struck by large arrows of many different forms. With their flags and riders, they were brought down, like mountains shattered by thunder. Those gold-tufted arrows afflicted and killed the giant elephants that had golden harnesses. They fell down, like mountains that were on fire. O lord of the earth! In that great roar, Gandiva's twang could be heard. Men, elephants and horses shrieked and lamented. O king! The elephants were killed and fled in different directions. With their riders slain, the horses ran away in the ten directions. O great king! Chariots were without their rathas and so were the steeds. Thousands of them were seen, like the cities of the gandharvas. O great king! Horse riders ran hither and thither. They were seen there, brought down by Partha's arrows. At that

[697]Meaning Arjuna.

[698]The yavanas and the mlecchas are being equated here.

time, Pandava showed the strength of his arms. Single-handedly, he defeated the riders, the elephants and the chariots in the battle.

'"O bull among the Bharata lineage! O king! Bhimasena saw that Kiriti was surrounded by a large army consisting of three kinds of forces.[699] O king! He abandonded the few remaining rathas who were left on your side and swiftly advanced towards Dhananjaya's chariot. On seeing that Bhima was advancing towards his brother Arjuna, the soldiers who had not been killed were distressed and fled. There were some extremely fast horses that had not been killed by Arjuna. In the great battle, with the club in his hand, Bhima slaughtered them. It[700] was as fierce as the night of destruction and fed on men, elephants and horses. It was extremely terrible and could shatter walls, mansions and the gates of cities. Bhima used that club against the men, elephants and horses who were around. O venerable one! He slew many horses and horse riders. Pandava crushed men and horses plated in bronze armour and terrified them. He uprooted them with the club. Slain, they fell down with a great noise. He then ascended his chariot again and followed Arjuna from the rear. The army of the enemy was slain or devoid of spirit and retreated. Those soldiers were immobile and distracted. On seeing this, Arjuna shrouded them with arrows that robbed lives. As they clung to each other, there were severe woes of lamentation. At that time, your soldiers whirled around like a circle of fire. With the armour shattered by arrows, the soldiers blazed. Overflowing with blood, they looked like a flowering grove of *ashoka* trees. On seeing Savyasachi's valour there, all the Kurus there lost all hope of Karna remaining alive. In the battle, they could not withstand the downpour of Partha's arrows. Having been defeated by the wielder of Gandiva, the Kurus retreated. Slaughtered by Partha's arrows, they abandoned the battle. They were terrified and fled in different directions, calling out to the son of a suta. Partha followed them, showering down many hundreds of arrows. The Pandava warriors, with Bhimasena at the forefront, were delighted.

[699]Only three, presumably because the chariots had been destroyed.
[700]The club.

'"O great king! Your sons advanced towards Karna's chariot. They were submerged in fathomless waters and Karna was like an island to them. O great king! The Kurus were like defanged serpents. Because of their fear of the wielder of Gandiva, they sought shelter with Karna. O descendant of the Bharata lineage! It was just as all beings, fearing death and because of their deeds, seek shelter with dharma. O lord of men! Karna, the great archer, was like that to your sons. Terrified of the great-souled Pandava, they sought refuge with him. They were overflowing with blood and severely distressed on account of the arrows, and Karna told them, 'Do not be frightened. Come to me.' He saw that your army had been destroyed because of Partha's strength. Wishing to kill the enemy, Karna stretched his bow and while Savyasachi looked on, attacked the Panchalas again. The lords of the earth possessed eyes that were as red as wounds. In a short while, Karna showered down torrents of arrows on them, like clouds pouring down on a large mountain. O venerable one! Thousands of arrows were shot by Karna. The supreme among all living beings robbed many Panchalas of their lives. O lord of the earth! In that battle, great sounds of lamentation arose among the Panchalas. To ensure the welfare of his friend,[701] the son of a suta, the slayer of enemies, slaughtered them."'

Chapter 1210(60)

'Sanjaya said, "O king! The Kurus[702] were driven away by Karna, whose chariot possessed white horses. Using great arrows, the son of a suta slew the sons of the Panchalas, like a storm dispelling large masses of clouds. With an *anjalika* arrow, he brought down Janamejaya's charioteer from his chariot and killed his horses. He enveloped Shatanika and Sutasoma with broad-headed arrows and

[701]Duryodhana.

[702]Meaning the Pandavas here. Kuru was a common ancestor, so the Pandavas could also be referred to as the Kurus.

severed their bows. In the battle, he pierced Dhrishtadyumna with six arrows and slew the horses that were on his right flank. The son of a suta next killed Satyaki's horses and also slew Vishoka, the son of Kekaya. When that prince was killed, Ugradhanva, the general of the Kekayas, attacked him. He used many arrows that were fierce and forceful and severely struck Karna's son, Sushena.[703] Karna laughed. Using three arrows that were in the shape of a half-moon, he severed his[704] arms and head. Having lost his life, he fell down from his chariot, like a decaying shala tree that is struck down with an axe. The horses of the foremost among the Shinis[705] had been slain. Sushena, the grandson of a suta, enveloped him with sharp arrows and seemed to be dancing around. However, he was struck by the arrows of Shini's descendant and fell down. When his son was killed, Karna became senseless with rage and wished to kill Shini's descendant, bull among men. He said, 'O descendant of Shini's lineage! You have been killed.' He released an arrow that was capable of killing all enemies. Shikhandi severed it with three arrows and struck Karna with three more. Using large arrows, he[706] severed Shikhandi's bow and standard and then pierced Shikhandi with six fierce arrows. He next severed the head of Dhrishtadyumna's son. Adhiratha's great-souled son then mangled Sutasoma with an extremely sharp arrow.

'"O lion among men! While that tumultuous battle was going on and Dhrishtadyumna's son had been killed, Krishna said, 'O Partha! He is eliminating the Panchalas. Go and kill Karna.' Thus addressed, that foremost of men laughed and advanced swiftly on his chariot towards the chariot of Adhiratha's son. The one with excellent arms wished to save those who were frightened and were being killed[707] by that leader of rathas. He stretched Gandiva with a twang that was loud and terrible. He rubbed the bowstring fiercely. He suddenly

[703]However, we have earlier been told that Uttamouja killed Sushena.

[704]Ugradhanva's.

[705]Satyaki. We don't know how Satyaki's horses were killed.

[706]Karna.

[707]The Panchalas.

created darkness with his arrows and destroyed elephants, horses, chariots and men. Bhimasena, the brave one among the Pandavas, followed him on his chariot and protected his rear. Those two princes quickly advanced on their chariots towards Karna, releasing arrows at the enemy.

'"During that time, the son of a suta fought mightily, crushing the Somakas in the battle. He destroyed large numbers of chariots, horses and elephants and enveloped the directions with his arrows. Uttamouja, Janamejaya, the enraged Yudhamanyu and Shikhandi united with Parshata.[708] They roared loudly and mangled Karna with many arrows. Those five Panchala rathas attacked Vaikartana Karna extremely well, but were incapable of dislodging him from his chariot, just as the senses cannot overpower a patient and self-controlled person. Karna severed their bows, standards, horses, charioteers, quivers and flags with his arrows and struck each of the five with arrows. He then roared like a lion. As he struck them and there were the sounds of his bowstring, arrows, palms and the bow, all beings were distressed. They thought that the earth, with its mountains and trees, was being shattered. His bow was like Shakra's bow. Using that, Adhiratha's son shot fierce arrows. He was resplendent in the battle, like the blazing solar disc, surrounded by a garland of rays. He pierced Shikhandi with twelve sharp arrows and the ratha Uttamouja with six. He pierced Yudhamanyu with three sharp arrows and the sons of Somaka and Prishata each with three arrows.[709] O venerable one! In the great battle, those five maharathas were defeated by the son of a suta. They were rendered immobile by that scorcher of enemies, just as the senses are vanquished by one with a controlled soul. They were submerged in the ocean that was Karna, like distressed merchants on an ocean. Droupadi's son rescued their maternal uncles[710] with well-prepared chariots, like providing boats on an ocean.

'"The bull among the Shini lineage used his sharp arrows to slice

[708]Dhrishtadyumna.

[709]Janamejaya is the son of Somaka and the son of Prishata (Drupada) is Dhrishtadyumna.

[710]Because these warriors were from Panchala.

down the many arrows that Karna shot. He struck Karna with sharp and iron arrows and pierced his eldest son[711] with eight arrows. Kripa, Bhoja,[712] your sons and Karna struck him back with sharp arrows. However, the supreme one amongst the Yadu lineage fought with them, like the guardians of the directions fighting with the lords of the daityas. His bow roared continuously and he showered down extremely fierce arrows. Satyaki became invincible, like the midday sun in the autumn sky. Those rathas[713] armoured themselves well and again attacked, desiring to protect the foremost one from the Shini lineage. The rathas from Panchala united in that great battle, like large numbers of Marut surrounding Shakra, when he was afflicting the enemy. An extremely terrible encounter commenced between them and those on your side who were engaged in your welfare. It was like an ancient one between gods and asuras and destroyed chariots, horses and elephants. Afflicted by many types of weapons, chariots, elephants, horses and foot soldiers wandered around. They struck each other and wavered. They uttered loud wails of lamentation and fell down, deprived of their lives.

'"At that time, without any fear, your son, the younger brother of the king,[714] showered arrows and advanced against Bhima. Vrikodara spiritedly encountered him, like a lion leaping on a large ruru deer. The battle between them was superhuman and was like a gambling match, with lives as stakes. They attacked each other fiercely and angrily, like Shakra and Shambara in earlier times. They severely struck each other with extremely energetic arrows that were capable of ending lives. They mangled each other, like two mighty elephants that are overcome with sexual desire and seek to indulge in intercourse.[715] With two kshurapra arrows, Vrikodara severed the bow and the standard of your son. He struck him in the forehead with an arrow and severed his charioteer's head from his body. The

[711]Vrishasena.

[712]Kritavarma.

[713]The five warriors from Panchala.

[714]Duhshasana.

[715]That is, they are fighting over the same she-elephant.

prince picked up another bow and struck Vrikodara with twelve arrows. He controlled the reins of the horses himself and again rained down arrows on Bhima."'

Chapter 1211(61)

'Sanjaya said, "Prince Duhshasana accomplished an extremely difficult task in that tumultuous battle. He severed Bhima's bow with a razor-sharp arrow and pierced his charioteer with six arrows. In an instant, the great-souled one then struck Bhimasena with many excellent arrows. Bhimasena hurled a fierce club towards him. It struck Duhshasana and flung him a distance of ten bow-lengths away, rendering him like a wounded elephant with shattered temples. He was struck and fell down, trembling. O Indra among kings! It[716] slew his horses and charioteer and having crushed the horses and the chariot, fell down. His armour, ornaments and garments were destroyed and, completely immobile, he shrieked in pain. The spirited Bhimasena remembered all the acts of enmity that had been performed by your sons. He jumped down from the chariot onto the ground and eagerly looked at him. He grasped an extremely sharp sword and placed it against the throat of the trembling one. He tore apart the breast of the one who had fallen down on the ground and drank the warm blood. He repeatedly savoured the taste. Then, excessively angry, he glanced at him and spoke these words. 'This is superior to mother's milk, honey, clarified butter, well-prepared liquor, celestial water and skimmed and churned milk. It is my view today, that the blood of my enemies is tastier than all of these.' He again repeated these cheerful and eloquent words. Whoever saw Bhimasena in that state then, fell down in distress and in fear. When the men fell down there, the weapons also fell down from their hands. Others were terrified and glanced at him with half-open eyes, uttering loud lamentations of woe. All those who saw Bhima drink

[716] The club.

Duhshasana's blood were terrified and miserable and ran away in different directions. They said, 'This one is not human.' In the hearing of the brave ones in the world, he[717] spoke these words. 'O worst of men! I am drinking the blood from your throat. In great rage, you repeatedly called us cattle. [718] When I was asleep in Pramanakoti, you fed me poison and made me suffer the hardship of being bitten by serpents.[719] You burnt us down in the house of lac. You robbed our kingdom through a gambling match and made us dwell in the woods. We were robbed of the happiness in our homes and suffered from weapons in battle. There were many other hardships and we have never known any joy. Dhritarashtra and his son have always acted maliciously towards us.' O king! O great king! Having spoken these words, Vrikodara, who had obtained victory, again spoke these words to Keshava and Arjuna. 'O brave ones! I had taken a vow about Duhshasana in the battle.[720] I have accomplished that today. I will accomplish the second vow now too, that of killing Duryodhana like a sacrificial animal. In the presence of the Kouravas, I will press down the evil-souled one's head with my foot and obtain peace.' Having spoken these words, he cheerfully roared, blood streaming from his body. The extremely powerful and great-souled one danced, like the one with one thousand eyes[721] after Vritra's death."'

Chapter 1212(62)

'Sanjaya said, "O king! Ten of your sons were brave and maharathas. They did not run away from the field of battle.

[717]Bhima.

[718]At the time of the gambling match, described in Section 27 (Volume 2).

[719]The Kouravas tried to poison Bhima in Pramanakoti. This has been described in Section 7 (Volume 1).

[720]At the time of the gambling match, Bhima took a pledge that he would kill Duhshasana in the battle and drink his blood.

[721]Indra has one thousand eyes.

When Duhshasana was slain, those immensely valiant ones were overcome with great rage and showered Bhima with arrows. Kavachi, Nishangi, Pashi, Dandadhara, Dhanurdhara, Alolupa, Shala, Sangha, Vatavega and Suvarchasa united and attacked together, overcome with grief on account of their brother. They enveloped the mighty-armed Bhimasena with arrows. He was restrained in every direction by the arrows of those maharathas. Bhima's eyes became red with rage and he looked like the wrathful Destroyer himself. Using ten immensely forceful broad-headed and sharp arrows that were gold-tufted and decorated with gold, Partha conveyed those ten to Yama's eternal abode. When those brave ones were killed, your soldiers ran away, afflicted by fear of the Pandavas, while the son of a suta looked on.

'"O great king! On witnessing Bhima's valour, like Yama amongst beings, Karna entered the great battle. O destroyer of enemies! On discerning what was going on in his mind, Shalya, the ornament of an assembly, realized that the time was right and spoke these words to Karna. 'O Radheya! Do not be distressed. This is not deserving of you. These kings are being driven away, afflicted by their fear of Bhimasena. Overcome with misery and grief on account of his brother, Duryodhana is numb. The great-souled one has drunk Duhshasana's blood. His mind is full of sorrow, and grief has robbed him of his senses. O Karna! Kripa and the others and the remaining brothers are tending to Duryodhana and have surrounded him from all directions. The brave Pandavas are unwavering in their aim. With Dhananjaya at the forefront, they are advancing towards you, stationing themselves in the battle. O tiger among men! Base yourself on your great manliness. Devoting yourself to the dharma of kshatriyas, fight against Dhananjaya. Dhritarashtra's son has placed the entire burden on you. O mighty-armed one! Shoulder it, to the best of your capacity and the best of your strength. If you are victorious, you will obtain great fame. If you are defeated, heaven is certain. O Radheya! The wrathful Vrishasena is your son. Since you are confused, he is advancing towards the Pandavas.' Hearing the words of the infinitely energetic Shalya, he came to the human conclusion that there was nothing to do but to base oneself well in the battle.

'"The angry Vrishasena was stationed on his chariot and wishing to slay the enemy, advanced against Vrikodara, who was like Yama with a staff in his hand, and with a club in his hand, was uprooting those on your side. Nakula, foremost among brave ones, was full of anger and attacked this enemy with arrows. He cheerfully attacked Karna's son in the battle, like Jishnu and Maghavan wishing to kill Jambha.[722] Using a razor-sharp arrow, the brave Nakula severed his standard, which had the complexion of a conch shell and sparkled like crystal. Karna's son possessed a colourful bow that was adorned with golden cloth. He severed this with a broad-headed arrow. Extremely quickly, Karna's son picked up another bow and pierced Pandava. Wishing to show his respect to Duhshasana, who had lost his life, the one who knew about great weapons, then struck Nakula with divine and great weapons. The great-souled Nakula was enraged and pierced him back with arrows that were like giant meteors. Karna's son was skilled in the use of weapons and pierced Nakula back with celestial weapons. O king! Karna's son slew all of Nakula's horses with supreme weapons. They were swift, delicate and pure, ornamented with gold, and were of the *vanayu* breed. When the horses were slain, he descended from his chariot and picked up a beautiful shield that was marked with the signs of eight moons. He also picked up a sword that sparkled like the sky. With these, he leapt up and roamed around, like a bird. He executed many wonderful motions in the air and sliced down the best of men, horses and elephants. They were struck by that sword and fell down on the ground, like animals at an *ashvamedha* sacrifice, struck by the executioner. There were two thousand warriors who found delight in battle. They were well trained and came from many different countries. They never missed their objective. The upper parts of their bodies were smeared with sandalwood paste. Quickly and single-handedly, Nakula brought them down. While they were falling down, he[723] attacked Nakula and pierced him from every direction with arrows. Nakula was thus struck by those arrows and angrily pierced

[722]Jambha was a demon killed by Vishnu and Indra.
[723]Vrishasena.

the brave one back in turn. Single-handedly, Karna's son struck men, horses, elephants and chariots. He pierced the brave one who seemed to be sporting[724] with eighteen arrows and was angrily pierced back in return. Wishing to kill him, Pandu's son, foremost among men, attacked Karna's son in that battle. In the great battle, Karna's son sliced down the shield, which was decorated with one thousand stars, with his arrows. The sword was extremely sharp, keen at the edges. It had been unsheathed and was capable of bearing a great load. It was extremely terrible and was being whirled around, used to sever the bodies of the enemy. It was as fierce in form as a serpent. With six sharp and extremely pointed arrows, he[725] shattered his enemy's sword. He then struck him again between the breasts with sharp and yellow arrows and pierced him grievously. Madri's son was tormented by Karna's son. His horses were slain. He jumped onto Bhimasena's chariot, like a lion leaping onto the summit of a mountain, while Dhananjaya looked on.

'"Nakula's bow and arrows had been severed. He was without a chariot and afflicted by arrows. He had been mangled by the weapons of Karna's son. On discerning this, the five foremost sons of Drupada, Shini's descendant as the sixth, and the five sons of Drupada's daughter, all destroyers of enemies, swiftly advanced against those on your side and devastated the elephants, chariots, men and horses. Those supreme men were cheerful and were on swift chariots drawn by speedy steeds. Their flags fluttered in the wind. They used hundreds of arrows and other weapons that resembled the lords of serpents. The foremost of rathas on your side, Hridika's son,[726] Kripa, Drona's son, Duryodhana, Shakuni, Shuka, Vrika, Kratha and Devavridha speedily countered them. They wielded bows and were on chariots that roared like elephants and clouds. Those best of men countered the eleven brave ones[727] and used supreme and fierce arrows to strike and repel them.

[724]Nakula.

[725]Vrishasena.

[726]Kritavarma.

[727]Five of Drupada's sons, Satyaki and five of Droupadi's sons.

'"Those on your side were in turn countered by Kunindas who were on elephants that were fierce in force and were like the summits of mountains, with complexions like that of newly formed clouds. They[728] had been prepared well, were crazy and were from the Himalaya regions. Accomplished riders who desired to fight were astride them. The elephants were beautifully covered with nets of gold and looked like clouds tinged with lightning. Using ten arrows that were completely made out of iron, the son of Kuninda[729] severely struck Kripa and his charioteer. However, slain by the arrows of Sharadvata's son, he fell down on the ground, together with his elephant. The younger brother of the son of Kuninda then struck, using javelins that were completely made out of iron and were as radiant as the sun's rays. He hurled these at his[730] chariot and roared loudly. But the lord of Gandhara[731] severed his head, while he was still roaring. When the Kunindas were slain, the maharathas on your side were delighted. They loudly blew on conch shells obtained from the ocean and with bows and arrows in their hands, attacked the enemy. An extremely terrible battle commenced again between the Kurus and the Pandus and Srinjayas. Arrows, swords, javelins, scimitars, clubs and battleaxes were fiercely used and men, horses and elephants destroyed. As they attacked and wounded each other, chariots, horses, elephants and foot soldiers fell down here and there. It was as if clouds tinged with lightining were stationed in the sky and were dispelled with fierce winds. Bhoja struck Shatanika, the mighty elephants, the chariots and the infantry on their side. Using his weapons, Kritavarma brought down the horses and the elephants. At that time, three elephants belonging to the enemy were struck by the arrows of Drona's son. All of them were ridden by warriors and sported flags. They lost their lives, shrieked and fell down, like large mountains shattered by the thunder. The third son of the king of Kuninda struck your

[728]The elephants.

[729]That is, the son of the king of Kuninda.

[730]Kripa's.

[731]Shakuni.

son[732] between the breasts with excellent arrows. Your son pierced his body and that of his elephant with sharp arrows. With the son of the king, that king of elephants fell down, with copious quantities of blood issuing forth. It was as if, at the onset of the moon, water mixed with red chalk was exuding from a mountain, when it had been struck by the vajra of Shachi's consort.[733] However, though struck, the son of Kuninda ascended another elephant and brought down Shuka, with his charioteer, horses and chariot. The lord Kratha[734] was afflicted by the arrows and fell down, like a mountain shattered by thunder. Seated astride an elephant, the invincible ratha from the mountainous regions[735] slew and brought down the lord of Kratha with arrows. He was brought down with his horses, charioteer and bow, like a giant tree struck by a mighty storm. Vrika used twelve arrows to severely strike the one who resided in the mountainous regions and was astride his elephant. However, using great speed in the battle, he brought down Vrika, with his four horses and chariot. But that king of elephants was severely struck and brought down by Babhru's son, together with its driver. Devavridha's son was also struck, slain and brought down by Sahadeva's son. The elephant of the son of Kuninda was capable of slaying the enemy with its tusks and body. It impetuously rushed towards Shakuni, wishing to kill him. The lord of Gandhara severed its head. Mighty elephants, horses, rathas and large numbers of infantry on your side were slain by Shatanika. They fell down on the ground, crushed and immobile, like trees devastated through a storm raised by Suparna.[736] The son of Kuninda smiled and shot many sharp arrows at Nakula's son.[737]

[732]Duryodhana.

[733]Indra is Shachi's consort.

[734]The text of the Critical edition confuses between Shuka and Kratha. In other editions, in this description, Kratha figures consistently.

[735]The prince of Kuninda.

[736]Suparna is Garuda and the storm is raised through his wings. The text uses the word naga, which can only be translated as tree. This is probably a typo and should read *naaga* or serpent. Given Garuda, that fits better.

[737]This entire section is replete with typos and this must be another one of those. Why should the son of Kuninda attack Nakula's son? It can only be

At this, Nakula's son used a razor-sharp arrow to sever his head, which was like a lotus, from his body.

'"Karna's son pierced Shatanika with three swift arrows and Arjuna with three more. He pierced Bhima with three arrows, Nakula with seven and Janardana with twelve. On witnessing that superhuman deed, all the Kurus were delighted and applauded him. But they also knew about Dhananjaya's valour and thought that he[738] was like an oblation that had been poured into the fire. Kiriti, the slayer of enemy heroes, saw that the best of men[739] was without his horses, which had been slain. In the battle, he attacked Vrishasena, who was stationed in front of the son of a suta. In that great battle, he descended, with thousands of arrows. On seeing him advance, Karna's maharatha son, fierce and foremost among men, also attacked, like Namuchi against Indra in ancient times.[740] The son of the son of a suta then pierced Partha with many wonderful arrows. The illustrious one roared loudly, like Namuchi in ancient times, after having pierced Shakra. Vrishasena used fierce arrows to again pierce Partha in his armpits. He struck Krishna with nine arrows and again struck Partha with ten sharp and fierce arrows. Kiriti became enraged in that field of battle and his forehead furrowed into three lines. The great-souled one shot arrows in the battle, designed to kill the son of a suta in the battle.[741] Kiriti pierced him violently in the inner organs with ten arrows. With four razor-sharp arrows, he severed his bow, his arms and his head. He was struck by Partha's arrows and fell down from the chariot onto the ground, deprived of his arms and head. He was like an extremely large and flowering shala tree, with a lot of leaves, which had been struck by a storm and brought down from the summit of a mountain. The son

rationalized, other than a typo, by presuming that some of the Kunindas also fought on the side of the Kouravas.

[738]Karna's son, Vrishasena.

[739]Nakula. The Critical edition excises a shloka where we are told that Vrishasena deprived Nakula of his horses.

[740]Namuchi was a demon killed by Indra.

[741]Meaning Vrishasena. Son is being used in the extended sense of a grandson.

of a suta saw that his son had been struck by arrows and had fallen down from his chariot. He was tormented because his son had been slain. Powerfully and violently, he advanced on his chariot towards the ratha Kiriti."'

Chapter 1213(63)

'Sanjaya said, "On seeing that Vrishasena had been killed, Karna was overcome by anger and rage. Sudden tears of sorrow flowed down from Vrisha's eyes. On his chariot, he spiritedly advanced towards the enemy. His eyes were coppery red with rage and he challenged Dhananjaya to a fight. Those two chariots were as radiant as the sun and were covered with tiger skins. When they encountered each other, it was as if two suns had clashed against each other. Those two men, scorchers of enemies, were like suns and were borne by white horses. Those two great-souled ones were as radiant as the sun and the moon in the sky. O venerable one! On seeing them, all the beings were astounded. They looked like Indra and Virochana's son,[742] embarking on a conquest of the three worlds. There was the clatter of chariots, the twang of bowstrings, the slapping of palms, the whizzing of arrows and the blare of conch shells. As they advanced on their chariots, all the lords of the earth looked on. As they clashed against each other, the standards generated great wonder. Karna's had the housing of an elephant and Kiriti's the ape. O descendant of the Bharata lineage! As the two chariots clashed against each other, the kings looked on. They emitted roars like lions and voiced loud words of applause. On hearing about the duel between them, the warriors gathered around there. They slapped their arms powerfully and forcefully waved their garments around. The Kurus assembled there. Wishing to cheer Karna, they blew loudly on their conch shells and instructed that musical instruments

[742] Virochana's son was the demon Bali.

should be played. All the Pandavas also cheered Dhananjaya. They caused trumpets and conch shells to be sounded in all the directions. The roars generated a tumultuous sound everywhere. As Karna and Arjuna clashed, the brave ones slapped their arms. They saw that those two tigers among men, supreme among rathas, were stationed on their chariots. They grasped their giant bows, arrows, javelins, clubs and other weapons. They were armoured and had girded their swords. They were borne on white horses that were as beautiful as conch shells. Both of them possessed the best of quivers and were handsome. They were smeared with red sandalwood paste on their limbs and were as crazy as bulls. They were like venomous serpents and like Yama, the Destroyer, in their rage. They were as wrathful as Indra and Vritra and as resplendent as the sun and the moon. They were as cruel as mighty planets that clash at the end of a yuga. They were born from gods. They were the equals of the gods. They were like the gods in their beauty. Those two tigers among men, Karna and Dhananjaya, clashed and it was a sight worth seeing. Both of them possessed the best of weapons and both of them were exhausted from fighting. Both of them made the sky resound with the slapping of their arms. Both of them were famous for their deeds, their manliness and their strength. In a battle, both of them were the equals of Shambara and the king of the immortals. In an encounter, both of them were the equals of Kartavirya[743] and Dasharatha's son. Both of them possessed valour that was like Vishnu's bravery and both were Bhava's[744] equal in a fight. O king! Both were borne on white horses and on supreme chariots. The charioteers of those immensely strong ones were the best. O great king! On seeing those two blazing maharathas, there was great amazement among the large numbers of siddhas and charanas. O bull among the Bharata lineage! The sons of Dhritarashtra quickly surrounded Karna, the ornament of a battle, with their army. In similar fashion, with Dhrishtadyumna at the forefront, the Pandavas joyfully surrounded the great-souled Partha, who was unmatched in a battle. O lord of the earth! For those

[743]Karavirya Arjuna.

[744]Bhava is Shiva.

on your side, Karna became the stake in the battle. In that way, for the Pandaveyas, Partha became the stake in the battle. The troops on both sides, and those who had assembled, were eager to witness the encounter. The stakes were determined and it was certain that there would be victory, or there would be defeat. Stationed on the field of battle, the gambling match between us and the Pandavas commenced, with the objective of victory, or its reverse. O great king! Those two, who were skilled in fighting, were stationed in the encounter. They were extremely angry towards each other and wished to defeat each other. Like Indra and Vritra, they wished to kill each other. They assumed fearful forms, like planets trailing a lot of smoke.

'"O bull among the Bharata lineage! As they took sides between Karna and Arjuna, there were differences, debates, dissension and arguments among those in the sky and among all beings. O venerable one! The directions and all the worlds also adopted different sides. When Karna and Arjuna clashed, the gods, the danavas, the gandharvas, the pishachas, the serpents and the rakshasas adopted different sides. O lord of the earth! The sky and the nakshatras became anxious on Karna's account.[745] O descendant of the Bharata lineage! The extensive earth was anxious on Partha's account, like a mother for her son.[746] O supreme among men! The rivers, the oceans, the mountains, the trees and the herbs took Kiriti's side. O scorcher of enemies! The asuras, the *yatudhanas*, the *guhyakas*, crows and others who travelled through the sky were on Karna's side. The stores of all gems, the Vedas and accounts as the fifth,[747] the minor Vedas, the Upanishads, with collections of their commentaries, Vasuki, Chitrasena, Takshaka, Upatakshaka, all the mountains, Kadru's offspring and immensely wrathful and virulent serpents were on Arjuna's side.[748] Airavata's

[745]Presumably because Karna was the son of the sun god.

[746]Presumably because Arjuna was the son of Pritha (Kunti) and earth is known as *prithvi*. Kunti personified the earth.

[747]Accounts (the two epics and the Puranas) are regarded as the fifth Veda.

[748]Kadru was married to the sage Kashyapa and was the mother of all the serpents. Since Arjuna burnt down the serpents in Khandava, the serpents

offspring, the offspring of Surabhi and Vaishali and the serpents were on Arjuna's side.[749] The smaller snakes were on Karna's side. O king! The wolves, jackals and all the auspicious animals and birds were on Partha's side, wishing for his victory. The Vasus, the Maruts, the Sadhyas, the Rudras, the Vishvas,[750] the Ashvins, Agni, Indra, the moon god, the wind god and the ten directions were on Dhananjaya's side, while the Adityas were on Karna's side.[751] The gods, together with the large number of ancestors, were on Arjuna's side. Yama, Vaishravana[752] and Varuna were also with Arjuna. The gods, the brahmanas, the kings and the large number of rishis were with Pandava. O king! The gandharvas, with Tumburu at the head, were with Arjuna. The descendants of Prava and Muni, the large numbers of gandharvas and apsaras,[753] wolves, predatory beasts, animals, birds, large numbers of chariots, different forms of clouds and winds, and sages assembled there to witness the clash between Karna and Arjuna. O great king! The gods, the danavas, the

should have been on Karna's side. However, as a succeeding shloka explains, the serpents were divided.

[749]Surabhi was married to the sage Kashyapa and was the mother of cattle. Vaishali is a reference to the princess Vaishali, daughter of King Vishala. Her story is recounted in the Puranas. She gave birth to the famous King Marut, who was an emperor who ruled over the entire earth. The reference to Vaishali's offspring is not obvious. Serpents mentioned again require an explanation. The earlier reference to serpents was to serpents in general. Here, the reference is to specific serpents who live in Bhogavati, the capital city of nagas.

[750]The Vishvadevas.

[751]In general, the Adityas are the sons of Aditi and Kashyapa, that is, the gods. There is no reason for the gods to be on Karna's side, especially because some of them (Vasus, Maruts, Sadhyas, Rudras, Vishvadevas, Agni, Indra, Soma (the moon god) and Pavana (the wind god) have just been mentioned to be on Arjuna's side. However, in a narrower sense, the twelve Adityas are the manifestations of the sun for the twelve months. It is these who were on Karna's side, Karna being the son of the sun god.

[752]Kubera.

[753]Prava is a typo. It should be Pradha. Kashyapa married Pradha and the gandharvas were the offspring. Kashyapa married Muni and the apsaras were the offspring.

gandharvas, the nagas, the yakshas, birds, maharshis learned in the Vedas, the ancestors who thrive on *svadha* oblations,[754] austerities, learning and the herbs, in many different forms and attires, took up their places in the firmament and this created a great noise. Brahma, with the *brahmarshi*s and the Prajapatis[755] and Bhava,[756] on his celestial chariot, also arrived at the spot.

'"On seeing that Prajapati,[757] the self-creating one, had arrived, the gods spoke to him. 'O god! Let this struggle for victory between these two lions among men be pacified.' Hearing this, Maghavan[758] prostrated himself before the grandfather and said, 'Let the entire universe not be destroyed because of Karna and Arjuna. O self-creating one! You had earlier said that Vijaya and the other one[759] are identical. O illustrious one! I am bowing down before you. Be pacified and let that be true.' Brahma and Ishana[760] spoke these words to the lord of the thirty gods. 'The victory of the great-souled Vijaya is certain. He is spirited, powerful and brave. He is skilled in the use of weapons and is rich in austerities. Great energy is manifested in him, especially in dhanurveda. Through his greatness, he is capable of overcoming destiny. He is capable of controlling and overcoming the worlds. When the two Krishnas are angered, no one is capable of standing before them. Those two bulls among men are truly the creators of the universe. They are the ancient and supreme rishis Nara and

[754]Svadha is the exclamation made when oblations are offered to the ancestors.

[755]Prajapati is a name for Brahma, as well as for guardians of the world. Since Brahma has been separately mentioned, the Prajapatis here are the guardians of the world.

[756]Shiva.

[757]This Prajapati means Brahma.

[758]Indra.

[759]Vijaya is Arjuna. The other one seems to be a reference to Krishna. It is difficult to make sense of these shlokas, especially because the Critical edition excises some shlokas where Indra sides with Arjuna and Surya with Karna. But the gist is that Indra wants Arjuna to win.

[760]Shiva.

Narayana.[761] Those two scorchers of enemies control everything and cannot be controlled by anyone. Karna, foremost in the worlds, is a bull among men. Vaikartana is brave and valiant. But let the two Krishnas be victorious. With Drona and Bhishma, let him[762] obtain the great world of heaven and the worlds of the Vasus and the Maruts.' Having heard the words spoken by those two gods of the gods and abiding by the instructions of Brahma and Ishana, the one with the one thousand eyes spoke these words to all the beings. 'You have heard what the two illustrious ones have said for the welfare of the universe. It must happen that way and cannot be countered. Therefore, do not be anxious.' O venerable one! O king! Having heard Indra's words, all the beings were astounded and honoured him. The gods showered down many kinds of fragrant flowers from the sky and sounded divine trumpets. To witness the unmatched duel between those two lions among men, all the gods, danavas and gandharvas waited.

'"The two chariots were yoked to white horses. They possessed standards and made a loud noise. The brave ones from the world assembled and separately blew on their conch shells. O descendant of the Bharata lineage! So did the brave Vasudeva and Arjuna and Karna and Shalya. The battle that generated terror among cowards commenced. They rivalled each other in their valour, like Shakra and Shambara. The two clear and radiant standards were fixed to the chariots. As they angrily prepared to fight each other, they[763] were thick. Karna's resplendent one was marked with an elephant's housing. It was bejewelled and firm, like Purandara's bow, and like a venomous serpent. The best of apes opened its terrible and gaping mouth on Partha's. It was extremely fierce and difficult to look at, like the sun. Stationed on the standard of the wielder of Gandiva, it desired a fight. It roared loudly and flung itself on Karna's standard. Having descended with great force, the ape used its nails and its teeth to destroy the elephant's housing, like Garuda

[761]Nara being identified with Arjuna and Narayana with Krishna.

[762]Karna.

[763]The standards.

against serpents. The elephant's housing was well decorated with bells. It was like Yama's noose and was hard as iron. It angrily attacked the giant ape. As those two excellent ones challenged each other to a duel, the standards began to fight each other, wishing to destroy each other.

'"Pundarikaksha pierced Shalya with the arrows of his sight and he also glanced back at Pundarikaksha in a similar way. Using the arrows of his sight, Vasudeva defeated Shalya. Kunti's son, Dhananjaya, also glanced at Karna with his sight and vanquished him. At this, the son of a suta smiled and told Shalya, 'O friend! If through some means, Partha slays me in the battle today, what will you do after that? Tell me truthfully.' Shalya replied, 'O Karna! If the one with the white horses kills you in the battle today, I will slay both Madhava and Pandava.' In that way, Arjuna also asked Govinda. However, Krishna laughed and spoke these supreme words to Partha. 'The sun may fall down from its place. The earth may shatter into many fragments. The fire may become cold. But Karna will not be able to kill Dhananjaya. However, if this does happen, the world will be destroyed. Using my arms in the battle, I will kill Karna and Shalya.' Having heard Krishna's words, the one with the ape on his banner laughed. Arjuna told Krishna, the performer of undecaying deeds, 'O Janardana! Karna and Shalya together are not sufficient for me. In the battle today, you will see Karna severed into many fragments with my arrows, with Karna's flags and standard, with Shalya, the chariot and the horses, with his umbrella and armour, and with his javelins, arrows and bow. In earlier times, he laughed at Krishna.[764] Today, you will see Karna uprooted by me, like a flowering tree brought down by a maddened elephant. O Madhusudana! After that, you will hear pleasant words today. Today, you will be able to comfort Abhimanyu's mother and repay her debt. O Janardana! Kunti, your father's sister, will be delighted. O Madhava! The tears on Krishna's[765] face will be comforted today. You will be able to speak immortal words to Dharmaraja Yudhishthira.'"'

[764]Krishnaa, Droupadi.

[765]Krishnaa's, that is, Droupadi's.

Chapter 1214(64)

'Sanjaya said, "With nagas, asuras, large numbers of siddhas, gandharvas, yakshas, large numbers of apsaras, brahmarshis, rajarshis and groups of birds, the sky was beautiful in form. There were pleasant sounds of musical instruments. There were sounds of praise. There was singing and dancing. All those in the sky, and men, were spectators. The sky assumed a beautiful form. Cheerfully, the warriors on the Kuru and Pandava sides made the earth and the directions resound with their musical instruments, the sounds of arrows and weapons and leonine roars. With that sound, they began to slaughter their enemies. The field of battle had many horses, elephants and chariots and it was extremely difficult to withstand, because of the descent of supreme swords, javelins and scimitars. As they attacked, bodies were slain and it was red and beautiful because of the blood. As the battle commenced, Dhananjaya and Adhiratha's son, supreme among wielders of weapons, used their sharp and swift arrows against the soldiers in all directions. They were armoured and showered these towards each other.[766] Because of the darkness that was created by the arrows, those on one's own side could not be distinguished from that of the enemy. Since they[767] were terrified, they sought refuge with those two rathas, who were like the extending rays of the sun at the end of darkness. Those two countered each other's weapons with their own, like the east wind clashing against the west wind. They were as radiant as two suns, dispelling the thick darkness after the sun has arisen. Each encouraged those on his side to take a stand against the enemy. The two maharathas were surrounded in every direction, like the gods and the asuras around Vasava and Shambara. O descendant of the Bharata lineage! Drums, smaller drums and battle drums were sounded. There was the blare of conch shells. This mingled with roars like lions. Those two supreme among men were dazzling, like the sun and the moon amidst a thick mass of clouds. Both of them possessed large bows

[766]Towards each other's soldiers.

[767]The soldiers on either side.

drawn into circles, like radiant solar discs, with thousands of arrows as the rays. They were extremely unassailable in battle and were like two suns that had arisen at the end of a yuga to destroy all mobile and immobile objects in the universe. They were both invincible and capable of destroying ill-wishers. They were accomplished and wished to kill each other. In the great battle, Karna and Pandava, supreme among brave ones, clashed, like Indra and Jambha. Those two great archers released great weapons and terrible arrows. As they sought to kill each other with supreme arrows, they slaughtered large numbers of men, horses and elephants. Terrified and afflicted again by those arrows, the Kurus and Pandavas sought refuge with those two supreme among men. Elephants, foot soldiers, horses and chariots fled in various directions, like residents of a forest out of fear for a lion.

'"Duryodhana, Bhoja, Soubala, Kripa and Sharadvata's son—these five maharathas attacked Dhananjaya and Achyuta with arrows that could destroy the body. Dhananjaya used his arrows to destroy their bows, arrows, horses, standards, chariots and charioteers. Having countered and defeated them, he struck the son of a suta with twelve supreme arrows. At this, one hundred chariots, one hundred elephants, riders from Shakas, Tukharas and Yavanas and the best of Kambojas attacked Arjuna, desiring to kill him. However, Dhananjaya used razor-sharp arrows to swiftly sever the supreme weapons in their hands, heads, horses, elephants and chariots of the large numbers of the enemy who were fighting against him. The assembled gods in the sky were delighted and applauded by sounding their trumpets. Showers of beautiful and fragrant flowers were rained down. Auspicious winds began to blow. O king! Gods, men and beings who witnessed that wonderful sight were amazed. However, your son and the son of a suta certainly felt neither pain, nor wonder. Drona's son grasped your son's hand in his own hand and comforted him. He said, 'O Duryodhana! Be pacified. Make peace with the Pandavas. There is no need for dissension. Shame on war. Your preceptor[768] was Brahma's equal and knew about great weapons. He

[768]Drona.

has been killed and so have bulls among men, with Bhishma as the foremost. I cannot be killed and neither can my maternal uncle.[769] Together with the Pandavas, enjoy the kingdom for a long time. Restrained by me, Dhananjaya will withdraw. Janardana does not desire a conflict either. Yudhishthira is always engaged in the welfare of beings. Vrikodara is obedient to him and so are the twins. If there is peace between you and Partha,[770] all the subjects will be fortunate and that seems to be your desire too. Let the remaining kings return to their own cities. Let the soldiers refrain from hostilities. O lord of men! If you do not listen to my words, you are certain to be slain by the enemies in the battle and will repent. This universe, and you, has seen what the one with the diadem and the garland[771] has single-handedly accomplished. This has not been accomplished by the destroyer of Bala,[772] Yama, the illustrious Prachetas[773] and the king of the yakshas.[774] There are many other qualities that Dhananjaya possesses. He will not transgress my words. He will act so as to follow you. O king! For the benefit of the world, be pacified. You have always shown me great honour and I have reciprocated. I am your great well-wisher and that is the reason I am speaking these words. If you are inclined towards affection, I will restrain Karna too. Those who are learned say that there are four kinds of friends—those who are natural friends, those who are made such through conciliation, those who are earned through riches and those who are subjugated through power. Towards you, the Pandavas are all four. O brave one! They are naturally your relatives. Make them that through conciliation. O Indra among kings! If they are pacified and become friends towards you, it is certain that you should also act in that

[769]Ashvatthama and Kripa were immortal. There are seven immortals. In addition to Ashvatthama and Kripa, these are Bali, Parashurama, Vibhishana, Vyasa and Hanumana.

[770]Yudhishthira.

[771]Arjuna.

[772]Indra.

[773]One of the guardians of the world (Prajapati), sometimes identified with Daksha.

[774]Kubera.

way.' Having heard the beneficial words spoken by his well-wisher, he[775] thought for some time. He sighed and, distressed in his mind, replied, 'O friend! It is as you have said. However, listen to the words that I will tell you. Vrikodara is evil-minded. He slew Duhshasana like a tiger, and laughing, spoke many words. Those are still lodged in my heart. They were uttered in your presence. How can there be peace? O son of my preceptor! O unblemished one! You should not speak to Karna and try to restrain him. Phalguna is overcome by great exhaustion. Karna will kill him in a short while.' Humbly and respectfully, your son repeatedly spoke these words and instructed his soldiers, 'Attack and kill those who seek to injure us. Why is the sound of arrows not heard and why is everything quiet?'"'

Chapter 1215(65)

'Sanjaya said, "The blare of conch shells and the beating of drums became loud. Those two best among men, Vaikartana, the son of a suta, and Arjuna, borne on white horses, clashed against each other. O king! This was because of the evil counsels of your son. They were like two elephants with shattered temples from the Himalayas, attacking each other with their tusks in a desire for intercourse.[776]The brave Dhananjaya and Adhiratha's son rushed against each other with fierce force, as they willed. It was like a cloud dashing against another cloud, or a mountain against another mountain. The twang of bowstrings and the sound of palms could be heard. The wheels of the chariots rattled. They clashed and showered down arrows. They were like large mountain tops, covered with trees and herbs and populated by many kinds of dwellers of mountains, dashing against each other. As they struck each other with great weapons, those two immensely strong ones were like mountains that had

[775]Duryodhana.

[776]Contending for the same she-elephant.

been dislodged. The clash between those two great ones was like that between the lord of the gods and Virochana's son[777] in ancient times. Arrows mangled their bodies and those of their charioteers and horses. This was impossible for others to withstand. Blood began to flow like water. It was as if there were two large ponds filled with lotuses, lilies, fish and turtles and resounding with the calls of a large number of birds. It was as if they were being gently stirred by the wind. Those two chariots, with standards, were like that and they approached each other. Each of them possessed a valour that was like that of the great Indra. Those two maharathas were as resplendent as the great Indra. Their arrows were like the vajra of the great Indra. They attacked each other, like the great Indra and Vṛitra. Both armies possessed elephants, foot soldiers, horses and chariots. There were diverse colourful ornaments and garments. Everyone, including those in the sky, trembled and was astounded at the clash between Karna and Arjuna. The spectators raised their arms, with diamonds on their fingers. They were delighted and roared like lions. Adhiratha's son attacked Arjuna, wishing to kill him, like a crazy elephant against another elephant. The Somakas roared and urged Partha on. 'O Arjuna! Speed up. Pierce Karna. Sever his sparkling head without any delay. This is because of the greed that Dhritarashtra's son has for the kingdom.' In similar fashion, many warriors from our side exclaimed, 'O Karna! Proceed. Advance. O Karna! Slay Arjuna without any delay. Let the Parthas again be banished to the forest for a long time.'

'"With ten great arrows, Karna struck Partha first. Extremely angry, Arjuna pierced him back in the flanks with ten sharp and fierce arrows. The son of a suta and Arjuna struck and wounded each other with extremely sharp arrows. So as to crush each other, they sought for a weakness in the adversary. Cheerfully, but fiercely, they attacked each other in the great conflict. In the great conflict, the great-souled Bhimasena became wrathful and intolerant. He squeezed his hands and bit his lips with his teeth. Dancing around like a musician, he asked, 'O Kiriti! How was it that the son of a

[777]Bali.

suta was able to pierce you first with ten great arrows? Do you remember the fortitude with which you defeated all beings and satisfied Agni in Khandava? Use that fortitude and kill the son of a suta. Otherwise, let me bring him down with a club.' On seeing that Partha's arrows were being repulsed, Vasudeva spoke to him. 'O Kiriti! How is it that in every way, your weapons today are being countered by Karna's weapons? O brave one! Why do you look like someone who is confused? The Kurus are cheerfully roaring. All of them are honouring Karna, knowing that all your weapons have been destroyed by his. In yuga after yuga, you have used fortitude to destroy the weapons of darkness and terrible rakshasas. You slew Dambhodbhava and other asuras in encounters.[778] Use that fortitude and slay the son of a suta. Or use this *sudarshana* chakra now and slice off his head. It is sharp at the edges and even the immortals cannot withstand it. It has been used by me earlier, like Shakra using the vajra to strike Namuchi. The illustrious one, in the form of a hunter, was pleased by your greatness and fortitude.[779] Resort to that fortitude again and slay the son of a suta, together with his relatives. Give this earth, right up to the frontiers of the ocean, prosperous with its towns and villages, to the king.[780] O Partha! Having slain large numbers of the enemy, obtain unlimited fame.' Having been thus urged by both Bhima and Janardana, he glanced towards his own self and remembered his spirit.

'"The great-souled one knew the reason for his birth and spoke to Keshava. 'I will release a great and fierce weapon for the welfare of the worlds and for the death of the son of a suta. Let me have your permission, that of the gods, Brahma, Bhava and all the ones who are knowledgeable about the brahman.' Having said this, he

[778]Dambhodbhava was a king who attacked the sages Nara and Narayana, the incident having been described in Section 54 (Volume 4). The name Dambhodbhava signifies someone who is inordinately insolent and proud. In some versions of the Mahabharata, Dambhodbhava is equated with Karna. Dambhodbhava was reborn as Karna.

[779]Arjuna fought with Shiva, who was in the disguise of a hunter, and pleased him. This has been described in Section 31 (Volume 2).

[780]Yudhishthira.

invoked the invincible brahmastra in his mind, in accordance with the prescribed rites. All the directions and sub-directions were covered by extremely energetic arrows. O bull among the Bharata lineage! Many hundreds of swift arrows were released from it. In the midst of this, Vaikartana also created many thousands of arrows. These descended on Pandava with a large roar, like showers of rain released from a cloud. He performed a superhuman deed and pierced Bhimasena, Janardana and Kiriti with three arrows each. Terrible in his strength, he then emitted a loud and fierce roar. Kiriti saw that Bhima and Janardana had also been struck by Karna's arrows. He became intolerant and shot eighteen arrows again. He pierced Sushena with one arrow, Shalya with four and Karna with three. He then shot ten excellent arrows and killed Sabhapati,[781] who was clad in golden armour. The head and the arms of that prince were severed. He was without his charioteer, bow and standard. He was mangled and fell down from the chariot, like a shala tree sliced down with an axe. He again pierced Karna with three, eight, two and fourteen arrows. He slew four hundred elephants, stocked with weapons, eight hundred rathas, one thousand horses and riders and eight thousand valiant foot soldiers. Karna and Partha fought on. They were the best of the brave and the slayers of enemies. The spectators, who were assembled in the sky and on earth, controlled their mounts and watched what was going on in the battle.

'"Pandava's bowstring was being drawn with great force and snapped, with a loud noise. At that moment, the son of a suta struck Partha with one hundred *kshudraka* arrows. He pierced Vasudeva with sixty sharp iron arrows that were washed in oil and were tufted with the feathers of birds. They were like snakes that had cast off their skins. At this, the Somakas ran away. Partha became extremely angry. His body was mangled by Karna's arrows. He stretched his bowstring and swiftly countered the arrows of Adhiratha's son. He made the Somakas return. The sky was darkened because of this release of weapons and birds were unable to fly. Partha pierced Shalya's body armour with ten arrows and laughed. He pierced

[781]A Kourava warrior.

Karna with twelve well-aimed arrows and pierced him again with another seven. He was firmly struck by Partha's forceful arrows. Those arrows were fierce in their power. His body was mangled and his limbs were wounded. Karna looked as beautiful as Rudra at the time of destruction. Dhananjaya was the equal of the lord of the gods. However, Adhiratha's son struck him with three arrows. Wishing to slay Achyuta, he next shot five arrows that were like flaming serpents. They were decorated with gold and were aimed well. They pierced Purushottama's armour with great force and passing through, entered the earth. Having bathed there, they returned to Karna. Quickly, with well-aimed and broad-headed arrows, Dhananjaya sliced each of them into three fragments and they fell down on the ground. They were mighty serpents that were on the side of Takshaka's son.[782] The one with the diadem and the garland flamed in rage, like a fire that burns down dead wood. He drew his bow all the way back to his ears and shot many flaming arrows that were capable of bringing an end to the body. They pierced him[783] in the inner organs and made him waver. However, he was extremely patient and used that fortitude to withstand the grief. O king! Dhananjaya angrily covered Karna's chariot, all the directions and the sub-directions with his torrents of arrows. These shrouded the radiance of the sun. The sky also seemed to disappear, as if it was covered in snow. On the instructions of Duryodhana, there were those who were guarding the chariot wheels, the feet, the front and the rear.[784] These were excellent rathas and the best. In the battle, Savyasachi slew all of them. He killed two thousand of the foremost Kurus, bulls among the Kuru lineage. O king! In a short instant, the brave one single-handedly destroyed all of them, with their chariots, horses and charioteers. They fled, abandoning Karna. And so did your son and the Kurus who were left. They abandoned those who were slain and wounded by the

[782]Much is left implicit. Takshaka's son was Ashvasena, who vowed revenge on Arjuna because Arjuna had burnt down the serpents in Khandava. The five serpents went to the nether regions, where the capital city of the nagas, Bhogavati, is located. They bathed in the waters there and returned to Karna.

[783]Karna.

[784]Of Karna.

arrows, including lamenting sons and fathers. All the directions were emptied and devoid of Kurus, because they were afflicted by fear. O descendant of the Bharata lineage! However, on seeing this, Karna wasn't distressed. Cheerfully, he attacked Arjuna."'

Chapter 1216(66)

'Sanjaya said, "They fled because of that descent of arrows. The soldiers of the Kurus were routed. However, they waited at a distance and glanced back, gazing at Dhananjaya's weapons, which were descending like lightning in all directions. In that great battle, the angry Partha quickly unleashed a weapon to slay Karna. However, while Arjuna's weapon was still travelling and roaring through the air, the brave one destroyed it with a great weapon that he had obtained from Atharvan Rama[785] and which was capable of destroying enemies. Having destroyed Arjuna's weapon, he struck Partha with innumerable sharp arrows. O king! The clash between Arjuna and Adhiratha's son assumed a great and dreadful form. They struck each other with arrows, like two fierce elephants goring each other with their tusks. Karna affixed an extremely sharp and flaming arrow that was capable of slaying the enemy. This had a serpent in its mouth.[786] That terrible arrow had been carefully preserved and washed well, protected well for Partha's destruction. It had been worshipped and laid down on a bed of sandalwood paste. That immensely virulent weapon was lying down in a golden quiver. It was generated from the lineage of Airavata[787] and flamed. Wishing to kill Phalguna in the battle, he aimed at his head. On seeing that

[785]Parashurama. Atharvan can simply be interpreted as wise. Alternatively, the Atharvan lineage was often mentioned in conjunction with the Bhrigu lineage, from which, Parashurama was descended.

[786]This was the serpent Ashvasena, desiring to take revenge on Arjuna.

[787]This means the serpent Airavata, from whom, Ashvasena was descended.

Vaikartana had affixed that arrow, the great-souled king of Madra said, 'O Karna! This arrow will not be able to reach his neck. Fix and aim another arrow that can sever his head.' With eyes that were red with rage, Karna affixed that arrow and told Shalya, 'O Shalya! Karna will not affix a second arrow. Someone like me does not engage in deceit.' Having said this, he released that arrow, the serpent which he had worshipped for many years. He said, 'O Phalguna! You have been slain,' and swiftly shot the arrow. On seeing that Karna had affixed the serpent, Madhava, supreme among strong ones, used his strength to press down on the chariot with his feet. The chariot sank down on the ground and the horses sank down on their knees.

'"The arrow struck down the intelligent one's diadem. The ornament that adorned Arjuna's head was famous throughout the earth, heaven and the waters. In his anger and through the strength of his weapon, the son of a suta used the arrow to bring it down from his head. It possessed the flaming radiance of the sun, the moon and the planets. It was decorated with nets of gold, pearls and gems. Using his austerities and efforts, this had been crafted for Purandara by the earth's son himself. [788] It was extremely expensive in form and generated terror amongst the enemy. It was fragrant and brought happiness to the one who wore it. When he killed the enemies of the gods, [789] the lord of the gods was delighted and himself gave it to Kiriti. It could not be destroyed by Hara, the lord of the waters or the protector of riches,[790] and by the *pinaka*, *pasha* or vajra[791] and the best of arrows. The supreme gods were incapable of withstanding it. However, using the serpent, Vrisha now destroyed it. The flame of the poison uprooted it from his head and brought the beloved crown, with flaming rays, down on the ground. Partha's supreme diadem fell down, like the blazing sun setting over Mount Asta. The crown was

[788]There is a typo here that is difficult to unravel. The crown was given by Purandara (Indra) to Arjuna. It had been constructed by Brahma, the earth's creator. Therefore, the text should probably read earth's creator and not earth's son. However, this is more than a simple typo.

[789]Described in Section 32 (Volume 2).

[790]Shiva, Varuna and Kubera respectively.

[791]Respectively the weapons of Shiva, Yama and Indra.

decorated with many gems. The serpent forcefully tore it down from Arjuna's head. It was as if an excellent mountain top, with shoots and blossoming trees, was struck down by the great Indra's vajra. O descendant of the Bharata lineage! The earth, the sky, heaven and the waters seemed to be whirled around by a tempest. Such a noise arose on earth then. Though they tried to control themselves, people were distressed and trembled. But Arjuna was not distressed. He tied the hair on his head with a white garment. The serpent released from Karna's arms was extremely radiant, like the rays of the sun. That giant serpent was firm in its enmity of Arjuna. It struck the diadem and fell down. It told him,[792] 'Know who I am. I am firm in my enmity of the two Krishnas, because they slew my mother.'[793] In the battle, Krishna then spoke to Partha. 'The giant serpent is firm in its enmity. Slay it.' Having been thus addressed by Madhusudana, the wielder of Gandiva, fierce in using the bow and arrow against enemies, asked, 'Who is the serpent who is advancing against me of his own accord, as if into Garuda's gaping mouth?' Krishna replied, 'In Khandava, you satisfied the blazing one[794] with the bow in your hand. You killed his mother, taking her to be a single snake. However, though her body was destroyed by the arrows, he was in the sky, covered by her.' The serpent was falling down from the sky. Jishnu severed the serpent with six sharp arrows. Mangled in its body, it fell down on the ground.

'"At the time, Karna, foremost among brave men, glanced sideways at Dhananjaya and pierced him with ten arrows that had been sharpened on stone and were tufted with the feathers of peacocks. Arjuna drew his bow all the way back up to his ears and struck him with twelve sharp arrows. Those iron arrows were like venomous serpents in their force. He drew his bow all the way back

[792]Karna.

[793]The Critical edition excises some shlokas. In those, Ashvasena returns and asks Karna to shoot the arrow again. More specifically, the first time, Karna shot the arrow without looking at Ashvasena and that was the reason it failed. Ashvasena asks him to shoot the arrow a second time, after taking a look at him. However, Karna refuses to use the same arrow a second time.

[794]The fire god.

up to his ears and shot them. They were released well. They shattered his supreme and colourful armour, as if they were robbing him of his life. Having drunk Karna's blood, they penetrated the ground, with the tufts smeared with blood. Vrisha became extremely angry at being struck by the arrows, like a giant serpent that has been beaten with a staff. He swiftly shot supreme arrows that were like giant serpents with excellent poison. He struck Janardana with twelve arrows and Arjuna with ninety-nine. Karna again pierced Pandava with terrible arrows and roared loudly. Pandava could not tolerate this joy. He was like Indra in his valour. He shot supreme arrows, like Indra energetically striking Bala. Arjuna shot ninety arrows at Karna and each of them was like Yama's staff. Those arrows severely mangled his body, like a mountain shattered by thunder. The crown on his head was decorated with gems and diamonds and he wore excellent earrings. These were severed by Dhananjaya's arrows and fell down. His radiant and excellent armour was carefully crafted by the best of craftsmen over a long period of time. It was extremely expensive. In an instant, Pandava shattered this into many fragments with his arrows. Having deprived him of his armour with those excellent arrows, he then angrily struck him with four arrows. Distressed and struck by his enemy, he was like a diseased person, suffering from bile, phlegm, wind and wounds. Arjuna spiritedly shot sharp arrows from the great circle of his bow. He made great efforts and struck with strength. Karna was struck by many supreme arrows and they penetrated his inner organs. Karna was struck by many of Partha's sharp arrows. He was severely wounded by those arrows that were fierce and forceful. He looked as beautiful as a mountain with red chalk, from which, streams of red water were flowing down the slopes. O descendant of the Bharata lineage! Kiriti struck Karna and his horses and his chariot with vatsadanta arrows. Making every effort, he used gold-tufted arrows to envelope the directions. When he was struck in his broad chest by those vatsadanta arrows, Adhiratha's son looked resplendent. He looked like a blossoming ashoka, *palasha* or *shalmali* tree, or like a trembling mountain with many sandalwood trees. O lord of the earth! With those many arrows stuck to his body, Karna looked beautiful in the battle. He looked like a valley in a mountain, covered with many large trees, or like a giant mountain, with sparkling *karnikara* trees.

'"Karna also shot a large number of arrows from his bow. With those nets of arrows as rays, he looked dazzling. He was like the sun advancing towards sunset, red and with a crimson solar disc. Those arrows were released from the arms of Adhiratha's son and blazed like giant serpents in the sky. In all the directions, they clashed with the sharp and fierce arrows released from Arjuna's arms and destroyed them. At that time, the earth trembled and the son of a suta became confused in the battle. Because of the brahmana's curse, the chariot was whirled around in the encounter.[795] Because of Rama's curse, the weapons no longer manifested themselves. Unable to tolerate this, he whirled his garments and his arms around and lamented, 'Those who know about dharma have always held that that dharma protects those who place dharma at the forefront. But instead of protecting one who is devoted, it is now bringing me down. I think that dharma does not always protect.' While he was speaking in this way, his horses and chariot were dislodged and he began to waver because of the downpour of Arjuna's weapons. He was struck in his inner organs and was incapable of acting. He repeatedly censured dharma. In the battle, having been struck by three fierce arrows in the arm, Karna then pierced Partha with seven. Arjuna struck him back with seventeen straight-flying and energetic arrows. They were as terrible as Indra's vajra and like fire to the touch. They pierced him with great force and then fell down on the surface of the earth.

'"Karna trembled. However, he exhibited great capacity. Using his strength, he invoked brahmastra. On seeing this, Arjuna invoked mantras and released *aindrastra*. Dhananjaya also invoked mantras on the bowstring of Gandiva and the arrows. He released showers of arrows, like Purandara pouring down rain. Those energetic arrows issued from the immensely valorous Partha's chariot and were about to destroy Karna's chariot. However, when they arrived in front of

[795]Disguised as a brahmana, Karna had studied under Parashurama. When this was discovered, Parashurama cursed Karna that his chariot would be swallowed up by the earth and the weapons wouldn't manifest themselves.

him, maharatha Karna repulsed all of them. When that weapon was destroyed, the brave one from the Vrishni lineage said, 'O Partha! Radheya is destroying your arrows. Release supreme weapons.' Using mantras, Arjuna released brahmastra. With those radiant arrows, Arjuna shrouded Karna. But Karna used extremely energetic arrows to angrily sever his bowstring. Fixing another bowstring, Pandava enveloped Karna with thousands of fiery arrows. In that battle, when Karna severed his bowstring, he fixed another one so quickly that no one could make this out. It was wonderful. Using his weapons, Radheya countered all of Savyasachi's weapons. At that time, his valour seemed to be greater than that of Partha. Krishna saw that Arjuna was afflicted because of Karna's weapons. He said, 'O Partha! Go closer and strike him with the best weapons.' Dhananjaya invoked an arrow with divine mantras. It was like a fire and the poison of a serpent. It was made completely out of iron. Kiriti united this with *roudrastra* and wished to shoot it. But, in that great battle, the earth swallowed up one of the wheels of Radheya's chariot.

'"Radheya wept in rage. He told Arjuna, 'O Pandava! Wait for an instant. You can see that because of destiny, my central wheel[796] has got submerged. O Partha! Abandon the thought[797] that only befits a coward. O Arjuna! One should not shoot a weapon at one with dishevelled hair, at one who doesn't wish to fight, at a brahmana, at someone who has joined his hands in salutation, at one who has sought refuge, at one who has cast aside his weapons, at someone who faces a calamity, at someone who doesn't have arrows, at a person whose armour has been destroyed, or at a person whose weapons have been shattered and broken. Brave ones do not strike at such people, nor do kings and lords of the earth. O Kounteya! You are brave. Wait for a short while. O Dhananjaya! Let me extricate the wheel from the ground. You are stationed on your chariot. You should not kill me when I am on the ground. O Pandaveya! You and Vasudeva are not frightened of me. You are a kshatriya and

[796]Some non-critical versions say left wheel.

[797]Of shooting the weapon.

you are the extender of a great lineage. O Pandava! Remember the instructions of dharma and wait for a short while.'"'

Chapter 1217(67)

'Sanjaya said, "Vasudeva was stationed on his chariot. He said, 'O Radheya! It is fortunate that you remember dharma. Quite often, when they are immersed in hardships, inferior ones censure destiny, but not their evil deeds. O Karna! When you, Suyodhana, Duhshasana and Shakuni Soubala brought Droupadi to the assembly hall in a single garment, did dharma not show itself to you? When, in the assembly hall, Yudhishthira, who was not skilled at dice, was defeated by Shakuni, who was skilled at dice, where did dharma go then? O Karna! During her season, Krishna[798] was under Duhshasana's subjugation in the assembly hall and you laughed at her. Where did dharma go then? O Karna! Resorting to the king of Gandhara and coveting the kingdom, you challenged the Pandavas.[799] Where did dharma go then?' When Vasudeva addressed Radheya in this way, Pandava Dhananjaya remembered all this and was overcome by great rage. Energetic flames of anger seemed to issue out from all the pores on his body and it was extraordinary.

'"On seeing this, Karna again invoked brahmastra against Dhananjaya. He showered down arrows and tried to extricate his chariot. Pandava countered those weapons with his own weapons. Kounteya then released another weapon, beloved of the fire god, towards Karna. It blazed fiercely. Karna pacified the fire through a varuna weapon. He covered all the directions with clouds and it was as dark as a rainy day. Pandaveya was not frightened. While Radheya looked on, the valiant one used the vayavya weapon and dispelled all the clouds. The supreme one's standard had the marks

[798]Krishnaa, Droupadi.

[799]To the gambling match.

of an elephant's housing. It was decorated with gold, pearls, jewels and diamonds. It had been crafted by excellent artisans over a long period of time. It was expensive and beautiful in form. It always inspired your soldiers and terrified and frightened the enemy. It was renowned in the world and blazed like the sun and the moon. Kiriti used a razor-sharp arrow that was gold-tufted and pointed. With that, he brought down the handsome and blazing standard of the great-souled maharatha, Adhiratha's son. O venerable one! When that standard was uprooted, fame, dharma, victory and everything that was dear to the hearts of the Kurus also fell down. Great sounds of lamentation arose.

'"To ensure Karna's death, Pandava took out an anjalika arrow. It was like the great Indra's vajra, or like a rod that was made out of fire. It blazed in its rays, like the one with one thousand rays.[800] It was capable of penetrating the inner organs and smearing itself with blood and flesh. It was extremely expensive and was like the fire and the sun. It could destroy men, horses and elephants and was three cubits long, with six tufts.[801] It travelled straight and possessed a great force. In its energy, it was like the vajra of the one with one thousand eyes. It was as difficult to withstand as predatory beasts. It was like the pinaka and Narayana's chakra. It was fearful and destructive of living beings. He invoked mantras and affixed that supreme and great weapon to Gandiva. He loudly said, 'I am grasping this great weapon, which is in the form of an arrow. It is extremely difficult to withstand and is capable of destroying the body. If I have tormented myself through austerities and have satisfied my seniors, if I have listened to what my well-wishers have told me, through that truth, let this arrow slay my armoured enemy, Karna, and bring me victory.' Having said this, for the sake of Karna's death, Dhananjaya released that terrible arrow. It was as fierce as rites performed by Atharvan and Angiras. It blazed and was impossible to be endured in a battle, even by Death itself. Kiriti cheerfully said, 'Let this arrow bring me victory.' Wishing to slay Karna, bring about his end and convey him

[800]The sun.

[801]*Ratni* is a measure of distance and is equal to one cubit.

to Yama, he released the arrow, which was as radiant as the sun and the moon. Cheerfully, so that he could be conveyed towards victory, the one with the diadem and the garland shot the arrow. It was as radiant as the sun and the moon. He harboured feelings of enmity and wished to slay his enemy. That weapon, blazing like the sun, was shot. Like the sun, it lit up the earth with its radiance. The head of the commander of the army was severed. Like the sun, with a red disc, it seemed to set. The body of the one who performed generous deeds was always reared in happiness. Like a person who is reluctant to leave a house filled with great riches, the head parted from the body with great difficulty. Without the armour, the body was mangled by arrows and lost its life. Karna's body was severed and fell down. Blood oozed from the wounds, like red chalk flowing from the slopes of a mountain, when the summit has been struck by thunder. When Karna's body fell down, a flaming mass of energy arose and rose up into the sky. O king! When Karna was slain, all the men and warriors witnessed this great wonder.

'"On seeing that he had been slain and was lying down, with their soldiers, the Somakas roared in delight. They joyfully blew on their trumpets and waved their garments and hands around. Other troops danced around. They embraced each other, roaring in delight. They saw that Karna had been destroyed and was lying down on the ground. The ratha had been slain and mangled by the arrows. It was as if the untainted and extinguished fire was lying down in the expansive sky, after the end of a sacrifice. All his limbs were mangled by arrows and torrents of blood flowed from them. Karna's body was beautiful, like the rays of the sun in the firmament. He had tormented the soldiers of the enemy with flaming arrows that were like the sun's rays. The powerful Karna was like the setting sun, conveyed to death by Arjuna. When the sun sets, all its radiance also departs. Like that, the arrow took away Karna's life. O venerable one! It was the late part of the afternoon then. Severed by the anjalika in the battle, the head and the body of the son of a suta fell down. While the soldiers of the enemy looked on, it swiftly severed Karna's head and body.

'"The brave Karna fell down on the ground. Mangled by arrows, blood flowed out from his body. On seeing that he was lying down on the ground and seeing that the standard had been severed, the king of Madra withdrew on the chariot. When Karna was slain, the Kurus fled. They were severely struck in the battle and were afflicted with fear. They repeatedly glanced at Arjuna's great standard, blazing in form. He[802] had performed deeds like those of the one with one thousand eyes. His face was as beautiful as one with one thousand petals.[803] He was like the one with one thousand rays, at the end of the day. Thus did his head fall down on the ground."'

Chapter 1218(68)

'Sanjaya said, "In the course of the encounter between Karna and Arjuna, the soldiers had been mangled with arrows. O descendant of the Bharata lineage! On seeing this, Shalya went to Duryodhana, who was glancing at the field of battle. Duryodhana saw that his army, with its chariots, horses and elephants, had been destroyed and the son of a suta had been killed. His eyes filled with tears and in great distress, he sighed repeatedly. The brave Karna had fallen down on the ground. His body had been mangled by arrows and blood flowed from it. It was as if the sun had fallen down from the sky. To see this, everyone came there and surrounded the body. There were those who belonged to your side and others who belonged to the enemy. Some were cheerful. Others were frightened. Some were distressed. Others were amazed. There were others who were completely overcome by grief. According to their natural traits, they looked towards each other. Karna had possessed armour, ornaments, garments and weapons. On seeing that he had been brought down by Dhananjaya and deprived of his energy, the Kurus fled. They were like a distressed herd of cattle, when the bull has been killed. By slaying Karna, like an elephant by a lion, Arjuna had struck them severely.

[802]Karna.

[803]A lotus.

'"On seeing that he was lying down on the ground, the king of Madra was terrified. He swiftly withdrew on his chariot. The lord of Madra was stupefied. He quickly departed on the chariot that was without a standard. He swiftly went to Duryodhana's side and spoke these sorrowful words. 'The elephants, horses and best of rathas in your army have been destroyed. It looks like Yama's kingdom. The large armies with men, horses and elephants that are like mountain tops have clashed against each other and have been killed. O descendant of the Bharata lineage! There has never been a battle like that fought between Karna and Arjuna today. Karna clashed against the two Krishnas and others who are your enemies and has been devoured. Destiny flows according to its own rules. That is the reason it is protecting the Pandavas and weakening us. All the brave ones sought to accomplish your objectives. They have been slain by the enemy. Those brave ones were the equals of Kubera, Vaivasvata and the lord of the waters in power. They possessed valour, bravery and strength. They possessed large stores of qualities. Those lords of men were unslayable. They sought to accomplish your objectives, fought against the Pandaveyas and have been slain. O descendant of the Bharata lineage! Do not grieve. This is destiny. There is no substitute for success. However, success cannot always be obtained.' Hearing the words of the lord of Madra, Duryodhana was miserable in his mind. He thought of his own evil deeds and looked within his heart. He was bereft of his senses. In great grief, he repeatedly sighed.

'"He reflected and was silent. He was extremely distressed. Artayani[804] spoke these words to him. 'O brave one! Behold this fierce field of battle. It is strewn around with slain men, horses and elephants. Giant elephants have fallen down, like giant mountains. They have been sliced down. Their inner organs have been pierced with arrows. They are unconscious and anxious. Some have lost their lives. The warriors have dislodged their body armour and their weapons. They are like fragmented mountains, with rocks, animals,

[804]Shalya.

trees and herbs, which have been shattered by Indra's vajra. The bells, goads, javelins and standards have been destroyed. They possessed golden harnesses, which are streaming with copious quantities of blood. Mangled by arrows, horses have fallen down. Some of them are finding it difficult to breathe and are vomiting blood. Some are shrieking loudly, with dilated eyes. Some are biting the ground with their teeth and neighing in distress. Warriors on horses and elephants have been struck. Some have a little bit of life left and others have lost their lives. Men, horses, elephants and chariots have been crushed. Like the great Vaitarani, the earth is difficult to behold. Elephants have had their trunks severed by the enemy. They are shrieking, trembling and falling down on the ground. There were illustrious elephants, chariots, horses, warriors and foot soldiers. Advancing against the enemy, they have been slain. Armour, ornaments, garments and weapons are strewn around. It is as if the earth is covered with many fires that have been extinguished. One can see that the mighty armies have been struck by the force of the arrows and soldiers have fallen down in thousands. They have lost their senses and are trying to regain their breath again. The earth is beautiful, as if with fires that have been extinguished. Flaming and sparkling planets seem to have fallen down from the sky. The arrows, released from the arms of Karna and Arjuna, have shattered the bodies of elephants, horses and men. The weapons have quickly deprived them of their lives and have entered the ground, like giant serpents looking for an abode. In the battle, men, horses and elephants have been killed. Chariots have been shattered by the arrows. The earth has become impassable because of the bodies of elephants that have been killed by the arrows of Dhananjaya and Adhiratha's son. The best of rathas and warriors have been uprooted by the arrows. Chariots, horses, the best of weapons and standards are strewn around. It is impassable because of shattered and destroyed weapons. Wheels, axles, yokes and trivenus have been shattered. The chariots are without charioteers, who have been killed. It is impassable because some are without yokes, while others have had their yokes broken. The seats were decorated with gold and jewels and have been shattered. They are strewn around on the ground, like clouds in the autumn sky. The swift and ornamented horses were yoked to excellent chariots and with riders slain, are dragging them around. Large numbers of men, elephants, chariots and horses are seen to speedily run away. They have been routed in many ways. Clubs tied in golden cloth, battleaxes, swords,[805] bludgeons, spears, sparkling and unsheathed scimitars, and maces tied up in golden pieces of cloth have fallen down. There are bows, golden armlets, ornaments, arrows with colourful tufts made out of gold, yellow and spotless swords that have been unsheathed, javelins and scimitars with golden complexions. There are umbrellas, fans, whisks, conch shells and garlands of flowers, embellished with gold. There are housings, flags and garments. There are radiant crowns, garlands and diadems. The housings are scattered and strewn around. There are necklaces decorated with pearls from the waters. There are guards, armlets and excellent bracelets. There are golden collars and golden threads for the necks. There are the best of gems, diamonds, gold, pearls and other jewels. There are auspicious signs, good and not that good, on the bodies, which have been reared in great happiness. The faces on the heads are like the full moon. The bodies have given up pleasure and garments, objects desired by the heart and happiness. They have resorted to their own dharma and obtained great merits. They have ascended to the worlds that bring fame.' Shalya spoke these words to Duryodhana and stopped.

'"His[806] mind was overcome with great grief. Bereft of his senses, he lamented, 'Alas! Karna! Alas! Karna!' His eyes overflowed with tears. All the kings, with Drona's son at the forefront, comforted him and departed.[807] They repeatedly glanced at Arjuna's great standard, which seemed to be blazing because of his glory. The bodies of men, horses and elephants were covered with blood. The earth was covered with blood. It looked like a woman attired in crimson and golden garments and garlands, who would go to everyone.[808] O king! Their

[805]Actually, the text says *kaddanga*. This is a kind of liquor made from molasses. This doesn't fit at all. So we have assumed that this is a typo and should actually read *khadga*.

[806]Duryodhana's.

[807]Towards their camp.

[808]Meaning that the woman was a courtesan.

terrible forms were covered with blood and could not be recognized. The Kurus were unable to look at all those who had departed for the world of the gods and could not stand there. Because Karna had been slain, they were extremely miserable. They lamented, 'Alas! Karna! Alas! Karna!' On seeing that the sun had assumed a reddish tinge, they rapidly left for their camps.

'"Gold-tufted and sharp arrows were released from Gandiva. Their tufts were smeared with blood. With those arrows on his limbs, Karna looked beautiful on the ground. Though slain, he looked like the sun, with its rays. Karna's body was covered with blood. It was as if the illustrious sun was showing compassion towards its devotee[809] and having touched the crimson form with its red hand, was proceeding beyond the ocean to have a bath. That is what the large numbers of gods and rishis thought. They returned to their respective abodes. The other beings also thought in the same way and left as they wished, to heaven or on earth. The foremost of brave ones among the Kurus had witnessed the terrible encounter between Dhananjaya and Adhiratha's son, destructive of lives. They were amazed. Now that it was over, they praised it and departed. The brave one's armour had been shattered by arrows. He had been slain in the battle. Radheya had lost his life. But his beauty[810] did not desert him. O king! He was adorned in many ornaments and his armlets were made out of gold. Vaikartana had been slain and was lying down, like a tree with branches and sprouts. He had the complexion of pure gold and blazed like a fire. With his son, the tiger among men was pacified by Partha's energy. O king! With his weapons and energy, he scorched the Pandavas and the Panchalas. Whenever he was asked to give, he always did and never said that he had nothing to give. The virtuous always regarded him as righteous. This Vrisha was killed in the duel. The great-souled one gave everything that he possessed to brahmanas. There was nothing, not even his own life, which he would not give away to brahmanas. He was always loved by men. He was generous. He loved giving. He went to heaven. He

[809]Karna was devoted to the sun god.

[810]The word used is Lakshmi. So it can also be translated as lustre or prosperity.

took away with him the hopes your sons cherished for victory and their comfort and armour. When Karna was killed, the rivers stopped flowing. The sun was tainted and set. The blazing planets coursed in a diagonal direction. O king! Yama's son arose.[811] The sky seemed to divide into two parts. The earth seemed to shriek. Extremely harsh and forceful winds began to blow. The directions seemed to blaze fiercely, with a lot of smoke. The giant oceans were agitated and roared loudly. O venerable one! The groves, mountains and large numbers of beings were distressed and trembled. Brihaspati afflicted Rohini[812] and assumed the complexion of the moon and the sun. When Karna was killed, the directions were covered in darkness and could not be distinguished. The firmament and the earth seemed to move. Flaming meteors showered down. Those who travel during the night[813] were seen to be delighted. Karna's head was as beautiful as the full moon and Arjuna brought it down with a razor-sharp arrow. Loud sounds of lamentation were heard among beings in heaven, in the sky and on the ground. In the battle, Arjuna killed his enemy, Karna, who was revered by the gods, the gandharvas and men.

'"Partha was resplendent in his supreme energy, like the one with the one thousand eyes, after Vritra had been killed. That chariot roared like a large mass of clouds. Its radiance was like the midday sun in the autumn sky. With its standard and flags, it clattered loudly. It was as radiant as snow, the moon, a conch shell or a crystal. It was ornamented with gold, pearls, jewels, diamonds and coral. It possessed the speed of thought. Those two supreme among men, Pandava and the slayer of Keshi[814] were as resplendent

[811]This must be a typo. Yama has no recorded son. It should probably read Soma, rather than Yama, as it does in some non-critical versions. Soma's (the moon) son is Budha (Mercury). So Mercury arose. Yama can also be interpreted as 'twin'. But one doesn't know what to make of the son of twins. Finally, Yama is a name for Pluto. But no Pluto was known then and Pluto's son makes no sense.

[812]Brihaspati is Jupiter and Rohini is the fourth of the twenty-seven nakshatras, known in English as Aldebaran.

[813]Demons.

[814]Krishna killed a demon named Keshi.

as the fire and the sun in that field of battle. They roamed around, without any fear. Astride the same chariot, they were like Vishnu and Vasava. The one with the ape on his banner created a tumult with the twang of his bowstring, the slapping of his palms and the clatter of his wheels. He destroyed and killed the enemy with his power. With the one with a bird on his banner[815] with him, he showered torrents of arrows on the Kurus. They held their conch shells, as white as snow, in their hands. These emitted a loud roar and were decorated with golden nets. Their minds filled with delight, they blew loudly on these conch shells. Placing those best of conch shells against their lips, those best of men, simultaneously blew on them with the best of mouths. Panchajanya and Devadatta[816] roared. That sound filled up the earth, the sky and heaven. At the sound of those conch shells, the forest, the mountains, the rivers and the directions were terrified, as were the soldiers of your son. However, those two brave ones delighted Yudhishthira. As soon as they heard the loud blare of those conch shells, the Kurus speedily departed. O descendant of the Bharata lineage! They abandoned the lord of Madra and Duryodhana, the lord of the Bharatas. In the great battle, a large number of beings assembled around the radiant Dhananjaya. They joyfully congratulated him and Janardana, each dazzling like a sun. In the battle, having been struck by Karna's arrows, those two scorchers of enemies, Achyuta and Arjuna, looked beautiful. They were like the sparkling moon and sun, garlanded with rays, arising after darkness has been destroyed. Taking out those large numbers of arrows, those valiant lords entered their own camps, surrounded by well-wishers. They were like Vasava and Achyuta,[817] invoked by officiating priests. When Karna was slain in that supreme battle, the gods, the gandharvas, men, charanas, maharshis, yakshas and giant serpents honoured them greatly and hoped that their victories might continue."'

[815]Krishna/Vishnu has a bird (Garuda) on his banner.

[816]Krishna and Arjuna's conch shell respectively.

[817]Vishnu.

Chapter 1219(69)

'Sanjaya said, "When Karna was brought down, your soldiers fled. Dasharha joyfully embraced Partha and said, 'O Dhananjaya! Through your strength, Karna, who was like Vritra, has been killed. Men will talk about the deaths of Karna and Vritra. The infinitely energetic one[818] used the vajra to slay Vritra in a battle. You have slain Karna with your bow's sharp arrows. Your fame will be renowned in this world and will bring you glory. O Kounteya! Go and tell this to the intelligent Dharmaraja. For a long time, this death of Karna in the battle has been desired. You should go and tell this to Dharmaraja and free yourself of the debt.' Having been thus addressed by Keshava, bull among the Yadu lineage, Partha agreed. The foremost chariot of the foremost among rathas was turned back. Govinda spoke these words to Dhrishtadyumna, Yudhamanyu, Madri's sons, Vrikodara and Yuyudhana, 'Remain here and carefully confront the enemy, until we have returned, after informing the king that Karna has been killed by Arjuna.' Having taken their leave of those brave ones, they departed for the king's abode.

'"With Partha, Govinda saw Yudhishthira. The tiger among kings was lying down on an excellent golden bed. Joyfully, they touched the king's feet. On discerning their joy and the superhuman marks of wounds, Yudhishthira deduced that Radheya must have been killed and arose. Vasudeva, the descendant of the Yadu lineage, pleasant in speech, told him everything about Karna's death. Joining his hands in salutation, Achyuta Krishna smiled a little and told Yudhishthira that his enemy had been killed. 'O king! It is through good fortune that the wielder of Gandiva, Pandava Vrikodara, you and the Pandavas who are the sons of Madri are safe. You have been freed from the battle that led to a destruction of heroes and made the body hair stand up. O king! Quickly undertake whatever tasks must be done next. The cruel and immensely strong Vaikartana, son of a suta, has been slain. O Indra among kings! It is through good fortune that

[818]Indra.

you have obtained victory. O Pandava! You are prospering through good fortune. The worst among men laughed at Krishna[819] when she had been won in the gambling match. The earth is now drinking the blood of that son of a suta. O bull among the Kuru lineage! With arrows mangling his limbs, that enemy of yours is now lying down. O tiger among men! Look at him. He has been shattered by many arrows.' Delighted, Yudhishthira honoured Dasharha back in return. O Indra among kings! He joyfully said, 'This is good fortune. It is fortunate. O mighty-armed one! O Devaki's son! This is all because of you. With you as a charioteer, Partha was able to exhibit this manliness today.' The best of the Kuru lineage grasped his[820] right hand, adorned with a bracelet, and addressed both Partha Arjuna, the upholder of dharma, and Keshava. 'Narada had said that you were the gods Nara and Narayana. You are the ancient and supreme men, united in establishing dharma. The revered and intelligent Krishna Dvaipayana also told me this. O mighty-armed ones! The lord told me about that divine account. O Krishna! It is because of your powers that Dhananjaya confronted his enemies with Gandiva and defeated them, not retreating before any of them. Our victory is certain and their defeat is certain. After all, when Partha fights in the battle, you have agreed to be his charioteer.' O great king! Having spoken these words, the maharatha ascended his gold-decorated chariot, which was yoked to horses with the complexion of ivory and with black tails. The tiger among men was surrounded by his own soldiers. The brave Krishna and Arjuna cheerfully followed him. Surrounded by many and conversing pleasantly with the brave and resplendent Madhava and Phalguna, he went to see the field of battle.

'"He saw Karna, bull among men, lying down in the battle. Arrows released from Gandiva had splintered all over his body. King Yudhishthira saw that Karna had been slain, together with his son. He praised those two tigers among men, Madhava and Pandava, and said, 'O Govinda! Today, with my brothers, I have become the king of the earth. This is because you are our protector and we are

[819]Krishnaa, Droupadi.

[820]Krishna's.

sheltered by your bravery and your learning. On seeing that the proud Radheya, tiger among men, has been slain, Dhritarashtra's evil-souled son will lose all hope today, both about remaining alive and about the kingdom. Maharatha Karna has been killed. O bull among men! It is because of your favours that we are successful. O descendant of the Yadu lineage! You have ensured that the wielder of Gandiva is victorious. O Govinda! It is through good fortune that you have been victorious. It is through good fortune that Karna has been brought down.' O Indra among kings! Delighted, Dharmaraja Yudhishthira praised Janardana, and also Arjuna, in many ways. The joy of the kings and the maharathas also increased. O great king! When the descendant of the suta lineage was killed, Nakula, Sahadeva, Pandava Vrikodara, Satyaki, the foremost rathas among the Vrishnis, Dhrishtadyumna, Shikhandi, the Pandus, the Panchalas and the Srinjayas honoured Kounteya.[821] They increased the desire of King Yudhishthira, Pandu's son, for victory. Those strikers delighted in fighting and wished to accomplish their objective. With eloquent words, they praised and honoured the two Krishnas, the scorchers of enemies. Then, filled with great delight, the maharathas left for their respective camps. In this way, there was a great destruction and it made the body hair stand up. O king! All of this was the consequence of your evil counsel. Why are you grieving?"'

Vaishampayana said, 'O king! On hearing the unpleasant news, Dhritarashtra, the lord of the earth, fell down unconscious on the ground. Kouravya was overcome by supreme distress. Queen Gandhari, who was devoted to the truth and knew about dharma, also fell down. Vidura and Sanjaya raised the king and comforted the monarch. The women of the king's household raised Gandhari. Comforted by them, the king regained his senses, but was silent.'

This ends Karna Parva.

[821]Arjuna.

Shalya Parva

Shalya Parva continues with the account of the war. After Karna's death, Shalya is instated as the commander of the Kourava army. Shalya is the commander for a single day, day eighteen. In the 18-parva classification, Shalya Parva is the nineth. In the 100-parva classification, this parva constitutes Sections 74 to 77. Shalya Parva has sixty-four chapters. In the numbering of the chapters in this parva, the first number is a consecutive one, starting with the beginning of the Mahabharata. And the second number, within brackets, is the numbering of the chapter within Shalya Parva.

Shalya Parva

Shalya Parva continues with the account of the war. After Karna's death, Shalya is instated as the commander of the Kourava army. Shalya is the commander for a single day, day eighteen. In the 18-parva classification, Shalya Parva is the ninth. In the 100-parva classification, this parva constitutes Sections 74 to 77. Shalya Parva has sixty-four chapters. In the numbering of the chapters in Shalya Parva, the first number is a consecutive one, starting with the beginning of the Mahabharata. And the second number, within brackets, is the numbering of the chapter within Shalya Parva.

SECTION SEVENTY-FOUR

Shalya-Vadha Parva

This parva has 844 shlokas and sixteen chapters.

Chapter 1220(1): 52 shlokas	*Chapter 1228(9): 65 shlokas*
Chapter 1221(2): 65 shlokas	*Chapter 1229(10): 56 shlokas*
Chapter 1222(3): 50 shlokas	*Chapter 1230(11): 63 shlokas*
Chapter 1223(4): 50 shlokas	*Chapter 1231(12): 45 shlokas*
Chapter 1224(5): 27 shlokas	*Chapter 1232(13): 45 shlokas*
Chapter 1225(6): 41 shlokas	*Chapter 1233(14): 41 shlokas*
Chapter 1126(7): 44 shlokas	*Chapter 1234(15): 67 shlokas*
Chapter 1227(8): 46 shlokas	*Chapter 1235(16): 87 shlokas*

Vadha means killing and the section is named after the killing of Shalya. Shalya is appointed the supreme commander of the Kourava army. Nakula kills Karna's sons. Duryodhana kills Chekitana, the prince of Chedi. Ashvatthama kills Suratha of Panchala. Yudhishthira kills Shalya and Shalya's younger brother.

Chapter 1220(1)

Janamejaya asked, 'O brahmana! In the battle, Karna was brought down by Savyasachi. What did the few Kurus who were left do then? The army of the Pandavas was swelling. On seeing this, what did Kourava, King Duryodhana, do? O supreme among brahmanas! I wish to hear all this in detail. I am not satisfied with listening to the great deeds of my ancestors.'

Vaishampayana replied, 'O king! When Karna was slain, Dhritarashtra's son, Suyodhana, was immersed in an ocean of great grief. In every possible way, he lost all hope. He repeatedly grieved, "Alas! Karna! Alas! Karna!" With a great deal of difficulty, he went to his own camp, together with the remaining kings. Remembering the death of the son of a suta, the king could find no peace of mind and was comforted by them, with citations from reasons given in the sacred texts. The king eventually decided that destiny was supremely powerful. He made up his mind to fight and again emerged for the battle. The bull among kings made Shalya the commander, in accordance with the decreed rites. With the kings who had not been slain, the king emerged to do battle. An extremely tumultuous battle commenced between the soldiers of the Kurus and the Pandavas. O best of the Bharata lineage! It was like that between the gods and the asuras. O great king! In the battle, Shalya created carnage among the Pandu soldiers and was slain by Dharmaraja at midday. In the field of battle, all of King Duryodhana's relatives were slain. Terrified of his enemies, he fled and entered into a terrible lake. During the later part of the afternoon, he was surrounded by maharathas. He was summoned from the lake and brought down by Bhimasena, who used yoga. When that great archer was killed, three rathas remained alive.[1] O Indra among kings! Overcome by rage, they slaughtered the Panchala soldiers in the night. Next morning, Sanjaya left the camp and entered the city,[2] distressed and overcome with grief. He swiftly entered the city, raising his hands in sorrow. Trembling, he entered

[1]Ashvatthama, Kripa and Kritavarma.

[2]Hastinapura.

the king's abode. O tiger among men! In sorrow, he wept and said, "O king! Alas! The great-souled one has been killed and all of us are agitated. Although it was not yet time, the extremely powerful one has attained the supreme objective. All the kings on our side were like Shakra in strength and they have been killed." O king! On seeing Sanjaya in the city, all the people were extremely anxious and wept in loud voices, saying, "O king! Alas!" O tiger among men! On hearing that the king had been killed, even the children surrounded the city from all sides and lamented loudly. We saw three bulls among men running around there.[3] They were deprived of their senses. They were mad with grief. They were severely afflicted.

'Entering, the distracted suta saw the king, who was without decay. He saw the lord, best among kings, who had wisdom as his sight.[4] He saw that the unblemished one, foremost among the Bharata lineage, was seated, surrounded by his daughters-in-law, Gandhari, Vidura and other well-wishers, relatives and friends. He was thinking about Karna's death. O Janamejaya! In a voice that was choking with tears, and distressed in his mind, the suta spoke these words to the king, weeping amidst the words. "O tiger among men! O bull among the Bharata lineage! I am Sanjaya. Shalya, the lord of Madra, and Shakuni Soubala have been slain. O tiger among men! So has Uluka, firm in his valour and the son of the one who played with dice.[5] All the samshaptakas have been slain, together with the Kambojas and the Shakas. The mlecchas, the ones from the mountainous regions and the Yavanas have been brought down. O great king! All those from the east and the south have been slain. O lord of men! All those from the north and the west have been killed. O king! All the kings and the princes have been killed. O king! Pandava has killed Duryodhana, as he had said he would. O great king! With his thigh broken, he is lying down in the dust,

[3]The 'three' is a typo, probably because Ashvatthama, Kripa and Kritavarma have been mentioned earlier. It should read *stri* (women) and not *tri* (three). That is, men and women were running around, not three men.

[4]Dhritarashtra was blind.

[5]Uluka was Shakuni's son.

covered with blood. O king! Dhrishtadyumna has been killed and also the unvanquished Shikhandi, Uttamouja and Yudhamanyu. O king! The Prabhadrakas, the Panchalas and the Chedis, tigers among men, are dead. O descendant of the Bharata lineage! Your sons, all of Droupadi's sons, have been slain. The immensely strong and brave Vrishasena, Karna's son, has been killed. All the men have been killed and the elephants have been brought down. O tiger among men! Rathas and horses have been slain in the battle. O lord! There are only a few who remain in your camp. Those brave ones and the Pandavas clashed against each other. They were confounded by destiny and only women are left in this world. There are seven left on the side of the Pandavas and three on the side of the sons of Dhritarashtra. There are the five brothers and Vasudeva and Satyaki. And there are Kripa, Kritavarma and Drona's son, supreme among victorious ones. O great king! O supreme among kings! Those are the only rathas who are left. O lord of men! O great king! Out of the akshouhinis that assembled, these are the only ones who are left. Everyone else has been killed. O bull among the Bharata lineage! The entire world has been slain by destiny. O descendant of the Bharata lineage! With Duryodhana at the forefront, this was the result of the enmity."

'O great king! Having heard these cruel words, Dhritarashtra, the lord of men, lost his senses and fell down on the ground. O great king! When he fell down on the ground, the immensely illustrious Vidura was touched by the king's grief and also fell down. O best of kings! On hearing those cruel words, Gandhari and all the Kuru women also suddenly fell down on the ground. All the servant-maids in the king's circle also lost their senses and fell down on the ground. They were overcome by a great delirium, as if they were figures on a painting. King Dhritarashtra, lord of the earth, was overcome by a great hardship. He was afflicted by hardship on account of his sons and slowly regained his senses. Having regained his senses, the king trembled in great grief. He glanced in all the directions and spoke these words to Kshatta.[6] "O learned Kshatta! O immensely wise one!

[6]Vidura.

O bull among the Bharata lineage![7] You are the refuge. I am in a grievous state, without a protector. I am without all my sons." Having said this, he lost his senses again and fell down. On seeing him fall down in this way, his relatives sprinkled cold water on him. They fanned him with fans. After a long time, the lord of the earth was comforted. Oppressed by grief on account of his sons, the lord of the earth remained silent. O lord of the earth! He sighed, like a snake that has been flung into a pot. On seeing that the king was so distressed, Sanjaya also wept. For a long time, so did all the women and the illustrious Gandhari. After repeatedly losing his senses, Dhritarashtra, tiger among men, spoke these words to Vidura. "Let all the women, and the illustrious Gandhari, depart, and all these well-wishers. My mind is greatly distracted." O bull among the Bharata lineage! Having heard these words, Vidura trembled repeatedly and gently asked the women to leave. O bull among the Bharata lineage! On seeing that the king was distressed, all the women and all the well-wishers departed. O scorcher of enemies! The king regained his senses and wept in great grief. The distressed Sanjaya looked at him. The lord of men was sighing repeatedly. Kshatta joined his hands in salutation and comforted him with gentle words.'

Chapter 1221(2)

Vaishampayana said, 'O great king! When the women had been sent away, Dhritarashtra, Ambika's son, lamented again, plunged into an even greater grief. His sighs seemed to be mixed with smoke and he repeatedly waved his arms around. O great king! Having reflected, he spoke these words. "O suta! Alas! What I have heard from you is a reason for great unhappiness. In the battle, the Pandavas are safe and have not suffered. It is certain that my heart is extremely firm, with an essence that is as tough as a diamond.

[7]Vidura was also born in the same lineage, though through a servant-maid.

Despite hearing that my sons have been killed, it has not shattered into a thousand fragments. O Sanjaya! I am thinking about their words and the sports they indulged in when they were children. Today, having heard that they have been killed, my mind is severely shattered. Because I was blind, I was never able to see their beauty. However, because of affection towards one's sons, I have always borne great love towards them. O unblemished one! They passed from childhood to youth and then attained middle age. On hearing this, I was delighted. Today, I have heard that they have been killed, deprived of their prosperity and robbed of their energy. Because of the calamity that has overtaken my sons, I cannot find any peace. O son! O Indra among kings![8] Come to me. I am without a protector now. O mighty-armed one! Without you, what will be my state now? O great king! You were the refuge of your relatives and your well-wishers. O brave one! I am old and blind. Abandoning me, where have you gone? O king! Where is your compassion, your affection and your honour? You were invincible in a battle. How could the Parthas have killed you? O son! Why have you abandoned all the assembled kings? Slain, you are now lying down on the ground, like an ordinary person, or a wicked king. When I arose at the appointed time, you always addressed me in such respectful words. 'O father! O father! O protector of the world!' You clasped my neck with moistened eyes and affectionately said, 'O Kouravya! Instruct me.' Address me in those excellent words. O son! I have heard these wonderful words from you. 'This extensive earth is mine, as much as it is of Partha. O supreme among kings! O lord! Bhagadatta, Kripa, Shalya, the two from Avanti,[9] Jayadratha, Bhurishrava, Somadatta, the great king Bahlika, Ashvatthama, Bhoja, the immensely strong Magadha, Brihadbala, the lord of Kashi, Shakuni Soubala, the many thousands of mlecchas, Shakas and Yavanas, Sudakshina of Kamboja, the lord of Trigarta,[10] grandfather Bhishma, Bharadvaja's son, Goutama, Shrutayu, Achyutayu, the valorous

[8]In his lamentations, Dhritarashtra is addressing Duryodhana.

[9]Vinda and Anuvinda.

[10]Susharma.

Shatayu, Jalasandha, Rishyashringa's son,[11] the rakshasa Alayudha, the mighty-armed Alambusa, maharatha Subahu—these and many other kings have taken up weapons for my sake. All of them are ready to give up their lives in the battle. I will be stationed amidst them in the battle, surrounded by my brothers. O tiger among kings! I will fight against all the Parthas, Panchalas, Chedis and Droupadi's sons in the battle and with Satyaki, Kuntibhoja and rakshasa Ghatotkacha. O great king! In the battle, even a single one amongst these is capable of angrily countering the rush of the advancing Pandaveyas. Need one say anything about these brave ones when they are united, firm in their enmity against the Pandavas? O Indra among kings! All of them will fight with the Pandavas and their followers in the battle and slay them. With me, Karna will single-handedly kill the Pandavas. All these brave kings will then be under my subjugation. Their adviser is the immensely strong Vasudeva. O king! But he has given me word that he will not don armour for their sake.' O suta! Thus did he often speak in my presence and believing this, I thought that the Pandavas would be killed in the battle. However, though they were stationed in their midst and strove in the battle, my sons have been killed. What can this be, other than destiny? The powerful Bhishma was the protector of the world and having clashed against Shikhandi, was slain, like a king of deer[12] by a jackal. The brahmana Drona was skilled in the use of all weapons.[13] He has been slain by the Pandavas in the battle. What can this be, other than destiny? Bhurishrava has been killed in the battle, and so have Somadatta and the great king, Bahlika. What can this be, other than destiny? Sudakshina has been killed, and Kourava Jalasandha and Shrutayu and Achyutayu. What can this be, other than destiny? Brihadbala has been slain and the immensely strong Magadha. The two from Avanti have been killed, the lord of Trigarta and many samshaptakas. What

[11]A rakshasa who fought on the side of the Kouravas.

[12]A lion.

[13]The text uses both the words astra and shastra. Both means weapons. Broadly, an astra is hurled, while a shastra is held in the hand.

can this be, other than destiny? O king![14] Alambusa, the rakshasa Alayudha and Rishyashringa's son have been killed. What can this be, other than destiny? The narayanas, the gopalas, invincible in battle, and many thousands of mlecchas have been killed. What can this be, other than destiny? The brave and immensely strong Shakuni Soubala, skilled with the dice, has been slain, along with his soldiers. What can this be, other than destiny? Many brave kings and princes, with arms like clubs, have been slain. What can this be, other than destiny? O Sanjaya! Kshatriyas assembled there from many countries. All of them have been killed in the battle. What can this be, other than destiny? My sons have been killed and my immensely strong grandsons. So have my friends and brothers. What can this be, other than destiny? There is no doubt that a man is born with his destiny. The man who has a good destiny is fortunate. O Sanjaya! I do not have a good destiny. Hence, I have been deprived of my sons. Therefore, in my aged state, I have now come under the subjugation of my enemies. O lord! I think that the best thing for me now is to resort to the forest. I am without relatives and my kin have been destroyed. I will go to the forest. O Sanjaya! For a person like me, who has been reduced to this state and whose wings have been clipped, there is nothing superior to retiring to the forest. Duryodhana has been slain. Shalya has been killed in the battle. So have Duhshasana, Vishasta and the immensely strong Vikarna. How can I bear to hear Bhimasena's supreme roars? In the battle, he has single-handedly killed one hundred of my sons. He will repeatedly speak about Duryodhana's death in my presence and tormented by grief and sorrow, I will not be able to bear those harsh words." The king's relatives had been slain and he was tormented by grief. He repeatedly lost his senses, overcome by sorrow on account of his sons.

'Dhritarashtra, Ambika's son, lamented for a long time. His sighs were warm and long and he thought about the defeat. O bull among the Bharata lineage! The king was tormented by great misery. Then

[14]This is a typo. Since Dhritarashtra is speaking, there is no king he can be addressing.

he again asked the suta, Gavalgana's son,[15] to tell him exactly what had transpired. "After Bhishma and Drona had been killed, and on hearing that the son of a suta had also been brought down, who did those on my side appoint as a commander? In the battle, whoever is appointed as a commander by those on my side, is slain in a short while by the Pandavas. In the forefront of the battle, while all of you looked on, Bhishma was killed by Kiriti. Drona was also killed in that way, while all of you looked on. In that fashion, Karna, the powerful son of a suta, was also killed by Kiriti, while all of you, and all the kings, looked on. This is exactly what the great-souled Vidura had told me earlier. Because of Duryodhana's crimes, the subjects would be annihilated. There are some who see well. But there are others who are so stupid that they cannot see what is in front of them. I was stupid and treated those words accordingly. The far-sighted Vidura has dharma in his soul and spoke to me. He spoke the truth and his words have now come to pass. Deluded by destiny, I paid no attention to them earlier. The fruits have now manifested themselves. O Gavalgana's son! Tell me again. When Karna was brought down, who became the leader of our soldiers? Which ratha advanced against Arjuna and Vasudeva? In the battle, who guarded the right wheel of the king of Madra? When he wished to fight, who was on his left? Who protected the brave one's rear? O Sanjaya! When all of you were assembled, how were the immensely strong king of Madra and my son killed by the Pandavas in the encounter? Tell me everything about the great destruction of the Bharatas in detail. How was my son, Duryodhana, slain in the battle? How were all the Panchalas, along with all their followers, Dhrishtadyumna, Shikhandi and Droupadi's five sons killed? How did the Pandavas, the two Satvata warriors,[16] Kripa, Kritavarma and the son of Bharadvaja's son[17] escape? I wish to hear about the battle exactly as it occurred. O Sanjaya! I wish to hear everything. You are skilled in recounting."'

[15]Sanjaya was the son of Gavalgana.

[16]Krishna and Satyaki.

[17]Ashvatthama. Ashvatthama was Drona's son and Drona was Bharadvaja's son.

Chapter 1222(3)

'Sanjaya said, "O king! Listen to the great destruction of the Kurus and the Pandavas that ensued when they clashed against each other. The son of a suta was slain by the great-souled Pandava. Your soldiers were repeatedly rallied and routed. The senses of your son were overcome by great sorrow and he retreated. On witnessing Partha's valour, the soldiers were extremely anxious. O descendant of the Bharata lineage! Confronted by that misery, the soldiers reflected about what should be done next. The troops were being crushed. Loud wails could be heard. In the battle, the kings were in disarray. The great-souled ones had fallen down from their seats on the chariots and from the chariots. O venerable one! In the battle, the elephants and the foot soldiers were being destroyed. An extremely terrible battle was going on, as if Rudra was sporting. Hundreds and thousands of kings confronted an inglorious death.

'"O king! On discerning all this, Kripa, aged and virtuous in conduct, was overcome with compassion. The energetic one approached King Duryodhana. Overcome with anger, the eloquent one spoke these words. 'O Duryodhana! O Kourava! Listen to the words that I am speaking to you. O great king! O unblemished one! Having heard me, act in accordance with those words, if you find them acceptable. O Indra among kings! There is no path that is superior to the dharma of fighting. O bull among kshatriyas! That is the reason kshatriyas resort to fighting. One who lives the life of a kshatriya fights with sons, brothers, fathers, sister's sons, maternal uncles, matrimonial allies and relatives. There is supreme dharma in being killed and adharma in retreat. That is the reason, if one wishes to remain alive, this kind of livelihood is terrible. However, I wish to tell you some beneficial words. O unblemished one! After the deaths of Bhishma, Drona, maharatha Karna and Jayadratha, and the death of your brothers and your son, Lakshmana, what is there left for us to do? They were the ones on whom we resolved to impose the burden of the kingdom. Those brave ones have given up their bodies and gone to the destination reserved for those who know about the brahman. Those maharathas possessed many qualities and we are deprived of them now. We have brought down many kings and are reduced to a miserable state. Even when all of them were alive, Bibhatsu remained unvanquished. Krishna is his eyes and the mighty-armed is extremely difficult to defeat, even by the gods. The ape sits astride his standard, which is like Indra's standard and Indra's bow, with the resplendence of the vajra. The large army trembles at this. Bhima's leonine roars, Panchajanya's blare and Gandiva's twang bring distress to our hearts. Gandiva's brilliance dazzles our eyes. As it is brandished, it is like a circle of fire and is seen to move around, like a giant flash of lightning. Colourful and decorated with gold, that giant bow is brandished around. It is seen in all the directions, like a mass of clouds tinged with lightning. O king! Arjuna is supreme among those who are skilled in weapons. Wielded by Krishna,[18] your troops are driven away, like clouds dispelled by the wind. He is like the great Indra in his radiance and is scorching your soldiers, like a fire that has arisen to burn down the dead wood in a forest during the winter. We have beheld Dhananjaya agitate your soldiers and terrify the kings, like an elephant with four tusks. We have beheld Dhananjaya, like an elephant amidst lotuses. The warriors have been terrified by the twang of Pandava's bow. We have repeatedly seen him, like a lion amidst herds of deer. Those two Krishnas are great archers in all the worlds. They are bulls among all archers. Clad in their armour, they are resplendent amidst all the people. O descendant of the Bharata lienage! This is the seventeenth day of the battle and warriors have been slaughtered in this extremely terrible battle. Your soldiers have been routed and scattered in all the directions, like the wind dispelling masses of clouds during the autumn. O great king! Your troops are trembling because of Savyasachi. They are like an overturned boat, being whirled around on the giant ocean. When we saw that Jayadratha was within the range of his arrows,[19] where were the ones on your side—the son of a suta, Drona and his followers,

[18]Arjuna.

[19]The slaying of Jayadratha has been described in Section 69 (Volume 6).

I, you, Hardikya, your brother Duhshasana, and his brothers? O king! While all the worlds looked on, he used his valour to cross all your relatives, brothers, aides and maternal uncles and placing his feet on their heads,[20] slew Jayadratha. What is left for us to do? Where is the man who can defeat Pandava? The great-souled one possesses many divine weapons. He robs our valour with the twang of Gandiva. With their leaders slain, the soldiers are like the night without the moon, or like a dried up river, with the trees along the banks destroyed by elephants. The mighty-armed one on the white horses is roaming around amidst the soldiers at will, consuming them like fire amidst dead wood. Both Satyaki and Bhimasena have a force that can shatter mountains and dry up all the oceans. O lord of the earth! Bhima uttered words in the midst of the assembly hall. He has accomplished them and will accomplish them again.[21] When Karna was fighting in the forefront, the army of the Pandavas, protected by the wielder of Gandiva, was so strongly protected that it was difficult to assail. You have performed many evil acts against those virtuous ones. Those deeds were unwarranted and the fruits have arrived. For your own sake, you carefully assembled all these people. O son![22] O bull among the Bharata lineage! Both they and you face a danger. O Duryodhana! Protect your own self, because your own self is the reservoir of everything. O son! If that reservoir is destroyed, everything in it is scattered in different directions. A weakened person should try to obtain peace through conciliation. War is meant for someone who is prospering. That is Brihaspati's[23] policy. In terms of the strength of our forces, we are now inferior to the sons of Pandu. O lord! Pardon me, but I think that peace with the Pandavas is indicated now. He who does not know what is beneficial for him, or disregards the beneficial, is quickly dislodged from his kingdom and does not obtain anything superior. O king!

[20]Metaphorically.

[21]This is a reference to Bhima's pledge of killing Duryodhana and his brothers.

[22]The word used is tata.

[23]Brihasapati is the preceptor of the gods.

If you are able to obtain the kingdom by bowing down before the king,[24] that would be superior to heading towards the folly of defeat. Yudhishthira is compassionate. On the instructions of Vichitravirya's son[25] and on Govinda's words, he will allow you to retain the kingdom. There is no doubt that the unvanquished king, Arjuna, Bhimasena and all of them will do what Hrishikesha asks them to. I think that Krishna will not be able to ignore the words of Kourava Dhritarashtra and the Pandavas will not cross Krishna. I think that a cessation of hostilities with the Parthas is for your own good. I am not saying this out of weakness, or because I wish to save my own life. O king! I am offering you medication and you will remember this later.'[26] The aged Kripa Sharadvata lamented in these words. His sighs were deep and warm and, in sorrow, he lost his senses."'

Chapter 1223(4)

'Sanjaya said, "O lord of the earth! Having been thus addressed by the illustrious Goutama, the king let out deep and warm sighs and was silent. Dhritarashtra's great-minded son thought for an instant. The scorcher of enemies then spoke these words to Kripa Sharadvata. 'You have spoken like a well-wisher and I have heard all those words. In the course of fighting, you were ready to give up your life and did everything. You have immersed yourself in the immensely energetic array of Pandava maharathas and fought with them. The worlds have seen this. Like a well-wisher, you have made me listen to your words. But they do not appeal to me, like medicine to a person who is about to die. Those supreme words are beneficial and full of reason. O mighty-armed one! O foremost among brahmanas!

[24]Yudhishthira.

[25]Dhritarashtra.

[26]On the assumption that Duryodhana will not listen to the advice.

However, they do not appeal to me. Having been deprived of his kingdom earlier, why will he[27] trust us now? The king was defeated by us in the great contest of gambling with the dice earlier. Why will he repose any trust in my words now? Engaged in the welfare of the Parthas, Krishna arrived as a messenger.[28] Because of our greed, we acted contrary to Hrishikesha's intent. O brahmana! Why will he pay heed to my words now? When Krishna[29] was summoned to the assembly hall, she lamented. Krishna will not forgive that, or the deprivation of the kingdom. O lord! We had earlier heard that the two Krishnas were united with each other and we have also seen it now. On hearing of the death of his sister's son,[30] Keshava slept in sorrow. We have injured him. Why will he forgive us now? When Abhimanyu died, Arjuna could obtain no peace. Even if he is requested, why will he endeavour for my good? The immensely strong Bhimasena, the second Pandava, is fierce. He has taken a terrible pledge. He will break, rather than bow down. The brave twins are like Yama. They have girded their swords and are clad in armour. They are firm in their enmity. Dhrishtadyumna and Shikhandi are firm in their enmity towards me. O supreme among brahmanas! Why will they endeavour for my good? Krishna[31] was in her season and was clad in a single garment. While all the worlds looked on, she was oppressed by Duhshasana in the midst of the assembly hall. The Pandavas remember the distress of the naked one. No one is capable of restraining those scorchers of enemies from fighting. To accomplish the objective of her husbands and ensure my destruction, the miserable Droupadi Krishna has tormented herself through severe austerities. Until the hostilities are over, Krishna always sleeps on the bare ground. Vasudeva's sister has cast aside her pride and her honour and always serves Krishna.[32] Thus, everything has flared up and can never be quenched. Because of

[27]Yudhishthira.

[28]Described in Section 54 (Volume 4).

[29]Krishnaa, Droupadi.

[30]Abhimanyu.

[31]Krishnaa, Droupadi.

[32]Vasudeva's sister is Subhadra and she serves Krishnaa, Droupadi. The reference to pride and honour is because Droupadi and Subhadra were Arjuna's co-wives.

Abhimanyu's death, how can there be peace with me? I have enjoyed the earth, right up to the frontiers on the ocean. How can I be satisfied with the pleasures of a small kingdom, obtained through the favours of the Pandavas? Like a sun, I have blazed above all the kings. How can I follow Yudhishthira, like a servant? I have myself enjoyed all the pleasures and have donated generously. How can I lead a miserable life, together with other miserable people? The words that you have spoken are gentle and beneficial and I do not hate them. But I do not think that the time has arrived for peace. O scorcher of enemies! I see good policy as one that involves fighting well. This is not the time to be a eunuch. This is the time to fight. I have performed many rites and sacrifices. I have given a lot of donations to brahmanas. In due order, I have listened to all the Vedas. I have placed myself on the heads of my enemies. O father![33] I have nurtured my servants well and also distressed ones who have resorted to me. I have gone to the kingdoms of enemies. I have ruled my own kingdom. I have enjoyed many kinds of objects of pleasure. Large numbers of women have served me. I have paid my debts to my ancestors and to the dharma of kshatriyas. It is certain that there is no happiness on earth. What is the kingdom? What is fame? Fame can only be obtained through battle and there is no other way. If a kshatriya dies at home, that is reprehensible. Death in one's home is great adharma. If a man gives up his body in a forest, or in a battle, he performs a great sacrifice and attains great glory. There are those who lament in distress and misery, overcome by age. They die among their weeping relatives and are not men. I will abandon various objects of pleasure and attain the supreme objective. I will engage in a good battle and go to the worlds of the virtuous. Brave ones, noble in conduct, do not retreat from the field of battle. They are wise and unwavering in their aim. All of them perform sacrifices that involve rites with weapons. It is certain that they reside in heaven. It is certain that large numbers of pure apsaras glance delightedly at them. It is certain that the ancestors see them honoured in Shakra's assembly. They find joy in heaven, surrounded by apsaras. That is the path followed by the immortals

[33]The word used is tata. It means father, but is used for anyone senior or older.

and by brave ones who do not retreat. We will now ascend along that virtuous path, followed by the aged grandfather, the intelligent preceptor, Jayadratha, Karna and Duhshasana. There are brave kings who strove for my sake and have been killed. They were mangled by arrows and lay down on the ground, their limbs covered with blood. They were brave and supreme in the knowledge of weapons. They performed the decreed sacrifices. They gave up their lives for another and now reside in Indra's home. They have constructed the path. It will be difficult to travel along, because there are large numbers who are travelling along it with great speed, advancing towards the virtuous end. I remember the brave ones who have been killed in my cause. I wish to repay my debt to them. I am not interested in the kingdom. When my friends, brothers and grandfathers have been brought down, it is certain that the worlds will censure me if I protect my life. In the absence of my relatives, friends and well-wishers, and bowing down to Pandava, what kind of a kingdom will I have? Someone like me has brought the entire earth under his subjugation. I will now attain heaven through a good fight. There is no other way.' When Duryodhana spoke in this way, everyone applauded these words. The kshatriyas praised the king.

'"They ceased to grieve over their defeat and set their minds on bravery. All of them made up their minds to place fighting at the forefront of their hearts. All of them were delighted at the prospect of battle and comforted their mounts. The Kouravas went to a spot that was two yojanas away. This was a sacred and auspicious spot on the slopes of the Himalayas, without any trees. The waters of the Sarasvati were red there and they bathed in it and drank it. Inspired by your son, they rallied. O king! Having again reassured themselves and each other, all the kshatriyas were driven by destiny and waited."'

Chapter 1224(5)

'Sanjaya said, "O great king! All those warriors were delighted at the prospect of battle and gathered together on the slopes of the

Himalayas. Shalya, Chitrasena, maharatha Shakuni, Ashvatthama, Kripa, Satvata Kritavarma, Sushena, Arishtasena, the valiant Dhritasena, Jayatsena and the kings spent the night there. When the brave Karna was killed in the battle, though your sons desired victory, they were terrified and could find no peace, other than on the slopes of the Himalayas. O king! Having resolved to make every effort in the battle, in the presence of the soldiers, they honoured the king[34] in the prescribed way and, united, said, 'You should fight with the enemy after having decided on a commander. All the well-wishers will then be protected by him and obtain victory.' Stationed on his chariot, Duryodhana went to the supreme among rathas,[35] who knew about all the kinds of warfare and was unmatched in a battle. He was pleasant in speech and his neck was like that of a conch shell. He possessed a sword and his head was covered. His face was like a blooming lotus. His mouth was like that of a tiger and he had the majesty of Meru. His shoulders, eyes, gait and voice was like that of Sthanu's[36] bull. His arms were thick and long, with excellent joints. His chest was extremely broad and well formed. In his speed and strength, he was like Aruna's younger brother.[37] He was like the sun in his splendour and like Ushanas[38] in his intelligence. He was like the moon in three respects—the beauty of his form, his face and his prosperity. The joints on his body seemed to be made out of golden lotuses. His thighs, waist and feet were formed well, and so were his fingers and nails. He was created by the creator with great care, after remembering all the qualities that should be remembered. He possessed all the auspicious marks. He was skilled and an ocean of learning. He was capable of winning speedily, but was incapable of being defeated by the forces of the enemy. He possessed knowledge about the science of fighting, with its four parts and ten divisions.[39]

[34]Duryodhana.

[35]Ashvatthama.

[36]Shiva's.

[37]Aruna's younger brother is Garuda. Aruna and Garuda were Vinata's sons, through the sage Kashyapa.

[38]Shukra, the preceptor of the demons.

[39]Dhanurveda (the science of fighting) had different classifications. The four

He knew the four Vedas and their *angas*, with accounts as the fifth.[40] Drona was not born in a womb. The immensely energetic one observed fierce and careful austerities, worshipping Tryambaka and obtained him through someone who was also not born in a womb.[41] His deeds and beauty were unmatched on earth. He was accomplished in all the forms of learning. He was unblemished and an ocean of qualities. He was immeasurable in his soul. Having approached this Ashvatthama, he said, 'O preceptor's son! For all of us, you are the supreme refuge. Whom should I appoint as a commander now? You should tell me. With him at the forefront, we will fight with the Pandavas and defeat them.'

'"Drona's son replied, 'Let Shalya be the commander of our army. He possesses lineage, bravery, energy, fame, prosperity and all the qualities. He has abandoned his sister's sons[42] and has gratefully come to our side. He possesses a large army and is mighty-armed. He is like Mahasena[43] to the enemy. O supreme among kings! Make that king the commander. We will then be able to obtain victory, like the triumphant gods after appointing Skanda.'

'"When Drona's son said this, all the lords of the earth surrounded

---

parts could mean chariots, cavalry, elephants and infantry. But it probably means four types of weapons—amukta (held in the hand while fighting), mukta (hurled from the hand), muktamukta (weapons that can either be held in the hand or hurled) and yantramukta (hurled through an implement). The ten divisions (anga) are more difficult to pin down. While each kind of weapon had different modes of fighting and different positions, described for example in the *Agni Purana*, there is no ready identification with the number ten.

[40]The four Vedas are Rig, Sama, Yajur and Atharva. Itishasa (the epics and the Puranas), that is, accounts, are regarded as the fifth Veda. The six vedangas are *shiksha* (articulation and pronunciation), *chhanda* (prosody), *vyakarana* (grammar), *nirukta* (etymology), *jyotisha* (astronomy) and *kalpa* (rituals).

[41]Drona was born in a pot from the sage Bharadvaja's semen. Kripa and Kripi were also born in weeds, not a womb, through the sage Sharadvat's semen. Drona married Kripi and their son was Ashvatthama. Drona obtained Asvatthama after worshipping Tryambaka or the three-eyed one, Shiva.

[42]Shalya's sister was Madri, Nakula and Sahadeva's mother.

[43]Kartikeya, the general of the gods. Skanda is also Kartikeya's name.

Shalya and stationed themselves around him, proclaiming his victory.[44] They set their minds on fighting and were filled with supreme delight. From his chariot, Duryodhana alighted on the ground. He joined his hands in salutation and told Shalya, who was like Rama[45] and Bhishma in battle, 'O one who is devoted to friends! The time has come for friendship. At such times, learned ones can differentiate between a friend and an enemy. You are brave. Station yourself at the forefront of our army. When you advance in the battle, the evil-minded Pandavas, with their advisers and the Panchalas, will lose enterprise.' Shalya replied, 'O king! O king of the Kurus! I will accomplish the task you have thought for me. Everything that I possess, my life, my kingdom and my riches, is for your pleasure.' Duryodhana said, 'O unmatched maternal uncle![46] I instate you as the commander. O foremost among warriors! Save us in this encounter, like Skanda saved the gods in battle. O Indra among kings! I consecrate you, like the gods did to Pavaki.[47] O brave one! Slay the enemies in the battle, like the great Indra against the danavas.'"'

Chapter 1225(6)

'Sanjaya said, "O king! On hearing the king's words, the powerful king of Madra spoke these words to Duryodhana. 'O Duryodhana! O mighty-armed one! O supreme among eloquent ones! Listen to my words. You think that the two Krishnas, stationed on

[44]Though not explicitly stated, this is Sanjaya speaking again.

[45]This could mean either Rama or Parashurama.

[46]Shalya was a maternal uncle by extension.

[47]Pavaki means Pavaka's son, Pavaka being Agni. Pavaki is another name for Kartikeya. There are different stories about Kartikeya's birth. In some, he is directly born from Agni. In others, he is born from Shiva, but the semen is conveyed by Agni. In either case, Kartikeya can be described as Agni's son.

their chariot, are supreme among rathas. However, though united, they are not my equal in strength of arms. Even if the entire earth were to arise, with gods, asuras and men, I will angrily fight with them in the forefront of the battle, not to speak of the Pandavas. In the battle, I will vanquish the assembled Parthas and Somakas. There is no doubt that I will protect your soldiers. I will construct a vyuha that the enemy will not be able to cross. O Duryodhana! I am telling you this truthfully. Entertain no doubt on this score.' O supreme among the Bharata lineage! O lord of the earth! The king was thus addressed by the lord of Madra and delightedly, in the midst of the soldiers, sanctified him with water, in accordance with the rites laid down in the sacred texts. When he was consecrated, a loud noise arose among the soldiers. O descendant of the Bharata lineage! They roared like lions and musical instruments were sounded. The maharatha Madraka warriors were delighted. All the kings praised Shalya, the ornament of a battle. 'O king! May you be victorious. May you live for a long time. Slay the assembled enemy. The immensely strong son of Dhritarashtra has obtained the strength of your arms. Let him slaughter the enemy and rule over the entire earth. You are capable of defeating the gods, the asuras and humans in a battle, not to speak of the Somakas and the Srinjayas, who must follow the dharma of mortals.' The powerful lord of the Madras was praised in this way. The brave one was filled with great joy, the likes of which cannot be obtained by those who have not controlled their souls. Shalya said, 'O Indra among kings! In the battle today, I will slay all the Panchalas and the Pandavas, or be slain and go to heaven. The worlds will see me roam around fearlessly today. Let all the sons of Pandu, Vasudeva, Satyaki, the Panchalas, the Chedis, all the sons of Droupadi, Dhrishtadyumna, Shikhandi and all the Prabhadrakas behold my valour and the great strength of my bow, in addition to the dexterity and valour of my weapons and the strength of my arms in the encounter. Let the Parthas, the siddhas and the charanas behold me today, with the strength of my arms and the wealth of my weapons. The maharatha Pandavas will witness my valour today. Let the enemy try out different means of countering me. Today, I will drive away the Pandu soldiers in every direction. O Kourava! For the sake of bringing you pleasure, I will roam around and fight in the battle today, surpassing Drona, Bhishma and the son of a suta.' O one who grants honours! Amidst your soldiers, Shalya was thus consecrated. O descendant of the Bharata lineage! No one felt any sorrow on account of Karna. The soldiers were happy and cheerful in their minds. They thought that the Parthas had already been killed and had come under the subjugation of the king of Madra. O bull among the Bharata lineage! Your soldiers were filled with great joy. They were assured and slept happily during the night.

'"On hearing the sounds made by your soldiers, while all the kshatriyas heard, King Yudhishthira spoke these words to Varshneya. 'O Madhava! Honoured by all the soldiers, Dhritarashtra's son has made the great archer, Shalya, the king of Madra, the commander. O Madhava! Having heard this, do what is beneficial. You are our leader and our protector. Do what must be done next.' O great king! Vasudeva told the king, 'O descendant of the Bharata lineage! I know everything about Artayani.[48] He is brave and immensely energetic. In particular, he is great-souled. He is accomplished and colourful in fighting. He also possesses dexterity. In an encounter, he is like Bhishma, Drona and Karna. The king of Madra may even be superior to them. That is my view. O descendant of the Bharata lineage! O lord of men! On thinking about it, I cannot find a warrior on your side who is his equal. O descendant of the Bharata lineage! In the battle, he possesses a strength that is superior to Shikhandi, Arjuna, Bhima, Satvata[49] and Dhrishtadyumna. O great king! The king of Madra is like a lion and an elephant in valour. He will roam around fearlessly, like a wrathful Destroyer among beings, when the time for destruction has arrived. O tiger among men! In the battle today, with the exception of you, I do not see any warrior who can fight against him. He is like a tiger in his bravery. Barring you, there is no other man in all of heaven or earth. O descendant of the Kuru lineage! In a battle, there is no one else who can kill the angry king of Madra. He has fought from one day to another, agitating your

[48]Shalya.
[49]Satyaki.

troops. Therefore, kill Shalya in the battle, like Maghavan against Shambara. The brave one is revered by Dhritarashtra's son. When the lord of Madra is killed in the battle, thereafter, victory will be certain. When he is slain, the large army of the son of Dhritarashtra will also be completely destroyed. O great king! O Partha! In the battle, having heard my words, advance against the large army of the king of Madra. O mighty-armed one! Slay him, like Vasava against Namuchi.[50] You should not think of him as your maternal uncle and show any compassion. With the dharma of kshatriyas at the forefront, kill the lord of Madra. The ocean of Bhishma and Drona and the nether region of Karna have been crossed. Having encountered the trifle[51] of Shalya, do not get submerged, with your followers. You possess austerities and valour and the strength of kshatriyas. Exhibit all of those in the battle. Kill the maharatha.' Having spoken these words, Keshava, the slayer of enemy heroes, was honoured by the Pandavas. In the evening, he went to his own camp. When Keshava had left, Dharmaraja Yudhishthira dismissed all his brothers and the Panchalas and the Somakas. He slept happily in the night, like an elephant from which stakes have been removed. All the Panchalas and the Pandavas, great archers, were delighted that Karna had been killed, and slept well during the night. The great archers were cured of their fever. The maharathas had reached a bank.[52] The Pandaveya soldiers rejoiced during the night. O venerable one! With the son of a suta slain, they had obtained victory."'

Chapter 1226(7)

'Sanjaya said, "When night was over, King Duryodhana asked all the maharathas on your side to arm themselves. On hearing the

[50]Namuchi was a demon killed by Indra.

[51]The text uses the word *goshpada*. This literally means the mark of a cow's foot in the soil and the small puddle of water that fills up such a mark, that is, a trifle.

[52]After crossing a river or an ocean.

king's command, the army armoured itself. Some quickly yoked the chariots. Others rushed here and there. The elephants were prepared. The foot soldiers were armoured. Thousands of others spread out coverlets on the horses. O lord of the earth! Musical instruments were sounded and a large roar arose. This was meant to enthuse the warriors and the soldiers. O descendant of the Bharata lineage! All the soldiers were seen to be properly arrayed in the army. They made up their minds to die, rather than retreat. The maharathas made Shalya, the king of Madra, their commander. They divided the army into divisions and stationed themselves. The time having arrived, all the soldiers, with Kripa, Kritavarma, Drona's son, Shalya and Soubala, approached your son, together with the kings who were still alive. They resolved, 'One who fights alone with the Pandavas, or one who abandons a co-warrior who is fighting single-handedly with the Pandaveyas, will commit a sin equal to the five great sins and all the minor sins.[53] We will protect each other and fight in a united way.' The time having arrived, all the maharathas adopted such a resolution. With the king of Madra at the forefront, they quickly advanced against the enemy. O king! In that fashion, in the great battle, the Pandavas also arranged their soldiers in a vyuha. Wishing to fight, all of them advanced against the Kouravas from every side. O foremost among the Bharata lineage! That army[54] made a sound like that of the agitated ocean. With the chariots and the elephants, it assumed a form like that of turbulent waves on an ocean."

'Dhritarashtra asked, "I have heard about the downfall of Drona, Bhishma and Radheya. Tell me now about the downfall of Shalya and my son. O Sanjaya! How was Shalya slain by Dharmaraja in the battle? And how was my mighty-armed son, Duryodhana, brought down by Bhima?"

[53]A great sin is *pataka* or *mahapataka*, while a minor sin is *upapataka*. While it is agreed that there are five great or major sins, the listing of those sins varies. But something like killing a brahmana or having intercourse with a preceptor's wife would figure in all such lists.

[54]The singular is used and it is not clear which of the two armies is being referred to.

'Sanjaya replied, "There was a destruction of the bodies of men, horses, elephants and chariots. O king! Be patient and listen. I will describe the battle that ensued to you. O king! At that time, hope became powerful among your sons. O venerable one! This was despite Bhishma, Drona and the son of a suta having been brought down. They thought that Shalya would kill all the Parthas in the battle. O descendant of the Bharata lineage! Resorting to this hope in their hearts, they were comforted. In the battle, they sought refuge with the maharatha king of Madra. Your son thought that he had found himself a protector. O king! When Karna was slain, the Parthas roared like lions. At that time, a great fear had overtaken the sons of Dhritarashtra. However, they now sought refuge with the powerful king of Madra. O great king! Having constructed a vyuha that was auspicious in every way,[55] the powerful king of Madra attacked the Parthas in the battle. He brandished his colourful bow, which was extremely forceful and capable of withstanding a great burden. The maharatha was on an excellent chariot, yoked to horses from the Sindhu region. O great king! The furrows created by the ratha's chariot were beautiful to behold. The brave one, afflicter of enemies, was surrounded by brave rathas. O great king! The valiant one dispelled the fears of your sons. Armoured and stationed at the head of the vyuha, the king of Madra advanced. He was accompanied by the brave Madrakas and Karna's invincible sons. Kritavarma, surrounded by the Trigartas, was on the left flank. With the Shakas and the Yavanas, Goutama[56] was on the right flank. Surrounded by the Kambojas, Ashvatthama was at the rear. Protected by the bulls among the Kurus, Duryodhana was in the middle. Soubala was surrounded by a large army of horses. The gambler's maharatha son advanced with all the soldiers.[57] The Pandavas, great archers and

[55]The word used is *sarvatobhadra*. Used as an adjective, this does mean auspicious in every way. But the word can also be interpreted as a noun. In that case, a *sarvatabhadra* vyuha would be one symmetrical in every direction, implying either a circle, or perhaps a square.

[56]Kripa.

[57]Shakuni is being described as the gambler. His son is Uluka.

scorchers of enemies, also arranged their soldiers into a vyuha. O great king! They divided themselves into three[58] and attacked your soldiers. In the battle, Dhrishtadyumna, Shikhandi and maharatha Satyaki quickly rushed against Shalya's army. O bull among the Bharata lineage! Wishing to kill, King Yudhishthira surrounded himself by his own troops and attacked Shalya. The great archer Arjuna, the slayer of enemy hordes, powerfully rushed against Hardikya and large numbers of samshaptakas. O Indra among kings! Wishing to kill the enemy in the battle, Bhimasena and the maharatha Somakas attacked Goutama. In the battle, maharatha Shakuni and Uluka were stationed with their forces, and Madri's two sons attacked them, with their soldiers. In that way, tens of thousands of your warriors angrily attacked the Pandavas in the battle, with many different kinds of weapons in their hands."

'Dhritarashtra asked, "O Sanjaya! The great archers and maharathas, Bhishma, Drona and Karna, were killed. In the battle, among the Kurus and the Pandavas, there were only a few left. The powerful Parthas again became enraged in the battle. What were the remaining forces on my side, and on the side of the enemy?"

'Sanjaya replied, "O king! The remaining forces on our side, and on that of the enemy, were stationed for battle again. Listen to who were left in the encounter. O bull among the Bharata lineage! Your side had eleven thousand rathas, ten thousand and seven hundred elephants and a complete complement of two hundred thousand horses. O bull among the Bharata lineage! There were also three crores of men. O descendant of the Bharata lineage! The forces of the Pandavas consisted of six thousand rathas, six thousand elephants, ten thousand horses and one crore of foot soldiers.[59] This is what was left to them in the battle. O bull among the Bharata lineage! These

[58]As described, the divisions amount to more than three. The threefold division probably means troops headed by Bhima, Arjuna and Yudhishthira.

[59]The Kouravas started the war with roughly 1.5 times the size of the Pandava army. The relative destruction of rathas and elephants was more or less proportionate on both sides. However, for cavalry and infantry, there was relatively greater destruction among the Pandavas.

were the ones who attacked each other. O Indra among kings! We followed the instructions of the king of Madra and divided ourselves. Desiring victory, we advanced against the Pandavas. In that way, the brave Pandavas also wished for victory in the battle. With the illustrious Panchalas, those tigers among men attacked. O lord! When it was dawn, thus did those tigers among men rush against each other, wishing to kill each other and rushing forward in strong waves. A fierce battle commenced and it was terrible in form. Those on your side, and the enemy, wished to kill each other."'

Chapter 1227(8)

'Sanjaya said, "O Indra among kings! The terrible battle between the Kurus and the Srinjayas commenced. It was like that between the gods and the asuras and increased one's fear. Men, chariots, crowds of elephants, thousands of riders and horses powerfully clashed against each other. Elephants that were terrible in form rushed forward, and a great noise was heard, like clouds roaring in the sky during the rains. Some rathas were struck by the elephants and fell down from their chariots. In the battle, those brave ones were routed and driven away by those crazy ones.[60] O descendant of the Bharata lineage! Large numbers of well-trained horses were stationed there, to guard the feet of the rathas. Because of the arrows, they were dispatched to the world of the hereafter. O king! Trained horse riders surrounded the maharathas and, roaming around in the battle, slew them with spears, javelins and swords. Some men used bows to repulse the maharathas. Many attacked one and dispatched him to Yama's eternal abode. Maharathas surrounded elephants and the best of chariots. They severed the heads of the warriors and drove them away, with a great roar. The rathas were enraged and shot many arrows. O great king! In every direction, they surrounded and slew the elephants. In

[60]The elephants were crazy.

the battle, elephants attacked elephants and rathas attacked rathas. Using spears, javelins and iron arrows, they killed each other. In the field of battle, foot soldiers, chariots, elephants and horses were seen to be driven away, creating a great tumult. Horses adorned with whisks were routed and drank up the earth[61] and were like swans on the slopes of the Himalayas. O lord of the earth! The earth was marked with the hooves of the horses and was as beautiful as a woman with the marks of nails on her body.[62] There were sounds from the hooves of the horses and the wheels of chariots. There were the sounds of foot soldiers and the trumpeting of elephants. Musical instruments were sounded and conch shells blared. O descendant of the Bharata lineage! The earth resounded, as if it had been struck by a storm. There was the twang of bows. Swords blazed and the armour was radiant. Nothing could be seen. Many arms were severed and were like the trunks of kings of elephants. They writhed fearfully with great force, or were immobile. O great king! Heads fell down on the surface of the earth and a sound was heard, like that when ripe palm fruit falls down. O descendant of the Bharata lineage! Because of the heads that fell down, the earth was red with blood and looked beautiful, as if adorned with golden lotuses in the right season. O great king! With lives lost, the eyes were dilated. With all those wounds, it looked beautiful, as if covered with lotuses. O Indra among kings! Severed hands fell down on the ground, smeared with sandalwood paste and adorned with extremely expensive armlets. They were as dazzling as Shakra's standard. In the great battle, the thighs of the kings were severed. They adorned the field of battle, like the trunks of elephants. Hundreds of headless torsos were strewn around, and umbrellas and fans. That forest of soldiers was as beautiful as a blooming forest. O great king! The warriors roamed around fearlessly. With blood flowing from their limbs, they were seen to be like flowering kimshukas. Elephants were seen there, afflicted by arrows and spears. They fell down in the battle, like dispersed clouds. O great king! The

[61]This is a reference to the speed of the flying horses. They seemed to drink up the earth and were as fast as swans.

[62]Marks left from a session of love.

great-souled ones slaughtered divisions of elephants. They drove them away in all the directions, like clouds dispelled by the wind. Those elephants were like clouds. In every direction, they shrieked and fell down. They were like mountains shattered by thunder, at the time of the destruction of a yuga. Horses fell down on the ground, together with their riders. With their harnesses, those heaps were seen to be like mountains. A river was created on the field of battle and it flowed towards the world hereafter. The water was made out of blood and the chariots were the eddies. The standards were like trees and the bones were the rocks. The arms were the crocodiles. The bows were the current. The elephants were the boulders. The horses were the stones. Fat and marrow constituted the mire. The umbrellas were the swans. The clubs were rafts. Armour and headdresses were scattered around. The flags were like beautiful trees. There were a large number of wheels, trivenus and poles. This delighted brave ones and generated terror among cowards. That terrible river, full of Kurus and Srinjayas, flowed along. That extremely horrible river flowed along to the world of the ancestors. Those brave ones possessed arms like clubs and used their mounts as boats to cross it. O lord of the earth! That cruel battle raged on. It was fierce and led to the destruction of the four kinds of forces,[63] like that in earlier times between the gods and the asuras. O scorcher of enemies! Relatives called out to each other. Other terrified ones returned, after being summoned by their relatives. That battle was cruel and fierce.

'"Arjuna and Bhimasena confounded the enemy. O lord of men! They slaughtered your large army. Your soldiers were confounded by Bhimasena and Dhananjaya. They lost their senses, like a woman under the influence of alcohol. They[64] blew on their conch shells and roared like lions. On hearing that loud noise, with Dharmaraja at the forefront, Dhrishtadyumna and Shikhandi attacked the king of Madra. O lord of the earth! It was terrible in form and we witnessed something that was extraordinary. Those brave ones, who were fighting in different segments, united and attacked Shalya. Madri's

[63]Chariots, elephants, infantry and cavalry.

[64]Bhima and Arjuna.

sons were proud, skilled in the use of weapons and invincible in battle. Wishing to slay your soldiers, they attacked spiritedly. O bull among the Bharata lineage! At this, your forces retreated. The Pandavas, desiring victory, used arrows to mangle them in many ways. While your sons looked on, the army was slaughtered. O great king! Afflicted by the ones who wielded firm bows, they were routed in different directions. O descendant of the Bharata lineage! A great sound of lamentation arose among your warriors. There were some other great-souled kshatriyas who still desired victory in the battle,[65] and they asked them to wait. However, your soldiers were shattered and routed by the Pandavas. In the battle, they abandoned their beloved sons, brothers, grandfathers, maternal uncles, sisters' sons, kin and relatives. Urging the horses and elephants to speed up, the warriors fled in different directions. O bull among the Bharata lineage! Those on your side were only interested in saving themselves."'

Chapter 1228(9)

'Sanjaya said, "On seeing that the army was shattered, the powerful king of Madra urged his charioteer, 'Quickly drive these extremely swift horses towards the spot where King Yudhishthira, Pandu's son, is stationed. He is resplendent, with a white umbrella held aloft his head. O charioteer! Take me there swiftly and behold my might. The Parthas are incapable of remaining stationed before me in the battle today.' Having been thus addressed, the charioteer of the king of Madra departed for the spot where Dharmaraja King Yudhishthira, unwavering in his aim, was. In the battle, Shalya violently descended on the large army of the Pandavas, like the shoreline holding back the rolling waves of the ocean. O venerable one! The Pandava troops clashed against Shalya and stationed themselves in that battle, like a mountain against a flood of

[65]On the Kourava side.

water. On seeing that the king of Madra was stationed in the battle, the Kurus returned, preferring death over retreat. O king! They returned and positioned themselves in different arrays. An extremely terrible battle commenced and blood flowed like water.

'"Nakula, invincible in battle, clashed against Chitrasena.[66] Wielding colourful bows, those two clashed against each other. They were like two clouds that had arisen to the south and the north, and showered down. In the battle, they rained down arrows on each other. I could not differentiate between Pandava and his adversary. Both of them were strong and skilled in the use of weapons. They were knowledgeable about the conduct of rathas. They endeavoured to kill each other and tried to seek out each other's weaknesses. O great king! Using a yellow, sharp and broad-headed arrow, Chitrasena severed Nakula's bow in his hand. Having severed his bow, he then used three gold-tufted arrows that had been sharpened on stone to fearlessly strike him on the forehead. He used sharp arrows to dispatch his horses to the land of the dead and then brought down his standard and charioteer with three arrows each. O king! The three arrows released from his enemy's arm were affixed to his forehead and Nakula looked as beautiful as a mountain with three peaks. His bow was severed and he was without a chariot. The brave one grasped a sword and a shield and jumped down from his chariot, like a lion from the summit of a mountain. As he advanced on foot, arrows were showered down on him. However, Nakula was fierce in his spirit and dexterous in his valour. He received them on his shield. He was colourful in fighting and conquered his exhaustion. While all the soldiers looked on, the mighty-armed one approached Chitrasena's chariot and climbed up. Pandava severed Chitrasena's head, with its earrings and crown, excellent nose and large eyes, from his head. Resplendent as the sun, he fell down from his chariot. On seeing that Chitrasena had been killed, all the maharathas there roared loudly like lions and uttered words of praise.

'"On seeing that their brother had been killed, Karna's maharatha sons, Sushena and Satyasena, released sharp arrows.[67] They swiftly

[66]Karna's son.

[67]There is an inconsistency, because both Sushena and Satyasena have been killed in Section 73.

attacked Pandava, supreme among rathas. O king! They wished to kill him, like two tigers against an elephant in the large forest. Both of them attacked the maharatha with sharp arrows. They flooded him with arrows, like clouds showering down rain. Though he was pierced with arrows all over, Pandava was cheerful. The valiant one grasped another bow and ascended his chariot. The brave one was stationed in the battle, like an enraged Yama. O king! O lord of the earth! Those two brothers used straight-tufted arrows to shatter his chariot. However, in the battle, Nakula laughed. He used four sharp and pointed arrows to slay Satyasena's four horses. O Indra among kings! Pandava affixed a gold-tufted iron arrow that had been sharpened on stone to sever Satyasena's bow. Satyasena grasped another bow and ascended another chariot. He and Sushena attacked Pandava. O great king! In the forefront of the battle, without any fear, Madri's powerful son pierced each of them with two arrows. Maharatha Sushena became enraged. He laughed in the battle and used a kshurapra arrow to sever Pandava's large bow. Nakula became senseless with rage and picked up another bow. He pierced Sushena with five arrows and severed his standard with another one. O venerable one! In the encounter, he spiritedly severed Satyasena's bow and arm-guard. At this, the people roared. He grasped another bow that was forceful and capable of bearing a great load. From every direction, he enveloped Pandu's descendant with arrows. Nakula, the slayer of enemy heroes, repulsed those arrows and pierced both Satyasena and Sushena with two arrows each. O Indra among kings! Each of them separately pierced him back with arrows. They next pierced his charioteer with sharp arrows. The powerful Satyasena displayed the dexterity of his hands. Using separate arrows, he severed Nakula's chariot and bow. However, the atiratha[68] remained stationed on his chariot. He picked up a spear[69] that possessed a golden handle and was sharp at the tip. It was washed in oil and was extremely bright. It was as radiant as the flickering tongue of an immensely poisonous serpent maiden. In the battle, having grasped it, he hurled

[68]Nakula.

[69]*Rathashakti.*

it towards Satyasena. O king! In the encounter, it pierced his heart and shattered it into one hundred fragments. Deprived of his life and bereft of his senses, he fell down from the chariot onto the ground. On seeing that his brother had been slain, Sushena became senseless with rage. He swiftly showered down arrows on Pandu's descendant, who was fighting on foot. On seeing that Nakula was without a chariot, Droupadi's immensely strong son, Sutasoma, wished to save his father[70] in the battle and attacked. Nakula climbed onto Sutasoma's chariot. The foremost among the Bharata lineage looked as beautiful as a lion on a mountain. He picked up another bow and started to fight with Sushena. They showered down arrows on each other and looked dazzling. Those two supreme maharathas made great efforts to slay each other. Sushena angrily struck Pandava with three arrows and pierced Sutasoma in the arms and the chest with twenty arrows. O great king! Nakula, the destroyer of enemy heroes, became angry at this. The valiant one covered all the directions with his arrows. In the battle, he grasped an extremely energetic arrow that was in the shape of a half-moon and was pointed at the tip. With great force, he shot it towards Karna's son. O supreme among kings! While all the soldiers looked on, it severed his head from his body and it was extraordinary. O king! He was slain by the great-souled Nakula and fell down, like a large tree on a bank that is destroyed by the force of a river. O bull among the Bharata lineage! On seeing that Karna's son had been killed and on beholding Nakula's valour, your soldiers were frightened and fled.

'"O great king! The powerful king of Madra saw that the soldiers were running away in the battle. The brave one, the commander who was a scorcher of enemies, sought to restrain the terrified troops. O great king! He roared loudly like a lion and fiercely twanged his bow. O king! The one with the firm bow protected those on your side in the battle. The ones who were running around in different directions returned. From every direction, they surrounded the king of Madra, the great archer. O king! The large army was stationed there, wishing to fight on every side. Satyaki, Bhimasena and the Pandavas who

[70]Father by extension.

were Madri's sons placed the modest Yudhishthira, the scorcher of enemies, at their head. Those brave ones surrounded him in the battle and roared like lions. There was the fierce sound of arrows whizzing. They let out many kinds of roars. In that way, all those on your side angrily surrounded the lord of Madra, desiring to fight again. A battle commenced and it increased the terror of cowards. Those on your side, and that of the enemy, preferred death to retreat and were without fear. O lord of the earth! It was like that between the gods and the asuras in earlier times. It extended Yama's kingdom.

'"O king! Having killed the samshaptakas in the battle, the descendant of the Pandu lineage, with the ape on his banner, attacked the Kourava soldiers. The remaining Pandavas, with Dhrishtadyumna at the forefront, attacked those soldiers and shot sharp arrows. They[71] were overwhelmed and confused by the Pandavas and could not distinguish the directions and the sub-directions. The Pandavas covered them with sharp arrows. In every direction, the foremost ones among the Kourava army were slaughtered and they were routed by the maharatha sons of Pandu. O king! In that way, in the battle, hundreds and thousands of Pandava soldiers were killed by your sons, who shot arrows from every direction. Those two armies slaughtered each other and were tormented. They were anxious and agitated, like rivers during the monsoon. O Indra among kings! In the great battle, those on your side were overcome by a sharp and great fear and so were the Pandavas."'

Chapter 1229(10)

'Sanjaya said, "The soldiers slaughtered each other and were agitated. The warriors were driven away and the tuskers shrieked. In the great battle, the foot soldiers lamented loudly. O great king! The horses ran away in many directions. For all living beings,

[71]The Kourava soldiers.

there was terrible destruction and carnage. Many weapons descended and chariots and elephants were mangled. Those who found joy in battle were delighted. The fear of cowards increased. Wishing to kill each other, the warriors immersed themselves in this. They gave up their lives in that extremely terrible gambling match. The fierce battle extended Yama's kingdom. The Pandavas slaughtered your soldiers with sharp arrows. In that way, your warriors killed the Pandava soldiers. The battle continued and terrified cowards. It was the morning, after the sun had arisen. Unwavering in their aim, the great-souled Pandavas protected the king[72] and killed the enemy. They were powerful and proud strikers and did not miss their objective. They fought against your soldiers, preferring death to retreat. O Kouravya! Your forces weakened, like deer when there is a fire.

'"The army was weakened, like a cow submerged in mud. On seeing this, Shalya wished to rescue it and advanced towards the Pandu army. The king of Madra was angry and picked up a supreme bow. In the battle, he rushed against the Pandava assassins. O great king! The Pandavas desired victory in the encounter. They attacked the king of Madra and pierced him with sharp arrows. While Dharmaraja looked on, the immensely strong king of Madra afflicted those soldiers with hundreds of sharp arrows. O king! At that time, many different kinds of portents manifested themselves. The earth, with its mountains, moved and made a noise. From the solar disc in the firmament, meteors descended on the earth in every direction. They were fierce at the tip, like spears with handles. O lord of the earth! O king! Many deer, buffaloes and birds kept your soldiers to the right.[73] O lord of men! As large numbers descended on each other and attacked with all their divisions, there was a fierce encounter. The Kouravas attacked the Pandava divisions.

'"Spirited in his soul, Shalya attacked Yudhishthira, Kunti's son, showering down arrows, like the one with one thousand

[72]Yudhishthira.

[73]That is, they were to the left of the army, an inauspicious omen, because the left is inauspicious.

eyes[74] pouring down rain. The immensely strong one used gold-tufted arrows that were sharpened on stone to pierce Bhimasena, all of Droupadi's sons, the two Pandavas who were Madri's sons, Dhrishtadyumna, Shini's descendant and Shikhandi, striking each of them with ten arrows. He rained down arrows, like Maghavan showering rain at the end of summer. O king! Because of Shalya's arrows, thousands of Prabhadrakas and Somakas were seen to fall down, or falling down. They were like flights of bees or locusts, driven by the wind. Shalya's arrows descended, like lightning from clouds. Elephants, horses, foot soldiers and rathas were distressed. Because of Shalya's arrows, they fell down, or wandered around, shrieking. They were afflicted by the lord of Madra's anger and manliness. In the battle, he enveloped the enemy, like Yama bestirred by destiny. The immensely strong lord of Madra roared, like lightning in the clouds. The Pandava soldiers were slaughtered by Shalya, with his dexterity and his sharp arrows, and ran towards Kounteya, Ajatashatru Yudhishthira. In the battle, they were oppressed by that great shower of arrows and sought refuge with Yudhishthira. On seeing that he[75] was angrily descending with foot soldiers and horses, King Yudhishthira countered him with sharp arrows, like a crazy elephant checked with a goad. Shalya released a terrible arrow that was like a venomous serpent. It pierced the great-souled one with force and fell down on the ground. At this, Vrikodara wrathfully pierced him with seven arrows, Sahadeva with five and Nakula with ten arrows. Droupadi's sons showered down arrows on Artayani, the immensely fortunate slayer of enemies, like clouds pouring down on a mountain. On seeing that Shalya was assailed from every side by the Parthas, Kritavarma and Kripa attacked angrily. Uluka attacked like a bird[76] and so did Shakuni Soubala. Maharatha Ashvatthama smiled gently. All your sons protected Shalya in the battle.

'"Kritavarma used three arrows with iron heads to pierce Bhimasena. Assuming an angry form, he repulsed him with a great

[74]Indra.

[75]Shalya.

[76]The text says *patatri*, bird. This may be a typo.

shower of arrows. Kripa angrily afflicted Dhrishtadyumna with a shower of arrows. Shakuni attacked Droupadi's son and Drona's son attacked the twins. Duryodhana, best of warriors, was fierce in his energy and strong. In the battle, he advanced against Keshava and Arjuna and attacked them with arrows. There were hundreds of duels between those on your side and the enemy at various spots. O lord of the earth! It was fierce in form and wonderful. In the battle, Bhoja slew Bhima's brown horses. When the horses were slain, Pandu's descendant descended from his chariot and fought with a club in his hand, like Yama with an upraised staff. In his sight, the king of Madra slew Sahadeva's horses. At this, Sahadeva killed Shalya's son with his sword. The preceptor, Goutama, again fought with Dhrishtadyumna. Both of them were fearless and made efforts against each other. The preceptor's son[77] wasn't very angry. He smiled and pierced each of Droupadi's brave sons with ten arrows. O king! Shalya angrily slaughtered the Somakas and the Pandavas. He again afflicted Yudhishthira with sharp arrows.

'"The valiant Bhima was angry in the battle and bit his lower lips in rage. To destroy him,[78] he hurled a club. It was like Yama's staff and was raised, like the night of destruction. It was capable of destroying the lives of elephants, horses and men. It was bound in golden cloth and blazed like a meteor. It was like the vajra to the touch and was completely made out of iron. It was as fierce as a she-serpent and was slung in a noose. It was smeared with sandalwood paste and unguents, like a desired woman. It was smeared with fat and marrow and it was like Yama's tongue. There were bells attached to it and it was like Vasava's vajra. It was smeared with the fat of elephants and it was like a snake that had cast off its skin. It frightened the enemy soldiers and delighted the soldiers on one's own side. It was famous in the world of men and was capable of shattering the summit of a mountain. It was one with which powerful Kounteya had challenged the lord of Alaka, Maheshvara's friend, in his abode in Kailasa.[79]

[77]Ashvatthama.

[78]Shalya.

[79]The lord of the yakshas is Kubera and his capital is Alaka, in Kailasa. Kubera is Maheshavara's (Shiva's) friend. Bhima fought with the yakshas. The

For the sake of the *mandara* flower, the immensely strong one had proudly killed many guhyakas, who used their powers of maya, in the abode of the lord of the riches. To ensure Droupadi's pleasure, he had countered many. It[80] was famous as the vajra and possessing eight sides, it was embellished with diamonds, gems and jewels. Raising it, the mighty-armed one attacked Shalya in the battle. He was skilled in fighting and grasped that fearful club. He brought down Shalya's four horses, which were extremely fast. At this, Shalya became angry in the battle. He hurled a javelin towards his broad chest and roared. It pierced the brave one's armour and penetrated. However, Vrikodara wasn't frightened. He plucked the javelin out and pierced the king of Madra's charioteer in the heart with it. With the armour penetrated, he was distressed in his mind and began to vomit blood. He fell downwards and the king of Madra looked on, in sorrow. On seeing that his own deed had been countered, Shalya wondered in his mind. Serene in his soul, he grasped a club and glanced towards his opponent. On beholding his deed in the battle, the Parthas were delighted in their minds and honoured Bhimasena, the performer of terrible and unblemished deeds."'

Chapter 1230(11)

'Sanjaya said, "O king! Shalya saw that his charioteer had been killed. He quickly picked up a club that was completely made out of iron and stood immobile, like a mountain. He was like the blazing fire of destruction, or like Yama with a noose in his hand. He was like the summit of Kailasa, or Vasava with the vajra. He was like the tawny-eyed one[81] with a trident, or like a crazy elephant in the forest. Bhima grasped a mighty club and swiftly dashed towards

---

incident has been described in Section 35 (Volume 3). Bhima went in search of a flower, because Droupadi wanted it.

[80]The club.

[81]Shiva.

him. At that time, thousands of conch shells and trumpets blared. The brave ones roared like lions and this increased one's delight. All the warriors saw them fight against each other, like giant elephants. Those on your side, and on the side of the enemy, uttered words of praise. With the exception of the lord of Madra, Rama[82] and the descendant of the Yadu lineage, who else was capable of withstanding Bhimasena's force in an encounter? With the exception of the great-souled lord of Madra and the force of his club, which other warrior was capable of fighting against Vrikodara? They roared like bulls and circled each other. With clubs in their hands, the king of Madra and Vrikodara wheeled around each other. In the circles that they executed, or in the way they roamed around with the clubs, there was nothing to differentiate those two lions among men in the encounter. Shalya's club was made of gold. It was radiant and sparkling and increased one's terror. It was tied in cloth that looked like a net of fire. The great-souled Bhima roamed around in circles with a radiant club that looked like clouds tinged with lightning. O king! The king of Madra struck Bhima's club with his club and this generated blazing sparks of fire. In that way, Bhima struck Shalya's club with his club and this released a shower of flames. It was extraordinary. They were like giant elephants with tusks, or gigantic bulls with horns. They struck each other with the tips of their clubs, wishing to kill each other. Struck by the clubs, in a short while, blood began to flow from their bodies. They were beautiful to behold, like two flowering kimshukas. Bhimsena was struck on the right and the left by the king of Madra's club. However, the mighty-armed one was immobile, like a mountain. O king! In that fashion, Shalya was repeatedly struck by the force of Bhima's club. But he did not waver, like a mountain struck by a tusker. The sounds generated by those two lions among men could be heard in all the directions. The clubs descended and struck, with a sound like that of the vajra. Those two immensely valorous ones stopped for a while and then again attacked with their clubs. They again roamed around, executing circular motions. Raising those iron staffs, they advanced eight steps forward and

[82]Parashurama.

struck each other, performing a superhuman deed. They roamed around, executing circular motions and seeking to strike each other. Those accomplished ones exhibited great deeds. They raised those terrible clubs, which were like the summits of mountains. They struck each other, like mountains at the time of an earthquake. They were severely struck from the force of each other's clubs. Both of those brave ones simultaneously fell down, like Indra's standards. Sounds of lamenation arose from the brave ones in both armies. They were severely struck in their inner organs and lost their senses. Shalya, bull among the Madras, was severely struck by the club and Kripa used his chariot to swiftly bear him away from the field of battle. Bhimasena was also weakened and senseless. However, he raised himself in an instant. With the club in his hand, he challenged the king of Madra.

'"The brave ones on your side raised many kinds of weapons. To the sound of diverse kinds of musical instruments, they fought with the Pandu soldiers. They held weapons in their hands and made a great noise. O great king! With Duryodhana at the forefront, they attacked. On seeing those soldiers, the sons of Pandu roared like lions and advanced, wishing to kill Duryodhana. O bull among the Bharata lineage! On seeing that they were swiftly descending, your son severely pierced Chekitana[83] in the heart with a javelin. Struck thus by your son, he fell down from his chariot. With blood flowing from his body, he was submerged in great darkness. On seeing that Chekitana had been killed, the maharatha Pandavas engaged and showered down arrows on the different divisions. O great king! The Pandavas could be seen to roam around and attacked your soldiers from every direction, desiring victory. With the king of Madra at the forefront, Kripa, Kritavarma and the immensely strong Soubala fought with Dharmaraja. O great king! Duryodhana fought with Dhrishtadyumna, who was the slayer of Bharadvaja's son and great in his valour and bravery. O king! Goaded by your son, with Drona's son at their head, three thousand rathas on your side fought Vijaya.

[83]The prince of Chedi, Dhrishtaketu's son.

'"O king! Setting their minds on victory and ready to give up their lives, those on your side penetrated, like swans into a large lake. As they sought to kill each other, an extremely terrible battle raged on. They wished to kill each other and were delighted at being able to strike each other. O king! The battle that led to the destruction of the best among brave ones continued. The earth was covered with a terrible dust that arose in the air. We could ascertain who the Pandavas were, only when they called out to each other. We fought fearlessly. O tiger among men! That dust was pacified by the blood. When the dust was pacified, the directions could clearly be seen. The fearful battle, terrible in form, continued between those on your side and the enemy. No one wished to retreat. With Brahma's world as the supreme objective, they wished for victory in the battle. Wishing to go to heaven, those brave men fought an excellent war. Setting their minds on the tasks of their masters, they wished to repay the debts of their masters. With their minds set on heaven, they fought and clashed against each other. The maharathas released many different kinds of weapons. They roared at each other and struck each other. 'Strike. Pierce. Seize. Hit. Sever.' These were the words that were heard amongst the armies on your side and that of the enemy.

'"O great king! Wishing to kill maharatha Dharmaraja Yudhishthira, Shalya pierced him with sharp arrows. O great king! However, Partha knew about the inner organs. He smiled and struck him in the inner organs with fourteen iron arrows. The immensely illustrious one wished to kill Pandava and repulsed him with arrows. In the battle, he angrily pierced him with many arrows tufted with the feathers of herons. O great king! While all the soldiers looked on, he again struck Yudhishthira with an arrow with a drooping tuft. Dharmaraja became extremely angry. The immensely illustrious one pierced the king of Madra with sharp arrows that were tufted with the feathers of herons and peacocks. The maharatha then struck Chandrasena with seventy arrows, his charioteer with nine and Drumasena with sixty-four.[84] O king! When the protectors of

[84]As the next sentence makes clear, Chandrasena and Drumasena were guarding Shalya's chariot wheels.

his chariot wheels were slain by the great-minded Pandava, Shalya killed twenty-five Chedis. He pierced Satyaki with twenty-five sharp arrows, Bhimasena with five and Madri's two sons with one hundred. O supreme among kings! While he was thus roaming around in the battle, Partha shot sharp arrows at him and these were like venomous serpents. In the battle, with a broad-headed arrow, Yudhishthira, Kunti's son, brought down the tip of his adversary's standard from his chariot, while he looked on. Severed by the great-souled son of Pandu, the standard was seen to fall down, like the summit of a mountain. On seeing that his standard had been brought down and on seeing Pandava stationed, the king of Madra angrily showered down arrows. Shalya showered down arrows, like Parjanya pouring down rain. The bull among the kshatriya lineage, immeasurable in his soul, showered down arrows on the kshatriyas—Satyaki, Bhimasena and the two Pandavas who were the sons of Madri. He pierced each of them with five arrows and afflicted Yudhishthira. O great king! We saw a net of arrows spread over Pandava's chest, like a mass of clouds that had risen. In the battle, maharatha Shalya angrily used straight-tufted arrows to envelop the directions and the sub-directions. King Yudhishthira was afflicted by that net of arrows. He seemed to have been deprived of his valour, like Jambha by the slayer of Vritra."'[85]

Chapter 1231(12)

'Sanjaya said, "O venerable one! When Dharmaraja was thus afflicted by the king of Madra, Satyaki, Bhimasena and the Pandavas who were Madri's sons surrounded Shalya with chariots and oppressed him in the battle. On seeing that the single-handed one was afflicted by the maharathas, great sounds of praise arose from the delighted siddhas.[86] The assembled sages also said that it

[85]Indra killed a demon named Jambha.

[86]The siddhas were delighted that he could fight with them single-handed.

was extraordinary. Shalya was like a dart in his valour[87] and in the battle, Bhimsena pierced him with an arrow. He then pierced him again with seven. Satyaki wished to rescue Dharma's son. He covered the lord of Madra with hundreds of arrows and roared like a lion. Nakula pierced him with five arrows. Sahadeva pierced him with seven and then swiftly pierced him again with another seven. While he endeavoured in the battle, the brave one was afflicted by those maharathas. He brandished his terrible bow, which was extremely forceful and capable of bearing a great load. O venerable one! Shalya pierced Satyaki with twenty-five arrows, Bhimasena with seventy-three and Nakula with seven. In the battle, he used broad-headed arrows to sever the archer Sahadeva's bow, with an arrow affixed to it, and pierced him with seventy-three arrows. Sahadeva strung another bow. In the encounter, he struck his greatly radiant maternal uncle with five arrows that were like virulent serpents and blazed like the fire. In the battle, extremely enraged, he struck his charioteer with arrows with drooping tufts and pierced him[88] again with three arrows. Bhimasena struck Shalya in his body with seventy-three arrows, Satyaki with nine and Dharmaraja with sixty. O great king! Shalya was pierced by those maharathas. Blood began to flow from his body, like red chalk from a mountain. O king! He spiritedly struck those great archers with five arrows each and it was wonderful. O venerable one! He then used another broad-headed arrow to sever the bow of Dharma's son in the battle. At this, Dharma's maharatha son picked up and strung another bow and shrouded Shalya, his horses, his charioteer, his standard and his chariot with arrows. He was thus enveloped in the encounter by the arrows of Dharma's son. He pierced Yudhishthira with ten sharp arrows. Satyaki was angry that Dharma's son was thus afflicted by arrows. He enveloped the brave lord of Madra with torrents of arrows. In Bhimasena's presence, he then used a kshurapra arrow to slice down Satyaki's large bow and struck him with three arrows. O great king! Satyaki, for whom truth was his valour, became wrathful. He hurled an extremely expensive

[87]There is a pun on the word shalya, which means arrow, spear or dart.
[88]Shalya.

spear with a golden handle. Bhimasena shot an iron arrow that was like a flaming serpent. In the battle, Nakula hurled a javelin and Sahadeva a sparkling club. Dharmaraja used a shataghni. All of them wished to kill Shalya in the battle.

'"They were swiftly released from the arms of those five.[89] Shalya severed the spear Satyaki had hurled with a broad-headed arrow. Bhima had shot an arrow decorated with gold. In the battle, the powerful one displayed the dexterity of his hands and severed it into two fragments. Nakula had hurled a fearful javelin with a golden handle and Sahadeva a club. He countered these with torrents of arrows. O descendant of the Bharata lineage! While the sons of Pandu looked on, he used a couple of arrows to sever the king's shataghni and roared like a lion. Shini's descendant could not tolerate that the enemy should be victorious in the battle. Senseless with rage, Satyaki picked up another bow. With two arrows, he pierced the lord of Madra and used another three to pierce his charioteer. O great king! Shalya became extremely angry. He severely pierced each of them with ten arrows, like a giant elephant being struck with a goad. In the encounter, those maharathas were repulsed by the king of Madra. Those slayers of enemies were incapable of remaining before him. King Duryodhana witnessed Shalya's valour and thought that the Pandavas, the Panchalas and the Srinjayas had been killed. O king! The mighty-armed and powerful Bhimasena made up his mind to give up his life and fought with the lord of Madra. Nakula, Sahadeva and maharatha Satyaki surrounded Shalya and showered down arrows on him. The powerful king of Madra was surrounded by those four Pandava maharathas and great archers. However, he fought with them. O king! In the great battle, Dharmaraja used a kshurapra arrow to swiftly slay the one who was guarding the chariot wheel of the king of Madra.[90] The king of Madra was extremely strong and enveloped the soldiers with arrows. O king! On seeing that the soldiers were enveloped in that battle, Dharmaraja Yudhisthira

[89]Satyaki, Bhima, Nakula, Sahadeva and Yudhishthira.

[90]However, we have earlier been told that the two who were guarding the chariot wheels had been killed.

began to think. 'The great words that were spoken by Madhava have really come true. I hope that the king will not angrily destroy my army in the battle.' O Pandu's elder brother! With their chariots, elephants and horses, the Pandavas approached the lord of Madra and afflicted him from every direction. They used many diverse kinds of weapons. A shower of arrows arose. O king! In the battle, he drove these away, like clouds dispelled by the wind. Shalya poured down gold-tufted arrows. We beheld that shower of arrows, like locusts descending. The king of Madra released those arrows in the field of battle. We saw them descend, like a flight of locusts. Gold-decorated arrows were shot from the king of Madra's bow. O lord of men! They did not leave a single bit of space in the sky. Nothing could be discerned there, the Pandavas, nor those on our side. He created a great darkness because of those arrows and there was great fear. The powerful king of Madra used his dexterity to shower down arrows. The Pandava army was seen to be agitated there, like the ocean. The gods, the gandharvas and the danavas were overcome by great wonder. O venerable one! Everyone who strove against him was afflicted by those arrows. He enveloped Dharmaraja and roared repeatedly, like a lion. The Pandava maharathas were shrouded by him in that battle. In the encounter, no one was capable of standing up to the maharatha and fighting against him. But those that had Dharmaraja at their head or the rathas who had Bhimasena at the forefront, did not retreat in the battle before the brave Shalya, the ornament of a battle."'

Chapter 1232(13)

'Sanjaya said, "In the battle, Drona's son pierced Arjuna with many iron arrows and so did his followers, the brave maharathas from Trigarta. In the encounter, he pierced Drona's son with three arrows sharpened on stone. Dhananjaya pierced the other great archers with two arrows each. The mighty-armed one showered down arrows again. O bull among the Bharata lineage! Those on your side were impaled with arrows, like thorns. But though they were slaughtered by those sharp arrows, they did not abandon Partha in that battle. With Drona's son at the forefront, in the battle, the maharathas surrounded Arjuna with an array of chariots and fought against him. O king! They shot arrows decorated with gold. They swiftly covered the seat of Arjuna's chariot. The two Krishnas were bulls among all archers. They were great archers. On seeing that their limbs were covered with arrows, the ones who found delight in battle rejoiced.[91] O lord! The pole, wheels, staff, harnesses and yoke of the chariot were completely covered with arrows and looked beautiful. O king! The likes of what those on your side did to Partha had not been seen earlier, nor heard of. Covered by those sharp arrows with colourful tufts, the chariot was dazzling. It was as if a celestial vehicle had come down on earth and was blazing because of a hundred torches. O great king! Arjuna used arrows with straight tufts to repel those soldiers, like a cloud pouring down rain on a mountain. In the battle, they were slaughtered by Partha's arrows, which were marked with his name. They thought that the entire field was full of many Parthas. Partha was like a fire. The arrows were flames. The great twang of the bow was the wind that fanned it. The soldiers on your side were the kindling. It was extraordinary. Wheels and yokes fell down on the ground, together with quivers, flags, standards and chariots. O descendant of the Bharata lineage! There were arrows, housings, trivenus, wheels, yokes and goads in every direction. Heads fell down, wearing earrings and headdresses. O great king! Arms and shoulders were strewn around everywhere. O descendant of the Bharata lineage! Along the path of Partha's chariot, umbrellas, whisks, crowns and reins could be seen. Because of the mire created by flesh and blood, the earth became impassable. O best of the Bharata lineage! It looked like Rudra's sporting ground. This generated fear among cowards and increased the delight of brave ones. O scorcher of enemies! Partha destroyed two thousand chariots in that encounter, together with their bumpers. He was like

[91]That is, the Kourava warriors rejoiced.

a flame without smoke. O king! Maharatha Partha was seen there, like the smokeless and illustrious Agni, consuming all mobile and immobile objects.

'"On witnessing Pandava's valour in the battle, Drona's son countered Pandava, on a chariot with many flags. Those two tigers among men were the best of archers and were borne on white horses. They swiftly clashed against each other, wishing to kill each other. O great king! O bull among the Bharata lineage! The extremely terrible shower of arrows was like rain pouring down from clouds. They rivalled each other with their straight-tufted arrows. Like two bulls with horns, they mangled each other in that encounter. O great king! The battle between them lasted for a long time. There was a great and terrible clash of weapons there. O descendant of the Bharata lineage! Drona's son pierced Arjuna with twelve gold-tufted arrows that were extremely energetic and Vasudeva with ten. In the great battle, Bibhatsu showed respect towards his preceptor's son for a short while. Then he laughed and stretched his Gandiva bow. Maharatha Savyasachi deprived him of his horses, charioteer and chariot and gently pierced him with three arrows. Though his horses had been slain, Drona's son remained stationed on that chariot. He smiled and hurled a club that was like a bludgeon towards Pandu's son. It was bound in golden cloth and descended with great violence. But the brave Partha, the destroyer of enemies, shattered it into seven fragments. On seeing that the club had been shattered, Drona's son became supremely angry. He picked up a terrible bludgeon that was like the summit of a king of mountains. Drona's son was skilled in fighting and hurled this towards Partha. Pandava saw that the bludgeon had been angrily flung towards him. Arjuna used five supreme arrows to swiftly slice it down. In the great battle, shattered by Partha's arrows, it fell down on the ground. O descendant of the Bharata lineage! That sound shattered the minds of the kings. Pandava then pierced Drona's son with three supreme weapons. The extremely strong one was severely and powerfully struck by Partha. However, Drona's son resorted to his manliness and wasn't frightened.

'"O king! While all the kshatriyas looked on, Bharadvaja's maharatha son covered Sudharma with a storm of arrows. At this, the Panchala maharatha Suratha attacked Drona's son on his chariot, making a sound like the roaring of clouds. He brandished his supreme bow, which was firm and was capable of bearing all loads. He shot flaming arrows that were like venomous serpents. In the battle, when maharatha Suratha angrily descended, Drona's son became wrathful, like a snake that has been struck with a staff. His brows furrowed into three lines and he licked the corners of his mouth. He glanced at Suratha in rage and rubbed his bowstring. He shot a sharp iron arrow that was like Yama's staff. It powerfully pierced and shattered his heart and then penetrated the ground, like Shakra's unleashed vajra. Slain by the iron arrow, he fell down on the ground. It was as if an extremely large mountain top had been shattered by thunder. When that brave one was killed, Drona's powerful son, supreme among rathas, swiftly climbed onto his chariot.[92] O great king! Drona's son was invincible in battle. Equipped and supported by the samshaptakas in the encounter, he fought with Arjuna. There was a great battle between Arjuna and the enemy. It extended Yama's kingdom. The sun reached midday. The valour that they exhibited was wonderful to see. Arjuna single-handedly fought with many enemies at the same time. The great clash between Arjuna and the enemy was like that in earlier times, between Shatakratu and the daitya soldiers."'

Chapter 1233(14)

'Sanjaya said, "O great king! Duryodhana and Parshata Dhrishtadyumna fought a great battle, with innumerable arrows and javelins. O great king! They shot thousands of torrents of arrows. It was like rain pouring down from clouds during the monsoon. The king pierced Parshata with five arrows that were made out of iron. He then again pierced the fierce one who had killed Drona with seven arrows. In the encounter, Dhrishtadyumna

[92]Ashvatthama climbed onto Suratha's chariot.

was powerful and firm in his valour. He struck Duryodhana with seventy arrows. O bull among the Bharata lineage! On seeing that the king was afflicted, his brothers surrounded Parshata with a large army. O king! Severely surrounded by those brave atirathas from all sides, he roamed around in the battle, exhibiting the dexterity of his hands. Shikhandi, supported by the Prabhadrakas, fought with the maharatha archers, Kritavarma and Goutama. O lord of the earth! There was a great battle there, fierce in form. They were ready to give up their lives in the battle and offered their lives as stakes in the gambling match.

'"Shalya showered down arrows in every direction. He afflicted the Pandavas, including Satyaki and Vrikodara. O Indra among kings! Using his valour and strength, he also fought in that encounter with the twins, who were like Yama in their prowess. When the Pandavas were afflicted by Shalya's arrows in the great battle, those maharathas could not find a protector. On seeing that Dharmaraja was oppressed, the brave Nakula, Madri's son, powerfully attacked his maternal uncle. Nakula, the destroyer of enemy heroes, enveloped Shalya in that battle. He smiled and struck him between the breasts with ten arrows. These arrows were completely made out of iron and had been polished by artisans. They were gold-tufted and sharpened on stone. They were propelled from the implement of the bow. Shalya was struck by his sister's great-souled son and pierced Nakula with straight-flying arrows. At this, King Yudhishthira, Bhimasena, Satyaki and Madri's son, Sahadeva, attacked the king of Madra. They descended swiftly and the directions and the sub-directions resounded with the roar of their chariots. The earth trembled. The conqueror of enemies, the commander, received them in the battle. He pierced Yudhishthira with three arrows, Bhimasena with seven, Satyaki with one hundred and Sahadeva with three arrows. O venerable one! The lord of Madra used a kshurapra arrow to slice down the great-souled Nakula's bow, with an arrow affixed to it. When his bow was shattered and destroyed by Shalya's arrows, Madri's maharatha son quickly picked up another bow and covered the king of Madra's chariot with arrows. O venerable one! Both Yudhishthira and Sahadeva pierced the lord of Madra in the chest with ten arrows each. Bhimasena attacked the king of Madra and struck him with sixty arrows shafted with the feathers of herons. Satyaki did the same with nine arrows. The king of Madra angrily struck Satyaki with nine arrows and pierced him again with seventy arrows with drooping tufts. O venerable one! He struck down the bow in his[93] hand, with an arrow affixed to it and, in the battle, dispatched his four horses to the land of the dead. Satyaki was deprived of his chariot by the immensely strong king of Madra, who struck him with one hundred arrows from every direction. O Kouravya! He then pierced Madri's angry sons, Pandava Bhimasena and Yudhishthira with ten arrows each. We witnessed the king of Madra's extraordinary manliness. Even though they were together, the Parthas could not counter him in the battle.

'"Satyaki, for whom truth was his valour, climbed onto another chariot. He saw that the Pandavas were afflicted and had come under the king of Madra's subjugation. The powerful one attacked the lord of Madra with force. On seeing that he was descending on his chariot, Shalya, the ornament of an assembly, countered him on his chariot, like a crazy elephant against another crazy elephant. The clash that ensued was tumultuous and wonderful to behold. The brave Satyaki and the lord of Madra fought, like the ancient battle between Shambara and the kind of the immortals. On seeing that the king of Madra was stationed in the battle, Satyaki asked him to wait and pierced him with ten arrows. The king of Madra was grievously pierced by the great-souled one. He pierced Satyaki back with sharp arrows that were colourfully tufted. The Parthas, great archers, saw that the king was assailed by Satvata. Wishing to kill their maternal uncle, they quickly attacked him on their chariots. In that supreme and tumultuous encounter, blood flowed like water. The brave ones fought and roared like lions. O great king! They mangled each other. In the encounter, they shot arrows and roared like lions. The earth was covered with thousands of torrents of arrows. The firmament was also suddenly covered with arrows. In every direction, those arrows created a great darkness. The arrows

[93]Satyaki's.

shot by the great-souled ones created a shadow, like that of clouds. O king! The arrows released there were like snakes that had cast off their skins. They were gold-tufted and made the directions blaze. Shalya, the destroyer of enemies, was supreme and wonderful. In the battle, he single-handedly fought against many brave ones. Arrows, shafted with the feathers of herons and peacocks, were released from the king of Madra's arms. That terrible torrent of arrows descended and covered the earth. O king! Shalya's chariot roamed around in the great battle there. We saw him, like Shakra in earlier times, when the asuras were being destroyed."'

Chapter 1234(15)

'Sanjaya said, "O lord! Your soldiers placed the king of Madra at their head. In that great battle, they again powerfully attacked the Parthas. Though they were afflicted, all those on your side were intoxicated at the prospect of war. In a short while, they agitated the Parthas in many ways. While Krishna and Partha looked on, the Pandavas were slaughtered by the Kurus and were incapable of remaining stationed there, though they were restrained by Bhima. Dhananjaya became angry at this. He covered Kripa and his followers and Kritavarma with a storm of arrows. Sahadeva countered Shakuni and his soldiers. Stationed on a flank, Nakula glanced at the king of Madra. Droupadi's sons repeatedly repulsed many kings. Panchala Shikhandi countered Drona's son. With the club in his hand, Bhimasena held back the kings. Kunti's son, Yudhishthira, countered Shalya and his soldiers. As those on your side and the enemy engaged, refusing to retreat from the battle, duels commenced here and there.

'"In the great battle, we witnessed Shalya's supreme deed. He single-handedly fought against all the soldiers on the Pandava side. We saw Shalya stationed near Yudhishthira in the battle, like the planet Saturn near the moon. He afflicted the king with arrows that were like venomous serpents. He again attacked Bhima and covered him with showers of arrows. On witnessing the lightness of his hands and his skill in the use of weapons, the soldiers on your side and those on the side of the enemy, applauded him. The Pandavas were severely oppressed and wounded by Shalya. Ignoring Yudhishthira's cries, they abandoned the field of battle. The Pandava soldiers were slaughtered by the king of Madra. Dharmaraja Yudhishthira was overcome with intolerance. He resorted to his manliness and oppressed the king of Madra. The maharatha made up his mind to win or be killed. He summoned all his brothers and Krishna Madhava and said, 'Bhishma, Drona, Karna and all the other brave kings fought in the battle for the sake of the Kouravas and went to their death. All of you have resorted to your manliness and used your enterprise to take care of your shares.[94] There is a single share that is left. Maharatha Shalya is mine. I wish to fight against the lord of Madra and defeat him today. I will tell all of you what is in my mind now. Madravati's[95] brave sons will guard my chariot wheels. They are revered as brave ones in battle and cannot be vanquished by Vasava. They will place the dharma of kshatriyas at the forefront and virtuously fight against their maternal uncle. They deserve honour and are devoted to the truth. They will fight back, for my sake. O fortunate ones! Either Shalya will be killed by me in the battle, or I will be killed by him. O brave ones in the world! Listen to my words. I am telling you truthfully. O kings! I will resort to the dharma of kshatriyas and fight against my maternal uncle today. I have determined that I will be victorious, or be defeated. Therefore, equip me with a larger store of weapons and all the implements. Let the chariot be quickly equipped for the battle, in accordance with the decrees of the sacred texts. Let Shini's descendant guard my right wheel and Dhrishtadyumna the left. Let Partha Dhananjaya protect my rear today. Let Bhima, supreme among wielders of weapons, advance in front of me today. In the great battle, I will then be superior to Shalaya and will drive him away.' Having been thus addressed by the king, all the well-wishers

[94]The Pandavas had apportioned out the Kouravas amongst themselves. Shalya was Yudhishthira's share.

[95]Madri's.

did as they had been asked to. O king! The soldiers were again filled with delight. This was especially true of the Panchalas, the Somakas and the Matsyas. Having taken the pledge, Dharmaraja set out to accomplish it in the battle.

'"Hundreds of conch shells, trumpets and drums were sounded by the Panchalas and they roared like lions. Spiritedly and angrily, they rushed towards the king of Madra. The bulls among the Kurus were also filled with great delight and roared. There was the noise of bells on elephants and the blare of conch shells. The earth resounded with the great sounds of trumpets. Your son and the valiant king of Madra received them. They were like large mountains, receiving rain pouring down from giant clouds. Shalya prided himself in battle and showered down arrows on Dharmaraja, the scorcher of enemies, like Maghavan pouring down rain. The great-minded king of the Kurus also grasped a beautiful bow and displayed the diverse kinds of learning that he had been taught by Drona. He showered down arrows, colourful, dexterous and skilled. As he roamed around in the battle, no weakness could be discerned in him. They wounded each other with many kinds of arrows. In the battle, those valorous ones were like tigers fighting over a piece of meat. Bhima clashed against your son, who found delight in a battle. In every direction, Shakuni and the other brave ones received Panchala,[96] Satyaki and the Pandavas who were the sons of Madri. They desired victory and fought tumultuously again. O king! The enemy and those on your side fought because of your evil policy.

'"In the battle, Duryodhana used an arrow with a drooping tuft to sever Bhima's gold-decorated standard. It was large and beautiful to see, adorned with nets of bells. Having brought Bhimasena's standard down, he roared like a lion. With a razor-sharp arrow, pointed at the tip, the lord of men then severed his[97] colourful bow, which was like the trunk of a king of elephants. When his bow was severed, the spirited one resorted to his prowess and hurled a javelin[98]

[96]Dhrishtadyumna.
[97]Bhima's.
[98]Rathashakti.

towards your son. It pierced his chest and made him sink down on his chariot. When he was bereft of his senses, Vrikodara again used a kshurapra arrow to sever his charioteer's head from his body. O descendant of the Bharata lineage! O king! When the charioteer was slain, the horses dragged the chariot away in different directions and loud sounds of lamentation arose. For the sake of rescuing your son, Drona's maharatha son, Kripa and Kritavarma followed. The soldiers were agitated and the followers were terrified. The wielder of Gandiva used his bow and arrows to slaughter them.

'"Yudhishthira intolerantly attacked the lord of Madra. He himself controlled his horses, which were as swift as thought and as white as ivory. When we saw Kunti's son, Yudhishthira, it was extraordinary. He was mild and controlled earlier, but assumed a fearful form. Kounteya dilated his eyes in rage and trembled in anger. He mangled hundreds and thousands of warriors with his arrows. Wherever the soldiers fought back, the eldest Pandava was there. O king! He brought them down with his arrows, like the best of mountains shattered by thunder. Many horses, charioteers, standards, chariots and rathas were brought down. He sported with them, like a violent wind toying with clouds. In the battle, he angrily brought down thousands of horse riders, horses and foot soldiers, like an enraged Rudra among animals. With showers of arrows shot in every direction, he emptied the field of battle of warriors. He attacked Shalya, the lord of Madra, and asked him to wait. On witnessing him roam around in the battle, terrible in his deeds, all those on your side were terrified. However, Shalya countered him. Extremely enraged, those two blew on their conch shells. They challenged each other and censured each other. Shalya countered Yudhishthira with a shower of arrows. Kounteya also countered the king of Madra with a shower of arrows. O king! In that battle, those two brave ones, the king of Madra and Yudhishthira, were seen to be covered with blood, because of the arrows shafted with the feathers of herons. They were as beautiful as flowering shalmali or kimshuka trees in the forest. Those great-souled ones blazed. They were ready to give up their lives and were unassailable in battle. On seeing them, none of the soldiers knew which one would be victorious, whether Partha would kill the lord of Madra and enjoy the earth today, or whether Shalya would kill Pandava and give the earth to Duryodhana. O descendant of the Bharata lineage! The warriors there could not make up their minds on this. As he fought, Dharmaraja kept all of them to his right.[99] Shalya swiftly shot one hundred arrows towards Yudhishthira. He severed his bow with an arrow that was sharp at the tip. He picked up another bow and piercing Shalya with three hundred arrows, severed his bow with a razor-sharp arrow. He then slew his four horses with arrows with drooping tufts. With two arrows that were sharp at the tips, he killed the two parshni charioteers. Stationed in front of him, he used a blazing, yellow, sharp and broad-headed arrow to sever his standard. O scorcher of enemies! At this, that army of Duryodhana's scattered. Drona's son rushed towards the king of Madra and picking him up on his chariot, swiftly fled. After they had travelled a short distance, they heard Yudhishthira roar. The lord of Madra stopped and ascended another chariot. It sparkled and had been duly prepared. It roared like the clouds. It had been equipped with all the implements and made the body hair of enemies stand up."'

Chapter 1235(16)

'Sanjaya said, "The lord of Madra picked up another bow that was more powerful and capable of bearing a greater load. He pierced Yudhishthira and roared like a lion. He showered down arrows, like Parjanya pouring down rain. The bull among the kshatriyas, immeasurable in his soul, showered arrows on the kshatriyas. He pierced Satyaki with ten arrows and Bhimasena with three. He pierced Sahadeva with three and afflicted Yudhishthira. He afflicted all the other great archers, with their horses, chariots and elephants. The supreme among rathas destroyed elephants and elephant riders, horses and horse riders and chariots and

[99]He placed the enemy on the right.

rathas. He severed arms, weapons and flags. He scattered the earth with warriors, like a sacrificial altar strewn with *kusha* grass. He slaughtered the soldiers, like Death, the Destroyer. The Pandus, Panchalas and Somakas angrily surrounded him. Bhimasena, Shini's grandson and Madri's sons, foremost among men, challenged him and clashed against him in turn, while he was fighting with the king, terrible in his strength. Those brave Indras among men, supreme among warriors, reached the lord of Madra. In the battle, those brave ones among men struck him with arrows that were fierce and powerful. The king was protected by Bhimasena, Madri's sons and Madhava. Dharma's son struck the lord of Madra between the breasts with fierce and powerful arrows. Those on your side saw that the lord of Madra was afflicted by arrows in the battle. On the instructions of Duryodhana, those supreme ones surrounded him with an array of chariots from all sides. In the encounter, the lord of Madra speedily pierced Yudhishthira with seven arrows. O king! In the tumultuous battle, the great-souled Partha pierced him with nine arrows. Those two maharathas, the lord of Madra and Yudhishthira, drew their bows back up to their ears and covered each other with arrows that had been washed in oil. The two maharathas swiftly glanced towards each other in the battle. Those two supreme among kings were immensely strong. They attacked the enemy and severely pierced each other. A great sound arose because of the twanging of bows and the slapping of palms. It was like the roar of the great Indra's vajra. Those two brave and great-souled ones, the lord of Madra and Pandu, showered down large numbers of arrows on each other. They circled around, like young tigers in a great forest in search of meat. They insolently gored each other, like the best of elephants using their tusks. The great-souled lord of Madra struck the brave Yudhishthira, whose valour was terrible, in the chest with a powerful arrow that was like the sun or the fire in its splendour. O king! Yudhishthira, the bull among the Kuru lineage, was grievously struck by that well-aimed arrow. He struck the great-souled lord of Madra back and was delighted. In a short instant, the Indra among kings regained his senses. His eyes were red with rage. He was like the one with one thousand eyes[100] in his prowess. He swiftly struck Partha with one hundred arrows. Dharma's great-souled son wrathfully struck Shalya with nine arrows. These pierced his golden armour and he struck him again with another six arrows. The lord of Madra was delighted at this. He stretched his bow and released two razor-sharp arrows towards the king, severing the bow of the bull among the Kuru lineage. The great-souled king picked up another bow in that encounter, one that was more terrible. From every direction, he pierced Shalya with sharp arrows that were pointed at the tip, like the great Indra against Namuchi. Shalya used nine arrows to sever the golden armour of Bhima and King Yudhishthira and then struck the great-souled ones in their arms. He then used another razor-sharp and flaming arrow, as resplendent as the sun, to sever the king's bow.

'"At this, Kripa used six arrows to slay his[101] charioteer, who fell down in front of him. The lord of Madra used his arrows to slay Yudhishthira's four horses. Having slain the horses, the great-souled one began to destroy the warriors who were on the side of the king, Dharma's son. When the king was reduced to this state, the great-souled Bhimasena quickly attacked the king of Madra and severed his bow with a powerful arrow. He then severely pierced that Indra among men with two arrows. With another arrow, he severed the head of his charioteer from his armoured body. Extremely enraged, Bhimasena swiftly killed his four horses. The foremost among all archers[102] was single-handedly roaming around in that field of battle, with great force. Bhima enveloped him with one hundred arrows and so did Madri's son, Sahadeva. On seeing that he was confounded by these arrows, Bhima severed Shalya's armour with his arrows. When his armour was severed by Bhimasena, the lord of Madra picked up a shield that was marked with the signs of one thousand stars. The great-souled one jumped down from his chariot. Grasping a sword, he dashed towards Kunti's son. Terrible in his strength, he destroyed

[100]Indra.
[101]Yudhishthira's.
[102]Shalya.

Nakula's chariot and advanced towards Yudhishthira. He angrily descended on the king, like an advancing Yama. Dhrishtadyumna, Droupadi's sons, Shikhandi and Shini's descendant swiftly advanced to the rescue. The great-souled Bhima used ten arrows to sever his unmatched shield. He used a broad-headed arrow to sever the sword in his hand and roared in the midst of the soldiers. On witnessing Bhima's deed, the foremost of the rathas on the Pandava side were delighted. They roared in applause and blew on conch shells that were as white as the moon. At that terrible sound, the soldiers on your side were tormented and distressed. They were covered in sweat and their limbs were covered in blood. They were miserable and lost all sense of enterprise.

'"However, the lord of Madra violently attacked the foremost of Pandava warriors, with Bhima at their head. He swiftly advanced against Yudhishthira, like a lion advancing in search of deer. Dharmaraja's horses and charioteer had been slain. He blazed in anger, like the fire. On seeing the lord of Madra advance swiftly, he also rushed forward with great force. He swiftly thought of Govinda's words and made up his mind to destroy Shalya. Though his horses and charioteer had been slain, Dharmaraja remained stationed on his chariot and wished to pick up a javelin. The great-souled one thought about Shalya's deeds and the remaining share that had been allotted to him. Remembering this, he set his heart on killing Shalya, just as Indra's younger brother[103] had asked him to.

'"Dharmaraja picked up a javelin that was golden in complexion. It was bejewelled and possessed a golden handle. His eyes blazed and were dilated. With an angry heart, he glanced towards the lord of Madra. The king was a god among men. He was pure in his soul and all his sins had been cleansed. O king! Though he glanced at the lord of Madra, he was not reduced to ashes.[104] This was extraordinary. That javelin possessed a beautiful tip and handle. With coral and gems, it flamed and dazzled. The great-souled one

[103]Vishnu, that is, Krishna.

[104]That is, Shalya could have been reduced to ashes because of Yudhishthira's sight alone.

flung it with great force towards the lord of Madra, foremost among the Kurus. It blazed as it was flung with great force. It descended violently, emitting sparks. While all the assembled Kurus looked on, it was like a giant meteor at the time of the destruction of a yuga. It was like the night of destruction and like Yama with a noose in his hand. It was fierce in form, like the midwife of destruction. It was like Brahma's staff and was invincible. Dharmaraja had preserved it carefully for the battle. The sons of Pandu had taken great care to worship it with the best of fragrances, garlands and seats, food and drink. It flamed like the fire of destruction. It was as fierce as rites performed by Atharvan and Angirasa. Tvashtra had created it for Ishana's use.[105] It was capable of consuming the lives and bodies of enemies. Through it, Isha[106] was capable of destroying all beings on earth, the firmament and bodies of water. It was adorned with bells, flags, jewels and diamonds. It was decorated with lapis lazuli and had a golden handle. Tvashtra had constructed it with great care, after controlling himself and observing rites. It was invincible and could destroy all those who hated brahmanas. He[107] hurled it with great force, strength and care, after having chanted terrible mantras over it. For the sake of destroying the lord of Madra, he dispatched it towards the enemy along the best of paths. Dharmaraja seemed to be dancing around in anger. He extended his firm arm, with the excellent hand. He loudly exclaimed, 'O wretched one! You are dead.' It was like Rudra shooting an arrow. That javelin was hurled by Yudishthira with force. Shalya roared loudly and used all his strength to try to seize and repulse it. It was as if a fire was leaping up to catch clarified butter over it. It pierced through his inner organs, his broad chest and his sparkling armour. It then penetrated the earth, as if it was slicing through water. The king's[108] great fame was taken away. Blood began to flow from his wounds and covered his nose, eyes, ears and mouth. His limbs were covered with blood. He was

[105]Ishana is Shiva and Tvashtra is Vishvakarma, the architect of the gods.

[106]Shiva.

[107]Yudhishthira.

[108]Shalya's.

like the giant mountain Krouncha, when it had been shattered by Skanda.[109] He stretched out his arms and fell down from his chariot onto the ground. His armour was shattered by the descendant of the Kuru lineage. The great-souled one was like the great Indra's mount. But he was like the summit of a mountain that had been shattered by thunder. The king of Madra extended his arms in Dharmaraja's direction. He then fell down on the ground, like Indra's standard. All his limbs were mangled and covered with blood. The bull among men fell down affectionately on the ground, like a beloved wife who falls down on the chest of her dear husband. The lord had enjoyed the earth for a long time, like a beloved wife. He seemed to go to sleep now, clasping her with all his limbs. The one with dharma in his soul had fought in accordance with dharma and was killed by Dharma's son. He was like a fire that had been pacified on a sacrificial altar. The javelin shattered his heart and he was deprived of his weapons and standard. Though he had been pacified, prosperity[110] did not desert the lord of Madra.

'"Yudhishthira picked up his bow, which was as dazzling as Indra's bow. In the battle, he began to slaughter the enemy, like the king of birds against serpents. In a short instant, he used sharp and broad-headed arrows to deprive the bodies of the enemies of their lives. Your soldiers were completely covered by Partha's arrows. With their eyes closed and distressed, they began to strike each other in fear. The armour was displaced from their bodies and they lost their weapons and their lives. The younger brother of the king of Madra was youthful. He was his brother's equal in all the qualities. When Shalya was brought down, the ratha attacked Pandava. He swiftly pierced that best of men with many iron arrows. He was invincible in battle and wished to observe the last rites of his brother. Dharmaraja quickly pierced him back with six swift arrows. With a couple of razor-sharp arrows, he severed his bow and his standard. While he was stationed in front of him, he used a blazing, extremely firm,

[109]Skanda (Kartikeya) shattered Mount Krouncha, when he killed the demons who hid there. The Krouncha mountain is in the Bellary district of Karnataka.

[110]Lakshmi, alternatively, beauty.

sharp and broad-headed arrow to sever his head. With the earrings, the head was seen to fall down from the chariot. This was like a resident of heaven falling down, after the store of good deeds has been exhausted. With the head severed, the torso fell down from the chariot. The limbs were covered with blood. On seeing this, the soldiers[111] ran away. The younger brother of the king of Madra was clad in colourful armour. On seeing that he had been slain, sounds of lamentation arose among the Kurus and they fled swiftly. On seeing that Shalya's younger brother had been killed, those on your side gave up all hope of remaining alive. They were terrified because of their fear of the Pandavas and, covered with dust, ran away.

'"O bull among the Bharata lineage! While the terrified Kouravas were running away, Satyaki, Shini's grandson, pursued them and shot arrows. He was a great archer and extremely difficult to withstand. O king! However, Hardikya received him fearlessly and spiritedly. Those two great-souled and unvanquished ones from the Vrishni lineage,[112] Hardikya and Satyaki, clashed against each other. They were like maddened lions. They showered down sparkling arrows, which were like the rays of the sun, on each other. Both of them were like the sun in their radiance. Those lions among the Vrishni lineage shot powerful arrows from the circles of their bows and they seemed to be like swift insects in the sky. Hardikya used ten arrows with drooping tufts to pierce Satyaki and struck his horses with three. He then severed his bow with a single arrow. The bull among the Shini lineage cast aside the best of bows that had been severed. He picked up another powerful weapon[113] that was even more forceful. Picking up the best of bows, the supreme among all archers pierced Hardikya back between the breasts with ten arrows. He used well-aimed broad-headed arrows to shatter his chariot and his yoke. He then swiftly slew his horses and his two parshni charioteers. O king! When the king of Madra was slain and Kritavarma deprived of his chariot, all of Duryodhana's soldiers again retreated from the battle. Because

[111]The Kourava soldiers.

[112]Both Satyaki and Kritavarma were from the Vrishni lineage.

[113]Another bow.

they were covered in dust, the soldiers could no longer distinguish the enemy. The troops who were still alive retreated from the battle. A dust had arisen from the earth. O bull among men! But in a short while, it was seen that this was pacified because of the several streams of blood that flowed.

'"From a close distance, Duryodhana saw that his troops had been shattered. He advanced with great speed and single-handedly countered all the Parthas. He saw the Pandavas on their chariots and Parshata Dhrishtadyumna and the invincible one from Anarta.[114] He countered them with his sharp arrows. At that time, the enemy did not attack him, like mortal beings avoiding death. Hardikya ascended another chariot and returned. Maharatha King Yudhishthira swiftly slew Kritavarma's four horses with four arrows. He pierced Goutama with six broad-headed arrows that were extremely energetic. Ashvatthama saw that Hardikya had been deprived of his chariot by the king and that his horses had been slain. He bore him away on his own chariot, away from Yudhishthira. Sharadvata pierced Yudhishthira back with eight arrows and also pierced his horses with eight other sharp arrows that had been sharpened on stone. O great king! At this time, the remnants of the battle raged on. O king! O descendant of the Bharata lineage! All this happened because of your evil policy, together with that of your sons. When Shalya, supreme among great archers, was slain in the midst of the battle by the bull among the Kuru lineage, all the assembled Parthas saw this and were greatly delighted. In a short while, they blew on their conch shells. They praised Yudhishthira, just as in ancient times, the gods had praised Indra after Vritra had been killed. They roared and sounded many kinds of musical instruments. This resounded, from every side of the earth."'

[114]Satyaki.

they were covered in dust, the soldiers could no longer distinguish the enemy. The troops who were still alive retreated from the battle. A dust had arisen from the earth. O bull among men! But in a short while, it was seen that the dust was pacified because of the several streams of blood that flowed.

From a close distance, Duryodhana saw that his troops had been shattered. He advanced with great speed and single-handedly countered all the Parthas. He saw the Pandavas on their chariots and Parshata Dhrishtadyumna and the invincible one from Anarta. He countered them with his sharp arrows. At that time, the enemy did not approach him, like mortal beings avoiding death. Hereafter, he ascended another chariot and returned. Maharatha King Yudhishthira swiftly slew Kritavarma's four horses with his arrows. He pierced Goutama with six broad-headed arrows that were extremely energetic. Ashvatthama saw that Hardikya had been deprived of his chariot by the king and that his horses had been slain. He bore him away on his own chariot, away from Yudhishthira. Sharadvata pierced Yudhishthira back with eight arrows and also pierced his horses with eight other sharp arrows that had been sharpened on stones. O great king! At this time, the remnants of the battle raged on. O king! O descendant of the Bharata lineage! All this happened because of your evil policy, together with that of your sons. When Shalya, supreme among great archers, was slain in the forefront of the battle by the bull among the Kuru lineage, all the assembled Parthas saw this and were greatly delighted. In a short while, they blew on their conch shells. They praised Yudhishthira, just as in ancient times, the gods had praised Indra after Vritra had been killed. They sounded and sounded many kinds of musical instruments. This resounded from every side of the earth."

SECTION SEVENTY-FIVE

Hrada-Pravesha Parva

This parva has 664 shlokas and twelve chapters.

Chapter 1236(17): 39 shlokas	*Chapter 1242(23): 64 shlokas*
Chapter 1237(18): 65 shlokas	*Chapter 1243(24): 56 shlokas*
Chapter 1238(19): 26 shlokas	*Chapter 1244(25): 37 shlokas*
Chapter 1239(20): 36 shlokas	*Chapter 1245(26): 54 shlokas*
Chapter 1240(21): 44 shlokas	*Chapter 1246(27): 63 shlokas*
Chapter 1241(22): 88 shlokas	*Chapter 1247(28): 92 shlokas*

*Satyaki kills Shalva, the king of the mlechhas, and Kshemadhurti. Bhima kills Duryodhana's remaining brothers. Arjuna kills warriors from Trigarta, including Susharma, the king of Trigarta. Sahadeva kills Shakuni and his son, Uluka. Duryodhana enters (*pravesha*) a lake (*hrada*) and hides there, the section being named after this. The survivors, including the women, flee to Hastinapura.*

Chapter 1236(17)

'Sanjaya said, "O king! When Shalya was killed, seven hundred brave rathas, followers of the king of Madra, advanced in a large army. Duryodhana was astride an elephant that was like a mountain. An umbrella was held aloft his head and he was fanned with whisks. He restrained the ones from Madra, 'Do not go. Do not advance.' Duryodhana repeatedly tried to restrain those brave ones. However, wishing to kill Yudhishthira, they penetrated the Pandu army. O great king! Those brave warriors had made up their minds to fight. They loudly twanged their bows and fought with the Pandavas. On hearing that Shalya had been killed, they afflicted Dharma's son. Those maharathas from Madra were devoted to ensuring the welfare of the king of Madra. Partha advanced there, stretching the bow Gandiva. The maharatha again filled the directions with the clatter of his chariot. Arjuna, Bhima, the Pandavas who were Madri's sons, Satyaki, tiger among men, all of Droupadi's sons, Dhrishtadyumna, Shikhandi, the Panchalas and the Somakas desired to protect Yudhishthira and surrounded him from every direction. Surrounding him, the bulls among the Pandavas agitated that army, like makaras in an ocean. It was as if the great river Ganga was agitated by a mighty wind. O king! But those maharathas were ready to give up their lives and again agitated the great army of the Pandus and their standards. Those on your side made it tremble, like trees by a giant storm. They loudly exclaimed, 'Where is King Yudhishthira? Why are his brave brothers not seen? Where are the immensely valorous Panchalas, maharatha Shikhandi, Dhrishtadyumna, Shini's descendant and all the sons of Droupadi?' While they were roaring in this way, Droupadi's brave and maharatha sons and Yuyudhana attacked the followers of the king of Madra. Some of them were crushed by the wheels. Others were mangled and the giant standards destroyed. In the battle, those on your side were seen to be slain by the enemy. O king! O descendant of the Bharata lineage! Though they were restrained by your son, on seeing the Pandavas in the battle, those warriors powerfully rushed against them from every side. Duryodhana tried to restrain and calm those brave ones. But not a single one of those maharathas would listen to him.

'"O great king! Shakuni, the son of the king of Gandhara, capable of speaking eloquently, spoke these words to Duryodhana. 'The army of the Madras is being slaughtered. Why are we looking on? O descendant of the Bharata lineage! While you are stationed in the battle, this is not proper. At that time, we took a decision that we would fight together. O king! The enemy is slaughtering us. Why are you tolerating this?' Duryodhana replied, 'I tried to restrain them earlier. But they did not listen to my words. Having penetrated the Pandu army, this is the reason they are being killed.' Shakuni said, 'When they are enraged in a battle, valiant ones do not listen to their master. You should not be angry with them. This is not the time to ignore this. All of us should advance with our horses, chariots and elephants and rescue the great archers who are the followers of the king of Madra. O king! We will take great care and protect each other. Let all of us think along those lines and ask the soldiers to advance.' Having been thus addressed, the king surrounded himself with a large army. He roared like a lion, made the earth tremble and advanced. O descendant of the Bharata lineage! Among your soldiers, there were tumultuous sounds like, 'Slay. Pierce. Seize. Strike. Sever.' In the battle, the Pandavas beheld the followers of the king of Madra. They advanced, uniting in a moderate formation.[1] O lord of the earth! In a short instant, those brave ones engaged in hand-to-hand combat in the battle and the followers of the king of Madra were seen to be killed. While we were advancing, we saw that the enemy had spiritedly killed their foes and were cheerfully uttering roars of delight. In every direction, headless torsos were seen to rise up and fall down, like giant meteors from the solar disc at midday. The chariots and yokes were shattered. The maharathas were slain. Horses fell down. The earth was strewn with these. O great king! Steeds that were as fleet as the wind were still yoked. In the battle, they were seen to drag the warriors around. In the encounter, some horses dragged around chariots with shattered wheels. Some others fled in the ten directions, dragging along halves of chariots. Here and

[1]The word used is *madhyama*, meaning mild or moderate. The word used for formation is *gulma*, not vyuha. The entire army is arrayed in the form of a vyuha, while a gulma is a smaller division, something like a battalion. The suggestion probably is that the Pandavas did not take this attack very seriously.

there, yokes were seen to be attached to the horses. O supreme among men! Rathas were seen to fall down. They were like siddhas dislodged from the sky, after their store of good deeds had been exhausted. The brave followers of the king of Madra were slaughtered.

'"The maharatha Parthas saw that we were advancing towards them.[2] Wielding weapons and desiring victory, they attacked powerfully. They created a whizzing sound with their arrows and this mixed with the blare of conch shells. Unwavering in their aim, those strikers again clashed against us. They brandished their bows and arrows and roared like lions. On seeing that the large army of the king of Madra had been slain and that the brave king of Madra had been brought down in the battle, all of Duryodhana's soldiers again retreated. O great king! They were slaughtered by the Pandavas, firm archers, who desired victory. Frightened and terrified, they fled in different directions."'

Chapter 1237(18)

'Sanjaya said, "The unassailable maharatha, the king of Madra, was brought down in the battle. Those on your side, and your sons, generally retreated. They were like merchants whose boats had been shattered, so that they were without a raft on the fathomless ocean. O great king! When the brave king of Madra was slain by the great-souled one,[3] they wished to find a shore, but could not reach one. They were frightened and mangled by arrows. They desired a protector, but were without a protector. They were like deer afflicted by a lion. They were like bulls with broken horns, or elephants with shattered tusks. They were defeated by Dharma's son and tormented at midday. O king! There was no one who could rally the soldiers, nor any valour among them. When Shalya was killed, there was no warrior who could resort to his own intelligence. O descendant of the Bharata

[2]The Kouravas who were trying to rescue the followers of the king of Madra.
[3]Yudhishthira.

lineage! O lord of the earth! When Bhishma, Drona and the son of a suta were killed, the warriors on your side suffered from sorrow and fear. That grief and terror manifested itself again. When maharatha Shalya was killed, all hope of victory was given up. The foremost of brave ones were slain and destroyed, mangled by sharp arrows. O king! When the king of Madra was slain, the warriors fled. Some of the maharathas resorted to horses, others to elephants, and still others to chariots. They speedily ascended on these, or fled on foot. There were two thousand elephants, accomplished in striking. They were like mountains. When Shalya was killed, goaded by goads and toes, they ran away. O best among the Bharata lineage! In the encounter, those on your side fled in different directions. They were seen to run away. They sighed and were afflicted by the arrows. On seeing that they were shattered and running away, vanquished and bereft of enthusiasm, the Panchalas and Pandavas attacked them, desiring victory. They created a whizzing sound with their arrows and roared loudly, like lions. The brave ones blew fiercely on their conch shells.

'"On seeing that the Kourava soldiers were terrified and were running away, the Panchalas and the Pandavas spoke to each other. 'King Yudhishthira is firm in his devotion to the truth and has vanquished the enemy today. King Duryodhana has been destroyed today and has lost his glory and prosperity. On hearing that his sons have been killed, Dhritarashtra, the lord of men, will fall down senseless on the ground and grieve. He will realize today, how capable Kounteya is, among all archers. The evil-minded one will today censure his evil deeds. Today, he will remember the truthful and beneficial words that were spoken by Kshatta earlier. Let him serve the Parthas today, with different kinds of objects. Let the king know the sorrow that the sons of Pandu had felt. Let the lord of the earth learn about Krishna's greatness today. Today, let him realize how terrible the twang of Arjuna's bow is in battle. Today, let him know the terrible strength of the great-souled Bhima, who possesses the strength of all weapons and the strength of his arms in battle. Duryodhana will be slain in the battle, like the asura Maya by Shakra.[4]

[4]There is no story that tells us that Maya was killed by Indra.

There is no one else in the world who could have performed the task that the immensely strong Bhima has. Bhimasena slew Duhshasana. Today, on hearing about the death of the king of Madra, who was extremely difficult for even the gods to withstand, let him know about the eldest Pandava's valour. In the encounter today, he will know about the great strength of the two sons of Madri, when the brave Soubala and all those from Gandara are killed. Why should victory not be on the side of those who have a warrior like Dhananjaya, or Satyaki, Bhimasena, Parshata Dhrishtadyumna, Droupadi's five sons, the Pandavas who are Madri's sons, the great archer, Shikhandi, and King Yudhishthira? Why should victory not be on the side of those who have Krishna Janardana, the protector of the universe, as their protector, and who have resorted to dharma? There were Bhishma, Drona, Karna, the king of Madra and hundreds and thousands of other brave kings. Who other than Partha Yudhishthira was capable of vanquishing them in battle? Hrishikesha, the store of dharma and fame, has always been his protector.' In great delight, these were the words they spoke to each other. O king! Those on your side were routed and the Srinjayas followed them from the rear. The brave Dhananjaya attacked the army of chariots[5] and Madri's sons and maharatha Satyaki attacked Shakuni.

'"On seeing that all of them were running away, afflicted by their fear of Bhimasena, Duryodhana smiled and spoke to his charioteer. 'Partha, stationed with the bow in his hand, will not be able to cross me. He is slaying all the soldiers. Take my horses to him. I will fight and kill Kounteya, or Dhananjaya will kill me. He will not be able to cross me, like the great ocean against the shoreline. O charioteer! Behold that large army, attacked by the Pandavas. Behold. In every direction, a dust has arisen because of the soldiers. Listen to the many leonine roars. They are terrible and fearful. O charioteer! Advance slowly there and protect the rear. If I station myself in battle and counter the Pandus, my energetic army will swiftly return again.' On hearing the words of your son, spoken like the best of brave ones, the charioteer gently goaded the horses, tied

[5]Belonging to the Kouravas.

to golden harnesses. There were twenty-one thousand foot soldiers who were ready to lay down their lives, though they were without elephants, horses and charioteers. They stationed themselves for the battle. They had come from diverse countries and were attired in garments of many colours. Desiring great fame, those warriors stationed themselves there. In great delight, they clashed against each other. There was an extremely great encounter. It was fierce in form and terrible. O king! Those four kinds of troops, who had come from many countries, countered Bhimasena and Parshata Dhrishtadyumna.[6] In the battle, other foot soldiers attacked Bhima. Desiring to ascend to the world of the brave, they roared cheerfully and slapped their armpits. Invincible in the battle, they angrily attacked Bhimasena. Those on the side of the sons of Dhritarashtra did not speak to each other. But they roared. They surrounded Bhima in the battle and struck him from all sides. O great king! When he was surrounded by that large number of foot soldiers in the battle, maharatha Pandava did not waver. He remained immobile on his chariot, like Mount Mainaka. He slaughtered them and they angrily attacked him, countering the other warriors who tried to repulse them. Thus attacked, Bhima became enraged in that battle. He quickly descended from his chariot and stood on the ground. He grasped a giant club that was decorated with gold. With this, like Yama with a staff in his hand, he began to slay those warriors. With his club, the powerful Bhima brought down twenty-one thousand foot soldiers, who were without chariots, horses or elephants. Bhima, for whom truth was his valour, slew that army of men. He was soon seen, with Dhrishtadyumna at the forefront. The slain foot soldiers lay down on the ground, their bodies covered with blood. They were like flowering karnikara trees shattered by a storm. They were adorned with garlands made out of different kinds of flowers. They wore many kinds of earrings. They were of different races and had assembled from different countries. That

[6]There is a contradiction and a possible typo, because we have been told there were only foot soldiers on the Kourava side. It should perhaps read that Bhimasena and Dhrishtadyumna countered them with four kinds of forces.

large army of foot soldiers was killed there. Flags and standards were scattered around. They were destroyed and it was beautiful, but fearful and terrible in form.

'"With Yudhishthira at the forefront, all the soldiers and maharathas attacked your great-souled son, Duryodhana. All the great archers on your side retreated. On seeing this, they attacked. But they could not cross your son, like the abode of makaras against the shoreline. We witnessed your son's extraordinary manliness. Though he was single-handed, all the united Parthas were incapable of withstanding him. Duryodhana spoke to his own soldiers, who were mangled with arrows. Though they had made up their minds to run away, they had not gone far. 'I do not see a country or mountain on earth, where the Pandavas will not follow and kill you. What is the point of running away? They have only a little bit of their army left and the two Krishnas have been severely wounded. If all of us take a stand, it is certain that there will be victory. If you run away, the Pandavas will destroy all of us. They will pursue and kill us. It is better to be stationed in battle. O kshatriyas! All of you listen to me, those who are still assembled here. Yama slays both cowards and brave ones. Which man calls himself a kshatriya and is stupid enough not to fight? It is better to be stationed before the angry Bhimasena. If we resort to the dharma of kshatriyas and fight, there will be happiness, even if there is death in the battle. If we win, we will obtain happiness. If we are slain, we will obtain great fruits in the world hereafter. O Kouravas! There is no greater path towards heaven than by resorting to the dharma of fighting. If we are killed in battle, we will soon obtain all those revered worlds.' On hearing these words, the kings applauded them. They returned and attacked the Pandava assassins. On seeing that they were swiftly attacking, the Parthas, who were strikers, arrayed themselves in battle formation. Desiring victory, those strikers counter-attacked. The valiant Partha attacked on his chariot. He brandished Gandiva bow, famous in the three worlds. Madri's sons and the immensely strong Satyaki attacked Shakuni. Cheerfully and quickly, they endeavoured to attack your army."'

Chapter 1238(19)

'Sanjaya said, "When that large army had returned, Shalva, the lord of large numbers of mlecchas, became extremely angry and attacked the large army of the Pandus. He was astride an extremely large elephant. It possessed shattered temples and was like a mountain. It was as proud as Airavata[7] and was capable of crushing large numbers of the enemy. It had been born in an extremely noble lineage and had always been worshipped, extremely well, by Dhritarashtra's son. O king! It was equipped well and had been well trained for fighting, by those who knew about war. The supreme among kings was resplendent astride it. He was like a rising sun, at the end of summer. O king! On that supreme elephant, he advanced against the sons of Pandu. From every direction, he enveloped them with sharp arrows that were extremely terrible, like the great Indra's vajra. O king! In the great battle, he shot arrows and conveyed warriors to Yama. No one, on his side or that of the enemy, could discern any weakness in him, like the daityas in ancient times, against the wielder of the vajra. The Pandavas, Somakas and Srinjayas seemed to see that elephant in every direction, as if the single elephant was roaming around and was actually one thousand. It was like the great Indra's elephant. The enemy's army was driven away. Failing to find protection, they ran away in different directions. They were incapable of remaining in the battle. Severely afflicted by fear, they crushed each other. That large army of the Pandavas was violently routed by that lord of men. Unable to withstand the force of that king of elephants, they swiftly fled in the four directions. On seeing that they were powerfully routed, all the warriors and supreme fighters on your side honoured that lord of men. They blew on conch shells that were as white as the moon. The delighted roars emitted by the Kouravas mingled with the blare of conch shells. On hearing this, the commander of the Pandavas and the Srinjayas[8] could not tolerate this

[7]Indra's elephant.

[8]Dhrishtadyumna.

and became angry. Desiring to obtain a quick victory, the great-souled one advanced against the elephant. He was like Jambha advancing against Airavata, the king of elephants and Indra's mount, during the clash with Shakra. O king! On seeing that the king of Panchala, Drupada's son, was violently attacking, the lion among men goaded the elephant, so as to kill him. The elephant attacked powerfully. He pierced it with three sharp iron arrows that were like the fire to the touch. They had been washed by artisans and were fierce and powerful. The great-souled one then used five other sharp and iron arrows to strike it on its frontal lobe. Having been severely pierced in the battle, that supreme elephant retreated and fled. While that king among elephants was speedily running away, Shalva restrained it. He swiftly used his goad to propel it towards the chariot of the king of Panchala. On seeing that the elephant was violently advancing, the brave Dhrishtadyumna quickly descended from his chariot. He swiftly grasped a club and stood on the ground, his limbs benumbed with fear. That giant elephant used its trunk to pick up his gold-decorated chariot, with the horses and the charioteer, and violently crushed it down on the ground. The charioteer of the king of Panchala was thus destroyed by that supreme elephant. On seeing this, Bhima, Shikhandi and Shini's grandson hastily rushed towards it. While they advanced against the elephant, he[9] afflicted them with powerful and forceful arrows. In the battle, those rathas restrained the elephant and it began to waver. The king continued to shower down arrows from every direction, like the sun with its net of rays. Struck by those arrows, a large number of rathas fled in every direction. O king! On beholding Shalva's deed in the battle, loud sounds of lamentation arose among all the Panchalas, Matsyas and Srinjayas. But those best of archers surrounded the elephant from all sides. The brave king of Panchala spiritedly grasped a club that was like a mountain top. O descendant of the Bharata lineage! Without any fear and with great speed, that brave slayer of enemies struck the elephant. The elephant was like a cloud and it was exuding musth. It fell down on the ground. The spirited son of the Panchala king struck it severely

[9]Shalva.

with the club. Its temples were violently shattered and it began to vomit blood from its mouth. The elephant fell down on the ground, like a mountain dislodged during an earthquake. When that king of elephants fell down, lamentations arose among your son's soldiers. The foremost among the Shini lineage then used a sharp and broad-headed arrow to sever King Shalva's head. The head was severed by Satvata in the battle and fell down on the ground, together with the king of elephants. It was as if a giant mountain peak had been shattered by the vajra, unleashed by the lord of the gods."'

Chapter 1239(20)

'Sanjaya said, "When the brave Shalva, the ornament of an assembly, was killed, that army was agitated, like a giant tree struck by a forceful storm. On seeing that the army was routed, the immensely strong and valiant maharatha Kritavarma resisted the soldiers of the enemy in the battle. O king! The descendant of the Satvata lineage[10] was stationed in the battle and was enveloped with arrows. On seeing this, the brave ones[11] returned and a battle between the Kurus and the Pandavas commenced. O great king! They did not retreat and preferred death over retreat. There was a wonderful battle between Satvata and the enemy. Single-handedly, he countered the Pandu soldiers, who were difficult to resist. On witnessing this, other well-wishers performed extremely difficult deeds. They cheerfully roared like lions and that great sound rose up to heaven. O bull among the Bharata lineage! The Panchalas were frightened by that noise. However, Shini's grandson, the mighty-armed Satyaki, attacked. He advanced against the immensely strong Kshemadhurti, and using seven sharp arrows, conveyed him to Yama's abode. The mighty-armed descendant of the Shini lineage tormented with sharp arrows. As he attacked, Hardikya rushed against him, terrible and

[10]Kritavarma.

[11]On the Kourava side.

fierce. Those two archers, best among rathas, roared like lions. They rushed against each other, wielding the best of weapons. The Pandavas, the Panchalas, other warriors and the best of kings became spectators to that clash between those two lions among men. The maharathas from the Vrishni and Andhaka lineages used vatsadantas and iron arrows. Like cheerful elephants, they tried to kill each other. Hardikya and the bull among the Shini lineage roamed around in diverse motions. They repeatedly struck each other with showers of arrows. Those lions from the Vrishni lineage stretched their bows with force and strength and shot arrows. We saw these in the sky, travelling fast, like insects. Hridika's son approached the one who was the performer of truthful deeds[12] and used four sharp arrows to pierce his four horses. The long-armed one became angry, like an elephant struck with a goad. He used eight supreme arrows to pierce Kritavarma. Kritavarma stretched his bow back all the way up to his ears. Piercing Satyaki with three arrows, he severed his bow with another one. When that best of bows was severed, the bull among the Shini lineage picked up another bow with an arrow affixed to it. Shini's descendant, best among all archers, picked up that best of bows with great speed. The immensely valorous, immensely intelligent and immensely strong one was unable to tolerate the fact that his bow had been severed by Kritavarma. Enraged, the atiratha speedily attacked Kritavarma. Using ten extremely sharp arrows, the bull among the Shini lineage struck Kritavarma's charioteer, horses and standard. His gold-decorated chariot, horses and charioteer were destroyed. O king! O venerable one! On seeing this, the great archer, maharatha Kritavarma, was overcome by great rage and picked up a javelin. With the force of his arms, he hurled this towards the bull among the Shini lineage, wishing to kill him. But Satvata shattered the javelin with his sharp arrows. Shattered, it fell down, and Madhava[13] was confused. His horses had been slain. His charioteer had been killed. In the encounter, Yuyudhana,[14] skilled in

[12]Satyaki.

[13]Kritavarma.All the Yadavas were descended from Madhu.

[14]Satyaki.

the use of weapons, used a broad-headed arrow to strike him in the chest. Kritavarma fell down on the ground. In the duel, the brave one was deprived of his chariot by Satyaki. At this, all the soldiers[15] were overcome by great fear and your sons were miserable, because Kritavarma had been deprived of his chariot and his horses and charioteer had been slain. The horses of that scorcher of enemies had been killed. His charioteer had been slain. O king! On seeing this, Kripa attacked the bull among the Shini lineage, wishing to kill him. While all the archers looked on, the mighty-armed one swiftly picked him up on his own chariot and bore him away from the field of battle. O king! Kritavarma had been deprived of his chariot and Shini's descendant remained stationed there. All of Duryodhana's soldiers again became reluctant to fight. Because they were covered in dust, the soldiers could no longer discern the enemy. O king! With the exception of King Duryodhana, those on your side ran away. Duryodhana was nearby and saw that his own army had been routed. O venerable one! Angered, he quickly attacked all the Pandus, Parshata Dhrishtadyumna, Shikhandi, Droupadi's sons, the large numbers of Panchalas, the Kekayas, the Somakas and the Panchalas[16] and countered them. He was fearless and unassailable and repulsed them with sharp weapons. Your immensely strong son endeavoured and remained stationed in the battle. He was as resplendent as the great fire on a sacrificial altar, invoked with mantras. In the battle, the enemy was incapable of approaching him, like mortal beings against Death. Hardikya ascended another chariot and attacked."'

Chapter 1240(21)

'Sanjaya said, "O great king! Your son, supreme among rathas, was stationed on his chariot in the battle. He was resplendent

[15]On the Kourava side.

[16]The Panchalas are mentioned twice.

and difficult to resist, like the powerful Rudra. The earth was covered with thousands of his arrows. He showered the enemy with arrows, like rain pouring down on a mountain. In the great battle, there wasn't a man among the Pandavas, or a horse, elephant or a ratha, who was not wounded by his arrows. O lord of the earth! O descendant of the Bharata lineage! Whichever warrior I saw in the encounter was struck by your son with his arrows. The soldiers in the army[17] were covered by dust and were seen to be mangled by the great-souled one's arrows. O lord of the earth! The earth seemed to be made out of arrows that were released by the archer Duryodhana, swift in the use of his hands. Among the thousands of warriors on your side, or that of the enemy, it seemed to me that Duryodhana was the only man. We beheld your son's wonderful valour. O descendant of the Bharata lineage! He was single-handed. But the united Parthas could not advance against him. O bull among the Bharata lineage! He pierced Yudhishthira with one hundred arrows, Bhimasena with seventy, Sahadeva with seven, Nakula with sixty-four, Dhrishtadyumna with five, Droupadi's sons with seven each and pierced Satyaki with three. O venerable one! He severed Sahadeva's bow with a broad-headed arrow. Casting aside the severed bow, Madri's powerful son picked up another great bow and attacked the king. In the battle, he pierced Duryodhana with ten arrows. The brave and great archer, Nakula, pierced the king with nine arrows and roared, assuming a terrible form. Satyaki struck the king with an arrow with drooping tufts. Droupadi's sons struck him with seveny-three and Dharmaraja with seven. Bhimasena struck the king with eighty arrows. He was afflicted from every direction by storms of arrows shot by those great-souled ones. O great king! However, while all the soldiers looked on, he did not waver. All the beings and all the men witnessed the dexterity, skill and prowess of the great-souled one. O Indra among kings! Some sons of Dhritarashtra had only fled a short distance away. On seeing the king, those armoured ones surrounded him. When they attacked, they created a tumultuous sound. It was like

[17]The Pandava army.

a turbulent ocean on a monsoon night. In the battle, those great archers approached the unvanquished king and counter-attacked the Pandava assassins.

'"In the encounter, Drona's son repulsed the enraged Bhimasena. O great king! Arrows were released in all the directions. The brave ones could not be distinguished in the battle, nor the directions or the sub-directions. O descendant of the Bharata lineage! Both of those resplendent ones[18] were the performers of cruel deeds and were extremely difficult to resist. They assumed fearful forms and fought, acting and neutralizing each other. The entire universe was terrified because of the twangs of their bows and their words. In the battle, the brave Shakuni attacked Yudhishthira. Subala's powerful son slew the four horses that belonged to the lord and roared. This made all the soldiers tremble. At that time, the powerful Sahadeva bore the brave and unvanquished king[19] away from the field of battle on his chariot. Dharmaraja Yudhishthira ascended another chariot. He pierced Shakuni with nine arrows and pierced him again with five. The best among all archers then roared loudly. O venerable one! The battle was wonderful and fearful in form. It generated delight among the spectators and was applauded by the siddhas and the charanas. Uluka, immeasurable in his soul, attacked the great archer, Nakula, invincible in battle, and showered him with arrows from every direction. In that way, the brave Nakula repulsed Soubala's son in the encounter and repulsed him with a great shower of arrows. They were brave maharathas, born in noble lineages. They were seen to fight with each other, enraged with each other. O king! In that way, Kritavarma fought against Shini's descendant, the tormentor of enemies, and was resplendent, like Shakra in an encounter against Bala. In the battle, Duryodhana severed Dhrishtadyumna's bow. When his bow had been severed, he pierced him with sharp arrows. While all the archers looked on, in that encounter, Dhrishtadyumna grasped a supreme weapon and fought against the king. O bull among the Bharata lineage! The clash between those two was exceedingly

[18]Ashvatthama and Bhima.

[19]Yudhishthira.

great. They were like two supreme and crazy elephants, with shattered temples, exuding musth. In the battle, the brave Goutama became angry and pierced Droupadi's immensely strong sons with many arrows with drooping tufts. That clash between them and him was like that between a being and the senses.[20] It assumed a fierce and terrible form and neither side was inclined to show mercy. They afflicted him, like senses oppressing a stupid person. He angrily fought against them in that battle. O descendant of the Bharata lineage! Thus the colourful battle between them and him raged on. O lord! It was like the one that always takes place between a being and the senses.

'"Men fought with men. Tuskers fought with tuskers. Horses clashed against horses and rathas against rathas. O lord of the earth! The battle became tumultuous and fearful in form. O lord! It was wonderful in one spot and terrible and fierce in another. O great king! There were many terrible clashes. Those scorchers of enemies clashed against each other in the encounter. They pierced, struck and killed each other in the great encounter. Because of the weapons, a terrible dust was seen to rise. O king! As they ran away, it was also created by the horses and the horse riders and was fanned by the wind. The dust was created by the chariots and the breaths of the tuskers. It was like a tawny cloud in the evening and obstructed the path of the sun. The sun was covered by the dust and lost its brilliance. The earth and the brave maharathas were shrouded. O supreme among the Bharata lineage! But in a short while, the earth was sprinkled with the blood of the brave ones and, in every direction, became free of the dust. That terrible dust, fierce in form, was pacified. O great king! O descendant of the Bharata lineage! Those extremely fearful duels could again be seen, as the best and the eldest fought against each other at midday. O Indra among kings! The armour was seen to blaze in resplendent brilliance. As arrows descended in that battle, a tumultuous sound was raised. It was as if a large forest of bamboos was being burnt in every direction."'

[20]There are five senses and Droupadi had five sons.

Chapter 1241(22)

'Sanjaya said, "That fierce battle continued, terrible in form. The army of your sons was shattered by the Pandavas. The maharathas made great efforts to restrain them and your sons fought against the Pandava soldiers. Wishing to ensure your son's pleasure, the warriors on your side suddenly returned. When they returned, the battle again assumed a fearful form. Those on your side and the enemy fought against each other in the battle, like the gods and the asuras. The soldiers on your side, and that of the enemy, were unwilling to retreat. They fought against each other through guessing and by means of signs.[21] As they fought against each other, there was a great destruction.

'"King Yudhishthira was overcome by great rage. In the battle, he wished to vanquish the sons of Dhritarashtra and the kings. He pierced Sharadvata with three arrows that were gold-tufted and had been sharpened on stone. He slew Kritavarma's four horses with injurious arrows. Ashvatthama bore the illustrious Hardikya away. Sharadvata pierced Yudhishthira back with eight arrows. In the battle, King Duryodhana dispatched seven hundred chariots towards the spot where King Yudhishthira, Dharma's son, was. Those chariots possessed the speed of thought or the wind and rathas rode them. In the encounter, they rushed against Kounteya's chariot. O great king! They surrounded Yudhishthira from all sides. With their arrows, they made him disappear, like clouds against the sun. Rathas, with Shikhandi at the forefront, were unwilling to tolerate this and became angry. They attacked with the best of swift chariots, decorated with nets of bells. They advanced to protect Yudhishthira, Kunti's sons. A terrible battle ensued between the Pandavas and the Kurus. Blood flowed like water and it extended Yama's kingdom. Having slain the seven hundred rathas that belonged to the Kuru assassins, the Pandavas and the Panchalas again countered them. A great battle was fought between your son and the Pandavas. Nothing

[21]Because of the dust.

like this had been seen earlier, nor heard of. That merciless battle continued in every direction. Warriors, on your side and that of the others, were slain. The warriors roared and blew on their conch shells. The archers roared like lions and shouted. O venerable one! As that battle extended, the inner organs were mangled. In search of victory, the warriors dashed in every direction. Every species on earth seemed to be destroyed and this generated sorrow. As the battle extended, the best of women were deprived of their partings in the encounter.[22] That merciless and extremely fearful battle continued. There was a sound, like that of the earth, with all its mountains and forests, during an earthquake. O king! Torches with handles fell down in every direction. From the solar disc, meteors descended from the firmament onto the ground. Harsh winds blew from every side and showered down stones underneath. The elephants shed tears and trembled severely. Disregarding these ominous portents, the extremely fearful battle raged on. Consulting each other, the kshatriyas weren't distressed and fought again on that beautiful and sacred region of Kurukshetra, desiring to go to heaven.

'"Shakuni, the son of the king of Gandhara, said, 'Station yourselves in the forefront of the battle. I will slay the Pandavas from the rear.' At this, the spirited warriors from Madra cheerfully advanced, uttering many sounds of delight and so did the enemy. Those invincible ones, unwavering in their aim, attacked us again. They brandished their bows and arrows and showered down arrows. The soldiers of the king of Madra were slain by the army there. On seeing this, Duryodhana's soldiers again retreated. The powerful king of Gandhara again spoke these words. 'O wicked ones! O ones who are ignoring dharma! Return and fight. Why are you running away?' O bull among the Bharata lineage! The king of Gandhara possessed an army of ten thousand horses, with warriors with sparkling lances. He used this army and his valour and there was a destruction of men. He attacked the Pandava soldiers from the rear and killed

[22]This requires explanation. *Simanta* is the parting of the hair and a marking on that indicates that the lady is married.The women were not deprived of the parting, but that marking. Stated simply, the women became widows.

them with his sharp arrows. O great king! In every direction, the extremely large army of the Pandus was destroyed and driven away, like clouds by the wind. From a close distance, Yudhishthira saw that his own army was being routed. The immensely strong Sahadeva was in front of him and he urged him. 'Subala's armoured son is afflicting our rear. O Pandava! Behold. The evil-minded one is slaying our soldiers. Advance with the sons of Droupadi and kill Shakuni Soubala. O unblemished one! Protect yourself with an army of Panchala chariots. Let all the elephants and horses go with you, and three thousand foot soldiers. Kill Shakuni Soubala.' At this, seven hundred elephants, with bows in the hands of the riders, five thousand horses, the valiant Sahadeva, three thousand foot soldiers and the sons of Droupadi combined and attacked Shakuni, invincible in a battle, in the encounter. O king! However, the powerful Soubala, desiring victory, overcame the Pandavas and slaughtered the soldiers from the rear. The spirited Pandava horse riders were angry. They penetrated Soubala's army and overcame his rathas. Those brave riders stationed themselves amidst elephants and enveloped Soubala's large army with showers of arrows. The brave men used clubs and javelins. O king! Because of your evil counsel, a great battle raged. As the rathas watched, the twang of bowstrings was no longer heard, because one could not distinguish those on one's own side from that of the enemy. O bull among the Bharata lineage! Javelins were hurled from the arms of the brave ones among the Kurus and the Pandavas and one could see them descend like stellar bodies. O lord of the earth! Sparkling swords were seen to descend there and covered the sky, rendering it exceedingly beautiful. O king! O supreme among the Bharata lineage! Beautiful javelins descended in every direction and were like locusts in the sky. The limbs of horses were covered with blood and because they were wounded, fell down in hundreds and thousands. They fell against each other and crowded together. Wounded, they were seen to vomit blood from their mouths. There was a terrible darkness and the soldiers were covered in dust. With wet eyes, those scorchers of enemies retreated from the spot. O king! Horses and men were covered with dust. Some fell down on the ground. Others vomited copious quantities of blood. The hair of some men got entangled with the hair of others and they could not move. The immensely strong ones dragged each other from the backs of their horses and, clashing like wrestlers, slew each other. Many lost their lives and were dragged away by the horses. There were many others who fell down on the ground, desiring victory. Those men, proud of their prowess, were seen here and there. Blood flowed from their wounds. Their arms were severed. Their hair was shorn. The earth was seen to be strewn with hundreds and thousands of them. Those who tried to use their horses could not travel a great distance away. Horse riders were slain and the earth was covered with horses. Armour was smeared with blood. And there were those who were armed with many terrible kinds of weapons, seeking to kill each other. They clashed against each other in the battle and many soldiers were killed. O lord of the earth! Soubala fought in that battle for a short while. He then retreated with the six thousand horses that still remained.

'"The horse riders on the Pandu side were also covered with blood. They engaged well in that battle, ready to give up their lives. They also retreated with the six thousand horses that still remained. They said, 'One can no longer use chariots or mighty elephants to fight here. Let chariots advance against chariots and elephants against elephants. Shakuni has now retreated and has stationed himself inside his formation. King Soubala will not advance in the battle again.' Droupadi's sons and those crazy elephants then went to the spot where maharatha Panchala Dhrishtadyumna was. O Kouravya! When that mighty cloud of dust arose, Sahadeva alone went to the spot where King Yudhishthira was. When they had departed, Shakuni Soubala again became enraged and attacked Dhrishtadyumna's army from the side. There was a dreadful battle again and they were ready to give up their lives. Those on your side, and that of the enemy, attacked each other, wishing to kill each other. O king! In that clash of brave warriors, they first glanced at each other, and then attacked, in hundreds and thousands. In that destruction of men, heads were severed with swords and fell down with a great noise, like palm fruit. Devoid of armour, bodies were mangled and fell down on the ground. O lord of the earth! Arms and thighs were severed with weapons. There were loud noises and the body hair stood up. With sharp weapons, brothers, sons and friends were killed. The warriors descended, like birds in search of meat. Extremely enraged, they attacked each other. 'I will be the first. I am the first.' Saying this, thousands were killed. Because of that clash, horse riders lost their lives and were dislodged from their seats. Horses fell down in hundreds and thousands. O lord of the earth! There was the neighing of swift horses. There were the roars of armoured men. A tumultuous sound was created by javelins and swords. O king! Because of your evil policy, they pierced each other's inner organs. The wrathful ones were overcome by exhaustion. The mounts were exhausted and thirsty. Wounded by sharp weapons, those on your side retreated. Many became crazy because of the scent of blood and lost their senses. They killed whomever they could approach, regardless of whether it was friend or foe. Many kshatriyas, desiring victory, lost their lives. O king! They were covered with showers of arrows and fell down on the ground. Wolves, vultures and jackals emitted fierce sounds of delight. While your son looked on, your army met with a terrible destruction. O lord of the earth! The earth was covered with the bodies of men and horses. It was colourful with flow of blood and increased the fear of cowards. O descendant of the Bharata lineage! Those on your side, as well as that of the Pandavas, were repeatedly struck by swords, javelins and spears and stopped attacking. As long as they had lives, they struck to the best of their capacity. The warriors then fell down, vomiting blood from their wounds. Headless torsos could be seen, grasping the hair[23] and raising sharp swords smeared with blood. O lord of men! Many such headless torsos rose up. Because of that scent of blood, the warriors were overcome by weakness.

'"When the sound became less, Soubala attacked the large army of the Pandavas with the few remaining horses. The Pandavas desired victory and spiritedly attacked back. The foot soldiers, elephant riders

[23]Their own hair. They grasped their own hair with one hand and wielded a sword in the other.

and horse riders raised their weapons. They protected themselves in every direction, by arranging themselves into an array. They struck him with many kinds of weapons, wishing to bring an end to the hostilities. On seeing this attack, those on your side rushed against the Pandavas, with horses, infantry, elephants and chariots. There were some foot soldiers who no longer possessed weapons. In the battle, those brave ones attacked and brought down each other with feet and fists. Rathas fell down from their chariots and elephant riders from their elephants. They were like siddhas falling down from celestial vehicles, after their store of good deeds has been exhausted. In the great battle, thus did the warriors kill each other, fathers, brothers, friends, sons and others. O supreme among the Bharata lineage! Thus did that fearful battle continue. It was extremely terrible and spears, swords and arrows were used."'

Chapter 1242(23)

'Sanjaya said, "When the sound became less and the Pandavas had slain some of that army, Soubala advanced with seven hundred well-trained horses that still remained. He swiftly approached the army[24] and said, 'O warriors! Make haste. Fight cheerfully.' The scorcher of enemies repeatedly said this. He asked the kshatriyas there, 'Where is the maharatha king?'[25] O bull among the Bharata lineage! Hearing Shakuni's words, they replied, 'The maharatha Kouravya is stationed in the midst of the battle. He is at the spot where the great umbrella is, as radiant as the full moon. That is where the armoured rathas are, with their arm-guards. A tumultuous sound can be heard there, like the roar of clouds. O king! Go there swiftly and you will be able to see Kouravya.' O lord of men! Having been thus addressed by those brave ones, Shakuni Soubala went to the

[24]His own army.
[25]Duryodhana.

spot where your son was. He was surrounded on all sides by valiant ones who were unwilling to retreat from the battle. Duryodhana was stationed there, in the midst of an array of chariots. O lord of the earth! Having seen him, Shakuni cheerfully spoke these words to Duryodhana, gladdening all the rathas on your side. He spoke to the king, as if he thought that his objective had already been achieved. 'O king! Slay this array of rathas.[26] All their horses have already been defeated by me. Yudhishthira is incapable of being defeated in the battle, unless one is prepared to give up one's own life. Slay this array of rathas, protected by Pandava. We will then kill these elephants, foot soldiers and horses.' On hearing these words, those on your side were cheered. Wishing for victory, they swiftly attacked the Pandava soldiers. They fixed their quivers and grasped their bows. They brandished their bows and roared like lions. O lord of the earth! The noise of twang of bowstrings and the slapping of palms was again heard. They shot extremely terrible arrows.

'"On seeing that they were joyfully and swiftly advancing, with upraised bows, Dhananjaya, Kunti's son, spoke these words to Devaki's son. 'Goad these horses without any fear and penetrate this ocean of soldiers. Using sharp arrows, I will bring an end to these enemies. O Janardana! This is the eighteenth day of the battle and we have engaged against each other in this great clash. The standard-bearers, the great-souled ones, were almost infinite. Behold. They have been destroyed in the battle, by destiny. O Madhava! The army of Dhritarashtra's son was like an ocean. O Achyuta! Having clashed against us, it has now become like a trifle.[27] O Madhava! It would have been well had there been peace after Bhishma was killed. But Dhritarashtra's stupid and extremely foolish son did not act accordingly. O Madhava! Bhishma spoke beneficial words that were like medicine. However, Suyodhana was beyond reason and did not listen to it. After Bhishma was dislodged and brought down

[26]On the Pandava side.

[27]The text uses the word goshpada. This literally means the mark of a cow's foot in the soil and the small puddle of water that fills up such a mark, that is, a trifle.

on the surface of the ground, I do not know the reason why the battle had to continue. I think that, in every way, Dhritarashtra's son is stupid and extremely foolish. They continued to fight even after Shantanu's son was brought down. After that, Drona, supreme among those who know about the brahman, was killed, and so were Radheya and Vikarna. But even then, there was no peace. When only a few of the soldiers were left and the son of a suta, tiger among men, was brought down with his sons, even then, there was no peace. When the brave Shrutayusha was killed, and Pourava Jalasandha, and King Shrutayudha, even then, there was no peace. O Janardana! Bhurishrava, Shalya, Shalva and the brave ones from Avanti[28] were killed. Even then, there was no peace. Jayadratha, the rakshasa Alayudha, Bahlika and Somadatta were slain. Even then, there was no peace. The brave Bhagadatta, Sudakshina from Kamboja and Duhshasana were killed. Even then, there was no peace. O Krishna! There were many brave kings, lords of their separate dominions. Even when those powerful ones were killed in the battle, there was no peace. Even when he[29] saw that an entire akshouhini was brought down by Bhimasena, either because of his delusion or because of his avarice, there still was no peace. Other than Kourava Suyodhana, who else would have been born in a noble lineage and generated this large and pointless enmity? Knowing that we were superior in qualities, strength and valour, which sensible person would attempt to fight, other than a foolish one unable to differentiate good from evil? He could not make up his mind that he should listen to your beneficial words and make peace with the Pandavas. Instead, he listened to the advice of another. Shantanu's son, Bhishma, Drona and Vidura spoke in favour of peace, but were disregarded. What medicine will he resort to today? O Janardana! Because of his stupidity, he rejected his aged father and mother's beneficial words, when they spoke about what was good for him. How can he accept good advice? O Janardana! It is evident that he was born to bring an end to his lineage. O lord of the earth! That

[28]Vinda and Anuvinda.

[29]Duryodhana.

is the direction his policy has followed. O Achyuta! It is my view that he will still not give us the kingdom. O father![30] On several occasions, the great-souled Vidura has told me that Dhritarashtra's son, as long as he is alive, will never give us a share. O venerable one! He also said, "As long as Dhritarashtra's son is alive, that wicked one will continue to act in evil ways towards you. You will not be able to defeat him, without engaging with him in battle." O Madhava! Vidura, who sees the truth, always spoke to me in this way. I now see that the evil-souled one's deeds have been exactly in accordance with the words of the great-souled Vidura. He also heard the beneficial and appropriate words spoken by Jamadagni's son.[31] But the evil-minded one disregarded them and set himself along a path of certain destruction. As soon as Suyodhana was born, many siddhas had said that this evil-souled one would bring about the destruction of kshatriyas. O Janardana! Those words have now been realized. Because of Duryodhana's deeds, the kings are headed towards fearful destruction. O Madhava! I will kill all the warriors in the battle today. When the kshatriyas have been speedily killed and their camps emptied, for the sake of his own destruction, Duryodhana will desire to fight with us. O Madhava! I think that will bring an end to the enmity. O Varshneya! Using my intelligence, on due reflection, I think this will be the end, borne out by Vidura's words and the evil-souled one's efforts. O brave one! Take me to the Bharata army, so that I can use my sharp arrows to slay the evil-souled Duryodhana's soldiers in the battle. O Madhava! Today, I will accomplish what Dharmaraja wants. While Dhritarashtra's son looks on, I will destroy this weakened army.' Thus addressed by Savyasachi, Krishna, with the reins in his hand, fearlessly penetrated the large army of the enemy in the battle.

'"The spot was terrible with the best of bows and arrows, and the javelins were like thorns.[32] Clubs and maces were the paths

[30]The word used is tata. This means father, but is affectionately used towards anyone who is older or superior.

[31]Parashurama.

[32]There is an imagery of a forest.

and chariots and elephants were the large trees. The immensely illustrious ones immersed themselves in horses and foot soldiers. Govinda roamed around there, on a chariot with several flags. O king! Those white horses bore Arjuna in the battle. Controlled by Dasharha, they were seen in every direction. Savyasachi, the scorcher of enemies, advanced on his chariot. He showered down hundreds of sharp arrows, like torrents of rain pouring down on a mountain. In the battle, Savyasachi shot and enveloped everything with arrows with drooping tufts, which made a loud noise. Torrents of arrows penetrated armour and fell down on the ground. Shot from Gandiva, those arrows were like Indra's vajra to the touch. O lord of the earth! Men, elephants and horses were struck. The arrows whizzed like insects and brought them down in the battle. Everything was covered by arrows shot from Gandiva. In the encounter, the directions and the sub-directions could not be distinguished. Everything was covered by arrows marked with Partha's name. They were gold-tufted, washed in oil and polished by artisans. They were consumed by Partha, like elephants by a fire. The Kouravas were afflicted and slaughtered by those sharp arrows. O descendant of the Bharata lineage! Wielding the bow and arrows, Partha blazed. In the battle, he consumed the warriors, like a flaming fire among dead wood. He was like a fire with black trails kindled on the outskirts of a forest by the residents of the forest, roaring loudly and consuming dead wood. Many trees and heaps of dry creepers seemed to be burnt by the blazing and powerful one. The innumerable iron arrows of the powerful one were like extremely energetic flames. The spirited one burnt all the soldiers of your son, swiftly and intolerantly. His gold-tufted arrows were shot well and could not be countered by armour. They robbed lives. He did not have to shoot a second arrow at a man, a horse, or a supreme elephant. The arrows were of many different kinds of forms and penetrated the arrays of the maharathas. He single-handedly killed the soldiers of your son, like the wielder of the vajra against the daityas."'

Chapter 1243(24)

'Sanjaya said, "Those brave ones were unwilling to retreat and made efforts. Their resolution was firm. But Dhananjaya's Gandiva was invincible. The touch of the immensely energetic one's arrows was like that of Indra's vajra. They were seen to be shot, like a torrent of rain released on a mountain. O foremost among the Bharata lineage! Those soldiers were slaughtered by Kiriti. While your son looked on, they fled from the battle. Some lost the yokes of their chariots. For others, the charioteers were slain. O lord of the earth! For some others, the poles and wheels of the chariots were shattered. Some no longer possessed any arrows. Others were afflicted by arrows. Some were not unwounded. Nevertheless, they collectively fled, afflicted by fear. With their mounts slain, some tried to rescue their sons. Others loudly called out to their fathers, or to others, for help. O tiger among men! O lord of the earth! Here and there, some fled, abandoning their relatives, brothers and allies. Many maharathas were severely wounded and benumbed. Men were seen to be immobile, struck by Partha's arrows. Others ascended their chariots and assured themselves for a short while. Having rested and quenched their thirst, they advanced towards the fight again. Some were invincible in battle. Acting in accordance with your son's instructions, they abandoned the wounded and set out to fight again. O supreme among the Bharata lineage! Others drank water and tended to their mounts. Having donned armour, they battled again. Others comforted their brothers, sons and fathers and conveyed them to the camps. Having done this, they desired to fight again. The brave ones were resplendent, decorated with nets of gold. They were like the daityas and the danavas, in pursuit of the conquest of the three worlds. Some violently advanced on chariots that were decorated with gold. They fought with the Pandava soldiers and with Dhrishtadyumna. Panchala Dhrishtadyumna, maharatha Shikhandi and Nakula's son, Shatanika, fought against that division of rathas.

'"The angry Panchala was surrounded by a large army. He wrathfully rushed against those on your side, wishing to kill them.

O lord of men! O descendant of the Bharata lineage! When he attacked, your son affixed and shot many arrows at him. O king! Dhrishtadyumna swiftly struck your archer son in the arms and the chest with many iron arrows. Severely pierced, the great archer was like an elephant struck by a goad. He used arrows to convey his[33] four horses to the land of the dead. With a broad-headed arrow, he severed his charioteer's head from his body. Having been deprived of his chariot, King Duryodhana ascended onto the back of a horse. The scorcher of enemies retreated a short distance away. O great king! On seeing that his immensely strong and valiant army had been destroyed, your son went to where Soubala was.

'"When the rathas were routed, three thousand giant elephants surrounded and attacked the five Pandava rathas[34] from all directions. O descendant of the Bharata lineage! In the battle, those five were surrounded by an army of elephants. Those tigers among men looked radiant, like planets surrounded by clouds. O great king! Arjuna was unwavering in his aim and mighty-armed. With Krishna as his charioteer, he advanced on a chariot drawn by white horses. Surrounded by elephants that were like mountains, he used sharp, sparkling and iron arrows to bring down that army of elephants. We saw each of those giant elephants killed by a single arrow. Mangled by Savyasachi, they fell down, or were falling down. On seeing those elephants, Bhimasena became like a crazy elephant. The powerful one grasped a giant club in his hand and swiftly descended from his chariot onto the ground, like Yama with a staff in his hand. On seeing the Pandava maharatha attack with his club, the soldiers on your side were frightened and excreted urine and excrement. On seeing Vrikodara with the club, the entire army was agitated. The elephants were as large as mountains and we saw them run away. Their frontal lobes were shattered by Bhimasena with the club, and blood began to flow. Struck by Bhimasena's club, the elephants fled, uttering shrieks of pain, like mountains with their wings lopped off.[35]

[33]Duryodhana's.

[34]The five Pandava brothers.

[35]According to belief, mountains once possessed wings.

There were many elephants that fled, with their frontal lobes shattered. On seeing that they were falling down, your soldiers were terrified. Yudhishthira and the Pandavas who were Madri's sons were enraged. They used sharp arrows that were tufted with the feathers of vultures to kill the warriors on elephants.

'"When the king, your son, had been defeated by Dhrishtadyumna in the battle, he retreated on the back of a horse. O great king! On seeing that all the Pandavas had been surrounded by elephants, Dhrishtadyumna, accompanied by all the Prabhadrakas, attacked. Your son climbed onto another elephant, wishing to kill the king of Panchala. On not seeing Duryodhana, scorcher of enemies, in the midst of that array of chariots, Ashvatthama, Kripa and Satvata Kritavarma asked the kshatriyas there, 'Where has Duryodhana gone?' On not seeing the king in that destruction of men, the maharathas thought that your son had been killed. Therefore, with distress written on their faces, they asked about your son. Some people told them that your son had gone to the spot where Soubala was. Other kshatriyas, who were severely wounded, said, 'What is the need to ask about Duryodhana and see if he is still alive? Fight unitedly. What can the king do?' Those kshatriyas were wounded in their limbs. Many of their mounts had been slain and they were afflicted with arrows. They softly said, 'Let us kill the army with which we have been surrounded. After having slain all the elephants, the Pandavas are advancing here.' On hearing their words, the immensely strong Ashvatthama penetrated that irresistible army of the king of Panchala. With Kripa and Kritavarma, they went to the spot where Soubala was. Those brave ones, firm archers, abandoned that array of chariots.[36]

'"O king! When they had left, with Dhrishtadyumna at the forefront, the Pandavas attacked and slaughtered those on your side. The maharathas descended cheerfully, powerful and brave. On seeing this, the faces of those in your army turned pale and they gave up all hope of remaining alive. They had few weapons left and they saw

[36]They wanted to find out if Duryodhana was well.

that they were surrounded. O king! Surrounded by those two kinds of forces, I abandoned all hope of remaining alive. With the five on our side, I fought with the Panchala soldiers. I stationed myself at the spot where Sharadvata was.[37] The five on our side were severely afflicted by Kiriti's arrows. However, we fought a great battle with Dhrishtadyumna's large army. When all of us were defeated, we retreated from the field of battle. We saw maharatha Satyaki advancing against us. With four hundred chariots, the brave one pursued me in the battle. With difficulty, I freed myself from Dhrishtadyumna, whose mounts were exhausted. But I now found myself in the midst of Madhava's army, like an evildoer who has descended into hell. For a short while, there was a fierce and extremely terrible battle. The mighty-armed Satyaki sliced off my armour. He seized me alive and I fell down on the ground, senseless. In a short instant, that army of elephants was slaughtered by Arjuna's iron arrows and Bhimasena's club. In every direction, those mangled and giant elephants fell down, like mountains. Consequently, the Pandavas found that their path was obstructed. O great king! The immensely strong Bhimasena dragged away those giant elephants and created a path for the Pandava chariots. On not seeing Duryodhana, the scorcher of enemies, in that army of chariots, Ashvatthama, Kripa and Satvata Kritavarma tried to search for the king, your maharatha son. They abandoned Panchala and went to the spot where Soubala was. In that destruction of men, they were anxious to see the king."'

Chapter 1244(25)

'Sanjaya said, "O descendant of the Bharata lineage! When that army of elephants was slain by Pandu's son[38] and when

[37]This is one of the rare and anomalous instances of Sanjaya personally fighting. The five on the Kourava side clearly are Ashvatthama, Kripa, Kritavarma, Shakuni and Duryodhana. The two kinds of forces probably means elephants and chariots.

[38]The singular is used, presumably meaning Bhima.

that army was slaughtered in the battle by Bhimasena, Bhimasena, the scorcher of enemies, was seen to be wandering around there. He was enraged as Yama with a staff in his hand, destroying all beings. O king! In the encounter, he clashed against and killed your remaining sons, while your son, Kouravya Duryodhana, could not be seen. Those and other brothers united and attacked Bhimasena. O great king! They were Durmarshana, Jaitra, Bhuribala and Ravi. These sons of yours united and attacked from every direction. They obstructed Bhimasena from all the directions. O great king! At this, Bhima again ascended his chariot. He shot sharp arrows towards the inner organs of your sons. In the great battle, your sons were afflicted by Bhima and tried to drag Bhimasena away, like an unwilling elephant. In the encounter, the wrathful Bhimsena swiftly used a kshurapra arrow to sever Durmarshana's head and it fell down on the ground. With another broad-headed arrow that was capable of penetrating all armour, Bhima slew your maharatha son, Shrutanta. The scorcher of enemies seemed to smile. He pierced Kouravya Jayatsena with an iron arrow and brought him down from his seat on the chariot. O king! He was quickly killed and fell down from his chariot onto the ground. O venerable one! At this, Shrutarva angrily pierced Bhima with one hundred arrows with drooping tufts that were shafted with feathers of vultures. In the encounter, Bhima angrily pierced Jaitra, Bhuribala and Ravi. Those three were struck with three arrows that were like the poison or the fire. Having been slain, those maharathas fell down from their chariots onto the ground. They were like blossoming kimshuka trees during the spring that had been struck down. With another sharp and iron arrow, the scorcher of enemies struck Durvimochana and sent him to the world of the dead. Having been slain, that supreme of rathas fell down from his chariot onto the ground. He was like a tree on a mountain top that had been struck down by a storm. In that battle, in the forefront of that army, he then struck two of your sons, Dushpradharsha and Sujata, with two arrows each. Those arrows had stone heads. Their limbs were struck by these and the supreme of rathas fell down. Bhima saw that Durvisaha, another of your sons, was impetuously advancing in the battle. He pierced him with a broad-headed arrow. While all the archers looked on, he was slain and fell down from his mount. On seeing that many of his brothers had been single-handedly killed in the battle, Shrutarva became intolerant and attacked Bhima. He brandished his giant bow, decorated with gold. He shot many arrows that were like poison and the fire. O king! In the battle, he severed Pandava's bow and when the bow was severed, struck him with twenty arrows. However, maharatha Bhimasena picked up another bow. Enveloping your son with arrows, he asked him to wait. The great duel that took place between the two of them was wonderful and fearful. Such a duel had earlier occurred between Jambha and Vasava. They shot sparkling arrows that were like Yama's staff and shrouded the entire earth, the sky and all the directions. O king! In the battle, Shrutarva angrily picked up his bow and struck Bhimasena in the arms and the chest with arrows. O great king! Thus severely pierced by your archer son, Bhima was angry and agitated, like the ocean during the new or the full moon. O venerable one! Overcome by anger, Bhima used his arrows to convey your son's charioteer and his four horses to Yama's eternal abode. On seeing that he was without a chariot, the one with an immeasurable soul showed the dexterity of his hands and covered him with tufted arrows. O king! Devoid of his chariot, Shrutarva picked up a sword and a shield. The sword was as radiant as the sun and was marked with the signs of one hundred moons. However, Pandava used a kshurapra arrow to sever his head from his body. The great-souled one severed his head with a kshurapra arrow and the headless torso fell down from the chariot onto the ground, making a loud noise.

'"When that brave one fell down, those on your side were overcome by fear. Despite this, they advanced against Bhimasena in the battle, wishing to fight with him. Those were the only ones left from the army that was like an ocean. When they speedily attacked, the armoured and powerful Bhimasena received them. They attacked him, surrounding him from all sides. Bhima enveloped those on your side with sharp arrows. He afflicted all of them, like the one with the one thousand eyes[39] against the asuras. He destroyed five hundred maharathas and destroyed the bumpers of their chariots. In the battle, he again slaughtered an army of seven hundred elephants. With supreme arrows, he slew ten thousand foot soldiers and eight hundred horses. Pandava was radiant. O lord! Having slain your sons in the battle, Bhimasena Kounteya thought that his task and the purpose of his birth had been accomplished. He slew all those on your side who battled. O descendant of the Bharata lineage! No one among your soldiers was capable of glancing towards him. All the Kurus were driven away and their followers slain. He then made a loud noise by slapping his armpits and terrified the giant elephants. O lord of the earth! There were many warriors in your army who were killed. O great king! The few who were left were overcome by distress."'

Chapter 1245(26)

'Sanjaya said, "O great king! In the battle, there were only two of your sons who had not been killed, Duryodhana and Sudarsha. They were stationed in the midst of the horses. On seeing that Duryodhana was stationed in the midst of the horses, Devaki's son spoke to Dhananjaya, Kunti's son. 'Many enemies, and relatives protected by them, have been killed. The bull among the Shini lineage is returning, having captured Sanjaya. O descendant of the Bharata lineage! Having fought in the battle against the wicked sons of Dhritarashtra and their followers, Nakula and Sahadeva are exhausted. Those three, Kripa, Kritavarma and Drona's maharatha son, have abandoned Suyodhana and stationed themselves elsewhere. Having slain Duryodhana's soldiers, the Panchalas, together with all the Prabhadrakas, are stationed here, supreme in their prosperity. O Partha! Duryodhana is stationed there, in the midst of the horses. The

[39]Indra.

umbrella is held aloft his head and he is repeatedly glancing here and there. He has arrayed his entire army in the form of a counter-vyuha and is stationed in the midst of the battle. If you kill him with your sharp arrows, you will be successful in your objective. O scorcher of enemies! Having seen that the army of elephants has been killed, they are not approaching you. While they are still running away, kill Suyodhana. Let someone else go to Panchala and ask him to quickly come here. O son![40] The army is exhausted and the wicked one will not be able to escape. Having destroyed a large army in the battle, Dhritarashtra's son thinks that the sons of Pandu have been defeated and has assumed an insolent form. Having seen that his own army has been destroyed by the Pandavas, he is distressed. It is certain that the king will advance in the battle and ensure his own destruction.' Having been thus addressed, Phalguna spoke these words to Krishna. 'O one who grants honours! O Krishna! All the sons of Dhritarashtra have been killed by Bhima and the two who are alive will also be killed today. Bhishma has been killed. Drona has been killed. Karna Vaikartana has been killed. Shalya, the king of Madra, has been killed. O Krishna! Jayadratha has been killed. O Janardana! Only five hundred horses remain from Shakuni Soubala's army and two hundred chariots. There are one hundred fierce tuskers and three thousand foot soldiers. O Madhava! Ashvatthama, Kripa, the lord of Trigarta, Uluka, Shakuni and Satvata Kritavarma—these are the ones who are left in Dhritarashtra's army. It is certain that no one on earth can ever escape from death. Behold. Though the soldiers have been killed, Duryodhana is still stationed there. However, all the enemies of the king[41] will be slain today. I think that no one amongst the enemy will be able to escape. O Krishna! Even if they are crazy in the battle and are superhuman, as long as they do not run away, I will slay all of them in the battle today. I will angrily bring down Gandhara with sharp arrows in the battle today. The king has not slept for a long time. I will win back the riches the evil-

[40]The word used is tata. This means son, but is affectionately used towards anyone who is younger or junior.

[41]Yudhishthira.

acting Soubala deceitfully won from us, when he again challenged us to a gambling match in the assembly hall. On hearing that their husbands and sons have been killed in the battle by the Pandavas, all the women of Nagapura[42] will weep today. O Krishna! All our tasks will be completed today. Today, Duryodhana will abandon his blazing prosperity and his life. O Krishna! O Varshneya! You can regard Dhritarashtra's stupid son as having been killed by me in the battle today, as long as he does not flee because of fear. O scorcher of enemies! Those horses cannot endure the twang of my bow and the slapping of my palms. Take me there.' O king! Thus addressed by the illustrious Pandava, Dasharha drove the horses towards Duryodhana's army.

'"O venerable one! On seeing that army, three maharathas—Bhimasena, Arjuna and Sahadeva—prepared themselves. They roared like lions and advanced, wishing to kill Duryodhana. All three united and raised their bows. In the battle, on seeing this, Soubala advanced against the Pandava assassins. Your son, Sudarshana, advanced against Bhimasena.[43] Susharma and Shakuni fought against Kiriti. Your son[44] was on the back of a horse and attacked Sahadeva. O lord of men! With care and speed, your son severely struck Sahadeva's head with a javelin. Struck by your son, he sank down on the floor of his chariot. His limbs were covered with blood and he sighed like a venomous serpent. O lord of the earth! Having regained his senses, Sahadeva angrily countered Duryodhana with sharp arrows. Partha Dhananjaya, Kunti's son, fought valiantly and severed the heads of many warriors who were seated on horses. Partha slaughtered that army with many arrows. Having brought down all the horses, he advanced against the chariots of the Trigartas. The maharathas from Trigarata united and covered Arjuna and Vasudeva with showers of arrows. Pandu's immensely illustrious son struck Satyakarma with a kshurapra arrow and shattered the yoke of his chariot. O lord! With

[42]Hastinapura.

[43]Since we have been told that all the other brothers have been killed, Sudarshana is the same as Sudarsha. That apart, the two words have the same meaning.

[44]Duryodhana.

a kshurapra arrow that had been sharpened on stone, the immensely illustrious one then laughingly severed his adversary's head, adorned with earrings made out of molten gold. O king! While all the warriors looked on, he then attacked Satyeshu, like a hungry lion in the forest going after deer. Having killed him, Partha pierced Susharma with three arrows and destroyed all the chariots that were decorated with gold. Partha then forcefully advanced against the lord of Prasthala,[45] harbouring an enmity nurtured over many years and angrily shooting arrows that were like poison. O bull among the Bharata lineage! Arjuna first enveloped him with one hundred arrows and then slew all the horses that belonged to that archer. Partha then affixed a sharp arrow that was like Yama's staff and smilingly, shot it towards Susharma. That arrow was shot by an archer who flamed with rage. In the battle, it struck and pierced Susharma's heart. O great king! Having lost his life, he fell down on the ground. All the Pandavas roared and those on your side were distressed. When Susharma had been killed in the battle, he used sharp arrows to dispatch forty-three of his[46] maharatha sons to Yama's eternal abode. He then used sharp arrows to kill all his followers. The maharatha then attacked the remaining soldiers in the Bharata army.

'"O lord of men! In the battle, Bhima was wrathful. He laughed and made your son, Sudarshana, invisible with arrows. Angry, but smiling, he severed his head from his body with an extremely sharp kshurapra arrow. Slain, he fell down on the ground. When that brave one was killed, his followers surrounded Bhima in the battle and covered him with sharp arrows. However, Vrikodara used sharp arrows that were like Indra's vajra to the touch to envelop that army in every direction. O bull among the Bharata lineage! In a short while, they were slaughtered by Bhima. O descendant of the Bharata lineage! When they were thus being slaughtered by that immensely strong one, many of those soldiers advanced against Bhimasena and fought with him. However, Pandava countered all of them with fierce arrows. O king! In that fashion, those on your side brought down

[45]Prasthala was the capital of Trigarta and Susharma was the king of Trigarta.

[46]Susharma's.

a great shower of arrows on the Pandaveya maharathas from every side. All the Pandavas, and the enemy, became anxious. Those on your side, and that of the Pandaveyas, fought in that battle. The warriors struck each other and fell down. O king! Both armies sorrowed over their relatives."'

Chapter 1246(27)

'Sanjaya said, "That battle, destructive of men, horses and elephants, continued. O king! Shakuni Soubala attacked Sahadeva. As he swiftly attacked, the powerful Sahadeva shot a torrent of arrows that were like swift insects. In the encounter, Uluka pierced Bhima with ten arrows. O great king! Shakuni pierced Bhima with three arrows and enveloped Sahadeva with ninety. O king! In the battle, those brave ones clashed against each other and pierced each other with sharp arrows that were tufted with the feathers of herons and peacocks. They were gold-tufted and sharpened on stone. O lord of the earth! Those showers of arrows were released from the bows in their hands. They covered the ten directions, like rain pouring down from clouds. O descendant of the Bharata lineage! In the battle, the enraged and extremely powerful Bhima and Sahadeva roamed around in the encounter and created great carnage. O descendant of the Bharata lineage! Those two shrouded your army with hundreds of arrows. Here and there, the sky became covered with darkness. O lord of the earth! Mangled by the arrows, the horses fled in a reverse direction and dragged around many slain ones in their paths. Horses and horse riders were killed. O venerable one! Armour was shattered and javelins were destroyed. The earth seemed to be strewn with coloured flowers. O great king! The warriors there clashed against each other. They angrily roamed around in the battle, slaying each other. The earth was strewn with beautiful heads that had the complexion of lotus filaments. The eyes were turned up and the lower lips were bit in anger. They were adorned with earrings.

O great king! Arms that were like the trunks of kings of elephants were severed. They were adorned with armlets and arm-guards and still wielded swords, javelins and battleaxes. Other bleeding and headless torsos seemed to rise up and dance around on the field of battle. O lord! The earth was frequented by a large number of carnivorous beasts and it was terrible. In the great battle, only a few of the Kouraveya soldiers were left. Having conveyed them to Yama's abode, the Pandavas were delighted.

'"At that time, the brave and powerful Soubala severely struck Sahadeva on the head with a javelin. O great king! Losing his senses, he sank down on the floor of his chariot. O descendant of the Bharata lineage! On seeing Sahadeva in that state, the powerful Bhimasena angrily restrained all the soldiers. He pierced hundreds and thousands with his iron arrows. Having pierced them, the scorcher of enemies roared like a lion. At that sound, all of Shakuni's followers were terrified and quickly fled in fear, together with their horses and elephants. On seeing that they had been routed, King Duryodhana said, 'O wicked ones! O those who do not know about dharma! Why are you running away from the battle? Deeds performed in this world by brave ones who give up their lives in the battle and do not show their backs, earn worlds in the hereafter.' Having been thus addressed, King Soubala's followers attacked the Pandavas, preferring death over retreat. O Indra among kings! As they advanced, they created an extremely terrible noise. All of them were agitated, like a turbulent ocean. O great king! On seeing that Soubala's followers were attacking, in their pursuit of victory, the Pandavas counter-attacked.

'"O lord of the earth! Having regained his assurance, the invincible Sahadeva pierced Shakuni with ten arrows and his horses with three. He seemed to smile as he severed Soubala's bow with his arrows. Shakuni, unassailable in battle, picked up another bow. He pierced Nakula with sixty arrows and Bhimasena with seven. O great king! Uluka also pierced Bhima with seven arrows. Wishing to save his father in the battle, he pierced Sahadeva with seventy. In the encounter, Bhimasena pierced Shakuni with sixty-four sharp arrows and those who were along the flanks with three arrows each. In the battle, having been struck by Bhima with arrows washed in oil, he[47] angrily covered Sahadeva with a shower of arrows. It was like clouds tinged with lightning pouring down rain on a mountain. O great king! The brave and powerful Sahadeva used a broad-headed arrow to sever and bring down Uluka's head. He was slain by Sahadeva and fell down from his chariot onto the ground. His limbs were covered with blood and the Pandava warriors were delighted. O descendant of the Bharata lineage! On seeing that his son had been killed there, Shakuni's voice choked with tears. He remembered Kshatta's words and sighed. Having thought for some time, with his eyes full of tears, he sighed and, approaching Sahadeva, he pierced him with three arrows. O great king! Countering the large number of arrows with his own arrows, the powerful Sahadeva severed his bow in the battle. O Indra among kings! When his bow was severed, Shakuni Soubala grasped a large sword and hurled it towards Sahadeva. O lord of the earth! It descended violently, terrible in form. But smilingly, he[48] severed Soubala's sword into two fragments in the encounter. When the sword was shattered into two fragments, he grasped a mighty club and hurled it towards Sahadeva. Though invincible, it too fell down on the ground. The angry Soubala then hurled an extremely terrible javelin towards Pandava. It was like the night of destruction. It descended violently in the encounter. However, Sahadeva seemed to smile. He used gold-decorated arrows to slice it into three fragments. Shattered into three fragments and decorated with gold, it fell down on the ground. It was as if blazing thunder had fallen from the sky, with flashes of lightning. On seing that the javelin had been destroyed, Soubala was overcome with fear. Because of their fright, all those on your side fled, and this included Soubala. The Pandavas, hoping for victory, roared loudly in delight. Almost all those on the side of the sons of Dhritarashtra retreated. On seeing that they were distressed, Madri's powerful son[49] restrained them with thousands of arrows in the battle.

[47]Uluka.

[48]Sahadeva.

[49]Sahadeva.

'"Sahadeva approached Soubala from the rear. He was still hoping for victory, though he was running away from the battle and was protected by those from Gandhara. O king! He remembered that Shakuni, his share, was still left.[50] Sahadeva pursued him on a chariot that was decorated with gold. He strung his large bow and repeatedly twanged it. He pursued Soubala and struck him with arrows that had been sharpened on stone and shafted with feathers of vultures. In rage, he struck him severely, like a mighty elephant being struck with a goad. Having struck him, the intelligent one addressed him, as if reminding him. 'Resort to the dharma of kshatriyas. Be a man and fight. O stupid one! You rejoiced a lot in the assembly hall. O evil-minded one! You will receive the fruits of that action now. All the evil-souled ones who disrespected us in earlier times have been killed. Duryodhana, who brings ill fame to his lineage, is the only one that is left, and his maternal uncle.[51] I will slay you and slice off your head with a razor-sharp arrow today. It will be like plucking fruit from a tree with a stick.' O great king! O tiger among men! Having said this, the immensely strong Sahadeva attacked him with great force. The invincible Sahadeva, the lord of warriors, attacked him. He seemed to be smiling, as he stretched his bow with great force and rage. He pierced Shakuni with ten arrows and his horses with four. He severed his umbrella, standard and bow and roared like a lion. Soubala's standard, bow and umbrella were severed by Sahadeva and he was pierced in all his inner organs by many arrows. O great king! Then, the powerful Sahadeva again shot a shower of invincible arrows towards Shakuni. Angrily, Subala's son rushed towards Madri's son, Sahadeva. He wished to kill him with a javelin that was decorated with gold. In the forefront of that battle, as he rushed swiftly ahead, Madri's son severed the upraised javelin and the two well-rounded arms with three broad-headed arrows. Having spiritedly severed them, he roared. Acting swiftly, he then used a broad-headed arrow that was gold-tufted and was capable of penetrating all armour. It was firm and was made out of iron.

[50]Shakuni was the share allotted to Sahadeva.

[51]Shakuni.

Aiming this well and with force, he severed his head from his body. That arrow was decorated with gold. It was extremely sharp and was as radiant as the sun. In the battle, Pandava used that to sever the head of Subala's son and he fell down on the ground. The arrow was gold-tufted and had been sharpened on stone and Pandu's enraged son powerfully severed the head with this. He[52] was the root of all the bad conduct of the Kurus. With the head severed, Shakuni was seen to lie down on the ground. His body was wet with blood.

'"The warriors on your side were dispirited and terrified. Still wielding weapons, they fled in different directions. Their mouths were dry and they ran away, bereft of their senses. They were afflicted by the twang of Gandiva. They were oppressed by fear. Together with the son of Dhritarashtra, the chariots, horses and elephants were routed. O descendant of the Bharata lineage! When Shakuni was brought down, the Pandaveyas were delighted. In the battle, they cheerfully blew on their conch shells. Together with Keshava, the soldiers rejoiced. All of them honoured the energetic Sahadeva and joyfully said, 'O brave one! It is through good fortune that the evil-souled gambler and his son have been killed by you in the battle.'"'

Chapter 1247(28)

'Sanjaya said, "O great king! Soubala's followers were enraged. Ready to give up their lives, they repulsed the Pandavas. Wishing to support Sahadeva in his victory, Arjuna and the spirited Bhimasena, who looked like an angry and virulent serpent, received them. They wished to kill Sahadeva, with javelins, swords and spears in their hands. But with Gandiva, Dhananjaya rendered their resolution unsuccessful. With weapons in their hands, those warriors attacked. However, with broad-headed arrows, Bibhatsu severed their heads and their horses. They were slain and lay down on the ground, deprived of their lives. Spiritedly, Savyasachi struck those brave men

[52]Shakuni.

of the world. King Duryodhana saw that his own army was being destroyed. O lord! He angrily rallied the one hundred chariots that still remained. O scorcher of enemies! He spoke these words to all the assembled army of the son of Dhritarashtra, the elephants, the horses and the foot soldiers. 'In the battle, attack all the Pandavas and their well-wishers, with Panchala and his army. Return after swiftly slaying them.' Unassailable in battle, they accepted those instructions. On your son's command, they attacked the Parthas back in that encounter. In the great battle, those who were left attacked swiftly. But the Pandavas countered them with arrows that were like venomous serpents. O foremost among the Bharata lineage! In a short instant, those great-souled ones slaughtered those soldiers in the battle and they could not find a protector. Though armoured and stationed, they were full of fear. The horses fled in a reverse direction and the soldiers were covered in dust. In the battle, the directions and the sub-directions could not be distinguished. O descendant of the Bharata lineage! In a short while, in that battle, many men emerged from the army of the Pandavas and slaughtered those on your side. O descendant of the Bharata lineage! Your soldiers were annihilated. O descendant of the Bharata lineage! O lord! Eleven akshouhinis had been mustered by your son and they were slaughtered in the battle by the Pandus and the Srinjayas. O king! Among the thousands of great-souled kings on your side, only Duryodhana remained and he was seen to be severely wounded. He glanced in all the directions and saw that the earth had been emptied. He was bereft of all warriors and glanced at the Pandavas in the battle, who were delighted that all their objectives had been accomplished. They roared in every direction. O great king! Hearing the whizzing of arrows shot by those great-souled ones, Duryodhana was overcome by depression. Devoid of soldiers and men, he resolved to retreat."

'Dhritarashtra asked, "O suta! When my soldiers and my camps were annihilated, what was the army that still remained with the Pandavas? I am asking you. O Sanjaya! You are skilled in recounting. Tell me. What did my unfortunate son, Duryodhana, the lord of the earth, do, when he saw that his army had been destroyed and he was the only one left?"

'Sanjaya replied, "O king! Two thousand chariots, seven hundred elephants, five thousand horses and ten thousand foot soldiers—this is what was left from the large army of the Pandavas. Dhrishtadyumna gathered them and remained stationed in the battle. O foremost among the Bharata lineage! King Duryodhana was alone. In the battle, he could not see any supreme ratha as his aide. He saw that his own army had been destroyed and that the enemy was roaring. He abandoned his horse, which had been slain. Out of fear, he retreated and fled in an eastern direction. Your son, Duryodhana, had been the lord of eleven hundred army divisions. With a club in his hand, the spirited one advanced on foot towards a lake. He had advanced on foot only for a short distance, when the lord of men remembered the words that the intelligent Kshatta, devoted to dharma, had spoken. 'The immensely wise Vidura had certainly foreseen all of this earlier. Our great destruction and that of the kshatriyas would occur in the battle.' Thinking in this way, the king entered the lake. O king! Having seen the destruction of his army, his heart was consumed with grief. O great king! With Dhrishtadyumna at the forefront, the Pandavas angrily attacked your soldiers. O king! They[53] wielded javelins, swords and spears in their hands and roared powerfully. With Gandiva, Dhananjaya rendered their resolutions unsuccessful. He slaughtered them with his sharp arrows, with their advisers and their relatives. Stationed on a chariot drawn by white horses, Arjuna was extremely radiant. Subala and his son were killed, with their horses, chariots and elephants. Your army was like a large forest that had been destroyed. There had been hundreds and thousands in Duryodhana's army. O king! But not a single maharatha was seen to remain alive. O king! The only exceptions were Drona's son, the brave Kritavarma, Goutama Kripa and the king, your son.

'"On seeing me, Dhrishtadyumna laughed. He spoke to Satyaki. 'What is the point of capturing this one? Nothing will be gained by keeping him alive.' On hearing Dhrishtadyumna's words, Shini's maharatha grandson raised his sharp sword, so as to kill me then. At that time, the immensely wise Krishna Dvaipayana arrived and

[53]The remaining Kourava soldiers.

said, 'Free Sanjaya alive. Under no circumstances should he be killed.' Hearing Dvaipayana's words, Shini's grandson joined his hands in salutation. Freeing me, he said, 'O Sanjaya! Depart in peace.' Obtaining his permission, I cast aside my armour. I was without weapons. In the evening, I set out for the city,[54] my limbs covered in blood. O king! When I had travelled one krosha,[55] I saw the solitary Duryodhana, with the club in his hand. He was severely wounded. His eyes were full of tears and he did not see me. Miserable, I stood before him. Though he saw me, he ignored me. On seeing him alone thus, alone after the battle, I was overcome with great grief and could not speak for a while. Then I told him everything about my capture in the battle and my release, alive, through the favours of Dvaipayana. Having thought for some time, he regained his senses. He asked me about his brothers and all the soldiers. I told him everything that I had directly witnessed, that all his brothers had been killed and the soldiers brought down. 'O lord of men! Only three rathas remain among those on your side. This is what Krishna Dvaipayana told me when I was about to leave.'[56] He sighed and glanced repeatedly at me. Then, touching me with his hands, your son replied, 'O Sanjaya! With your exception, no one else has been left alive in this battle. I do not see a second one, though the Pandavas have their aides. O Sanjaya! Tell the lord, the king, who has wisdom for his sight.[57] Tell him, your son, Duryodhana, has entered the lake. He is without well-wishers, without direction and without sons and brothers. When the Pandavas have obtained the kingdom, what is the point of someone like me remaining alive? Tell him everything and tell him that I have escaped from the great battle. I am alive, but am severely wounded. I will rest in this lake.' O great king! Having said this, the king entered the lake. Through his maya, that lord of men created a passage in the water.

'"When he had entered that lake, I was alone and saw that the

[54]Hastinapura.

[55]Measure of distance, between 2 and 3 miles.

[56]Sanjaya knew it too and didn't need Vyasa to tell him this.

[57]Dhritarashtra.

three rathas arrived at the spot, with their exhausted mounts. They were Sharadvata Kripa, Drona's son, supreme among rathas, and Kritavarma, from the Bhoja lineage. They were wounded with arrows. All of them glanced towards me and swiftly urged their horses. Having approached me, they said, 'O Sanjaya! It is through good fortune that you are alive.' All of them asked me about your son, the lord of men. 'O Sanjaya! Where is King Duryodhana? Is he alive?' I told them that the king was well. I told them everything that Duryodhana had told me. I also showed them the lake that the king had entered. O king! Having heard my words, Ashvatthama glanced towards the large lake. He lamented in grief and said, 'Alas! The king does not know that we are still alive. With him, we are sufficient to fight with the enemy.' For a long time, those maharathas lamented there. Then, on seeing the sons of Pandu in the battle, those best of rathas fled.[58] Kripa took me up on his well-prepared chariot. Those three rathas, all that was left of our army, departed for the camp. The sun had set. On hearing that all your sons had been killed, those who guarded the outposts lamented.

'"O great king! They were aged men who had been employed to take care of the women. With the wives of the king, they set out for the city. All of them lamented and wept loudly. On hearing about the destruction of your army, great sounds of woe arose. O king! The women wept repeatedly. They made the earth resound with that noise, like female ospreys. They scratched their bodies with their nails. They struck their heads with their hands. They tore out their hair. The wept loudly. They beat on their breasts with loud sounds of lamentation. O lord of the earth! With those sounds of lamentation, they wept loudly. Duryodhana's advisers were extremely miserable and their voices choked with tears. Taking the king's wives with them, they left for the city. O lord of the earth! With staffs in their hands, those who were in charge of the gates and those who guarded the gates also swiftly fled towards the city. They took with them beautiful beds that were spread with expensive

[58]The Pandava soldiers were approaching.

covers. Other men placed their wives on carts that were drawn by mules and left towards the city. O great king! Those noble women had earlier lived in palaces and were not seen, even by the sun. As they departed for the city, they were seen by ordinary men. O foremost among the Bharata lineage! Those women were delicate and noble. With their kin and relatives slain, they swiftly departed for the city. The cowherds and other herdsmen also fled towards the city. The men were terrified, afflicted by their fear of Bhimasena. They were overcome by an extremely terrible fear of the Parthas too. As they fled towards the city, they glanced at each other. There was an extremely terrible exodus that took place.

'"At that time, Yuyutsu was senseless because of his grief. Nevertheless, he thought about what should be done at the time. 'Duryodhana has been defeated in the battle by the terrible valour of the Pandavas. He was the lord of eleven army divisions. His brothers have been slain. All the Kurus, with Bhishma and Drona as the foremost, have been killed. Through the wishes of destiny, I am the only one who has been spared. In every direction, all of them are running away from the camps. There are only a few who are left from among Duryodhana's advisers. Taking the king's wives with them, they have run away towards the city. O lord![59] I think that the time has come for me to also enter with them, after having taken Yudhishthira and Bhima's permission.'[60] For this purpose, the mighty-armed one presented himself before them. The king, who was always compassionate, was pleased. The mighty-armed one[61] embraced the son of a vaishya[62] and granted him leave. Ascending his chariot, he swiftly urged the horses and also tended to the task of conveying the wives of the king to the city. With them, he entered Hastinapura, his voice choking with tears and his eyes full of tears. The sun was swiftly setting. He saw the immensely wise Vidura, who also had tears in his eyes. His senses overcome with grief, he had

[59]Yuyutsu is addressing himself.

[60]Because these two were older than him.

[61]Yudhishthira.

[62]Yuyutsu was the son of a vaishya lady.

come away from the king.[63] He bowed down before him and stood before him. The one who upheld the truth spoke to him.[64] 'O son! It is through good fortune that you are alive amidst this destruction of the Kurus. Why have you entered and come here without the king?[65] Tell me, in detail, the reason for this.' Yuyutsu replied, 'O father![66] Shakuni has been slain, with his kin and his relatives. When his relatives had been killed, King Duryodhana abandoned his horse. He retreated and fled in an eastern direction. When the king had run away, all those in the camps and abodes were terrified and anxious and fled towards the city. The guards in charge also fled, having placed the wives of the king and his brothers on the mounts. At this, I took the permission of the king and Keshava[67] and entered Hastinapura, wishing to protect the people who were running away.' Having heard the words spoken by the son of a vaishya, Vidura, knowledgeable about all forms of dharma, thought that the right decision had been taken at the time. The one who was eloquent with words, immeasurable in his soul, applauded Yuyutsu. 'When all those of the Bharata lineage were being destroyed, you acted in accordance with what should have been done at the time. You should rest now. Tomorrow, you can return to Yudhishthira.' Having heard the words of Vidura, knowledgeable about all forms of dharma, Yuyutsu took his permission and entered, after the destruction of the king had taken place. Yuyutsu spent the night in his own house."'

[63]That is, Vidura had come away from Dhritarashtra.

[64]Vidura spoke to Yuyutsu.

[65]Duryodhana.

[66]The word used is tata. It means father, but is affectionately used towards anyone who is senior or elder.

[67]However, earlier, Bhima rather than Krishna has been mentioned.

come away from the king?" He bowed down before him and stood before him. The one who upheld dharma said to him, "O son! It is through good fortune that you [illegible] amidst the destruction of the Kurus. Why have you returned and come here without the king? Tell me in detail." He answered the queries. "O father! Shakuni has been slain, with his kin and his relatives. When his [illegible] had been killed, King Duryodhana abandoned his horse. He was scared and fled in an eastern direction. When the king fled, all those in the camps and [illegible] were terrified and fled towards the city. The guards of the [illegible] having placed the wives of the king and his brothers on the mounts, [illegible]. At this, I took the permission of the king and Keshava and entered Hastinapura, wishing to protect the people who [illegible]." Having heard the words spoken by the son of a vaishya, Vidura, knowledgeable about all forms of dharma, thought that the man [illegible] had been [illegible]. The one who was supreme with words, immeasurable in his soul, applauded Yuyutsu. "When all those of the Bharata lineage were being destroyed, you acted with compassion and did what should have been done at the time. You should rest now. Tomorrow, you can return to Yudhishthira." He heard the words of Vidura, knowledgeable about all forms of dharma. Yuyutsu took his permission and entered [illegible] where [illegible] had taken place. Yuyutsu spent the night in his own house.

[illegible] who had come away from Dhritarashtra.
[illegible] Vidura, [illegible].
[illegible] Yuyutsu.
The word used is [illegible]. It means [illegible] father [illegible] towards [illegible] who is [illegible].
Shame on [illegible]. Kunti [illegible] Gandhari's [illegible].

SECTION SEVENTY-SIX

Tirtha Yatra Parva

This parva has 1261 shlokas and twenty-five chapters.

Chapter 1248(29): 66 shlokas
Chapter 1249(30): 68 shlokas
Chapter 1250(31): 60 shlokas
Chapter 1251(32): 52 shlokas
Chapter 1252(33): 18 shlokas
Chapter 1253(34): 81 shlokas
Chapter 1254(35): 53 shlokas
Chapter 1255(36): 63 shlokas
Chapter 1256(37): 50 shlokas
Chapter 1257(38): 33 shlokas
Chapter 1258(39): 32 shlokas
Chapter 1259(40): 35 shlokas
Chapter 1260(41): 39 shlokas
Chapter 1261(42): 41 shlokas
Chapter 1262(43): 52 shlokas
Chapter 1263(44): 110 shlokas
Chapter 1264(45): 95 shlokas
Chapter 1265(46): 29 shlokas
Chapter 1266(47): 61 shlokas
Chapter 1267(48): 23 shlokas
Chapter 1268(49): 65 shlokas
Chapter 1269(50): 51 shlokas
Chapter 1270(51): 26 shlokas
Chapter 1271(52): 21 shlokas
Chapter 1272(53): 37 shlokas

It is discovered that Duryodhana is hiding in Lake Dvaipayana. Bhima and Duryodhana prepare to fight. Balarama returns from his pilgrimage to witness the encounter. This parva has a description of places of pilgrimage (tirtha). Yatra *means travel or journey and this section is accordingly named after a journey to places of pilgrimage.*

Chapter 1248(29)

'Dhritarasthra asked, "O Sanjaya! When all the soldiers had been killed by the sons of Pandu in the field of battle, what did my remaining soldiers do? What about Kritavarma, Kripa and Drona's valiant son? What did evil-souled King Duryodhana do then?"

'Sanjaya replied, "When the wives of those great-souled kshatriyas had fled and the camp was empty, those three rathas were extremely anxious. They heard the sounds made by the victorious Pandavas. In the evening, they saw that the camp was empty. They no longer wished to stay there and wishing to save the king, went towards the lake. O king! Yudhishthira, with dharma in his soul, and his brothers were delighted in the battle. They roamed around, wishing to kill Duryodhana. Desiring victory, they angrily sought to follow him. But though they endeavoured to search for him, they could not see that king of men. With the club in his hand, he had run away with great speed and with his maya, had entered the lake and had made the waters solid.[1] The mounts of all the Pandavas became extremely tired. They returned to their camp and with their soldiers, rested there.

'"After the Parthas had left, Kripa, Drona's son and Satvata Kritavarma slowly went to the lake. They approached the lake where the lord of men was lying down. They addressed the invincible king who was sleeping in the waters. 'O king! Arise! With us, fight against Yudhishthira. Triumph and enjoy the earth, or be slain and enjoy heaven. O Duryodhana! All their soldiers have also been slain by you. O lord of the earth! The soldiers who are left will also not be able to withstand your impetuosity. You will also be protected by us. O descendant of the Bharata lineage! Therefore, arise.' Duryodhana replied, 'O bulls among men! This clash between the Pandus and the Kouravas has been destructive for men. It is through good fortune that I see that you have escaped with your lives. We will defeat all of them, but after we have got rid of our tiredness and our exhaustion.

[1]That is, after Duryodhana had entered the lake, he used his powers to make the waters solid, so that, it no longer looked like a lake.

You are also exhausted and we are severely wounded. Their army is prospering. Therefore, I do not think we should fight now. O brave ones! Since your hearts are large, the words that you have spoken are not surprising. You are also supremely devoted to us. However, this is not the time for valour. I will rest for one night. Then, in the battle tomorrow, I will fight with you against the enemy. There can be no doubt about that.' Having been thus addressed, Drona's son spoke to the king, who was unassailable in battle. 'O king! O fortunate one! Arise. We will defeat the enemy in the battle. O king! I swear on my religious rites, my donations, my truthfulness and my meditation that I will slay the Somakas today. Virtuous people obtain delight from performing sacrifices. If I do not slay the enemy in the battle before the night is over, let me not obtain that delight. O lord! Without slaying all the Panchalas, I will not take off my armour. I am telling you this truthfully. O lord of men! Listen to me.' While they were conversing in this way, some hunters came to the spot.

'"They were exhausted from carrying their burden of meat and wished to drink some water. O great king! O lord! Every day, with supreme devotion, those hunters used to carry a load of meat to Bhimasena. While they were concealed there, they heard all the words that were exchanged between them and Duryodhana. On finding that Kourava was unwilling to fight, those great archers, who wished to fight, made great efforts to persuade him. They[2] saw the Kourava maharathas there. Situated in the water, the king was unwilling to fight. O Indra among kings! On hearing the conversation between them and the king, who was in the waters, the concealed hunters realized that it was Suyodhana who was inside the water. Some time earlier, while searching for the king, Pandu's son[3] had arrived there and had asked them about your son. O king! On remembering the words of Pandu's son, those hunters of deer softly spoke to each other. 'If we tell Pandava about Duryodhana, he will give us riches. It is evident that King Duryodhana is inside this lake. Therefore, let all of us go to the spot where King Yudhishthira is. We will tell him

[2]The hunters.

[3]Meaning Bhima.

that the intolerant Duryodhana is sleeping in the waters. Let us tell the intelligent Bhimasena, the wielder of the bow, everything about Dhritarashtra's son sleeping in the waters. He will be extremely pleased with us and will give us a lot of riches. Why should we exhaust ourselves with this dried out meat?' Having said this, the hunters were delighted. Desiring wealth, they abandoned that burden of meat and headed towards the camp.

'"O great king! The Pandavas, strikers, had accomplished their objectives. But they did not see Duryodhana in the battle. Desiring to ascertain the final destination of that wicked and deceitful one, they had dispatched spies in every direction of the field of the battle. But all those soldiers had returned and told Dharmaraja that King Duryodhana could not be found. O bull among the Bharata lineage! On hearing the words of the messengers, the king was anxious and breathed heavily. O bull among the Bharata lineage! The Pandus were thus distressed. O lord! At that time, the hunters swiftly arrived at the camp, delighted because they had seen King Duryodhana. Though they were restrained,[4] while Bhimasena looked on, they entered. They approached the immensely strong Pandava Bhimasena and told him everything that they had seen and heard. O king! At this, Vrikodara gave them a lot of riches. The scorcher of enemies went and told Dharmaraja everything. 'O king! Duryodhana has been discovered by my hunters. You have been tormented because of him. He is sleeping in the waters and has turned them into stone.' O lord of the earth! On hearing Bhimasena's pleasant words, Kounteya Ajatashatrua, together with his brothers, was delighted. On hearing that the great archer had entered the waters of a lake, with Janardana at the forefront, he[5] swiftly went there. O lord of the earth! Loud sounds of joy arose among all the Pandavas and the Panchalas. O bull among the Bharata lineage! They roared loudly, like lions. O king! All the kshatriyas swiftly rushed towards Lake Dvaipayana. In every direction, the cheerful Somakas roared, 'Dhritarashtra's wicked son withdrew from the battle and has been found out.' O lord of the earth! Speedily and swiftly, the chariots

[4]Presumably by the guards.

[5]Yudhishthira.

proceeded there and the tumultuous sound that they made reached heaven. Yudhishthira wished to seek out Duryodhana and wherever he went, the kings spiritedly followed him, although their mounts were exhausted. O descendant of the Bharata lineage! There were Arjuna, Bhimasena, the two Pandavas who were Madri's sons, Panchala Dhrishtadyumna, the unvanquished Shikhandi, Uttamouja, Yudhamanyu, the unvanquished Satyaki, the remaining Panchalas and Droupadi's sons. There were all the horses and elephants and hundreds of foot soldiers. O great king! All of them went with Dharma's son.

'"Yudhishthira reached the lake known as Dvaipayana, where Duryodhana was. The waters were clear, cool and pleasant to the heart and it was as large as the ocean. Through his maya, your son had solidified the waters and was inside them. O descendant of the Bharata lineage! This was a wonderful act and could only be performed with divine powers. The lord of men was lying down inside the waters and was extremely difficult to see. O Indra among men! The lord of men still held the club in his hand. King Duryodhana was residing inside the water and heard a tumultuous sound, like the roar of a cloud. O Indra among kings! O great king! It was made by Yudhishthira and his brothers, when they arrived to kill Duryodhana. There was the great roar of conch shells and the wheels of chariots. A great cloud of dust arose and the earth trembled. O hearing the noise made by Yudhishthira's soldiers, maharathas Kritavarma, Kripa and Drona's son rushed towards the king and said, 'Desiring victory, the cheerful Pandavas are advancing here on their horses. Therefore, you should know that we are withdrawing ourselves from this spot.' On hearing the words of those illustrious ones, the lord agreed, from inside the waters that he had turned solid with his maya. O great king! Having obtained the king's permission, Kripa and the other rathas, severely oppressed by grief, went some distance away. O venerable one! Having travelled some distance, they saw a banyan tree. They were extremely tired and rested under it, thinking about the king. 'Dhritarashtra's immensely strong son is sleeping inside the waters, having solidified them. Desiring to fight, the Pandavas will reach that spot. How will the fight take place?

What will happen to the king? How will the Pandavas discover the Kourava king?' Thinking about these and other things, they unyoked their horses from their chariots. O king! Kripa and the other rathas prepared to rest there."'

Chapter 1249(30)

'Sanjaya said, "When those three rathas had withdrawn, the Pandavas arrived at the lake where Duryodhana was. O best of the Kuru lineage! They reached Lake Dvaipayana. They saw that the abode of the waters had been turned to stone by Dhritarashtra's son. The descendant of the Kuru lineage[6] spoke these words to Vasudeva. 'Behold. Dhritarashtra's son has used his powers of maya on the water. He has turned the waters to stone and is lying down, without any fear from humans. He has used divine powers of maya and is inside the water now. He is skilful in deceit and has used deceit. However, he will not escape from me with his life. O Madhava! Even if the wielder of the vajra himself helps him in the fight, the worlds will see that he is slain in the battle today.' Vasudeva replied, 'He is skilled in the use of maya. O descendant of the Bharata lineage! Slay his maya with maya. O Yudhishthira! Maya must be destroyed with maya. That is the truth. Use many different deeds and means to apply maya to these waters. O best among the Kuru lineage! Slay Suyodhana, who is evil in his soul. It is through different deeds and means that Indra slew the daityas and the danavas. It is through many different deeds and means that Bali was bound down by the great-souled one.[7] It is through deeds and means that the great asura Hiranyaksha was slain in earlier times

[6]Meaning, Yudhishthira.

[7]This great-souled one means Vishnu in his dwarf (vamana) incarnation, when he deprived Bali of the three worlds in three steps.

and deeds were also used to slay Hiranyakashipu.[8] O king! There is no doubt that Vritra was slain through deeds. O king! Poulastya's son, the rakshasa named Ravana, was slain by Rama, together with his relatives and followers.[9] Resort to deeds and yoga and show your valour. O king! In ancient times, I used deeds and means to slay the great daityas Taraka and the valiant Viprachitti.[10] O lord! It is through deeds that Vatapi, Ilvala, Trishira and the asuras Sunda and Upasunda were killed.[11] O lord! Indra enjoys the three worlds through deeds and means. O King Yudhishthira! Deeds are powerful. There is nothing else. Daityas, danavas, rakshasas and kings have been killed through deeds and means. Therefore, resort to deeds.' Pandava, rigid in his vows, was thus addressed by Vasudeva.

'"O descendant of the Bharata lineage! Kounteya laughed and addressed your immensely strong son, who was inside the water. 'O Suyodhana! O lord of the earth! After having caused the destruction of all the kshatriyas and your own lineage, why have you entered the water? Today, you have entered the water, wishing to save your own life. O king! O Suyodhana! Arise and fight with us. O best of men! O king! Where have your insolence and your sense of pride gone now, since you are terrified and are inside the waters, having turned them to stone? In assemblies, everyone has spoken of you as a hero. I think all of that is in vain, since your prowess is now lying down inside the water. O king! Arise and fight. You have been born

[8]Hiranyaksha and Hiranyakashipu were brothers. Hiranyakashipu was slain by Vishnu in his half-man half-lion (*narasimha*) incarnation and Hiranyaksha was slain by Vishnu in his boar (*varaha*) incarnation.

[9]Ravana was the son of the sage Vishrava, and Vishrava (Poulastya) was the son of the sage Pulastya.

[10]Vishnu's role in the slaying of Taraka and Viprachitti can only have been indirect. Taraka was slain by Kartikeya, though there are some references to Taraka having been killed by Indra. There are also references to Viprachitti having been killed by Indra.

[11]Ilvala and Vatapi were killed by the sage Agastya. The story has been recounted in Section 33 (Volume 3). The Sunda-Upasunda story has been recounted in Section 16 (Volume 1). Trishira was killed by Indra. The story has been recounted in Section 49 (Volume 4).

in a kshatriya lineage. In particular, remember that you have been born in the lineage of Kouraveyas. How can you praise your birth in the lineage of Kouravas? You have run away from the battle and have entered and stationed yourself inside these waters. Stationing oneself away from a battle is not eternal dharma. O king! It is not like an arya to run away from a battle. That does not lead to heaven. How is it that you wish to remain alive, without having seen the end of this war? You have seen your sons, brothers, fathers, matrimonial allies, friends, maternal uncles and relatives brought down. O son![12] Having caused their destruction, how can you station yourself inside this lake? O descendant of the Bharata lineage! Though you have spoken of yourself as brave, you are not brave. O evil-minded one! In everyone's hearing, you have said that you are brave. On seeing enemies, brave ones do not run away. O brave one! Tell us about the fortitude that has led you to run away from the encounter. Arise and fight and abandon the fear in you. O Suyodhana! You have caused the destruction of all the soldiers and your brothers. You should not turn your mind to the dharma of remaining alive now. O Suyodhana! This is not indicated for someone who has resorted to the dharma of kshatriyas. You depended on Karna and Shakuni Soubala and in your delusion, thought yourself to be immortal. You were not intelligent. O descendant of the Bharata lineage! Having performed that extremely evil deed, fight back now. In your confusion, how can something like flight appeal to someone like you? O Suyodhana! Where have your manliness and your pride gone now? Where have your valour and your extremely swollen insolence gone now? Where has your skill with weapons gone? Why have you resorted to this store of water? O descendant of the Bharata lineage! Following the dharma of kshatriyas, arise and fight. O descendant of the Bharata lineage! Defeat us and rule over the entire earth, or be killed by us and lie down on the ground. That is the foremost dharma, ordained by the great-souled creator. O maharatha! Act in accordance with that and be a king.'

[12]The word used is tata. This means son, but is used towards anyone who is younger or junior. Duryodhana was younger to Yudhishthira.

'"Duryodhana replied, 'O great king! It is not surprising that fear should enter all living beings. O descendant of the Bharata lineage! But I have not retreated because I am frightened for my life. I was without a chariot and without quivers. The parshni charioteers were killed. I was without a single follower in the battle and wished to retreat. O lord of the earth! I did not enter these waters because I was frightened of being killed or because I was grieving, but because I was exhausted. O Kounteya! With those that follow you, rest for some time. I will arise and fight with all of you in this battle.'

'"Yudhisthira said, 'All of us are sufficiently rested. We have been looking for you for a long time. O Suyodhana! Arise and fight with us now. Kill the Parthas in the battle and obtain this prosperous kingdom, or be killed in the battle and obtain the worlds of heroes.'

'"Duryodhana replied, 'O descendant of the Kuru lineage! O lord of men! Those among the Kurus for whose sake I desired the kingdom, all my brothers, are dead. Those bulls among kshatriyas have been killed and the earth is devoid of her jewels. I am not interested in enjoying her. She is like a widowed lady. O Yudhishthira! O bull among the Bharata lineage! However, I still wish to defeat and subjugate you and am interested in breaking the Panchalas and the Pandus. But I do not think there is any need for battle when Drona and Karna have been pacified and the grandfather has been slain. O king! This bare earth is now only for you. Which king wishes to rule over a kingdom without any aides? Well-wishers have been killed by me and so have sons, brothers and fathers. When the kingdom has been robbed, who like me would wish to remain alive? I will clad myself in deerskin and leave for the forest. O descendant of the Bharata lineage! With those on my side slain, I have no desire for the kingdom. Many relatives have been killed. Horses have been killed. Elephants have been killed. O king! Devoid of fever, enjoy this kingdom. I will clad myself in deerskin and go to the forest. O lord! Now that I have been vanquished, I have no desire to remain alive any more. O Indra among kings! Go and enjoy the earth, which is devoid of kings, destitute of warriors, robbed of riches and bereft of fortifications, as you please.'

'"Yudhishthira said, 'O son! Do not utter such woes of lamentation from inside the water. O king! In my mind, there is no desire like that of a bird.[13] O Suyodhana! You may be capable of giving it to me, but I do not wish to rule over something that has been given by you. If you give this earth to me, its acceptance will be adharma. O king! The learned texts say that it is not dharma for a kshatriya to receive gifts. I do not desire this entire earth, when it has been given by you. I will enjoy this earth after having defeated you in battle. Why do you want to give an earth that has no kings? O king! Why do you want to give an earth that is not yours to give? We asked for it in accordance with dharma, for the sake of peace and for the sake of our lineage. O king! You first refused the immensely strong Varshneya. Why do you want to give it now? What is this delusion in your mind? When he is accused, which king wishes to give away the earth? O descendant of the Kourava lineage! You are not the lord of this earth that you can give it away. O king! Why do you wish to give something that you have no powers over? Defeat me in the battle and rule over the earth. O descendant of the Bharata lineage! In earlier times, you were not prepared to give me even that much which could be held up on the point of a needle. O lord of the earth! Why do you then wish to gift me the entire earth? If you were earlier not prepared to give up that much which could be held up on the point of a needle, why do you want to give up the earth now? This earth is prosperous and you have ruled over it. Which foolish person will be prepared to give this earth to enemies? You are not only stupid and foolish, you possess no intelligence. Though you wish to give up the earth, you will not escape with your life. Defeat us and rule over the earth, or be killed by us and roam in the supreme worlds. O king! If, between the two of us, both of us remain alive, all beings will be uncertain about who has emerged victorious. You are of limited intelligence and your life now depends on me. If I wish, I can grant you life. But you are not capable of remaining alive. In particular, you had made efforts to burn us. You tried to kill us by drowning us and making us consume virulent

[13]The sense is that a bird is given crumbs that it has not earned.

poison.[14] Deceived by you, we were deprived of the kingdom. Because of these and other evil deeds, you should not remain alive. Arise. Arise. Fight. That will be beneficial for you.'"

'Sanjaya said, "O lord of men! Those brave and victorious ones spoke these and many other words there."'

Chapter 1250(31)

'Dhritarashtra asked, "Thus, my son, the lord of the earth, was censured. The scorcher of enemies is naturally intolerant. What did he do? He has never heard reprimands like these earlier. He has been revered by all the worlds with the respect that is due to a king. O Sanjaya! You have seen how the entire earth, with mlecchas and those who live in mountainous regions, depended on him for favours. Such a person was censured, especially by the sons of Pandu. He was alone and without servants, in a secluded spot. On hearing the words repeatedly spoken by the victorious ones, what did he tell the Pandaveyas? O Sanjaya! Tell me everything about that."

'Sanjaya replied, "O king! O Indra among kings! Your son was thus censured by Yudhishthira and his brothers. The lord of men heard those words, which were like poison. Inside the water, he repeatedly let out long and hot sighs. Inside the water, the king repeatedly wrung his hands. Then, having made up his mind to fight, he replied to the king.[15] 'O Parthas! All of you are served by well-wishers. You possess chariots and mounts. I am alone and miserable. I have been deprived of a chariot. My mounts have been slain. I am without weapons and am surrounded by many rathas. Without weapons, even if I wish to fight, how can I single-handedly fight on foot? O Yudhishthira! Fight with me one at a time. It is not

[14]This is a reference to the attempt made to poison Bhima, described in Section 7 (Volume 1).

[15]Yudhishthira.

appropriate that one should single-handedly fight with many warriors simultaneously, especially when one is without armour, exhausted and miserable. I am severely wounded in my limbs. My soldiers and mounts are exhausted. O king! I am not frightened of you, or Partha Vrikodara, or Phalguna, or Vasudeva, or the Panchalas, or the twins, or Yuyudhana, or of any of the other soldiers. Single-handedly and wrathfully, I am interested in fighting against all of you. O lord! The deeds of all virtuous men have a source in dharma. Fame follows dharma and I will observe this. I am telling you that I will arise and fight against all of you in the battle. Like a year encounters all the seasons, I will encounter all of you in due course. This is despite you possessing chariots and weapons and me not possessing weapons and a chariot. When night is over, the sun destroys the radiance of all the nakshatras. O Pandavas! Wait. O bull among the Bharata lineage! Today, I will free myself of the debt I owe to the illustrious kshatriyas[16]—Bahlika, Drona, Bhishma, the great-souled Karna, the brave Jayadratha and Bhagadatta, Shalya, the king of Madra, Bhurishrava, my sons, Shakuni Soubala, my friends, well-wishers and kin. I will kill you and your brothers and free myself of that debt today.' Having said this, the lord of men stopped.

'"Yudhisthira said, 'O Suyodhana! It is through good fortune that you have learnt about the dharma of kshatriyas. O great-armed one! It is through good fortune that your mind has turned towards fighting. O Kouravya! It is good fortune that you are brave and it is good fortune that you know about fighting, since you have single-handedly decided to engage all of us in an encounter. Fight with us one at a time, with whatever weapon you wish. While you fight thus, all the others will remain as spectators. O brave one! I am also granting your desire. If you kill any one of us, the kingdom will be yours. Otherwise, be slain and obtain heaven.'

'"Duryodhana replied, 'If you are granting me the boon of fighting one at a time, as a weapon, I am choosing the club that I am wielding. Let any one of the brothers come forward, whoever thinks he is capable of fighting me with a club on foot. Let him fight

[16]The ones who have been killed.

with me. There are many wonderful battles that are fought through circular motions of chariots. This wonderful and great duel on foot, with clubs, will be the only one of its kind. As a fight progresses, men often wish to change weapons. But with your permission, let that not be the case.[17] O mighty-armed one! With a club, I will defeat you and your younger brothers, the Panchalas, the Srinjayas and your other soldiers.'

'"Yudhisthira said, 'O Gandhari's son! O Suyodhana! Arise! Arise and fight with me. O powerful one! With the club, fight with us one at a time. O Gandhari's son! Be a man and fight well. Even if you are as fast as thought, you will not remain alive today.'"

'Sanjaya said, "Your son, tiger among men, could not tolerate this. From inside the waters, he sighed like an immense serpent. He was repeatedly urged by the goad of the words. He could not tolerate those words, like an intelligent horse cannot bear a whip. The valiant one agitated the waters and forcefully grasped the club, which was heavy, with the essence of stone and decorated with gold. He arose from inside the waters, like an Indra of serpents that was sighing. He penetrated the waters that had been converted to stone, with the iron club on his shoulder. Your son arose, like the sun scorching with its rays. The club was heavy and made out of iron. It was decorated with molten gold. Dhritarashtra's immensely strong son grasped it. With the club in his hand, he looked like a mountain with a peak. He was like the enraged wielder of the trident,[18] stationed among subjects. With the club in his hand, the descendant of the Bharata lineage was as resplendent as the scorching sun. The mighty-armed scorcher of enemies arose, with the club in his hand. All the beings thought that he was Yama, with a staff in his hand. He was like Shakra with the vajra in his hand, or like Hara with the trident in his hand. O lord of men! All the Panchalas saw your son. When they saw him arise, all the Panchalas and Pandaveyas were delighted and grasped each other's palms. Your son, Duryodhana, thought that this was a mark of disrespect. He dilated his eyes in rage and glanced towards the

[17]That is, the entire fight will be with clubs.

[18]Shiva.

Pandavas. There were three lines on his forehead and he bit his lower lip. He addressed the Pandavas and Keshava. 'O Pandavas! I will reply to your taunts today. With the Panchalas, I will soon slay you and convey you to Yama's eternal abode.' Having arisen from the water, your son, Duryodhana, stood there, with the club in his hand and with blood flowing from his body. He was drenched in blood and water and his body was as beautiful as an exuding mountain.[19] When the brave one arose with the club, the Pandavas thought that he was an enraged Vaivasvata, with Kimkara in his hand.[20] His voice thundered like the clouds, or like the bellows of a delighted bull. With the club, the valiant one challenged the Parthas to battle.

'"Duryodhana said, 'O Yudhishthira! You will fight with me one at a time. O brave one! It is not appropriate that one should single-handedly fight with many warriors, especially when one is devoid of armour, exhausted, covered with water, severely wounded in the limbs and without mounts and soldiers.'

'"Yudhishthira replied, 'O Suyodhana! Where did this wisdom of yours disappear, when many maharathas united and slew Abhimanyu in the battle? O brave one! Don armour and tie your hair. O descendant of the Bharata lineage! Take everything else that you need. O brave one! I will grant you another of your wishes. If you can kill any of the five Pandavas with whom you wish to fight, you will be king. Otherwise, be slain and obtain heaven. O brave one! With the exception of your life in battle, what else do you desire?'"

'Sanjaya said, "O king! Your son then picked up golden armour and a colourful helmet that was decorated with gold. He fastened the helmet and the sparkling and golden armour. O king! Your son dazzled like a golden mountain. O king! In the field of battle, he was armoured and wielded the club. Your son, Duryodhana, spoke to all the Pandavas. 'Among all the brothers, let anyone fight with me with a club. O bull among the Bharata lineage![21] I am willing to fight with Sahadeva, Bhima, Nakula, Phalguna, or with you.

[19]A mountain exuding minerals.

[20]Vaivasvata is Yama and Kimkara is the name of Yama's club.

[21]Yudhishthira.

Having obtained an opportunity to fight, I will be victorious in the field of battle. Today, I will accomplish the extremely difficult task of bringing an end to the hostilities. O tiger among men! I will use my club, tied in golden cloth. I think that there is no one who is equal to me in fighting with a club. With the club, I will kill all those who advance against me. Let the one who wishes to fight against me, pick up a club.'"'

Chapter 1251(32)

'Sanjaya said, "O king! Duryodhana roared repeatedly. Vasudeva angrily spoke these words to Yudhishthira. 'O Yudhishthira! In this encounter, if he had named you, Arjuna, Nakula or Sahadeva, what would have happened? O king! How could you show rashness like this? "If you can kill any one of us, you will be king!" O king! With the desire of killing Bhimasena, for thirteen years he has practised against a man made out of iron.[22] O bull among the Bharata lineage! How will our task be accomplished? O supreme among kings! Because of compassion, you have committed an act of rashness. With the exception of Vrikodara, I do not see anyone who can fight against him in the encounter and Partha has not made a great deal of effort.[23] O lord of the earth! It is almost as if the ancient and unequal gambling match between you and Shakuni is being enacted again. Bhima is powerful and capable, but King Suyodhana is accomplished. O king! When there is a contest between strength and skill, skill is always superior. O king! You have placed such an enemy on an even path. You have also placed us in an extremely difficult and hazardous state. Having vanquished all the enemies and with only a single foe remaining, who desires to give that up in a single act of gambling? I do not see the man in this world who can

[22]Duryodhana has practised against an iron statue.

[23]Bhima has not practised as much as Duryodhana has.

fight, with a club in his hand in an encounter, against Duryodhana, supreme among men, especially because he is skilled. With a club in the hand in a battle, I do not think Phalguna, Madri's sons or you are capable. How did you tell the enemy to fight with a club? "O descendant of the Bharata lineage! If you kill any one of us, you will be the king!" Even if Vrikodara fights against him, our victory is not certain, especially not in a fair encounter. He is extremely strong and skilled.' Bhima said, 'O Madhusudana! O descendant of the Yadu lineage! Do not grieve. Even if it is extremely difficult, I will bring an end to this enmity today. There is no doubt that I will kill Suyodhana in the battle. O Krishna! It is evident that Dharmaraja's victory is certain. In qualities, this club of mine is one-and-a-half times heavier than that of Dhritarashtra's son. O Madhava! Do not be distressed. I can cheerfully fight with the three worlds, including the immortals, even if they are armed with many weapons, not to speak of Suyodhana.' When Vrikodara spoke these words, Vasudeva joyfully honoured him and spoke these words. 'O mighty-armed one! Depending on you, there is no doubt that Dharmaraja Yudhishthira will slay his enemies and obtain his blazing prosperity. All the sons of Dhritarashtra have been killed by you in the battle. You have brought down kings, princes and elephants. O descendant of the Pandu lineage! Kalingas, Magadhas, those from the east, Gandharas and Kurus have clashed against you in the great battle and have been slain. O Kounteya! Having also slain Duryodhana, bestow the earth, with all its oceans, to Dharmaraja, like Vishnu to Shachi's lord.[24] Having obtained you in the battle, Dhritarashtra's wicked son will be destroyed. Having shattered the bones of his thigh, you will accomplish your pledge.[25] O Partha! However, you must always fight carefully with Dhritarashtra's son. He is skilled and strong and always revels in a fight.' O king! At this, Satyaki honoured Pandava. The eloquent Madhava[26] honoured him in various ways. With

[24]Shachi's lord (husband) is Indra, that is, just as Vishnu gave the lordship of the three worlds to Indra.

[25]Bhima had taken a vow that he would break Duryodhana's thigh in the battle.

[26]Meaning Satyaki.

Dharmaraja at the forefront, all the Panchalas and the Pandaveyas applauded Bhimasena's words.

'"Bhima, terrible in his strength, spoke these words to Yudhishthira, who was stationed amidst the Srinjayas, like the scorching sun. 'I am interested in establishing you and fighting this one in the battle. This worst of men is not capable of defeating me in the encounter. Today, I will free myself of the terrible anger that is lodged in my heart against Suyodhana, Dhritarashtra's son. I will be like Arjuna, offering Khandava to Agni. O Pandava! Today, I will uproot the stake that is lodged in your heart. O king! Today, I will kill this wicked one with my club. Be happy. O unblemished one! Today, I will regain your garland of fame. Today, Suyodhana will be freed of his life, his prosperity and his kingdom. Today, King Dhritarashtra will hear that his son has been killed by me and remember all the evil deeds he did because of Shakuni's advice.' Having spoken thus, the valiant and best of the Bharata lineage raised his club up and stationed himself for battle, like Shakra challenging Vritra. Dhritarashtra's immensely strong son advanced alone to the clash, like an elephant that has been separated from the herd. At this, the Pandavas were delighted. They saw him raise his club, like the summit of Kailasa.

'"O king! Bhimasena spoke these words to Duryodhana. 'Remember all the evil deeds that King Dhritarashtra and you have done towards us and what happened in Varanavata.[27] Droupadi was in her season and was oppressed in the midst of the assembly hall. Through Shakuni's advice, the king was vanquished in the gambling match. O evil-souled one! You have performed many other wicked deeds towards the innocent Parthas. Behold the grave consequences of that. It is because of your deeds that Gangeya, best of the Bharata lineage and a grandfather to all of us, has been brought down and is lying down on a bed of arrows. Drona has been slain. Karna has been slain, and so has the powerful Shalya. Shakuni, the creator of the enmity, has also been killed in the battle. Your brave brothers and sons have been killed, together with the soldiers. Brave kings, who

[27]This is a reference to the attempt to burn the Pandavas down, described in Section 8 (Volume 1).

did not retreat from the battle, have been slain. Many other bulls among kshatriyas have been killed. The wicked Pratikami, who seized Droupadi by the hair, has been slain.[28] You alone are left, destroyer of your lineage and worst among men. There is no doubt that I will slay you with the club today. O king! I will destroy all your insolence in the encounter today and your hopes of the kingdom. O king! I will repay the grave misdeeds towards the Pandavas.' Duryodhana replied, 'What is the need to speak a lot? Fight with me now. O Vrikodara! I will today destroy your love for fighting. O wicked one! Do you not see me, stationed for the encounter with a club? I have grasped a gigantic club that is like a summit of the Himalayas. O wicked one! When I wield the club today, where is the enemy who wishes to slay me? If it is a fair fight, not even the god Purandara can do that. O Kounteya! Do not roar in vain, like a cloud without water, during the autumn. Show me your strength in the battle today, everything that you possess.' On hearing his words, all the Panchalas and the Srinjayas honoured his words, desiring victory. O king! The men were like crazy elephants and clapped their hands repeatedly, delighting King Duryodhana. The elephants there trumpeted and the horses neighed. Desiring victory, the weapons of the Pandavas seemed to blaze."'

Chapter 1252(33)

'Sanjaya said, "O great king! That extremely terrible battle was about to commence. All the great-souled Pandavas were seated. O king! On hearing about the clash between his disciples, Rama,[29]

[28]Pratikami is a messenger. This isn't a proper name. In Section 27 (Volume 2), after the gambling match, the Pratikami was sent to summon Droupadi to the assembly hall. However, the Pratikami didn't seize Droupadi by the hair, Duhshasana did. Nor, before this, have we been told anything about the Pratikami being killed.

[29]Balarama.

with the mark of the palm tree on his banner and with the plough as his weapon, arrived at the spot where the encounter was to take place.[30] On seeing him, the lords among men were extremely delighted and honoured him. They said, 'O Rama! Behold the skill of your disciples in the encounter.' On beholding Krishna and Pandava[31] and Kouravya Duryodhana, stationed with the club in his hand, Rama said, 'Since I departed, forty-two days have elapsed. I left at the time of Pushya and have returned at the time of Shravana.[32] O Madhava![33] I wish to witness this duel with the clubs between my two disciples.' King Yudhishthira embraced the one who has a plough as his weapon, welcomed him and in proper fashion, asked about his welfare. The illustrious and great archers, the two Krishnas, were delighted. They joyfully honoured and embraced him. O king! Madri's sons and Droupadi's five brave sons also honoured Rohini's immensely strong son[34] and stood there. O lord of men! The powerful Bhimasena and your son raised their clubs and honoured the powerful one. The kings repeatedly welcomed and worshipped Rohini's great-souled son and told Rama, 'O mighty-armed one! Witness this encounter.' The infinitely energetic Rama embraced the Pandavas and the Srinjayas and asked all the Pandavas about their welfare. He also greeted and asked all the others about their welfare. The great-minded one, who wields the plough, honoured all the kshatriyas back. In accordance with age, he asked each of them about their welfare. He affectionately embraced Janardana and Satyaki. Inhaling the fragrance of their heads, he asked about their welfare. O king! In accordance with the prescribed rites, those two honoured their superior. They were delighted, like Indra, lord of the gods, and Upendra, honouring Brahma.

[30]Both Bhima and Duryodhana had studied under Balarama. Balarama's weapon was the plough.

[31]Bhima.

[32]Though listings of the twenty-seven nakshatras sometimes differ, Pushya is usually the eighth, while Shravana is usually the twenty-second. Three days per nakshatra gives that total of forty-two days.

[33]Krishna.

[34]Balarama was Rohini's son.

'"O descendant of the Bharata lineage! Dharma's son spoke to Rohini's son, the scorcher of enemies. 'O Rama! Witness this great battle between the two brothers.' Keshava's mighty-armed elder brother was resplendent. Honoured by the maharathas, he was supremely delighted and seated himself among them. Amidst those kings, he was clad in blue garments and, with a fair complexion, looked dazzling. He was like the moon in the firmament, surrounded by a large number of stars. O king! That tumultuous battle between your two sons commenced and it made the body hair stand up. It would bring an end to the enmity."'

Chapter 1253(34)

Janamejaya said, 'Before the war started, with Keshava's permission, the lord Rama had left with the Vrishnis, saying, "O Keshava! I will not help the sons of Dhritarashtra, or the sons of Pandu. I will go where I wish." Having spoken those words, Rama, the destroyer of enemies, had departed. O brahmana! You should again tell me everything about his return. Tell me in detail about Rama's arrival. How did he witness the battle? You are a supremely skilled narrator.'

Vaishampayana replied, 'O mighty-armed one! The great-souled Pandavas set themselves up in Upaplavya and sent Madhusudana to Dhritarashtra, for the sake of peace and for the welfare of all beings.[35] He went to Hastinapura and met Dhritarashtra. In particular, he spoke truthful and beneficial words to him. As you have already been told, the king did not pay any attention to these words. O lord of men! Unable to obtain peace, the mighty-armed Krishna Purushottama returned to Upaplavya. O tiger among men! Dismissed by Dhritarashtra's son, Krishna returned unsuccessful and spoke

[35]This is a reference to Krishna's mission of peace, described in Section 54 (Volume 4).

to the Pandavas. "Goaded by destiny, the Kurus have not acted in accordance with my words. O Pandaveyas! With me, set out under the nakshatra Pushya." Armies were being arrayed on both sides. Rohini's great-minded son, supreme among strong ones, spoke to his brother, Krishna. "O mighty-armed one! O Madhusudana! Let us help them."[36] However, Krishna did not act in accordance with these words. At this, the immensely illustrious descendant of the Yadu lineage, the wielder of the plough, was overcome by supreme rage and set out on a pilgrimage towards the Sarasvati. With all the Yadavas, he set out when the conjunction of nakshatras known as Maitra[37] occurred. Bhoja, scorcher of enemies,[38] was on Duryodhana's side. With Yuyudhana, Vasudeva was on the side of the Pandavas. When Rohini's brave son set out under Pushya, Madhusudana placed the Pandaveyas at the forefront and advanced towards the Kurus.

'While setting out on his route, Rama instructed his servants, "Bring all the objects and equipment that will be needed for a pilgrimage. Bring the fire from Dvaraka[39] and the priests. Bring gold, silver, cows, garments, horses, elephants, chariots, mules, camels and carts. Swiftly bring all the garments that are required for a pilgrimage. Let us quickly go towards the flow of the Sarasvati. Bring officiating priests and hundreds of bulls among brahmanas." O king! Having given these instructions to his servants, the immensely strong Baladeva set out on a pilgrimage at a time when the Kurus confronted a calamity. O bull among the Bharata lineage! Along the flows of the Sarasvati, he proceeded towards the ocean, with officiating priests, well-wishers, supreme among brahmanas, chariots, elephants, horses and servants. He was surrounded by many carts that were drawn by cattle, mules and camels. O descendant of the Bharata lineage! In many countries along the path, large donations were given to the weary, tired of limb,

[36]The text leaves it as 'them'. Balarama meant helping the Kouravas.

[37]Maitra or Mitra is more a *muhurta*, rather than a conjunction of nakshatras. Depending on when the sun rises, it is usually between 7.30 a.m. and 8.30 a.m.

[38]Kritavarma.

[39]A sacred fire burns in every household. That is carried at the time of a pilgrimage.

children, the hungry and those who were distressed and waited for alms in different ways. O king! In all those places, brahmanas were instantly given food and whatever objects they desired. O king! On the instructions of Rohini's son, men were stationed, with large quantities of food and drink. To brahmanas who desired happiness, extremely expensive garments, beds, covers and objects of worship were given. O descendant of the Bharata lineage! Whenever a brahmana or a kshatriya wanted anything, it was seen that the object was unhesitatingly given. All those who advanced, or stayed, were happy. O bull among the Bharata lineage! Vehicles were given to those who wished to travel, drinks to those who were thirsty and tasty food to those who were hungry. The men there obtained garments and ornaments. O king! The path along which they advanced was happy in every possible way. O brave one! The men who travelled seemed to be in heaven. They were always happy and tasty and good food was always available. There were shops and stalls with merchandise, frequented by hundreds of men. There were many kinds of trees and beings, decorated with many kinds of jewels. The great-souled one was unwavering in his soul and observed rites. O king! The foremost among the Yadu lineage, the wielder of the plough, gave riches and sacrificial donations to brahmanas at sacred places of pilgrimage. He also gave away one thousand cows that yielded milk. They were covered in excellent garments and their horns were encased in gold. There were diverse horses that had been born in many countries. These, and servant-maids, were given to the brahmanas. There were gems, pearls, jewels, diamonds and the best of sparkling gold and silver. Rama gave the best of brahmanas iron and copper vessels. In this way, in the best of tirthas along the Sarasvati, the great-souled one gave away a large quantity of riches. His deeds and power were unlimited. Eventually, he cheerfully returned to Kurukshetra.'

Janamejaya asked, 'O best among men! Tell me about the qualities and origins of tirthas along the Sarasvati, their fruits and the deeds that must be done when one is there. O illustrious one! Tell me about these tirthas in due order. O brahmana! O supreme among those who know about the brahman! My curiosity is great.'

Vaishampayana replied, 'O king! The qualities and origins of all the tirthas will be extensive. O Indra among kings! However, I will tell you about these sacred spots in entirety. Listen. O great king! With the officiating priests, well-wishers and large numbers of brahmanas, the foremost among the Yadu lineage first went to the sacred Prabhasa. O Indra among men! The lord of the stars[40] was afflicted by tuberculosis and was freed of his curse there. Having regained his energy, he lights up the entire universe. This is the foremost tirtha on earth. Because he obtained his radiance there, it is known as Prabhasa.'[41]

Janamejaya asked, 'Why was the illustrious Soma afflicted by tuberculosis? How did Chandra[42] bathe in that supreme of tirthas? Having bathed there, how did Shashi regain his energy? O great sage! Tell me everything about this in detail.'

Vaishampayana replied, 'O lord of the earth! Daksha had twenty-seven maidens as daughters and Daksha gave them to Soma.[43] O descendant of the Bharata lineage! They are always united with the nakshatras and are used for computing time. O Indra among kings! Those auspicious ones became the wives of Soma. All of them were large-eyed and were unmatched on earth in terms of their beauty. But in the richness of her beauty, Rohini was superior.[44] Therefore, the illustrious moon god was especially affectionate towards her. She was in his heart and he always enjoyed her alone. O Indra among kings! In those ancient times, Soma dwelt with Rohini for a long time. At this, the other nakshatras became angry with the great-souled one. They quickly went to their father, Prajapati,[45] and said, "Soma does not dwell with us. He always resides with Rohini. O lord of beings! Therefore, all of us will live with you. We will live here, be restrained in our diet and perform supreme austerities." On hearing

[40]The moon.

[41]The word *prabha* means radiance.

[42]Chandra, Soma and Shashi are names for the moon god.

[43]These were the twenty-seven nakshatras, married to Soma, the moon.

[44]Rohini is Aldebaran and is brighter than the others.

[45]Daksha.

their words, Daksha told Soma, "Treat all your wives equally, so that a great adharma does not touch you." Daksha told all of them, "Go to Soma. On my instructions, Chandra will treat all of you equally." Dismissed by him, all of them went to Shitamshu's abode.[46] O lord of the earth! However, as earlier, the illustrious Soma repeatedly dwelt only with Rohini and pleased her alone. The others united and again went and told their father, "We will serve you and dwell under your refuge. Soma does not dwell with us and has not acted in accordance with your words." On hearing their words, Daksha told Soma, "O Virochana![47] Treat all your wives equally, so that I do not have to curse you." However, the illustrious Shashi paid no attention to Daksha's words. He continued to live with Rohini. The others were enraged and went to their father. They lowered their heads in salutation and said, "Soma does not dwell with us. Grant us refuge. The illustrious Chandra always dwells with Rohini. Therefore, save us, so that Soma accepts all of us." O lord of the earth! On hearing these words, the illustrious one became angry. In his rage, he inflicted tuberculosis on Soma and the lord of the stars became afflicted. Overcome by tuberculosis, Shashi decayed from one day to another. O king! He made many efforts to free himself from the tuberculosis. O great king! The moon performed many different kinds of sacrifices. However, he could not free himself of the curse and was immersed in decay. As Soma began to decay, herbs ceased to grow. All of them were tasteless and without juices. All of them lost their energy. When the herbs decayed, the destruction of beings started. When the moon decayed, all the subjects became emaciated. O lord of the earth! At this, all the gods assembled and went to Soma. They asked, "Why is your form like this, without any radiance? Tell us everything about the reason behind this great fear. Having heard your words, we will think of a means." Having been thus addressed, the one with the mark of a hare[48] replied to all of

[46]Shitamshu is another name for the moon, meaning the one with the cool rays.

[47]Another name for the moon god.

[48]*Shasha* or *shashaka* is a rabbit or hare. Because the moon bears the mark of a hare, it is known as Shashi or Shashanka.

them. He told them about the reason behind the curse and about his own tuberculosis. Having heard his words, the gods went to Daksha and said, "O illustrious one! Be pacified. Take away your curse from Soma. Chandra has decayed and only a little bit of him can be seen. O lord of the gods! Because of his decay, all the subjects have been overcome by decay. Many different kinds of creepers, herbs and seeds are wasting. O preceptor of the worlds! You should be pacified." Having been thus addressed, Prajapati thought and spoke these words. "My words cannot be transgressed. It cannot be otherwise. O immensely fortunate ones! However, there is a means whereby this can be withdrawn. Let Shashi always treat all of his wives equally. Let the one with the mark of the hare bathe in the supreme tirtha along the Sarasvati. The god will then wax again. These words of mine are true. For one half of the month, Soma will always wane. But for another half of the month, Soma will always wax. These words of mine are true." On the instructions of the rishi,[49] Soma went to the Sarasvati. Along the Sarasvati, he went to the supreme tirtha of Prabhasa. The immensely energetic and immensely radiant one bathed there on the day of the new moon. He obtained his cool rays back and radiated the world again. O Indra among kings! All the gods also went to Prabhasa. With Soma, they presented themselves before Daksha. Prajapati gave all the gods permission to leave. Pleased with Soma, the illustrious one again spoke these words to him. "O son! Never disregard women. Never disregard brahmanas. Depart and always follow my instructions." O great king! Having taken his leave, he again returned to his own abode.[50] All the subjects were delighted and lived as they had earlier. This is the entire account about how the moon was cursed. This is how the tirtha of Prabhasa came to be the foremost among all tirthas. O great king! The one with the mark of the hare always bathes there on the day of the new moon. Having bathed in the supreme tirtha of Prabhasa, he obtains his handsomeness back. O lord of the earth! That spot is known as Prabhasa, because bathing there, Chandra obtained his supreme radiance back.

[49]Daksha.

[50]Chandra took Daksha's leave.

'After this, the undecaying and powerful one[51] went to Chamasodbheda. People know that spot as Chamasodbheda. The one with the plough as his weapon gave away many precious donations there. He spent a night there and bathed in accordance with the prescribed rituals. Keshava's elder brother then quickly went to Udapana. Great fruits are obtained from observing rites there. O Janamejaya! The herbs and the earth are cool there. O Indra among kings! Though the Sarasvati has been destroyed there,[52] the siddhas know this.'

Chapter 1254(35)

Vaishampayana said, 'O great king! The one with the plough as his weapon then went to Udapana, associated with the illustrious Trita. He gave away a lot of objects and honoured the brahmanas. The one with the club as his weapon bathed there and was delighted. The extremely great ascetic Trita, devoted to supreme dharma, had lived there. The great-souled one had dwelt in a pit and had drunk *soma* juice. His two brothers had abandoned him there and had returned home. At this, Trita, supreme among brahmanas, had cursed them.'

Janamejaya asked, 'O brahmana! How did the extremely great ascetic fall down in Udapana? Why did his brothers abandon that supreme among brahmanas? Why did the brothers leave him in the pit and return home? O brahmana! If you think that this can be heard, please tell me all this.'

Vaishampayana replied, 'O king! In an earlier yuga, there were three brothers who were sages. They were Ekata, Dvita and Trita[53] and they were as radiant as the sun. All of them were like Prajapati

[51]Balarama.

[52]The Sarasvati has been destroyed in the sense of becoming invisible and flowing underground.

[53]Literally, first, second and third.

and they had offspring. All of them were ascetics who knew about the brahman and they had attained Brahma's world. Their father, Goutama, was always devoted to dharma. Because of their austerities, rituals and self-control, they always pleased him. After having been pleased by them for a long time, the illustrious one went to the regions that were appropriate for him.[54] There were kings for whom the great-souled one had been an officiating priest. After he had gone to heaven, all of them continued to honour his sons. Trita was the best among them and was just like his father. All the immensely fortunate and auspicious sages worshipped the immensely fortunate one, as they had the learned one[55] before him. O king! Once, the brothers Ekata and Dvita thought of performing a sacrifice and in particular, were concerned about the wealth required for this. O scorcher of enemies! They thought that they would take Trita and go to the houses of those who performed sacrifices.[56] They would collect the required animals. They would cheerfully drink soma juice and obtain the great merits of a sacrifice. O king! The three brothers did as they had deciced. They visited all the *yajamana*s to collect the animals. From the yajamanas, they received a large number of animals for the sacrifice. For performing the act of sacrifice, they also obtained all the decreed gifts. The great-souled maharshis then went towards an eastern direction. O great king! Trita was cheerfully walking in front and Ekata and Dvita were following him from the rear, herding the animals. On seeing that large number of animals, they began to think about how they could appropriate all the cattle, without giving a share to Trita. O lord of men! Listen to what the cunning and wicked Ekata and Dvita said to each other, as they conversed. "Trita is skilled in performing sacrifices. Trita is established in the Vedas. Trita is capable of obtaining many other cattle. Let us go away, taking these cattle with us. Let Trita go wherever he wishes. We do not have to be with him." As they proceeded along the path, it became night and they saw a wolf before them. Not very far from the spot, there was a

[54]That is, Goutama died.

[55]Goutama.

[56]Yajamanas, that is, the kings.

pit along the banks of the great Sarasvati. Trita was in the front. On seeing the wolf along the path, he ran in fear and fell down into the pit. It was extremely deep and extremely terrible and was the cause of great fright to all beings. The immensely fortunate Trita, supreme among sages, began to scream from inside the pit. From this, the brothers realized that the sage had fallen into the pit, but they were frightened of the wolf. They were frightened of the wolf and also driven by avarice. They abandoned him and went on. O great king! The brothers were greedy for the animals and abandoned the great ascetic in Udapana,[57] in a spot that was full of dust and without any water. Trita found that he was inside a pit, covered with creepers and herbs. O foremost among the Bharata lineage! He thought that he was submerged, like a wicked person in hell. However, the wise one was scared of dying, since he had not yet drunk soma juice. He began to think about how he might be able to drink soma juice there. That is what the immensely ascetic one thought about in the pit. He then saw that a creeper was hanging down there. Though the pit was covered with dust, the sage imagined that there was water there. He also thought of a fire there and thought of himself as the officiating priest. The immensely ascetic one thought of the creeper as soma. In his mind, the sage thought of the mantras of the Rig, Yajur and Sama Vedas. O king! He imagined the pebbles to be grains of sugar. He thought the water to be clarified butter and allotted shares to the residents of heaven. Having drunk the soma,[58] he created a tumultuous noise. O king! Those sounds created by Trita rose up into heaven. The sacrifice had been performed in accordance with the norms laid down by those who know about the brahman. While the extremely great-souled Trita performed the sacrifice, heaven was agitated. But no one knew the reason. Brihaspati heard the tumultuous sound. On hearing this, the priest of the gods spoke to all the gods. "O gods! Trita is performing a sacrifice and all of us must go there. If he is enraged, the great ascetic is capable of creating other

[57]The word *udapana* means well.
[58]Mentally.

gods."[59] Hearing his words, all the gods were frightened. Together, they went to the spot where Trita was performing his sacrifice. The gods went to the pit where Trita was. They saw the great-souled one, consecrated in the task of performing the sacrifice. They saw the great-souled one, supreme in his resplendence. They told the immensely fortunate one, "We have come for our shares." On seeing the gods, the rishi replied, "O residents of heaven! Look at me. I am submerged in this fearful pit and am devoid of my senses." O great king! However, Trita gave them their shares, in accordance with the decreed rites, uttering the mantras. They accepted these and were delighted. The residents of heaven obtained their shares, in accordance with the decreed rites. Pleased with him, they gave him the boons that he desired. He asked the gods for the boon that he should be freed from his distressful state. He also said, "Let a person who bathes in this pit obtain the same end as one who drinks soma." With her waves, Sarasvati then descended into the pit. Trita was raised up by the waters and worshipped by the thirty gods. O kings! The gods agreed to what he had said and returned to where they had come from. Trita cheerfully returned to his own house. He met his brothers, the rishis, and angrily spoke harsh words to them. The immensely ascetic one cursed them. "Because of your greed for the animals, you abandoned me and ran away. You will therefore adopt their forms[60] and roam around, with sharp teeth. Because of your wicked deeds, this is how you will be cursed by me. The offspring that you have will be leopards, bears and apes." O lord of the earth! As soon as he spoke these words, because his words were always truthful, they were seen to assume these forms. The one with the plough as his weapon touched the waters there. He gave away many kinds of donations and honoured the brahmanas. Having seen Udapana, he praised it repeatedly. The one whose soul was never distressed then went to Vinashana, which was also on the river.'

[59]If the gods do not turn up.

[60]The forms of predatory beasts like wolves.

Chapter 1255(36)

Vaishampayana said, 'O king! The one with the plough as his weapon then went to Vinashana. The Sarasvati became invisible there, because of her hatred for the shudras and the *abhiras*.[61] O foremost among the Bharata lineage! Because the Sarasvati disappeared there, as a consequence of her hatred, the rishis speak of that place as Vinashana. Having touched the waters of the Sarasvati there, the immensely strong Bala[62] went to Subhumika, also located on the supreme banks of the Sarasvati. Pure apsaras are always engaged in sporting there. Their faces are fair and the innocent ones sport there. O lord of men! Every month, the gods and the gandharvas go there. That sacred tirtha is frequented by the brahmanas. Gandharvas and large numbers of apsaras can be seen there. O king! They unite happily in that spot. Amidst the creepers there, the gods and the ancestors find delight. Divine and sacred flowers repeatedly shower down there. O king! That is the sporting ground of the beautiful apsaras. Along the supreme banks of the Sarasvati, Subhumika is famous. Madhava[63] bathed there and donated riches to the brahmanas. He heard the songs and the sounds of celestial musical instruments. He saw a large number of shadows of gods, gandharvas and rakshasas. Rohini's son then went to the tirtha of the gandharvas. With Vishvavasu at their head, the gandharvas are engaged in austerities there. They are engaged in beautiful dancing, singing and the playing of musical instruments. The wielder of the plough gave away many riches to brahmanas there and also goats, cattle, mules, camels, gold and silver. He fed the brahmanas and satisfied them with extremely expensive gifts that they desired. Praised by the brahmanas, Madhava then departed with them. The mighty-armed one, the scorcher of enemies, adorned with a single earring, left the tirtha of the gandharvas. He went to the extremely great tirtha of Gargasrota. The aged Garga, cleansed in

[61] Abhiras are cowherds and *vinashana* means disappearance.

[62] Balarama.

[63] Balarama.

his soul, performed austerities there. O Janamejaya! He got to know about the reckoning of time, the movements of stellar bodies and about favourable and unfavourable portents.[64] The auspicious tirtha along the Sarasvati is known by the name of the great-souled one. That is the reason that tirtha is known by the name of Gargasrota. O king! Wishing to know about the reckoning of time, the immensely fortunate rishis, rigid in their vows, always worshipped the lord Garga there. O great king! Bala, smeared with white sandalwood paste, went there and, in accordance with the rites, gave away riches to the sages who were cleansed in their souls. He gave away many kinds of rich foodstuff to the brahmanas who were there. Attired in blue garments, the immensely illustrious one then went to the tirtha known as Shankha. He saw Mahashanka[65] there. It was as large as Meru and was like a white mountain. It was frequented by large numbers of rishis. The powerful one, with the palm tree on his banner, saw it rise on the banks of the Sarasvati. Yakshas, *vidyadhara*s, immensely strong pishachas, thousands of siddhas—all of them were seen there, giving up the fruits of that tree. They only enjoyed those at the right time, observing vows and rituals. They obtained those after following rules and wandered around separately. O bull among men! They roamed around, invisible to men. O lord of men! That tree is famous in this world. It is the source of the sacred tirtha of the Sarasvati, renowned in the world. The illustrious tiger of the Yadu lineage donated copper and iron vessels and many garments at that tirtha. He worshipped the brahmanas and was honoured back by those stores of austerities. O king! The one with the plough as his weapon then went to the sacred Dvaitavana. Having gone there, Bala saw sages attired in many different kinds of garments. He worshipped the brahmanas and bathed in those waters. He donated all the objects of pleasure to the brahmanas. O king! Bala then went to the region south of the Sarasvati. The mighty-armed and greatly illustrious one, with dharma in his soul, went only a short distance

[64]The sage Garga is believed to have been a pioneer in astronomy and astrology.

[65]A large tree or mountain. The word used is naga, so it could mean either. However, subsequently, a tree is indicated.

away. The one without decay went to the tirtha of Nagadhanva. That was the abode of Vasuki, king of the serpents. O great king! There, the immensely radiant one[66] was surrounded by many serpents. There were fourteen thousand rishis and siddhas there. The gods went there and instated Vasuki, supreme among serpents, as the king of all the serpents, in accordance with the proper rites. O Kourava! There is no fear from serpents there. According to the decrees, he gave away many stores of jewels to the brahmanas there. O king! Radiant in his own energy, he then set out in an eastern direction. Joyfully, the one with the plough bathed in many tirthas. He donated riches to the brahmanas and met the ascetics. The one with the plough as his weapon honoured large numbers of rishis there. Rama then went to the tirtha that was frequented by a large number of rishis, at the spot where the Sarasvati returns in an eastern direction. The great-souled one wished to see Naimisharanya of the rishis. The one with the plough saw the great river retrace course there. O king! Bala, smeared with white sandalwood paste, was astounded.'

Janamejaya asked, 'O brahmana! Why did Sarasvati retrace course in an eastern direction? O supreme among all officiating priests! I wish to hear this recounted. For what reason was the descendant of the Yadu lineage astounded? O supreme among brahmanas! Why did the best of rivers retrace course?'

Vaishampayana replied, 'O king! In an earlier era, in *krita yuga*, the large number of ascetics in Naimisha performed an extremely large sacrifice that went on for twelve years. O king! Many rishis came to that sacrifice. The immensely fortunate ones performed that sacrifice, in accordance with the prescribed rites. After the sacrifice had been performed for twelve years, they returned. The rishis went to visit the large number of tirthas that were there. O lord of the earth! Because of the large number of rishis, the tirthas along the southern banks of the Sarasvati seemed to look like cities. O tiger among men! Because of their love for tirthas, the supreme among brahmanas resided along the banks of the river, all the way up to Samantapanchaka. The sages, cleansed in their souls, offered oblations there and the loud

[66]Vasuki.

sounds of incantations filled the directions. The great-souled ones offered oblations in *agnihotra* sacrifices there. In every direction, the best of rivers was beautiful and radiant. O great king! Valakhilyas, Ashmakutta ascetics, Dantolukhalinas and others, Samprakshalas[67] and others, those who lived on air, those who lived on water, those who lived on leaves, many others who observed diverse kinds of rituals and those who used the bare earth as their beds—all these sages came there, near the Sarasvati. The best of rivers was radiant, like Ganga frequented by the residents of heaven.[68] After this, the rishis, wishing to perform sacrifices and rigid in their vows, could not find a bare spot in Kurukshetra. They measured out small tirthas with their sacrificial threads and offered oblations to agnihotras and other kinds of sacrifices. O Indra among kings! Sarasvati saw that the large number of rishis was finding the situation hopeless and began to think about a means for their sake. O Janamejaya! The supreme of rivers retraced her course and created many abodes for herself, for the sake of the rishis and the pious ascetics. The supreme of rivers again flowed in a western direction. "I must go there, so that their[69] arrival is not rendered futile." O king! The great river performed this great and wonderful deed there. O Indra among kings! Those abodes of hers are famous as Naimisha. O best of the Kuru lineage! You must perform great rites in Kurukshetra. When the river retraced her course, she created many abodes for herself. On seeing these there, the great-souled Rama was overcome by great wonder. In accordance with the rites, the descendant of the Yadu lineage bathed there. He gave away gifts and diverse vessels to the brahmanas. He also gave the brahmanas many kinds of food and drink. O king! Worshipped by the brahmanas, Bala then went to the supreme of tirthas on the Sarasvati, frequented by tens of thousands of many kinds of birds.

[67]Valakhilyas are sages who are as small as the thumb. Ashmakuttas are sages who pound their bodies with stone. Dantolukhalinas (or Dantolukhalikas) are sages who use their teeth as mortar, that is, they only eat grain that has not been ground. Samprakshalas are sages who incessantly wash themselves in water.

[68]Meaning that part of the Ganga (Mandakini) that flows in heaven.

[69]The rishis'.

There are *badari*, *inguda*, *kashmarya*, *plaksha*, *ashvattha*, *vibhitaka*, *panasa*, *palasha*, *karira*, *pilu* and other kinds of trees there.[70] They bind down the banks of the Sarasvati and make it look like a chariot. It is adorned with groves of *parusha*s, *bilva*s, *amrataka*s, *atimukta*s, *kashanda*s and *parijata*s.[71] There are also beautiful groves of plantains, beautiful and charming. There were those who lived on air, those who lived on water, those who lived on fruit and those who lived on leaves. The Dantolukhalinas were there too, as were the Ashmakuttas, Vaneyas[72] and many other kinds of sages. There were the sounds of chanting and the place teemed with herds of animals. It was a place frequented by those who were without malice and devoted to dharma. The one with the plough as his weapon went to the tirtha of Sapta-Sarasvata. The great sage, Mankanaka, had performed austerities there and attained success.'

Chapter 1256(37)

Janamejaya asked, 'Why is it called Sapta-Sarasvata? Who was the sage Mankanaka? How did that illustrious one observe rituals and become successful? O supreme among brahmanas! What lineage was he born in and what did he study? O supreme among brahmanas! In accordance with the proper way, I wish to hear all this.'

Vaishampayana replied, 'O king! The seven Sarasvatis cover this entire universe. Wherever she was powerfully summoned, Sarasvati manifested herself there—Suprabha, Kanchanakshi, Vishala,

[70]Badari is the Indian *ber* tree, inguda is the desert date, kashmarya is the barberry, plaksha is pipal, ashvattha is the religious fig tree, vibhitaka is myrobalan, panasa is jackfruit, palasha is flame of the forest, karira is *capparis deciduas* and pilu is *salvadora oleoides*.

[71]Parusha is difficult to identify, Bilva is *bel*, Amrataka is wild mango, atimukta is madhumalati, Kashanda is difficult to identify and parijata is the night jasmine or coral jasmine.

[72]Vaneyas are those who live in forests.

Manashrada, Sarasvati, Oghavati, Suvenu and Vimalodaka.[73] The grandfather[74] performed a great sacrifice on the surface of the earth and all the brahmanas assembled there. Sacred incantations from the unblemished Vedas resounded there. At that great sacrifice, performed in accordance with the indicated rites, the gods were also agitated.[75] O great king! The great grandfather consecrated himself at that sacrifice. That sacrifice yielded every object of desire, everything that one could mentally think of. It yielded the objectives of dharma and artha. O Indra among kings! All of these manifested themselves before the brahmanas who were there. The gandharvas went there and large numbers of apsaras danced. Divine musical instruments were played upon. At the richness of the sacrifice, even the gods were satisfied, not to speak of the supreme wonder that arose among those who were human. In the grandfather's presence, the sacrifice was held in Pushkara. O king! However, the rishis said, "This sacrifice will not lead to great fruits. The best of rivers, Sarasvati, cannot be seen here." On hearing this, the illustrious one cheerfully summoned Sarasvati. O Indra among kings! Summoned by the grandfather to the sacrifice in Pushkara, Sarasvati came there as Suprabha. On seeing the swift flows of the Sarasvati, the sages were satisfied and showed a great deal of respect to the grandfather's sacrifice. Thus, for the sake of the grandfather and to satisfy the learned ones, Sarasvati, supreme among rivers, manifested herself in Pushkara.

'O king! The sages assembled in Naimisha. O lord of men! They conversed colourfully amongst themselves. In diverse ways, the sages there talked about the study of the Vedas. The sages who were assembled there remembered Sarasvati. O great king! The rishis, who wanted to perform a sacrifice, thought of her. O Indra among kings!

[73]It is not clear whether Vimalodaka is a proper name or not. If it is a proper name, the seven names of Sarasvati are in addition to the name of Sarasvati. If Sarasvati is also one of the seven names, Vimalodaka is an adjective, meaning the one with clear waters. However, since the seven names occur separately later, Sarasvati is not one of the seven names.

[74]Brahma.

[75]Because the sacrifice was so spectacular.

To aid the assembled great-souled ones, the immensely fortunate and sacred Sarasvati arrived there in Naimisha, as Kanchanakshi, for the sake of the sages who wished to perform a sacrifice. O descendant of the Bharata lineage! The best of rivers arrived there and was worshipped.

'Gaya performed a great sacrifice in Gaya. Sarasvati, the best of rivers, was summoned to Gaya's sacrifice. In Gaya, the rishis, rigid in their vows, named her Vishala.

'The river originates from the flanks of the Himalayas and is swift in flow. O descendant of the Bharata lineage! Ouddalaka performed a sacrifice there. From every direction, a large number of sages assembled there. O king! This was a sacred spot towards the north of the region of Kosala. Before the great-souled Ouddalaka had performed his sacrifice there, he had thought of Sarasvati. For the sake of that rishi, the best of rivers had arrived at that spot. She was honoured by the large number of sages, clad in bark and deerskin. Because she had been summoned mentally, she came to be known as Manashrada.[76]

'There is a sacred region known as Suvenurishabha, frequented by rajarshis. There, the great-souled Kuru performed a sacrifice in Kurukshetra. The immensely fortunate Sarasvati, best among rivers, arrived there. O Indra among kings! Sarasvati, with divine waters, was summoned to Kurukshetra as Oghavati by the great-souled Vasishtha.

'Daksha performed a sacrifice in Gangadvara.[77]

'Brahma again performed a sacrifice on the sacred slopes of the Himalaya mountains. The illustrious one was summoned there as Vimaloda.[78]

'All of these come together as one flow at the tirtha of Sapta-

[76]Here, the text actually says Manohrada, but the two words mean the same thing. Literally, both mean something that has been summoned by the mind.

[77]The Critical edition abruptly excises a shloka here. The missing shloka tells us that Sarasvati appeared there as Suvenu. Gangadvara is the gate of the Ganga, meaning the opening in the Himalayas, through which, Ganga descends into the plains. This is in Haridvara.

[78]The same as Vimalodaka.

Sarasvata. That tirtha is famous on earth. These are the seven names of Sarasvati that are recounted. The tirtha of Sapta-Sarasvata is sacred and famous. Now hear about the young Mankanaka, who observed *brahmacharya*. O descendant of the Bharata lineage! While he was bathing, he saw a woman sporting a lot in the waters, as she pleased. She was also bathing and was beautiful in her limbs. She was unblemished and was naked. O great king! At this, his semen fell into the waters of the Sarasvati. The great ascetic picked it up and placed it in a pot. Collected in the pot, it became divided into seven parts. Seven rishis were born from these and gave birth to the large number of Maruts.[79] Vayuvega, Vayubala, Vayuha, Vayumandala, Vayujvala, Vayureta and the valiant Vayuchakra—these were the ones who gave birth to the Maruts.

'O Indra among kings! Other than this, listen to another wonderful account on earth. This is about the conduct of the maharshi, famous in the three worlds. O king! It has been heard that, in earlier times, after Mankanaka obtained success, his hand was wounded by a blade of kusha grass. The juice of vegetables began to flow from this. On seeing the flow of vegetable juice, he was delighted and began to dance around. O brave one! He was overwhelmed by his own energy and began to dance. On seeing him dance, all mobile and immobile objects also began to dance. O king! Brahma and the other gods and the rishis, rich in their austerities, went to Mahadeva and told him about the rishi. O lord of men! They said, "O god! You should do something to prevent him from dancing." On seeing that the sage was extremely delighted, for the sake of the welfare of the gods, the god Mahadeva spoke to him. "O brahmana! You know about dharma. Why are you dancing around in this way? O supreme among sages! What is the reason for your delight? Tell me. O supreme among brahmanas! You are an ascetic and should be stationed on the path of dharma." The rishi replied, "O brahmana![80]

[79]The Maruts are gods of the storm and the wind, sometimes identified with Indra and sometimes with Shiva. While the number of Maruts varies, it is often given as forty-nine, which fits the notion of seven times seven.

[80]Shiva was in the disguise of a brahmana.

Can you not see that vegetable juice is flowing from this wound in my hand? O lord! On seeing this, I am overcome with great delight and am dancing." The god laughed at the sage who was overcome by such emotion and said, "O brahmana! I am not astounded at all. Look at me." O Indra among kings! Having spoken thus to the best of sages, the intelligent Mahadeva pierced his thumb with one of his fingernails. O king! Ashes, white as snow, began to flow from that wound. O king! On seeing this, the sage was ashamed and fell down at his feet. The rishi said, "I think that you are no other than the god Rudra, great and supreme. O wielder of the trident! You are the refuge of the universe, the gods and the asuras. The learned ones say that the universe has been created by you. At the time of the destruction of a yuga, everything enters into you again. Even the gods are incapable of comprehending you. How can I? O unblemished one! Everything, Brahma and the other gods, are seen in you. You are all the gods. You are the actor and the one who causes action. It is through your favours that the gods enjoy happiness, free from fear." Thus did the rishi prostrate himself and worship Mahadeva. He said, "O illustrious one! Through your favours, let there be no decline in my store of austerities." The god was pleased and spoke again to the rishi. "O brahmana! Through my favours, your austerities will multiply a thousandfold. I will always dwell with you in this hermitage. If a man worships me in Sapta-Sarasvata, there is nothing that cannot be attained by him, in this world or in the next. There is no doubt that he will go to the world known as Sarasvata."[81] Such was the infinitely energetic conduct of Mankanaka. He was the son of Sajanya, born from the wind god.'

Chapter 1257(38)

Vaishampayana said, 'Rama spent a night there and was worshipped by the residents of the hermitage. The pious one,

[81]After death.

with the plough as his weapon, showed his affection for Manakanka. He gave gifts to the brahmanas and spent a night there. The one with the plough was worshipped by a large number of sages and arose in the morning. O descendant of the Bharata lineage! He touched the waters and took his leave of all the sages. For the sake of tirthas, the immensely strong Rama departed quickly. The one with the plough as his weapon went to the tirtha known as Oushanasa. O king! This is also known as Kapalamochana, where the great sage, Mahodara, was freed from the large head that stuck to his thigh. O great king! In earlier times, Rama hurled a rakshasa's head a great distance. Before this, the extremely great-souled Kavya[82] had tormented himself through austerities there. It was there that the great-souled one thought about all kinds of policies. It was there that he thought about the conflict of the daityas and the danavas.[83] O king! Bala reached that supreme of tirthas. In due form, he donated riches to the great-souled brahmanas.'

Janamejaya asked, 'O brahmana! Why is it known as Kapalamochana? How was the great sage freed from the head? Why did it stick to him?'

Vaishampayana replied, 'O tiger among kings! Earlier, the great-souled Raghava dwelt in Dandakaranya, to bring an end to the rakshasas who lived there. In Janasthana, with a razor-sharp arrow that was sharp at the edges, he severed the head of an evil-souled rakshasa. This fell down in a great forest. O king! Mahodara was roaming around in the forest at will. It fell down, pierced his bones and stuck to his thigh. Because it was stuck to his thigh, the immensely wise brahmana could not go to any of the other tirthas. The great sage was in pain and pus exuded from the wound. It has been heard that he went to all the tirthas on earth. The immensely ascetic one went to all the rivers and the oceans. He spoke to all the rishis who had cleansed their souls. He bathed in all the tirthas, but was not freed.

[82]Shukra, the preceptor of the demons. The wise Shukra laid down many kinds of policy (*niti*).

[83]Not a conflict between the daityas and the danavas, but their conflict with the gods.

The Indra among brahmanas then heard the great words of the sages about the famous and supreme tirtha on the Sarasvati. It could free from all sins and was the supreme spot for obtaining success. The brahmana went to that tirtha of Oushanasa. He touched the waters of Oushanasa tirtha. The head was freed from his leg and fell down into the water there. O king! The one with the pure soul was freed from the taint. Having been successful, Mahodara delightedly went to his hermitage. The great ascetic brahmana became pure and was freed from his exhaustion. He told all the rishis, who had cleansed their souls, about this. O one who grants honours! On hearing his words, all the assembled ones named that tirtha Kapalamochana.[84] Madhava honoured the brahmanas there and gave them many gifts.

'The foremost among the Vrishni lineage then went to the hermitage of Rishangu. O descendant of the Bharata lineage! Arshtishena had tormented himself through terrible austerities there. The great sage Vishvamitra was able to become a brahmana there.[85] O Indra among kings! The handsome wielder of the plough was surrounded by brahmanas there and departed from the spot known as Rishangu. O descendant of the Bharata lineage! Rishangu was an aged brahmana who was always engaged in austerities. Having made up his mind to cast aside his body, he thought a lot. Rishangu summoned all his immensely ascetic sons and told them to take him to a spot where there was a lot of water. Knowing about Rishangu's age, those great ascetics took that store of austerities to a tirtha on the Sarasvati. Those intelligent sons took him to the Sarasvati, where there were hundreds of tirthas, frequented by large numbers of brahmanas. O king! The immensely ascetic one bathed there, in accordance with the prescribed rites. O tiger among men! The supreme among rishis knew about the qualities of tirthas and delightedly told all his sons, who were worshipping him, "The northern bank of the Sarasvati has a lot of water. He who makes up his mind to cast aside his body there and engages in meditation and austerities, will never suffer from death." The one with the plough as his weapon, with dharma

[84]*Kapala* means a skull and *mochana* means release. Thus, release from a skull.

[85]Vishvamitra was born as a kshatriya and wanted to become a brahmana.

in his soul, touched the water there and bathed. He was devoted to brahmanas and gave a lot of gifts to brahmanas.

'O Kouravya! He then went to Lokaloka, created by the illustrious grandfather. Arshtishena, rigid in his vows and supreme among rishis, had performed great austerities there and become a brahmana. O king! Rajarshi Sindhudvipa, the great ascetic Devapi and the great sage Vishvamitra had also become brahmanas there. They were illustrious and great ascetics. They were fierce in their energy and great in their austerities. The strong and powerful Balabhadra[86] went there.'

Chapter 1258(39)

Janamejaya asked, 'Why did the illustrious Arshtishena torment himself through great austerities? How did Sindhudvipa become a brahmana? How did Devapi and the supreme Vishvamitra become brahmanas? O illustrious one! Tell me all this. I am supremely curious.'

Vaishampayana replied, 'O king! Earlier, in krita yuga, there was a supreme among brahmanas, known as Arshtishena. He always resided in the house of his preceptor and was always engaged in studying. O king! He always lived in the house of his preceptor. O lord of the earth! But his learning of the Vedas never became complete. O king! Depressed, the great ascetic tormented himself through austerities. Because of his austerities, he obtained the supreme Vedas.[87] The supreme among rishis obtained learning of the Vedas and attained success. The immensely great ascetic granted three boons to that tirtha. "From today, a man who bathes in the tirtha on this great river,[88] will obtain all the fruits of a horse sacrifice. From today, there will be no fear here from predatory beasts.[89] From a little bit

[86]Another name for Balarama.
[87]That is, knowledge of the Vedas.
[88]Sarasvati.
[89]Alternatively, snakes.

of effort, all the fruits will be obtained." Having spoken thus, the immensely energetic sage went to heaven. Thus did the illustrious and powerful Arshtishena attain success. O great king! In that tirtha, the powerful Sindhudvipa and Devapi obtained the exalted status of being a brahmana.

'O son![90] In that way, Koushika controlled his senses and always engaged in austerities. Severely tormenting himself through austerities, he attained the status of a brahmana. There was a great kshatriya, famous everywhere on earth by the name of Gadhi. O king! His son was the powerful Vishvamitra. O son! King Koushika performed a great sacrifice[91] and obtained the immensely ascetic Vishvamitra as his son. Having decided to cast aside his body, he decided to instate his son. The subjects bowed down and said, "O immensely wise one! Do not go. Save us from a great fear." Having been thus addressed, Gadhi replied to the subjects, "My son will be the protector of the entire universe." O king! Saying this and instating Vishvamitra, Gadhi went to heaven. Vishvamitra became the king. However, despite making efforts, he could not protect the earth. The king heard that there was a great fear from the rakshasas. With four kinds of forces, he went out of the city. Having gone a long distance, he reached Vasishtha's hermitage. O king! His soldiers created a lot of nuisance there. When the illustrious brahmana Vasishtha returned to his hermitage, he saw that the entire large forest was being destroyed. O great king! Vasishtha, supreme among sages, became angry at this. He instructed his cow to create a large number of terrible mountainous hunters. Thus instructed, the cow created men who were terrible in form. From every direction, they clashed against those soldiers and caused carnage. On seeing that the soldiers were driven away, Gadhi's son, Vishvamitra, made up his mind that austerities were

[90]The word used is tata. This means son, but is affectionately used towards anyone younger or junior.

[91]The use of the word Koushika causes a problem, since it is being used for both Vishvamitra and his father. The entire family was descended from Kusha. Vishvamitra's father was Gadhi. Hence, both Gadhi and Vishvamitra are Koushika.

supreme. O king! He meditated in that supreme tirtha along the Sarasvati. He observed vows and fasted. He emaciated his own body. He lived on water. He lived on air. He lived on leaves. He slept on the bare ground and observed many other separate rules. The gods made many attempts to dislodge him from his vows. But the great-souled one's mind never deviated from those rules. He made supreme efforts and tormented himself through many kinds of austerities. In his energy, Gadhi's son became as radiant as the sun. When Vishvamitra was thus engaged in austerities, the grandfather, the granter of boons, thought that he would grant the immensely ascetic one a boon. O king! He asked for the boon that he might become a brahmana. Brahma, the grandfather of all the worlds, agreed. The immensely illustrious one thus became a brahmana through his fierce austerities. Successful in his objective, he roamed around the entire earth, like a god. O king! In that supreme tirtha, Rama cheerfully gave away many riches, milk-yielding cows, carts, beds, garments, ornaments and the best of food and drink to the best of brahmanas, after having worshipped them. O king! Rama then went to the hermitage of Baka, which was not that far away. It has been heard that Dalbhya Baka tormented himself through fierce austerities there.'

Chapter 1259(40)

Vaishampayana said, 'O king! The descendant of the Yadu lineage then went to see the spot where Dalbhya Baka, the extremely great ascetic, offered the kingdom of Dhritarashtra, Vichitravirya's son, as an oblation. The place was full of brahmanas. Deciding to torment his body, he performed austerities that were extremely terrible in form. The powerful one, with dharma in his soul, was overcome by great rage. In earlier times, those who lived in Naimisha performed a sacrifice for twelve years. When the sacrifice named Vishvajita was completed, the rishis set out for Panchala. The learned ones asked for a *dakshina*[92]from the lord there.[93] They wanted twenty-one strong and healthy calves. The aged Baka told them, "Divide these animals among you.[94] I am giving up these animals and will ask for some more from the best of kings." O king! Having told all the rishis this, the powerful one, supreme among brahmanas, went to Dhritarashtra's abode. Having approached King Dhritarashtra, Dalbhya begged him for some animals. The best of kings saw that some of his cattle had died and angrily told him, "O one who is united with the brahman! If you want, take these animals." The rishi knew about dharma and hearing these words, he thought, "The words that have been spoken to me in this assembly are cruel. Having thought for an instant, the best of brahmanas was overcome with rage. He made up his mind to ensure King Dhritarashtra's destruction. The best of brahmanas sliced off flesh from the dead animals. He went to the tirtha on the banks of the Sarasvati and lit a fire there. Into that, in those ancient times, he offered King Dhritarashtra's kingdom as an oblation.[95] O great king! Dalbhya Baka was supremely devoted to rituals. The immensely ascetic one used the flesh to offer the kingdom as an oblation. In accordance with the rituals, that extremely terrible sacrifice started. At this, King Dhritarashtra's kingdom began to decay. O lord! It was as if a large forest was being sliced down with an axe. On seeing that the kingdom was thus afflicted, losing its vitality and afflicted by a hardship, the lord of men was distressed. O king! The lord began to think. In those earlier times, to free himself, the king made endeavours with brahmanas. O king! The king asked those brahmanas. O king! However, he was incapable of freeing his kingdom. O Janamejaya! He asked his advisers and those advisers said, "A wicked deed has been committed by you concerning those animals. In the form of flesh, the sage Baka is offering your kingdom as an oblation. It is because of those oblations that the kingdom is facing this great decay. It is because of his austere deeds that this great calamity has come about.

[92]Donation given to priests for performing a sacrifice.

[93]That is, the king of Panchala.

[94]Baka offered them his animals.

[95]The flesh was offered as an oblation, intending the destruction of the kingdom.

O king! There is a grove with water along the Sarasvati. Go and seek his favours there." The king went to the Sarasvati and spoke to Baka. O bull among the Bharata lineage! He lowered his head down on the ground and joined his hands in salutation. "O illustrious one. Grant me your favours. Pardon my offence. I am distressed and greedy. I am stupid and devoid of intelligence. You are my refuge. You are my protector. You should show me your favours." He lamented in this way, senseless with grief. On seeing this, the rishi felt compassion and freed his kingdom. He was pleased and abandoned his wrath. To free the kingdom, he again offered oblations into the fire. Having freed the kingdom, he received many animals in return. Delighted, he again went to Naimisharanya. The great-minded Dhritarashtra, with dharma in his soul, was also relieved. The king returned to his greatly prosperous city.

'O great king! In that tirtha, the immensely intelligent Brihaspati offered oblations of flesh for the decay of the asuras and the prosperity of the denizens of heaven. At this, the asuras began to decay. The gods desired victory and shattered them in a battle. In accordance with the prescribed rites, the immensely illustrious one[96] gave brahmanas horses, elephants, vehicles with horses and mules yoked to them, extremely expensive jewels, riches and grain. O lord of the earth! The mighty-armed one then went to the tirtha known as Yayata. O great king! The great-souled Yayati, Nahusha's son, performed a sacrifice there and Sarasvati produced milk and clarified butter.[97] Having performed the sacrifice, King Yayati, tiger among men, cheerfully ascended upwards and obtained all the worlds. O king! Because Yayati performed the sacrifice there, Sarasvati flowed and gave all the objects of desire to the great-souled brahmanas. In whatever spot the brahmanas desired whichever object of desire, in those spots, the best of rivers flowed and gave those in abundance. The gods and the gandharvas were pleased at this prosperous sacrifice. On beholding the prosperity at the sacrifice, men were astounded. The great-souled one, cleansed in his

[96]Balarama.

[97]Instead of water.

soul,[98] always gave away a lot of gifts. He possessed a palm tree on his banner and was the source of great dharma. He had fortitude and had conquered his soul. He then went to Vasishthapavaha, which had a great and terrible current.'

Chapter 1260(41)

Janamejaya asked, 'Why does Vasishthapavaha have a great and terrible current? Why did the best of rivers bear the rishi away?[99] O lord! What was the reason for the enmity between them?[100] O immensely wise one! I am asking you. Please tell me. I am not satisfied from hearing these stories.'

Vaishampayana replied, 'O descendant of the Bharata lineage! There was an extremely terrible enmity between the rishis Vishvamitra and Vasishtha. This was because they greatly rivalled each other in austerities. Vasishtha's great hermitage was in the tirtha known as Sthanu. This was on the east and the intelligent Vishvamitra's was on the west.[101] O great king! Sthanu had performed great austerities there.[102] Learned ones speak about the terrible deeds he performed there. O lord! Having performed a sacrifice there and having worshipped Sarasvati, the illustrious Sthanu established a tirtha there, known as Sthanu-tirtha. O lord of men! All the gods had instated Skanda, the destroyer of the enemies of the gods, as the great general of their army there. Through his fierce austerities, the great sage, Vishvamitra, brought Vasishtha to that tirtha on the Sarasvati. Listen

[98]Balarama.

[99]We haven't been told this yet, nor has Janamejaya heard it yet. Janamejaya has inferred this from the name Vasishthapavaha. *Apavaha* means to bear or carry away, so Vasishthapavaha means something that carries off Vasishtha.

[100]Vasishtha and Vishvamitra.

[101]The eastern and western banks of the river Sarasvati.

[102]Sthanu means one who is fixed and immobile and is one of Shiva's names. The tirtha got its name because of this.

to that account. O descendant of the Bharata lineage! Vishvamitra and Vasishtha, rich in austerities, rivalled and challenged each other through the fierce austerities that they performed. Vishvamitra, the great sage, saw that Vasishtha was superior to him in energy. He was tormented by this and began to think. O descendant of the Bharata lineage! The sage formed a resolution. "This Sarasvati will swiftly and forcefully bring Vasishtha, store of austerities and supreme among those who meditate, to my presence. Once he is here, there is no doubt that I will kill that foremost of brahmanas." Having decided this, Vishvamitra, the great sage, remembered the best of rivers, his eyes red with rage. When she was thus thought of, the beautiful one anxiously went to the sage, who was great in energy and great in wrath. Sarasvati trembled and was pale. She joined her hands in salutation and presented herself before Vishvamitra, supreme among sages. She was extremely miserable and was like a lady whose husband had been killed. She asked that supreme of sages, "What do I have to do? Tell me." The sage angrily replied, "Quickly bring Vasishtha here, so that I can kill him today." On hearing this, the river was distressed. The one with eyes like a lotus joined her hands in salutation. She trembled, like a climbing creeper shaken by the wind. Vishvamitra saw that she had arrived and that she was trembling, joining her hands in salutation. Extremely angry, he said, "Quickly bring Vasishtha here." O descendant of the Bharata lineage! Terrified, the best of rivers began to think. She was frightened that either one would curse her and did not know what to do.

'Realizing the purport of the words, the best of rivers went to Vasishtha and told him what the intelligent Vishvamitra had said. She was scared that either one would curse her and trembled repeatedly. She was grievously frightened that the rishis would impose a grave curse on her. O king! Vasishtha was supreme among men and had dharma in his soul. He saw that she was wan and pale and was worried. He said, "O best of rivers! Save yourself. O fast-flowing one! Bear me there. Otherwise, Vishamitra will curse you. Do not think unnecessarily." The river heard the words of the compassionate one. O Kouravya! She began to think about the best course of action for herself. She thought and arrived at the conclusion, "Vasishtha has always shown compassion for me. What he has asked me to do will be beneficial for me." O king! She saw that the supreme of rishis was meditating along her banks. She saw that Koushika[103] was also offering oblations. Sarasvati, supreme among rivers, decided that this was her opportunity. With great force, the river washed away one of her banks. When the bank was broken, Maitra Varuni's son was also borne away.[104] O king! As he was borne away, he was satisfied and praised Sarasvati. "O Sarasvati! You are a river that has arisen from the grandfather.[105] This entire universe is pervaded by your wonderful waters. O goddess! You flow through the sky and pass on your waters to the clouds. All the waters are yours and it is through you that we obtain our learning.[106] You are nourishment, radiance, fame, success, expansion and splendour.[107] You are speech and *svaha*.[108] You pervade the entire universe. It is through you that the four kinds of beings find life."[109] O king! Sarasvati was praised thus by the maharshi. With great force, she bore the brahmana along towards Vishvamitra's hermitage and told the sage Vishvamitra that he had been brought. On seeing that Vasishtha had been brought by Sarasvati, he[110] was overcome by rage and looked for a weapon so that he might be slain. On seeing that he was angry, the river was scared that a brahmana might be killed. Without any delay, she swiftly bore Vasishtha away to the eastern bank again. She acted in accordance with both their words, but deceived Gadhi's son. On seeing that Vasishtha, supreme among rishis, had been borne away,

[103]Vishvamitra.

[104]There was a sage named Maitra Varuni. According to some accounts, Vasishtha was the son of the sage Maitra Varuni and Urvashi. Thus, Vasishtha is being referred to as Maitra Varuni's son.

[105]As a goddess, Sarasvati was born from Brahma's mental powers.

[106]Sarasvati is the goddess of learning.

[107]Pushti, Dyuti, Kirti, Siddhi, Vriddhi and Uma respectively.

[108]The incantation made when oblations are offered into the fire for the gods.

[109]Those born from wombs, those born from eggs, those that are trees/plants and those that are born from sweat (insects).

[110]Vishvamitra.

Vishvamitra was overcome by intolerance and wrathfully told her, "O supreme among rivers! You have gone away again and have deceived me. O fortunate one! Your waters will change to blood, acceptable only to the foremost among rakshasas." Sarasvati was thus cursed by the intelligent Vishvamitra. For an entire year, Sarasvati flowed, with blood instead of water. The rishis, the gods, the gandharvas and the apsaras were extremely miserable to see the Sarasvati in that state. O lord of men! That is the reason that spot is famous in this world as Vasishthapavaha. However, the supreme among rivers again returned to her original course.'

Chapter 1261(42)

Vaishampayana said, 'The intelligent and enraged Vishvamitra cursed her. In that supreme tirtha, the auspicious one's flows were made out of blood. O king! O descendant of the Bharata lineage! Rakshasas went there. In delight, all of them drank that blood. They were extremely satisfied, delighted and devoid of anxiety. They danced and laughed, as if they had won heaven for themselves. O lord of the earth! After some time had passed, rishis, rich in austerities, went on a visit of tirthas to the Sarasvati. Those bulls among sages went and bathed in all the tirthas. Those accomplished ones were supremely delighted and wished to obtain greater austerities. O king! They went to the other tirthas. Those immensely fortunate ones went to the terrible tirtha.[111] O supreme among kings! They saw that the waters of the Sarasvati were covered in blood and that these were being drunk by a large number of rakshasas. O king! On seeing this, the sages, rigid in their vows, made supreme efforts to save Sarasvati from the rakshasas. Those immensely fortunate ones, great in their vows, assembled and jointly summoned the river with these best of words. "O fortunate one! Tell us the reason why this lake of

[111]Vasishthapavaha, where the river flowed in the form of blood.

yours has been reduced to this plight.[112] We have heard the reason behind your state of hardship. We will try to rescue you." Having been addressed, she looked at them. Trembling and miserable, she told them what had transpired. Those stores of austerities said, "O unblemished one! We have heard about the reason. We know why you have been cursed. All of us, rich in austerities, will make the best of efforts." Having thus spoken to the best of rivers, they consulted among themselves. "All of us will free Sarasvati from the curse." O king! They gave their word that Sarasvati would be returned to her natural state and indeed, the waters became clean, as they had been earlier. Freed, the best of rivers became as resplendent as she had been earlier.

'O king! Seeing what the sages had done to the waters of the Sarasvati, the rakshasas were overcome by hunger. They joined their hands in salutation and repeatedly requested all the sages for compassion. "All of us are hungry. We have been dislodged from our eternal dharma.[113] It is not of our own desire that we are the performers of wicked deeds. It is because you do not show us favours that we perform these wicked deeds. Those among us who are especially bad become brahma-rakshasas.[114] In a similar way, those among vaishyas, shudras and kshatriyas, who hate brahmanas, also become rakshasas. Those beings who disrespect preceptors, officiating priests, elders and the aged, also become rakshasas. Wickedness increases through the sexual transgressions of women.[115] O supreme among brahmanas! You should therefore act so as to show us compassion. You are capable of saving all the worlds." On hearing these words, the sages praised the great river. They controlled their minds. To save the rakshasas, they said, "Food

[112]*Saras* means lake or pool and Sarasvati was so named because the river had many lakes or pools.

[113]Of feeding on blood.

[114]A wicked brahmana becomes a brahma-rakshasa. In this, a varna-based classification is being made of rakshasas.

[115]The text uses the word *yonidosha*. More literally, this is sexual defilement, or a defect in the female genital organ.

in which there are insects and worms, food that has been mixed with leftovers, food that is mixed with hair, food that is mixed with grain that has not been broken and food that has been touched by dogs—these will constitute the share of rakshasas. Knowing this, the learned will always avoid such kinds of food. Those who partake of such food will eat food that is meant for rakshasas." Thus did those stores of austerities purify that tirtha. They instructed the river to save those rakshasas. O bull among men! Knowing the views of the maharshis, that supreme of rivers thought of a new form in her body, known as Aruna. Bathing there, the rakshasas gave up their bodies and went to heaven. O great king! He who bathes in Aruna is saved from the crime of killing a brahmana. Knowing the purport of all this, Shatakratu, the king of the gods, bathed in that best of tirthas and was freed from a great sin.'

Janamejaya asked, 'How did the illustrious Shakra commit the offence of killing a brahmana? How was he freed from his sin by bathing in that tirtha?'

Vaishampayana replied, 'O lord of men! Listen to that account, exactly as it happened. In ancient times, Vasava broke his treaty of peace with Namuchi. Because of his fear of Vasava, Namuchi hid inside one of the sun's rays. Indra entered into a pledge of friendship with him and told him, "O best of asuras! O friend! I will not kill you with anything that is wet, or with anything that is dry, nor during the day or during the night. I swear this to you truthfully." Having thus entered into an agreement, the lord created a mist. O king! Vasava severed his head with the foam of water.[116] Namuchi's severed head pursued Shakra from the rear and said, "O friend! You have committed a crime." He was repeatedly spoken to by the head. In torment, he went to the grandfather and told him what had happened. The preceptor of the worlds said, "O Indra of the gods! You have committed the crime of killing a brahmana.[117] Perform a sacrifice in accordance with the decreed rites and bathe in Aruna."

[116]Foam is neither wet, nor dry. Because of the mist, it was neither day, nor night.

[117]Because Namuchi was descended from the sage Kashyapa.

O Janamejaya! Having been thus addressed, the slayer of Bala performed a sacrifice in the grove of Sarasvati and bathed in Aruna. He was freed from the crime of killing a brahmana. Cheerfully, the lord of the thirty gods returned to heaven. O descendant of the Bharata lineage! O supreme among kings! Namuchi's head was submerged in those waters and he[118] obtained many eternal worlds that grant every object of desire.

'The great-souled Bala bathed there and gave away many different kinds of gifts. Devoted to dharma and the performer of supreme and noble deeds, he then went to the great tirtha of Soma. O Indra among kings! In earlier times, in accordance with the prescribed rites, Soma had himself performed a royal sacrifice there. In that best of sacrifices, the intelligent and great-souled Atri was chief among the officiating priests. When it was over, there was a great clash between the danavas, daityas and rakshasas on one side and the gods on the other. That extremely terrible battle is known as Taraka and in this, Skanda killed Taraka. Mahasena,[119] the destroyer of the daityas, became the commander of the gods there. Kartikeya himself lives at that spot. Kumara always dwells there and there is a king of plaksha trees there.'

Chapter 1262(43)

Janamejaya asked, 'O supreme among brahmanas! You have told me about the powers of Sarasvati. O brahmana! You should tell me about Kumara's consecration. O supreme among eloquent ones! Tell me about the time and the place where it happened. O illustrious one! How was the lord consecrated according to the proper rites? How did Skanda create great carnage among the daityas? Tell me everything about this. I have great curiosity.'

[118]Namuchi.

[119]Skanda or Kartikeya's name. Kumara is another of his names.

Vaishampayana replied, 'Your curiosity is characteristic of someone belonging to the Kuru lineage. O Janamejaya! My words will generate delight in you. O lord of men! I will tell you about that wonderful account, about the great-souled Kumara's consecration and powers. Listen. In earlier times, Maheshvara's seed fell down into fire.[120] The illustrious one who devours everything[121] was incapable of destroying that eternal seed. Instead, because he was bearing that energetic seed, the one who bears oblations became energetic and radiant. On Lord Brahma's instructions, he went to the Ganga and flung that divine seed, as energetic as the sun, there. However, Ganga was also not capable of bearing that seed and flung it on the beautiful slopes of the Himalayas, worshipped by the immortals. Agni's son[122] began to grow there, pervading the worlds. The Krittikas saw the blazing womb there.[123] The lord, the great-souled son of the fire god, was lying down in a clump of reeds. Desiring a son, all of them exclaimed, "This is mine." Discerning the sentiments of the mothers, the illustrious lord assumed six mouths and drank milk from all their breasts. Seeing the powers of the child, the divine goddesses, the Krittikas, celestial in their forms, were filled with great wonder. O supreme among the Kuru lineage! Since Ganga had cast the illustrious one on the peak of the mountain, that mountain is beautiful and golden everywhere. The child began to grow and made the earth beautiful. It is because of this that all the mountains began to yield gold. The immensely valorous Kumara is known by the name of Kartikeya.[124] Before this, with his great powers of yoga, he had been known by the

[120]*Skanna* means something that has trickled down or fallen. The word Skanda is derived from that. The story is left implicit. Shiva was interrupted by the god of love. The seed fell down and was conveyed by Agni.

[121]Meaning Agni.

[122]Because Agni had borne the seed.

[123]Krittika (Pleiades) is the third of the twenty-seven nakshatras. Krittika is actually a star cluster, not a single star. There are believed to be six Krittikas in that cluster.

[124]After the Krittikas.

name of Gangeya. The god possessed prowess and austerities. O Indra among kings! He began to grow and was as handsome as the moon. Surrounded by prosperity, he lay down on that divine and golden clump of reeds. As he lay down there, he was praised by the gandharvas and the sages. Thousands of celestial maidens danced around him. They were beautiful and skilled in dancing. They played on divine musical instruments and praised him. The celestial river Ganga, supreme among rivers, also worshipped him. The earth, assuming the most beautiful of forms, bore him. Brihaspati performed the rites, including those connected with birth. The four Vedas presented themselves before him, hands joined in salutation. The four branches of dhanurveda and collections of weapons, not just arrows, presented themselves before him.

'The immensely valorous one saw that Uma's consort, the lord of the gods, was seated, surrounded by a large number of *bhuta*s.[125] The daughter of the mountains was with him.[126] Those large numbers of bhutas were without bodies and were extremely wonderful to behold. They were hideous, with distorted bodies. Their ornaments and standards were ugly. Their faces were like tigers, lions and bears. Some of them had faces like cats and makaras. There were those with faces like cats.[127] There were others with faces like elephants and camels. Some had faces like owls. Others looked like vultures and jackals. Others had faces like curlews, pigeons and herons. Others had bodies like those of dogs, porcupines, lizards and mules. They assumed all these kinds of forms. Some were like mountains, others were like oceans. Some held chakras, maces and other weapons. Some looked like large masses of collyrium. Others possessed the complexion of white mountains. O lord of the earth! The seven *matrika*s and their

[125]They had come to see Skanda.

[126]Uma's consort is Shiva. The daughter of the mountains is Uma or Parvati. The bhutas are demons, Shiva's followers.

[127]Cats have already been mentioned. The text uses the word *vrishadamsha*. *Vrisha* means rat or mouse. Therefore, vrishadamsha is something that bites rats/mice, hence it means cat. However, the word can be used for any animal that has strong teeth.

followers were also there.[128] So were the Sadhyas, the Vishvadevas, the Maruts, the Vasus and the ancestors. The Rudras, the Adityas, the Siddhas, the serpents, the danavas, the birds, the illustrious and self-creating Brahma and his sons,[129] Vishnu and Shakra went there, desiring to see the supreme and undecaying Kumara. There were the best of gods and gandharvas, with Narada at their head. There were the devarshis and the Siddhas, with Brihaspati at their head. There were the lords of creation, supreme among the gods. Aryama[130] and all the worlds went there. Though he was yet a child, the illustrious one possessed great powers of yoga. He advanced towards the lord of the gods,[131] who wielded the trident and pinaka in his hands. On seeing him advance, Shiva, the daughter of the mountain, Ganga and Agni simultaneously wondered, "Whom will the child approach and show honours to first? He will come to me."[132] All of them thought in this way. Discerning their thoughts, he simultaneously divided himself into four bodies. The illustrious lord assumed these four bodies in an instant—Skanda, Shakha, Vishakha and Naigamesha as the last. Thus did the illustrious lord divide himself into four parts. Skanda, extraordinary in form, went to where Rudra was. Vishakha went to the goddess who was the daughter of the mountain. Shakha, the illustrious one's form as the wind, went to Vibhavasu.[133] Naigamesha, Kumara's form that was as radiant as the fire, went to Ganga. All the four blazing bodies were similar in appearance. They advanced forward and it was wonderful. On beholding this great and wonderful sight, which made the body hair stand up, great

[128]The matrikas are mother goddesses, originally identified with the Krittikas. They have both malign and benign aspects, vis-à-vis infants. Usually, the matrikas are said to be seven—Brahmani, Vaishnavi, Maheshvari, Indrani, Koumari, Varahi and Chamundi (or Narasimhi).

[129]The sages who were created through Brahma's mental powers.

[130]The sun god.

[131]Shiva.

[132]All four had some claim to parentage. There are varying stories about Kartikeya's birth. In some of these, Parvati is the mother.

[133]Agni.

sounds of lamentation arose among the gods, the danavas and the rakshasas. Rudra, the goddess,[134] Agni and Ganga—all of them bowed down before the grandfather, the lord of the worlds. O bull among kings! O king! Having bowed down in different ways and to ensure Kartikeya's welfare, they said, "O illustrious one! O lord of the gods! For the sake of our pleasure, grant this child some kind of sovereignty that is appropriate for him." The illustrious and wise one, grandfather of all the worlds, thought about this. What could be given to him? All the riches had already been given away to the gods, the gandharvas, the rakshasas, the bhutas, the yakshas, the birds, the serpents and great-souled ones without any bodies. The immensely intelligent one thought about what prosperity might be bestowed on him. With the welfare of the gods in mind, he thought for an instant. O descendant of the Bharata lineage! He then made him the general of all the beings. The grandfather of all the beings instructed all the gods, and the lords among them, to serve him. Together with Kumara, all the gods, led by Brahma, went to the king of the mountains, so as to consecrate him there. That sacred spot was on the slopes of the Himalayas, where the goddess Sarasvati, best among rivers, flowed. It is famous in the three worlds by the name of Samantapanchaka. That sacred bank of the Sarasvati possesses all the qualities. Cheerful in their minds, all the gods and the gandharvas seated themselves there.'

Chapter 1263(44)

Vaishampayana said, 'In accordance with the sacred texts, they collected everything that was required for a consecration. In accordance with the decreed rites, Brihaspati kindled a fire and offered oblations. The Himalayas provided a celestial, golden and supreme seat, decorated with the best of jewels and divine gems. All

[134]Parvati.

the auspicious objects were brought by the masses of gods, objects required for the consecration. The required mantras were chanted. The immensely valorous Indra, Vishnu, the sun god, the moon god, Dhata, Vidhata, the wind god, the fire god, Pusha, Bhaga, Aryama, Amsha, Vivasvat,[135] the immensely wise Rudra, Mitra, Varuna, the Rudras, the Vasus and the Adityas surrounded the handsome lord. With the ancestors, there were the Vishvadevas, the Maruts and the Sadhyas. There were gandharvas, apsaras, yakshas, rakshasas, serpents and large numbers of devarshis and brahmarshis. There were Vaikhanasas,[136] Valakhilyas, those that lived on air and those that lived on the rays of the sun. There were great-souled sages descended from Bhrigu and Angiras. There were all the Vidyadharas,[137] surrounded by Siddhas with sacred powers of yoga. O lord of the earth! The grandfather was there and Pulastya, the immensely ascetic Pulaha, Angiras, Kashyapa, Atri, Marichi, Bhrigu, Kratu, Hara, Prachetas, Manu, Daksha, the seasons, the planets and the stellar bodies. O lord of men! In personified form, the rivers were there and the eternal Vedas, the oceans, the lakes, the many kinds of tirthas, the earth, the firmament, the directions and all the trees. Aditi, the mother of the gods, Hri, Shri, Svaha, Sarasvati, Uma, Shachi, Sinivali, Anumati, Kuhu, Raka, Dhishana and all the wives of the residents of heaven were there.[138] The Himalayas, the Vindhyas, Meru and many other mountains were there. O king! Airavata and his followers were there and Kala, Kashtha,[139] the fortnights, the months, the seasons, night and day. Ucchaihshrava, best among horses, was there and Vamana, king among elephants. They were with Aruna, Garuda, the trees and the herbs. The illustrious god Dharma came there, with Destiny, Yama, Death and Yama's followers. There were many

[135]The sun god.

[136]Hermits.

[137]Semi-divine species.

[138]Hri is modesty personified. Shri can be interpreted as prosperity personified, or Lakshmi. Sinivali is the first day of the new moon, when the crescent is barely visible. Anumati is the fifteenth day of the moon. Kuhu is the day of the new moon. Raka is the day of the full moon. Dhishana is intellect personified.

[139]Kala and Kashtha are small measures of time.

others from the large numbers of gods that I have not named. They arrived there, for the purpose of Kumara's consecration. O king! All the residents of heaven came there. They carried many auspicious vessels for the consecration. O king! There were golden pots filled with divine objects. They came to the divine and sacred waters of the Sarasvati. The residents of heaven were delighted that the great-souled Kumara, a terror to the asuras, would be consecrated as the general. O great king! In that ancient age, the illustrious Brahma, the grandfather of the worlds, consecrated him by pouring Varuna, the lord of the waters, over him. So did the immensely ascetic Kashyapa and the others who have been named.

'The lord Brahma was delighted and gave him great companions who were powerful and as swift as the wind. They were successful and possessed valour that could be increased at will. They were Nandisena, Lohitaksha and Ghantakarna. The fourth companion was known by the name of Kumudamali. Sthanu gave him a great companion by the name of Kratu. He was immensely forceful and could summon a hundred different kinds of maya at will. He possessed valour and strength that could be increased at will. O Indra among kings! He was the destroyer of the enemies of the gods and he gave him to Skanda. In the battle between the gods and the asuras, he[140] angrily killed fourteen million terrible daityas with his bare hands alone. The god also gave him soldiers that were full of demons.[141] They destroyed and defeated the enemies of the gods and possessed all kinds of earthy forms. With Vasava, all the gods uttered roars of victory. So did the gandharvas, the yakshas, the rakshasas, the sages and the ancestors. Yama gave him two companions who were like Death and Destiny. They were Unmatha and Pramatha. They were immensely valorous and greatly radiant. Surya cheerfully gave the powerful Kartikeya two companions who were Surya's followers. They were Subhraja and Bhaskara. Soma gave him companions named Mani and Sumani. They were like peaks of Kailasa. They wore white garlands and were smeared with white unguents.

[140]Kratu.

[141]*Nairritas*.

Hutashana[142] gave him two brave companions named Jvalajihva and Jyoti. They were ones who crushed enemy soldiers. Amsha gave the intelligent Skanda five companions—Parigha, Vata, the immensely strong Bhima, Dahati and Dahana. They were fearsome and full of valour. Vasava, the destroyer of enemy heroes, gave Agni's son two companions named Utkrosha and Pankaja. They were armed with the vajra and a staff. In battle, they had killed many enemies of the great Indra. The immensely famous Vishnu gave Skanda three companions named Chakra, Vikrama and Samkrama. They were immensely strong. O bull among the Bharata lineage! The Ashvins cheerfully gave Skanda companions named Vardhana and Nandana. They were skilled in all the arts. The immensely illustrious Dhata gave the great-souled one companions named Kundana, Kusuma, Kumuda, Dambara and Adambara. Tvastha gave Skanda supreme companions named Vakra and Anuvakra. They were strong, proud of their valour and had mouths like those of sheep. They had great powers of maya. The lord Mitra gave the great-souled Kumara two great-souled companions, Suvrata and Satyasandha. They possessed austerities and learning. Vidhata gave Kartikeya two handsome companions who were famous in the three worlds. They were Suprabha and the great-souled Shubhakarma. They were the granters of boons and the performers of auspicious deeds. O descendant of the Bharata lineage! Pusha gave Kartikeya two companions, Palitaka and Kalika. They possessed great powers of maya. O supreme among the Bharata lineage! Vayu gave Kartikeya Bala and Atibala. They were immensely powerful and possessed large mouths. Varuna, devoted to the truth, gave Kartikeya Ghasa and Atighasa. They had faces like whales and were immensely strong. O king! The Himalayas gave Hutashana's son the great-souled Suvarchasa and Ativarchasa. O descendant of the Bharata lineage! Meru gave Agni's son two companions—the great-souled Kanchana and Meghamali. Meru also gave Agni's great-souled son two others—Sthira and Atisthira. They were immensely strong and powerful. The Vindhyas gave Agni's son two companions named Ucchrita and Atishringa. They fought with

[142]Agni.

large boulders. The ocean gave Agni's son two great companions, Samgraha and Vigraha. They were the wielders of clubs. The beautiful Parvati gave Agni's son Unmada, Pushpadanta and Shankukarna. O tiger among men! Vasuki, the lord of serpents, gave the son of the fire two serpents named Jaya and Mahajaya.

'In that way, the Sadhyas, the Rudras, the Vasus, the ancestors, the oceans, the rivers and the immensely strong mountains gave him the leaders of soldiers, armed with spears and battleaxes. They wielded divine weapons and were attired in many kinds of garments. Listen to the names of the other soldiers that Skanda obtained. They were armed with many kinds of weapons and attired in colourful ornaments and armour. O king! O Indra among kings! O descendant of the Bharata lineage! They were[143] Shankukarna, Nikumbha, Padma, Kumuda, Ananta, Dvadashabhuja, Krishna, Upakrishna, Dronashrava, Kapskandha, Kanchanaksha, Jalamdhama, Akshasamtarjana, Kunadika, Tamobhrakrit, Ekaksha, Dvadashaksha, the lord Ekajata, Sahasrabahu, Vikata, Vyaghraksha, Kshitikampana, Punyanama, Sunama, Suvaktra, Priyadarshana, Parishruta, Kokanada, Priyamalyanulepana, Ajodira, Gajashira, Skandhaksha, Shatalochana, Jvalajihva, Karala, Sitakesha, Jati, Hari, Chaturdamshtra, Ashtajihva, Meghanada, Prithushrava, Vidyutaksha, Dhanurvaktra, Jathara, Marutashana, Udaraksha, Jhashaksha, Vajranama, Vasuprabha, Samudravega, Shailakampi, Putramesha, Pravaha, Nanda, Upanandaka, Dhumra, Shveta, Kalinga, Siddhartha, Varada, Priyaka, Nanda, the powerful Gonanda, Ananda, Pramoda, Svastika, Dhruvaka, Kshemavapa, Sujata, Siddha, Govraja, Kanakapida, the lord of great companions, Gayana, Hasana, Bana, the valiant Khadga, Vaitali, Atitali, Katika, Vatika, Hamsaja, Pankadigdhanga, Samudronmada, Ranotkata, Prahasa, Shvetashirsha, Nandaka, Kalakantha, Prabhasa, Kumbhabhandaka, Kalakaksha, Sita, Bhutalonmatha, Yajnavaha, Pravaha, Devayaji, Somapa, Sajala, Mahateja, Krathakratha, Tuhana, Tuhana,[144] the valiant Chitradeva, Madhura, Suprasada, the immensely strong Kiriti,

[143]Some names are repeated more than once.

[144]Tuhana and Tuhaana.

Vasana, Madhuvarna, Kalashodara, Ghamanta, Manmathakara, the valiant Suchivakrta, Shvetavaktra, Suvaktra, Charuvaktra, Pandura, Dandabahu, Subahu, Raja, Kokila, Achala, Kanakaksha, the lord Balanamayika, Samcharaka, Kokanada, Gridhravaktra, Jambuka, Lohashvavaktra, Jathara, Kumbhavaktra, Kundaka, Madgugriva, Krishnouja, Hamsavaktra, Chandrabha, Panikurma, Shambuka, Shakavaktra and Kundaka. There were other great-souled ones who possessed powers of yoga and were always devoted to brahmanas. O Janamejaya! These great companions were given to him by the great-souled grandfather and they were children, youths and the aged. Thousands of companions presented themselves before Kumara.

'O Janamejaya! They had many different kinds of faces. Listen to this. Some had faces like tortoises and cocks, others mouths like hares and owls. Some had faces like asses and camels, others faces like boars. Some had mouths like men and sheep, others faces like jackals. Some had terrible faces like makaras, others mouths like alligators.[145] O descendant of the Bharata lineage! Some had faces like cats and rabbits, others had long faces. Some had faces like mongooses and owls, others faces like dogs. Some had mouths like rats, others faces like peacocks. Others had faces like fish and sheep, while still others had faces like goats and buffaloes. Some had faces like bears and tigers, others faces like leopards and tigers. Some had terrible faces like elephants, others mouths like crocodiles. Some had faces like Garuda, others mouths like rhinoceros, wolves and crows. Others had mouths like cows and mules, still others mouths like cats.[146] O descendant of the Bharata lineage! Some had large stomachs and feet, with eyes like stars. Others had mouths like pigeons, and still others mouths like bulls. There were those with faces like cuckoos and others with faces like hawks and partridges. Some had mouths like partridges,[147] others were dressed in white garments. Some had faces like serpents, others mouths like porcupines. Some had terrible mouths, others one hundred faces. Some were attired in snakeskin.

[145]*Shishumara*, alternatively, dolphins or porpoises.

[146]Vrishadamsha again.

[147]*Tittira* and *krikala* are mentioned. Both are types of partridges.

Others wore snakes as garments. There were large stomachs and thin bodies, as there were thin stomachs and large bodies. There were short necks and large ears, dressed in many kinds of snakeskin. Some wore garments made out of elephant skin, others were attired in black deerskin. O great king! Some had mouths on their shoulders, others had mouths on their stomachs. Some had mouths on their backs. Some had mouths on their cheeks. Some had mouths on their thighs. Many had faces on their flanks and others had mouths all over the body. There were other lords of *ganas*[148] who looked like worms and insects. There were those with mouths like carnivorous beasts. They had many arms and many heads. Some had arms like trees. Others had heads around their waists. Some had faces like the bodies of snakes, others dwelt on many creepers. Some covered their bodies with deerskin, others attired themselves in bark. There were many different kinds of garments, including those made of hides. There were headdresses and crowns. They had necks like conch shells and were extremely radiant. Some were diademed. Some had five tufts of hair on their heads. Some had stiff hair. There were those with three, two or seven tufts of hair on their heads. Some had tufts, others wore crowns. Some were shaved, others had matted hair. Some were adorned in colourful garments. Some others had hair on their faces. Some donned divine garlands and garments and always loved the prospect of fighting. Some were dark, with no flesh on their faces. Some had long backs, without stomachs. Some had long backs, others had short backs. Some had elongated stomachs. Some were long-armed, others were short-armed. Some were short in stature and were dwarfs. Some were hunchbacked. There were those with long thighs and ears and heads like those of elephants. There were noses like elephants and noses like tortoises. Others had noses like wolves. Some had long lips and long tongues. Others had terrible visages and their faces looked downwards. There were long teeth and short teeth. Some only had four teeth. O king! There were thousands who were as terrible as the kings of elephants. Some had proportionate bodies that blazed and were ornamented.

[148]Followers of Shiva.

O descendant of the Bharata lineage! There were those with tawny eyes, with conical ears and bent noses. There were broad teeth, large teeth, stout lips and tawny hair. There were many kinds of feet, lips and teeth. There were many kinds of hands and heads. O descendant of the Bharata lineage! There were many kinds of armour and many kinds of speech. Those lords were skilled in the languages of different countries and spoke to each other. Those great companions were seen to cheerfully descend there. They were long in the neck, long in the nails and long in the feet, heads and arms. O descendant of the Bharata lineage! They were tawny-eyed, blue in the throat and long in the ear. Some had stomachs like wolves. Others were like masses of collyrium. Others had white limbs, red necks and tawny eyes. O king! O descendant of the Bharata lineage! Many were dappled in colourful hues. There were ornaments that were like whisks, white, red and silver. These were of many different colours. Some were golden, or had the complexion of peacocks.

'Let me recount the weapons that were grasped and wielded by the companions who came last. Listen. Some wielded nooses in their hands. Others had faces like asses, with gaping mouths. Some had large eyes, blue throats and arms like clubs. They had shataghnis and chakras in their hands. Others had clubs in their hands. There were bludgeons and catapults in their hands. Some had spears in their hands. O descendant of the Bharata lineage! While some had spears and swords in their hands, others held staffs in their hands. Those great-souled ones possessed many kinds of terrible weapons. They were swift in speed. They were immensely strong and immensely forceful. Such were the great companions who were seen at Kumara's consecration. They were cheerful and loved to fight. Nets of bells were fastened to their bodies and they were immensely energetic. O king! There were many other great companions like these. They presented themselves before the great-souled and illustrious Kartikeya. They were from heaven, the firmament and earth and some were like the wind. Instructed by the gods, those brave ones became the companions of Skanda. There were many others like them, in thousands, millions and tens of millions. They surrounded the great-souled one at his consecration.'

Chapter 1264(45)

Vaishampayana said, 'O king! Listen to the large number of matrikas who became Kumara's followers. O brave one! I will recount the names of the ones who slay large numbers of the enemy. O descendant of the Bharata lineage! Listen to the names of those illustrious matrikas. O descendant of the Bharata lineage! O Indra among kings! O king! O Kouravya! Those fortunate ones pervade the three worlds and everything that is mobile and immobile[149]—Prabhavati, Vishalakshi, Palita, Gonasi, Shrimati, Bahula, Bahuputrika, Apsujata, Gopali, Brihadambalika, Jayavati, Malatika, Dhruvaratna, Bhayankari, Vasudama, Sudama, Vishoka, Nandini, Ekachuda, Mahachuda, Chakranemi, Uttejani, Jayatsena, Kamalakshya, Shobhana, Shatrunjaya, Krodhana, Shalabhi, Khari, Madhavi, Shubhravaktra, Tirthanemi, Gitapriya, Kalyani, Kadrula, Amitashana, Meghasvana, Bhogavati, Subhru, Kanakavati, Alatakshi, Viryavati, Vidyutjihva, Padmavati, Sunakshatra, Kandara, Bahuyojana, Santanika, Bahudama, Suprabha, Yashasvini, Nrityapriya, Shatolukhalamekhala, Shataghanta, Shatananda, Bhagananda, Bhamini, Vapushmati, Chandrashita, Bhadrakali, Samkarika, Nishkutika, Bhrama, Chatvaravasini, Sumangala, Svastimati, Vriddhikama, Jayapriya, Dhanada, Suprasada, Bhavada, Jaleshvari, Edi, Bhedi, Samedi, Vetalajanani, Kanduti, Kalika, Devamitra, Lambasi, Ketaki, Chitrasena, Bala, Kukkutika, Shankhanika, Jarjarika, Kundarika, Kokalika, Kandara, Shatodari, Utkrathini, Jarena, Mahavega, Kankana, Manojava, Kantakini, Praghasa, Putana, Khashaya, Churvyutirvama, Kroshanatha, Taditprabha, Mandodari, Tunda, Kotara, Meghavasini, Subhaga, Lambini, Lamba, Vasuchuda, Vikatthini, Urddhvavenidhara, Pingakshi, Lohamekhala, Prithuvaktra, Madhurika, Madhukumbha, Pakshalika, Manthanika, Jarayu, Jarjaranana, Khyata, Dahadaha, Dhamadhama, Khandakhanda, Pushana, Manikundala, Amocha, Lambopayodhara, Venuvinadhara, Pingakshi, Lohamekhala, Shasholukamukhi,

[149]Some names are repeated more than once.

Krishna, Kharajhangha, Mahajava, Shishumaramukhi, Shveta, Lohitakshi, Vibhishana, Jatalika, Kamachari, Dirghajihva, Balotkata, Kaledika, Vamanika, Mukuta, Lohitakshi, Mahakaya, Haripindi, Ekakshara, Sukusuma, Krishnakarni, Kshurakarni, Chatushkarni, Karnapravarana, Chatushpathaniketa, Gokarni, Mahishanana, Kharakarni, Mahakarni, Bherisvanamahasvana, Shankhakumbhasvana, Bhangada, Mahabala, Gana, Sugana, Bhiti, Kamada, Chatushpatharata, Bhutitirtha, Anyagochara, Pashuda, Vittada, Sukhada, Mahayasha, Poyada, Gomahishada, Suvishana, Pratishtha, Supratishtha, Rochamana, Surochana, Gokarni, Sukarni, Sasira, Stherika, Ekachakra, Megharava, Meghamala, Virochana. O king! O Indra among kings! O lord of the earth! O descendant of the Bharata lineage! There were these and many other matrikas. O bull among the Bharata lineage! Thousands of them followed Kartikeya, in many different forms. They had long nails and long teeth. O descendant of the Bharata lineage! Their mouths were long. They were simple, sweet, youthful and ornamented. They were full of greatness and could assume any form at will. O descendant of the Bharata lineage! Some didn't have any flesh on their bodies. Some were fair. Others possessed the complexion of gold. O bull among the Bharata lineage! Some were like dark clouds. Others were like smoke. Some immensely fortunate ones were red in hue, long in the hair and dressed in white garments. Some were in braids that were held up. Others were tawny-eyed and were attired in long girdles. Some had long stomachs and long ears. Others possessed drooping breasts. There were others who were coppery-eyed and green-eyed, with complexions like copper. O descendant of the Bharata lineage! They were the ones who granted boons. They could travel anywhere at will and were always cheerful. O scorcher of enemies! O bull among the Bharata lineage! O descendant of the Bharata lineage! Some assumed the traits of Yama, Rudra, Soma, the immensely strong Kubera, Varuna, the great Indra, Agni, Vayu, Kumara and Brahma. They were like apsaras in their beauty and like the wind in speed. They were like cuckoos in their voice and like the lord of riches in prosperity. They were like Shakra in their valour and like the fire in their resplendence. They lived on trees and open plains. Others made their abodes at crossroads. Some lived in caves and cremation grounds. Others made their abodes in mountains and springs. They wore many kinds of ornaments. They were attired in diverse kinds of garlands and garments. They were dressed in many kinds of clothing. They spoke many different kinds of languages. There were large numbers of others, terrifying to enemies. On the instructions of Indra of the gods, they followed the great-souled one.

'O tiger among kings! The illustrious chastiser of Paka[150] gave Guha[151] a javelin, for the destruction of the enemies of the gods. O bull among the Bharata lineage! It possessed large bells and made a loud noise. It blazed and was sparkling in complexion. He also gave him a flag, with the complexion of the rising sun. Pashupati gave him a large army consisting of all kinds of beings who were fierce and wielded many kinds of weapons. They possessed austerities, valour and strength. Vishnu gave him a garland that ensured victory and increased one's powers. Uma gave him two garments that were as resplendent as the sun. Ganga gave him a supreme and celestial water pot that was created from amrita. In delight, Brihaspati gave Kumara a staff. Garuda gave him his beloved son, a peacock with colourful feathers. Aruna gave him a red-crested cock, which used its feet as weapons. King Varuna gave him a noose that possessed strength and valour. The lord Brahma gave him, devoted as he was to brahmanas, a black antelope skin. The creator of the worlds also granted him victory in battles. Having become the general of the large numbers of gods, Skanda blazed in radiance. He was like the rays of a second fire god. He was accompanied by the companions and the matrikas and the terrible army of the nairrtas.[152] The flags were decorated with bells. There were penants and weapons. There were drums, conch shells and larger drums. The army looked like the autumn sky, decorated with stars. That army of the gods and army of the bhutas advanced. They fiercely played on their musical

[150]Indra.
[151]Kartikeya's name.
[152]Demons.

instruments, the drums and the conch shells. A large sound was created by the tambourines, *jharjharas*,[153] *krakachas*,[154] trumpets made of cow horn, trumpets,[155] *gomukhas*[156] and smaller drums.[157] All the gods, together with Vasava, praised Kumara. The gods and gandharvas sang and large numbers of apsaras danced.

'Delighted, Mahasena[158] granted a boon to the gods. "In the battle, I will kill the enemies who desire to slay you." Having obtained this boon from that god, all the gods were delighted. The great-souled ones thought that their enemies had already been killed. All the large numbers of bhutas raised a roar of delight. Once they had been granted this boon by the great-souled one, this roar filled the three worlds. Mahasena advanced, surrounded by a large army, for the sake of the protection of the gods and the destruction of the daityas. O lord of men! Resolution, Victory, dharma, Success, Prosperity, Fortitude and Learning[159] advanced ahead of Mahasena's terrible army, who were armed with spears, clubs, maces, bludgeons, iron arrows, javelins and spikes in their hands. They roared like proud lions. The god Guha advanced.

'On seeing him, all the daityas, rakshasas and danavas became anxious and frightened. They fled in all the directions. With diverse weapons in their hands, the gods pursued them. On seeing this, Skanda, energetic and powerful, became enraged. The illustrious one repeatedly used the javelin as a weapon.[160] He displayed his energy, like a fire into which oblations have been poured. The infinintely energetic Skanda repeatedly used the javelin as a weapon. O great king! Like a blazing meteor, it fell down on the ground. Lightning and thunder also descended on the earth. O king! Everything was terrible, like at the time of destruction. O bull among the Bharata

[153]Kind of drum.
[154]Kind of musical instrument.
[155]*Adambara*. Alternatively, drum.
[156]Kind of musical instrument.
[157]*Dindimas*.
[158]Kartikeya.
[159]All in personified form.
[160]The one he received from Indra.

lineage! Whenever, Agni's son hurled the extremely terrible javelin, crores of javelins issued from it. The Indra among the daityas was named Taraka. He was extremely strong and brave. The illustrious lord used the weapon of the javelin to slay him[161] in the battle and also another ten thousand brave and powerful daityas who were around him. In the battle, he slew Mahisha and eight *padma*s who surrounded him.[162] He slew Tripada and ten million who surrounded him. The lord then killed Hradodara and ten billion who surrounded him. He also slew his followers, who had diverse weapons in their hands. O king! As they slaughtered the enemy, Kumara's followers roared loudly and filled the ten directions. O Indra among kings! The weapon of the javelin generated flames in every direction and consumed thousands of daityas. Others were killed because of Skanda's roars. Some enemies of the gods were killed by the flags. Some were frightened by the bells and fell down on the ground. Some were mangled by the weapons and fell down, deprived of their lives. There were many such who hated the gods, powerful assassins. The immensely strong and valiant Kartikeya slaughtered them in the encounter.

'Bali's son was the immensely strong daitya named Bana. He resorted to Mount Krouncha and fought against the large numbers of the gods. The intelligent Mahasena advanced against that enemy of the gods. Terrified of Kartikeya, he hid inside Krouncha. The illustrious Kartikeya was overcome by great rage. He shattered Krouncha with the javelin that had been given to him by Agni and because of the shriek, it was called Krouncha.[163] The mountain had shala and *sarala*[164] trees and the apes and elephants that lived on

[161]Taraka.

[162]Mahisha is a demon in the form of a buffalo. In some accounts, he was killed by Durga/Parvati. In others, he was killed by Skanda. A padma is a large number.

[163]There is a slight anomaly, because we have been told that the javelin was given by Indra, not Agni. Krouncha is a curlew/snipe. When it was shattered, the mountain shrieked like a curlew/snipe and got its name. Mount Krouncha is believed to be in Bellary district of Karnataka.

[164]Pine.

it were terrified. The birds rose up in terror and the serpents fell down. Large numbers of monkeys[165] and bears shrieked in fear and fled. The place echoed with the sounds of antelopes running away. When the mountain was shattered and fell down, *sharabhas*[166] and lions were overtaken by a calamity and suddenly ran away. But it was very beautiful. Vidyadharas who dwelt on the peak rose up into the air. The kinnaras were anxious, because they were struck by the descent of the javelin. Hundreds and thousands of daityas were crushed. They emerged from that blazing mountain, attired in excellent and colourful ornaments and garlands. Kumara's followers proved to be superior and killed them in the battle. Pavaka's son,[167] the destroyer of enemy heroes, shattered Krouncha with the javelin. The great-souled one divided himself into one, and also many forms. In the encounter, he repeatedly hurled the javelin from his hands. Thus, did Pavaka's son repeatedly show his powers. He shattered Krouncha and killed hundreds of daityas.

'Thus did the illustrious god slaughter the enemies of the gods. The gods were supremely delighted. O king! O descendant of the Bharata lineage! They sounded drums and blew on conch shells. The wives of the gods showered down excellent flowers. An auspicious breeze, mixed with celestial fragrances, began to blow. Some describe the lord as the eldest of all of Brahma's sons, Sanatkumara.[168] Some describe him as the son of Maheshvara, others as the son of Vibhavasu. Others speak of him as the son of Uma, the Krittikas or Ganga. The immensely strong one is in one form, or two forms, or four forms. The god, who is the lord of yoga, is in hundreds and thousands of forms.

'O king! I have thus told you about Kartikeya's consecration. Now listen to the most sacred of tirthas along the Sarasvati. O great king! After the enemies of the gods had been killed by Kumara, it became foremost among the tirthas and was like heaven itself. Pavaka's

[165]*Golangula*, the cow-tailed black monkey.

[166]Mythical animal similar to a lion, which feeds on lions.

[167]Pavaka is one of Agni's names.

[168]Usually, it is said that four sons were born to Brahma through his mental powers—Sanatkumara, Sanaka, Sanatana and Sanandana, though seven sons are sometimes also mentioned. Sanatkumara is believed to have reappeared as Kartikeya.

son gave the foremost of nairrtas separate dominions and riches in different parts of the three worlds. O great king! The illustrious destroyer of the lineage of the daityas was consecrated by the gods as the general of the celestials in that tirtha. O bull among the Bharata lineage! Earlier, large number of gods had consecrated Varuna as the lord of the waters in that tirtha and it had been known by the name of Oujasa. Having bathed in that tirtha and having worshipped Skanda, the wielder of the plough donated gold, garments and ornaments to the brahmanas. Madhava, the destroyer of enemy heroes, spent a night there. The wielder of the plough worshipped that supreme of tirthas and touched the waters there. The best of the Madhava lineage was cheerful and delighted. I have told you everything that you had asked me, about how the illustrious Skanda was consecrated by the assembled gods.'

Chapter 1265(46)

Janamejaya said, 'O brahmana! What I have heard from you is exceedingly wonderful. You have told me in detail about how Kumara was duly consecrated. O one rich in austerities! After hearing this, I know that I have been purified. My body hair has stood up and my mind is delighted. After hearing about Kumara's consecration and the slaughter of the daityas, I am supremely happy. However, I am still curious. How was the lord of the waters consecrated by the gods and the asuras? O immensely wise one! O supreme one! You are skilled in narrating. Tell me about this.'

Vaishampayana replied, 'O king! Listen to this wonderful account, exactly as it happened in another kalpa.[169] During that original

[169]We have deliberately retained the word kalpa, since a kalpa is much more than an era (yuga). It is more like an aeon or epoch. A cycle of *satya* (or krita) yuga, *treta* yuga, *dvapara* yuga and *kali* yuga constitutes a *mahayuga* and 1000 mahayugas constitute a kalpa, one of Brahma's days. A kalpa is divided into fourteen *manvantara*, with a Manu presiding over each of these.

krita yuga, all the gods assembled, went to Varuna in the proper fashion and said, "Just as Shakra, lord of the gods, always protects us from fear, in that way, you become the lord of all the rivers. O god! Always dwell in the ocean, the abode of makaras. May the ocean, the lord of the rivers, be under your control. Together with Soma,[170] you will also wax and wane." Varuna spoke to the gods, signifying his acceptance. All of them assembled and made Varuna, whose abode was the ocean, the lord of the waters, in accordance with the decreed rites. Having consecrated Varuna as the lord of the waters, the gods worshipped the lord of the waters and returned to their respective abodes. The immensely illustrious Varuna was thus consecrated by the gods. In accordance with what was required, he protected flowing water, oceans, rivers and lakes, like Shatakratu protects the gods. The immensely wise destroyer of Pralamba[171] touched the waters there and gave away many riches. He then went to Agnitirtha. The fire god was destroyed there and became invisible inside shami. O unblemished one! When the lord and light-giver of the worlds disappeared in this way, the great-souled gods presented themselves before the grandfather of all the worlds and said, "The illustrious Agni has disappeared and we do not know the reason. Let all the worlds not be destroyed. Please create fire again."'

Janamejaya asked, 'Why was the illustrious Agni, the creator of all the worlds, destroyed? How did the gods discover him again? Please tell me everything about this.'

Vaishampayana replied, 'The powerful fire god was extremely frightened because of Bhrigu's curse.[172] The illustrious one sought refuge inside a shami tree and could no longer be seen. When the fire god disappeared, all the gods, together with Vasava, were extremely

[170]The moon.

[171]Name of a demon killed by Balarama.

[172]The sage Bhrigu's wife was Puloma. A demon was enamoured of her and asked Agni who she was. To avoid telling a lie, Agni said that she was the sage Bhrigu's wife. The demon abducted her. At that time, Puloma was pregnant and had a miscarriage. Though the child (Chyavana) survived, Bhrigu cursed Agni for revealing Puloma's identity. The curse was that Agni would devour everything. The story has been recounted in Section 1 (Volume 1).

unhappy. They searched for the fire that had vanished. Having reached Agnitirtha, they found Agni inside a shami tree. They found the fire god dwelling there. O tiger among men! With Brihaspati at the forefront, and with Vasava, all the gods were delighted at having found the fire god. They returned to the places that they had come from and he became the devourer of everything. O lord of the earth! Bhrigu was knowledgeable about the brahman and this happened because of his curse. Having bathed there, the intelligent one[173] went to Brahmayoni. In earlier times, the illustrious lord Brahma, the grandfather of all the worlds, had bathed there, with the gods, in accordance with the rites that are laid down for the gods. Having bathed there, he[174] gave away many riches. He then went to the tirtha named Koubera. O king! The lord Ailabila tormented himself through great austerities there and became the lord of riches. O king! O best of men! At that spot, many stores of riches manifested themselves before him.[175] The one with the plough presented himself at that tirtha. Having gone and bathed there, in the prescribed way, he gave away riches to the brahmanas. He saw the place known as Koubera, with the best of groves. In earlier times, the extremely great-souled King Kubera tormented himself through great austerities there and obtained a large number of boons. He became the lord of riches and became a friend of the infinitely energetic Rudra. He became a god and a guardian of the world there. He also obtained a son named Nalakubara. O mighty-armed one! The lord of riches swiftly obtained all these things there. Large numbers of Maruts assembled there and consecrated him. He also obtained a vehicle there, yoked to beautiful horses. This was the celestial vimana Pushpaka. He also got the riches of the gods. O king! Having bathed there, Bala gave away many kinds of gifts. Smearing himself with white sandalwood paste, Rama quickly went to the tirtha known as Badarapachana. It

[173]Balarama.

[174]Balarama.

[175]According to some accounts, Vishrava was the son of Pulastya and Vishrava's wife was Ilavida or Ilavila. The son of this union was Ailavida or Ailabila. Ailabila performed austerities and became Kubera, the lord of riches.

was inhabited by all kinds of living beings. Auspicious flowers and fruit are always found in the groves there.'

Chapter 1266(47)

Vaishampayana said, 'Rama then went to the supreme tirtha of Badarapachana. Many ascetics and Siddhas roamed around there. Bharadvaja's daughter was unmatched on earth in beauty. The maiden was firm in her vows. O lord! Her name was Sruchavati and the maiden observed brahmacharya. O king! She performed severe austerities and observed many rules. The beautiful one had made up her mind to obtain the king of the gods as her husband. O extender of the Kuru lineage! A long period of time passed. She continued to observe those terrible rituals, which are extremely difficult for women to observe. O lord of the earth! The illustrious chastiser of Paka was supremely delighted because of her conduct, austerities and devotion. The lord, the king of the thirty gods, arrived at the hermitage, assuming the form of the great-souled brahmana rishi, Vasishtha. O descendant of the Bharata lineage! On seeing Vasishtha, supreme among ascetics and the performer of fierce austerities, she worshipped him. The fortunate one, knowledgeable about rules and sweet in speech said, "O illustrious one! O tiger among sages! O lord! What is your command? O one who is excellent in vows! I will give you everything, in accordance with my capacity. However, because I am devoted to Shakra, I will not be able to give you my hand. O one who is rich in austerities! My vows, rules and austerities are an attempt to satisfy Shakra, the lord of the three worlds." Having been thus addressed, the illustrious god smiled and glanced at her. O descendant of the Bharata lineage! He assured the one who knew about rules and said, "O one good in vows! I know that you are performing fierce austerities. O fortunate one! O one with a beautiful face! All the objectives that you have in your heart will be obtained. Everything can be obtained through austerities.

Everything is established in austerities. O one with an auspicious face! All the celestial states of the gods can be obtained through austerities. Austerities are the source of great happiness. Those men, who perform great austerities and cast aside their bodies on earth, obtain the status of gods. O fortunate one! Listen to these words of mine! O immensely fortunate one! O one who is auspicious in vows. Cook these berries."[176] Having asked her to boil them, the illustrious slayer of Bala went away. Having asked the fortunate one, he went to an excellent spot that was not far from that hermitage, so as to chant and meditate there. O great king! This is famous in the three worlds as Indratirtha.

'The illustrious chastiser of Paka wished to test her. Hence, the lord of the gods asked her to boil those berries. O king! Cleansed of sin, the humble one tried to do this. She purified herself and offered kindling into a fire. O tiger among kings! The one who was great in her vows began to boil those berries. O bull among men! As she boiled them, a long period of time passed. The berries were not boiled and the day was over. The wood that she had stored was consumed by the fire. On seeing that the fire no longer had any wood, she began to burn her body. At first, the beautiful one thrust her feet into the fire. As her feet were repeatedly burnt, the unblemished one paid no attention to this. The unblemished one did not think about her feet being burnt. So as to please the maharshi, the lotus-eyed one bore this misery. Her face was cheerful. On witnessing her deed, the lord of the three worlds was pleased. He displayed his own self to the maiden. The best of the gods spoke these words to the maiden, who was extremely firm in her vows. "O fortunate one! I am pleased with your devotion, austerities and rituals. O beautiful one! Everything that you wish for will be obtained. O immensely fortunate one! You will cast aside this body and live with me in heaven. This supreme tirtha will be established in this world. O one with the beautiful brows! It will clean all sins and be known by the name of Badarapachana. It will

[176]A berry or jujube is *badara* and *pachana* is to cook, in this case, boil. Hence the name Badarapachana.

be famous in the three worlds and will be praised by brahmarshis. O immensely fortunate one! O beautiful one! In ancient times, in this supreme tirtha, the *saptarshi*s had left Arundhati[177] and gone to the Himalayas. Those immensely fortunate ones, rigid in their vows, went there to collect fruits and roots for their sustenance. For the sake of their sustenance, they dwelt in the forests of the Himalayas and there was a drought that lasted for twelve years. Having constructed a hermitage for themselves, the ascetics dwelt there. The fortunate Arundhati always performed austerities. On seeing that Arundhati was observing fierce rituals, the three-eyed one, the granter of boons, the immensely illustrious Mahadeva, was extremely pleased. Assuming the form of a brahmana, he arrived there. The god approached her and said, 'O fortunate one! I am looking for alms.' The beautiful one replied to the brahmana, 'O brahmana! Our store of food has been exhausted. Eat these berries.' Mahadeva said, 'O one who is good in vows! Cook these berries.' Having been thus addressed, wishing to please the brahmana, she began to cook those berries. The illustrious one offered kindling in the fire and placed the berries on that. She listened to divine, beautiful and sacred accounts.[178] Those twelve years of terrible drought passed. She was without food and was cooking, listening to those auspicious accounts. That extremely terrible period passed, as if it was a single day. Having obtained fruits, the sages returned from the mountain. The illustrious one[179] was pleased with Arundhati and spoke to her. 'O one who knows about dharma! Approach the rishis, as you used to do earlier. O one who knows about dharma! I am pleased with your austerities and your rituals.' The illustrious Hara then showed himself in his own form. He spoke to them[180] about the greatness of her conduct. 'You have earned merit from the austerities you have performed on the slopes of the Himalayas. O brahmanas! But it is my view that what she has earned through

[177]Vasishtha's wife.

[178]Shiva told her these, while the berries were being cooked.

[179]Shiva.

[180]The rishis.

her austerities is equal to that. This ascetic has tormented herself through extremely difficult austerities. While fasting, she has spent twelve years in cooking.' The illustrious one then spoke to Arundhati again. 'O fortunate one! Ask for the boon that is in your heart.' In the presence of the saptarshis, the one with the large and coppery eyes addressed the god. 'O illustrious one! If you are pleased with me, let this spot become an excellent tirtha. Let it be loved by the siddhas and the devarshis and let it be known by the name of Badarapachana. O god! O lord of the gods! If a person purifies himself[181] and fasts here for three days, let him obtain the fruits that are obtained from fasting for twelve years.' Hara agreed to this and returned to heaven. On seeing this, and on seeing the virtuous Arundhati, who was capable of withstanding hunger and thirst and was yet not exhausted or pale, the rishis were astounded. Thus did the pure Arundhati attain supreme success. O immensely fortunate one! O one who is good in vows! You have done the same for my sake. O fortunate one! Your vows have been dedicated to me. Therefore, pleased with your observance of rules, I will grant you this special boon today. O fortunate one! Ask for a special and supreme boon, which is superior to the boon granted to Arundhati by the great-souled one. Through his favours and because of your energy, in accordance with the prescribed rites, I will grant you another boon. Whoever controls himself[182] and spends a night in this tirtha and bathes here, will, after casting aside his body, obtain worlds that are extremely difficult to get." Having spoken to Sruchavati, the thousand-eyed god, the illustrious and powerful one, returned again to heaven. O king! O foremost among the Bharata lienage! When the wielder of the vajra had left, celestial flowers, with divine fragrances, showered down there. In every direction, drums sounded with a loud roar. O lord of the earth! A breeze, laced with auspicious scents, began to blow. Having cast aside her body, the sacred one became Indra's wife. She obtained him through her fierce austerities and pleasured with the undecaying one.'

[181]The text is gender neutral. But that is difficult to render in English.

[182]Gender neutral again.

Janamejaya asked, 'Who was the illustrious mother of that beautiful one? How was she reared? O brahmana! I wish to hear this. My curiousity is supreme.'

Vaishampayana replied, 'On seeing the large-eyed apsara Gritachi, the seed of the great-souled brahmana rishi, Bharadvaja, fell. The one who was supreme among those who meditate, picked that seed up in his hand. It was kept in a cup made of leaves and the beautiful one was born from this.[183] All her birth rites were performed by the one who was rich in austerities. The great sage, Bharadvaja, also named her. In the presence of a large number of rishis, the great-souled one gave her the name of Sruchavati. Leaving her in that hermitage, he returned to the slopes of the Himalayas. The immensely generous one[184] bathed there and gave away riches to the great brahmanas. Extremely controlled in his soul, the foremost of the Vrishni lineage then went to Shakra's tritha.'

Chapter 1267(48)

Vaishampayana said, 'The strong and foremost one among the Yadu lineage then went to Indratirtha. In accordance with the prescribed rites, having given riches and jewels to the brahmanas, he bathed there. The king of the immortals had performed a hundred horse sacrifices there. The lord of the gods had also given a large quantity of riches to Brihaspati. As instructed by those who are learned about the Vedas, he had incessantly performed sacrifices there and given away all the indicated gifts. O foremost among the Bharata lineage! The immensely radiant one had performed one hundred sacrifices. Having performed them in the prescribed way, he had become famous as Shatakratu.[185] That sacred, auspicious

[183]The word *srijana* means something that is shed, explaining the name Sruchavati.

[184]Balarama.

[185]*Shata* is one hundred and *kratu* is sacrifice.

and eternal tirtha is named after him. It is famous as Indratirtha and cleanses from all sins. The one with the club as his weapon bathed there, in accordance with the prescribed rites. He honoured the brahmanas and gave them food, drink and garments.

'He then went to the auspicious and supreme tirtha known as Ramatirtha. The immensely fortunate Bhargava Rama,[186] the extremely great ascetic, subjugated the earth, slaying all the bulls among the kshatriyas. With his preceptor Kashyapa, supreme among sages, at the forefront, he performed a *vajapeya*[187] and one hundred horse sacrifices there. As a gift, he gave him[188] the entire earth, with all its oceans. O Janamejaya! Rama[189] gave riches to the brahmanas there. He bathed there and duly honoured the brahmanas. In that sacred tirtha in that auspicious land, the fair-complexioned one gave away riches and honoured the sages.

'He then went to Yamunatirtha. O lord of the earth! Fair in his complexion, the immensely fortunate Varuna, Aditi's son, had performed a rajasuya sacrifice there. Varuna, the slayer of enemy heroes, had performed that supreme sacrifice there, after defeating men and the gods in a battle. While that supreme sacrifice was going on, a battle commenced between the gods and the danavas and this led to destruction in the three worlds. O Janamejaya! After that excellent rajasuya sacrifice was over, there was a great and terrible clash among the kshatriyas. Madhava Rama, with the plough as his weapon, bathed in that supreme tirtha and gave away riches to the brahmanas. The delighted brahmanas praised Vanamali.[190]

'The lotus-eyed one then went to Adityatirtha. O supreme among kings! The illustrious and radiant sun god performed a sacrifice there and obtained power and lordship over the stellar bodies. O lord of the earth! All the gods, together with Vasava, the Vishvadevas and the Maruts, the gandharvas and the apsaras, Dvaipayana, Shuka,

[186]Parashurama.

[187]Kind of sacrifice.

[188]Kashyapa.

[189]This means Balarama now.

[190]Balarama's name. Literally, the one who wears a garland of wild flowers.

Madhusudana Krishna, the yakshas, the rakshasas and the pishachas are always there, on the banks of that river. O scorcher of enemies! That apart, many thousands of others who are successful in yoga are always present, in the sacred and auspicious tirtha on the Sarasvati. O foremost among the Bharata lineage! In earlier times, having slain the asuras Madhu and Kaitabha, Vishnu had bathed in that supreme and excellent tirtha. O descendant of the Bharata lineage! Dvaipayana, with dharma in his soul, had also bathed there and had obtained supreme success in yoga, accomplishing the ultimate objective. The great ascetics, rishis powerful in yoga, Asita and Devala, had resorted to supreme yoga there.'

Chapter 1268(49)

Vaishampayana said, 'In earlier times, Asita-Devala dwelt there.[191] He was a store of austerities and had dharma in his souls. He resorted to the dharma of a householder. He was pure and controlled and always devoted to dharma. The great ascetic never punished anyone. He treated all beings equally, in his deeds, thoughts and speech. O great king! He never resorted to anger and treated the pleasant and the unpleasant as equal. The great ascetic treated gold and stones equally. He honoured gods, guests and brahmanas. He was always devoted to brahmacharya and always devoted to dharma. O great king! Once, while that intelligent sage was controlled and engaged in *yoga* in that tirtha, a mendicant named Jaigishavya came to him. O king! The immensely radiant one began to dwell in Devala's hermitage. O great king! Always devoted to yoga, the great ascetic[192] attained success there. While the great sage Jaigishavya dwelt there, Devala always looked towards his

[191]Asita-Devala is sometimes described as a single sage and sometimes as two different sages. This is true of this section too. While the singular is generally used, in some shlokas, there is the dual too.

[192]Jaigishavya.

needs and never deviated from dharma. O great king! They spent a long period of time in this way. There was an occasion when Devala did not see the sage Jaigishavya. O Janamejaya! However, when it was time to take food, the intelligent mendicant, learned in dharma, presented himself before Devala. On seeing the great sage appear in the form of a mendicant, he honoured him greatly and was full of great delight. O descendant of the Bharata lineage! Devala honoured him to the best of his capacity, controlling himself in many ways and following the rites indicated by the rishis. O king! However, on one occasion, on seeing the immensely radiant sage, a grave thought arose in the mind of the great-souled Devala. "I have spent a long time, honouring him in many ways. However, this idle mendicant never speaks to me." Having thought this, Devala travelled through the sky and went to the great ocean, carrying a handsome pot with him. The one with dharma in his soul went to the ocean, the lord of the rivers. O descendant of the Bharata lineage! Having gone there, he found that Jaigishavya had reached before him. Seeing this, the lord Asita was supremely astounded. He thought, "How could the mendicant have arrived at the ocean and bathed here?"[193] Maharshi Asita thought in this way. Having bathed in the ocean in accordance with the rites and purifying himself, he chanted. O Janamejaya! The handsome one chanted, performed the daily rituals and returned to the hermitage, filling the pot with water. As the sage entered his hermitage, he saw Jaigishavya seated in the hermitage. Jaigishavya never spoke a word. The immensely ascetic one lived in that hermitage, as if he was a piece of wood. He was like an ocean. He[194] had seen him bathe in the waters of the ocean and now saw him enter the hermitage before him. O king! On seeing the powers of the ascetic Jaigishavya, immersed in yoga, the intelligent Asita-Devala began to think. O Indra among kings! The supreme among sages reflected. "How could I see him in the ocean and again in the hermitage?" O lord of the earth! The sage, learned in the use of mantras, thought in this way and then rose up

[193]Before Asita-Devala reached there.

[194]Asita-Devala.

into the sky from his hermitage. Devala wished to find out who the mendicant Jaigishavya was.

'As he travelled through the sky, he saw many controlled siddhas. He saw that those siddhas were worshipping Jaigishavya. Asita made efforts to be firm in his vows and was enraged at this. Devala next saw Jaigishavya ascend to heaven. He next saw him roaming around in the world of the ancestors. From the world of the ancestors, he saw him travel to Yama's world. From Yama's world, he rose to Soma's world. He saw the great sage Jaigishavya travel around in this way, ascending to the sacred worlds of those who perform special sacrifices. He next arose to the world of those who perform agnihotra sacrifices and worlds of ascetics who perform *darsha* and *pournamasa* sacrifices.[195] The intelligent one saw him in the worlds meant for those who sacrifice with animals and roaming around in the unblemished worlds revered by the gods. He went to the regions meant for ascetics who perform many *chaturmasya* sacrifices,[196] those who perform *agnishtoma* sacrifices and also ascetics who perform *agnishtuta* sacrifices. Devala saw him reach all those regions. He saw him in the worlds meant for the immensely wise ones who perform vajapeya, the best of sacrifices, and give away a lot of gold. Devala also saw Jaigishavya in the worlds meant for the performers of *pundarika* and rajasuya sacrifices. He saw him in the worlds meant for the best of men who perform the best of sacrifices, ashvamedha and *naramedha*.[197] Devala saw Jaigishavya in the worlds meant for those who sacrifice everything that is difficult to obtain and for those who perform *soutramani* sacrifices.[198] O king! There are those who perform *dvadashaha*[199] and diverse other sacrifices. Devala saw Jaigishavya in the worlds meant for them. Asita next saw him

[195]Different kinds of sacrifices. Agnihotra sacrifices are performed with fire, darsha sacrifices on the day of the new moon and pournamasa sacrifices on the day of the full moon.

[196]Performed once every four months.

[197]Ashvamedha is a horse sacrifice, in which, a horse is sacrificed. In a naramedha sacrifice, a human being is sacrificed.

[198]Sacrifice in Indra's honour.

[199]Sacrifices that go on for twelve days.

attain the worlds of Mitra, Varuna, Adityas, the Rudras, the Vasus and Brihaspati's region. Asita saw him transcend all these worlds and go to Goloka[200] and the world meant for those who know about the brahman. Asita saw Jaigishavya go to all these worlds. Through his energy, he rose up, beyond the three worlds and was seen to travel to the worlds meant for those who are devoted to their husbands. O scorcher of enemies! However, then Asita could no longer see Jaigishavya, the supreme sage. Using his powers of yoga, he disappeared.

'The immensely fortunate Devala began to think about Jaigishavya's powers, the discipline of his vows and his unmatched success in the use of yoga. Asita controlled himself. He joined his hands in salutation and asked the supreme ones who were in the worlds of the siddhas and the revered ones who knew about the brahman. "I do not see Jaigishavya, the greatly energetic one. I wish to hear about him. My curiousity is great." The siddhas replied, "O Devala! O one who is firm in vows! Listen to the truth. Jaigishavya has gone to the eternal and undecaying world of the brahman. On hearing the words of the siddhas, who are knowledgeable about the brahman, Asita-Devala also tried to rise up, but swiftly fell down. At this, the siddhas again spoke to Devala. "O Devala! You cannot go where the one who is rich in austerities has gone. The brahmana Jaigishavya has attained the abode of the brahman." On hearing the words of the siddhas, Devala descended from those worlds, one after the other. Like an insect, he descended to his own sacred hermitage. As he entered, Devala saw Jaigishavya there. Devala, devoted to dharma, comprehended the powers of Jaigishavya, who was immersed in yoga.

'Having understood, Devala spoke to the great-souled Jaigishavya. O king! Bowing in humility, he approached the great sage. "O illustrious one! I wish to resort to the dharma that brings *moksha*."[201] On hearing these words, he[202] instructed him about

[200]Vishnu's world.

[201]Release, liberation, salvation, emancipation.

[202]Jaigishavya.

the rites of supreme yoga and about what the sacred texts say about what should be done and what should not be done. On seeing that he[203] had made up his mind about *sannyasa*,[204] the great ascetic told him about all the rites and the ordained tasks. On seeing that he had made up his mind about sannyasa, all the beings and the ancestors started to lament. "Who will henceforth feed us?" Having made up his mind to seek moksha, Devala heard the piteous lamentations of the beings in the ten directions. O descendant of the Bharata lineage! At this, the sacred fruits and roots and the flowers and the herbs began to lament, in their thousands. "The evil-minded and inferior Devala will sever us again. He has offered to save all the beings, but does not know what he is doing."[205] The supreme among sages used his intelligence to reflect on this again. "Which is superior, moksha or the dharma of a householder?" O supreme among kings! Having thought about this, Devala made up his mind. He abandonded the dharma of a householder and adopted the dharma of moksha. Having thought in this way, Devala made up his mind. O descendant of the Bharata lineage! Resorting to supreme yoga, he obtained supreme success. With Brihaspati at the forefront, the gods approached Jaigishavya and praised the ascetic's austerities. Narada, supreme among rishis, addressed the gods then. "Since he has astounded Asita, there are no austerities left in Jaigishavya."[206] The residents of heaven replied to the resolute one.[207] "Do not speak about the great sage Jaigishavya in this way." The great-souled wielder of the plough bathed there and gave away riches to the brahmanas. Having performed that supreme act of dharma, he then went to Soma's great tirtha.'

[203]Asita-Devala.

[204]Sannyasa cannot be satisfactorily rendered in English. Literally, it means resorting to the path of virtue. Loosely, it is the path of an ascetic who renounces the world. But it also means casting aside one's body.

[205]In case Asita-Devala gives up his pursuit of mokṣha and continues to feed the beings by plucking fruit, roots, flowers and herbs.

[206]Presumably because the austerities have been inappropriately used.

[207]Narada.

Chapter 1269(50)

Vaishampayana said, 'O descendant of the Bharata lineage! The lord of the stars performed a rajasuya sacrifice there. This was after the great Tarakamaya battle[208] had been fought. Having bathed there, the controlled Bala gave away gifts. The one with dharma in his soul then went to the tirtha of the sage Sarasvata. In ancient times, when a drought had lasted for twelve years, the sage Sarasvata, had taught the Vedas to many supreme brahmanas.'

Janamejaya asked, 'In ancient times, during the twelve years of drought, why did the sage Sarasvata, rich in austerities, teach the Vedas?'

Vaishampayana replied, 'O great king! In earlier times, there was an intelligent sage who was a great ascetic. He was known by the name of Dadhicha. He was a *brahmachari* and had control over his senses. Because of his austerities, the lord Shakra was always frightened.[209] But he could not tempt him by offering him many kinds of fruits.[210] To tempt him, the chastiser of Paka sent a celestial, sacred and beautiful apsara named Alambusa. O great king! The great-souled one was worshipping the gods on the banks of the Sarasvati and the beautiful one approached him there. Though the rishi was controlled in his senses, on seeing her beautiful form, his seed fell down into the Sarasvati and the river held it. O bull among men! On seeing the seed, the great river held it inside her, hoping that a son might be born in her womb. When it was time, the best of rivers gave birth to a son. O lord! With the son, she went to the rishi. The river saw that the supreme sage was in an assemblage of rishis. O Indra among kings! Handing over the son, she said, "O brahmarshi! This is your son. Out of my devotion towards you, I have borne him. When you saw Alambusa, your seed fell down into the water. O brahmarshi! Out of my devotion towards you, I bore it inside me. I had decided that your energy should not be destroyed. I am giving you this unblemished son. Accept him." Having been thus

[208]Famous battle fought between the gods and the demons.

[209]In case those powers were used to dislodge Indra.

[210]Indra could not tempt him away from his austerities.

addressed, he was supremely delighted and accepted him. Uttering mantras, the supreme among brahmanas inhaled the fragrance of his head. O supreme among the Bharata lineage! He embraced him for a long time. Delighted, the great sage granted Sarasvati a boon. "O immensely fortunate one! When your waters are offered as oblations, the Vishvadevas, the ancestors and large numbers of gandharvas and apsaras will be satisfied." Having said this, he praised the great river in these words. He was happy and supremely delighted. O king! Listen to this. "O immensely fortunate one! In earlier times, you have arisen from Brahma's lake. O best of rivers! Sages, rigid in their vows, know about you. O one who is beautiful to behold! You have always done that which brings me pleasure. O one with a beautiful complexion! This great son of yours will be known by the name of Sarasvata. This son of yours will be known by that name and will be the creator of worlds. He will be known by the name of Sarasvata and will be a great ascetic. O immensely fortunate one! When there is a drought for twelve years, he will teach the Vedas to bulls among the brahmanas. O beautiful one! Your waters will always be sacred. You will be the most sacred one. O immensely fortunate one! O Sarasvati! This is what you will obtain through my favours." The great river was thus praised and obtained that boon. O bull among the Bharata lineage! Taking the son with her, she cheerfully went away.

'At this time, there was a conflict between the gods and the danavas. In search of weapons, Shakra travelled around the three worlds. The illustrious Shakra could not find a weapon through which he could slay the enemies of the gods. Shakra told the gods, "I am incapable of slaying the great asuras who are the enemies of the thirty gods, without the bones of Dadhicha." The supreme gods then went to the best of rishis and said, "O Dadhicha! Give us the bones in your body, so that we can slay our enemies." Having been asked by the gods, the best of rishis did not hesitate. He carefully gave up his body and gave them the bones. Having performed an act that was beneficial to the gods, he obtained the eternal worlds. Shakra was delighted. He fashioned many celestial weapons with those bones—vajras, chakras, clubs and large staffs. Prajapati's son was Bhrigu, the creator of worlds, and that supreme rishi had obtained him[211] through his fierce austerities. He was large and energetic and had been created with the essence of the worlds. The lord[212] was famous and was as tall as the Himalayas, the greatest of mountains. The chastiser of Paka had always been anxious on account of his energy. O descendant of the Bharata lineage! The vajra was fashioned from that illustrious one[213] and invoked with mantras. It was created with great anger and possessed the energy of the brahman. With this, he[214] slaughtered ninety-nine brave ones among the daityas and the danavas.

'A long and fearful period passed since that time. O king! There was a drought that lasted for twelve years.[215] O king! Because of the twelve years of drought, the maharshis could not sustain themselves. Hungry, they fled in all the directions. On seeing that they were running away in different directions, the sage Sarasvata also made up his mind to leave. However, Sarasvati spoke to him. "O son! You need not go away. I will always give you food. I will always give you large fish. Stay here." O descendant of the Bharata lineage! Having been thus addressed, he remained there and offered oblations to the ancestors and the gods. He always sustained himself through this food and sustained the Vedas. When the period of drought was over, the maharshis wished to study again and asked each other. When they were afflicted by hunger, the proper knowledge of the Vedas had been destroyed. O Indra among kings! There was not a single one among them who could understand them. Some of those rishis came upon Sarasvata, supreme among rishis, when he had controlled his soul and was engaged in studying. They went to the others and told them about the unmatched Sarasvata, who was like an immortal. Alone in a solitary spot, he was studying. O king! All the maharshis arrived at that spot. The assembled ones spoke to Sarasvata, best

[211]Dadhicha.

[212]Dadhicha.

[213]From his bones.

[214]Indra.

[215]Indra killed Vritra with the vajra. Because of the crime of killing a brahmana, Indra hid for twelve years and a drought ensued.

among sages. They said, "Teach us." The sage replied, "Become my disciples in the ordained way." At this, the large number of rishis said, "O son! You are only a child." He replied to the sages, "I must act so that my dharma is not diminished. Those who teach without following dharma and those who learn without following dharma are quickly destroyed and come to hate each other. Rishis cannot claim to follow dharma on the basis of grey hair, riches or the number of relatives. One who can teach is alone great." Having heard his words, the sages duly[216] learnt the Vedas from him and began to practise dharma again. Sixty thousand sages became his disciples. Those brahmana rishis desired to study under Sarasvata. Though he was yet a child, each of those brahmana rishis brought a fistful of *darbha* grass to him,[217] offered him a seat and obeyed him. Rohini's immensely strong son, Keshava's elder brother, gave away riches there. Joyfully, and in due order, he then went to another great and famous tirtha, where an aged maiden had once lived.'

Chapter 1270(51)

Janamejaya asked, 'O illustrious one! In earlier times, why did the maiden dwell there, engaging in austerities? Why did she torment herself through austerities? What was her vow? O brahmana! I have heard supreme accounts of difficult deeds from you. Tell me everything. Why was she engaged in austerities?'

Vaishampayana replied, 'There was an immensely illustrious rishi. He was immensely energetic and his name was Kuni-Gargya. O king! His austerities were great and in austerities, he was supreme among ascetics. Through the powers of his mind, the lord generated a fair-browed daughter. On seeing her, the immensely illustrious Kuni-Gargya was extremely happy. O king! He gave up his body and went to heaven. The fortunate and fair-browed one had eyes

[216]They formally became his disciples.

[217]As a token of becoming a disciple.

like a lotus. The unblemished one undertook great hardships and performed fierce austerities. She fasted and worshipped and satisfied the ancestors and the gods. O king! While she was engaged in these terrible austerities, a long period of time elapsed. Her father had desired that she should be given away to a husband. However, she could not see a husband who was equal to her own self. She oppressed her mind and her body through those fierce austerities. In that deserted forest, she was devoted to worshipping the ancestors and the gods. O Indra among kings! Though she afflicted herself through austerities and was also overcome by old age, she did not regard herself to be exhausted. Finally, she was no longer capable of taking even a single step on her own. Therefore, she resolved to depart to the world hereafter.

'On seeing that she wished to free herself of her body, Narada told her, "O unblemished one! Which worlds can a maiden who has not been married go to? O one who is great in vows! This is what we have heard in the world of the gods. Though you have performed supreme austerities, you have not obtained any worlds for yourself." On hearing his words, she spoke in an assembly of rishis. "O supreme ones! I will give half of my austerities to anyone who accepts my hand." Hearing this, a rishi named Sringavan, Galava's son, accepted her hand. He proposed a pledge and told her, "O beautiful one! I will accept your hand with this pledge. You will live with me for only one night." Accepting this pledge, she gave him her hand. Galava's son accepted her hand and married her. O king! That night, she became young and as beautiful as a goddess. She was adorned in celestial ornaments and garments and adorned with divine garlands and unguents. On seeing her blazing beauty, Galava's son was delighted. He spent a night with her. In the morning, she told him, "O brahmana! O supreme among ascetics! The pledge that I had taken with you is over. O fortunate one! Since that has been accomplished, may you be at peace. I will leave." Obtaining his permission, she again said, "Anyone who controls himself and spends a night at this tirtha, offering oblations to the gods, will obtain the fruits that are obtained from observing brahmacharya for sixty-four years." Having said this, the virtuous one gave up her body and went to heaven. The rishi was distressed and thought of her beauty. Because of the agreement, though he found it difficult, he accepted half of her austerities. O foremost among the Bharata lineage! He was miserable because of the power of her beauty. He cast off his own body and followed her. This is the great account about the conduct of the aged maiden. While the one with the plough as his weapon was there, he heard about Shalya's death. O scorcher of enemies! He gave away gifts to the brahmanas there. He sorrowed that Shalya had been killed by the Pandavas in the battle. Madhava Rama then emerged through the gates of Samantapanchaka and asked the large number of rishis about what had transpired in Kurukshetra. O lord! Asked by the lion among the Yadu lineage, those great-souled ones told him everyting that had transpired in Kurukshetra, exactly as it had occurred.'

Chapter 1271(52)

'The rishis said, "O Rama! Samantapanchaka has been spoken of as Prajapati's eternal northern altar. In earlier times, the residents of heaven, the granters of great boons, performed a great sacrifice there. The intelligent and great-souled Kuru, best among royal sages and infinite in his energy, cheerfully cultivated this field. That is the reason this is known as Kurukshetra."[218]

'Rama asked, "Why did the great-souled Kuru cultivate this field? O stores of austerities! I wish to hear this. Tell me."

'The rishis replied, "O Rama! In earlier times, Kuru was always engaged in tilling this. On seeing this, Shakra came from heaven and asked him the reason. 'O king! Why are you making this supreme effort? O rajarshi! What is the reason for you to till this field?' Kuru said, 'O Shatakratu! Men who die in this field will go to the worlds reserved for those with meritorious deeds. They will be cleansed of their sins.' Laughing at this, the lord Shakra returned to heaven.

[218]*Kshetra* means field, Kurukshetra is Kuru's field.

The rajarshi was not distressed and continued to plough the earth. Shatakratu repeatedly came to him and repeatedly received the same reply. Disgusted, he repeatedly went away. The king continued to till the earth with great perseverance. Shakra told the other gods what the rajarshi was up to. On hearing this, the gods spoke these words to the one with one thousand eyes. 'O Shakra! If you can, grant the rajarshi a boon and stop him. If men can die here and go to heaven, without dutifully giving us a share in the sacrifices, we will have no existence left.' Shakra came to the rajarshi and told him, 'Do not make any more efforts. Listen to my words. O king! Men who fast here and give up their bodies, with all their senses intact, or those who are killed in battle, will certainly go to heaven. O Indra among kings! O immensely intelligent one! They will enjoy heaven.' King Kuru agreed to the words that Shakra had spoken. Having taken his leave and delighted in his mind, the slayer of Bala swiftly returned to heaven. O best among the Yadu lineage! In ancient times, this was thus ploughed by the rajarshi. Shakra promised great merits to those who give up their lives here. Shakra, the lord of the gods, himself composed a song about Kurukshetra and sang it. O one with the plough as his weapon! Listen to this. 'The dust of Kurukshetra, when blown away by the wind, will convey even those who perform wicked deeds to the supreme objective.' Bulls among the gods, supreme among the brahmanas, Nriga[219] and the best among kings, lions among men, have performed extremely expensive sacrifices here. They have given up their bodies and attained excellent ends. The region between Tarantuka and Arantuka, between Rama's lakes and Machakruka, is Kurukshetra Samantapanchaka.[220] It is known

[219]King famous for his generosity.

[220]There were believed to be four yakshas on the four corners of Kurukshetra. Tarantuka was on the north-east, now identified as Pipli. Arantuka was in the north-west, now identified as Behar Jaka, partly in Patiala and partly in Kaithal. Machakruka was in the south-east, now identified as Sinkh, in Panipat. Kapila yaksha was in the south-west, near Jind. This is also where Rama's lakes are. Parashurama is believed to have created five (pancha) lakes of blood, after killing the kshatriyas, one reason for the name Samantapanchaka. Another reason for the name Samantapanchaka is that it was five yojanas in every direction.

as Prajapati's northern altar. It is sacred, extremely auspicious and is revered by the residents of heaven. It possesses all the qualities of heaven. Therefore, all the lords of the earth who are slain here obtain the ends earmarked for great-souled ones."'

Chapter 1272(53)

Vaishampayana said, 'O Janamejaya! Having seen Kurukshetrra and having given away gifts, Satvata went to an extremely great and divine hermitage. It had groves of *madhuka* and mango trees and also plakshas and *nyagrodha*s. It had sacred *bilva*s, jackfruit and *arjuna*s.[221] On seeing that supreme place, marked with all the auspicious signs, the foremost among the Yadava lineage asked all the rishis whom that excellent hermitage belonged to. O king! All those great-souled ones told the one with the plough as his weapon, "O Rama! Listen to whom this hermitage belonged to in earlier times. In earlier times, the god Vishnu observed supreme austerities here. It is here that he performed all the eternal sacrifices, according to the prescribed rites. It was here that the brahmana lady observed brahmacharya from her youth and was immersed in yoga. Having attained success through her austerities, the ascetic lady went to heaven. O king! The great-souled Shandilya obtained a beautiful daughter. She was virtuous and firm in her vows. She always followed brahmacharya. Having achieved supreme yoga, she went to the excellent place of heaven. In this hermitage, the auspicious one obtained the fruits that can be got through the performance of a horse sacrifice. The immensely fortunate one was controlled in her soul. She was revered and went to heaven." The bull among the Yadu lineage went to the sacred hermitage and saw it. Having greeted the rishis who dwelt along the slopes of the Himalayas, Achyuta began to climb that mountain.

[221]Madhuka is a kind of tree. Plaksha is the religious fig tree. Nyagrodha is the Indian fig tree. Bilva is bel and arjuna is a tall tree.

'The powerful one, with the palm tree on his banner, had only advanced a short distance along that mountain. He then saw a supreme and sacred tirtha and was overcome by great wonder. Bala saw the powers of the Sarasvati at Plakshaprasravana. He reached the supreme and excellent tirtha of Karapachana. The immensely strong wielder of the plough gave away gifts there. He bathed in the cool waters and, extremely happy, went to the hermitage of Mitra and Varuna. This was the region of Karapachana, along the Yamuna. It was the place where Indra, Agni and Aryama had obtained great happiness. The one with dharma in his soul went and bathed there. He obtained supreme satisfaction. The immensely strong bull among the Yadu lineage seated himself with the rishis and the siddhas and listened to their sacred accounts.

'While Rama was seated among them at that spot, the illustrious rishi Narada arrived there. He had matted hair. The great ascetic was attired in garments with a golden complexion. O king! He had a golden staff and a water pot in his hands. The lute, the melodious veena that made a pleasant noise, was in his hands.[222] He was skilled in dancing and singing and was worshipped by the gods and the brahmanas. However, he was also one who provoked quarrels and always loved dissension.[223] He came to the spot where the handsome Rama was. All of them stood up and honoured the one who was careful in his vows. He[224] asked the devarshi about what had happened to the Kurus. O king! Narada knew about all forms of dharma and told him everything as it had occurred and about the destruction of the Kurus. Rohini's son was distressed and asked Narada, "How are the kshatriyas? How are the kings? O one who is rich in austerities! I have heard everything about this earlier. But I wish to hear it in detail. I am curious."

'Narada replied, "Bhishma, Drona and the lord of Sindhu have

[222]The text uses the word *kacchapi*. This means a lute, which is the sense in which we have translated it. However, this could also mean that the veena was made of tortoise shell.

[223]Narada liked to incite quarrels.

[224]Balarama.

been killed earlier. Vaikartana Karna and his maharatha sons have been slain. O Rohini's son! So have Bhurishrava and the valiant king of Madra. So have many other extremely strong ones. For the sake of pleasing the Kouravas, they have given up their lives. The kings and princes refused to retreat in the battle. O mighty-armed one! O Madhava! Listen to the ones who have not been killed. Dhritarashtra's powerful son, Kripa, the valiant Bhoja and the brave Ashvatthama are left. But with the soldiers routed, they have fled in different directions. When the soldiers were slain and Kripa and the others ran away, Duryodhana was overcome by great grief and has entered the lake Dvaipayana. Dhritarashtra's son is lying down there, having turned the waters to stone. O Rama! The Pandavas and Krishna approached and, from every direction, have tormented the powerful one with harsh and eloquent words. The brave one has arisen and has grasped a mighty club. O Rama! The extremely terrible encounter with Bhima is about to commence and will take place today. O Madhava! If you are curious, go there without any delay. If you so desire, witness that extremely terrible encounter between your two disciples."'

Vaishampayana said, 'Hearing Narada's words, he[225] honoured the bulls among the brahmanas and took their leave. He asked all those who had come with him to leave. He requested his attendants to return to Dvaraka. He descended from the best of mountains and from the sacred Plakshaprasravana. Having heard about the great fruits that could be obtained from that tirtha, Rama was delighted. In the presence of the brahmanas, Achyuta also sang a shloka. "Where can one obtain delight like the one obtained from dwelling along the Sarasvati? Where can one obtain qualities like those obtained from dwelling along the Sarasvati? Having approached Sarasvati, people go to heaven. The river Sarasvati should always be remembered. Sarasvati is the most sacred of rivers. Sarasvati always bestows happiness on the worlds. Even those who have performed extremely wicked deeds approach Sarasvati and do not have to sorrow, in this

[225]Balarama.

world or in the next." In delight, he repeatedly glanced towards Sarasvati. The scorcher of enemies then ascended an excellent chariot to which horses had been yoked. The bull among the Yadu lineage ascended the chariot that could travel fast. He wished to witness the encounter that was going to take place between his two disciples.'

SECTION SEVENTY-SEVEN

Gada Yuddha Parva

This parva has 546 shlokas and eleven chapters.

Chapter 1273(54): 44 shlokas
Chapter 1274(55): 44 shlokas
Chapter 1275(56): 67 shlokas
Chapter 1276(57): 59 shlokas
Chapter 1277(58): 24 shlokas
Chapter 1278(59): 44 shlokas
Chapter 1279(60): 65 shlokas
Chapter 1280(61): 40 shlokas
Chapter 1281(62): 73 shlokas
Chapter 1282(63): 43 shlokas
Chapter 1283(64): 43 shlokas

Gada *means a club and* yuddha *means a fight or encounter. This section is named after Bhima and Duryodhana's encounter with the clubs, where, Bhima strikes Duryodhana unfairly and brings him down. Krishna goes to Hastinapura and pacifies Dhritarashtra and Gandhari.*

Chapter 1273(54)

Vaishampayana said, 'O Janamejaya! Thus did that terrible encounter take place. In misery, King Dhritarashtra spoke these words. "Rama[1] reached the spot where the duel with the clubs was to take place. O Sanjaya! On seeing this, how did my son fight back against Bhima?"

'Sanjaya said, "Seeing that Rama was present, your son, the mighty-armed and valiant Duryodhana, who desired to fight, was delighted. O descendant of the Bharata lineage! On seeing the wielder of the plough, the king[2] stood up, filled with great delight. He[3] told Yudhishthira, 'O lord of the earth! I will swiftly go to Samantapanchaka. In the world of the gods, it is known as Prajapati's northern sacrificial altar. It is eternal and the most sacred spot in the three worlds. It is certain that someone who is killed there will attain heaven.'[4] O great king! Yudhishthira, Kunti's son, agreed to these words. The brave lord[5] advanced in the direction of Samantapanchaka. At this, King Duryodhana also picked up a gigantic club. The immensely radiant and intolerant one advanced on foot, with the Pandavas. As he advanced on foot, armoured and mailed, and with the club in his hand, the gods in the firmament uttered words of praise and honoured him. On seeing this, the men who were bards were also filled with joy. Surrounded by the Pandavas, the king of the Kurus, your son, advanced—adopting the gait of a crazy king of elephants. Conch shells sounded and there was the great roar of drums. The brave ones roared like lions and filled all the directions. With your son, they went to the western direction that had been appointed. Having gone there, they spread themselves out in all the directions. This was a supreme tirtha on the southern banks of the Sarasvati. At that spot, the ground was not sandy and they chose this for the encounter.

'"Bhima was armoured and grasped an extremely thick club. O great king! In that resplendent form, he looked like Garuda. O king!

[1]Balarama.

[2]Yudhishthira.

[3]Balarama.

[4]That is, they would go to Samantapanchaka. The encounter would take place there, rather than near Lake Dvaipayana.

[5]Yudhishthira.

For the encounter, your son fixed a helmet and was clad in golden armour. He was as dazzling as a golden mountain. The brave Bhima and Duryodhana were both attired in armour. In that encounter, they were as resplendent as angry elephants. Those two brothers, bulls among men, were stationed in that field of battle. O great king! They were as beautiful as the rising moon and the sun. They glanced towards each other, like two angry and giant elephants. O king! Wishing to kill each other, they burnt each other down with their eyes. O king! Delighted, Kourava[6] grasped the club. O king! His eyes were red with anger. He sighed and licked the corners of his mouth. The valiant King Duryodhana also grasped a club. He glanced towards Bhimasena, like an elephant towards another elephant. The valiant Bhima also picked up one[7] that possessed the essence of stone and challenged the king, like a lion against another lion in the forest. Duryodhana and Vrikodara raised the clubs in their hands. In that encounter, they looked like mountains with peaks. Both of them were extremely angry and were terrible in their valour. In battling with clubs, both of them were the disciples of Rohini's intelligent son. They were the equals of each other in their deeds, like Yama and Vasava. In their deeds, they were the equals of the immensely strong Varuna. O great king! As warriors, they were the equals of Madhu and Kaitabha.[8] In their deeds in a battle, they were the equals of Sunda and Upansunda.[9] Those scorchers of enemies were like Destiny and like Death. They rushed towards each other, like two crazy and giant elephants, as if they were proud and maddened in the autumn season, desiring to have intercourse.[10] O bull among the Bharata lineage! They were like crazy elephants that wished to defeat each other. Like blazing serpents, they seemed to vomit out the poison of wrath towards each other. Those scorchers of enemies angrily glanced towards each other. Both those tigers of the Bharata

[6]Meaning Bhima.

[7]A club.

[8]Demons killed by Vishnu.

[9]Famous demons.

[10]The image is of two bull elephants, contending over the same she-elephant.

lineage were full of valour. In fighting with clubs, those two destroyers of enemies were as unassailable as lions. Those two brave warriors were difficult to withstand, like tigers armed with claws and teeth. They were like two agitated oceans, impossible to cross, that were about to destroy beings. The angry maharathas scorched, like the one with the red limbs and rays.[11] The great-souled and immensely strong ones blazed. The best ones among the Kuru lineage were like two suns that had arisen at the time of destruction. They were as angry as tigers and roared like monsoon clouds. The mighty-armed ones were as cheerful as lions with manes. They were as angry as elephants and flamed like the fire. The great-souled ones were seen to be like mountains with peaks. Their lips were swollen in rage and they glanced towards each other. With clubs in their hands, those best of men clashed against each other. Both of them were extremely delighted and also revered each other.[12] They seemed to neigh like well-trained horses and trumpet like elephants. Duryodhana and Vrikodara bellowed like bulls. Those two best of men were as strong as daityas.

'"O king! Duryodhana spoke to Yudhishthira, who was stationed with the Srinjayas, like a scorching sun. 'O best of kings! Be seated and witness this encounter that will take place between me and Bhima.' At this, that large circle of kings sat down. They were seen to be as beautiful as a collection of gods in the firmament. O great king! Honoured by them from every direction, Keshava's mighty-armed and handsome elder brother seated himself in their midst. The fair-complexioned one with the blue garments was beautiful in the midst of the kings, like the full moon in the night, surrounded by the stars. O great king! With clubs in their hands, they[13] were unassailable. They were stationed there and censured each other with fierce words. Having spoken those unpleasant words towards each other, those two brave bulls of the Kuru lineage glanced towards each other, like Vritra and Shakra in a battle."'

[11]The sun.

[12]As worthy adversaries.

[13]Bhima and Duryodhana.

Chapter 1274(55)

Vaishampayana said, 'O Janamejaya! There was a terrible battle of words between them. Miserable, King Dhritarashtra spoke these words. "Shame on a man—since he is reduced to such a state. O lord! My son was the master of eleven armies.[14] All the kings followed his commands and he enjoyed the earth. With a club and on foot, he now has to advance forcefully in an encounter. Having been the protector of the earth, my son is now without a protector. Since he has to advance with a club, what can this be, other than destiny? O Sanjaya! My son must have suffered from great misery." Having said this, the grieving king stopped.

'Sanjaya replied, "The valiant one[15] was cheerful. He roared like a cloud and bellowed like a bull. The warrior challenged Partha in that battle. When the great-souled king of the Kurus challenged Bhima, many extremely terrible portents of different types manifested themselves. Fierce winds began to blow and showers of dust fell down. All the directions were enveloped in darkness. Tumultuous thunder descended with a loud roar and the body hair stood up. Hundreds of meteors fell down, roaring in the sky. O lord of the earth! Though it was not the right time, Rahu devoured the sun.[16] The earth, with all its forests and trees, trembled, as if in a giant quake. Harsh winds began to blow, showering stones and dragging them along the ground. The summits of mountains fell down on the ground. Many kinds of animals were seen to run away in the ten directions. Extremely terrible jackals howled in fierce tones, their mouths blazing. Extremely fearful and strong sounds were heard and it made the body hair stand up. O Indra among kings! The directions blazed and animals uttered inauspicious noises. In every direction, the water in wells increased. O king! At that time, invisible and loud sounds were heard.

'"On seeing these evil portents, Vrikodara spoke to his elder brother, Dharmaraja Yudhishthira. 'The evil-souled Suyodhana is

[14] The eleven akshouhinis.

[15] Duryodhana.

[16] Rahu is the demon who devours the sun and causes a solar eclipse.

incapable of defeating me in this battle. Today, I will free myself of the anger that has been lodged deep in my heart for a long time. Suyodhana, Indra among Kouravas, will be like Khandava before the fire god. O Pandava! Today, I will uproot the stake that has been lodged in your heart. I will slay the wicked one, the worst of the Kuru lineage, with the club. Today, I will free you and place a garland of fame around you. In the field of battle, I will kill the performer of evil deeds with my club. With the club, I will shatter his body into a hundred fragments. He will not enter the city of Varanasahvya[17] again. He released snakes while I was sleeping and mixed poison in my food in Pramanakoti. He tried to burn us down in the house of lac. He robbed us of everything and disrespected us in the assembly hall. O unblemished one! He exiled us in the forest, with one year of concealment. O supreme among the Bharata lineage! I will bring an end to all those hardships today. I will kill him and, in a single day, free ourselves of those debts. O best among the Bharata lineage! Today, this evil-minded son of Dhritarashtra, whose soul is not clean, will come to an end. He will not see his mother and father again. This Kuru king is the worst of Shantanu's lineage. He will abandon his life and his kingdom today and lie down on the ground. King Dhritarashtra will hear that his son has been slain by me and remember the wicked deeds that were performed because of Shakuni's advice.' O tiger among kings! Having said this, the valiant one grasped his club. He stationed himself in the battle, like Shakra challenging Vritra.

'"Duryodhana also raised his club, like Kailasa with its summit. On seeing this, Bhimasena again angrily spoke to Duryodhana. 'Remember the extremely wicked deeds and conduct that you and King Dhritarashtra exhibited towards us in Varanavata.[18] Droupadi was in her season and was oppressed in the assembly hall. In the gambling match, the king was deceived by you and Soubala. Because of your deeds, we confronted a great hardship in the forest and also in the city of Virata, as if we had entered into another

[17]Hastinapura.

[18]The attempt to burn the Pandavas down in the house of lac.

womb.[19] I will pay back all that today. O evil-minded one! It is through good fortune that I have met you. It is because of your deeds that powerful Gangeya, best among rathas, was brought by Yajnasena's son[20] and brought down, is lying down on a bed of arrows. Drona, Karna and the powerful Shalya have been slain. Shakuni Soubala, the source of this fire of enmity, has been killed. The wicked Pratikami, who seized Droupadi by the hair, and all your brave brothers, valiant warriors, have been slain.[21] There are many other kings who have been killed because of your deeds. There is no doubt that I will kill you with this club today.' O Indra among kings! Having been thus addressed by Vrikodara, your son was not frightened. O king! Truth was his valour and he replied, 'O Vrikodara! Why speak a lot? Fight. O worst of your lineage! Today, I will kill you and destroy your love for fighting. Know that Duryodhana is not inferior and is not like an ordinary man. He is incapable of being frightened by someone like you. For a long time, I have harboured a desire in my heart that I will engage in a duel with clubs with you. Through good fortune and the favours of the thirty gods, the opportunity has presented itself. O evil-minded one! What is the point of speaking a lot? Do what you have promised in your words. Do not delay.' On hearing these words, everyone applauded him, the kings, the Somakas and all the others who were assembled there. Having been thus honoured by all of them, his body hair stood up in joy. The steadfast descendant of the Kuru lineage made up his mind to fight. As if they were cheering a crazy elephant, the kings slapped their palms and delighted the intolerant Duryodhana. The great-souled Pandava raised his club and rushed at the great-souled one. Vrikodara forcefully attacked Dhritarashtra's son. The elephants present there trumpeted and the horses neighed. The Pandavas desired victory and their weapons blazed."'

[19]This was the year of concealment in Virata's kindom. Since the Pandavas and Droupadi were in disguise, they were pretending to be other people. In that sense, it was as if they had been reborn as other people.

[20]Yajnasena is Drupada and the son in question is Shikhandi.

[21]As we have mentioned earlier, there is no mention of the Pratikami seizing Droupadi by the hair, or of the Pratikami being killed.

Chapter 1275(56)

'Sanjaya said, "On seeing that Bhimasena had approached, Duryodhana was not distressed in his soul. He roared loudly and attacked him with force. Like horned bulls, they clashed against each other. As they struck each other, there were great and thunderous sounds. That tumultuous battle commenced and it made the body hair stand up. Wishing to triumph, they fought each other in that battle, like Indra and Prahlada.[22] The spirited ones fought with clubs and blood covered all their limbs. The great-souled ones looked like flowering kimshukas. That great and extremely terrible battle raged on. As they roamed around, the sky was beautiful, as if covered with swarms of fireflies.[23] That fierce and tumultuous clash raged on for some time. As they fought, both scorchers of enemies were exhausted. Having rested for a short while, those scorchers of enemies again grasped their sparkling clubs and attacked each other. Those immensely valorous bulls among men looked like strong elephants, intolerant with pride and wishing to indulge in intercourse. With clubs in their hands, those infinitely valorous ones glanced towards each other. The gods, the gandharvas and the danavas were overcome by supreme wonder. On seeing Duryodhana and Vrikodara wield those clubs, all the beings were uncertain about who would be victorious. The brothers, supreme among strong ones, attacked each other again. They circled around each other, seeking to detect a weakness in each other. O king! The spectators saw that they raised those heavy and terrible clubs, which were like Yama's staff or Indra's vajra.

'"In that encounter, when Bhimasena struck with his club, in an instant, it produced a terrible and fierce sound. Dhritarashtra's son saw that Pandava was striking dexterously and powerfully with his club and was astounded. O descendant of the Bharata

[22]Prahlada was a virtuous demon and Vishnu's devotee. There are no stories about Indra and Prahlada having fought each other.

[23]Presumably, the sparks of fire from the clubs are being compared with fireflies.

lineage! As the brave Vrikodara roamed around, executing many different kinds of motions, he looked resplendent. They protected themselves and attacked each other. They repeatedly wounded each other, like hungry cats over food. Bhimasena moved around in many different kinds of motions. He executed circular motions in different spots, wonderful zigzag movements, advancing and retreating. He countered strikes, struck, avoided and chased. He adopted positions that were meant for attack. He defended, restrained himself, leapt up and leapt down. Both of them were skilled in fighting with clubs and wielded them, high and low. The best among the Kuru lineage roamed around in this way, striking each other and avoiding each other. The extremely strong ones sported, executing circular motions. With clubs in their hands, those powerful ones whirled around. O king! Dhritarashtra's son struck from the right side. Bhimasena struck from the left side. O great king! As Bhima strode around in that field of battle, Duryodhana struck him on his flank. O descendant of the Bharata lineage! When Bhima was thus struck by your son, he whirled his heavy club, thinking about how he should strike. O great king! Bhimasena's upraised and terrible club was seen to be like Indra's vajra or like Yama's staff. On seeing that Bhimasena was whirling his club around, your son, the scorcher of enemies, raised his terrible club and struck him again. O descendant of the Bharata lineage! Your son's club descended with the violence of a storm. A tumultuous sound was raised and sparks were generated. Suyodhana was energetic and radiant. As he roamed around and executed many kinds of circular motions, he again got the better of Bhima. When Bhima used his gigantic club to strike with great force, smoke and sparks of fire were generated and there was also a loud and terrible sound. On seeing that Bhimasena was whirling his club, the radiant Suyodhana whirled his heavy club, which possessed the essence of stone. The great-souled one's club had the violence of a storm. Beholding this, all the Pandus and the Somakas were terrified. They were seen in that encounter, as if they were sporting in the field of battle. Those two scorchers of enemies violently struck each other with their clubs. They were like elephants, goring each other with their tusks. O great king! With blood flowing down, they were beautiful. Thus did the battle, terrible in form, rage on. At the end of the day, it was cruel, like that between Vritra and Vasava.

'"On seeing that Bhima was stationed, your immensely strong son executed wonderful and colourful motions and attacked Kounteya. Bhima became angry. With great force, he struck that gold-decorated club.[24] O great king! Sparks began to fly and there was a clap, as if lightning was mixed with thunder. O great king! Hurled powerfully by Bhimasena, the club descended and made the earth tremble. Kouravya could not tolerate that his club should be countered in the clash. He was like a crazy elephant, angered at the sight of another elephant. O king! Enraged and having made up his mind, from the left, he powerfully struck Kounteya on the head with the club. O great king! Struck in this way by your son, Pandava Bhima did not tremble and it was extraordinary. O king! It was wonderful and all the soldiers honoured him. Despite being struck by the club, Bhima did not waver and did not retreat a step. Bhima, terrible in his valour, picked up a flaming club, decorated with gold, which was heavier and hurled this towards Duryodhana.[25] However, displaying his dexterity, the immensely strong Duryodhana freed himself from that thrust and it was extremely wonderful. O king! The club hurled by Bhima was baffled and fell down with the loud noise of a storm and made the earth tremble. Repeatedly resorting to the *koushika*[26] technique of jumping up and circling, he[27] discerned when Bhimasena would strike down with the club and deceived him. Having thus deceived Bhima, the immensely strong one, supreme among the Kuru lineage, angrily struck him in the chest with the club. Struck by the club in that great encounter, Bhima was stupefied. Having been struck by your son, he did not know what he should do. O king! At that time, the Somakas and the Pandavas were severely distressed and miserable in their minds. Having been struck, he[28] became as enraged as an

[24]Duryodhana's club.
[25]The earlier club had already been hurled.
[26]Technique of fighting with a club.
[27]Duryodhana.
[28]Bhima.

elephant and attacked your son, like an elephant against another elephant. The proud Bhima attacked your son with the club. He rushed forward with force, like a lion against a wild elephant. O king! He was skilled in releasing the club. Approaching the king, he used the club to strike in your son's direction. Duryodhana was struck in the flank by Bhimasena. He was stupefied by this blow and sank down on his knees on the ground. O lord of the earth! At this, the Srinjayas let out a loud roar. O best of the Bharata lineage! On hearing the roar of the Srinjayas, your son, bull among men, became angry. The mighty-armed one raised himself, like an angry serpent that was sighing. He glanced towards Bhimasena and burnt him down with his sight. With the club in his hand, the great-souled one, best among the Bharata lineage, attacked and, in that clash, struck the great-souled Bhimasena on his head. Bhima was terrible in his valour. Though he was struck on his head, he did not waver, like a mountain. O king! Struck by the club in that encounter, blood began to flow from Partha and he was as beautiful as an elephant with a shattered temple.

'"Dhananjaya's brave elder brother then picked up a club that was made out of iron and was capable of slaying heroes. It made a sound like that of the vajra. The destroyer of enemies struck powerfully with this. Struck in this way by Bhimasena, your son fell down, with his body trembling. He was like a blossoming shala tree in a large forest, whirled around by the force of a storm. On seeing that your son had fallen down on the ground, the Pandavas roared in delight. Your son recovered his senses and rose, like an elephant from a lake. The king was always intolerant. He skilfully circled around and struck Pandava, who was stationed before him, making him lose control over his limbs and fall down on the ground. In that encounter, on seeing that the infinitely energetic Bhima had fallen down on the ground, Kourava roared like a lion. Though he[29] was like the thunder in his energy, the descent of the club shattered his body armour. At this, a loud roar was heard in the firmament, made

[29]Bhima.

by the residents of heaven and the apsaras. The immortals showered down many kinds of excellent flowers. On seeing that the supreme among men had fallen down on the ground, great fear entered the hearts of the enemies. Because of the force of Kourava's blow, the firm armour had been shattered. However, he[30] recovered his senses in a short while and wiped away the blood from his face. Resorting to his fortitude and recovering his strength, Vrikodara dilated his eyes and steadied himself."'

Chapter 1276(57)

'Sanjaya said, "On seeing the clash between the two foremost ones of the Kuru lineage, Arjuna spoke to the illustrious Vasudeva. 'Between those two brave ones who are fighting, who do you think is superior? O Janardana! Who possesses the greater qualities? Tell me.'

'"Vasudeva replied, 'They are equal in what they have learnt, but Bhima is stronger. However, Dhritarashtra's son is superior to Vrikodara because of the efforts that he has undertaken. Using dharma, Bhimasena will not be able to win this encounter. He will be able to kill Suyodhana only if he fights through unfair means. It has been heard that the gods defeated the asuras through the use of maya. The slayer of Bala robbed Vritra of his energy through maya. O Dhananjaya! At the time of gambling with the dice, Bhima took a pledge that in the encounter, he would shatter Suyodhana's thighs with a club. This destroyer of enemies needs to accomplish that pledge. The king uses maya[31] and has to be brought down through maya. If he uses his strength and fights through fair means, King Yudhishthira will face a hardship. O Pandava! I am saying this again. Listen to me. It is because of Dharmaraja's transgression that this

[30]Bhima.

[31]The word is being used here in the sense of deception.

fear has again confronted us. Having performed the great deed of slaying the Kurus, with Bhishma as the leader, he had obtained victory and fame and an end to the enmity with the adversary. However, having obtained the victory, he has once again placed himself in a situation of uncertainty. O Pandava! This has been great stupidity on Dharmaraja's part. He has staked the entire victory on the outcome of a single encounter. Suyodhana is accomplished and brave. He is firm in his resolution. There is an ancient song by Ushanas[32] and we have heard it. I will recite the shloka, with its deep meaning. Listen. "Those who have been routed, wishing to protect their lives, but rally and return, must be feared. They will be single-minded in their resolution." Suyodhana was routed. With his soldiers slain, he had immersed himself in a lake. He had been defeated. Hopeless about obtaining the kingdom, he had wished to go to the forest. Which wise one would challenge such a person to a duel again? Suyodhana may now obtain the kingdom that we had won. Having made up his mind, he has practised with the club for thirteen years. Wishing to kill Bhimasena, he leaps up and moves diagonally. If the mighty-armed one does not slay him through unfair means, Kourava, Dhritarashtra's son, will be the king.'

'"Hearing Keshava's words, the great-souled Dhananjaya glanced in Bhimasena's direction and slapped his thigh with his hand.[33] Understanding the sign, Bhima roamed around with his club in the battle. He executed wonderful circular motions and doubled back. He circled to the right and the left and alternated between the two. O king! Pandava roamed around confounding the enemy. In that fashion, your son was also skilled in executing motions with the club. Wishing to kill Bhimasena, he roamed around, executing dexterous and wonderful motions. They whirled terrible clubs that had been smeared with sandalwood paste and unguents. They were like two angry Yamas, wishing to bring an end to the hostility. Those foremost ones, bulls among men, wished to kill each other. They fought like two Garudas who were after the same serpent. O king! Both of them

[32]Shukra, the preceptor of the demons.

[33]Though not explicitly stated, this is Sanjaya speaking again.

executed wonderful circular motions. Because of the descent of the clubs, sparks of fire were generated there. In the encounter, those brave and powerful ones struck each other equally. O king! They were like two oceans agitated by storms. Like crazy elephants, they struck each other equally. Thunderous sounds were generated from the blows of the clubs. That fierce and terrible clash continued. As they fought, both scorchers of enemies were exhausted. Having rested for some time, those scorchers of enemies again angrily grasped their giant clubs and attacked. O Indra among kings! They fought a terrible battle with the descending clubs and severely wounded each other. With eyes like bulls, they spiritedly rushed towards each other. Those brave ones fiercely struck each other, like buffaloes stuck in mud. All their limbs were mangled and they were covered with blood. They looked like two flowering kimshukas on the Himalayas.

'"Partha showed Duryodhana a weakness and smiling, he suddenly extended himself forwards.[34] Vrikodara was learned about fighting. On seeing the advance, the strong one powerfully hurled the club. O lord of the earth! Seeing that the club had been hurled, your son moved from the spot and baffled, it fell down on the ground. Having respectfully warded off that blow, your son, supreme among the Kuru lineage, struck Bhimasena with the club. Struck severely by that blow and with blood flowing down, the infinitely energetic one was stupefied. However, in that encounter, Duryodhana did not realize that Pandava was afflicted. Though his body suffered great pain, Bhima bore himself. He[35] thought that he was still steady and ready to strike back in the encounter. That is the reason your son did not strike him again. O king! Having rested for a while, the powerful Bhimasena attacked Duryodhana, who was stationed before him, with force. O bull among the Bharata lineage! On seeing that the angry and infinitely energetic one was attacking, he wished to save himself from the blow. Your great-minded son made up his mind to take a stand. O king! He leapt up, wishing to deceive Vrikodara.

[34]Duryodhana extended forwards. There was no real weakness and Bhima tempted Duryodhana to attack.

[35]Duryodhana.

However, Bhimasena understood what the king wished to do. He dashed forward, roaring like a lion. O king! As the king leapt up to avoid the blow, Pandava powerfully struck him on the thighs with the club. He was terrible in his deeds and struck with a force like that of the vajra. Duryodhana's handsome thighs were fractured. The tiger among men fell down, making the earth resound. O lord of the earth! Your son's thighs were fractured by Bhimasena.

'"Fierce winds began to blow and showers of dust fell down. The earth, with its trees, shrubs and mountains, began to tremble. The brave one was the lord of all the kings on earth. When he fell down, a great sound was heard and there were blazing and fearful winds. When the lord of the earth fell down, giant meteors descended. O descendant of the Bharata lineage! There were showers of blood and showers of dust. When your son was brought down, Maghavan[36] showered these down. O bull among the Bharata lineage! Large roars were heard in the firmament, made by the yakshas, the rakshasas and the pishachas. Because of that terrible roar, animals and birds emitted many more terrible sounds in all the directions. When your son was brought down, the remaining horses, elephants and men emitted loud roars. When your son was brought down, there were the loud sounds of drums, conch shells and cymbals and a sound seemed to emerge from inside the ground. O king! In all directions, headless torsos, fearful in form, with many feet and many legs, were seen to dance around, generating fear. O king! When your son was brought down, those who held standards, weapons and arms trembled. O supreme among kings! Lakes and wells vomited blood. Extremely swift-flowing rivers began to flow in a reverse direction. Men looked like women and women looked like men. O king! This is what happened when your son, Duryodhana, was brought down. O bull among the Bharata lineage! On seeing these evil portents, all the Panchalas and the Pandavas were anxious in their minds. O descendant of the Bharata lineage! The gods, the gandharvas and the apsaras went away, wherever they wished to go, after that wonderful encounter between your sons was over. O Indra among kings! So

[36]Indra.

did the siddhas, the bards and the charanas. Having praised those two lions among men, the brahmanas went away, to wherever they had come from."'

Chapter 1277(58)

'Sanjaya said, "On seeing that he had fallen down, like a giant shala tree uprooted by the wind, all the Pandavas present there were delighted. He was like a crazy elephant that had been brought down by a lion. On seeing this, the body hair of the Somakas stood up and they were joyful. Having struck and brought down Duryodhana, the powerful Bhimasena approached the Indra among the Kouravas and said, 'O wicked one! In earlier times, when Droupadi was in a single garment, you addressed us as cattle.[37] O evil-minded one! When we were in the assembly hall, you laughed at us. Suffer the consequences of that disrespect now.' Having said this, he kicked his head with his left foot. He struck the head of that lion among kings with his foot. Bhima was the destroyer of enemy forces and his eyes were red with rage. O lord of men! He again spoke these words. Listen to them. 'In earlier times, there were those who danced around and repeatedly called us cattle. We will dance back at them now and repeatedly address them as cattle. There is no guile, no fire[38] and no deception in gambling with the dice in us. We resort to the strength of our own arms and counter our enemies.' Having attained the other shore of the enmity, Vrikodara laughed and softly spoke these words to Yudhishthira, Keshava, the Srinjayas, Dhananjaya and Madri's two sons. 'Droupadi was in her season and they disrespected her. They deprived her of her garment there. Behold. Through Yajnaseni's[39] austerities, in the battle, the sons of Dhritarashtra have been slain by the Pandavas. In earlier times, King Dhritarashtra's wicked sons

[37]At the time of the gambling match, described in Section 27 (Volume 2).

[38]A reference to the attempt to burn the Pandavas down in the house of lac.

[39]Yajnaseni is Droupadi's name.

called us sterile sesamum seeds. They have been slain by us, with their followers and their relatives. We are indifferent as to whether we go to heaven or to hell.' He again raised the club that was on his shoulder. Glancing towards the deceitful King Duryodhana, who had fallen down on the ground, he kicked his head with his left foot and spoke these words. The foremost among the Somakas had dharma in their souls. O king! On seeing that Bhimasena, inferior in his soul, was kicking the Kuru king on the head with his foot, they did not approve.

'"Having brought down your son, Vrikodara was bragging. As he danced around in different ways, Dharmaraja spoke to him. 'O Bhima! Do not crush his head with your foot. Do not greatly transgress dharma. He is a king and your relative. He has been brought down. O unblemished one! This conduct is not proper. He has been destroyed. His advisers have been slain. His brothers have been slain. His subjects have been slain. His funeral cakes have been destroyed.[40] He is our brother. This conduct of yours is inappropriate. In earlier times, people used to say that Bhimasena followed dharma. How can Bhimasena then disrespect the king in this way?' Having spoken these words, the king who was Kunti's son approached and saw Duryodhana. With his eyes full of tears, he spoke these words. 'It is certain that destiny, ordained by the great-souled Creator, is powerful. O supreme among the Kuru lineage! Otherwise, why should you harbour violence towards us and we towards you? It is because of your own misdeeds that you have faced this great calamity. O descendant of the Bharata lineage! You have reaped it because of your avarice, insolence and folly. You have slain your friends, your brothers and your fathers. The sons, grandsons and preceptors have also been slain. It is because of your crimes that your maharatha brothers and other relatives have been killed. I think that destiny is irresistible. Dhritarashtra's daughters-in-law and grand-daughters-in-law are miserable. Oppressed by grief, those widows will certainly censure us.' Having spoken in this way, the

[40]The sons who would have offered Duryodhana funeral cakes have been killed.

king was extremely miserable and sighed. Yudhishthira, Dharma's son, lamented for a long time."'

Chapter 1278(59)

'Dhritarashtra asked, "O suta! On seeing that the king had been brought down through adharma, what did the immensely strong Baladeva, the best of the Madhava lineage, say? He knew about the rules of fighting with clubs. He was skilled in fighting with clubs. O Sanjaya! What did Rohini's son do?"

'Sanjaya replied, "On seeing that Bhimasena had kicked your son in the head, Rama, supreme among strikers and strongest among the strong, became angry. In the midst of those kings, the one with the plough as his weapon raised up his arms. In terrible words of lamentation, he spoke words of shame. 'Shame that one should exhibit the valour of a shudra and strike below the navel. In a duel with clubs, the likes of what Vrikodara has done have never been seen. It is certain that the sacred texts have said that one should not strike below the navel. But he is stupid and ignorant of the sacred texts. He has easily done what he wanted.' While speaking in this way, he was overcome by great rage. The powerful one raised his plough and advanced towards Bhima. As he raised his arms, the form of the great-souled one was like that of the great mountain Shveta, coloured with many minerals. However, as he descended, Keshava humbly seized him. The powerful one grasped the powerful one in his thick arms. The fair and the dark one,[41] best among the Yadu lineage, looked even more radiant. O king! They were like the sun and the moon in the sky, at the end of the day. To pacify the angry one, Keshava said, 'One can have six kinds of prosperity—one's own prosperity, the prosperity of friends, the decay of enemies, the decay of the friends of enemies, the decay of the friends of friends of enemies and the prosperity of the enemies of

[41]Balarama was fair and Krishna was dark.

enemies.[42] When there are reversals to one's own self or that of friends, the learned know that one should quickly strive for peace. The Pandavas are pure men and are our natural friends. They are the sons of our father's sister.[43] They have been severely oppressed by the enemy. The accomplishment of a vow is the dharma of kshatriyas. Earlier, in the assembly hall, Bhima had taken the pledge that in a great battle, he would shatter Suyodhana's thighs with a club. O scorcher of enemies! Earlier, maharshi Maitreya had cursed him that his thighs would be shattered by Bhima with a club.[44] O slayer of Pralamba![45] Therefore, I do not see a transgression. Do not be angry. Our alliance with the Pandavas is based on birth and bonds of affection. Their prosperity is our prosperity. O bull among men! Therefore, do not be angry.'

'"Rama said, 'Dharma is followed by the virtuous. But dharma is also followed for two reasons—artha, for those who are addicted to artha, and kama, for those who are addicted to it. Those who obtain great happiness follow dharma, artha and kama, without oppressing dharma and artha, or dharma and kama, or kama and artha.[46] Bhimasena has not followed all of them and has oppressed dharma. O Govinda! This is despite what you have told me.'

'"Vasudeva replied, 'In this world, you have always been spoken of as one without rage, one with dharma in your soul and one who is devoted to dharma. Therefore, be pacified and do not yield to anger. Know that kali yuga has almost arrived and also remember Pandava's pledge. Pandava has paid his debts to the enmity and accomplished his pledge.'"

'Sanjaya said, "O lord of the earth! Hearing this deceptive exposition of dharma on Keshava's part, Rama was not happy and

[42]The shloka is slightly cryptic. The six types have to be deduced and are not obvious.

[43]Pritha (Kunti) was from the Yadava lineage and Vasudeva's (Krishna's father) sister.

[44]The sage Maitreya had cursed Duryodhana. This has been described in Section 29 (Volume 2).

[45]Pralamba was a demon killed by Balarama.

[46]The idea is that all three must be followed. One must not follow one at the expense of the other two objectives.

spoke these words in the assembly. 'King Suyodhana had dharma in his soul and was slain through adharma. Pandava will be known in this world as someone who fought deceitfully. Duryodhana, with dharma in his soul, will obtain the eternal end. Dhritarashtra's son, king among men, fought fairly and has been slain. He consecrated himself for the encounter and entered the sacrifice that was the duel. He offered himself as an oblation into the fire and has obtained fame.' Speaking these words, Rohini's powerful son, who was like the crest of a white cloud, ascended his chariot and left towards Dvaraka. O lord of the earth! When Rama left for Dvaravati, the Panchalas, the Varshneyas and the Pandavas were cheerless.

'"Yudhishthira was miserable and with his head hanging down, was immersed in thought. Immersed in grief, he thought about what should be done. Vasudeva told him, 'O Dharmaraja! Why did you permit such an act of adharma? His relatives had been killed. He had been brought down, bereft of his senses. Yet, Bhima struck Duryodhana's head with his foot. O one who knows about dharma! O lord of men! Why did you ignore this?' Yudhishthira replied, 'O Krishna! I did not like what Vrikodara did to the king. Because of anger, he kicked his head with his foot and I am not happy at this extermination of my lineage. Dhritarashtra's sons have always deceived us and acted fraudulently. They have spoken many harsh words towards us and exiled us to the forest. That has led to great unhappiness in Bhimasena's heart. O Varshneya! Thinking about all this, I ignored it. He slew the deceitful and avaricious one who was always overcome by his passion. Pandava has accomplished his desire. How does it matter whether it was dharma or adharma?' Having been thus addressed by Dharmaraja, Vasudeva, the extender of the Yadu lineage, agreed with a considerable amount of difficulty. With Bhima's welfare in mind, Vasudeva spoke, approving of everything Bhima had done in the battle.

'"The intolerant Bhimasena brought down your son. He stood there cheerfully, his hands joined in salutation. The immensely energetic one spoke to Dharmaraja Yudhishthira. O lord of the earth! He[47]

[47]Bhima.

had wished for victory and his eyes were dilated with joy. 'O king! The pacified earth is now yours, without any thorns. O great king! Rule over it and follow your own dharma. O lord of the earth! He was the source of the enmity. He was fraudulent and loved deceit. He has been brought down and is lying down on the ground. All the enemies, Duhshasana, Radheya, Shakuni and the others, harsh in words, have been slain. The earth, with its many jewels, forests and mountains, is yours again now. O great king! The enemies have been killed.' Yudhishthira replied, 'With King Suyodhana brought down, the enmity is over. We have conquered the earth because of Krishna's advice. It is through good fortune that you have paid off your debts to your mother and to your anger. O invincible one! It is through good fortune that you have triumphed. It is through good fortune that your enemy has been brought down.'"'

Chapter 1279(60)

'Dhritarashtra asked, "O Sanjaya! On seeing that Duryodhana had been brought down by Bhimasena in the encounter what did the Pandavas and the Srinjayas do?"

'Sanjaya replied, "O great king! On seeing that Duryodhana had been brought down by Bhimasena in the encounter, like a crazy and wild elephant brought down by a lion in the forest, Krishna and the Pandavas were delighted. When the descendant of the Kuru lineage was brought down, the Panchalas and the Srinjayas waved their upper garments around and roared like lions. It was as if the earth was no longer able to bear those cheerful ones. Some brandished their bows. Others drew on their bowstrings. Others blew on their giant conch shells and sounded drums. Some sported. Other enemies of yours laughed. The brave ones spoke these words to Bhimasena. 'You have performed an extremely difficult and great task in the battle today. You have brought down the Indra among Kouravas in the encounter, one who had undertaken great exertions with the club. This is like

Indra killing Vritra in a supreme encounter. These people think that your deed of slaying the enemy is like that. You have roamed around in different ways and have executed all the circular motions. Who other than Vrikodara could have brought down a brave one like Duryodhana? You have reached the end of the hostilities, something so difficult that no one but you could have achieved that. No one else could have done that. O brave one! In the field of battle, you were like a crazy elephant. It is through good fortune that you have kicked Duryodhana's head with your foot. O unblemished one! It is through good fortune that you have performed the wonderful task of drinking Duhshasana's blood, like a lion against a buffalo. It is through good fortune and your deeds that you have placed your foot on the heads of those who injured King Yudhishthira, one with dharma in his soul. O Bhima! It is through good fortune that you have triumphed over the enemies and brought down Suyodhana. Your great fame will spread throughout the earth. Bards praised Shakra's slaying of Vritra. O descendant of the Bharata lineage! In that way, we are praising your slaying of the enemy. Since Duryodhana has been brought down, our body hair is standing up and we are delighted. O descendant of the Bharata lineage! Know that our joy has not diminished.'[48] The assembled bards spoke in this way to Bhimasena.

'"The Panchalas and the Pandavas, tigers among men, were delighted and also spoke in a similar way. Madhusudana spoke to them. 'O lords of men! It is not proper to again kill an enemy who has been brought down. This evil-minded one has already been killed. One should not address fierce words towards him. This wicked one has been slain by destiny. Destiny has afflicted the shameless one. He was avaricious and had wicked aides. He followed the advice of those well-wishers. Several times, Vidura, Drona, Kripa, Gangeya and the Srinjayas asked him to give the Pandus their paternal share. But he did not give it. The worst of men does not deserve to be called a friend or a foe now. One should not waste words on someone who has become a piece of wood. O lords of the earth! Ascend your chariots and let

[48]This is probably a reference to the act of adharma not having diminished the joy.

us leave swiftly. It is through good fortune that this evil-souled one has been brought down, with his advisers, kin and allies.'

'"O lord of the earth! Hearing Krishna's censorious words, King Duryodhana was overcome by intolerance and tried to rise. He used his two arms to support himself on the ground. He frowned and glanced towards Vasudeva. O descendant of the Bharata lineage! With his body half raised, the king's form was like that of an angry and virulent serpent, with a severed tail. He paid no attention to the terrible pain that was about to take away his life. Duryodhana spoke these harsh words to Vasudeva. 'You are the son of Kamsa's slave and you have no shame.[49] In this encounter with the clubs, I have been brought down through adharma. Bhima falsified the injunctions of the sacred texts and shattered my thighs. Do you think I do not know what you told Arjuna? You have slaughtered thousands of kings through unfair means. You have used many crooked means. But you suffer no shame or abhorrence on account of that. From one day to another, you have caused a great carnage of brave ones. Placing Shikhandi at the forefront, you brought down the grandfather. O evil-minded one! You caused an elephant named Ashvatthama to be killed and made the preceptor lay down his weapons. Do you think that this is not known to me? When that valiant one was cruelly brought down by Dhrishtadyumna, you witnessed it. But you did not restrain him. A javelin was obtained[50] for the destruction of Pandu's son. You wasted it on Ghatotkacha. Is there anyone more wicked than you? The powerful Bhurishrava's arms were severed and he was ready to give up his life. When Shini's evil-souled descendant[51] killed him, you were behind that act. Karna performed the excellent deed of triumphing over Partha. But you caused Ashvasena, the son of the king of the serpents, to be countered. In the battle, Karna's wheel was submerged in the ground. He was defeated and overtaken

[49]Krishna was the son of Vasudeva. Vasudeva married Devaki, Kamsa's (alternatively Kansa) sister. Vasudeva was never Kamsa's slave or servant, but was imprisoned by him. Eventually, Krishna killed Kamsa.

[50]By Karna, from Indra and for Arjuna's destruction.

[51]Satyaki.

by a hardship. That foremost among men was trying to extricate it and you had him killed. Had you fought me, Karna, Bhishma and Drona through fair means, it is certain that you would not have been victorious. However, you adopted ignoble and deceitful methods. There were many kings who followed their own dharma. But you caused them to follow you and thus to be killed.'

'"Vasudeva replied, 'O Gandhari's son! You have been brought down, with your brothers, sons, relatives, followers and well-wishers. That is because you resorted to a wicked path. It is because of your evil deeds that the brave Bhishma and Drona have been brought down. It is because he followed your conduct that Karna has been slain in the battle. O stupid one! Though I asked you, you did not give the Pandavas half of your kingdom, their paternal share. This is because of your avarice and Shakuni's advice. You gave poison to Bhimasena. O evil-minded one! You tried to burn down all the Pandavas, and their mother, in the house of lac. Yajnaseni was in her season. Despite this, at the time of the gambling match, she was oppressed in the assembly hall. O shameless one! That is the reason someone like you should be killed. The one who follows dharma[52] was unskilled and Soubala was knowledgeable about the heart of dice. He was defeated through deceit. For that reason, you should be slain in the battle. The wicked Jayadratha afflicted Krishna[53] in the forest, in Trinabindu's hermitage, when they[54] had gone out on a hunt. Abhimanyu was a child and though he was single-handed, many fought him in the battle. O evil one! He was killed because of your deeds. For that reason, you should be slain in this battle.'

'"Duryodhana said, 'I have studied and given the ordained gifts. I have ruled the earth, up to the frontiers of the ocean. I have placed my foot on the heads of enemies. Who is as fortunate as I am? It is through good fortune that I have seen my kshatriya relatives established in their own dharma. Even if I am slain, who can be more fortunate than I am? There are human objects of pleasure

[52]Yudhishthira.

[53]Krishnaa, that is, Droupadi. This has been described in Section 42 (Volume 3).

[54]The Pandavas.

that gods deserve. These are difficult for kings to obtain. But I have obtained that supreme prosperity. Who can be more fortunate than I am? O unblemished one! I will go to heaven, with my well-wishers and my relatives. Your objectives are yet unaccomplished. You will sorrow here.'"

'Sanjaya said, "O descendant of the Bharata lineage! When the king of the Kurus concluded these words, a large shower of flowers, with auspicious fragrances, rained down. Gandharvas and large numbers of apsaras played on musical instruments. O descendant of the Bharata lineage! Siddhas uttered words of praise. Fragrant, delicate and pleasant winds began to blow, mixed with sacred scents. The sky became beautiful and clear, with the complexion of lapis lazuli. On seeing these wonderful sights, they,[55] with Vasudeva at the forefront, were ashamed and honoured Duryodhana. On hearing that Bhishma, Drona, Karna and Bhurishrava had been slain through adharma, they grieved and wept in sorrow. The Pandavas were distressed and immersed in thought. On seeing this, Krishna spoke these words, in a voice that rumbled like clouds and drums. 'All of them were swift in the use of weapons and were maharathas. In a fair fight, even if we fought bravely, we were incapable of defeating them in the battle. That is the reason I thought of means to slay those lords of men. Otherwise, the Pandaveyas would never have obtained victory. Those four great-souled ones were atirathas on earth.[56] Following dharma, even the guardians of the world themselves would not have been able to kill them. Even when he is exhausted, Dhritarashtra's son, with the club in his hand, is incapable of being killed through the means of dharma, even by Yama with a staff in his hand. You should not sorrow that the king has been slain in this way. When enemies are many and numerous, they have to be killed through falsehood and other means. Earlier, this was the path followed by the gods, when they killed the asuras. That good route that they followed is one which everyone can follow. We

[55]The Pandavas.

[56]An atiratha is a great warrior, superior to a maharatha. The four in question are Bhishma, Drona, Karna and Bhurishrava.

have accomplished our objective. It is evening. We should go to our abodes. Let all the kings, the horses, the elephants and the chariots, rest.' On hearing Vasudeva's words, the Pandavas and the Panchalas became extremely cheerful and roared like a pride of lions. They blew on their conch shells and Madhava blew on Panchajanya. On seeing that Duryodhana had been brought down, the bulls among men were delighted."'

Chapter 1280(61)

'Sanjaya said, "All those kings left for their abodes. With arms that were like clubs, they cheerfully blew on their conch shells. O lord of the earth! The Pandavas proceeded towards our camp. The great archer, Yuyutsu Satyaki, followed them. Dhrishtadyumna, Shikhandi, all of Droupadi's sons and all the other great archers also proceeded towards our camp. The Parthas entered Duryodhana's camp, bereft of its radiance and with its lord slain. It looked like an arena devoid of men. It looked like a city deprived of life and like a lake without elephants. There were only a large number of women, eunuchs and aged advisers. O king! Earlier, with clean garments dyed in ochre, Duryodhana and the others used to wait on them,[57] with hands joined in salutation. The Pandavas reached the camp of the king of the Kurus. O great king! Those supreme of rathas descended from their chariots.

'"O bull among the Bharata lineage! Keshava was always engaged in bringing pleasure to the wielder of Gandiva and spoke to him. 'Take down Gandiva and the two great and inexhaustible quivers. O supreme among the Bharata lineage! I will get down after you have dismounted. O unblemished one! Descend. It is for your own good.' Dhananjaya, Pandu's brave son, did as he had been asked. Thereafter, the intelligent Krishna discarded the reins of the horses and got

[57]The aged advisers.

down from the chariot that belonged to the wielder of Gandiva. The extremely great-souled one, the lord of all beings, descended. The celestial ape, stationed on the standard of the wielder of Gandiva, disappeared. Earlier, it[58] had been burnt by the divine weapons of the maharathas, Drona and Karna. O lord of the earth! It blazed amidst a fire and was swiftly burnt. The chariot of the wielder of Gandiva was burnt, with its yokes, its harnesses, its horses and its lovely joints. O lord! On seeing that it had been reduced to ashes, Pandu's sons were astounded. O king! Arjuna joined his hands in salutation and bowing down affectionately, asked, 'O Govinda! O illustrious one! Why has the chariot been burnt down by the fire? O descendant of the Yadu lineage! What is this extremely wonderful thing that has occurred? O mighty-armed one! If you think that I deserve to hear it, tell me.' Vasudeva replied, 'O Arjuna! This has earlier been burnt by many different kinds of weapons. O scorcher of enemies! It is because I was seated that it was not destroyed in the battle. It has now been destroyed, consumed by the energy of brahmastra. O Kounteya! Now that you have accomplished your objective, I have abandoned it.' The illustrious Keshava, the destroyer of enemies, smiled a little, in pride.

'"He embraced King Yudhishthira and said, 'O Kounteya! It is through good fortune that you have become victorious. It is through good fortune that you have defeated your enemies. O king! It is through good fortune that the wielder of Gandiva, Pandava Bhimasena, you and the Pandavas who are Madri's sons are hale. You have slain your enemies and have escaped from a battle that has been destructive of heroes. O descendant of the Bharata lineage! Swiftly do the tasks that must be done next. When I earlier arrived in Upaplavya, with the wielder of Gandiva, you approached me and greeted me with *madhuparka*.[59] You spoke these words to me. "O Krishna! Dhananjaya is your brother and friend too. O mighty-armed one! O lord! You must therefore protect him from all dangers." When you spoke those words to me, I replied in words

[58]The chariot.

[59]A mixture of honey and milk, offered to a guest.

of assent. O lord of men! Savyasachi has been protected and you have become victorious. O Indra among kings! He is brave and truth is his valour. With his brothers, he has escaped from this battle that led to the destruction of brave ones and made the body hair stand up.' O great king! Having been thus addressed by Krishna, Dharmaraja Yudhishthira replied to Janardana, with his body hair standing up. 'O crusher of enemies! Who other than you, and Purandara, the wielder of the vajra himself, could have escaped from the brahmastras of Drona and Karna? It is through your many favours that we have triumphed in this battle and Partha never had to retreat, even from the greatest of battles. O mighty-armed one! In that fashion, it is through your favours and instructions that I have performed many deeds and attained objectives with auspicious energy. In Upaplavya, maharshi Krishna Dvaipayana told me, "Where there is dharma, Krishna is there. Where there is Krishna, victory is there."' O descendant of the Bharata lineage! These were the words the brave ones spoke in your camp.

'"They then entered and obtained the treasure chests, with many kinds of riches and gems—silver, gold, jewels, pearls, the best of ornaments, blankets, hides—many female and male slaves and other objects required for kingship. O bull among the Bharata lineage! O Indra among men! Having obtained access to your inexhaustible riches, those great archers roared in delight, having defeated their enemies. Those brave ones approached their mounts and unyoked them. All the Pandavas, with Satyaki, remained there for some time. O great king! The immensely illustrious Vasudeva then said, 'To ensure that everything is auspicious, we should dwell outside this camp.' All the Pandavas and Satyaki agreed to this. For the sake of ensuring the auspicious, with Vasudeva, they went outside. O king! They approached the sacred river Oghavati.[60] Having slain their enemies, the Pandavas spent the night there. When the sun arose, they[61] quickly sent the powerful Vasudeva to Nagasahvya. Daruka[62]

[60]Oghavati is that part of Sarasvati that flows through Kurukshetra.

[61]The Pandavas.

[62]Krishna's charioteer.

ascended the chariot. The king who was Ambika's son[63] was there. When he was about to leave, with Sainya and Sugriva[64] yoked, they told him, 'Comfort the illustrious Gandhari, whose sons have been slain.' Thus spoken to by the Pandavas, the best of the Satvata lineage set out for that city. He quickly approached Gandhari, whose sons had been killed."'

Chapter 1281(62)

Janamejaya asked, 'Why did Dharmaraja Yudhishthira, tiger among kings, send Vasudeva, the scorcher of enemies, to Gandhari? Krishna had earlier gone to the Kouravas, seeking peace. He was not successful and the battle followed. The warriors were slain and Duryodhana was also brought down. In the battle, the Pandaveyas eliminated their rivals from the earth. The camp[65] was emptied and everyone fled. They obtained supreme fame. O brahmana! Why did Krishna go again? O brahmana! It seems to me that the reason must have been a grave one, since Janardana, immeasurable in his soul, himself went. O supreme among officiating priests! Tell me everything about this. O brahmana! What was the reason behind deciding on such a course of action?'

Vaishampayana replied, 'O king! The question that you have asked me is one that is deserving of you. O bull among the Bharata lineage! I will tell you everything, exactly as it occurred. O king! Dhritarashtra's immensely strong son was brought down in the battle by Bhimasena, in contravention of the rules. O descendant of the Bharata lineage! In the duel with the clubs, he was brought down by unfair means. O great king! On seeing this, Yudhishthira was overcome by a great fear. He thought of the immensely fortunate and ascetic Gandhari. Because of her terrible austerities, she was

[63]Dhritarashtra.

[64]The names of Krishna's horses.

[65]Of the Kouravas.

capable of burning down the three worlds. Thinking about this, he arrived at this conclusion. "The flame of Gandhari's anger must first be pacified. Otherwise, on hearing about her son being killed by the enemies in this way, she can use the fire of her mind to angrily reduce us to ashes. How will Gandhari tolerate such fierce misery? She will hear that her son has been brought down through deceit and fraudulent means." Thinking about this in many ways, he was overcome by fear and sorrow. Therefore, Dharmaraja spoke these words to Vasudeva. "O Govinda! Through your favours, the kingdom has been deprived of its thorns. O Achyuta! We have obtained that which our minds thought was unattainable. O mighty-armed one! O descendant of the Yadava lineage! In the battle that made the body hair stand up, I have witnessed the extremely great blows that you have had to bear. In earlier times, you rendered your help in slaying the enemies of the gods. O mighty-armed one! O Achyuta! You have aided us in that way. O Varshneya! By agreeing to be our charioteer, you have supported us. If you had not been Phalguna's protector in the great battle, how would we have been capable of defeating this ocean of soldiers in the encounter? For the sake of our welfare, you have borne great blows with the club, strikes with bludgeons, spears, catapults, javelins, battleaxes and harsh words. O Achyuta! Now that Duryodhana has been brought down, all of that has become fruitful. O mighty-armed one! O Madhava! But you know about Gandhari's anger. The immensely fortunate one has always tormented herself through fierce austerities. On hearing about the slaughter of her sons and grandsons, there is no doubt that she will consume us. She will be oppressed with grief on account of her sons and her eyes will blaze in anger. O brave one! I think the time has come to seek your favours. O Purushottama! Which man, other than you, is capable of glancing at her? O Madhava! I think it is a good idea for you to go there, so that you can pacify the anger of Gandhari's wrath. O scorcher of enemies! You are the creator, the agent and the pervading power in the worlds. You will use words full of reason, appropriate for the occasion. O immensely wise one! Pacify Gandhari quickly. Krishna, the illustrious grandfather, will be there.[66] O mighty-armed one! O best of the Satvata lineage! For the sake of the welfare of the Pandavas, it is your duty to destroy Gandhari's rage in every possible way." On hearing Dharmaraja's words, the extender of the Yadu lineage sent for Daruka and asked him to prepare the chariot in the proper way. Hearing Keshava's words, Daruka quickly prepared the chariot and came and told the great-souled Keshava that it was ready. The scorcher of enemies, best of the Yadava lineage, ascended the chariot. The lord Keshava swiftly left for Hastinapura. O great king! The illustrious ratha, Madhava, departed. The valiant one approached and entered Nagasahvya.

'The brave one's chariot wheels clattered as he entered the city. Having sent word to Dhritarashtra, he alighted from that supreme chariot. Distressed in his mind, he entered Dhritarashtra's abode. He saw that the supreme among rishis[67] had arrived there before him. Janardana embraced Krishna's[68] feet and the king's. Keshava showed his honours to Gandhari, who was before him. Adhokshaja,[69] best among the Yadava lineage, held King Dhritarashtra by the hand and wept in a melodious voice. For some time, overcome by sorrow, he shed warm tears. Following the proper rites, he then washed his eyes with water. The scorcher of enemies then spoke these flowing words to Dhritarashtra. "O descendant of the Bharata lineage! Nothing is unknown to you, about what has happened and what will happen. O lord! You know everything about the passage of time extremely well. O descendant of the Bharata lineage! Because their hearts are devoted to you, all the Pandavas sought to prevent the destruction of the lineage and that of the kshatriyas. They are peaceful and devoted to dharma. Having contracted an agreement with their brothers, after being deceitfully defeated in the gambling match, they bore the hardship of dwelling in the forest. Attiring themselves in different garments, they spent the period of concealment. They

[66]Meaning Krishna Dvaipayana Vedavyasa.

[67]Vedavyasa.

[68]Krishna Vedavyasa's.

[69]Krishna and Vishnu's name.

always bore many other hardships, as if they were incapable. When the time for war presented itself, I myself arrived and in everyone's presence, asked for five villages.[70] Driven by destiny and because of your avarice, you did not accept this. O king! It is because of your crimes that all the kshatriyas have confronted destruction. Bhishma, Somadatta, Bahlika, Kripa, Drona and his son and the intelligent Vidura have always asked for peace. But you did not act accordingly. O descendant of the Bharata lineage! It was as if everyone was confounded by destiny. In so far as this is concerned, you also acted foolishly. What can this be, other than the dictate of destiny? Destiny is supreme. O great king! Do not ascribe any fault to the Pandavas. O scorcher of enemies! The great-souled Pandavas did not commit a trifling transgression, in dharma, fairness and affection. You know everything about this and about the fruits of your own deeds. Therefore, you should not harbour any malice towards the sons of Pandu. For both you and Gandhari, the family, the lineage, funeral oblations and the fruits obtained from begetting sons now vest on the Pandavas. Think about all this and about your own transgressions. Think peacefully about the Pandavas. O bull among the Bharata lineage! I salute you. O mighty-armed one! O tiger among the Bharata lineage! You know about Dharmaraja's natural devotion and affection towards you. Having caused this carnage amongst the enemy, even though they injured him, day and night, he is tormented and cannot find any peace. O best of the Bharata lineage! The tiger among men sorrows for you and the illustrious Gandhari and can find no peace. Knowing that you are tormented by sorrow on account of your sons and that your intelligence and senses are agitated, he is overcome by supreme shame and has not come before you." O great king! The supreme among the Yadu lineage spoke these words to Dhritarashtra.

'He then spoke these supreme words to Gandhari, who was afflicted by sorrow. "O Subala's daughter! O one who is excellent in vows! Listen to the words.that I tell you. O beautiful one! There

[70]Described in Section 54 (Volume 4).

is no woman[71] like you in this world now. O queen! You know the words that you spoke in the assembly hall in my presence. Those words, full of dharma and artha, were for the benefit of both sides. O fortunate one! You spoke those words, but your sons did not listen. Duryodhana desired victory and you spoke harsh words to him. 'O foolish one! Listen to my words. Victory exists where there is dharma.' O daughter of a king! Those words of yours have now come to pass. O fortunate one! Knowing all this, do not harbour any sorrow in your mind. Do not think about the destruction of the Pandavas. O immensely fortunate one! Through the blazing anger in your eyes and through the strength of your austerities, you are capable of burning down the earth, with everything that is mobile and immobile." On hearing Vasudeva's words, Gandhari spoke these words. "O mighty-armed one! O Keshava! It is exactly as you have described it. My heart is burning and my mind is agitated. O Janardana! But after hearing your words, I have steadied myself. O Keshava! The king is aged and blind and his sons have been slain. You are his refuge, with the brave Pandavas, best among men." Having spoken these words, Gandhari was tormented by sorrow on account of her sons. She covered her face with her garment and wept. The lord, the mighty-armed Keshava, comforted the one who was afflicted by sorrow, speaking words that were full of reason.

'Having comforted Gandhari and Dhritarashtra, Keshava got to know[72] what Drona's son was planning. O Indra among kings! He swiftly arose. He bowed down before Dvaipayana and touched his feet with his head. He then told Kourava, "O best among the Kuru lineage! I must take your leave. Do not sorrow in your mind. Drona's son has a wicked intention. That is the reason I have suddenly got up. He has decided to kill the Pandavas in the night." On hearing these words, Dhritarashtra and Gandhari spoke to Keshava, the slayer of Keshi.[73]

[71]The word used is *simantini*. While this means woman, in particular, it means a married woman, with the sign of marriage on the parting of the hair.

[72]Mentally.

[73]Demon killed by Krishna.

"O mighty-armed one! Go quickly and protect the Pandavas. O Janardana! Let us meet again, soon." With Daruka, Achyuta left swiftly. O king! When Vasudeva had departed, Dhritarashtra, the lord of men, was comforted by Vyasa, revered by the world and immeasurable in his soul. O king! Having been successful, Vasudeva, with dharma in his soul, departed from Hastinapura, wishing to see the Pandavas in their camp. Having arrived in the camp in the night, he met the Pandavas and seated with them, told them everything that had happened.'

Chapter 1282(63)

'Dhritarashtra asked, "O Sanjaya! My son's head was kicked with the foot and his thighs were shattered. He was lying down on the ground. He was extremely proud. What did he say? The king was extremely wrathful and firm in his enmity towards the Pandus. In that great battle, when that great calamity overtook him, what did he say?"

'Sanjaya replied, "O king! Listen. O lord of men! I will tell you exactly what happened and what the king spoke, when he was shattered and he was overtaken by that calamity. O king! The king's thighs were shattered and he was covered with dust. He gathered his flowing locks and glanced in the ten directions. Having carefully collected his locks, he sighed like a serpent. He was angry. With tears flowing from his eyes, he glanced towards me. For a short while, like a crazy elephant, he struck the earth with his hands. Then he shook his locks and gnashed his teeth. He censured the eldest Pandava and sighing, spoke these words.[74] 'As my protector, I had Bhishma, Shantanu's son, Karna, supreme among the wielders of weapons, Goutama, Shakuni, Drona, supreme among the wielders of weapons, Ashvatthama, the brave Shalya and Kritavarma. However, I have been reduced to this state. Destiny is difficult to cross. I was the lord

[74]As will become clear, Duryodhana is actually speaking to Sanjaya.

of eleven armies.[75] But I have been reduced to this state. O mighty-armed one! When the time comes, no one can cross it. Those on my side who are still alive should be informed about how I have been brought down by Bhimasena, violating rules of fairness. The Pandavas have indeed performed many cruel deeds—Bhurishrava, Karna, Bhishma and the prosperous Drona. This is yet another infamous and cruel deed that the Pandavas have perpetrated. On this account, it is my view that they will be reprimanded by virtuous ones. If victory is obtained unfairly, what pleasure can virtuous men obtain from that? Which learned one will approve this violation of rules? Having obtained victory through adharma, learned ones do not rejoice in the way that the wicked Vrikodara, Pandu's son, is delighted. My thighs have been shattered. What can be more extraordinary than the angry Bhimasena kicking my head with his foot? O Sanjaya! If a man acts in such a way towards a powerful and prosperous person who still has relatives, will he be honoured? My mother, my father and I are not ignorant about the dharma of kshatriyas. O Sanjaya! They will be miserable. Tell them my words. I have performed sacrifices. I have sustained servants. I have ruled the earth, up to the oceans. When my enemies were alive, I placed my feet on their heads. I have given gifts, to the best of my capacity. I have done pleasant deeds towards my friends. I have countered all my enemies. Who can be more fortunate than I am? I have advanced against the kingdoms of enemies and have subjugated those kings, like slaves. I have truly acted well towards virtuous ones. Who can be more fortunate than I am? I have honoured all my relatives and have been honoured and revered by men. I have served the three objectives.[76] Who can be more fortunate than I am? I have commanded the foremost among kings. I have obtained honour that is extremely difficult to get. I have gone to my place of birth. Who can be more fortunate than I am? I have studied and donated, in accordance with the prescribed rites. I have lived a long and healthy life. Based on my own dharma, I have conquered the worlds. Who can be more fortunate than I am? It is through good fortune that I

[75]Akshouhinis.

[76]Dharma, artha and kama.

have not been defeated in the battle and made to serve my enemies. It is through good fortune that my great prosperity goes to another one only after my death. Based on their own dharma, my kshatriya relatives attained their desired objective. That same death has been obtained by me. Who can be more fortunate than I am? An ordinary person is subjugated in the course of an enmity. It is through good fortune that I have not been subjugated by the enemy in that way. It is through good fortune that I have not been vanquished after performing a despicable act—like killing one who is asleep, one who is mad, or killing someone through the use of poison. I have been slain through adharma, through the contravention of fair rules. The immensely fortunate Ashvatthama, Satvata Kritavarma and Kripa Sharadvata should be told these words of mine. "The Pandavas have engaged in many acts of adharma. You should not trust them. They violate the rules."'

'"The king, your son, for whom truth was his valour, then addressed the bards. 'In the encounter, I have been brought down by Bhimasena through the use of adharma. I will now go to heaven, like Drona, Shalya, Karna, the immensely valorous Vrishasena, Shakuni Soubala, the immensely valorous Jalasandha, King Bhagadatta, the great archer who was Somadatta's son,[77] Saindhava Jayadratha, my brothers who were my equal, with Duhshasana as the foremost, Duhshasana's valiant son and my son, Lakshmana. There were many thousand of others on my side. They followed me from the rear. But I am now like a traveller without any riches. On hearing about the death of her brothers and her husband, how will my sister, Duhshala,[78] be? She will weep in sorrow. When they are overcome by sorrow, what will become of my father, the aged king, and Gandhari, and their daughters-in-law and granddaughters-in-law? There is no doubt that with her son and her husband slain, Lakshmana's mother,[79] fortunate and large-eyed, will swiftly die. The immensely fortunate mendicant, Charvaka, is eloquent in the use of words. If he

[77]Bhurishrava.

[78]She was married to Jayadratha.

[79]Duryodhana's wife, Bhanumati.

learns about this, he will certainly exact vengeance on my account.[80] The sacred Samantapanchaka is famous in the three worlds. By dying here today, I will obtain the eternal worlds.' O venerable one! On hearing the lamentations of the king, thousands of men fled in the ten directions, their eyes full of tears. The earth, with its oceans and forests, and mobile and immobile objects, trembled violently and made a loud noise. The directions were clouded.

'"They[81] went to Drona's son and told him how the king had been brought down in the duel with the clubs. O descendant of the Bharata lineage! When they had reported the account to Drona's son, all of them remained immersed in thought for a long time. Then, sorrowfully, they[82] went to wherever they had come from."'

Chapter 1283(64)

'Sanjaya said, "O king! The remaining Kourava maharathas heard from the bards that Duryodhana had been brought down. They were mangled with sharp arrows, clubs, spears and javelins. Ashvatthama, Kripa and Satvata Kritavarma ascended swift steeds and quickly arrived at the field of the encounter. There, they saw Dhritarashtra's great-souled son, who had been brought down. He was like a giant shala tree in the forest, shattered by the force of a storm. He was like a giant elephant in the forest, slain by a hunter. He was writhing and was covered by copious quantities of blood. It was as if the solar disc had been brought down. It was as if a giant tempest had arisen and had dried up the ocean. It was as if the disc of the full moon in the sky had been covered by mist. He was mighty-armed and like an elephant in valour, but was covered

[80]There was a famous Charvaka, the founder of a materialist and atheist school of philosophy. This is not the famous Charvaka. The word Charvaka means someone who is beautiful in speech.

[81]The messengers.

[82]The messengers.

in dust. He was surrounded by a large number of fierce demons and predatory beasts in every direction, as if they were servants greedy for riches, surrounding the best of kings. There was a frown on his face and his eyes were dilated in rage. That tiger among men was like a tiger that had been brought down. They saw the great archer, the king, lying down on the ground. Kripa and the other rathas were extremely stupefied. They descended from their chariots and rushed towards the king. They saw Duryodhana and sat down on the ground, around him.

'"O great king! Drona's son's eyes were full of tears and he sighed. He spoke to the best of the Bharata lineage, the lord of all the kings on earth. 'There is no doubt that there is nothing that is permanent in the world of men. O tiger among men! You are lying down thus, covered in dust. O king! You had earlier commanded the earth. O Indra among kings! How is it that you are alone in this deserted forest now? I do not see Duhshasana, or maharatha Karna. O bull among the Bharata lineage! All your well-wishers aren't here either. It is a great sorrow that the ways of Yama can never be known. You possessed all the worlds. Yet you are lying down, covered in dust. This scorcher of enemies was foremost among those whose heads had been consecrated.[83] Behold the course of destiny. He is covered with grass and dust now. O king! Where is your sparkling umbrella and whisk now? O supreme among kings! Where has your large army gone? It is indeed impossible to fathom the course and cause and effect, since you, who were the preceptor of all the worlds, have now been reduced to this state. Everything on earth is temporary. It is seen that only prosperity and beauty are permanent.[84] You used to rival Shakra and we now see you reduced to this terrible state.' O king! On hearing his words, which were especially full of sorrow, you son spoke these words, appropriate to the occasion. He shed tears of sorrow and wiped them away from his eyes with his hands. The lord of men spoke to those brave ones, Kripa and the others. 'It has been said that the creator has ordained such a dharma for those

[83]That is, kings.

[84]Prosperity and beauty in the hereafter.

who are mortal. In the course of time, death confronts all beings. In the presence of all of you, it now confronts me. I have ruled over the earth and have now been reduced to this state. It is through good fortune that I have not been defeated by the enemy in battle. It is through good fortune that I have been brought down, especially through wickedness and deception. It is through good fortune that, while engaged in fighting, I have always exhibited enterprise. After my relatives and allies have been slain in the battle, it is through good fortune that I have been brought down. It is through good fortune that I see that you have escaped from this destruction of men, and are well and hale. This is great delight for me. Because you are my well-wishers, do not torment yourself at my death. If the Vedas are proof, I have obtained eternal worlds. I know about the powers of the infinitely energetic Krishna. He has ensured that I did not deviate from following the dharma of kshatriyas. I have obtained him. Therefore, I have nothing to sorrow about. You have done what those like you should have done. You have always sought to ensure my victory. But destiny is impossible to cross.' O Indra among kings! Having spoken these words, with tears in his eyes, the king became silent. He was severely agitated by agony.

'"Drona's son blazed up in anger, like the fire at the time of the destruction of the universe. Overcome by rage, he pressed one hand with the other hand. His voice choking with tears, he spoke these words to the king. 'My father was slain by those inferior ones, through an extremely cruel deed. O king! But that did not torment me as much as I am suffering now. O lord! Listen to these words. I am swearing this truthfully, on the sacrifices I have performed, the donations, the dharma and the good deeds. While Vasudeva looks on, I will use every means possible to convey all the Panchalas to the abode of the lord of the dead today. O great king! You should grant me the permission.' Having heard the words of Drona's son, which brought pleasure to his mind, Kourava spoke these words to Kripa. 'O preceptor! Quickly bring a pot full of water.' On hearing the king's words, the supreme among brahmanas followed his instructions. He brought a pot full of water and approached the king. O great king! O lord of the earth! Your son spoke these words. 'O foremost among brahmanas! On my instructions, let Drona's fortunate son be consecrated as the commander, if you wish to do that which brings me pleasure. On the instructions of a king, even a brahmana can fight, especially one who follows the dharma of kshatriyas. That is what those who are learned about dharma say.' On hearing the king's words and following the king's instructions, Kripa Sharadvata consecrated Drona's son as the commander. O great king! Having been thus consecrated, he embraced the best of kings. Roaring like a lion and making the directions resound, he departed. O Indra among kings! Duryodhana was covered with blood. He passed the night, which was dreadful to all beings. O king! Those warriors quickly left. Their minds were overcome with grief and they were immersed in their thoughts."'

This ends Shalya Parva.

With the war over, the eighth volume is on the aftermath of the war and covers Souptika Parva, Stri Parva and a large chunk of Shanti Parva of the 18-parva classification, and parvas 78 through 85, with a part of 86, of the 100-parva classification. In the night, Ashvatthama kills all the remaining Pandavas—with the exception of the five Pandava brothers—and Panchalas. The funeral ceremonies for the dead warriors are performed. Shanti Parva (Bhishma's teachings after Yudhishthira is crowned) is about duties to be followed under different circumstances.

About the Translator

Bibek Debroy is a member of NITI Aayog, the successor to the Planning Commission. He is an economist who has published popular articles, papers and books on economics. Before NITI Aayog, he has worked in academic institutes, industry chambers and for the government. Bibek Debroy also writes on Indology and Sanskrit. Penguin published his translation of the Bhagavad Gita in 2006 and *Sarama and Her Children: The Dog in Indian Myth* in 2008. The 10-volume unabridged translation of the Mahabharata was sequentially published between 2010 and 2014 and he is now translating the Hari Vamsha, to be published in 2016. Bibek Debroy was awarded the Padma Shri in 2015.